高三同學要如何準備「升大學考試」

考前該如何準備「學測」呢？「劉毅英文」的同學很簡單，只要熟讀每次的模考試題就行了。每一份試題都在7000字範圍內，就不必再背7000字了，從後面往前複習，越後面越重要，一定要把最後10份試題唸得滾瓜爛熟。根據以往的經驗，詞彙題絕對不會超出7000字範圍。每年題型變化不大，只要針對下面幾個大題準備即可。

準備「詞彙題」最佳資料：

背了再背，背到滾瓜爛熟，讓背單字變成樂趣。

考前不斷地做模擬試題就對了！

你做的題目愈多，分數就愈高。不要忘記，每次參加模考前，都要背單字、背自己所喜歡的作文。考壞不難過，勇往直前，必可得高分！

練習「模擬試題
公司」最新出版
擬試題詳解」。
①以「高中常用7
對，不會學錯。③
明確交待。

稿專家多次校

用詳細解答，對錯答案均有

「克漏字」如何答題

　　第二大題綜合測驗（即「克漏字」），不是考句意，就是考簡單的文法。當四個選項都不相同時，就是考句意，就沒有文法的問題；當四個選項單字相同、字群排列不同時，就是考文法，此時就要注意到文法的分析，大多是考連接詞、分詞構句、時態等。克漏字是考生最弱的一環，你難，別人也難，只要考前利用這種答題技巧，勤加練習，就容易勝過別人。

準備「綜合測驗」（克漏字）可參考「學習出版公司」最新出版的「7000字克漏字測驗詳解」。

本書特色：

1. 取材自大規模考試，英雄所見略同。
2. 不超出7000字範圍，不會做白工。
3. 每個句子都有文法分析。一目了然。
4. 對錯答案都有明確交待，列出生字，不用查字典。
5. 經過「劉毅英文」同學實際考過，效果極佳。

「文意選填」答題技巧

　　在做「文意選填」的時候，一定要冷靜。你要記住，一個空格一個答案，如果你不知道該選哪個才好，不妨先把詞性正確的選項挑出來，如介詞後面一定是名詞，選項裡面只有兩個名詞，再用刪去法，把不可能的選項刪掉。也要特別注意時間的掌控，已經用過的選項就劃掉，以免重複考慮，浪費時間。

準備「文意選填」，可參考「學習出版公司」最新出版的「7000字文意選填詳解」。

特色與「7000字克漏字測驗詳解」相同，不超出7000字的範圍，有詳細解答。

「閱讀測驗」的答題祕訣

① 尋找關鍵字——整篇文章中，最重要就是第一句和最後一句，第一句稱為主題句，最後一句稱為結尾句。每段的第一句和最後一句，第二重要，是該段落的主題句和結尾句。從「主題句」和「結尾句」中，找出相同的關鍵字，就是文章的重點。因為美國人從小被訓練，寫作文要注重主題句，他們給學生一個題目後，要求主題句和結尾句都必須有關鍵字。

② 先看題目、劃線、找出答案、標號——考試的時候，先把閱讀測驗題目瀏覽一遍，在文章中掃瞄和題幹中相同的關鍵字，把和題目相關的句子，用線畫起來，便可一目了然。通常一句話只會考一題，你畫了線以後，再標上題號，接下來，你找其他題目的答案，就會更快了。

③ 碰到難的單字不要害怕，往往在文章的其他地方，會出現同義字，因為寫文章的人不喜歡重覆，所以才會有難的單字。

④ 如果閱測內容已經知道，像時事等，你就可以直接做答了。

準備「閱讀測驗」，可參考「學習出版公司」最新出版的「7000字閱讀測驗詳解」，本書不超出7000字範圍，每個句子都有文法分析，對錯答案都有明確交待，單字註明級數，不需要再查字典。

「中翻英」如何準備

可參考劉毅老師的「英文翻譯句型講座實況DVD」，以及「文法句型180」和「翻譯句型800」。考前不停地練習中翻英，翻完之後，要給外籍老師改。翻譯題做得越多，越熟練。

「英文作文」怎樣寫才能得高分？

① 字體要寫整齊，最好是印刷體，工工整整，不要塗改。

② 文章不可離題，尤其是每段的第一句和最後一句，最好要有題目所說的關鍵字。

③ 不要全部用簡單句，句子最好要有各種變化，單句、複句、合句、形容詞片語、分詞構句等，混合使用。

④ 不要忘記多使用轉承語，像 *at present*（現在），*generally speaking*（一般說來），*in other words*（換句話說），*in particular*（特別地），*all in all*（總而言之）等。

⑤ 拿到考題，最好先寫作文，很多同學考試時，作文來不及寫，吃虧很大。但是，如果看到作文題目不會寫，就先寫測驗題，這個時候，可將題目中作文可使用的單字、成語圈起來，寫作文時就有東西寫了。但千萬記住，絕對不可以抄考卷中的句子，一旦被發現，就會以零分計算。

⑥ 試卷有規定標題，就要寫標題。記住，每段一開始，要內縮5或7個字母。

⑦ 可多引用諺語或名言，並注意標點符號的使用。文章中有各種標點符號，會使文章變得更美。

⑧ 整體的美觀也很重要，段落的最後一行字數不能太少，也不能太多。段落的字數要平均分配，不能第一段只有一、兩句，第二段一大堆。第一段可以比第二段少一點。

準備「英文作文」，可參考「學習出版公司」出版的：

序 言

　　「學科能力測驗」開辦至今，已經有二十四年的歷史。再加上另外舉行的兩次補考，一共有二十六份珍貴的英文試題。這些試題內容，是命題教授們的心血結晶，每一道題目都具有代表性，非常重要。這些題目是未來考生們準備學測時，不可或缺的參考資料。

　　「學科能力測驗」實施以來，考試的題型和方向大抵已有脈絡可循。就題型來說，選擇題部分沒有太大的變動，基本上包含：（一）詞彙題、（二）克漏字、（三）文意選填、（四）閱讀測驗；而非選擇題部分，則出現過簡答題、中翻英、看圖說故事等。至於出題方向，來自國外的網站文章、雜誌、期刊，內容多元，考生可以參照本書每年附加的「出題來源」作為課外閱讀。要應付層出不窮的考題，多做最新試題是不二法門，像「劉毅英文家教班」的學生，每週都參加模擬考試，每次考試都考世界最新動態的相關文章，不管學測題目再怎麼變，「劉毅英文家教班」的學生，永遠是最後的贏家。

　　「**歷屆大學學測英文試題詳解②**」，特別將近八年歷屆學測英文試題全部收錄在內，且針對每一道題目，都有最完善的講解，讀者們不需另外花時間查字典。只要把本書列出的單字和片語熟記，就能把英文這一科，變成幫助你得高分的秘密武器。

　　本書編校製作過程嚴謹，但仍恐有疏失之處，尚祈各界先進不吝指正。

編者 謹識

目　錄

106 年大學入學學科能力測驗試題
英文考科

第壹部分：單選題（占 72 分）

一、詞彙題（占 15 分）

說明： 第 1 題至第 15 題，每題有 4 個選項，其中只有一個是正確或最適當的選項，請畫記在答案卡之「選擇題答案區」。各題答對者，得 1 分；答錯、未作答或畫記多於一個選項者，該題以零分計算。

1. John's clock is not functioning _____. The alarm rings even when it's not set to go off.
   (A) tenderly　　(B) properly　　(C) solidly　　(D) favorably

2. Michael has decided to _____ a career in physics and has set his mind on becoming a professor.
   (A) pursue　　(B) swear　　(C) reserve　　(D) draft

3. Peter plans to hike in a _____ part of Africa, where he might not meet another human being for days.
   (A) native　　(B) tricky　　(C) remote　　(D) vacant

4. People in this community tend to _____ with the group they belong to, and often put group interests before personal ones.
   (A) appoint　　(B) eliminate　　(C) occupy　　(D) identify

5. I mistook the man for a well-known actor and asked for his autograph; it was really _____.
   (A) relaxing　　(B) embarrassing　　(C) appealing　　(D) defending

6. After spending most of her salary on rent and food, Amelia _____ had any money left for entertainment and other expenses.
   (A) barely　　(B) fairly　　(C) merely　　(D) readily

7. In the Bermuda Triangle, a region in the western part of the North Atlantic Ocean, some airplanes and ships were reported to have mysteriously disappeared without a _____.
   (A) guide　　(B) trace　　(C) code　　(D) print

8. Shouting greetings and waving a big sign, Tony _____ the passing shoppers to visit his shop and buy the freshly baked bread.
   (A) accessed   (B) edited   (C) imposed   (D) urged

9. With a continuous 3 km stretch of golden sand, the beach attracts artists around the world each summer to create amazing _____ with its fine soft sand.
   (A) constitutions   (B) objections   (C) sculptures   (D) adventures

10. The clouds parted and a _____ of light fell on the church, through the windows, and onto the floor.
    (A) dip   (B) beam   (C) spark   (D) path

11. Instead of a gift, Tim's grandmother always _____ some money in the birthday card she gave him.
    (A) enclosed   (B) installed   (C) preserved   (D) rewarded

12. While winning a gold _____ is what every Olympic athlete dreams of, it becomes meaningless if it is achieved by cheating.
    (A) signal   (B) glory   (C) medal   (D) profit

13. The thief went into the apartment building and stole some jewelry. He then _____ himself as a security guard and walked out the front gate.
    (A) balanced   (B) calculated   (C) disguised   (D) registered

14. Due to numerous accidents that occurred while people were playing Pokémon GO, players were advised to be _____ of possible dangers in the environment.
    (A) aware   (B) ashamed   (C) doubtful   (D) guilty

15. Sherlock Holmes, a detective in a popular fiction series, has impressed readers with his amazing powers of _____ and his knowledge of trivial facts.
    (A) innocence   (B) estimation   (C) assurance   (D) observation

二、綜合測驗（占 15 分）

說明： 第 16 題至第 30 題，每題一個空格，請依文意選出最適當的一個選項，
　　　請畫記在答案卡之「選擇題答案區」。各題答對者，得 1 分；答錯、未
　　　作答或畫記多於一個選項者，該題以零分計算。

第 16 至 20 題為題組

You begin to notice a bit of pain on your eyelid each time you blink. You ___16___ the mirror to find a tiny red spot on the base of your lower lashes. These ___17___ are probably the beginning of an eye stye.

An eye stye is a small bump, resembling a pimple, that develops when an oil gland at the edge of an eyelid becomes infected by bacteria. These bacteria are found in the nose and are easily ___18___ to the eye when you rub your nose, then your eye. Pus will build up in the center of the stye, causing a yellowish spot. Usually a stye is accompanied by a swollen eye.

___19___ a stye can look unpleasant at times, it is usually harmless and doesn't cause vision problems. Most styes heal on their own within a few days. You might speed up healing time by gently pressing a warm washcloth ___20___ your eyelid for 10 minutes, 3 or 4 times a day. Make sure you don't squeeze or pop a stye like you would a pimple. Doing so may cause a severe eye infection.

16. (A) check out　(B) look into　(C) watch over　(D) see through
17. (A) incidents　(B) measures　(C) symptoms　(D) explanations
18. (A) attracted　(B) contributed　(C) exposed　(D) transferred
19. (A) As　(B) If　(C) Unless　(D) Although
20. (A) against　(B) among　(C) about　(D) after

第 21 至 25 題為題組

Shoes are hugely important for protecting our feet, especially in places like Africa, where healthcare provision is limited. Unfortunately, shoes are not always readily available for people living in poverty, ___21___ shoes that are the right size. Almost as soon as a child receives shoes to wear, he/she is likely to have grown out of them. Then the child has to ___22___ with shoes that are too small. *The Shoe That Grows*, created by a charity called Because International, changes all this. It allows children to ___23___ their shoes' size as their feet grow.

The innovative footwear resembles a common sandal and is made of leather straps and rubber soles, a material similar to that used in tires. They come ___24___ two sizes, and can expand in three places. The straps on the heel and toe control the length of the shoe, ___25___ the two on either side allow for different widths. With this special design, the shoes can "grow" up to five sizes and last for at least five years.

21. (A) except for   (B) provided with   (C) far from   (D) let alone
22. (A) get done   (B) get lost   (C) make do   (D) make believe
23. (A) adjust   (B) explore   (C) insert   (D) overlook
24. (A) by   (B) in   (C) from   (D) down
25. (A) whether   (B) while   (C) with   (D) for

第 26 至 30 題為題組

Research has proven that weather plays a part in our moods: Warmer temperatures and exposure to sunshine increase positive thinking, whereas cold, rainy days bring anxiety and fatigue. ___26___, many people believe that bad weather can reduce productivity and efficiency.

There is, however, a significant ___27___ between such beliefs and the actual effect of weather on people's performance at work. Using empirical data from laboratory experiments ___28___ observations of a mid-sized Japanese bank in real life, researchers find that weather conditions indeed influence a worker's focus. When the weather is bad, individuals tend to focus more on their work rather than thinking about activities they could ___29___ outside of work. But photos showing outdoor activities, such as sailing on a sunny day or walking in the woods, can greatly distract workers and thus ___30___ their productivity. The findings conclude that workers are actually most productive when the weather is lousy—and only if nothing reminds them of good weather.

26. (A) At most   (B) In contrast   (C) Literally   (D) Accordingly
27. (A) gap   (B) link   (C) clue   (D) ratio
28. (A) out of   (B) as well as   (C) in case of   (D) due to
29. (A) break off   (B) approve of   (C) engage in   (D) take over
30. (A) reform   (B) lower   (C) switch   (D) demand

三、**文意選填**（占 10 分）

說明： 第 31 題至第 40 題，每題一個空格，請依文意在文章後所提供的 (A) 到
(J) 選項中分別選出最適當者，並將其英文字母代號畫記在答案卡之「選
擇題答案區」。各題答對者，得 1 分；答錯、未作答或畫記多於一個選
項者，該題以零分計算。

第 31 至 40 題爲題組

　　The widespread popularity of onions is not limited to modern-day
kitchens. There is evidence of onions being used for culinary and
medicinal purposes all over the ancient world. Nonetheless, no culture
___31___ onions quite as much as the ancient Egyptians. For them, the
onion was not just food or medicine; it held significant ___32___ meaning.
Onions were considered to be ___33___ of eternal life. The circle-within-
a-circle structure of an onion, for them, ___34___ the eternity of existence.
According to certain documents, ancient Egyptians also used onions for
medicinal purposes, but they likely would have viewed the ___35___ power
of the vegetable as magical, rather than medical.

　　Onions are depicted in many paintings ___36___ inside pyramids and
tombs that span the history of ancient Egypt. They ___37___ as a funeral
offering shown upon the altars of the gods. The dead were buried with
onions and onion flowers on or around various ___38___ of their bodies.
Mummies have also been found with onions and onion flowers ___39___
their pelvis, chest, ears, eyes, and feet.

　　Some scholars theorize that onions may have been used for the dead
because it was believed that their strong scent would ___40___ the dead
to breathe again. Other researchers believe it was because onions were
known for their special curative properties, which would be helpful in
the afterlife.

(A) reflected　　(B) parts　　　　(C) admired　　(D) functioned
(E) prompt　　　(F) decorating　　(G) spiritual　　(H) discovered
(I) symbols　　　(J) healing

四、閱讀測驗（占 32 分）

說明： 第 41 題至第 56 題，每題請分別根據各篇文章之文意選出最適當的一個
選項，請畫記在答案卡之「選擇題答案區」。各題答對者，得 2 分；答
錯、未作答或畫記多於一個選項者，該題以零分計算。

第 41 至 44 題為題組

Is your dog an Einstein or a Charmer? For US $60, a recently-founded company called Dognition will help you learn more about your dog's cognitive traits. It offers an online test telling you about the brain behind the bark.

Dognition's test measures a dog's intellect in several aspects—from empathy to memory to reasoning skills. But don't expect it to measure your pet's IQ. Dr. Hare, one of the **venture**'s co-founders, says a dog's intelligence can't be described with a single number. Just as humans have a wide range of intelligences, so do dogs. The question is what type your dog relies on more.

After you plunk your money down, Dognition's website will take you through a questionnaire about your dog: For example, how excited does your dog get around other dogs, or children? Do fireworks scare your pup? Then, Dognition guides you through tests that are as fun as playing fetch or hide-and-seek. At the end, you get a report of your dog's cognitive profile.

Your dog could fall into one of nine categories: Ace, Stargazer, Maverick, Charmer, Socialite, Protodog, Einstein, Expert, or Renaissance Dog. That can give you something to brag about on Dognition's Facebook page. It also can shed new light on why dogs do the things they do. For example, a Charmer is a dog that trusts you so much that it would prefer to solve problems using information you give it rather than information it can get with its own eyes.

Dognition helps people understand their dogs in ways that they have never been able to do. This new understanding can enrich the relationship between dogs and their owners.

41. What is the third paragraph mainly about?
   (A) The theory behind the questionnaire used in the Dognition test.
   (B) The procedure for evaluating a dog's intellect on Dognition.
   (C) The products one can get by paying a fee to Dognition.
   (D) The characteristics of the activities Dognition offers.

42. According to the passage, which of the following statements is true?
   (A) Different dogs display strengths in different intelligences.
   (B) A dog's cognitive profile is composed of nine cognitive skills.
   (C) The purpose of Dognition's testing is to control a dog's behavior.
   (D) A dog's intelligence can be ranked based on the score of a Dognition's test.

43. Which of the following is closest in meaning to the word "**venture**" in the second paragraph?
   (A) Creative measurement.　　　(B) Risky attempt.
   (C) Non-profit organization.　　(D) New business.

44. According to the passage, what would a Charmer most likely do?
   (A) Stay away from people whenever possible.
   (B) Imitate how other dogs solve problems.
   (C) Rely on its owner to point out where a treat is.
   (D) Follow its own senses to get what it wants.

第 45 至 48 題為題組

　　Capoeira is a martial art that combines elements of fight, acrobatics, drumming, singing, dance, and rituals. It involves a variety of techniques that make use of the hands, feet, legs, arms, and head. Although Capoeira appears dancelike, many of its basic techniques are similar to those in other martial arts.

　　Capoeira was created nearly 500 years ago in Brazil by African slaves. It is believed that the martial art was connected with tribal fighting in Africa, in which people fought body to body, without weapons, in order to acquire a bride or desired woman. In the sixteenth century, when the Africans were taken from their homes to Brazil against their will and kept in slavery, Capoeira began to take form among the community of slaves for self-defense. But it soon became a strong weapon in the life-or-death struggle against their oppressors. When the slave owners realized the power of Capoeira, they began to punish those who practiced it. Capoeiristas learned to camouflage the forbidden fights with singing, clapping, and dancing as though it were simply entertainment.

At first, Capoeira was considered illegal in Brazil. However, a man known as Mestre Bimba devoted a great deal of time and effort to convincing the Brazilian authorities that Capoeira has great cultural value and should become an official fighting style. He succeeded in his endeavor and transformed the martial art into Brazil's national sport. He and Mestre Pastinha were the first to open schools, and the Capoeira tree grew, spreading its branches across the world. Nowadays, it is performed in movies and music clips. Capoeira is also believed to have influenced several dancing styles like breaking and hip-hop.

45. What is the passage mainly about?
    (A) The history of Capoeira.
    (B) The values of Capoeira.
    (C) The contribution of Capoeira.
    (D) The techniques of Capoeira.

46. Which of the following will probably **NOT** be found in the performance of Capoeira?
    (A) Singing with drums.　　　(B) Sweeping with the legs.
    (C) Stabbing with swords.　　(D) Striking with the hands.

47. What is the author's attitude toward Capoeira as a sport?
    (A) Admiring.　　　　　　　(B) Objective.
    (C) Doubtful.　　　　　　　(D) Harsh.

48. According to the passage, which of the following statements is true
   about Capoeira?
   (A) It was greatly influenced by modern dancing styles.
   (B) It was initially created as a type of dance and ritual.
   (C) It was mainly performed to protect a bride or desired woman.
   (D) It was officially recognized in Brazil through the effort of
   Mestre Bimba.

第 49 至 52 題為題組

　　Winslow Homer (1836-1910) is regarded by many as the greatest
American painter of the nineteenth century. Born and raised in Boston,
he began his career at age eighteen in his hometown, working as an
apprentice at a printing company. Skilled at drawing, he soon made a
name for himself making illustrations for novels, sheet music, magazines,
and children's books.

　　He then moved to New York City, where he worked as a freelance
illustrator with *Harper's Weekly*, a popular magazine of the time, and
began painting. Homer was assigned to cover the inauguration of
President Lincoln and, later, the Civil War. His pictures of the Union
troops won international recognition. Homer moved to England and,
after a two-year stay, returned to America. He settled permanently in
Maine in 1883.

　　From the late 1850s until his death in 1910, Winslow Homer
produced a body of work distinguished by its thoughtful expression and
its independence from artistic conventions. A man of multiple talents,
Homer excelled equally in the arts of illustration, oil painting, and
watercolor. Many of his works—depictions of children at play and in
school, farm girls attending to their work, hunters and their prey—have
become classic images of nineteenth-century American life. **Others**
speak to more universal themes such as the primal relationship of humans
to nature.

　　This two-week exhibition highlights a wide and representative range of Homer's art. It shows his extraordinary career from the battlefields, farmland, and coastal villages of America, to the North Sea fishing village of Cullercoats, the rocky coast of Maine, the Adirondacks, and the Caribbean. The exhibition offers viewers an opportunity to experience and appreciate the breadth of his remarkable artistic achievement.

49. Where does this passage most likely appear?
    (A) On an ad featuring contemporary arts.
    (B) On a website of an art gallery.
    (C) In a booklet on American-born British artists.
    (D) In an encyclopedia on the art of printing.

50. Which of the following is true about Homer's career?
    (A) He achieved international fame with his vivid paintings of England.
    (B) He is considered the greatest illustrator in the history of American art.
    (C) He is better known for his watercolors than his illustrations and oil paintings.
    (D) He first established his reputation as an illustrator in his hometown of Boston.

51. According to the passage, which of the following best characterizes Homer's art?
    (A) His pictures vividly portrayed the life of nineteenth-century Americans.
    (B) His art thoughtfully expressed the voices of people suffering from war.
    (C) His style faithfully conformed to the artistic traditions of his time.
    (D) His paintings constantly reflected his desire to escape from society.

52. What does "**Others**" in the third paragraph refer to?
    (A) Other artists.   (B) Other themes.
    (C) Other works.   (D) Other images.

第 53 至 56 題爲題組

　　Tea, the most typical English drink, became established in Britain because of the influence of a foreign princess, Catherine of Braganza, the queen of Charles II. A lover of tea since her childhood in Portugal, she brought tea-drinking to the English royal court and set a trend for the beverage in the seventeenth century. The fashion soon spread beyond the circle of the nobility to the middle classes, and tea became a popular drink at the London coffee houses where people met to do business and discuss events of the day. Many employers served a cup of tea to their workers in the middle of the morning, thus inventing **a lasting British institution**, the "tea break." However, drinking tea in social settings outside the workplace was beyond the means of the majority of British people. It came with a high price tag and tea was taxed as well.

　　Around 1800, the seventh Duchess of Bedford, Anne Maria, began the popular practice of "afternoon tea," a ceremony taking place at about four o'clock. Until then, people did not usually eat or drink anything between lunch and dinner. At approximately the same time, the Earl of Sandwich popularized a new way of eating bread—in thin slices, with something (e.g., jam or cucumbers) between them. Before long, a small meal at the end of the afternoon, involving tea and sandwiches, had become part of the British way of life.

　　As tea became much cheaper during the nineteenth century, its popularity spread right through all corners of the British society. Thus, tea became Britain's favorite drink. In working-class households, it was served with the main meal of the day, eaten when workers returned home after a day's labor. This meal has become known as "high tea."

Today, tea can be drunk at any time of the day, and accounts for over two-fifths of all beverages consumed in Britain—with the exception of water.

53. How is this passage organized?
   (A) By cause and effect.
   (B) In the order of importance.
   (C) In the sequence of time.
   (D) By comparison and contrast.

54. What does the phrase "**a lasting British institution**" in the first paragraph mean?
   (A) The most popular British organization.
   (B) A long-standing tradition in the UK.
   (C) The last tea company in London.
   (D) A well-established British business.

55. According to the passage, why was tea **NOT** a common drink of everyday life in the seventeenth century?
   (A) It was only served at coffee houses in London.
   (B) It was taxed as an alcoholic drink.
   (C) It was forbidden outside of the business setting.
   (D) It was too expensive for most people.

56. According to the passage, which of the following is true?
   (A) High tea was served later in the day than afternoon tea in the nineteenth century.
   (B) British people had tea breaks twice a day in the eighteenth century.
   (C) Princess Catherine brought tea to England after visiting Portugal.
   (D) The Earl of Sandwich started the afternoon tea ceremony.

第貳部份：非選擇題（占 28 分）

說明： 本部分共有二題，請依各題指示作答，答案必須寫在「答案卷」上，並標明大題號（一、二）。作答務必使用筆尖較粗之黑色墨水的筆書寫，且不得使用鉛筆。

一、中譯英（占 8 分）

說明： 1. 請將以下中文句子譯成正確、通順、達意的英文，並將答案寫在「答案卷」上。

2. 請依序作答，並標明題號。每題 4 分，共 8 分。

1. 玉山（Jade Mountain）在冬天常常覆蓋著厚厚的積雪，使整個山頂閃耀如玉。

2. 征服玉山一直是國內外登山者最困難的挑戰之一。

二、英文作文（占 20 分）

說明： 1. 依提示在「答案卷」上寫一篇英文作文。

2. 文長至少 120 個單詞（words）。

提示： 請仔細觀察以下三幅連環圖片的內容，並想像第四幅圖片可能的發展，然後寫出一篇涵蓋每張圖片內容且結局完整的故事。

106年度學科能力測驗英文科試題詳解

第壹部分：單選題

一、詞彙題：

1. (**B**) John's clock is not functioning <u>properly</u>. The alarm rings even when it's not set to go off.
   約翰的時鐘不能<u>適當地</u>運作。即使沒有設定，鬧鈴也會響。
   (A) tenderly〔'tɛndəlɪ〕*adv.* 溫和地
   (B) ***properly***〔'prapəlɪ〕*adv.* 適當地   (C) solidly〔'salɪdlɪ〕*adv.* 堅固地
   (D) favorably〔'fevərəblɪ〕*adv.* 順利地；適宜地
   function〔'fʌŋkʃən〕*v.* 起作用；運作   alarm〔ə'lɑrm〕*n.* 鬧鈴
   ring〔rɪŋ〕*v.*（鈴）響   set〔sɛt〕*v.* 設定   ***go off*** 響起

2. (**A**) Michael has decided to <u>pursue</u> a career in physics and has set his mind on becoming a professor.
   麥克已決定<u>從事</u>物理學的職業，並下定決心要成爲一名教授。
   (A) ***pursue***〔pə'su〕*v.* 追求；從事   (B) swear〔swɛr〕*v.* 發誓
   (C) reserve〔rɪ'zɝv〕*v.* 保留；預訂   (D) draft〔dræft〕*v.* 草擬
   career〔kə'rɪr〕*n.*（終身的）職業   physics〔'fɪzɪks〕*n.* 物理學
   set one's ***mind on*** 對⋯下決心   professor〔prə'fɛsə〕*n.* 教授

3. (**C**) Peter plans to hike in a <u>remote</u> part of Africa, where he might not meet another human being for days. 彼得計劃在非洲一個<u>偏遠的</u>地區健行，他在那裡可能好幾天都不會見到另一個人。
   (A) native〔'netɪv〕*adj.* 本地的；本國的
   (B) tricky〔'trɪkɪ〕*adj.* 狡猾的；棘手的
   (C) ***remote***〔rɪ'mot〕*adj.* 偏遠的   (D) vacant〔'vekənt〕*adj.* 空的
   hike〔haɪk〕*v.* 健行；遠足   Africa〔'æfrɪkə〕*n.* 非洲   ***human being*** 人

4. (**D**) People in this community tend to <u>identify</u> with the group they belong to, and often put group interests before personal ones. 這個社區的人傾向於<u>認同</u>他們所屬的團體，經常把團體利益置於個人利益之前。
   (A) appoint〔ə'pɔɪnt〕*v.* 指派   (B) eliminate〔ɪ'lɪmə,net〕*v.* 除去

(C) occupy〔'ɑkjə,paɪ〕v. 佔據

(D) ***identify***〔aɪ'dɛntə,faɪ〕v. 認同＜ *with* ＞

community〔kə'mjunətɪ〕n. 社區　　***tend to V*.** 易於；傾向於
belong to 屬於　　interest〔'ɪntrɪst〕n. 利益
personal〔'pɜsn̩l〕adj. 個人的

5. (**B**) I mistook the man for a well-known actor and asked for his autograph;
it was really <u>embarrassing</u>. 我把這位男士誤認成一位知名的男演員，
還跟他要親筆簽名；這真的很<u>尷尬</u>。

(A) relaxing〔rɪ'læksɪŋ〕adj. 輕鬆的

(B) ***embarrassing***〔ɪm'bærəsɪŋ〕adj. 令人尷尬的

(C) appealing〔ə'pilɪŋ〕adj. 吸引人的

(D) defending〔dɪ'fɛndɪŋ〕adj. 保護的

mistake〔mə'stek〕v. 誤認＜ *for* ＞　well-known〔'wɛl'non〕adj. 有名的
ask for 要求　　autograph〔'ɔtə,græf〕n.（尤指名人的）親筆簽名

6. (**A**) After spending most of her salary on rent and food, Amelia <u>barely</u> had
any money left for entertainment and other expenses. 將她大部分的
薪水花在房租和食物後，艾蜜莉亞<u>幾乎沒</u>有錢留給娛樂和其他花費。

(A) ***barely***〔'bɛrlɪ〕adv. 幾乎不

(B) fairly〔'fɛrlɪ〕adv. 公平地；相當地

(C) merely〔'mɪrlɪ〕adv. 僅僅

(D) readily〔'rɛdɪlɪ〕adv. 欣然；容易地

salary〔'sælərɪ〕n. 薪水　　rent〔rɛnt〕n. 房租
entertainment〔,ɛntə'tenmənt〕n. 娛樂　　expense〔ɪk'spɛns〕n. 花費

7. (**B**) In the Bermuda Triangle, a region in the western part of the North
Atlantic Ocean, some airplanes and ships were reported to have
mysteriously disappeared without a <u>trace</u>. 在北大西洋西部地帶的百
慕達三角，有些飛機和船據報神秘消失，沒有留下一點<u>蹤跡</u>。

(A) guide〔gaɪd〕n. 指引　　　(B) ***trace***〔tres〕n. 蹤跡

(C) code〔kod〕n. 密碼　　　(D) print〔prɪnt〕n. 印刷

Bermuda〔bə'mjudə〕n. 百慕達【位於北大西洋的英國屬地】
triangle〔'traɪ,æŋgl〕n. 三角形　　***Bermuda Triangle*** 百慕達三角
region〔'ridʒən〕n. 地帶　　western〔'wɛstən〕adj. 西部的
Atlantic〔ət'læntɪk〕adj. 大西洋的　　report〔rɪ'port〕v. 報導
mysteriously〔mɪs'tɪrɪəslɪ〕adv. 神秘地　　disappear〔,dɪsə'pɪr〕v. 消失

8. (**D**) Shouting greetings and waving a big sign, Tony <u>urged</u> the passing shoppers to visit his shop and buy the freshly baked bread.
大聲問候並且揮舞著一個大牌子，東尼<u>力邀</u>經過的顧客去他的店買剛出爐的麵包。

(A) access (ˈæksɛs) v. 存取（資料）　(B) edit (ˈɛdɪt) v. 編輯
(C) impose (ɪmˈpoz) v. 強加　　　(D) ***urge*** (ɝdʒ) v. 力邀；力勸
greeting (ˈgritɪŋ) n. 問候　　wave (wev) v. 揮舞
sign (saɪn) n. 告示；牌子　　passing (ˈpæsɪŋ) adj. 經過的
freshly (ˈfrɛʃlɪ) adv. 新近地　　bake (bek) v. 烘烤

9. (**C**) With a continuous 3 km stretch of golden sand, the beach attracts artists around the world each summer to create amazing <u>sculptures</u> with its fine soft sand. 這座海灘有著綿延三公里的金沙，每年夏天吸引世界各地的藝術家，用它細微柔軟的沙子來創造驚人的<u>雕刻</u>。

(A) constitution (ˌkɑnstəˈtjuʃən) n. 憲法
(B) objection (əbˈdʒɛkʃən) n. 反對
(C) ***sculpture*** (ˈskʌlptʃɚ) n. 雕刻
(D) adventure (ədˈvɛntʃɚ) n. 冒險
continuous (kənˈtɪnjuəs) adj. 連續的　　stretch (strɛtʃ) n. 延伸
attract (əˈtrækt) v. 吸引　　***around the world*** 世界各地
create (krɪˈet) v. 創造　　amazing (əˈmezɪŋ) adj. 驚人的
fine (faɪn) adj. 細微的　　soft (sɔft) adj. 柔軟的

10. (**B**) The clouds parted and a <u>beam</u> of light fell on the church, through the windows, and onto the floor. 雲朵分離，一<u>束</u>光落在教堂上，穿過窗戶，照到地板上。

(A) dip (dɪp) n. 浸；泡　　　(B) ***beam*** (bim) n. 光束
(C) spark (spɑrk) n. 火花　　(D) path (pæθ) n. 小徑
part (pɑrt) v. 分離　　　through (θru) prep. 穿過

11. (**A**) Instead of a gift, Tim's grandmother always <u>enclosed</u> some money in the birthday card she gave him. 提姆的奶奶總是在給他的生日卡片中<u>隨函附上</u>一些錢，而不會送禮物。

(A) ***enclose*** (ɪnˈkloz) v. （隨函）附寄
(B) install (ɪnˈstɔl) v. 安裝　　(C) preserve (prɪˈzɝv) v. 保存
(D) reward (rɪˈwɔrd) v. 獎賞
instead of 而不是

12. (**C**) While winning a gold <u>medal</u> is what every Olympic athlete dreams of, it becomes meaningless if it is achieved by cheating. 雖然贏得一面金牌是所有奧運選手的夢想，但若是靠作弊達成，一切將變得沒有意義。

(A) signal〔ˈsɪgnḷ〕*n.* 信號　　　(B) glory〔ˈglorɪ〕*n.* 榮耀

(C) ***medal***〔ˈmɛdḷ〕*n.* 獎牌　　(D) profit〔ˈprɑfɪt〕*n.* 利潤；利益

while〔hwaɪl〕*conj.* 雖然　　Olympic〔oˈlɪmpɪk〕*adj.* 奧運的
athlete〔ˈæθlit〕*n.* 運動員　　***dream of*** 夢想
meaningless〔ˈminɪŋlɪs〕*adj.* 毫無意義的
achieve〔əˈtʃiv〕*v.* 達成　　cheat〔tʃit〕*v.* 作弊

13. (**C**) The thief went into the apartment building and stole some jewelry. He then <u>disguised</u> himself as a security guard and walked out the front gate. 那名小偷進入公寓大樓偷走一些珠寶。然後他把自己偽裝成一名保全，從正門走出去。

(A) balance〔ˈbæləns〕*v.* 使平衡　(B) calculate〔ˈkælkjə͵let〕*v.* 計算

(C) ***disguise***〔dɪsˈgaɪz〕*v.* 偽裝　(D) register〔ˈrɛdʒɪstə〕*v.* 登記；註冊

thief〔θif〕*n.* 小偷　　jewelry〔ˈdʒuəlrɪ〕*n.* 珠寶
security〔sɪˈkjurətɪ〕*n.* 安全　　guard〔gɑrd〕*n.* 守衛
security guard 保全　　gate〔get〕*n.* 大門

14. (**A**) Due to numerous accidents that occurred while people were playing Pokémon GO, players were advised to be <u>aware</u> of possible dangers in the environment. 由於民眾在玩寶可夢遊戲時發生了許多意外，所以玩家們被勸告要注意到環境中可能的危險。

(A) ***aware***〔əˈwɛr〕*adj.* 知道的；察覺到的 < *of* >

(B) ashamed〔əˈʃemd〕*adj.* 感到慚愧的

(C) doubtful〔ˈdautfəl〕*adj.* 懷疑的

(D) guilty〔ˈgɪltɪ〕*adj.* 有罪的；內疚的

due to 由於　　numerous〔ˈnjumərəs〕*adj.* 許多的
accident〔ˈæksədənt〕*n.* 意外　　occur〔əˈkɝ〕*v.* 發生
advise〔ədˈvaɪz〕*v.* 勸告　　environment〔ɪnˈvaɪrənmənt〕*n.* 環境

15. (**D**) Sherlock Holmes, a detective in a popular fiction series, has impressed readers with his amazing powers of <u>observation</u> and his knowledge of trivial facts. 夏洛克・福爾摩斯，一名很受歡迎的系列小說中的偵探，以他驚人的觀察力以及有關細微事實的知識令讀者印象深刻。

(A) innocence〔'ɪnəsn̩s〕n. 無罪;天眞

(B) estimation〔ˌɛstə'meʃən〕n. 估計

(C) assurance〔ə'ʃʊrəns〕n. 保證

(D) **observation**〔ˌɑbzə'veʃən〕n. 觀察

Sherlock Holmes 夏洛克・福爾摩斯【一個由 19 世紀末的英國偵探小説家亞瑟・柯南・道爾所塑造的一名才華洋溢的虛構偵探】

detective〔dɪ'tɛktɪv〕n. 偵探   fiction〔'fɪkʃən〕n. 小說

series〔'sɪrɪz〕n. 系列   impress〔ɪm'prɛs〕v. 使印象深刻

amazing〔ə'mezɪŋ〕adj. 驚人的   trivial〔'trɪvɪəl〕adj. 瑣碎的

二、綜合測驗:

第 16 至 20 題爲題組

You begin to notice a bit of pain *on your eyelid* **each time** *you blink*. You look into the mirror to find a tiny red spot on the base of your lower lashes.
16

These symptoms are *probably* the beginning *of an eye stye*.
  17

　你開始注意到,每當你眨眼時,眼皮就會有點痛。你照鏡子發現,在你下睫毛的底部有個小紅點。這些症狀可能就是開始要長針眼了。

notice〔'notɪs〕v. 注意到   **a bit of** 有點   pain〔pen〕n. 疼痛

eyelid〔'aɪˌlɪd〕n. 眼皮   blink〔blɪŋk〕v. 眨眼

mirror〔'mɪrə〕n. 鏡子   tiny〔'taɪnɪ〕adj. 微小的

spot〔spɑt〕n. 斑點   base〔bes〕n. 底部

lower〔'loə〕adj. 較低的;下層的   lash〔læʃ〕n. 睫毛

stye〔staɪ〕n. 麥粒腫;針眼(= *sty*)

16. (**B**) 依句意,選 (B) **look into the mirror**「照鏡子」(= *look in the mirror* = *look at yourself in the mirror*)。
　　　而 (A) check out「結帳退房;察看」, (C) watch over「看守;監視」, (D) see through「看透」,則不合句意。

17. (**C**) 依句意,選 (C) **symptoms**〔'sɪmptəmz〕n. pl. 症狀。
　　　而 (A) incident〔'ɪnsədənt〕n. 事件, (B) measure〔'mɛʒə〕n. 措施, (D) explanation〔ˌɛksplə'neʃən〕n. 解釋;說明,則不合句意。

An eye stye is a small bump, resembling a pimple, that develops when an oil gland at the edge of an eyelid becomes infected by bacteria. These bacteria are

found in the nose and are easily <u>transferred</u> to the eye when you rub your nose,
18
then your eye. Pus will build up in the center of the stye, causing a yellowish
spot. Usually a stye is accompanied by a swollen eye.

針眼是個很像青春痘的小腫塊，當眼皮邊緣的皮脂腺被細菌感染時，就會形成。
這些細菌可以在鼻子裡被發現，當你用手揉完鼻子再揉眼睛時，就很容易轉移到
眼睛。針眼的中央會化膿，形成淡黃色的斑點。通常長針眼的同時，眼睛會很腫。

bump〔bʌmp〕*n.* 腫塊　　resemble〔rɪˋzɛmbl̩〕*v.* 像
pimple〔ˋpɪmpl̩〕*n.* 青春痘　　develop〔dɪˋvɛləp〕*v.* 形成
gland〔glænd〕*n.* 腺　***oil gland*** 油腺；皮脂腺　　edge〔ɛdʒ〕*n.* 邊緣
infect〔ɪnˋfɛkt〕*v.* 感染　　bacteria〔bækˋtɪrɪə〕*n. pl.* 細菌
rub〔rʌb〕*v.* 摩擦；（用手）揉　　pus〔pʌs〕*n.* 膿
build up 增加；累積　　cause〔kɔz〕*v.* 造成
yellowish〔ˋjɛlo‧ɪʃ〕*adj.* 略帶黃色的；微黃的
accompany〔əˋkʌmpənɪ〕*v.* 伴隨；與…同時發生
swollen〔ˋswolən〕*adj.* 腫起的

18. (**D**) 依句意，選 (D)***transferred***。　　transfer〔trænsˋfɝ〕*v.* 轉移
而 (A) attract〔əˋtrækt〕*v.* 吸引，(B) contribute〔kənˋtrɪbjʊt〕*v.* 貢獻，
(C) expose〔ɪkˋspoz〕*v.* 暴露；使接觸，則不合句意。

Although *a stye can look unpleasant at times*, it is *usually* harmless and
19
doesn't cause vision problems. Most styes heal on their own within a few days.
You might speed up healing time by gently pressing a warm washcloth <u>against</u>
20
your eyelid for 10 minutes, 3 or 4 times a day. Make sure you don't squeeze or
pop a stye like you would a pimple. Doing so may cause a severe eye infection.

雖然針眼可能有時看起來很討厭，但通常是無害的，不會造成視力問題。大
多數針眼會在幾天之內自行痊癒。你可以將熱毛巾輕輕地壓在眼皮上，一天三或
四次，每次十分鐘，加速痊癒的時間。千萬不要像對青春痘一樣，擠壓針眼或使
它爆開，這樣做可能會造成嚴重的眼睛感染。

unpleasant〔ʌnˋplɛzn̩t〕*adj.* 令人不愉快的；令人討厭的
at times 有時候　　harmless〔ˋhɑrmlɪs〕*adj.* 無害的
vision〔ˋvɪʒən〕*n.* 視力　　heal〔hil〕*v.* 痊癒
on one's own 憑自己；獨自　　within〔wɪðˋɪn〕*prep.* 在…之內
speed up 加速　　gently〔ˋdʒɛntlɪ〕*adv.* 溫和地；輕輕地

press〔prɛs〕v. 壓；按　　warm〔wɔrm〕adj. 溫暖的；熱的
washcloth〔'waʃ,klɔθ〕n. 毛巾　　time〔taɪm〕n. 次　　**make sure** 確定
squeeze〔skwiz〕v. 擠壓　　pop〔pɑp〕v. 使啪的一聲爆裂
severe〔sə'vɪr〕adj. 嚴重的　　infection〔ɪn'fɛkʃən〕n. 感染

19. (**D**) 依句意，選 (D) *Although*「雖然」。而 (A) As「因為；當…的時候」，
　　　(B) If「如果」，(C) Unless「除非」，則不合句意

20. (**A**) *press A against B* 把 A 壓在 B 上（ = *press A on B* = *press A to B* ）

第 21 至 25 題為題組

　　Shoes are *hugely* important *for protecting our feet*, especially in places like
Africa, where healthcare provision is limited.　Unfortunately, shoes are not
always readily available for people living in poverty, <u>let alone</u> shoes that are
the right size.
　　　　　　　　　　　　　　　　　　　　　　　21

　　鞋子對於保護我們的腳而言，非常重要，尤其是在像是非洲這樣的地方，醫
療資源很有限。遺憾的是，對於生活貧困的人而言，要獲得鞋子不一定很容易，
更不用說尺寸正確的鞋子了。

hugely〔'hjudʒlɪ〕adv. 極大地；非常地　　protect〔prə'tɛkt〕v. 保護
especially〔ə'spɛʃəlɪ〕adv. 尤其；特別是
healthcare〔'hɛlθ,kɛr〕n. 醫療保健（服務）
provision〔prə'vɪʒən〕n. 供給；提供　　limited〔'lɪmɪtɪd〕adj. 有限的
unfortunately〔ʌn'fɔrtʃənɪtlɪ〕adv. 不幸地；遺憾地
not always 未必；不一定（ = *not necessarily* ）
readily〔'rɛdɪlɪ〕adv. 容易地；輕易地　　available〔ə'veləbḷ〕adj. 可獲得的
poverty〔'pɑvətɪ〕n. 貧窮　　**live in poverty** 過貧窮的生活

21. (**D**) 依句意，選 (D) *let alone*「更不用說」(= *not to mention* = *not to speak of*
　　　= *to say nothing of*)。【詳見「文法寶典」p.417「不定詞的獨立法」】
　　　而 (A) except for「除了」，(B) provided with「被提供了…」，(C) far from
　　　「一點也不」，則不合句意。

*Almost **as soon as** a child receives shoes to wear*, he/she is likely to have grown

out of them.　Then the child has to <u>make do</u> with shoes that are too small.　The

Shoe That Grows, created by a charity called Because International, changes
all this. It allows children to <u>adjust</u> their shoes' size as their feet grow.
23

幾乎孩子一收到可以穿的鞋子時，他或她可能就因為已經長
大，穿不下了。然後孩子就必須將就穿這些太小的鞋。有個
叫作Because International的慈善團體所創造的「會長大的鞋
子」改變了這一切。這能讓孩子隨著自己的腳逐漸成長，而
調整鞋子的尺寸。

> ***as soon as*** 一…就　　***be likely to V.*** 可能…
> ***grow out of*** （因長大而）穿不下　　create〔krɪ'et〕*v.* 創造
> charity〔'tʃærətɪ〕*n.* 慈善機構；慈善團體　　allow〔ə'laʊ〕*v.* 讓

22. (**C**) 依句意，選 (C) ***make do with*** 「將就使用」。We will make do with
what we have in the refrigerator.（我們會將就使用冰箱裡的東西。）
而 (A) get done with「做完；結束」，(B) get lost「迷路」，(D) make believe
「假裝」，則不合句意。

23. (**A**) 依句意，選 (A) ***adjust*** 〔ə'dʒʌst〕*v.* 調整。而 (B) explore〔ɪk'splor〕*v.*
探險；探討，(C) insert〔ɪn'sɝt〕*v.* 插入；加入，(D) overlook〔‚ovɚ'lʊk〕
v. 忽視，則不合句意。

The innovative footwear resembles a common sandal and is made of leather
straps and rubber soles, <u>a material similar to that used in tires</u>. They come <u>in</u>
　　　　　　　　　　　　　　　同　位　語　　　　　　　　　　　　24
two sizes, and can expand in three places. The straps on the heel and toe
control the length of the shoe, <u>while</u> the two on either side allow for different
　　　　　　　　　　　　　　　　25
widths. With this special design, the shoes can "grow" up to five sizes and
last for at least five years.

這種創新的鞋很像普通的涼鞋，是用皮製的帶子和橡膠鞋底
製成，和輪胎所使用的材料很類似。鞋子有兩種尺寸，而且
有三個地方可以擴大。在鞋後跟和腳尖上的帶子能控制鞋子
的長度，而兩邊的帶子，可以為不同的寬度預留空間。有了
這種特殊的設計，這些鞋子就可以「長」成五種尺寸，並且至少可以穿五年。

> innovative〔'ɪnə‚vetɪv〕*adj.* 創新的　　footware〔'fʊt‚wɛr〕*n.*（總稱）鞋類
> resemble〔rɪ'zɛmbḷ〕*v.* 像　　common〔'kɑmən〕*adj.* 普通的；常見的
> sandal〔'sændḷ〕*n.* 涼鞋　　***be made of*** 由…製成

leather〔ˈlɛðə〕adj. 皮（製）的　　　strap〔stræp〕n. 帶子
rubber〔ˈrʌbə〕n. 橡膠　　sole〔sol〕n. 鞋底
material〔məˈtɪrɪəl〕n. 原料；材料
similar〔ˈsɪmələ〕adj. 類似的 < to >　　tire〔taɪr〕n. 輪胎
expand〔ɪkˈspænd〕v. 擴大；擴充　　heel〔hil〕n. 鞋後跟；腳後跟
toe〔to〕n. 鞋尖；腳趾　　length〔lɛŋθ〕n. 長度
either〔ˈiðə〕adj.（兩者）任一　　**allow for** 考慮到；為…預留空間
width〔wɪdθ〕n. 寬度　　design〔dɪˈzaɪn〕n. 設計
last〔læst〕v. 持續；持久；支撐　　**at least** 至少

24.（**B**）依句意，選 (B) **come in**「有（…尺寸、形狀、顏色等）」。

25.（**B**）依句意，表對比，選 (B) **while**「然而」（= whereas ）。

第 26 至 30 題為題組

　　Research has proven that weather plays a part in our moods: Warmer temperatures and exposure to sunshine increase positive thinking, whereas cold, rainy days bring anxiety and fatigue. <u>Accordingly</u>, many people believe
26
that bad weather can reduce productivity and efficiency.

　　研究已經證實，天氣會影響我們的心情：較溫暖的氣溫及接觸到陽光，能促進正向思考，而寒冷、有雨的日子，則會帶來焦慮及疲勞。因此，很多人認為，壞天氣可能會降低生產力和效率。

research〔ˈrisɝtʃ〕n. 研究　　prove〔pruv〕v. 證實
weather〔ˈwɛðə〕n. 天氣　　part〔pɑrt〕n. 角色（= role ）
play a part 扮演一個角色；起作用　　mood〔mud〕n. 心情
temperature〔ˈtɛmpərətʃə〕n. 溫度　　exposure〔ɪkˈspoʒə〕n. 接觸 < to >
sunshine〔ˈsʌnˌʃaɪn〕n. 陽光　　increase〔ɪnˈkris〕v. 增加
positive〔ˈpɑzətɪv〕adj. 正面的；樂觀的
whereas〔hwɛrˈæz〕conj. 然而（= while ）
rainy〔ˈrenɪ〕adj. 下雨的　　anxiety〔æŋˈzaɪətɪ〕n. 焦慮
fatigue〔fəˈtig〕n. 疲勞　　reduce〔rɪˈdjus〕v. 降低；減少
productivity〔ˌprodʌkˈtɪvətɪ〕n. 生產力　　efficiency〔əˈfɪʃənsɪ〕n. 效率

26.（**D**）依句意，選 (D) **Accordingly**〔əˈkɔrdɪŋlɪ〕adv. 因此（= Therefore ）。而
　　(A) At most「最多」，(B) In contrast「對比之下」，(C) Literally〔ˈlɪtərəlɪ〕
　　adv. 確實地；照字面意義地，則不合句意。

There is, however, a significant <u>gap</u> *between such beliefs **and** the actual*
　　　　　　　　　　　　　　　　27

effect of weather on people's performance at work.　Using empirical data from laboratory experiments <u>as well as</u> observations of a mid-sized Japanese bank in
　　　　　　　　　　　　　　28
real life, researchers find that weather conditions indeed influence a worker's focus.

　　然而，這樣的想法，和天氣對人們工作表現真正的影響之間，有很大的差距。
用實驗室的實驗所得到的資料，以及在現實生活中，對一間中型的日本銀行所做的觀察，研究人員發現，天氣狀況的確會影響員工的專注力。

significant〔sɪg'nɪfəkənt〕*adj.* 相當大的；顯著的
belief〔bɪ'lif〕*n.* 信念；看法　　actual〔'æktʃuəl〕*adj.* 真實的；實際上的
effect〔ɪ'fɛkt〕*n.* 影響＜ on ＞　　performance〔pɚ'fɔrməns〕*n.* 表現
empirical〔ɪm'pɪrɪkl〕*adj.* 經驗主義的；以科學實驗爲根據的
data〔'detə〕*n. pl.* 資料　　laboratory〔'læbərə,torɪ〕*n.* 實驗室
experiment〔ɪk'spɛrəmənt〕*n.* 實驗　　observation〔,abzɚ'veʃən〕*n.* 觀察
mid-sized〔'mɪd,saɪzd〕*adj.* 中型的　　*in real life* 在現實生活中
researcher〔rɪ'sɝtʃɚ〕*n.* 研究人員　　condition〔kən'dɪʃən〕*n.* 狀況
indeed〔ɪn'did〕*adv.* 的確；眞地　　influence〔'ɪnfluəns〕*v.* 影響
focus〔'fokəs〕*n.* 專注；注意

27. (**A**) 依句意，選 (A) *gap*〔gæp〕*n.* 差距。而 (B) link〔lɪŋk〕*n.* 連結；關聯，
　　　(C) clue〔klu〕*n.* 線索，(D) ratio〔'reʃo〕*n.* 比率，則不合句意。

28. (**B**) 依句意，選 (B) *as well as*「以及」。而 (A) out of「出於」，(C) in case of
　　　「如果發生」，(D) due to「因爲；由於」，則不合句意。

***When** the weather is bad*, individuals tend to focus more on their work rather than thinking about activities they could <u>engage in</u> outside of work.　But photos
　　　　　　　　　　　　　　　　　　　　29
showing outdoor activities, such as sailing on a sunny day or walking in the woods, can greatly distract workers and thus <u>lower</u> their productivity.　The
　　　　　　　　　　　　　　　　　　　　　　30
findings conclude that workers are actually most productive when the weather is lousy—and only if nothing reminds them of good weather.

當天氣不好時，人就容易更專注於工作，而不是想著那些他們能從事的，工作以外的活動。但是，像在晴天坐船旅行或在森林中散步，這種戶外活動的照片，很可能會使員工分心，因而降低生產力。這些研究結果斷定，當天氣很不好時，員工事實上是非常有生產力的——只要沒有東西使他們想起好天氣的話。

individual 〔ˌɪndəˈvɪdʒuəl 〕 *n.* 個人　　　***tend to V.*** 易於…；傾向於…
focus on 專注於　　　***rather than*** 而不是
activity 〔 ækˈtɪvətɪ 〕 *n.* 活動　　　***outside of*** 在…之外
photo 〔ˈfoto 〕 *n.* 照片　　　show 〔 ʃo 〕 *v.* 顯示
outdoor 〔ˈautˌdor 〕 *adj.* 戶外的　　　***such as*** 像是
sailing 〔ˈselɪŋ 〕 *n.* 航海；坐船旅行　　　sunny 〔ˈsʌnɪ 〕 *adj.* 晴朗的
woods 〔 wudz 〕 *n. pl.* 森林　　　greatly 〔ˈgretlɪ 〕 *adv.* 大大地；非常地
distract 〔 dɪˈstrækt 〕 *v.* 使分心　　　thus 〔 ðʌs 〕 *adv.* 因此 (= *therefore*)
findings 〔ˈfaɪndɪŋz 〕 *n. pl.* 研究的結果
conclude 〔 kənˈklud 〕 *v.* 下結論；斷定
actually 〔ˈæktʃuəlɪ 〕 *adv.* 事實上　　　most 〔 most 〕 *adv.* 非常地
productive 〔 prəˈdʌktɪv 〕 *adj.* 有生產力的　　　lousy 〔ˈlauzɪ 〕 *adj.* 差勁的
only if 只要　　　remind 〔 rɪˈmaɪnd 〕 *v.* 提醒；使想起 < *of* >

29. (**C**) 依句意，選 (C) ***engage in*** 「從事；參與」。而 (A) break off 「突然停止；斷絕 (關係)」，(B) approve of 「贊成」，(D) take over 「接管」，則不合句意。

30. (**B**) 這種戶外活動的照片，很可能會使員工分心，因而「降低」生產力，選 (B) ***lower***。而 (A) reform 〔 rɪˈfɔrm 〕 *v.* 改革，(C) switch 〔 swɪtʃ 〕 *v.* 轉變；轉換，(D) demand 〔 dɪˈmænd 〕 *v.* 要求，則不合句意。

三、文意選填：

第 31 至 40 題為題組

　　The widespread popularity of onions is not limited to modern-day kitchens. There is evidence of onions being used for culinary and medicinal purposes all over the ancient world. Nonetheless, no culture [31.] **(C) admired** onions quite as much as the ancient Egyptians. For them, the onion was not just food or medicine; it held significant [32.] **(G) spiritual** meaning. Onions were considered to be [33.] **(I) symbols** of eternal life. The circle-within-a-circle structure of an onion, for them, [34.] **(A) reflected** the eternity of existence. According to certain documents, ancient Egyptians also used onions for medicinal purposes, but they likely would have viewed the [35.] **(J) healing** power of the vegetable as magical, rather than medical.

　　洋蔥廣受歡迎並不限於現代的廚房。有證據顯示，洋蔥在古代世界被用於烹飪和醫療。不過，沒有其他文化像古埃及人一樣崇拜洋蔥。對他們來說，洋蔥不只是食物或藥；它還有重要的宗教意義。洋蔥被認為是永生的象徵。它一圈環繞一圈的結構，對埃及人來說，反映了存在的永恆。根據某些文件，古埃及人也用洋蔥作為醫療的用途，但是他們可能把這蔬菜的治癒能力視為魔力，而非療效。

　　widespread〔'waɪd'sprɛd〕adj. 廣泛的；普遍的
　　popularity〔,pɑpjə'lærətɪ〕n. 流行；受歡迎　　onion〔'ʌnjən〕n. 洋蔥
　　be limited to 僅限於　　modern-day adj. 現代的
　　evidence〔'ɛvədəns〕n. 證據　　culinary〔'kjulə,nɛrɪ〕adj. 烹飪的
　　medicinal〔mə'dɪsn̩l〕adj. 醫藥的　　purpose〔'pɝpəs〕n. 目的；用途
　　all over 遍及　　ancient〔'enʃənt〕adj. 古代的
　　nonetheless〔,nʌnðə'lɛs〕adv. 然而　　culture〔'kʌltʃɚ〕n. 文化
　　admire〔əd'maɪr〕v. 讚賞；崇拜　　Egyptian〔ɪ'dʒɪpʃən〕n. 埃及人
　　hold〔hold〕v. 擁有　　significant〔sɪg'nɪfəkənt〕adj. 重要的
　　spiritual〔'spɪrɪtʃʊəl〕adj. 精神的；宗教上的
　　consider〔kən'sɪdɚ〕v. 認為　　symbol〔'sɪmbl̩〕n. 象徵
　　eternal〔ɪ'tɝnl̩〕adj. 永恆的　　structure〔'strʌktʃɚ〕n. 結構
　　reflect〔rɪ'flɛkt〕v. 反映；表達　　eternity〔ɪ'tɝnətɪ〕n. 永恆
　　existence〔ɪg'zɪstəns〕n. 存在；生存　　certain〔'sɝtn̩〕adj. 某些
　　document〔'dɑkjəmənt〕n. 文件　　likely〔'laɪklɪ〕adv. 可能
　　view A as B 視 A 為 B　　healing〔'hilɪŋ〕adj. 有治療功用的
　　magical〔'mædʒɪkl̩〕adj. 神奇的；不可思議的　　**rather than** 而非
　　medical〔'mɛdɪkl̩〕adv. 醫學的；醫療的

Onions are depicted in many paintings [36.] **(H) discovered** inside pyramids and tombs that span the history of ancient Egypt. They [37.] **(D) functioned** as a funeral offering shown upon the altars of the gods. The dead were buried with onions and onion flowers on or around various [38.] **(B) parts** of their bodies. Mummies have also been found with onions and onion flowers [39.] **(F) decorating** their pelvis, chest, ears, eyes, and feet.

　　洋蔥在很多畫中都有被描繪到，在跨越古埃及歷史的金字塔和墳墓中可以發現這些畫。它們被當作葬禮的供品放在神壇上。死者和洋蔥共葬，並在他們的屍體各個部分上面或是周圍放洋蔥和洋蔥花。也發現木乃伊有洋蔥或洋蔥花裝飾他們的骨盆、胸部、耳朵、眼睛和腳。

　　depict〔dɪ'pɪkt〕v. 描述；描繪　　painting〔'pentɪŋ〕n. 畫
　　pyramid〔'pɪrəmɪd〕n. 金字塔　　tomb〔tum〕n. 墳墓；墓穴
　　span〔spæn〕v. 跨越；擴及　　history〔'hɪstrɪ〕n. 歷史
　　Egypt〔'idʒɪpt〕n. 埃及　　function〔'fʌŋkʃən〕v. 起作用；產生功能

function as 充當；當作　　funeral〔'fjunərəl〕*adj.* 葬禮的
offering〔'ɔfərɪŋ〕*n.* 祭品；供品　　show〔ʃo〕*v.* 陳列
altar〔'ɔltə〕*n.* 祭壇；神壇　　*the dead* 死者（= *dead people*）
bury〔'bɛrɪ〕*v.* 埋葬　　various〔'vɛrɪəs〕*adj.* 各種的　　part〔part〕*n.* 部位
mummy〔'mʌmɪ〕*n.* 木乃伊　　decorate〔'dɛkə,ret〕*v.* 裝飾
pelvis〔'pɛlvɪs〕*n.* 骨盆　　chest〔tʃɛst〕*n.* 胸部

Some scholars theorize that onions may have been used for the dead because it was believed that their strong scent would **40.** **(E) prompt** the dead to breathe again. Other researchers believe it was because onions were known for their special curative properties, which would be helpful in the afterlife.

有些學者提出理論說，當時洋蔥用於死者身上，可能是因為人們相信洋蔥強烈的氣味會促使死者再次呼吸。其他的研究人員相信，這是因為洋蔥以其特殊的療癒性質而聞名，這對來生是有益的。

scholar〔'skalə〕*n.* 學者　　theorize〔'θiə,raɪz〕*v.* 提出理論；推測
scent〔sɛnt〕*n.* 氣味　　prompt〔prampt〕*v.* 促使；刺激
breathe〔brið〕*v.* 呼吸　　researcher〔rɪ'sɜtʃə〕*n.* 研究人員
be known for 因…而聞名　　curative〔'kjurətɪv〕*adj.* 治療的
property〔'prapətɪ〕*n.* 特性；特質　　helpful〔'hɛlpfəl〕*adj.* 有益的
afterlife〔'æftə,laɪf〕*n.* 來生

四、閱讀測驗：

第 41 至 44 題為題組

Is your dog an Einstein or a Charmer? For US $60, a recently-founded company called Dognition will help you learn more about your dog's cognitive traits. It offers an online test telling you about the brain behind the bark.

你的狗是愛因斯坦型，還是巫師型的？花六十美元，最近成立的一間叫「狗識」的公司，將幫助你更了解你家狗的認知特質。它提供線上測試，告訴你狗吠聲背後的狗腦在想什麼。

Einstein〔'aɪnstaɪn〕*n.* 愛因斯坦型
Charmer〔'tʃarmə〕*n.* 巫師型；有魅力的人　　found〔faʊnd〕*v.* 建立
recently-founded〔'risn̩tlɪ'faʊndɪd〕*adj.* 最近成立的
Dognition〔dag'nɪʃən〕*n.* 狗識【公司名稱取自於 cognition〔kag'nɪʃən〕
　　n. 認知，此公司主要是在幫助飼主了解自己的狗】
cognitive〔'kagnətɪv〕*adj.* 認知的　　trait〔tret〕*n.* 特質；特點
offer〔'ɔfə〕*v.* 提供　　online〔'an,laɪn〕*adj.* 線上的；網路上的
brain〔bren〕*n.* 頭腦　　bark〔bark〕*n.* 吠叫

Dognition's test measures a dog's intellect in several aspects—from empathy to memory to reasoning skills. But don't expect it to measure your pet's IQ. Dr. Hare, one of the **venture**'s co-founders, says a dog's intelligence can't be described with a single number. Just as humans have a wide range of intelligences, so do dogs. The question is what type your dog relies on more.

「狗識」的測試，是要測量狗在好幾個方面的智力——從同理心、記憶力，到推理技巧。但不要指望它能衡量你家寵物的智商。此企業的共同創立人之一的黑爾博士說，狗的智力不能用單一數字來描述。正如人類具有各種才智，狗也是如此。問題是你的狗依賴哪種類型的才智較多。

measure〔ˈmɛʒɚ〕v. 測量　　intellect〔ˈɪntl̩ˌɛkt〕n. 智力
aspect〔ˈæspɛkt〕n. 方面　　empathy〔ˈɛmpəθɪ〕n. 同理心
memory〔ˈmɛmərɪ〕n. 記憶力
reasoning〔ˈriznɪŋ〕n. 推論；推理　　skill〔ˈskɪl〕n. 技能；技巧
expect〔ɪkˈspɛkt〕v. 期望　　venture〔ˈvɛntʃɚ〕n.（冒險）事業
IQ〔ˈaɪˈkju〕n. 智商（= Intelligence Quotient）
co-founder〔koˈfaʊndɚ〕n. 共同創立人
intelligence〔ɪnˈtɛlədʒəns〕n. 聰明才智；智慧　　*rely on* 依靠；依賴

After you plunk your money down, Dognition's website will take you through a questionnaire about your dog: For example, how excited does your dog get around other dogs, or children? Do fireworks scare your pup? Then, Dognition guides you through tests that are as fun as playing fetch or hide-and-seek. At the end, you get a report of your dog's cognitive profile.

在投下你的錢後，「狗識」網站將帶你做一份關於你家狗的問卷：例如，你的狗與其他的狗或孩子在一起時，會有多興奮？煙火會嚇到你家的幼犬嗎？然後，「狗識」會引導你做測驗，像是玩你丟我撿或捉迷藏一樣有趣。最後，你會得到你家狗的認知概況的報告。

plunk〔plʌŋk〕v. 用力丟下　　*plunk down*（啪地）扔下（錢）付款
questionnaire〔ˌkwɛstʃənˈɛr〕n. 問卷　　firework〔ˈfairˌwɝk〕n. 煙火
pup〔pʌp〕n. 小狗；幼犬　　guide〔gaɪd〕v. 引導；帶領
fetch〔fɛtʃ〕n. 拿；取　　hide-and-seek〔ˈhaɪdˌənˈsik〕n. 捉迷藏
report〔rɪˈport〕n. 報告　　profile〔ˈprofaɪl〕n. 簡介；概況

Your dog could fall into one of nine categories: Ace, Stargazer, Maverick, Charmer, Socialite, Protodog, Einstein, Expert, or Renaissance Dog. That can give you something to brag about on Dognition's Facebook page. It also can shed new light on why dogs do the things they do. For example, a Charmer is a dog that trusts you so much that it would prefer to solve problems using information you give it rather than information it can get with its own eyes.

你的狗可能是屬於九個類型中的其中之一：王牌型、夢想家型、獨行俠型、巫師型、社會名流型、模範生型、愛因斯坦型、專家型，或博學多聞型。這可以給你一些東西在「狗識」的臉書專頁上誇耀。它也可以解釋，為什麼狗會有某些行為。例如，巫師型是極度信任主人的狗，牠會比較喜歡用你給牠的資訊來解決問題，而不是用自己的眼睛能得到的資訊。

> ***fall into*** 屬於　　category〔'kætəˌgorɪ〕*n.* 種類
> Ace〔es〕*n.* 王牌型　　Stargazer〔'starˌgezɚ〕*n.* 夢想家型；占星師
> Maverick〔'mævərɪk〕*n.* 獨行俠型；不服從的人
> Socialite〔'soʃəˌlaɪt〕*n.* 社會名流型
> Protodog〔'protəˌdog〕*n.* 模範狗；模範生型
> expert〔'ɛkspɝt〕*n.* 專家
> renaissance〔ˌrɛnə'zɑns〕*adj.* 博學多才的；文藝復興的
> ***brag about*** 誇耀　　***shed light on*** 闡明；解釋清楚

Dognition helps people understand their dogs in ways that they have never been able to do. This new understanding can enrich the relationship between dogs and their owners.

「狗識」能幫助人們，以他們無法做到的方式，去理解他們的狗。這種新的理解可以豐富狗與牠們主人之間的關係。

> ***be able to V.*** 能夠…　　enrich〔ɪn'rɪtʃ〕*v.* 使豐富
> relationship〔rɪ'lessenˌʃɪp〕*n.* 關係　　owner〔'onɚ〕*n.* 物主；所有人

41.(**B**) 本文的第三段主要是關於什麼？
　　(A) 「狗識」測試所使用的問卷背後的理論。
　　(B) 在「狗識」網站上評估狗的智力的流程。
　　(C) 藉由付費給「狗識」可得到的產品。
　　(D) 「狗識」提供的活動的特色。

> theory〔'θɪərɪ〕*n.* 理論　　procedure〔prə'sidʒɚ〕*n.* 程序
> evaluate〔ɪ'væljuˌet〕*v.* 評估　　fee〔fi〕*n.* 費用
> characteristic〔ˌkærɪktə'rɪstɪk〕*n.* 特色

42.(**A**) 根據本文，下列敘述何者為真？
　　(A) 不同的狗會展現不同的智能強項。
　　(B) 狗的認知概況是由九種認知技能所組成。
　　(C) 「狗識」測試的目的是要控制狗的行為。
　　(D) 狗的聰明才智可以根據「狗識」測驗的分數來排名。

display〔dɪˈsple〕v. 展現　　strength〔strɛŋθ〕n. 強項；優點
be composed of 由…組成　rank〔ræŋk〕v. 把…分等級
based on 根據

43.(**D**) 下列何者最接近在本文第二段 "venture" 的意思？
　　(A) 創意測量法。　　　　　　(B) 冒險嘗試。
　　(C) 非營利組織。　　　　　　(D) 新事業。

44.(**C**) 根據文章，巫師型的狗最有可能會做什麼？
　　(A) 儘可能遠離人類。　　　　(B) 模仿其他狗解決問題。
　　(C) 依靠主人指出牠的美食在哪裡。
　　(D) 靠自己的感覺來得到牠想要的。
imitate〔ˈɪmə͵tet〕v. 模仿　solve〔sɑlv〕v. 解決　　**point out** 指出
treat〔trit〕n. 難得的樂事　sense〔sɛns〕n. 感覺

第 45 至 48 題為題組

Capoeira is a martial art that combines elements of fight, acrobatics, drumming, singing, dance, and rituals. It involves a variety of techniques that make use of the hands, feet, legs, arms, and head. Although Capoeira appears dancelike, many of its basic techniques are similar to those in other martial arts.

卡波耶拉武術是一種結合了格鬥、特技、擊鼓、歌唱、舞蹈，以及儀式等元素的武術。它包含了各式各樣使用手、腳、腿、手臂，以及頭的技巧。雖然卡波耶拉武術看起來像舞蹈，它的許多基本技巧和其他的武術很相似。

Capoeira〔͵kɑpəˈwerɪə〕n. 卡波耶拉武術【源自十六世紀，由非洲黑奴發明，是一種結合舞蹈與武術的藝術】
martial〔ˈmɑrʃəl〕adj. 戰爭的；武打的　**martial art** 武術
combine〔kəmˈbaɪn〕v. 結合　element〔ˈɛləmənt〕n. 元素
fight〔faɪt〕n. 格鬥；武打　acrobatics〔͵ækrəˈbætɪks〕n. 特技
drumming〔ˈdrʌmɪŋ〕n. 擊鼓　ritual〔ˈrɪtʃuəl〕n. 儀式
involve〔ɪnˈvɑlv〕v. 包含　**a variety of** 各式各樣的
technique〔tɛkˈnik〕n. 技術　**make use of** 使用；利用
appear〔əˈpɪr〕v. 看起來　dancelike〔ˈdæns͵laɪk〕adj. 像舞蹈的
basic〔ˈbesɪk〕adj. 基本的　**be similar to** 和…相似

Capoeira was created nearly 500 years ago in Brazil by African slaves. It is believed that the martial art was connected with tribal fighting in Africa, in which people fought body to body, without weapons, in order to acquire a bride or desired woman. In the sixteenth century, when the Africans were taken from their homes to Brazil against their will and kept in slavery,

Capoeira began to take form among the community of slaves for self-defense. But it soon became a strong weapon in the life-or-death struggle against their oppressors. When the slave owners realized the power of Capoeira, they began to punish those who practiced it. Capoeiristas learned to camouflage the forbidden fights with singing, clapping, and dancing as though it were simply entertainment.

　　卡波耶拉武術是在大約五百年前，由巴西的非洲奴隸創造出來的。一般認爲，這項武術和非洲的部落戰爭有關，在這些戰鬥中，人們會近身肉搏，不使用武器，爲的是要獲得新娘或想要的女人。在十六世紀，當非洲人被迫從家鄉被帶到巴西，並且被當作奴隸時，卡波耶拉武術漸漸在奴隸社群中，爲了自我防衛而成形。但很快地，它在對抗壓迫者的生死存亡搏鬥中，變成一項強而有力的武器。當奴隸的擁有者了解到卡波耶拉武術的威力後，開始處罰所有練習這項武術的人。卡波耶拉武術的習武者會學習用歌唱、拍手，以及舞蹈，來僞裝被禁止的格鬥，讓它看起來好像只是娛樂一樣。

nearly〔'nırlı〕adv. 大約　　Brazil〔brə'zıl〕n. 巴西
African〔'æfrıkən〕adj. 非洲的　　slave〔slev〕n. 奴隸
It is believed that… 一般認爲…　　*be connected with* 和…有關
tribal〔'traıbl̩〕adj. 部落的　　fighting〔'faıtıŋ〕n. 戰爭
fight body to body 近身肉搏　　weapon〔'wεpən〕n. 武器
in order to 爲了　　acquire〔ə'kwaır〕v. 獲得
bride〔braıd〕n. 新娘　　desired〔dı'zaırd〕adj. 想得到的
century〔'sεntʃərı〕n. 世紀　　against〔ə'gεnst〕prep. 違反
will〔wıl〕n. 意願　　slavery〔'slevərı〕n. 奴隸身份
be kept in slavery 被當作奴隸蓄養　　*take form* 成形
among〔ə'mʌŋ〕prep. 在…之中　　community〔kə'mjunətı〕n. 社群；社區
self-defense〔'sεlf͵dı'fεns〕n. 自我防衛
life-or-death adj. 生死存亡的；非生即死的　　struggle〔'strʌgl̩〕n. 搏鬥
oppressor〔ə'prεsə〕n. 壓迫者　　realize〔'rıəl͵aız〕v. 了解
power〔'pauə〕n. 力量　　punish〔'pʌnıʃ〕v. 處罰
capoeirista〔͵kapəı'rıstə〕n. 從事卡波耶拉武術者（= *a practitioner*
　of capoeira）　　camouflage〔'kæmə͵flɑʒ〕v. 僞裝；掩飾
forbidden〔fə'bıdn̩〕adj. 被禁止的　　clapping〔'klæpıŋ〕n. 拍手
as though 就好像　　simply〔'sımplı〕adv. 僅僅是
entertainment〔͵εntə'tenmənt〕n. 娛樂

At first, Capoeira was considered illegal in Brazil. However, a man known as Mestre Bimba devoted a great deal of time and effort to convincing the Brazilian authorities that Capoeira has great cultural value and should become an official fighting style. He succeeded in his endeavor and transformed the martial art into Brazil's national sport. He and Mestre Pastinha were the first to open schools, and the Capoeira tree grew, spreading its branches across the world. Nowadays, it is performed in movies and music clips. Capoeira is also believed to have influenced several dancing styles like breaking and hip-hop.

　　起初，卡波耶拉武術在巴西被認爲是非法的。然而，一位名叫賓巴大師的人，奉獻了大量的時間和努力，說服巴西官方卡波耶拉武術有極大的文化價值，應該成爲一種官方的武術類型。他的努力成功了，而且將這項武術轉變成巴西的全國性的運動。他和巴斯奇亞大師首先創立了學校，接著卡波耶拉武術的樹成長苗壯，在全世界開枝散葉。如今，它在電影和音樂短片中被演出，同時它也被認爲影響了好幾種舞蹈的風格，像是地板霹靂舞和嘻哈舞蹈。

> ***at first*** 起初　　illegal〔ɪˈligḷ〕*adj.* 非法的　　***be known as*** 被稱爲
> ***Mestre Bimba*** 賓巴大師【卡波耶拉武術的著名代表人物。他建立了一系列
> 　　系統化的卡波耶拉武術教育方式，對於推廣與延續卡波耶拉武術有莫大的貢
> 　　獻，被譽爲現代卡波耶拉武術之父】　　devote〔dɪˈvot〕*v.* 奉獻
> ***a great deal of*** 大量的　　effort〔ˈɛfət〕*n.* 努力
> convince〔kənˈvɪns〕*v.* 說服；使確信
> Brazilian〔brəˈzɪljən〕*adj.* 巴西的
> authorities〔əˈθɔrətɪz〕*n. pl.* 當局　　cultural〔ˈkʌltʃərəl〕*adj.* 文化的
> value〔ˈvælju〕*n.* 價值　　official〔əˈfɪʃəl〕*adj.* 官方的；正式的
> style〔staɪl〕*n.* 樣式；類型　　endavor〔ɪnˈdɛvə〕*n.* 努力
> ***transform A into B*** 把A轉變成B　　national〔ˈnæʃənḷ〕*adj.* 全國性的
> ***Mestre Pastinha*** 巴斯奇亞大師　　spread〔sprɛd〕*v.* 伸展；張開
> branch〔bræntʃ〕*n.* 樹枝　　nowadays〔ˈnaʊəˌdez〕*adv.* 現在
> perform〔pəˈfɔrm〕*v.* 表演　　clip〔klɪp〕*n.* 短片
> influence〔ˈɪnfluəns〕*v.* 影響
> breaking〔ˈbrekɪŋ〕*n.* 地板霹靂舞【街舞的一種，也是第一種嘻哈舞種。
> 　　1970年代起源於美國紐約市的布朗克斯區】
> hip-hop〔ˌhɪpˈhap〕*n.* 嘻哈【是1970年代源自紐約市南布朗克斯與哈林區的
> 　　非洲裔及拉丁裔青年之間的一種邊緣性次文化，繼而發展壯大成爲新興藝術
> 　　型態，並席捲全球】

45.(**A**) 本文主要是關於什麼？
　　(A) 卡波耶拉武術的歷史。　　(B) 卡波耶拉武術的價值。
　　(C) 卡波耶拉武術的貢獻。　　(D) 卡波耶拉武術的技術。
　　contribution〔ˌkɑntrəˈbjuʃən〕*n.* 貢獻

46. (**C**) 以下何者不可能在卡波耶拉武術的表演中被找到？
    (A) 擊鼓歌唱。 　　　　　　　　(B) 掃腿。
    (C) <u>用劍刺。</u> 　　　　　　　　(D) 以手搏擊。

    sweep〔swip〕*v.* 掠過；掃過　　　stab〔stæb〕*v.* 刺
    sword〔sord〕*n.* 劍　　　　　　strike〔straɪk〕*v.* 敲打；襲擊

47. (**B**) 作者對於卡波耶拉武術作為一項運動的態度為何？
    (A) 佩服的。 　　　　　　　　　(B) <u>客觀的。</u>
    (C) 懷疑的。 　　　　　　　　　(D) 嚴厲的。

    attitude〔'ætə,tud〕*n.* 態度　　　admiring〔əd'maɪrɪŋ〕*adj.* 佩服的
    objective〔əb'dʒɛktɪv〕*adj.* 客觀的
    doubtful〔'dautfəl〕*adj.* 懷疑的　　harsh〔harʃ〕*adj.* 嚴厲的

48. (**D**) 根據本文，以下關於卡波耶拉武術的敘述，何者為真？
    (A) 它受到現代的舞蹈風格很大的影響。
    (B) 它最初被創造出來時，是一種舞蹈和儀式。
    (C) 它主要是被用來保護新娘或是想要的女人。
    (D) <u>透過賓巴大師的努力，它在巴西被官方認可。</u>

    modern〔'madən〕*adj.* 現代的　　inilially〔ɪ'nɪʃəlɪ〕*adv.* 起初
    mainly〔'menlɪ〕*adv.* 主要地
    perform〔pə'fɔrm〕*v.* 實行；做（ = *do* ）
    officially〔ə'fɪʃəlɪ〕*adv.* 官方地　　recognize〔'rɛkəg,naɪz〕*v.* 承認

第 49 至 52 題為題組

　　Winslow Homer (1836-1910) is regarded by many as the greatest American painter of the nineteenth century. Born and raised in Boston, he began his career at age eighteen in his hometown, working as an apprentice at a printing company. Skilled at drawing, he soon made a name for himself making illustrations for novels, sheet music, magazines, and children's books.

　　溫斯洛・荷馬（1836-1910），被許多人認為是十九世紀最偉大的美國畫家。出生並成長於波士頓，他十八歲時在家鄉展開他的職業生涯，在一間印刷公司工作擔任學徒。他精通畫畫，很快就用繪製小說、樂譜、雜誌，和童書上的插圖，替自己博得名聲。

　　　　Winslow Homer〔'wɪnslo'homə〕*n.* 溫斯洛・荷馬【美國畫家】
　　　　regard〔rɪ'gɑrd〕*v.* 認為　　　great〔gret〕*adj.* 偉大的
　　　　painter〔'pentə〕*n.* 畫家　　　born〔bɔrn〕*adj.* 出生的
　　　　raised〔rezd〕*adj.* 成長的

Boston〔'bɔstn̩〕*n.* 波士頓【美國東岸的城市】
career〔kə'rɪr〕*n.* 職業生涯　　hometown〔'hom,taun〕*n.* 家鄉
work as 擔任　　apprentice〔ə'prɛntɪs〕*n.* 學徒
printing〔'prɪntɪŋ〕*n.* 印刷
skilled〔skɪld〕*adj.* 熟練的；精於…的 < at >
drawing〔'drɔɪŋ〕*n.* 繪畫　　illustration〔,ɪləs'treʃən〕*n.* 插圖
novel〔'nɑvl̩〕*n.* 小說　　sheet〔ʃit〕*n.*（紙）一張
sheet music（單張）樂譜　　magazine〔,mægə'zin〕*n.* 雜誌

He then moved to New York City, where he worked as a freelance
illustrator with Harper's Weekly, a popular magazine of the time, and began
painting. Homer was assigned to cover the inauguration of President Lincoln
and, later, the Civil War. His pictures of the Union troops won international
recognition. Homer moved to England and, after a two-year stay, returned to
America. He settled permanently in Maine in 1883.

他接著搬到紐約市，在當時深受好評的哈潑週刊擔任自由插畫家，然後開始
畫畫。荷馬被指派去報導林肯總統的就職典禮，以及後來的南北戰爭。他的北方
軍圖畫贏得國際認可。荷馬搬到英格蘭，待了兩年之後，回到美國。他於1883年
永久定居在緬因州。

move〔muv〕*v.* 搬家　　***New York Ctiy*** 紐約市【位於美國東岸】
freelance〔'fri'læns〕*n.* 自由職業者　　illustrator〔'ɪləs,tretɚ〕*n.* 插畫家
weekly〔'wiklɪ〕*n.* 週刊　　popular〔'pɑpjəlɚ〕*adj.* 受歡迎的；深受好評的
assign〔ə'saɪn〕*v.* 指派　　cover〔'kʌvɚ〕*v.* 報導
inauguration〔ɪn,ɔgjə'reʃən〕*n.* 就職典禮
president〔'prɛzədənt〕*n.* 總統　　civil〔'sɪvl̩〕*adj.* 國內的
Civil War（美國）南北戰爭
the Union（美國南北戰爭時支持聯邦政府的）北部各州
troop〔trup〕*n.* 部隊　　***the Union troops*** 北方軍
win〔wɪn〕*v.* 贏得　　international〔,ɪntɚ'næʃənl̩〕*adj.* 國際上的
recognition〔,rɛkəg'nɪʃən〕*n.* 認可　　England〔'ɪŋglənd〕*n.* 英格蘭
stay〔ste〕*n.* 停留　　return〔rɪ'tɝn〕*v.* 返回
settle〔'sɛtl̩〕*v.* 定居　　Maine〔men〕*n.* 緬因州【位於美國東北部】

From the late 1850s until his death in 1910, Winslow Homer produced a
body of work distinguished by its thoughtful expression and its independence
from artistic conventions. A man of multiple talents, Homer excelled equally
in the arts of illustration, oil painting, and watercolor. Many of his
works—depictions of children at play and in school, farm girls attending to

their work, hunters and their prey—have become classic images of nineteenth-century American life. **Others** speak to more universal themes such as the primal relationship of humans to nature.

從1850年代後期到他於1910年逝世，溫斯洛‧荷馬創作了大量的作品，以其深思熟慮的表達手法和不落俗套的畫法而聞名。荷馬是一位有多項才能的人，他同樣擅長插畫、油畫和水彩畫等藝術。他的許多作品——描繪在玩耍和在學校的孩童、專注工作的農場女孩、獵人和他們的獵物——已經變成十九世紀美國生活的經典圖像。其他作品提到更多普遍的主題，像是人對自然的最初關係。

> produce〔prəˋdjus〕v. 製造；畫（畫）　　***a body of*** 很多的
> work〔wɝk〕n. 作品　　distinguish〔dɪˋstɪŋgwɪʃ〕v. 出名
> thoughtful〔ˋθɔtfəl〕adj. 體貼的；表達思想的
> expression〔ɪkˋsprɛʃən〕n. 表達　　independence〔͵ɪndɪˋpɛndəns〕n. 獨立
> ***independence from*** 脫離…而獨立　　artistic〔ɑrˋtɪstɪk〕adj. 藝術的
> convention〔kənˋvɛnʃən〕n.（藝術上的）傳統手法
> multiple〔ˋmʌltəpḷ〕adj. 多重的　　talent〔ˋtælənt〕n. 才能
> excel〔ɪkˋsɛl〕v. 擅長　　equally〔ˋikwəlɪ〕adv. 同樣地
> ***oil painting*** 油畫　　watercolor〔ˋwɔtɚ͵kʌlɚ〕n. 水彩
> depiction〔dɪˋpɪkʃən〕n. 描畫　　***at play*** 在玩　　***attend to*** 專心於
> hunter〔ˋhʌntɚ〕n. 獵人　　prey〔pre〕n. 獵物
> classic〔ˋklæsɪk〕adj. 經典的　　image〔ˋɪmɪdʒ〕n. 形象；畫像
> ***speak to*** 提及　　universal〔͵junəˋvɝsḷ〕adj. 普遍的
> theme〔θim〕n. 主題　　primal〔ˋpraɪmḷ〕adj. 最初的
> nature〔ˋnetʃɚ〕n. 自然

This two-week exhibition highlights a wide and representative range of Homer's art. It shows his extraordinary career from the battlefields, farmland, and coastal villages of America, to the North Sea fishing village of Cullercoats, the rocky coast of Maine, the Adirondacks, and the Caribbean. The exhibition offers viewers an opportunity to experience and appreciate the breadth of his remarkable artistic achievement.

這場為期兩週的展覽，強調荷馬很多各種具有代表性的藝術作品。這場展覽表現出他從戰場、農地，和美國沿岸村莊，到克勒庫茲的北海漁村、緬因州的岩岸、阿第倫達克山脈，和加勒比海的非凡生涯。展覽提供觀展者一個機會，能體驗和欣賞他廣闊、卓越的藝術成就。

> exhibition〔͵ɛksəˋbɪʃən〕n. 展覽　　highlight〔ˋhaɪ͵laɪt〕v. 強調
> wide〔waɪd〕adj. 廣泛的
> representative〔͵rɛprɪˋzɛntətɪv〕adj. 代表性的

range〔rendʒ〕 n.（變動的）範圍；幅度
a wide range of 很多各式各樣的　　show〔ʃo〕 v. 表現；展示
extraordinary〔ɪk'stɔrdn̩,ɛrɪ〕 adj. 不尋常的
battlefield〔'bætl̩,fild〕 n. 戰場　　farmland〔'farm,lænd〕 n. 農地
coastal〔'kostl̩〕 adj. 海岸的　　village〔'vɪlɪdʒ〕 n. 村莊
the North Sea 北海　　fishing〔'fɪʃɪŋ〕 n. 漁業
Cullercoats〔'kʌlɚ,kots〕 n. 克勒庫茲【位於英國東北部】
rocky〔'rakɪ〕 adj. 多岩石的　　coast〔kost〕 n. 海岸
Adirondack〔,ædɪ'randæks〕 n. pl. 阿第倫達克山脈【位於美國東北部】
Caribbean〔,kærə'biən〕 adj. 加勒比海的　　offer〔'ɔfɚ〕 v. 提供
viewer〔'vjuɚ〕 n. 參觀者；觀眾　　opportunity〔,apɚ'tjunətɪ〕 n. 機會
experience〔ɪk'spɪrɪəns〕 v. 體驗　　appreciate〔ə'priʃɪ,et〕 v. 欣賞
breadth〔brɛdθ〕 n. 寬（闊）　　remarkable〔rɪ'markəbl̩〕 adj. 卓越的
achievement〔ə'tʃivmənt〕 n. 成就

49.（ **B** ）本文最有可能出現在哪裡？
(A) 當代藝術為特色的廣告。　　(B) 美術館網站。
(C) 美籍英裔藝術家的小冊子。　　(D) 探討印刷藝術的百科全書。

ad〔æd〕 n. 廣告（= *advertisement*）　　feature〔'fitʃɚ〕 v. 以…為特色
contemporary〔kən'tɛmpə,rɛrɪ〕 adj. 當代的
gallery〔'gælərɪ〕 n. 美術館　　booklet〔'bʊklɪt〕 n. 小冊子
on〔an〕 prep. 關於；論…　　encyclopedia〔ɪn,saɪklə'pidɪə〕 n. 百科全書

50.（ **D** ）關於荷馬的職業生涯，下列何者為真？
(A) 他用生動的英格蘭圖畫獲得國際名聲。
(B) 他被認為是美國藝術史上最偉大的插畫家。
(C) 他的水彩畫比他的插圖和油畫更有名。
(D) 他首先在他的家鄉波士頓以插畫家的身分建立名聲。

achieve〔ə'tʃiv〕 v.（經努力而）獲得
vivid〔'vɪvɪd〕 adj. 生動的；栩栩如生的
be better known for 以…而更有名
establish〔ə'stæblɪʃ〕 v. 建立　　reputation〔,rɛpjə'teʃən〕 n. 名聲

51.（ **A** ）根據本文，以下何者最能說明荷馬藝術作品的特色？
(A) 他的圖畫生動地描繪十九世紀美國人的生活。
(B) 他的藝術作品深切表達受戰爭所害的人們的心聲。
(C) 他的風格確實遵循了他那個時代的藝術傳統。
(D) 他的繪畫經常反映他想逃離社會的渴望。

characterize〔ˈkærɪktəˌraɪz〕v. 敘述…的特性
portray〔porˈtre〕v. 描繪　　express〔ɪkˈsprɛs〕v. 表達
voice〔vɔɪs〕n. 聲音　***suffer from*** 受…所苦　***conform to*** 遵守
tradition〔trəˈdɪʃən〕n. 傳統　constantly〔ˈkɑnstəntlɪ〕adv. 經常
reflect〔rɪˈflɛkt〕v. 反映　　escape〔əˈskep〕v. 逃走

52. (**C**) 在第三段的 "Others" 指的是什麼？
(A) 其他的藝術家。　　　　(B) 其他的主題。
(C) <u>其他的作品。</u>　　　　(D) 其他的圖像。

<u>第 53 至 56 題為題組</u>

　　Tea, the most typical English drink, became established in Britain because of the influence of a foreign princess, Catherine of Braganza, the queen of Charles II. A lover of tea since her childhood in Portugal, she brought tea-drinking to the English royal court and set a trend for the beverage in the seventeenth century.

　　茶是英國最具代表性的飲品，在英國變得普及，是因為受到一位異國公主的影響，她是布拉干薩王朝的凱薩琳，查理二世的皇后。她從小在葡萄牙的時候就喜愛喝茶，她把喝茶的習慣帶到英國皇室，並在十七世紀創下飲茶的潮流。

typical〔ˈtɪpɪkl̩〕adj. 典型的；有代表性的　　drink〔drɪŋk〕n. 飲料
established〔əˈstæblɪʃt〕adj. 確立的；被接受的；普遍的
Britain〔ˈbrɪtn̩〕n. 英國　　influence〔ˈɪnfluəns〕n. 影響
foreign〔ˈfɔrɪn〕adj. 外國的　　princess〔ˈprɪnsɪs〕n. 公主
Braganza〔brəˈgænzə〕n. 布拉干薩王朝【1640–1910 年間統治葡萄牙王國
　　的葡萄牙最後的王朝，包括兩位巴西帝國的皇帝】
Charles II 查理二世【1630–1685 年蘇格蘭及英格蘭、愛爾蘭國王】
Portugal〔ˈportʃəgl̩〕n. 葡萄牙　　royal〔ˈrɔɪəl〕adj. 王室的；皇家的
court〔kɔrt〕n. 宮廷　***royal court*** 皇室　trend〔trɛnd〕n. 趨勢；流行
set a trend 創造流行　　beverage〔ˈbɛvərɪdʒ〕n. 飲料

　　The fashion soon spread beyond the circle of the nobility to the middle classes, and tea became a popular drink at the London coffee houses where people met to do business and discuss events of the day. Many employers served a cup of tea to their workers in the middle of the morning, thus inventing **a lasting British institution**, the "tea break." However, drinking tea in social settings outside the workplace was beyond the means of the majority of British people. It came with a high price tag and tea was taxed as well.

　　這樣的流行很快就從貴族圈傳到了中產階級，而茶也變成倫敦的咖啡廳熱門的飲品，人們都在這裡見面做生意和討論當天發生的事。很多雇主會在早晨期間提供一杯茶給員工，因此創造了一個**英國長久以來的習俗**——「茶點時間」。然而，喝茶在工作場合以外的社交場所，並不是大多數英國人可以負擔得起的。茶的價格很高，而且要課稅。

fashion〔ˈfæʃən〕n. 時尚；流行　　spread〔sprɛd〕v. 擴散；散播
circle〔ˈsɝkl̩〕n. 圈；範圍　　nobility〔noˈbɪlətɪ〕n. 貴族
middle class 中產階級　　***coffee house*** 咖啡廳
do business 做生意　　event〔ɪˈvɛnt〕n. 事情；事件
employer〔ɪmˈplɔɪɚ〕n. 雇主；老闆　　serve〔sɝv〕v. 供應
in the middle of 在…的中間　　thus〔ðʌs〕adv. 因此
invent〔ɪnˈvɛnt〕v. 發明　　lasting〔ˈlæstɪŋ〕adj. 持久的
institution〔ˌɪnstəˈtjuʃən〕n. 設立；慣例　　***tea break*** 茶歇；茶點時間
social〔ˈsoʃəl〕adj. 社會的；社交的　　setting〔ˈsɛtɪŋ〕n. 環境；地點
outside〔ˈaʊtˈsaɪd〕prep. 在…之外　　workplace〔ˈwɝkˌples〕n. 工作場所
means〔minz〕n. pl. 收入；財富　　majority〔məˈdʒɔrətɪ〕n. 大多數
come with 附帶；伴隨　　tag〔tæg〕n. 標籤
price tag 價格　　tax〔tæks〕v. 對…課稅　　***as well*** 也（= *too*）

Around 1800, the seventh Duchess of Bedford, Anne Maria, began the popular practice of "afternoon tea," a ceremony taking place at about four o'clock. Until then, people did not usually eat or drink anything between lunch and dinner. At approximately the same time, the Earl of Sandwich popularized a new way of eating bread—in thin slices, with something (e.g., jam or cucumbers) between them. Before long, a small meal at the end of the afternoon, involving tea and sandwiches, had become part of the British way of life.

　　大約在1800年，貝德福第七任的公爵夫人，安・瑪麗亞，開創了「下午茶」這個非常受歡迎的習俗，這儀式大約在下午四點舉行。在那之前，人們通常不會在午餐和晚餐之間吃或喝任何東西。大約在同一個時間，三明治伯爵也使一項吃麵包的新方式變得普及——將麵包切成薄片，中間夾東西（例如果醬或黃瓜）。不久，在下午結束的時候，吃個小餐點，包含茶和三明治，已經變成英國生活方式的一部分。

around〔əˈraʊnd〕prep. 大約　　duchess〔ˈdʌtʃɪs〕n. 公爵夫人
Bedford〔ˈbɛdfəd〕n. 貝德福【位於東英格蘭】
Anne Maria〔ˈænməˈraɪə〕n. 安・瑪麗亞

practice〔'præktɪs〕*n.* 風俗；習慣   ***afternoon tea*** 下午茶
ceremony〔'sɛrə,monɪ〕*n.* 儀式；典禮   ***take place*** 舉行；發生
until then 在那之前   approximately〔ə'prɑksəmɪtlɪ〕*adv.* 大約
at the same time 同時   earl〔ɝl〕*n.* 伯爵
Sandwich〔'sændwɪtʃ〕*n.* 三明治【位於英格蘭東南方，或翻譯成「桑威治」】
popularize〔'pɑpjələ,raɪz〕*v.* 使普及；推廣   slice〔slaɪs〕*n.* 片
e.g. 例如（= *exempli gratia*）   jam〔dʒæm〕*n.* 果醬
cucumber〔'kjukʌmbɚ〕*n.* 黃瓜   ***before long*** 不久
meal〔mil〕*n.* 一餐   involve〔ɪn'vɑlv〕*v.* 包含

As tea became much cheaper during the nineteenth century, its popularity spread right through all corners of the British society. Thus, tea became Britain's favorite drink. In working-class households, it was served with the main meal of the day, eaten when workers returned home after a day's labor. This meal has become known as "high tea."

隨著茶在十九世紀變得更便宜，英國社會的各個角落都流行喝茶。因此，茶變成英國最喜愛的飲品。在勞工階級的家庭，茶是伴隨著當天的主餐一起上的，在勞工工作一整天後，回家的時候吃的。這一餐就變成所謂的「傍晚茶」。

popularity〔,pɑpjə'lærətɪ〕*n.* 流行   right〔raɪt〕*adv.* 完全
through〔θru〕*prep.* 遍及   corners〔'kɔrnɚz〕*n. pl.* 角落；地方；各處
working-class *adj.* 勞工階級的   household〔'haʊs,hold〕*n.* 家庭
main〔men〕*adj.* 主要的   ***main meal*** 主餐
labor〔'lebɚ〕*n.* 勞動   ***be known as*** 被稱為   ***high tea*** 傍晚茶

Today, tea can be drunk at any time of the day, and accounts for over two-fifths of all beverages consumed in Britain—with the exception of water.

現在，茶可以在一天的任何時候喝，而且佔了英國除了水以外，所有飲料的五分之二強。

account for 佔…   consume〔kən'sum〕*v.* 吃；喝
exception〔ɪk'sɛpʃən〕*n.* 例外
with the exception of 除了…之外（= *except*）

53. (**C**) 本文的段落是如何安排的？
　　(A) 藉由因果關係。　　　　　(B) 以重要性排列。
　　(C) 以時間順序。　　　　　　(D) 比較跟對比。

organize〔'ɔrgən,aɪz〕*v.* 組織；安排   ***cause and effect*** 因果關係

in the order of 以…的順序　　sequence〔'sikwəns〕*n.* 順序
comparison〔kəm'pærəsn〕*n.* 比較；對照
contrast〔'kɑntræst〕*n.* 對照；對比

54. (**B**) 第一段的片語 "**a lasting British institution**" 是什麼意思？
　　(A) 最受歡迎的英國機構。　　　　(B) <u>在英國存在已久的傳統。</u>
　　(C) 倫敦最後的一家茶葉公司。　　(D) 一間歷史悠久的英國公司。

phrase〔frez〕*n.* 片語
organization〔,ɔrgənə'zeʃən〕*n.* 組織；機構
long-standing *adj.* 存在已久的
the UK 英國（ = *the United Kingdom* ）
well-established *adj.* 歷史悠久的；久負盛名的

55. (**D**) 根據本文，爲何在十七世紀，茶「不」是日常生活普遍的飲品？
　　(A) 茶只在倫敦的咖啡廳有供應。
　　(B) 茶和含酒精的飲料一樣，都要課稅。
　　(C) 在商業場合以外，茶是被禁止的。
　　(D) <u>對大多數的人來說，茶太貴了。</u>

common〔'kɑmən〕*adj.* 常見的；普遍的
everyday life 日常生活　　alcoholic〔,ælkə'hɔlɪk〕*adj.* 含酒精的

56. (**A**) 根據本文，下列何者爲眞？
　　(A) <u>在十九世紀，傍晚茶比下午茶供應的時間晚。</u>
　　(B) 英國人在十八世紀時，一天有兩次的茶點時間。
　　(C) 凱薩琳公主在拜訪葡萄牙後把茶帶到英國。
　　(D) 三明治伯爵開創了下午茶的傳統。

第貳部分：非選擇題

一、中譯英

1. 玉山（ Jade Mountain ）在冬天常常覆蓋著厚厚的積雪，使整個山頂閃耀如玉。

Jade Mountain is often covered $\begin{Bmatrix} \text{by} \\ \text{with} \end{Bmatrix}$ thick snow $\begin{Bmatrix} \text{in winter} \\ \text{in the winter} \end{Bmatrix}$,

making its whole $\begin{Bmatrix} \text{peak} \\ \text{top} \end{Bmatrix}$ sparkle like jade.

2. 征服玉山一直是國內外登山者最困難的挑戰之一。

Conquering Jade Mountain has been one of the $\left\{\begin{array}{l}\text{greatest} \\ \text{toughest} \\ \text{most difficult}\end{array}\right\}$

challenges for climbers $\left\{\begin{array}{l}\text{at home} \\ \text{domestically}\end{array}\right\}$ and $\left\{\begin{array}{l}\text{abroad.} \\ \text{overseas.}\end{array}\right\}$

二、英文作文：

A Trip to the Amusement Park

The Martin family had been planning their trip to the amusement park for a long time. They were very excited as they packed up their van to make the long drive. *However*, once they hit the road, they were greeted by heavy traffic on the highway. The drive took three times longer than it should have. *To make matters worse*, arriving at the amusement park, they found the place was swarming with crowds of people waiting to enter. And more people were arriving *by the minute!*

Mr. Martin was furious for a couple of reasons, *but* mainly that they hadn't anticipated the crowds and the bad traffic, and left earlier in the morning. *After all*, it was a holiday weekend. *On the other hand*, the Martin kids were simply too excited about the trip to turn back now. Now, the only thing to do would be wait in line with everybody else.

Fortunately, the park manager recognized the situation and opened both gates to speed up the entrance process. *In the end*, the Martins gained access to the park and had a wonderful time.

去遊樂園玩

　　長久以來，馬丁一家人一直計畫要去遊樂園玩。當他們將行李打包好裝上廂型車，準備要長途開車時，覺得非常興奮。不過，當他們一上路，就遇到公路上大量的車潮。這趟車程所花的時間是平常的三倍。更糟的是，到達遊樂園時，他們發現那裡擠滿了人潮，等著要入園。而且每時每刻都湧入更多的人！

　　馬丁先生非常憤怒，原因有好幾個，不過最主要的是，他們沒預料到會有大批人潮和擁擠的交通而早一點出門。畢竟，這是個連假週末。另一方面，馬丁家的小孩對這趟行程感到非常興奮，不可能現在回去。現在唯一能做的，就是跟其他人一樣排隊。幸好，遊樂園的經理認清了這個情況，所以把兩個大門都打開，加快入場的過程。最後，馬丁一家人進入了樂園，並且玩得很愉快。

amusement〔ə'mjuzmənt〕*n.* 娛樂　　***amusement park*** 遊樂園
pack up 打包；收拾　　van〔væn〕*n.* 廂型車
drive〔draɪv〕*n.* 開車出遊；車程　　***hit the road*** 上路；出發
greet〔grit〕*v.* 迎接　　***be greeted by*** 遭遇
heavy traffic 擁擠的交通；塞車
highway〔'haɪ,we〕*n.* 公路　　time〔taɪm〕*n.* 倍
to make matters worse 更糟的是（= *what's worse*）
swarm〔swɔrm〕*v.* 充滿著＜*with*＞　　crowd〔kraʊd〕*n.* 人群；群眾
by the minute 每時每刻；以每分鐘計算
furious〔'fjʊrɪəs〕*adj.* 憤怒的　　***a couple of*** 幾個（= *several*）
anticipate〔æn'tɪsə,pet〕*v.* 預料　　***after all*** 畢竟
holiday weekend 連假週末　　***on the other hand*** 另一方面
simply〔'sɪmplɪ〕*adv.* 真正地；確實　　***turn back*** 往回走
wait in line 排隊　　fortunately〔'fɔrtʃənɪtlɪ〕*adv.* 幸運地
recognize〔'rɛkəg,naɪz〕*v.* 認出；認清
gate〔get〕*n.* 大門；出入口　　***speed up*** 加速
entrance〔'ɛntrəns〕*n.* 入場　　process〔'prɑsɛs〕*n.* 過程
in the end 最後　　gain〔gen〕*v.* 得到
access〔'æksɛs〕*n.* 進入　　***gain access to*** 進入
have a wonderful time 玩得很愉快（= *have fun* = *have a good time*）

106 年學測英文科試題出題來源

題　號	出　　　　　　　　　　　處
一、詞彙 第 1～15 題	所有各題對錯答案的選項，均出自大考中心編製的「高中常用 7000 字」。
二、綜合測驗 第 16～20 題	改寫自 Stye: A Painful Bump on the Eyelid（針眼：眼皮上的腫痛），描述針眼的原因和症狀，以及如何治療。
第 21～25 題	改寫自 Shoe That Grows gives poor kids footwear that fits for years（伴隨貧窮孩童長大的鞋，可穿好幾年），描寫在非洲地區，隨著孩子的成長，鞋子不敷使用，而新設計的鞋，可以伸縮長度和寬度，可以穿至少五年。
第 26～30 題 【WHO】	改寫自 Rainmakers: Why Bad Weather Means Good Productivity（祈雨者：為何壞天氣代表好的生產力），描述雖然好天氣可以帶來正面思考，雨天帶來焦慮和疲憊，但是事實上，根據實驗結果，壞天氣反而促使工人專注在工作，不去想好天氣的活動。。
三、文意選填 第 31～40 題	改寫自 Onions in Ancient Egypt（古埃及的洋蔥），描寫洋蔥在古埃及如何受到重視，除了作為食物和藥品，它的外觀被看成永生的象徵，因此具有神奇宗教力量。
四、閱讀測驗 第 41～44 題 【CBSNEWS】	改寫自 "Dognition" asks, how smart is your dog?（犬認知，問你家狗狗有多聰明？），描述一個叫「犬認知」的網站，可以用美金 60 元來測試狗的智商和分類。
第 45～48 題	改寫自 Let's explain what Capoeira is!（讓我們來解釋什麼是卡波耶拉），敘述卡波耶拉作為一項武術，其像舞蹈的特色，以及起源，曾經是非法的，而現在是巴西的國家運動。
第 49～52 題	改寫自 Winslow Homer (1836–1910)（溫斯洛‧霍默），描述美國十九世紀的畫家霍默，其身平和功績，擅長插畫、油畫，以及水彩畫。
第 53～56 題	改寫自 A Social History of the Nation's Favourite Drink（該國最受歡迎飲料的社會歷史），描述茶如何被凱薩琳公主普及於英國，成為國民飲品，以及下午茶演變的歷史。

【106 年學測】綜合測驗：16-20 出題來源

—— https://www.verywell.com/what-is-an-eye-stye-symptoms-treatment-3422082

Stye
A Painful Bump on the Eyelid

You begin to notice a bit of pain or heaviness in your eyelid each time you blink. You look into the mirror and you barely see a tiny red spot on the base of your lower lashes. If you've ever had a stye, you probably know these symptoms as the beginning of a miserable eye stye.

Although the appearance of a stye can be unsightly at times, it is usually harmless. A stye is a small bump that sometimes appears on the outside or inside of the eyelid.

A stye is also referred to as a hordeolum. A stye develops from an eyelash follicle or an eyelid oil gland that becomes clogged from excess oil, debris or bacteria. Styes can be a complication of blepharitis but also seem to be brought on by stress.

Stye Symptoms

If you have a stye, you may be suffering from watery eyes, pain, tenderness, itching, or redness. Your eye may feel bruised and sensitive to light. You may notice your blinking rhythm, as each blink feels a little different than usual. You may also notice a reddish bump on your eyelid. If your stye is severe, you may develop an internal hordeolum. Pus will build up in the center of the stye, causing a yellowish spot that looks similar to a pimple. If the stye is painful, it will feel better once it ruptures and the pus drains.

⋮

【106 年學測】綜合測驗：21-25 出題來源

——http://newatlas.com/shoe-that-grows/37145/

Shoe That Grows gives poor kids footwear that fits for years

For children living in poverty, footwear is one of many problems. Almost as soon as children have received shoes to wear, they're likely to have grown out of them and have to make do with them being too small. The Shoe That Grows changes this. It allows children to adjust its size as their feet grow.

Shoes are hugely important for protecting our feet, especially in places where healthcare provision is limited. In bare feet, an innocuous cut or graze can easily become infected or pick up soil-transmitted diseases. Unfortunately, shoes are not always readily available for those living in poverty, let alone shoes that are the right size. Kenton Lee, founder of poverty charity Because International, saw this first-hand during a trip to Nairobi, Kenya, in 2007. Lee says he saw young children wearing shoes that were way too small for them, with their their toes poking out of the ends. The experience led to the development of The Shoe That Grows. The shoe has a flexible compressed rubber sole and adjustable leather straps that fit over the top of the foot and around the rear of the heel.

⋮

【106 年學測】綜合測驗：26-30 出題來源

——http://www.hbs.edu/faculty/Publication%20Files/13-005.pdf

Rainmakers: Why Bad Weather Means Good Productivity

People believe that weather conditions influence their everyday work life, but to date, little is known about how weather affects individual productivity. Most people believe that bad weather conditions reduce productivity. In this research, we predict and find just the opposite. Drawing on cognitive psychology research, we propose that bad weather increases individual productivity by eliminating potential cognitive distractions resulting from good weather. When the weather is bad, individuals may focus more on their work rather than thinking about activities they could engage in outside of work. We tested our hypotheses using both field and lab data. First, we use field data on employees' productivity from a mid-size bank in Japan, which we then match with daily weather data to investigate the effect of bad weather conditions (in terms of precipitation, visibility, and temperature) on productivity. Second, we use a laboratory experiment to examine the psychological mechanism explaining the relationship between bad weather and increased productivity. Our findings support our proposed model and suggest that worker productivity is higher on bad rather than good weather days. We discuss the implications of our findings for workers and managers.

⋮

【106 年學測】文意選填：31-40 出題來源

—http://classroom.synonym.com/onions-ancient-egypt-13802.html

Onions in Ancient Egypt

The widespread popularity of the onion is not limited to modern-day kitchens. There is evidence of onions being used for culinary and medicinal purposes all over the ancient world. No culture revered the onion quite as much as the ancient Egyptians. For them, the onion was not just food or medicine; it held deep spiritual power and purpose.

Evidence of Ancient Egyptian Onions

Onions are depicted in many paintings found inside pyramids and tombs that span the history of ancient Egypt. The paintings show onions being consumed at feasts, as funeral offerings, on altars and in the hands of priests. Various types of onions are shown, from young, green onions to large yellow ones, and both the leaves and the roots were used. Onions themselves do not leave a large archeological footprint, as they are small and leave little residue after decomposing. But traces of onions have been found in ancient Egyptian tombs.

Culinary Uses

Along with bread and fish, onions were a basic dietary staple for all ancient Egyptians, rich and poor alike. Kitchen gardens were common in most ancient Egyptian households, where vegetables, including onions, were grown year-round to sustain the family. Onions were a very easy vegetable to cultivate, and they had a long shelf life and were easily preserved, making them a food source that ancient Egyptians could always count on.

Medical Uses

Onions have antiseptic and antibacterial compounds that many ancient cultures discovered and made use of. The ancient Egyptians used onions for medicinal purposes, but they likely would have viewed the vegetable's curative power as magical, rather than medical. One unique use of the onion devised by the ancient Egyptians is in a test for pregnancy. A woman would insert an onion in her vagina, and if her breath smelled like onions the next day, it would indicate pregnancy. This test has not been replicated in modern times, so its accuracy is unknown.

Spiritual Significance

Ancient Egyptians worshiped onions as symbols of eternal life. The concentric layers of an onion reflected the eternity of existence. The dead were buried with onions and onion flowers on or around various parts of their bodies, and mummies have been found with onions adorning their pelvis, chest, ears, eyes and feet. King Ramses IV was found with onions in his eye sockets. Ancient Egyptians may have seen the healing properties of onions as helpful in the afterlife.

【106 年學測】閱讀測驗：41-44 出題來源

——http://www.cbsnews.com/news/dognition-asks-how-smart-is-your-dog/

"Dognition" asks, how smart is your dog?

Is your doggy a dummy? Probably not. Most dogs are adept at simple problem solving and recognizing commands. But if you want to put your pet to the test, a new company has you covered. Started by a professor at Duke University,Dognition is a web app that allows you to test your dog's cognitive skills and record the results.

Purchasing the app allows users to run their dogs through a series of what Dr. Brian Hare calls "fun, science-based games." The tests are playful ways to measure a dog's intellect on several fronts -- from empathy to memory to reasoning skills.

"We've had a revolution in our understanding of animal psychology," Dr. Hare told CBS News. He and his team have been using the tests offered by Dognition for years to analyze canine intelligence. "We wanted to give people the same opportunity to play these games with their dogs."

Just as humans have a wide array of intelligences, so too do dogs. Dr. Hare and his team hope to gather the data from Dognition and analyze why some dogs are, say, better communicators than others. It could also help to answer broader questions, such as whether intelligence varies with breeds of dogs.

Of course, even the smartest Fido is only so smart. Compared to chimpanzees or bonobos, who are genetically closer to humans, dogs have a hard time with most fields of intelligence. It's why, for example, dogs are stumped when their leash gets tangled in a tree. But dogs excel at understanding humans' intent to communicate.

For $60, dog owners are being offered "a set of games that help people look at how their dogs solve problems in each of these different ways of intelligence," according to Hare.

【106 年學測】閱讀測驗：45-48 出題來源

——http://www.capoeira-world.com/about-capoeira/what-is-capoeira/

Let's explain what Capoeira is!

Capoeira is a martial art that combines elements of fight, acrobatics, music, dance and rituals in a very elegant and magnetic way. Performed by two people, it is often called the "Capoeira game" and is played, not a fought. Capoeira is always played with a smile on one's face, symbolizing that the capoeiristas are not afraid of the danger that is coming.

The uniqueness of Capoeira will give your body physical strength, power and flexibility and your mind self-confidence, concentration, courage and creativity. I've heard many people say that Capoeira is one of the best things that happened in their life. However, the only way to truly understand the magnetism of Capoeira is to see it and try it yourself.

Capoeira History

Although there are few official history records, it is known that Capoeira was created nearly 500 years ago in Brazil by African slaves (mainly from Angola). Taken from their homes against their will and kept in slavery, they started inventing fighting techniques for self-defense. To hide their combats from their captors, the African slaves used their traditional music, singing and dancing. Thus, Capoeira continued its development and soon became not only for self-defense but for rebellion.

Capoeira Through the Years

At first, Capoeira was considered illegal in Brazil and anyone who played was arrested. However, a man known as Mestre Bimbadid not let Capoeira down. He put great efforts into convincing the Brazilian authorities that Capoeira has a great cultural value and should become an official fighting style. He succeeded in his endeavor and created the Capoeira Regional style. In 1932 he created the first Capoeira School – Academia-escola de Capoeira Regional at the Engenho de Brotas in Salvador-Bahia. Thus, Mestre Bimba made what was once considered illegal an official martial art.

In 1942 the first Capoeira Angola school – Centro Esportivo de Capoeira – was createdby Mestre Pastinha. At this time, Capoeira was still practiced by poor black Brazilians. A few years later, however, a few Capoeira Mestres began to teach Capoeira in the United States and Europe.

Capoeira Today

Nowadays, Capoeira is a well known and very popular martial art all over the world. It is often included in school and university programs. You will see it in movies, music clips, etc. It is also known that Capoeira has influenced several dancing styles like break and hip-hop.

Although, Capoeira has changed over the years, the two main Capoeira styles – Capoeira Angola and Capoeira Regional continue to be practiced in the today's Capoeira Schools.

【106 年學測】閱讀測驗：49-52 出題來源

——http://www.metmuseum.org/toah/hd/homr/hd_homr.htm

Winslow Homer (1836–1910)

Winslow Homer (1836–1910) is regarded by many as the greatest American painter of the nineteenth century. Born in Boston and raised in rural Cambridge, he began his career as a commercial printmaker, first in Boston and then in New York, where he settled in 1859. He briefly studied oil painting in the spring of 1861. In October of the same year, he was sent to the front in Virginia as an artist-correspondent for the new illustrated journal, *Harper's Weekly*. Homer's earliest Civil War paintings, dating from about 1863, are anecdotal, like his prints. As the war drew to a close, however, such canvases as *The Veteran in a New Field* (67.187.131) and *Prisoners from the Front* (22.207) reflect a more profound understanding of the war's impact and meaning.

For Homer, the late 1860s and the 1870s were a time of artistic experimentation and prolific and varied output. He resided in New York City, making his living chiefly by designing magazine illustrations and building his reputation as a painter, but he found his subjects in the increasingly popular seaside resorts in Massachusetts and New Jersey, and in the Adirondacks, rural New York State, and the White Mountains of New Hampshire. Late in 1866, motivated probably by the chance to see two of his Civil War paintings at the Exposition Universelle, Homer had begun a ten-month sojourn in Parisand the French countryside.

⋮

【106 年學測】閱讀測驗：53-56 出題來源

——https://www.tea.co.uk/a-social-history

A Social History of the Nation's Favourite Drink

The origins of tea in UK society

A cup of tea is a vital part of everyday life for the majority of people in modern Britain - in fact tea is so integral to our routine, that it is difficult to imagine life without it! But it was not always so; tea was once a luxury product that only the rich could afford, and at one time there was even a debate about whether it might be bad for the health. It was over the course of several hundred years that tea gained its place as our national drink, and only relatively recently that its health-giving properties have been recognised.

Tea first became established in Britain because of the influence of a foreign princess, Catherine of Braganza, the queen of Charles II. A lover of tea since her childhood in Portugal, she brought tea-drinking to the English royal court, and set a trend for the beverage among the aristocracy of England in the seventeenth century.

Tea at seventeenth century London Coffee Houses

The fashion soon spread beyond these elite circles to the middle classes, and it became a popular drink at the London coffee houses where wealthy men met to do business and discuss the events of the day. But the tea that was being drunk in those seventeenth century coffee houses would probably be considered undrinkable now. Between 1660 and 1689, tea sold in coffee houses was taxed in liquid form. The whole of the day's tea would be brewed in the morning, taxed by a visiting excise officer, and then kept in barrels and reheated as necessary throughout the rest of the day. So a visitor to the coffee house in the late afternoon would be drinking tea that had been made hours before in the early morning! The quality of the drink improved after 1689, when the system of taxation was altered so that tea was taxed by the leaf rather than by the liquid.

Tea for the wealthy and the advent of tea parties

Some coffee houses also sold tea in loose leaf form so that it could be brewed at home. This meant that it could be enjoyed by women, who did not frequent coffee houses. Since it was relatively expensive, tea-drinking in the home must have been largely confined to wealthier households, where women would gather for tea parties. Such a party would be a genteel social occasion, using delicate china pots and cups, silver tea kettles and elegantly carved tea jars and tea tables. All the equipment would be set up by the servants, and then the tea would be brewed by the hostess (aided by a servant on hand to bring hot water) and served by her to her guests in dainty cups. Both green and black teas were popular, and sugar was frequently added (though like tea, this was an expensive import); in the seventeenth century though, it was still unusual for milk to be added to the beverage. We can imagine then that while seventeenth century men were at the coffee houses drinking tea and exchanging gossip, their wives gathered at one another's homes to do exactly the same thing - just in a more refined atmosphere!

:

105 年大學入學學科能力測驗試題 英文考科

第壹部分：單選題（占 72 分）

一、詞彙題（占 15 分）

說明：第 1 題至第 15 題，每題有 4 個選項，其中只有一個是正確或最適當的選項，請畫記在答案卡之「選擇題答案區」。各題答對者，得 1 分；答錯、未作答或畫記多於一個選項者，該題以零分計算。

1. Posters of the local rock band were displayed in store windows to promote the sale of their _____ tickets.
   (A) journey　　(B) traffic　　(C) concert　　(D) record

2. Maria didn't want to deliver the bad news to David about his failing the job interview. She herself was quite _____ about it.
   (A) awful　　(B) drowsy　　(C) tragic　　(D) upset

3. The newcomer speaks with a strong Irish _____; he must be from Ireland.
   (A) accent　　(B) identity　　(C) gratitude　　(D) signature

4. Although Maggie has been physically _____ to her wheelchair since the car accident, she does not limit herself to indoor activities.
   (A) ceased　　(B) committed　　(C) confined　　(D) conveyed

5. All passengers riding in cars are required to fasten their seatbelts in order to reduce the risk of _____ in case of an accident.
   (A) injury　　(B) offense　　(C) sacrifice　　(D) victim

6. The principal of this school is a man of exceptional _____. He sets aside a part of his salary for a scholarship fund for children from needy families.
   (A) security　　(B) maturity　　(C) facility　　(D) generosity

7. The science teacher always _____ the use of the laboratory equipment before she lets her students use it on their own.
   (A) tolerates   (B) associates   (C) demonstrates   (D) exaggerates

8. Most of the area is covered by woods, where bird species are so _____ that it is a paradise for birdwatchers.
   (A) durable   (B) private   (C) realistic   (D) numerous

9. In most cases, the committee members can reach agreement quickly. _____, however, they differ greatly in opinion and have a hard time making decisions.
   (A) Occasionally   (B) Automatically
   (C) Enormously   (D) Innocently

10. Many people try to save a lot of money before _____, since having enough money would give them a sense of security for their future.
    (A) isolation   (B) promotion
    (C) retirement   (D) announcement

11. In winter, our skin tends to become dry and _____, a problem which is usually treated by applying lotions or creams.
    (A) alert   (B) itchy   (C) steady   (D) flexible

12. Benson married Julie soon after he had _____ her heart and gained her parents' approval.
    (A) conquered   (B) estimated   (C) guaranteed   (D) intensified

13. The recent flood completely _____ my parents' farm. The farmhouse and fruit trees were all gone and nothing was left.
    (A) ruined   (B) cracked   (C) hastened   (D) neglected

14. The results of this survey are not reliable because the people it questioned were not a typical or _____ sample of the entire population that was studied.
    (A) primitive   (B) spiritual   (C) representative   (D) informative

15. In line with the worldwide green movement, carmakers have been
    working hard to make their new models more ＿＿＿＿ friendly to
    reduce pollution.
    (A) liberally　(B) individually　(C) financially　(D) environmentally

二、綜合測驗（占 15 分）

說明： 第 16 題至第 30 題，每題一個空格，請依文意選出最適當的一個選項，
　　　　請畫記在答案卡之「選擇題答案區」。各題答對者，得 1 分；答錯、未
　　　　作答或畫記多於一個選項者，該題以零分計算。

第 16 至 20 題為題組

　　　Bill and Sam decided to kidnap the son of a banker to compensate
for their business loss. They kidnapped the boy and hid him in a cave.
They asked for a ransom of $2,000 to return the boy.　＿＿16＿＿, their
plan quickly got out of control. Their young captive ＿＿17＿＿ to be a
mischievous boy. He viewed the kidnapping as a wonderful camping trip.
He demanded that his kidnappers play tiring games with him, such as
riding Bill as a horse for nine miles. Bill and Sam were soon desperate
and decided to ＿＿18＿＿ the little terror. They lowered the price to $1,500.
Yet, knowing perfectly well ＿＿19＿＿ a troublemaker his son was, the
father refused to give them any money.　＿＿20＿＿, he asked the kidnappers
to pay him $250 to take the boy back. To persuade the boy to return
home, Bill and Sam had to tell him that his father was taking him
bear-hunting. The kidnappers finally handed over the boy and $250 to
the banker and fled town as quickly as they could.

16. (A) However　　　(B) Otherwise　　(C) Furthermore　(D) Accordingly
17. (A) made believe　(B) got along　　(C) turned out　　(D) felt like
18. (A) hold on to　　　　　　　　　　(B) get rid of
　　(C) make fun of　　　　　　　　　(D) take advantage of
19. (A) how　　　　　(B) that　　　　(C) why　　　　　(D) what
20. (A) Namely　　　(B) Altogether　(C) Simply　　　　(D) Instead

第 21 至 25 題爲題組

A polygraph machine, also known as a "lie detector," is a common part of criminal investigations. The instrument is used to measure ___21___ a person's body reacts to questions. The theory underlying it is that lying is stressful, and that this stress can be measured and recorded on a polygraph machine.

When a person takes a polygraph test, four to six wires, called sensors, are ___22___ to different parts of his body. The sensors pick up signals from the person's blood pressure, pulse, and perspiration. ___23___ the process of questioning, all the signals are recorded on a single strip of moving paper. Once the questions are finished, the examiner analyzes the results to determine if the person tested ___24___ truthful.

Well-trained examiners can usually detect lying with a high degree of ___25___ when they use a polygraph. However, because different people behave differently when lying, a polygraph test is by no means perfect.

21. (A) what   (B) when   (C) how   (D) why
22. (A) adapted   (B) attached   (C) related   (D) restricted
23. (A) Before   (B) Among   (C) Without   (D) Throughout
24. (A) was being   (B) would be   (C) was to be   (D) would have been
25. (A) quantity   (B) accuracy   (C) possibility (D) emergency

第 26 至 30 題爲題組

International trade is the exchange of goods and services between countries. Trade is driven by different production costs in different countries, making ___26___ cheaper for some countries to import goods rather than make them. A country is said to have a comparative advantage over another when it can produce a commodity more cheaply. This comparative advantage is ___27___ by key factors of production such as land, capital, and labor.

While international trade has long been conducted in history, its economic, social, and political importance has been ___28___ in recent centuries. During the 1990s, international trade grew by nearly 8.6% each year. In the year 1990 alone, the growth in trade in services was as high as 19%.

Today, all countries are involved in, and to varying degrees dependent on, trade with other countries. ___29___ international trade, nations would be limited to the goods and services produced within their own borders. Trade is certainly a main ___30___ force for globalization. It is also the subject of many international agreements that aim to govern and facilitate international trade, such as those negotiated through the World Trade Organization (WTO).

26. (A) them　　　(B) such　　　(C) what　　　(D) it
27. (A) installed　(B) reserved　(C) opposed　(D) determined
28. (A) to the point　(B) on the rise　(C) off the hook　(D) for the record
29. (A) Despite　　(B) Between　　(C) Without　　(D) Under
30. (A) driving　　(B) pulling　　(C) riding　　(D) bringing

三、文意選填（占 10 分）

說明：　第 31 題至第 40 題，每題一個空格，請依文意在文章後所提供的 (A) 到 (J) 選項中分別選出最適當者，並將其英文字母代號畫記在答案卡之「選擇題答案區」。各題答對者，得 1 分；答錯、未作答或畫記多於一個選項者，該題以零分計算。

第 31 至 40 題為題組

Are forests always created by nature? A man from rural India proves that this is not necessarily ___31___.

Abdul Kareem, who used to be an airline ticketing agent, has a great love for the woods. Though he never went to college, he can talk about plants and trees like an expert. In 1977, he bought a piece of rocky wasteland with the ___32___ of growing trees on it. In the beginning,

people thought he was ___33___ to waste his time and money on the land.
But he simply ___34___ them and kept working on the soil and planting
trees there. The land was so ___35___ that it had to be watered several
times a day. Kareem had to fetch the water from a source that was a
kilometer away. In the first two years, none of the trees he planted
___36___. However, in the third year, several young trees started growing.
Greatly ___37___ by the result, Kareem planted more trees and his
man-made forest began to take shape.

Kareem let his forest grow naturally, without using fertilizers or
insecticides. He believed in the ability of nature to renew itself without
the ___38___ of humans. That's why he did not allow fallen leaves or
twigs from the forest to be removed.

After years of hard work, Kareem has not only realized his dream
but also transformed a piece of ___39___ property into a beautiful forest.
Today, his forest is home to 1,500 medicinal plants, 2,000 varieties of
trees, rare birds, animals, and insects. Now, scientists from all over the
world come to visit his ___40___. They hope to find the secret of his
success.

(A) deserted   (B) interference   (C) vision   (D) crazy

(E) creation   (F) encouraged   (G) ignored   (H) survived

(I) dry   (J) true

四、閱讀測驗（占 32 分）

說明： 第 41 題至第 56 題，每題請分別根據各篇文章之文意選出最適當的一個
選項，請畫記在答案卡之「選擇題答案區」。各題答對者，得 2 分；答
錯、未作答或畫記多於一個選項者，該題以零分計算。

第 41 至 44 題為題組

In Japan, a person's blood type is popularly believed to decide his/
her temperament and personality. Type-A people are generally considered
sensitive perfectionists and good team players, but over-anxious. Type

Os are curious and generous but stubborn. Type ABs are artistic but mysterious and unpredictable, and type Bs are cheerful but eccentric, individualistic, and selfish. Though lacking scientific evidence, this belief is widely seen in books, magazines, and television shows.

The blood-type belief has been used in unusual ways. The women's softball team that won gold for Japan at the Beijing Olympics is reported to have used blood-type theories to customize training for each player. Some kindergartens have adopted teaching methods along blood group lines, and even major companies reportedly make decisions about assignments based on an employee's blood type. In 1990, Mitsubishi Electronics was reported to have announced the formation of a team composed entirely of AB workers, thanks to "their ability to make plans."

The belief even affects politics. One former prime minister considered it important enough to reveal in his official profile that he was a type A, while his opposition rival was type B. In 2011, a minister, Ryu Matsumoto, was forced to resign after only a week in office, when a bad-tempered encounter with local officials was televised. In his resignation speech, he blamed his failings on the fact that he was blood type B. The blood-type craze, considered simply harmless fun by some Japanese, may manifest itself as prejudice and discrimination. In fact, this seems so common that the Japanese now have a term for it: *bura-hara*, meaning blood-type harassment. There are reports of discrimination leading to children being bullied, ending of happy relationships, and loss of job opportunities due to blood type.

41. What is the speaker's attitude toward the blood-type belief in Japan?
    (A) Negative.　(B) Defensive.　(C) Objective.　(D) Encouraging.

42. According to the examples mentioned in the passage, which blood type can we infer is the **LEAST** favored in Japan?
    (A) Type A.　(B) Type B.　(C) Type O.　(D) Type AB.

43. Why did Prime Minister Ryu Matsumoto resign from office?
    (A) He revealed his rival's blood type.
    (B) He was seen behaving rudely on TV.
    (C) He blamed his failings on local officials.
    (D) He was discriminated against because of blood type.

44. Which field is **NOT** mentioned in the passage as being affected
    by blood-type beliefs?
    (A) Education.　　　(B) Sports.　　　(C) Business.　　　(D) Medicine.

第 45 至 48 題爲題組

　　Like many other five-year-olds, Jeanie Low of Houston, Texas, would use a stool to help her reach the bathroom sink. However, the plastic step-stool she had at home was unstable and cluttered up the small bathroom shared by her whole family. After learning of an invention contest held by her school that year, Jeanie resolved to enter the contest by creating a stool that would be a permanent fixture in the bathroom, and yet could be kept out of the way when not in use.

　　Jeanie decided to make a stool attached to the bathroom cabinet door under the sink. She cut a plank of wood into two pieces, each about two feet wide and one foot long. Using metal hinges, Jeanie attached one piece of the wood to the front of the cabinet door, and the second piece to the first. The first piece was set just high enough so that when it swung out horizontally from the cabinet door, the second piece would swing down from the first, just touching the ground, and so serving as a support for the first piece of the wood. This created a convenient, sturdy platform for any person too short to reach the sink. When not in use, the hinges allowed the two pieces of wood to fold back up tightly against the cabinet, where they were held in place by magnets. Jeanie called her invention the "Kiddie Stool."

　　Jeanie's Kiddie Stool won first place in her school's contest. Two years later, it was awarded first prize again at Houston's first annual Invention Fair. As a result, Jeanie was invited to make a number of public appearances with her Kiddie Stool, and was featured on local TV as well as in newspapers. Many people found the story of the Kiddie Stool inspiring because it showed that with imagination, anyone can be an inventor.

45. Why did Jeanie Low invent the Kiddie Stool, according to the passage?
    (A) Many other five-year-olds had problems reaching the bathroom sink.
    (B) She did not think that plastic stools were tall enough for her.
    (C) The stool in her bathroom was not firm and often got in the way.
    (D) She was invited to enter an invention contest held by her school.

46. Which of the following statements is true about how the Kiddie Stool works?
    (A) The Kiddie Stool will swing out only when the cabinet door opens.
    (B) It uses hinges and magnets to keep the wooden pieces in place.
    (C) It swings from left to right to be attached to the cabinet door.
    (D) The platform is supported by two pieces of metal.

47. What are the characteristics of Jeanie's Kiddie Stool?
    (A) Permanent and foldable.　　(B) Fragile and eye-catching.
    (C) Conventional and touching.　(D) Convenient and recyclable.

48. Which of the following sayings best captures the spirit of Jeanie Low's story?
    (A) Failure is the mother of success.
    (B) There's nothing new under the sun.
    (C) Necessity is the mother of invention.
    (D) Genius is 1% inspiration and 99% perspiration.

第 49 至 52 題為題組
　　Ongoing conflicts across the Middle East have prevented more than 13 million children from attending school, according to a report published by **UNICEF**, the United Nations Children's Fund.

The report states that 40% of all children across the region are currently not receiving an education, which is a result of two consequences of violence: structural damage to schools and the displacement of populations, also called "forced migration." Both issues result from the tide of violence that has crossed the region in recent years. The report examines nine countries where a state of war has become the norm. Across these countries, violence has made 8,500 schools unusable. In certain cases, communities have relied on school buildings to function as shelters for the displaced, with up to nine families living in a single classroom in former schools across **Iraq**.

The report pays particularly close attention to Syria, where a bloody civil war has displaced at least nine million people since the war began in 2011. With the crisis now in its fifth year, basic public services, including education, inside Syria have been stretched to breaking point. Within the country, the quality and availability of education depends on whether a particular region is suffering violence.

The report concludes with an earnest request to international policymakers to distribute financial and other resources to ease the regional crisis. With more than 13 million children already driven from classrooms by conflict, it is no exaggeration to say that the educational prospects of a generation of children are **in the balance**. The forces that are crushing individual lives and futures are also destroying the prospects for an entire region.

49. What is this article mainly about?
    (A) Why people are moving away from their own countries.
    (B) Why there are civil wars and violence in the Middle East.
    (C) Why many schools have become shelters for displaced families.
    (D) Why many children in the Middle East are not attending school.

50. Why is "**Iraq**" mentioned in the second paragraph?
    (A) To convince people that temporary housing can be easily found.

(B) To prove that classrooms there are big enough to host many families.

(C) To give an example of why schools are not usable for children's learning.

(D) To show how structural damages of school can affect the quality of education.

51. What does the phrase "**in the balance**" in the last paragraph most likely mean?

(A) Being well taken care of.

(B) In an uncertain situation.

(C) Under control by the authority.

(D) Moving in the wrong direction.

52. According to the passage, which of the following statements is true?

(A) The war in Syria has been going on since 2011.

(B) More than nine thousand schools have been destroyed by wars.

(C) Thirteen million people have been forced to leave their homes in the Middle East.

(D) Forty percent of all children in the world are not attending schools due to ongoing conflict.

第 53 至 56 題爲題組

Many marine animals, including penguins and marine iguanas, have evolved ways to get rid of excess salt by using special salt-expelling glands around their tongue. However, the sea snake's salt glands cannot handle the massive amounts of salt that would enter their bodies if they actually drank seawater. This poses a serious problem when it comes to getting enough water to drink. If seawater is not an option, how does this animal survive in the ocean?

An international team of researchers focused on a population of yellow-bellied sea snakes living near Costa Rica, where rain often does not fall for up to seven months out of the year. Because yellow-bellied sea snakes usually spend all of their time far from land, rain is the animals' only source of fresh water. When it rains, a thin layer of fresh water forms on top of the ocean, providing the snakes with a fleeting opportunity to lap up that precious resource. But during the dry season when there is no rain, snakes presumably have nothing to drink. Thus, the team became interested in testing whether sea snakes became dehydrated at sea.

The researchers collected more than 500 yellow-bellied sea snakes and weighed them. They found that during the dry season about half of the snakes accepted fresh water offered to them, while nearly none did during the wet season. A snake's likelihood to drink also correlated with its body condition, with more withered snakes being more likely to drink, and to drink more. Finally, as predicted, snakes captured during the dry season contained significantly less body water than those scooped up in the rainy season. Thus, it seems the snake is able to endure certain degrees of dehydration in between rains. Scientists believe that dehydration at sea may explain the declining populations of sea snakes in some parts of the world.

53. What is the purpose of the study described in this passage?
    (A) To test if sea snakes lose body water at sea.
    (B) To see whether sea snakes drink water offered to them.
    (C) To find out if sea snakes are greatly reduced in population.
    (D) To prove that sea snakes drink only water coming from rivers.

54. Which of the following is true about sea snakes?
    (A) Their salt glands can remove the salt in the seawater.
    (B) They can drink seawater when it mixes with rainwater.
    (C) The ocean is like a desert to them since they don't drink seawater.
    (D) They usually live near the coastal area where there is more fresh water.

55. Which of the following is one of the findings of the study?
    (A) If a sea snake was dried and weak, it drank more fresh water.
    (B) If captured in the wet season, sea snakes drank a lot of fresh water.

(C) Most of the sea snakes had lost a lot of body water when captured.
(D) Dehydration is not a problem among sea snakes since they live at sea.

56. What can be inferred from the study?
(A) Sea snakes can easily survive long years of drought.
(B) Evolution will very likely enable sea snakes to drink seawater.
(C) Sea snakes will be the last creature affected by global warming.
(D) The sea snakes' population distribution is closely related to rainfall.

第貳部份：非選擇題（占 28 分）

說明： 本部分共有二題，請依各題指示作答，答案必須寫在「答案卷」上，並標明大題號（一、二）。作答務必使用筆尖較粗之黑色墨水的筆書寫，且不得使用鉛筆。

一、中譯英（占 8 分）

說明： 1. 請將以下中文句子譯成正確、通順、達意的英文，並將答案寫在「答案卷」上。
　　　 2. 請依序作答，並標明題號。每題 4 分，共 8 分。

1. 相較於他們父母的世代，現今年輕人享受較多的自由和繁榮。
2. 但是在這個快速改變的世界中，他們必須學習如何有效地因應新的挑戰。

二、英文作文（占 20 分）

說明： 1. 依提示在「答案卷」上寫一篇英文作文。
　　　 2. 文長至少 120 個單詞（words）。

提示： 你認為家裡生活環境的維持應該是誰的責任？請寫一篇短文說明你的看法。文分兩段，第一段說明你對家事該如何分工的看法及厘由，第二段舉例說明你家中家事分工的情形，並描述你自己做家事的經驗及感想。

105年度學科能力測驗英文科試題詳解

第壹部分：單選題

一、詞彙題：

1. (**C**) Posters of the local rock band were displayed in store windows to promote the sale of their <u>concert</u> tickets. 商店的櫥窗裡展示著當地搖滾樂團的海報，用以促進<u>演唱會</u>門票的銷售量。

    (A) journey〔'dʒɝnɪ〕*n.* 旅行   (B) traffic〔'træfɪk〕*n.* 交通

    (C) *concert*〔'kɑnsɝt〕*n.* 音樂會；演唱會

    (D) record〔'rɛkəd〕*n.* 紀錄

    poster〔'postə〕*n.* 海報   local〔'lokl〕*adj.* 當地的

    rock〔rɑk〕*n.* 搖滾樂   band〔bænd〕*n.* 樂團

    display〔dɪ'sple〕*v.* 展示   promote〔prə'mot〕*v.* 促進

2. (**D**) Maria didn't want to deliver the bad news to David about his failing the job interview. She herself was quite <u>upset</u> about it.. 瑪麗亞不想告訴大衛關於他面試不利的消息。瑪麗亞本身就爲此很<u>心煩</u>了。

    (A) awful〔'ɔful〕*adj.* 可怕的

    (B) drowsy〔'draʊzɪ〕*adj.* 想睡的

    (C) tragic〔'trædʒɪk〕*adj.* 悲劇的

    (D) *upset*〔ʌp'sɛt〕*adj.* 心煩意亂的

    deliver〔dɪ'lɪvə〕*v.* 遞送；傳遞   interview〔'ɪntə,vju〕*n.* 面試

    quite〔kwaɪt〕*adv.* 相當地

3. (**A**) The newcomer speaks with a strong Irish <u>accent</u>; he must be from Ireland. 那個新來的人員講話有很重的愛爾蘭<u>腔</u>；他一定是來自愛爾蘭。

    (A) *accent*〔'æksɛnt〕*n.* 腔調   (B) identity〔aɪ'dɛntətɪ〕*n.* 身分

    (C) gratitude〔'grætə,tjud〕*n.* 感謝   (D) signature〔'sɪgnətʃə〕*n.* 簽名

    newcomer〔'nju,kʌmə〕*n.* 新人   Irish〔'aɪrɪʃ〕*adj.* 愛爾蘭的

    Ireland〔'aɪrlənd〕*n.* 愛爾蘭

4. (**C**) Although Maggie has been physically <u>confined</u> to her wheelchair since the car accident, she does not limit herself to indoor activities.
雖然瑪姬自從車禍以來一直都被迫於坐輪椅，她並不限制自己只能進行室內活動。

(A) cease〔sis〕*v.* 停止
(B) commit〔kə'mɪt〕*v.* 承諾；犯（罪）
(C) ***confine***〔kən'faɪn〕*v.* 限制　　(D) convey〔kən've〕*v.* 傳達
physically〔'fɪzɪklɪ〕*adv.* 身體上地　　wheelchair〔'hwil,tʃɛr〕*n.* 輪椅
indoor〔'ɪn,dor〕*adj.* 室內的

5. (**A**) All passengers riding in cars are required to fasten their seatbelts in order to reduce the risk of <u>injury</u> in case of an accident.
所有乘車的乘客都被要求繫緊安全帶，以減少車禍發生時受傷的風險。

(A) ***injury***〔'ɪndʒərɪ〕*n.* 傷害　　(B) offense〔ə'fɛns〕*n.* 違反
(C) sacrifice〔'sækrə,faɪs〕*n.* 犧牲
(D) victim〔'vɪktɪm〕*n.* 受害者

require〔rɪ'kwaɪr〕*v.* 要求　　fasten〔'fæsn̩〕*v.* 繫牢
in case of 萬一發生

6. (**D**) The principal of this school is a man of exceptional <u>generosity</u>. He sets aside a part of his salary for a scholarship fund for children from needy family. 這間學校的校長是個非常慷慨的人。他會保留部分薪水，作為窮困家庭小孩的獎學金基金。

(A) security〔sɪ'kjurətɪ〕*n.* 安全
(B) maturity〔mə'tʃurətɪ〕*n.* 成熟
(C) facility〔fə'sɪlətɪ〕*n.* 設施
(D) ***generosity***〔,dʒɛnə'rɑsətɪ〕*n.* 慷慨

principal〔'prɪnsəpḷ〕*n.* 校長　　exceptional〔ɪk'sɛpʃənḷ〕*adj.* 特別的
set aside 保留　　salary〔'sælərɪ〕*n.* 薪水
scholarship〔'skɑlə,ʃɪp〕*n.* 獎學金　　fund〔fʌnd〕*n.* 基金
needy〔'nidɪ〕*adj.* 窮困的

7. (**C**) The science teacher always <u>demonstrates</u> the use of the laboratory equipment before she lets her students use it on their own.
那位科學教師總是會先示範實驗室的設備如何使用，才讓她的學生自己操作。

(A) tolerate〔'tɑlə,ret〕*v.* 容忍

(B) associate〔ə'soʃɪ,et〕*v.* 聯想

(C) ***demonstrate***〔'dɛmən,stret〕*v.* 示範；示威

(D) exaggerate〔ɪg'zædʒə,ret〕*v.* 誇大

laboratory〔'læbrə,torɪ〕*n.* 實驗室
equipment〔ɪ'kwɪpmənt〕*n.* 裝備；設備
on *one's* ***own*** 靠自己；獨自

8. (**D**) Most of the area is covered by woods, where bird species are so <u>numerous</u> that it is a paradise for birdwatchers.

這個地區大部分被森林所覆蓋，禽鳥的種類非常<u>多</u>，所以這是賞鳥者的天堂。

(A) durable〔'djʊrəbl̩〕*adj.* 耐用的

(B) private〔'praɪvɪt〕*adj.* 私人的

(C) realistic〔,riə'lɪstɪk〕*adj.* 現實的

(D) ***numerous***〔'njumərəs〕*adj.* 許多的

cover〔'kʌvɚ〕*v.* 覆蓋　　woods〔wʊdz〕*n. pl.* 樹林
species〔'spiʃiz〕*n. pl.* 種類　　***so…that***~ 如此…以至於~
paradise〔'pærə,daɪs〕*n.* 天堂　　birdwatcher〔'bɝd,watʃɚ〕*n.* 賞鳥者

9. (**A**) In most cases, the committee members can reach agreement quickly. <u>Occasionally</u> , however, they differ greatly in opinion and have a hard time making decisions.

在大多數情況下，委員會的成員們可以很快達成共識。然而，<u>偶爾</u>，他們的意見非常不同，要做出決定很困難。

(A) ***occasionally***〔ə'keʒənl̩ɪ〕*adv.* 偶爾

(B) automatically〔,ɔtə'mætɪklɪ〕*adv.* 自動地

(C) enormously〔ɪ'nɔrməslɪ〕*adv.* 龐大地

(D) innocently〔'ɪnəsn̩tlɪ〕*adv.* 天真地

in most cases 在大多數情況下　　committee〔kə'mɪtɪ〕*n.* 委員會
agreement〔ə'grimənt〕*n.* 同意；共識
reach agreement 達成共識
quickly〔'kwɪklɪ〕*adv.* 迅速地　　differ〔'dɪfɚ〕*v.* 不同
greatly〔'gretlɪ〕*adv.* 極其；非常　　opinion〔ə'pɪnjən〕*n.* 意見
have a hard time + V-ing 做某事很困難
make a decision 做決定

10. (**C**) Many people try to save a lot of money before <u>retirement</u>, since having enough money would give them a sense of security for their future. 許多人試著在<u>退休</u>前存很多錢，因為有足夠的錢可以在未來帶給他們安全感。

(A) isolation〔͵aɪsḷˋeʃən〕*n.* 隔離

(B) promotion〔prəˋmoʃən〕*n.* 升遷

(C) ***retirement***〔rɪˋtaɪrmənt〕*n.* 退休

(D) announcement〔əˋnaʊnsmənt〕*n.* 宣布

try〔traɪ〕*v.* 試圖　　save〔sev〕*v.* 儲蓄

sense〔sɛns〕*n.* 感覺　　security〔sɪˋkjʊrətɪ〕*n.* 安全

future〔ˋfjutʃɚ〕*n.* 未來

11. (**B**) In winter, our skin tends to become dry and <u>itchy</u>, a problem which is usually treated by applying lotions or creams.
在冬天，我們的皮膚容易變得乾癢，這問題通常可藉由塗抹乳液或乳霜來處理。

(A) alert〔əˋlɝt〕*adj.* 警覺的

(B) ***itchy***〔ˋɪtʃɪ〕*adj.* 發癢的

(C) steady〔ˋstɛdɪ〕*adj.* 穩固的

(D) flexible〔ˋflɛksəbḷ〕*adj.* 可彎曲的；有彈性的

skin〔skɪn〕*n.* 皮膚　　***tend to* + *V*** 有～傾向；容易～

dry〔draɪ〕*adj.* 乾燥的　　treat〔trit〕*v.* 處理

apply〔əˋplaɪ〕*v.* 塗抹　　lotion〔ˋloʃən〕*n.* 乳液

cream〔krim〕*n.* 乳霜

12. (**A**) Benson married Julie soon after he had <u>conquered</u> her heart and gained her parents' approval.
班森一<u>征服</u>了茱莉的心，以及得到她父母的許可後，便娶了茱莉。

(A) ***conquer***〔ˋkɑŋkɚ〕*v.* 征服

(B) estimate〔ˋɛstə͵met〕*v.* 估計

(C) guarantee〔͵gærənˋti〕*v.* 保證

(D) intensify〔ɪnˋtɛnsə͵faɪ〕*v.* 加強

gain〔gen〕*v.* 獲得　　approval〔əˋpruvḷ〕*n.* 認可

13. (**A**) The recent flood completely <u>ruined</u> my parents' farm. The farmhouse and fruit trees were all gone and nothing was left.

最近的洪水整個<u>毀掉</u>了我父母的農場。農舍及果樹全沒了，什麼都不剩。

(A) ***ruin*** 〔ˋrʊɪn〕*v.* 毀滅　　　(B) crack 〔kræk〕*v.* 破裂

(C) hasten 〔ˋhesn̩〕*v.* 催促；加快　　(D) neglect 〔nɪˋglɛkt〕*v.* 忽略

recent 〔ˋrisn̩〕*adj.* 最近的　　　flood 〔flʌd〕*n.* 洪水

completely 〔kəmˋplitlɪ〕*adv.* 完全地

14. (**C**) The results of this survey are not reliable because the people it questioned were not a typical or <u>representative</u> sample of the entire population that was studied.　這份調查的結果並不可靠，因爲該調查所詢問的人，並不是典型或<u>有代表性的</u>研究人口樣本。

(A) primitive 〔ˋprɪmətɪv〕*adj.* 原始的

(B) spiritual 〔ˋspɪrɪtʃʊəl〕*adj.* 精神上的

(C) ***representative*** 〔͵rɛprɪˋzɛntətɪv〕*adj.* 代表性的；典型的

(D) informative 〔ɪnˋfɔrmətɪv〕*adj.* 給予知識的；教育性的

result 〔rɪˋzʌlt〕*n.* 結果　　　survey 〔ˋsɝve〕*n.* 調查

reliable 〔rɪˋlaɪəbl̩〕*adj.* 可靠的　　question 〔ˋkwɛstʃən〕*v.* 詢問

typical 〔ˋtɪpɪkl̩〕*adj.* 典型的　　sample 〔ˋsæmpl̩〕*n.* 樣本

entire 〔ɪnˋtaɪr〕*adj.* 全部的

population 〔͵pɑpjəˋleʃən〕*n.* 人口　　study 〔ˋstʌdɪ〕*v.* 研究；調查

15. (**D**) In line with the worldwide green movement, carmakers have been working hard to make their new models more <u>environmentally</u> friendly to reduce pollution.

因應全世界的環保運動，汽車製造業者一直持續努力，使他們新的車款對<u>環境</u>更友善，以降低污染。

(A) liberally 〔ˋlɪbərəlɪ〕*adv.* 慷慨地；充分地

(B) individually 〔͵ɪndəˋvɪdʒʊəlɪ〕*adv.* 個別地

(C) financially 〔faˋnænʃəlɪ〕*adv.* 財政上

(D) ***environmentally*** 〔ɪn͵vaɪrənˋmɛntl̩ɪ〕*adv.* 環境上地

　　environmentally friendly 對環境友善的；環保的

in line with 和…一致；符合　　worldwide 〔ˋwɝld͵waɪd〕*adj.* 全世界的

green 〔grin〕*adj.* 綠色的；環保的

movement 〔ˋmuvmənt〕*n.* 運動；活動

carmaker 〔ˋkɑr͵mekɚ〕*n.* 汽車製造業者　　model 〔ˋmɑdl̩〕*n.* 款式

reduce 〔rɪˋdjus〕*v.* 降低；減少　　pollution 〔pəˋluʃən〕*n.* 污染

二、綜合測驗：

第 16 至 20 題爲題組

　　Bill and Sam decided to kidnap the son of a banker to compensate for their business loss. They kidnapped the boy and hid him in a cave. They asked for a ransom of $2,000 to return the boy. <u>However</u>, their plan quickly
16
got out of control.

　　比爾和山姆決定要綁架一位銀行家的兒子，來補償他們生意上的損失。他們綁架了小男孩，把他藏在洞穴中。他們要求要兩千元的贖金才肯釋放小男孩，然而，這項計畫很快就失控了。

　　　　decide〔dɪ'saɪd〕v. 決定　　　kidnap〔'kɪdnæp〕v. 綁架；勒贖
　　　　banker〔'bæŋkɚ〕n. 銀行家　　***compensate for*** 補償；彌補
　　　　compensate〔'kɑmpən,set〕v. 彌補　　cave〔kev〕n. 洞穴
　　　　ask for 要求　　　ransom〔'rænsəm〕n. 贖金
　　　　plan〔plæn〕n. 計畫；方法　　***out of control*** 失去控制

16. (**A**) 依句意，應選 (A) ***However***〔haʊ'ɛvɚ〕adv. 然而。
　　　　(B) Otherwise〔'ʌðɚ,waɪz〕adv. 否則
　　　　(C) Furthermore〔'fɝðɚ,mor〕adv. 再者；此外
　　　　(D) Accordingly〔ə'kɔrdɪŋlɪ〕adv. 因此，皆不合句意。

　　Their young captive <u>turned out</u> to be a mischievous boy. He viewed the
17
kidnapping as a wonderful camping trip. He demanded that his kidnappers play tiring games with him, such as riding Bill as a horse for nine miles.

　　這個年幼的俘虜結果是一個調皮的小男孩。他把綁架看成一場美好的野營之旅。他要求綁匪跟他玩相當累人的遊戲，像是把比爾當馬騎九哩。

　　　　captive〔'kæptɪv〕n. 俘虜　　mischievous〔'mɪstʃɪvəs〕adj. 調皮的
　　　　view A as B 視 A 爲 B　　kidnapping〔'kɪdnæpɪŋ〕n. 綁架
　　　　camping〔'kæmpɪŋ〕n. 野營　　demand〔dɪ'mænd〕v. 要求
　　　　tiring〔'taɪrɪŋ〕adj. 令人疲倦的

17. (**C**) 依句意，選 (C) ***turned out (to be)*** 結果是
　　　　而 (A) make believe 假裝，(B) get along 和睦相處，(D) feel like 想要，皆不合句意。

　　Bill and Sam were soon desperate and decided to <u>get rid of</u> the little terror.

　　　　　　　　　　　　　　　　　　　　　　　　　　　18

They lowered the price to $1,500. Yet, knowing perfectly well <u>what a</u>

　　　　　　　　　　　　　　　　　　　　　　　　19

troublemaker his son was, the father refused to give them any money.

　　比爾和山姆很快就絕望了，決定要擺脫這個小夢魘。他們把贖金降低到1500
元。然而，男孩的父親深知他兒子是個搗蛋鬼，所以拒絕給他們贖金。

> desperate〔'dɛspərɪt〕*adj.* 絕望的
> terror〔'tɛrɚ〕*n.* 麻煩的傢伙　　　lower〔'loɚ〕*v.* 降低
> perfectly〔'pɝfɪktlɪ〕*adv.* 十分；非常
> troublemaker〔'trʌblˌmekɚ〕*n.* 惹麻煩的人
> refuse〔rɪ'fjuz〕*v.* 拒絕

18.(**B**) 依句意，選 (B) ***get rid of*** 擺脫。
　　　(A) hold on to　抓住；堅持，(C) make fun of　取笑；嘲弄，
　　　(D) take advantage of　利用，皆不合句意

19.(**D**) 此處感歎句為名詞子句，做 knowing 的受詞，要用「***what*** a + (形) +
　　　單 N + S + V」，選 (D)。
　　　(A) 要用 how + 形/副 + S + V，(B) 應改成 that his son was a
　　　troublemaker，不倒裝，文法均錯誤。

　　<u>Instead,</u> he asked the kidnappers to pay him $250 to take the boy back.
　　　20

To persuade the boy to return home, Bill and Sam had to tell him that his
father was taking him bear-hunting. The kidnappers finally handed over the
boy and $250 to the banker and fled town as quickly as they could.

　　他反而要求綁匪付他250元，他才肯帶回小男孩。為了說服小男孩回家，比爾
和山姆還必須跟小男孩說，他的父親要帶他去獵熊。最後，綁匪終於把小男孩和
250元交付給銀行家，並且盡快逃離城鎮。

> ask〔æsk〕*v.* 要求　　　persuade〔pɚ'swed〕*v.* 說服
> hunt〔hʌnt〕*v.* 狩獵　　　***hand over*** 交出
> ***hand over A to B***　把 A 交付給 B
> ***as ~ as one can***　盡可能~
> flee〔fli〕*v.* 逃走【三態變化：flee-fled-fled】

20. (**D**) 依句意，選 (D) ***Instead*** 〔 ɪnˈstɛd 〕 *adv.* 反而；代替。

而 (A) Namely 〔ˈnemlɪ 〕 *adv.* 也就是，

(B) Altogether 〔͵ɔltəˈgɛðɚ 〕 *adv.* 完全地；總計

(C) Simply 〔ˈsɪmplɪ 〕 *adv.* 簡單地，皆不合句意

第 21 至 25 題爲題組

A polygraph machine, also known as a "lie detector," is a common part of criminal investigations. The instrument is used to measure <u>how</u> a person's

21

body reacts to questions. The theory underlying it is that lying is stressful, and that this stress can be measured and recorded on a polygraph machine.

測謊器又稱作「謊言偵測器」，是犯罪調查很常見的一部分。這個儀器是用來測量一個人的身體，對問題會有怎麼樣的反應。它的理論基礎，就是說謊會有很大的壓力，而這個壓力可以被測量並記錄在測謊器上。

> polygraph 〔ˈpolɪ͵græf 〕 *n.* 測謊器　　***be known as*** 被稱爲
> lie 〔 laɪ 〕 *n.* 謊言　*v.* 說謊　　detector 〔 dɪˈtɛktɚ 〕 *n.* 偵測器
> ***lie detector*** 測謊器　　common 〔ˈkamən 〕 *adj.* 常見的
> criminal 〔ˈkrɪmənḷ 〕 *adj.* 犯罪的
> investigation 〔 ɪn͵vɛstəˈgeʃən 〕 *n.* 調查
> instrument 〔ˈɪnstrəmənt 〕 *n.* 儀器；工具
> measure 〔ˈmɛʒɚ 〕 *v.* 測量
> react 〔 rɪˈækt 〕 *v.* 反應 < *to* >　　theory 〔ˈθiərɪ 〕 *n.* 理論
> underlie 〔͵ʌndɚˈlaɪ 〕 *v.* 位於…之下；成爲…的基礎
> stressful 〔ˈstrɛsfəl 〕 *adj.* 壓力大的　　stress 〔 strɛs 〕 *n.* 壓力

21. (**C**) 依句意，測量一個人的身體對問題會有「怎麼樣的」反應，選 (C) ***how***。

When a person takes a polygraph test, four to six wires, called sensors, are <u>attached</u> to different parts of his body. The sensors pick up signals from

22

the person's blood pressure, pulse, and perspiration. <u>Throughout</u> the process

23

of questioning, all the signals are recorded on a single strip of moving paper. Once the questions are finished, the examiner analyzes the results to determine if the person tested <u>was being</u> truthful.

24

當一個人接受測謊，會有四到六條叫作感應器的電線，被貼在他身體不同的部位。這些感應器會接收到來自那人的血壓、脈搏，以及流汗的信號。在整個詢問的過程中，所有的信號都被記錄在一長條會移動的紙上。一當問題結束，審查人員會分析結果，以判定接受測謊的人當時是否有說實話。

> ***take a test*** 接受測驗　　wire〔waɪr〕n. 電線
> sensor〔ˈsɛnsɚ〕n. 感應器　　***pick up*** 接收到；探測到；發現
> signal〔ˈsɪgnl̩〕n. 信號　　***blood pressure*** 血壓
> pulse〔pʌls〕n. 脈搏　　perspiration〔͵pɚspəˈreʃən〕n. 流汗
> process〔ˈprɑsɛs〕n. 過程　　question〔ˈkwɛstʃən〕v. 詢問；質問
> single〔ˈsɪŋl̩〕adj. 單一的　　strip〔strɪp〕n. 細長的一條
> moving〔ˈmuvɪŋ〕adj. 正在動的；會移動的
> examiner〔ɪgˈzæmɪnɚ〕n. 審查人員　　analyze〔ˈænl̩͵aɪz〕v. 分析
> determine〔dɪˈtɝmɪn〕v. 決定；判定
> truthful〔ˈtruθfəl〕adj. 說實話的；誠實的

22.(**B**) 依句意，選 (B)***attached***。　　attach〔əˈtætʃ〕v. 附上；貼上 < *to* >
而 (A) adapt〔əˈdæpt〕v. 適應；改編，(C) relate〔rɪˈlet〕v. 使有關連，
(D) restrict〔rɪˈstrɪkt〕v. 限制，則不合句意。

23.(**D**) 依句意，「在整個」詢問的過程「中」，選 (D)***Throughout***。
throughout〔θruˈaut〕prep. 在…期間一直

24.(**A**) 依句意，判定接受測謊的人「當時」是否有說實話，動詞應用「過去式」或「過去進行式」，故選 (A)***was being***。

Well-trained examiners can usually detect lying with a high degree of
<u>accuracy</u> when they use a polygraph. However, because different people
　25
behave differently when lying, a polygraph test is by no means perfect.

　　訓練有素的審查人員使用測謊器時，通常能非常準確地查出是否有說謊。不過，因為不同的人說謊時會有不同的行為表現，所以測謊絕對不是百分之百正確。

> well-trained〔ˈwɛlˈtrend〕adj. 訓練有素的
> detect〔dɪˈtɛkt〕v. 查出　　degree〔dɪˈgri〕n. 程度
> behave〔bɪˈhev〕v. 行為舉止；表現
> ***by no means*** 絕不　　perfect〔ˈpɝfɪkt〕adj. 完美的；正確的

25. (**B**) 依句意，選 (B) *accuracy* 〔ˋækjərəsɪ〕*n.* 準確性。而 (A) quantity
〔ˋkwɑntətɪ〕*n.* 數量，(C) possibility 〔͵pɑsəˋbɪlətɪ〕*n.* 可能性，
(D) emergency 〔ɪˋmɝdʒənsɪ〕*n.* 緊急情況，則不合句意。

第 26 至 30 題爲題組

　　International trade is the exchange of goods and services between
countries. Trade is driven by different production costs in different countries,
making <u>it</u> cheaper for some countries to import goods rather than make them. A
　　　26
country is said to have a comparative advantage over another when it can
produce a commodity more cheaply. This comparative advantage is <u>determined</u>
　　　　　　　　　　　　　　　　　　　　　　　　　　　　　　27
by key factors of production such as land, capital, and labor.

　　國際貿易指的是國與國之間的商品和服務交換。貿易是因爲不同國家的不同
生產成本產生的，這會使得對某些國家來說，進口商品比自己生產更便宜。當一
個國家可以在生產某樣商品上更便宜時，和另一國相比便被稱爲擁有比較利益。
比較利益由生產的關鍵要素決定，像是土地、資金和勞力。

　　international 〔͵ɪntəˋnæʃənḷ〕*adj.* 國際的；國際間的
　　trade 〔tred〕*n.* 貿易　　exchange 〔ɪksˋtʃendʒ〕*n.* 交換
　　goods 〔gudz〕*n.* 商品；貨物　　service 〔ˋsɝvɪs〕*n.* 服務
　　drive 〔draɪv〕*v.* 推動；產生　　production 〔prəˋdʌkʃən〕*n.* 生產
　　cost 〔kɔst〕*n.* 成本　　import 〔ɪmˋport〕*v.* 輸入；進口
　　rather than 而不是　　***be said to*** 被稱爲
　　comparative 〔kəmˋpærətɪv〕*adj.* 比較的
　　advantage 〔ədˋvæntɪdʒ〕*n.* 優點；利益
　　comparative advantage 比較利益　　produce 〔prəˋdus〕*v.* 生產；製造
　　commodity 〔kəˋmɑdətɪ〕*n.* 商品　　key 〔ki〕*adj.* 基本的；關鍵的
　　factor 〔ˋfæktə〕*n.* 要素　　capital 〔ˋkæpətḷ〕*n.* 資金
　　labor 〔ˋlebə〕*n.* 勞力

26. (**D**) 本題考 make *it* + *adj.* + to V 句型，讓做某事變得…，此處的 it 爲虛受
詞，應選 (D)。

27. (**D**) 依句意，選 (D)，determine 〔dɪˋtɝmɪn〕*v.* 決定，在此爲被動「由～決
定」。而 (A) install 〔ɪnˋstɔl〕*v.* 安置；安裝，(B) reserve 〔rɪˋzɝv〕*v.* 預
訂；保留，(C) oppose 〔əˋpoz〕*v.* 反對，皆不合句意。

　　While international trade has long been conducted in history, its economic, social, and political importance has been <u>on the rise</u> in recent centuries. During
28
the 1990s, international trade grew by nearly 8.6% each year. In the year 1990 alone, the growth in trade in services was as high as 19%.

　　雖然國際貿易已經在歷史上行之有年，但它在經濟、社會和政治上的重要性在近幾個世紀來持續地上升。在 1990 年代，國際貿易每年成長將近 8.6%。而光是在 1990 年這一年，貿易服務的成長就高達 19%。

> conduct〔kən'dʌkt〕v. 執行；進行
> economic〔,ikə'nɑmɪk〕adj. 經濟的
> social〔'soʃəl〕adj. 社會的
> political〔pə'lɪtɪkḷ〕adj. 政治的
> importance〔ɪm'pɔrtns〕n. 重要性　　recent〔'risnt〕adj. 最近的
> century〔'sɛntrɪ〕n. 世紀　　nearly〔'nɪrlɪ〕adv. 將近
> alone〔ə'lon〕adv. 單單；僅僅
> growth〔groθ〕n. 成長　　***as high as*** 高達

28. (**B**) 依句意，選 (B) ***on the rise*** 增加中，而 (A) to the point　中肯的；切中要點的，(C) off the hook　脫離困境，(D) for the record　為準確起見；供記錄存檔的，皆不合句意。

　　Today, all countries are involved in, and to varying degrees dependent on, trade with other countries. <u>Without</u> international trade, nations would be
29
limited to the goods and services produced within their own borders. Trade is certainly a main <u>driving</u> force for globalization. It is also the subject of
30
many international agreements that aim to govern and facilitate international trade, such as those negotiated through the World Trade Organization (WTO).

　　時至今日，所有的國家都參與其中，而且在不同程度上仰賴和其他國家進行貿易。若沒有國際貿易，各國將會受限於自己國內生產的產品以及服務。貿易毫無疑問是一個全球化的主要動力。這也是許多國際協議的主題，目標是要管理和促進國際貿易，像是那些透過世界貿易組織談判的協議。

> ***be involved in*** 參與其中　　***to varying degrees*** 不同程度上
> dependent〔dɪ'pɛndənt〕adj. 依賴的　　nation〔'neʃən〕n. 國家
> ***be limited to*** 受限於　　within〔wɪð'ɪn〕prep. 在…之內

border〔'bɔrdɚ〕 *n.* 國界
certainly〔'sɝtn̩lɪ〕 *adv.* 確實地；毫無疑問地
main〔men〕 *adj.* 主要的　　globalization〔,globəlɪ'zeʃən〕 *n.* 全球化
subject〔'sʌbdʒɪkt〕 *n.* 主題　　agreement〔ə'grimənt〕 *n.* 協議
aim to 旨在；目標在　　govern〔'gʌvɚn〕 *v.* 管理
facilitate〔fə'sɪlə,tet〕 *v.* 促進；幫助
negotiate〔nɪ'goʃɪ,et〕 *v.* 談判
organization〔,ɔrgənə'zeʃən〕 *n.* 組織

29. (**C**) 依後文的 "would be limited to the goods and services produced within their own borders"，可知是指「沒有」國際貿易的狀況，故選 (C) ***Without***。而 (A) Despite 儘管，(B) Between 在…之間，(D) Under 在…之下，皆不合句意。

30. (**A**) 依句意，選 (A) ***driving***，***driving force*** 動力。而 (B) pulling 拉，(C) riding 騎，(D) bringing 帶，皆不合句意。

三、文意選填：

第 31 至 40 題為題組

Are forests always created by nature? A man from rural India proves that this is not necessarily [31.] **(J) true**.

Abdul Kareem, who used to be an airline ticketing agent, has a great love for the woods. Though he never went to college, he can talk about plants and trees like an expert. In 1977, he bought a piece of rocky wasteland with the [32.] **(C) vision** of growing trees on it. In the beginning, people thought he was [33.] **(D) crazy** to waste his time and money on the land. But he simply [34.] **(G) ignored** them and kept working on the soil and planting trees there. The land was so [35.] **(I) dry** that it had to be watered several times a day. Kareem had to fetch the water from a source that was a kilometer away. In the first two years, none of the trees he planted [36.] **(H) survived**. However, in the third year, several young trees started growing. Greatly [37.] **(F) encouraged** by the result, Kareem planted more trees and his man-made forest began to take shape.

　　森林總是由大自然創造的嗎？一個來自印度鄉村的男子證明了，這未必是正確的。

　　阿卜杜勒·卡里姆，過去是一個航空公司票務員，對於森林有極大的熱愛。雖然他從沒上過大學，卻能夠像個專家一樣談論植物和樹木。1977 年，他買了一塊都是岩石的荒地，並懷著要在上面種樹的夢想。一開始，人們認為他非常的瘋狂，竟然浪費他的時間和金錢在這塊地上。但他就是不理他們，持續致力於這塊土壤，並且在那裡種樹。這塊土地非常的乾燥，以致於它一天必須要被灌溉好幾次。卡里姆必須要從一公里以外的水源取水。在前兩年，他種的樹沒有一棵存活。然而，在第三年，許多年幼的樹苗開始生長。卡里姆受到這個結果極大的鼓勵，他種植了更多的樹，他的人造森林也開始成形。

forest〔ˋfɔrɪst〕n. 森林　　create〔krɪˋet〕v. 創造
nature〔ˋnetʃɚ〕n. 自然　　rural〔ˋrʊrəl〕adj. 鄉村的
India〔ˋɪndɪə〕n. 印度　　prove〔pruv〕v. 證明
necessarily〔ˋnɛsəˏsɛrəlɪ〕adv. 必定；一定
not necessarily 未必；不一定　　**used to be** 過去是
airline〔ˋɛrˏlaɪn〕n. 航空公司　　ticketing〔ˋtɪkɪtɪŋ〕n. 票務
agent〔ˋedʒənt〕n. 代理人；經紀人
plant〔plænt〕n. 植物　v. 種植
expert〔ˋɛkspɝt〕n. 專家　　rocky〔ˋrɑkɪ〕adj. 多岩石的
wasteland〔ˋwestˏlænd〕n. 荒地
vision〔ˋvɪʒən〕n. 夢想；憧憬　　grow〔gro〕v. 種植；生長
simply〔ˋsɪmplɪ〕adv. 僅僅；只是
ignore〔ɪgˋnor〕v. 忽視；不理　　**work on** 致力於
soil〔sɔɪl〕n. 土壤　　dry〔draɪ〕adj. 乾燥的
water〔ˋwɑtɚ〕v. 灌溉　　fetch〔fɛtʃ〕v. 取得；拿來
source〔sors〕n. 水源　　kilometer〔ˋkɪləˏmitɚ〕n. 公里
survive〔sɚˋvaɪv〕v. 存活　　greatly〔ˋgretlɪ〕adv. 極大地
encourage〔ɪnˋkɝɪdʒ〕v. 鼓勵　　result〔rɪˋzʌlt〕n. 結果
man-made 人造的　　**take shape** 成形

　　Kareem let his forest grow naturally, without using fertilizers or insecticides.　He believed in the ability of nature to renew itself without the **38. (B)** interference of humans.　That's why he did not allow fallen leaves or twigs from the forest to be removed.

　　卡里姆讓他的森林自然地生長，沒有使用肥料或是殺蟲劑。他相信自然在沒有人類干擾下的自我修復能力。這也是爲什麼他不允許森林裡的落葉或小樹枝被清除。

　　naturally〔'nætʃərəlɪ〕*adv.* 自然地
　　fertilizer〔'fɜtl̩,aɪzə〕*n.* 肥料
　　insecticide〔ɪn'sɛktə,saɪd〕*n.* 殺蟲劑　　***believe in*** 相信
　　ability〔ə'bɪlətɪ〕*n.* 能力　　renew〔rɪ'nu〕*v.* 修復；更新
　　interference〔,ɪntə'fɪrəns〕*n.* 干擾　　human〔'hjumən〕*n.* 人類
　　twig〔twɪg〕*n.* 小樹枝　　remove〔rɪ'muv〕*v.* 移除

After years of hard work, Kareem has not only realized his dream but also transformed a piece of [39.] **(A) deserted** property into a beautiful forest. Today, his forest is home to 1,500 medicinal plants, 2,000 varieties of trees, rare birds, animals, and insects. Now, scientists from all over the world come to visit his [40.] **(E) creation**. They hope to find the secret of his success.

　　在多年的努力後，卡里姆不只實現了他的夢想，還將一塊荒廢的地產轉變成一座美麗的森林。時至今日，他的森林是 1500 株藥用植物、2000 種樹木、稀有的鳥類、動物以及昆蟲的家園。現在，來自世界各地的科學家都去拜訪他的創造結晶。他們希望可以找到他成功的秘訣。

　　not only A but also B 不只 A，還有 B
　　realize〔'rɪə,laɪz〕*v.* 實現　　***transform A into B*** 將 A 轉變成 B
　　deserted〔dɪ'zɜtɪd〕*adj.* 廢棄的　　property〔'prɑpətɪ〕*n.* 地產
　　be home to 是…的家園　　medicinal〔mə'dɪsn̩l〕*adj.* 藥用的
　　variety〔və'raɪətɪ〕*n.* 種類　　rare〔rɛr〕*adj.* 稀有的
　　all over the world 遍及全世界
　　creation〔krɪ'eʃən〕*n.* 創造；創造物　　secret〔'sikrɪt〕*n.* 秘訣

四、閱讀測驗：

第 41 至 44 題爲題組

In Japan, a person's blood type is popularly believed to decide his/her temperament and personality. Type-A people are generally considered sensitive perfectionists and good team players, but over-anxious. Type Os are curious and generous but stubborn. Type ABs are artistic but mysterious and unpredictable, and type Bs are cheerful but eccentric, individualistic, and selfish. Though lacking scientific evidence, this belief is widely seen in books, magazines, and television shows.

在日本，普遍認爲一個人的血型決定他/她的性情和人格特質。A型的人通常被認爲是敏感的完美主義者，也是很有團隊精神的人，但過於焦慮。O型的人是好奇和慷慨但頑固。AB型的人有藝術天分但神秘莫測，而B型的人性情開朗，但古怪、個人主義、自私。雖然缺乏科學依據，但此看法廣泛可見於書本、雜誌和電視節目。

> **blood type** 血型　　popularly〔'pɑpjələlɪ〕adv. 普遍地
> temperament〔'tɛmprəmənt〕n. 氣質；性情
> personality〔,pɜsn̩'ælətɪ〕n. 人格；品格
> generally〔'dʒɛnərəlɪ〕adv. 通常；一般地
> consider〔kən'sɪdə〕v. 認爲　　sensitive〔'sɛnsətɪv〕adj. 敏感的
> perfectionist〔pə'fɛkʃənɪst〕n. 完美主義者
> **team player** 有團隊精神的人　　anxious〔'æŋkʃəs〕adj. 焦慮的
> curious〔'kjurɪəs〕adj. 好奇的　　generous〔'dʒɛnərəs〕adj. 慷慨的
> stubborn〔'stʌbən〕adj. 頑固的
> artistic〔ɑr'tɪstɪk〕adj. 有藝術天賦的
> mysterious〔mɪs'tɪrɪəs〕adj. 神祕的
> unpredictable〔,ʌnprɪ'dɪktəbl̩〕adj. 不可預料的
> cheerful〔'tʃɪrfəl〕adj. 情緒好的；開朗的
> eccentric〔ɪk'sɛntrɪk〕adj.（人、行爲等）古怪的
> individualistic〔,ɪndə,vɪdʒuəl'ɪstɪk〕adj. 個人主義（者）的
> selfish〔'sɛlfɪʃ〕adj. 自私的　　evidence〔'ɛvədəns〕n. 證據
> belief〔bɪ'lif〕n. 信念；看法　　widely〔'waɪdlɪ〕adv. 廣泛地

The blood-type belief has been used in unusual ways. The women's softball team that won gold for Japan at the Beijing Olympics is reported to have used blood-type theories to customize training for each player. Some kindergartens have adopted teaching methods along blood group lines, and even major companies reportedly make decisions about assignments based on an employee's blood type. In 1990, Mitsubishi Electronics was reported to have announced the formation of a team composed entirely of AB workers, thanks to "their ability to make plans."

　　血型看法被運用在一些不尋常的地方。在北京奧運會中為日本奪下金牌的女子壘球隊，據報導使用血型理論去客製化每位球員的訓練。一些幼兒園採用血型分組教學法，而且據傳甚至連大公司都依據員工血型做出分派工作的決定。1990年，三菱電機被報已經公佈，公司裡一個團隊的形成全部是AB型的員工，由於他們具有企劃能力。

unusual〔ʌnˈjuʒʊəl〕*adj.* 不平常的　　softball〔ˈsɔftˌbɔl〕*n.* 壘球
Olympics〔oˈlɪmpɪks〕*n.* 奧林匹克運動會（= *Olympic Games*）
theory〔ˈθiərɪ〕*n.* 理論　　customize〔ˈkʌstəˌmaɪz〕*v.* 訂做
training〔ˈtrenɪŋ〕*n.* 訓練　　kindergarten〔ˈkɪndəˌgartn̩〕*n.* 幼稚園
adopt〔əˈdɑpt〕*v.* 採取；採納　　method〔ˈmɛθəd〕*n.* 方法；辦法
reportedly〔rɪˈpɔrtɪdlɪ〕*adv.* 據傳聞；據報導
assignment〔əˈsaɪnmənt〕*n.* （分派的）任務；工作
employee〔ˌɛmplɔɪˈi〕*n.* 員工
Mitsubishi Electronics 三菱電機【公司官網拼法為：Mitsubishi Electric】
announce〔əˈnaʊns〕*v.* 宣布；發布　　formation〔fɔrˈmeʃən〕*n.* 形成
compose〔kəmˈpoz〕*v.* 組成；構成　　entirely〔ɪnˈtaɪrlɪ〕*adv.* 完全地
thanks to 由於；託…福

The belief even affects politics. One former prime minister considered it important enough to reveal in his official profile that he was a type A, while his opposition rival was type B. In 2011, a minister, Ryu Matsumoto, was forced to resign after only a week in office, when a bad-tempered encounter with local officials was televised. In his resignation speech, he blamed his failings on the fact that he was blood type B.

　　此看法甚至影響政治。一位前首相認為在他官方簡介上，透露他是A型非常重要，而他的對手是B型的。2011年，一位首相松本龍在上任僅一週後被迫辭職，因為他有一次與地方官員發脾氣被電視播出來。在他的辭職談話中，他把他的缺失怪到他是血型B這件事上。

affect〔əˈfɛkt〕*v.* 影響　　politics〔ˈpɑləˌtɪks〕*n.* 政治
former〔ˈfɔrmə〕*adj.* 以前的　　***prime minister*** 首相
reveal〔rɪˈvil〕*v.* 揭露　　official〔əˈfɪʃəl〕*adj.* 官方的　*n.* 官員
profile〔ˈprofaɪl〕*n.* 人物簡介
opposition〔ˌɑpəˈzɪʃən〕*n.* 反對；對抗
rival〔ˈraɪvl̩〕*n.* 對手；敵手　　minister〔ˈmɪnɪstə〕*n.* 部長；大臣
force〔fors〕*v.* 強迫；迫使

resign〔rɪ'zaɪn〕v. 辭職　　***in office*** 在職；在位
bad-tempered〔'bæd'tɛmpəd〕adj. 脾氣不好的；易怒的
encounter〔ɪn'kaʊntə〕n. 遭遇　　televise〔'tɛlə,vaɪz〕v. 電視播送
resignation〔,rɛzɪg'neʃən〕n. 辭職
blame〔blem〕v. 責怪；怪罪　　failing〔'felɪŋ〕n. 缺失

The blood-type craze, considered simply harmless fun by some Japanese, may manifest itself as prejudice and discrimination.　In fact, this seems so common that the Japanese now have a term for it: *burahara*, meaning blood-type harassment.　There are reports of discrimination leading to children being bullied, ending of happy relationships, and loss of job opportunities due to blood type.

這種血型熱潮，有些日本人認為只是無害的樂趣，但可能顯現出偏見和歧視。事實上，血型熱潮似乎非常普遍，以致於日本現在有這個詞：burahara，意味著「血型騷擾」。而一些有關歧視的報告，導致兒童被霸凌，幸福關係的結束，以及就業機會的喪失，都是因為血型的因素。

craze〔krez〕n. 狂熱；風尚　　manifest〔'mænə,fɛst〕v. 表明；顯示
prejudice〔'prɛdʒədɪs〕n. 偏見
discrimination〔dɪ,skrɪmə'neʃən〕n. 不公平待遇；歧視
term〔tɝm〕n. 名詞；術語　　harassment〔hə'ræsmənt〕n. 煩擾；騷擾
lead to 導致　　bully〔'bʊlɪ〕v. 霸凌
relationship〔rɪ'leʃən,ʃɪp〕n. 人際關係
opportunity〔,ɑpə'tjunətɪ〕n. 機會；良機　　***due to*** 因為；由於

41.（**C**）對於日本的血型看法，說話者的態度為何？
　　(A) 負面的。　　(B) 防禦的。　　(C) 客觀的。　　(D) 鼓勵的。
　　negative〔'nɛgətɪv〕adj. 負面的；否定的
　　defensive〔dɪ'fɛnsɪv〕adj. 防禦的；保護的
　　objective〔əb'dʒɛktɪv〕adj. 客觀的；無偏見的
　　encouraging〔ɪn'kɝɪdʒɪŋ〕adj. 鼓勵的

42.（**B**）根據文章中所提及的例子，我們可以推斷出哪一種血型在日本是「最不」受到喜愛的？
　　(A) A 型。　　(B) B 型。　　(C) O 型。　　(D) AB 型。
　　infer〔ɪn'fɝ〕v. 推論　　least〔list〕adv. 最不
　　favor〔'fevə〕v. 喜愛

43. (**B**) 為什麼松本龍首相辭去職務？
　　(A) 他揭露了對手的血型。
　　(B) 他被看到在電視上行為粗魯。
　　(C) 他把自己的缺失怪到地方官員身上。
　　(D) 他因為血型而被歧視。

behave〔bɪ'hev〕v. 表現；行為舉止
rudely〔'rudlɪ〕adv. 無禮地；粗暴地
discriminate〔dɪ'skrɪmə,net〕v. 差別待遇；歧視 < *against* >

44. (**D**) 在文中「沒有」提及哪一項領域受到血型看法的影響？
　　(A) 教育。　　　　　　　　　(B) 運動。
　　(C) 商業。　　　　　　　　　(D) 醫藥。

第 45 至 48 題為題組

　　Like many other five-year-olds, Jeanie Low of Houston, Texas, would use a stool to help her reach the bathroom sink. However, the plastic step-stool she had at home was unstable and cluttered up the small bathroom shared by her whole family. After learning of an invention contest held by her school that year, Jeanie resolved to enter the contest by creating a stool that would be a permanent fixture in the bathroom, and yet could be kept out of the way when not in use.

　　就像許多其他的五歲兒童，德州休士頓的珍妮·羅，會使用板凳來幫助她碰到浴室的洗手槽。然而，她在家裡的塑膠階梯凳並不牢固，而且把她全家人共享的小型浴室弄得亂七八糟。那一年，在聽說她的學校有舉辦發明競賽後，珍妮決心參加比賽創造一個板凳，可以永久固定在浴室裡，但是在沒有使用的時候，又可以不佔空間。

Houston〔'hjustən〕n. 休士頓【美國南方城市】
Texas〔'tɛksəs〕n. 德州【美國南方一州】
stool〔stul〕n. 凳子　　reach〔ritʃ〕v.（伸手）接觸到
sink〔sɪŋk〕n. 水槽；洗手槽　　plastic〔'plæstɪk〕adj. 塑膠（製）的
step〔stɛp〕n. 階梯　　unstable〔ʌn'stebḷ〕adj. 不穩固的
clutter〔'klʌtɚ〕v. 把…弄亂　　share〔ʃɛr〕v. 分享
whole〔hol〕adj. 全部的　　learn〔lɜn〕v. 獲悉
invention〔ɪn'vɛnʃən〕n. 發明　　contest〔'kɑntɛst〕n. 競賽
hold〔hold〕v. 舉辦　　resolve〔rɪ'zɑlv〕v. 決心（做…）
enter〔'ɛntɚ〕v. 進入　　create〔krɪ'et〕v. 創造
permanent〔'pɝmənənt〕adj. 永久的　　fixture〔'fɪkstʃɚ〕n. 固定物
and yet 但是　　***out of the way*** 讓路；不妨礙

　　Jeanie decided to make a stool attached to the bathroom cabinet door under the sink. She cut a plank of wood into two pieces, each about two feet wide and one foot long. Using metal hinges, Jeanie attached one piece of the wood to the front of the cabinet door, and the second piece to the first. The first piece was set just high enough so that when it swung out horizontally from the cabinet door, the second piece would swing down from the first, just touching the ground, and so serving as a support for the first piece of the wood. This created a convenient, sturdy platform for any person too short to reach the sink. When not in use, the hinges allowed the two pieces of wood to fold back up tightly against the cabinet, where they were held in place by magnets. Jeanie called her invention the "Kiddie Stool."

　　珍妮決定做一個裝在洗手槽下方浴櫃的凳子。她將厚木板切成兩片，每一片大約兩英呎寬、一英呎長。利用金屬鉸鏈，珍妮將一片木板裝在櫥門的正面，然後第二片鎖住第一片。第一片設得剛好夠高，所以當它從櫥門水平拉出來時，第二片會從第一片盪下，正好接觸到地面，如此當作第一片木板的支撐用。這創造出一個方便、堅固的平台，給任何太矮小而碰不到洗手槽的人。在沒有使用的時候，鉸鏈會讓這兩片木板往回摺疊緊緊靠著櫥櫃，用磁鐵吸附在適當的位置。珍妮稱她的發明爲「小孩板凳」。

attach〔ə'tætʃ〕*v.* 裝上	cabinet〔'kæbənɪt〕*n.* 櫥櫃
plank〔plæŋk〕*n.* 厚板	wood〔wʊd〕*n.* 木材
foot〔fʊt〕*n.* 英呎	metal〔'mɛtḷ〕*n.* 金屬
hinge〔hɪndʒ〕*n.* 鉸鏈	set〔sɛt〕*v.* 設置
swing〔swɪŋ〕*v.* 擺動；搖動	
horizontally〔ˌhɔrə'zɑntḷɪ〕*adv.* 水平地	
touch〔tʌtʃ〕*v.* 碰觸	ground〔graʊnd〕*n.* 地面
serve as 當作	support〔sə'port〕*n.* 支撐
convenient〔kən'vinjənt〕*adj.* 方便的	
sturdy〔'stɝdɪ〕*adj.* 堅固的	platform〔'plæt,fɔrm〕*n.* 平台
too…to~ 太…而不~	allow〔ə'laʊ〕*v.* 允許；使能夠
fold〔fold〕*v.* 摺疊	tightly〔'taɪtlɪ〕*adv.* 緊緊地
against〔ə'gɛnst〕*prep.* 靠著	
hold〔hold〕*v.* 保持…的狀態	*in place* 在適當的位置
magnet〔'mægnɪt〕*n.* 磁鐵	kiddie〔'kɪdɪ〕*n.* 小孩

Jeanie's Kiddie Stool won first place in her school's contest. Two years later, it was awarded first prize again at Houston's first annual Invention Fair. As a result, Jeanie was invited to make a number of public appearances with her Kiddie Stool, and was featured on local TV as well as in newspapers. Many people found the story of the Kiddie Stool inspiring because it showed that with imagination, anyone can be an inventor.

珍妮的小孩板凳在她學校的競賽中獲得第一名。兩年後，小孩板凳又在休士頓的第一屆年度發明展上獲頒首獎。因此，珍妮和她的小孩板凳受邀出席一些公開場合，並且上了當地電視台和報紙的特別報導。許多人認為小孩板凳的故事很有啓發性，因為它說明了有想像力，任何人都能是一位發明者。

place〔ples〕n. 名次　　　award〔ə'wɔrd〕v. 頒發
prize〔praɪz〕n. 獎　　　annual〔'ænjuəl〕adj. 年度的
fair〔fɛr〕n. 展覽會　　**as a result** 因此　　invite〔ɪn'vaɪt〕v. 邀請
a number of 一些　　public〔'pʌblɪk〕adj. 公開的
appearance〔ə'pɪrəns〕n. 出現　　feature〔'fitʃə〕v. 特別報導
local〔'lokḷ〕adj. 當地的
inspiring〔ɪn'spaɪrɪŋ〕adj. 有啓發性的
imagination〔ɪ,mædʒə'neʃən〕n. 想像（力）
inventor〔ɪn'vɛntə〕n. 發明者；發明家

45. (**C**) 根據本文，為什麼珍妮・羅發明小孩板凳？
　　(A) 許多其他的五歲兒童很難碰到浴室洗手槽。
　　(B) 她不認為塑膠凳對她來說夠高。
　　(C) <u>在她浴室的板凳不穩固並且常常擋到路。</u>
　　(D) 她受邀進入她學校所舉辦的發明競賽。

invent〔ɪn'vɛnt〕v. 發明　　　**have problems + V-ing** 做～有困難
firm〔fɝm〕adj. 穩固的　　　**get in the way** 擋路；妨礙

46. (**B**) 關於小孩板凳如何運作，以下敍述何者為員？
　　(A) 小孩板凳只有在櫥門開啓時才會擺盪出來。
　　(B) <u>它使用鉸鏈和磁鐵來維持木板的適當位置。</u>
　　(C) 它被裝在櫥門上，由左邊擺動到右邊。
　　(D) 平台是由兩片金屬所支撐。

statement〔'stetmənt〕n. 敍述　　　work〔wɝk〕v. 作用；運作
wooden〔'wʊdṇ〕adj. 木（製）的
support〔sə'port〕v. 支撐

47. (**A**) 珍妮的小孩板凳特色是什麼？
    (A) 永久並且可摺疊。   (B) 易碎並且吸睛。
    (C) 傳統並且令人感動。   (D) 方便並且可回收。

characteristic〔ˌkærɪtəˈrɪstɪk〕*n.* 特色
foldable〔ˈfoldəbḷ〕*adj.* 可摺疊的   fragile〔ˈfrædʒəl〕*adj.* 易碎的
eye-catching〔ˈaɪˌkætʃɪŋ〕*adj.* 引人注目的
conventional〔kənˈvɛnʃənḷ〕*adj.* 傳統的
touching〔ˈtʌtʃɪŋ〕*adj.* 令人感動的
recyclable〔riˈsaɪkləbḷ〕*adj.* 可回收的

48. (**C**) 以下諺語，何者最能捕捉到珍妮・羅的故事的精神？
    (A) 失敗爲成功之母。   (B) 太陽底下沒有新鮮事。
    (C) 需要爲發明之母。
    (D) 天才是百分之一的靈感和百分之九十九的努力。

saying〔ˈseɪŋ〕*n.* 諺語；俗語   capture〔ˈkæptʃɚ〕*v.* 捕捉
spirit〔ˈspɪrɪt〕*n.* 精神   failure〔ˈfeljɚ〕*n.* 失敗
success〔səkˈsɛs〕*n.* 成功   necessity〔nəˈsɛsətɪ〕*n.* 需要
genius〔ˈdʒinjəs〕*n.* 天才   inspiration〔ˌɪnspəˈreʃən〕*n.* 靈感
perspiration〔ˌpɝspəˈreʃən〕*n.* 流汗；努力

第 49 至 52 題爲題組

    Ongoing conflicts across the Middle East have prevented more than 13 million children from attending school, according to a report published by **UNICEF**, the United Nations Children's Fund.

    根據一份UNICEF「聯合國兒童基金會」出版的報告指出，遍及中東的持續衝突已經使超過一千三百萬名孩童無法去上學。

ongoing〔ˈɑnˌgoɪŋ〕*adj.* 進行中的   conflict〔ˈkɑnflɪkt〕*n.* 衝突
across〔əˈkrɔs〕*prep.* 遍及   prevent〔prɪˈvɛnt〕*v.* 阻止
attend〔əˈtɛnd〕*v.* 上（學）   publish〔ˈpʌblɪʃ〕*v.* 出版
UNICEF〔ˈjunɪˌsɛf〕*n.* 聯合國兒童基金會
the United Nations 聯合國   fund〔fʌnd〕*n.* 基金會

    The report states that 40% of all children across the region are currently not receiving an education, which is a result of two consequences of violence: structural damage to schools and the displacement of populations, also called "forced migration." Both issues result from the tide of violence that has crossed the region in recent years.　The report examines nine countries where a state of war has become the norm.　Across these countries, violence has made 8,500 schools unusable.　In certain cases, communities have relied on school buildings to function as shelters for the displaced, with up to nine families living in a single classroom in former schools across **Iraq**.

這份報告陳敘，這整個地區百分之40的孩童目前沒有接受教育，這是兩種戰爭暴力結果下的後果：學校的結構性破壞及人口的離開。人口離開也被稱爲「被迫遷移」。這兩個問題都起因於近年整個地區的戰爭暴力狂潮。這份報告檢視了九個戰爭狀態已成常態的國家。在這些國家中，戰爭暴力已經使8500間學校不能被使用。在某些案例中，社區依賴學校建築物來充作難民的避難所，而在全伊拉克之前的學校裡，高達九個家庭住在單一個教室中。

state〔stet〕v. 陳述　　n. 狀態　　region〔'ridʒən〕n. 地區
currently〔'kɜəntlɪ〕adv. 目前地　　result〔rɪ'zʌlt〕n. 結果；後果
consequence〔'kɑnsəkwəns〕n. 結果　　violence〔'vaɪələns〕n. 暴力
structural〔'strʌktʃərəl〕adj. 結構性的　　damage〔'dæmɪdʒ〕n. 損害
displacement〔dɪs'plesmənt〕n. 取代；離開
forced〔fɔrst〕adj. 強迫的　　migration〔maɪ'greʃən〕n. 移民
issue〔'ɪʃu〕n. 問題　　***result from*** 起因於　　tide〔taɪd〕n. 潮
cross〔krɔs〕v. 橫越；遍及　　recent〔'risn̩t〕adj. 最近的
examine〔ɪg'zæmɪn〕v. 檢視　　norm〔nɔrm〕n. 規範；常態
unusable〔ʌn'juzəbəl〕adj. 不能使用的　　certain〔'sɜtn̩〕adj. 某些
community〔kə'mjunətɪ〕n. 社區　　***rely on*** 依賴
function〔'fʌŋkʃən〕v. 起作用　　shelter〔'ʃɛltə〕n. 避難所
the displaced （被迫離家的）難民　　single〔'sɪŋl̩〕adj. 單一的
former〔'fɔrmə〕adj. 之前的　　***up to*** 高達　　Iraq〔ɪ'rɑk〕n. 伊拉克

The report pays particularly close attention to Syria, where a bloody civil war has displaced at least nine million people since the war began in 2011.　With the crisis now in its fifth year, basic public services, including education, inside Syria have been stretched to breaking point.　Within the country, the quality and availability of education depends on whether a particular region is suffering violence.

這份報告特別關注敘利亞，在該國自從2011年開始內戰，血腥的內戰已經使至少九百萬人被迫遷移。戰爭危機現在已經第五年了，敘利亞國內的基本公共服務，包括教育，已經被拉長到爆發點了。在這個國家內，教育的品質及可及性取決於某個區域是否正飽受戰爭暴力之苦。

pay attention to 注意　　particularly〔pəˈtɪkjələlɪ〕adv. 特別地
close〔klos〕adj. 密切的　　Syria〔ˈsɪrɪə〕n. 敘利亞
bloody〔ˈblʌdɪ〕adj. 血腥的　　civil〔ˈsɪvḷ〕adj. 市民的；國內的
civil war 內戰　　crisis〔ˈkraɪsɪs〕n. 危機　　stretch〔strɛtʃ〕v. 拉長
availability〔əˌveləˈbɪlətɪ〕n. 可及性　　suffer〔ˈsʌfɚ〕v. 受…之苦

The report concludes with an earnest request to international policymakers to distribute financial and other resources to ease the regional crisis. With more than 13 million children already driven from classrooms by conflict, it is no exaggeration to say that the educational prospects of a generation of children are **in the balance**. The forces that are crushing individual lives and futures are also destroying the prospects for an entire region.

這份報告以一個誠摯的請求做爲結論，希望國際政策制定者能夠分配財務及其他資源，去舒緩這個區域危機。已有超過一千三百萬的孩童因戰爭衝突被趕出教室，說這世代孩童的教育前景是無法確定的一點也不誇張。這些正在壓碎個人生命及未來的力量，也正在破壞整個區域的前景。

conclude〔kənˈklud〕v. 下結論　　earnest〔ˈɝnɪst〕adj. 誠摯的
request〔rɪˈkwɛst〕n. 請求　　policymaker〔ˈpɑləsɪˌmekɚ〕n. 政策制定者
distribute〔dɪˈstrɪbut〕v. 分配　　financial〔faɪˈnænʃəl〕adj. 財務的
resource〔rɪˈsors〕n. 資源　　ease〔iz〕v. 減輕
regional〔ˈridʒənḷ〕adj. 區域性的
exaggeration〔ɪɡˌzædʒəˈreʃən〕n. 誇張
prospect〔ˈprɑspɛkt〕n. 前景；希望
generation〔ˌdʒɛnəˈreʃən〕n. 世代　　***in the balance*** 在不確定中
crush〔krʌʃ〕v. 壓碎　　entire〔ɪnˈtaɪr〕adj. 整個的

49.(**D**) 這篇文章主要是關於什麼？
　　(A) 人民離開他們國家的原因。
　　(B) 中東地區有內戰及暴力的原因。
　　(C) 許多學校已經變成難民家庭避難所之原因。
　　(D) 許多中東兒童沒有上學的原因。

50.(**C**) 爲什麼「伊拉克」在第二段中被提到？
　　(A) 使人相信臨時住宅可以輕易被找到。
　　(B) 證明教室夠大能接待很多家庭。
　　(C) 給一個例子，說明爲什麼學校不能用來讓學生學習。
　　(D) 顯示出學校的結構性破壞如何影響教育品質。

convince〔kən'vɪns〕*v.* 說服

temporary〔'tɛmpə,rɛrɪ〕*adj.* 臨時的

housing〔'hɑʊzɪŋ〕*n.* 住宅　　prove〔pruv〕*v.* 證明

host〔host〕*v.* 擔任主人；接待　　affect〔ə'fɛkt〕*v.* 影響

51. (**B**) 最後一段的片語 "in the balance" 最可能的意思是什麼？

(A) 被好好照顧。

(B) <u>在一個不確定的情況中。</u>

(C) 在當局的控制之下。

(D) 朝錯誤方向移動。

take care of 照顧　　uncertain〔ʌn'sɝtn̩〕*adj.* 不確定的

authority〔ə'θɔrətɪ〕*n.* 權威；當局　　direction〔də'rɛkʃən〕*n.* 方向

52. (**A**) 根據這個文章，哪一個陳述是正確的？

(A) <u>敘利亞的戰爭從 2011 年開始進行到現在。</u>

(B) 超過九千間學校已經被戰爭摧毀。

(C) 在中東有一千三百萬人已經被迫離開家園。

(D) 由於持續的戰爭衝突，全世界有百分之四十的孩童沒有上學。

<u>第 53 至 56 題爲題組</u>

　　Many marine animals, including penguins and marine iguanas, have evolved ways to get rid of excess salt by using special salt-expelling glands around their tongue. However, the sea snake's salt glands cannot handle the massive amounts of salt that would enter their bodies if they actually drank seawater. This poses a serious problem when it comes to getting enough water to drink. If seawater is not an option, how does this animal survive in the ocean?

　　很多海洋生物，包含企鵝和海鬣蜥，已經演化出去除多餘鹽分的方法，藉由利用牠們舌頭周圍能排出鹽分的特殊腺體。然而，海蛇如果確實喝到了海水，牠們的鹽腺不能夠處理大量進入身體的鹽分，這造成了一個嚴重的問題。若談到要獲取足夠的飲用水。如果海水不是個選擇，那這種動物要如何在海洋中生存呢？

marine〔mə'rin〕*adj.* 海洋的　　including〔ɪn'kludɪŋ〕*prep.* 包含

penguin〔'pɛngwɪn〕*n.* 企鵝　　iguana〔ɪ'gwɑnə〕*n.*鬣鱗蜥【美洲熱帶
　　地方所產的一種大蜥蜴】　　***marine iguana*** 海鬣蜥

evolve〔ɪ'vɑlv〕*v.* 演化；發展　　***get rid of*** 去除

excess〔ɪk'sɛs〕*adj.* 多餘的；額外的　　salt〔sɔlt〕*n.* 鹽

expel〔ɪkˋspɛl〕v. 吐出；排出
gland〔glænd〕n. 腺　　tongue〔tʌŋ〕n. 舌頭
sea snake 海蛇　　*salt gland* 鹽腺【排出體內多餘的鹽分藉以保持體液
　的滲透平衡】　　handle〔ˋhændl〕v. 處理
massive〔ˋmæsɪv〕adj. 大量的　　amount〔əˋmaʊnt〕n. 量
actually〔ˋæktʃʊəlɪ〕adv. 實際上；事實上；確實
seawater〔ˋsiˏwɔtɚ〕n. 海水　　pose〔poz〕v. 引起；造成
when it comes to V-ing 一提到～　　option〔ˋapʃən〕n. 選擇
survive〔səˋvaɪv〕v. 存活；生存

　　An international team of researchers focused on a population of yellow-
bellied sea snakes living near Costa Rica, where rain often does not fall for
up to seven months out of the year.　Because yellow-bellied sea snakes
usually spend all of their time far from land, rain is the animals' only source
of fresh water.　When it rains, a thin layer of fresh water forms on top of the
ocean, providing the snakes with a fleeting opportunity to lap up that precious
resource.　But during the dry season when there is no rain, snakes presumably
have nothing to drink.　Thus, the team became interested in testing whether
sea snakes became dehydrated at sea.

　　一個國際的研究團隊人員專注在一群位於在哥斯大黎加的黃腹海蛇，這裡一
年之中有高達七個月沒有降雨。因為黃腹海蛇通常大多時間在遠離陸地的地方，
雨是牠們唯一淡水的來源。當下雨的時候，一層薄薄的淡水會在海洋的表面上形
成，提供黃腹海蛇短暫舔飲那珍貴水資源的機會。但是在乾季沒雨的時候，海蛇
可能沒有東西可以喝。因此，該團隊變得有興趣測試，海蛇在海上是否會脫水。

researcher〔riˋsɝtʃɚ〕n. 研究員　　*focus on* 專注於
population〔ˏpapjəˋleʃən〕n. 人口；（生物的）群體
belly〔ˋbɛlɪ〕n. 腹部
Costa Rica〔ˋkɔstə ˋrikə〕n. 哥斯大黎加【哥斯大黎加共和國，通稱哥斯大
　黎加，是中美洲國家】
up to 高達　　*out of* ⋯之中　　*far from* 遠離
source〔sors〕n. 來源　　*fresh water* 淡水
thin〔θɪn〕adj. 薄的　　layer〔ˋleɚ〕n. 一層
form〔fɔrm〕v. 形成　　*on top of* 在⋯的上面
provide〔prəˋvaɪd〕v. 提供　　fleeting〔ˋflitɪŋ〕adj. 短暫的
opportunity〔ˏapɚˋtunətɪ〕n. 機會　　*lap up* 喝掉；舔飲
precious〔ˋprɛʃəs〕adj. 珍貴的　　resource〔rɪˋsors〕n. 資源

> ***dry season*** 乾季　　presumably〔prɪˈzjuməblɪ〕*adv.* 或許；可能
> **thus**〔ðʌs〕*adv.* 因此　　***be interested in*** 對…感興趣
> **test**〔tɛst〕*v.* 測試　　**dehydrated**〔diˈhaɪdretɪd〕*adj.* 脫水的
> ***at sea*** 在海上

The researchers collected more than 500 yellow-bellied sea snakes and weighed them. They found that during the dry season about half of the snakes accepted fresh water offered to them, while nearly none did during the wet season. A snake's likelihood to drink also correlated with its body condition, with more withered snakes being more likely to drink, and to drink more. Finally, as predicted, snakes captured during the dry season contained significantly less body water than those scooped up in the rainy season. Thus, it seems the snake is able to endure certain degrees of dehydration in between rains. Scientists believe that dehydration at sea may explain the declining populations of sea snakes in some parts of the world.

研究人員收集了超過五百隻黃腹海蛇，並秤重。他們發現在乾季的時候，大約一半的海蛇接受提供給牠們淡水，然而在雨季的時候，幾乎沒有蛇接受水。蛇喝水的可能性和牠的身體狀況相關，越脫水的蛇越可能喝水，並喝更多水。最後，如所預測，在乾季捕捉到的蛇，身體所含的水分遠遠低於在雨季捕捉到的蛇。因此，看似蛇能夠忍受在雨季之間某個程度的脫水。科學家相信，海上的脫水可能解釋了為何在世界上某些地方，海蛇的數量為何逐漸減少。

> **collect**〔kəˈlɛkt〕*v.* 收集　　**weigh**〔we〕*v.* 給…秤重
> **nearly**〔ˈnɪrlɪ〕*adv.* 幾乎；將近　　***wet season*** 濕季；雨季
> **likelihood**〔ˈlaɪklɪˌhʊd〕*n.* 可能性
> **correlate**〔ˈkɔrəˌlet〕*v.* （與…）相關 < *with* >
> **condition**〔kənˈdɪʃən〕*n.* 身體狀況
> **withered**〔ˈwɪðəd〕*adj.* 枯萎的；乾枯的；脫水的
> **predict**〔prɪˈdɪkt〕*v.* 預測　　**capture**〔ˈkæptʃə〕*v.* 捕捉
> **contain**〔kənˈten〕*v.* 包含；容納
> **significantly**〔sɪgˈnɪfəkəntlɪ〕*adv.* 相當地；顯著地（= *considerably*）
> **scoop**〔skup〕*v.* 舀取；抓取（= *capture*）　　***rainy season*** 雨季
> ***be able to V.*** 能夠　　**endure**〔ɪnˈdʊr〕*v.* 忍受
> **certain**〔ˈsɝtn̩〕*adj.* 某些的　　**degree**〔dɪˈgri〕*n.* 程度
> **dehydration**〔ˌdihaɪˈdreʃən〕*n.* 脫水　　***in between*** 在…的期間
> **rains**〔renz〕*n.* 雨季（= *a rainy season*）　　**explain**〔ɪkˈsplen〕*v.* 解釋
> **declining**〔dɪˈklaɪnɪŋ〕*adj.* 逐漸減少的；逐漸衰退的
> **parts**〔pɑrts〕*n. pl.* 地區

53.(**A**) 本文中所描述的研究目的是什麼？
　　(A) 測試是否海蛇在海上失去身體的水分。
　　(B) 看看是否海蛇喝提供給牠們的水。
　　(C) 找出是否海蛇數量大大減少。
　　(D) 證明海蛇只喝來自河流的水。

purpose〔'pɝpəs〕*n.* 目的　　study〔'stʌdɪ〕*v.* 研究
describe〔dɪ'skraɪb〕*v.* 描述
passage〔'pæsɪdʒ〕*n.*（文章的）一段
reduce〔rɪ'djus〕*v.* 減少

54.(**C**) 關於海蛇以下何者為真？
　　(A) 牠們的鹽腺可以去除海水的鹽份。
　　(B) 當海水和淡水混在一起時，牠們可以喝海水。
　　(C) 海洋對牠們來說像是一片沙漠，因為牠們不喝海水。
　　(D) 牠們通常生活在鄰近海岸的地方，這裡比較多淡水。

remove〔rɪ'muv〕*adj.* 去除　　mix〔mɪks〕*v.* 混合
rainwater〔'ren,wɔtə〕*n.* 雨水
desert〔'dɛzət〕*n.* 沙漠
costal〔'kostḷ〕*adj.* 沿岸的；臨海的

55.(**A**) 以下何者是該研究的調查結果？
　　(A) 如果海蛇脫水且虛弱，牠會喝較多的淡水。
　　(B) 如果在濕季被捕捉到，海蛇喝很多的淡水。
　　(C) 大多的海蛇被捕捉時失去了很多身體的水分。
　　(D) 脫水對海蛇不是問題，因為牠們生活在海上。

findings〔'faɪndɪŋz〕*n. pl.* 調查結果；研究發現
dried〔draɪd〕*adj.* 乾燥的；脫水的
weak〔wik〕*adj.* 虛弱的

56.(**D**) 從這研究中可以推論出什麼？
　　(A) 海蛇可以輕易地從長年的乾旱中生還。
　　(B) 演化很可能使海蛇能夠喝海水。
　　(C) 海蛇將會是最後一個受全球暖化影響的生物。
　　(D) 海蛇數量的分佈和降雨息息相關。

infer〔ɪn'fɝ〕*v.* 推論　　survive〔sə'vaɪv〕*v.* 從～生還；存活
drought〔draʊt〕*n.* 乾旱　　evolution〔,ɛvə'luʃən〕*n.* 演化

enable〔ɪn'ebḷ〕*v.* 使能夠　　creature〔'kritʃə〕*n.* 生物；動物
global warming 全球暖化
distribution〔,dɪstrə'bjuʃən〕*n.* 分配；分佈
closely〔'kloslɪ〕*adv.* 緊密地；密切地　　*be related to* 和…相關
rainfall〔'ren,fɔl〕*n.* 降雨；降雨量

第貳部分：非選擇題

一、中譯英

1. 相較於他們父母的世代，現今年輕人享受較多的自由和繁榮。

Compared with
In comparison with } their parents' generation, { young people
the youth }
nowadays enjoy more freedom and prosperity.

2. 但是在這個快速改變的世界中，他們必須學習如何有效地因應新的挑戰。

But
However, } in this fast-changing world, they { have to
must } learn how to

{ adapt to
respond to
deal with } new challenges effectively.
cope with
handle }

二、英文作文：

Household Chores

　　The sharing of household chores should be based on each family member's contribution to their overall living conditions and situations. *For instance*, if my father works a full-time job and a part-time job on the weekends, he shouldn't be expected to come home and wash the dishes. *Likewise*, my mother also has a full-time job, so her commitment to household chores is limited to what she feels comfortable with. *At the same time*, anybody in the household who is not making a contribution to the family is much more likely to be responsible for household chores. My family doesn't do a lot of cooking at home, so *fortunately*, washing the dishes is rarely if ever necessary.

In my house, the two main chores——cleaning and laundry——are shared between me and my older brother, mainly because we are students and contribute absolutely nothing to the family. *So* we take turns and maintain a chore schedule that is posted on the refrigerator each morning. Every day, following our studies, we have a list of tasks which must be completed before we can go outside, or watch TV, or play video games. We *also* do the laundry on alternate weekends, usually on Sunday. *Neither* my brother *nor* I mind doing these chores, and in fact, we have our preferences. My brother hates scrubbing the toilet bowls and I can't stand the noise of the vacuum cleaner, so we have an agreement. *And* we're happy to be contributing something to the family.

household〔'haʊs,hold〕*adj.* 家庭的　　*n.* 家庭；全家人

chores〔tʃɔrz〕*n. pl.* 雜事　　*household chores* 家事

be based on 根據　　overall〔'ovɚ,ɔl〕*adj.* 全部的；整體的

living conditions 生活條件　　situation〔,sɪtʃʊ'eʃən〕*n.* 情況

for instance 舉例來說（＝*for example*）

expect〔ɪk'spɛkt〕*v.* 期待　　dishes〔'dɪʃɪz〕*n. pl.* 餐具；碗盤

likewise〔'laɪk,waɪz〕*adv.* 同樣地

commitment〔kə'mɪtmənt〕*n.* 奉獻；付出

contribution〔,kɑntrə'bjuʃən〕*n.* 貢獻　　*be likely to V.* 可能～

be responsible for 對…負責　　*do a lot of V-ing* 做很多的…

fortunately〔'fɔrtʃənɪtlɪ〕*adv.* 幸運地；幸虧

rarely〔'rɛrlɪ〕*adv.* 罕見地；很少　　*rarely if ever* 就算有也很少

laundry〔'lɔndrɪ〕*n.* 待洗衣物

contribute〔kən'trɪbjut〕*v.* 貢獻＜*to*＞

absolutely〔'æbsə,lutlɪ〕*adv.* 絕對地；完全地

take turns 輪流　　maintain〔men'ten〕*v.* 維持

schedule〔'skɛdʒul〕*n.* 預定表；計畫　　post〔post〕*v.* 張貼

task〔tæsk〕*n.* 工作；任務　　*do the laundry* 洗衣服

alternate〔'ɔltə-nɪt〕*adj.* 隔一的　　preference〔'prɛfərəns〕*n.* 偏好

scrub〔skrʌb〕*v.* 刷洗　　toilet〔'tɔɪlɪt〕*n.* 廁所；馬桶

toilet bowl 抽水馬桶　　stand〔stænd〕*v.* 忍受

vacuum〔'vækjʊəm〕*n.* 真空；吸塵器

vacuum cleaner 吸塵器（＝*vacuum*）

agreement〔ə'grimənt〕*n.* 協議

105 年學測英文科試題出題來源

題　　號	出　　　　　　　　　處
一、詞彙 第 1～15 題	所有各題對錯答案的選項，均出自大考中心編製的「高中常用7000 字」。
二、綜合測驗 第 16～20 題	改寫自 The Ransom of Red Chief（紅酋長的贖金），改寫自歐·亨利幽默短文，敘述比爾和山姆綁架小孩的過程和最後諷刺的結果。
第 21～25 題	改寫自 Lie Detector and Polygraph Tests: Are They Reliable?（測謊機和測謊測驗：他們可靠嗎？），描寫測謊機的運作理論和方式。
第 26～30 題 【WHO】	改寫自 Trade（貿易），選自世界衛生組織（WHO）的網站，描述貿易的影響層面遍及國際，影響各國進出口品，以及其經濟、社會，和政治的重要性。
三、文意選填 第 31～40 題	改寫自 Abdul Kareem's Forest（阿卜杜卡里姆的森林），描寫一位來自印度鄉村而深深愛好森林的阿卜杜卡里姆如何創造森林。
四、閱讀測驗 第 41～44 題 【BBC】	改寫自 Japan and blood types: Does it determine personality?（日本和血型：這眞的能決定個性嗎？），描述日本人看待血型和個性的關係，以及在其應用的層面和後果。
第 45～48 題 【MIT】	改寫自 Jeannie Low（吉妮·羅），敘述一位五歲小女孩發明浴室用小板凳的故事。
第 49～52 題 【TIME】	改寫自 13 Million Middle Eastern Children Are Unable to Attend School（一千三百萬的中東孩童無法上學），描述超過一千三百萬中東的孩童因爲戰爭而無法上學，未來的狀況依然懸而未知。
第 53～56 題	改寫自 Some Sea Snakes Can Go Seven Months Without Drinking Water（有些水蛇可以七個月不喝水），描述在海上的水蛇何以在雨季和乾季高達七個月的間隔中，喝淡水而存活。

105 年學測英文科試題修正意見

※ 105 年學測英文試題出得很嚴謹，只有八個地方建議修正：

題 號	修 正 意 見
第 16～20 題 第 6 行	*Yet*, knowing perfectly well…. → *Yet* knowing perfectly well…. * yet 後面不須加逗點。
第 26～30 題 第二段第 1 行	While international trade has long been conducted *in history*, …. → 去掉 in history，或改成：While international trade *has been conducted for hundreds of years*, …. * in history 是多餘的。
第 43 題 (D)	He was discriminated against because of *blood type*. → He was discriminated against because of *his blood type*. * 依句意，應該是因為「他的」血型所以受人歧視，故須加 his。
第 45～48 題 第二段第 5 行	…, and so serving as a support for the first piece of *the* wood. → 去掉 the。 * the first piece of wood（第一塊木頭），不須加 the。
第 49～52 題 第三段第 2 行	With the crisis now in its fifth year, basic public services, *including education, inside Syria* have been….. → With the crisis now in its fifth year, basic public services *inside Syria*, *including education*, have been….. * inside Syria（敘利亞境內的）應該緊接在所修飾的 basic public services 之後。
第 53～56 題 第 2 行	…, around their *tongue*. → …, around their *tongues*. * 「牠們的」舌頭，應該是複數形，所以 tongue 要加 s。 However, the sea snake's salt glands cannot handle the massive amounts of salt that would enter *their bodies* if *they* actually drank seawater. → However, the sea snake's salt glands cannot handle the massive amounts of salt that would enter *its body* if *it* actually drank seawater. * the sea snake 是單數，所以 their bodies 要改成 its body，代名詞要用 it。
第 55 題 (A)	If a sea snake was dried *and weak*, it drank more fresh water. → 去掉 and weak。 * 因為內文沒有提到 weakness（虛弱），所以應該把 and weak 去掉。

【105 年學測】綜合測驗：16-20 出題來源

—— http://www.balancepublishing.com/ransyn.htm

"The Ransom of Red Chief"

Synopsis of the play.

Sam and Bill, a couple of down-on-their-luck con men, decide to kidnap the young son of a prosperous banker in Summit, a small Alabama town, to finance one of their crooked land deals in Illinois. They kidnap the boy and hide him in a cave a few miles from Summit. At the cave, they finalize their scheme to write a ransom letter asking for $2,000 ransom to return the boy. The boy, an eight-year old freckle-faced red-headed hellion, loves living in the cave. He treats the kidnapping as a wonderful adventure. Calling himself "Red Chief" he makes believe his kidnappers are really his captives. He plans to burn Sam at the stake and scalp Bill at daybreak. On the first night, the boy actually attempts to scalp Bill, using a sharp kitchen knife.

Throughout the story, Red Chief terrorizes Bill, whose job it is to placate the boy while Sam handles the various details of collecting the ransom. They write the ransom letter, but Bill convinces Sam that $2,000 is too much for a kid like Red Chief. They lower the ransom to $1500. Sam returns the carriage they had rented, and mails their ransom note.

The strain on Bill continues to worsen. Red Chief uses his sling shot to knock Bill out, making him fall across the campfire and puts a hot baked potato down Bill's back smashing it with his foot. Bill is made to play the horse in Red Chief's Black Scout game and is ridden ninety miles to the stockade and forced to eat sand for oats.

At last the reply from the boy's father arrives, but it is not what the kidnapers expect. Ebenzer Dorset answers the kidnappers' note with a counter-proposal. He'll accept his son back only if they pay him. To get the boy to return home with them, Sam tells Red Chief that his father has bought him a silver-mounted rifle and is planning to take him bear hunting.

Sam and Bill gladly hand over Red Chief and $250.00 to the banker and flee town, poorer and wiser men.

【105 年學測】綜合測驗：21-25 出題來源

——http://www.nolo.com/legal-encyclopedia/lie-detector-tests-tell-truth-29637. html

Lie Detector and Polygraph Tests: Are They Reliable?

Lie detector tests -- or polygraph tests, in more scientific terms -- are rarely used in criminal trials. The theory underlying a lie detector test is that lying is stressful, and that this stress can be measured and recorded on a polygraph machine.

Lie detectors are called polygraphs because the test consists of simultaneously monitoring several of the suspect's physiological functions -- breathing, pulse, and galvanic skin response -- and printing out the results on graph paper. The printout shows exactly when, during the questioning period, the biologic responses occurred. If the period of greatest biologic reaction lines up with the key questions on the graph paper -- the questions that would implicate the person as being involved with the crime -- stress is presumed. And along with this presumption of stress comes a second presumption: that the stress indicates a lie.

Arguments For and Against

Supporters of lie detector tests claim that the test is reliable because:

- very few people can control all three physiological functions at the same time, and
- polygraph examiners run preexamination tests on the suspect that enable the examiners to measure that individual's reaction to telling a lie.

On the other hand, critics of polygraph testing argue that:

- many subjects can indeed conceal stress even when they are aware that they are lying, and

- there is no reliable way to distinguish an individual's stress generated by the test and the stress generated by a particular lie.

The courts in most jurisdictions doubt the reliability of lie detector tests and refuse to admit the results into evidence. Some states do admit the results of polygraph tests at trial if the prosecution and defendant agree prior to the test that its results will be admissible.

⋮

【105 年學測】綜合測驗：26-30 出題來源

——http://www.who.int/trade/glossary/story090/en/

International trade is the exchange of goods and services between countries. Trade is driven by different production costs in different countries, making it cheaper for some countries to import commodities rather than make them. Today, all countries are involved in, and to varying degrees dependent on, trade with other countries.

A country is said to have a comparative advantage over another when it can produce a commodity more cheaply. A country's comparative advantage is determined by key factors of production such as land, capital and labour; more recently, information and communications capacity has become important.

National trade policies and practice tend to waver between protecting national interests and domestic industry to limit the import of goods and services (known as protectionism), and promoting free trade. When the international exchange of goods is neither hindered nor encouraged, trade is referred to as being free trade. Neo-liberals argue that a free trade system is most efficient because it allows countries to use their resources to best advantage, producing the goods they are best placed to produce, and importing others, thus driving economic growth. Others argue that even under a system with limited trade barriers or none at all, "free trade" is hampered by restrictions on labour mobility, monopolies on production and, not least, political imperatives (for example countries wanting to maintain self-sufficiency in key production areas such as food).

⋮

【105 年學測】文意選填：31-40 出題來源

—http://www.pitara.com/non-fiction-for-kids/features-for-ki
ds/abdul-kareems-forest/

Abdul Kareem's Forest

A lush green forest in the middle of a rocky wasteland. No, this paradise is not an illusion. Abdul Kareem has created it with his own hands.

Kareem's 30-acre forest is in Kasargode district, Kerala. It is home to 1,500 medicinal plants, 2,000 varieties of trees, rare birds, animals and insects. Agricultural scientist, MS Swaminathan, has called the forest a "wonderful example of the power harmony with nature."

So, how did Kareem manage to convert a wasteland into a forest? Let us go back 24 years, to 1977, when Kareem purchased a five-acre rocky wasteland. Kareem was an airlines ticketing agent with a craze for the woods. Though he never went to college, he could talk about the properties of plants and trees like an expert botanist, reports The Hindustan Times.

Kareem dug a huge well and began to toil in the rocky, arid terrain. In the beginning, people thought he was crazy to waste his time and money on wasteland. But, Kareem has 'green fingers' (a term used for people who love nature). Soon, he began investing more and more of his savings to add land and amenities.

Today, the 'wasteland' is the haven of nature-lovers – from students wanting to explore the woods, to agricultural scientists. Kareem has been honoured by several organisations, including the United Nations, for his work.

He just let his forest grow naturally, without insecticides or fertilisers. He believed in the ability of nature to replenish itself without the interference of humans. That's why he does not allow fallen leaves or twigs from the forest to be removed.

Recently, Kareem even refused an offer by a well-known resort to launch an Ayurveda (ancient Hindu practice of holistic medicine) centre in the forest.

"I wanted to spread the message that if trees, animals and birds survive, only then human beings have a future," Kareem said in an interview.

Shouldn't we be listening?

【105 年學測】閱讀測驗：41-44 出題來源

——http://www.bbc.com/news/magazine-20170787

Japan and blood types: Does it determine personality?

Are you A, B, O or AB? It is a widespread belief in Japan that character is linked to blood type. What's behind this conventional wisdom?

Blood is one thing that unites the entire human race, but most of us don't think about our blood group much, unless we need a transfusion. In Japan, however, blood type has big implications for life, work and love.

Here, a person's blood type is popularly believed to determine temperament and personality. "What's your blood type?" is often a key question in everything from matchmaking to job applications.

According to popular belief in Japan, type As are sensitive perfectionists and good team players, but over-anxious. Type Os are curious and generous but stubborn. ABs are arty but mysterious and unpredictable, and type Bs are cheerful but eccentric, individualistic and selfish.

About 40% of the Japanese population is type A and 30% are type O, whilst only 20% are type B, with AB accounting for the remaining 10%.

⋮

【105 年學測】閱讀測驗：45-48 出題來源

——http://lemelson.mit.edu/resources/jeannie-low

Jeannie Low

The Kiddie Stool

Jeanie Low of Houston, Texas created her best known invention, the Kiddie Stool, while she was still in kindergarten.

At that time, Jeanie was using a plastic step-stool in order to reach the bathroom sink. But step-stools were inconvenient, unstable and breakable, and cluttered up the room. Hearing about an invention contest at her school, Jeanie resolved to make a stool that would be a permanent but inconspicuous fixture in the bathroom.

She went to a local hardware store for supplies. The employees gladly provided wood, screws, hinges and magnets, but they were skeptical about Jeanie's idea. She proved them wrong.

Jeanie had cut a plank of wood into two pieces, each about as wide as a sheet of notebook paper, and half again as long. Using hinges, Jeanie attached one piece to the front of the bathroom vanity, and the second piece to the first. The first piece was set just high enough so that when it swung out horizontally from the face of the vanity, the second piece would swing down perpendicular to the first, just touching the ground, and so serving as a support for the platform above. This created a convenient, sturdy step-up for any person too short to reach the sink otherwise. When not in use, the hinges allowed the two platforms to fold back up flush against the vanity, where they were held in place by magnets.

Jeanie's Kiddie Stool won first place in her school's contest. Two years later, at age seven, Jeanie won first prize again at Houston's first annual Invention Fair. As a result, she was featured on local TV and in the Houston Post. Soon thereafter, Jeanie discovered the Houston

Inventors Association. Encouraged by her fellow inventors, and helped by a member who was a patent attorney, Jeanie applied for a patent, which was granted in 1992 (#5,094,515, "Folding step for cabinet doors").

【105 年學測】閱讀測驗：49-52 出題來源

——http://time.com/4021101/middle-east-children-education-unicef-report/

13 Million Middle Eastern Children Are Unable to Attend School

At least 8,500 schools are unusable, and millions of people have been displaced

Ongoing conflicts across the Middle East have prevented more than 13 million children from attending school, according to a report published Thursday by UNICEF, the U.N.'s Children's Fund.

The report states that 40% of all children across the region are currently not receiving an education, a crisis it attributes to two repercussions of violence: the displacement of populations and structural damages to the schools themselves. Both issues stem from the tide of violence that has crossed the region in recent years.

The report examines nine countries — Syria, Palestine, Libya, Yemen, Sudan, Iraq, Lebanon, Turkey, and Jordan — where a state of war has become the norm. Across the region, violence has rendered 8,500 schools unusable. In certain cases, communities have relied on school buildings to function as makeshift shelters for the displaced, with up to nine families living in a single classroom in former schools across Iraq. The document's authors pay particularly close attention to Syria, where a bloody civil war has displaced at least 9 million people since the war began in 2011.

【105 年學測】閱讀測驗：53-56 出題來源

——http://www.smithsonianmag.com/science-nature/some-sea-snakes-can-go-seven-months-without-drinking-water-180950157/?no-ist

Some Sea Snakes Can Go Seven Months Without Drinking Water

To survive the dry season, yellow-bellied sea snakes severely dehydrate until the wet season brings freshwater for them to lap up from the ocean's surface Sea snakes—as their name implies—spend all of their time at sea. On land, these marine creatures are virtually helpless, unable to slither or move about. With their paddled tails, narrow heads and thin, fish-like bodies, a sea snake slinking through a coral reef could easily be mistaken for an eel. Yet for all of their sea faring finesse, sea snakes—which evolved from terrestrial snakes—are not completely at home beneath the waves. For starters, like sea turtles and marine mammals, they do not have gills and so must regularly surface for air. And like other marine animals with terrestrial roots, including penguins and marine iguanas, sea snakes had to evolve ways to excrete excess salt, which they accomplish special salt-expelling glands around their tongue. Unlike animals like sea turtles, however, the sea snakes' salt glands cannot handle the massive amounts of salt that would enter their bodies if they actually drank seawater.

This poses a serious problem when it comes to getting enough water to drink. If seawater is off limits, how do these animals survive in the ocean?

An international team of researchers decided to investigate this question by studying yellow-bellied sea snakes, which live in warm, open waters around the world. In a paper published in *Proceedings of the Royal Society B*, the team focused on a population of animals living near Costa Rica, where rain oftentimes does not fall for up to seven months out of the year. "Rainfall is more likely to occur over land, so the open ocean can be a virtual 'desert' especially during the dry season," the researchers explain.

⋮

104年大學入學學科能力測驗試題
英文考科

第壹部分：單選題（占72分）

一、詞彙題（占15分）

說明： 第1題至第15題，每題有4個選項，其中只有一個是正確或最適當的選項，請畫記在答案卡之「選擇題答案區」。各題答對者，得1分；答錯、未作答或畫記多於一個選項者，該題以零分計算。

1. Nowadays many companies adopt a ＿＿＿＿＿＿ work schedule which allows their employees to decide when to arrive at work—from as early as 6 a.m. to as late as 11 a.m.
   (A) relative　　(B) severe　　(C) primitive　　(D) flexible

2. To teach children right from wrong, some parents will ＿＿＿＿＿＿ their children when they behave well and punish them when they misbehave.
   (A) settle　　(B) declare　　(C) reward　　(D) neglect

3. To stick to a tight budget, Robert bought a more ＿＿＿＿＿＿ LED TV instead of a fancy, expensive 3D TV.
   (A) technical　　(B) significant　　(C) affordable　　(D) expressive

4. David's new book made it to the best-seller list because of its beautiful ＿＿＿＿＿＿ and amusing stories.
   (A) operations　(B) illustrations　(C) engagements　(D) accomplishments

5. The airport was closed because of the snowstorm, and our ＿＿＿＿＿＿ for Paris had to be delayed until the following day.
   (A) movement　(B) registration　(C) tendency　　(D) departure

6. The moment the students felt the earthquake, they ran ＿＿＿＿＿＿ out of the classroom to an open area outside.
   (A) swiftly　　(B) nearly　　(C) loosely　　(D) formally

7. The _____ capacity of this elevator is 400 kilograms. For safety reasons, it shouldn't be overloaded.

   (A) delicate   (B) automatic   (C) essential   (D) maximum

8. An open display of _____ behavior between men and women, such as hugging and kissing, is not allowed in some conservative societies.

   (A) intimate   (B) ashamed   (C) earnest   (D) urgent

9. When taking medicine, we should read the instructions on the _____ carefully because they provide important information such as how and when to take it.

   (A) medals   (B) quotes   (C) labels   (D) recipes

10. The angry passengers argued _____ with the airline staff because their flight was cancelled without any reason.

   (A) evidently   (B) furiously   (C) obediently   (D) suspiciously

11. To _____ the new product, the company offered some free samples before they officially launched it.

   (A) contribute   (B) impress   (C) promote   (D) estimate

12. I was worried about my first overseas trip, but my father _____ me that he would help plan the trip so that nothing would go wrong.

   (A) rescued   (B) assured   (C) inspired   (D) conveyed

13. The recent cooking oil scandals have led to calls for tougher _____ of sales of food products.

   (A) tolerance   (B) guarantee   (C) regulation   (D) distribution

14. John should _____ more often with his friends and family after work, instead of staying in his room to play computer games.

   (A) explore   (B) interact   (C) negotiate   (D) participate

15. To prevent the spread of the Ebola virus from West Africa to the rest of the world, many airports have begun Ebola _____ for passengers from the infected areas.

   (A) screenings   (B) listings   (C) clippings   (D) blockings

二、綜合測驗（占 15 分）

說明： 第 16 題至第 30 題，每題一個空格，請依文意選出最適當的一個選項，
　　　請畫記在答案卡之「選擇題答案區」。各題答對者，得 1 分；答錯、未
　　　作答或畫記多於一個選項者，該題以零分計算。

<u>第 16 至 20 題為題組</u>

　　Tai Chi Chuan is a type of ancient Chinese martial art.　People
___16___ Tai Chi mainly for its health benefits.　This centuries-old
Chinese mind-body exercise is now gaining popularity in the United
States.

　　The most familiar aspect of Tai Chi Chuan is the hand form, which
is a series of slow-flowing movements with poetic names ___17___
"dragons stirring up the wind" and "wave hands like clouds."　These
movements, forming an exercise system, ___18___ one to effortlessly
experience the vital life force, or the Qi energy, in one's body.

　　Tai Chi Chuan is not only a physical but also a ___19___ exercise.
Psychologically, this exercise may increase communication between the
body and the mind and enable one to deal with other people more
effectively.　It ___20___ stress and creates calmness and confidence.
Relaxation and a feeling of joy are among the first noticeable differences
in a Tai Chi student.

16. (A) practice　　　(B) consult　　　(C) display　　　(D) manage
17. (A) from　　　　　(B) like　　　　　(C) between　　　(D) regarding
18. (A) allow　　　　　(B) allows　　　 (C) allowed　　　 (D) allowing
19. (A) formal　　　　 (B) mental　　　 (C) social　　　　(D) global
20. (A) imposes　　　　(B) offends　　　(C) reduces　　　 (D) disturbs

<u>第 21 至 25 題為題組</u>

　　Much like the dove and robin, the bluebird is considered a very
lucky sign in most cultures, particularly when seen in the spring.

___21___, a woodpecker, when seen near the home, is regarded as a good
sign. In contrast, the peacock is not ___22___ seen as lucky. In places
like India, the peacock is considered lucky because the great many
"eyes" on its feathers are said to alert it to ___23___ evil. Peacocks are
also highly valued in China and Japan, where they are kept as symbols
by the ruling families to ___24___ their status and wealth. However, the
peacock receives only scorn from the rest of the world. The feathers of
peacocks are considered the most ___25___ part of the bird because the
eye-shaped markings on them are associated with "evil eyes." To bring
the evil eye into the home is thus believed to invite trouble and sorrow.

21. (A) Therefore   (B) Nevertheless   (C) Roughly   (D) Similarly
22. (A) officially   (B) mutually   (C) universally   (D) eventually
23. (A) approach   (B) approaching
    (C) approached   (D) be approaching
24. (A) replace   (B) disguise   (C) distinguish   (D) represent
25. (A) unlucky   (B) illogical   (C) impossible   (D) unnecessary

第 26 至 30 題為題組

   Nutritional products that can be collected from trees include fruits,
nuts, seeds, leaves, and bark. Tree products have been an important part
of diets for thousands of years, from early humans ___26___ fruits and
nuts to the first cultivation of important trees, such as mango and apple.

   The apple is one of the world's most cultivated fruit trees, ___27___
over 7,000 different kinds in existence. Despite their great ___28___,
however, most domesticated apples can be traced back to a common
ancestor, the wild apple of Central Asia, *Malus sieversii*. Apples have
been grown for thousands of years in Asia and Europe, and ___29___ to
North America by European colonists in the 17th century. Today, apples
are ___30___ eaten the world over and form the basis for multi-million
dollar industries. In 2005, at least 55 million tons of apples were grown
worldwide, which generated a value of about $10 billion.

26. (A) to gather　(B) gather　(C) gathered　(D) gathering
27. (A) all　(B) with　(C) around　(D) still
28. (A) variety　(B) harvest　(C) condition　(D) discovery
29. (A) bring　(B) have brought
　　(C) were brought　(D) have been brought
30. (A) regularly　(B) particularly　(C) permanently　(D) barely

三、文意選填（占 10 分）

說明：　第 31 題至第 40 題，每題一個空格，請依文意在文章後所提供的 (A) 到
　　　　(J) 選項中分別選出最適當者，並將其英文字母代號畫記在答案卡之「選
　　　　擇題答案區」。各題答對者，得 1 分；答錯、未作答或畫記多於一個選
　　　　項者，該題以零分計算。

第 31 至 40 題為題組

　　A paperclip, made of steel wire bent into a hooped shape, is an
instrument used to hold sheets of paper together. This common ___31___
is a wonder of simplicity and function. But where did this simple,
cheap, and indispensable invention come from?

　　In the late 19th century, the most common way to hold papers
together was by using a pin. Although the pin was an inexpensive tool
and was easily ___32___, it would leave holes in the paper. Later, as
steel wire became more common, inventors began to notice its elastic
feature. With this feature, it could be stretched and ___33___ various
clip-like objects. In the years just prior to 1900, quite a few paperclip
designs emerged. The name most frequently ___34___ the paperclip
invention is Johan Vaaler, a Norwegian inventor. However, Vaaler's
clips were not the same as the paperclips currently in use. Specifically,
they did not have the interior loop we see today. The ___35___ looped
design was invented by Gem Manufacturing Ltd. in England. This clip
is therefore sometimes ___36___ the Gem clip.

　　Because of Vaaler, the paperclip played an important ___37___ role
in Norway. During World War II, Norway was occupied by the Nazis.

Norwegians were prohibited from wearing any ___38___ of their national unity, such as buttons with the initials of their king. Thus, in ___39___, they started wearing paperclips to show their solidarity. The reason for doing this was simple: Paperclips were a Norwegian invention whose original function was to bind together. After the war, a giant paperclip statue was erected in Oslo to ___40___ Vaaler—even though his design was never actually manufactured.

(A) familiar   (B) honor   (C) device   (D) removable
(E) known as   (F) protest   (G) symbol   (H) twisted into
(I) associated with (J) historical

四、閱讀測驗（占 32 分）

說明： 第 41 題至第 56 題，每題請分別根據各篇文章之文意選出最適當的一個
　　　選項，請畫記在答案卡之「選擇題答案區」。各題答對者，得 2 分；答
　　　錯、未作答或畫記多於一個選項者，該題以零分計算。

第 41 至 44 題為題組

　　In 2009, the Taiwu Elementary School Folk Singers were invited to perform in Belgium, France, Germany, and Luxemburg. In 2011, they were voted as one of the world's top five performance groups by audiences of Japan Broadcasting Corporation's Amazing Voice program.

　　Recalling the group's first tour in Europe, Camake Valaule, a physical education teacher and the founder of the Taiwu Elementary School Folk Singers, admitted that he felt very nervous. He was worried that the audience would fall asleep since most of the 75-minute performance was a cappella, that is, singing without instrumental sound. Surprisingly, the audience listened with full focus and high spirits. Camake said, "They told me afterward that through our performance, they had a vision of our country, our village, without having to visit it. This experience greatly boosted our confidence."

According to Camake Valaule, singing traditional ballads has helped students and their parents to re-understand their culture. "It used to be that the only ones who could sing these songs were tribal elders aged between 50 and 60. Now with the children performing the pieces, parents are beginning to ask, 'Why do we not know how to sing these ballads?' Many times nowadays, it is the children who teach the songs to their parents, putting back **the pieces of a blurred memory**."

Winning international fame, however, was neither the original intention nor the main reason why Camake founded the group in 2006. The most important thing was to make children understand why they sing these songs and to preserve and pass on their culture. Referring to the relocation of Taiwu Elementary School and Taiwu Village following Typhoon Morakot in August 2009, Camake said, "We could not take the forest or our houses in the mountains with us; but we were able to bring our culture along. As long as the children are willing to sing, I will always be there for them, singing with them and leading them to experience the meaning of the ballads."

41. Which of the following is true about Taiwu Elementary School Folk Singers?
   (A) The group was first established in 2009.
   (B) The group was founded by a PE teacher.
   (C) The singers usually sing popular folk songs.
   (D) The singers learn to sing from their parents.

42. On his first trip to Europe, why did Camake think the audience might fall asleep?
   (A) The average age of the audience was between fifty and sixty.
   (B) Most of the performance was not accompanied by any instrument.
   (C) Nobody could understand the language and the meaning of the songs.
   (D) The audience could not visualize the theme sung by the school children.

43. What does "**the pieces of a blurred memory**" in the third paragraph most likely refer to?
    (A) The children's ignorance of their own culture.
    (B) The fading memories about old tribal people.
    (C) The broken pieces of knowledge taught at school.
    (D) The parents' vague understanding of their own tradition.

44. What did Camake realize after the incident of Typhoon Morakot?
    (A) The significance of the relocation of Taiwu Elementary School.
    (B) The need to respect nature to avoid being destroyed by it.
    (C) The importance of passing on the traditional culture.
    (D) The consequence of building houses in the forest.

第 45 至 48 題為題組

When it comes to medical care, many patients and doctors believe "more is better." But what they do not realize is that overtreatment— too many scans, too many blood tests, too many procedures—may pose harm. Sometimes a test leads you down a path to more and more testing, some of which may be invasive, or to treatment for things that should be left alone.

Terrence Power, for example, complained that after his wife learned she had Wegener's disease, an uncommon disorder of the immune system, they found it difficult to refuse testing recommended by her physician. The doctor insisted on office visits every three weeks, even when she was feeling well. He frequently ordered blood tests and X-rays, and repeatedly referred her to specialists for even minor complaints. Even when tests came back negative, more were ordered, and she was hospitalized as a precaution when she developed a cold. She had as many as 25 doctor visits during one six-month period. The couple was spending about $30,000 a year for her care.

After several years of physical suffering and near financial ruin from the medical costs, the couple began questioning the treatment after consulting with other patients in online support groups. "It's a really hard thing to determine when **they**'ve crossed the line," Mr. Power said. "You think she's getting the best care in the world, but after a while you start to wonder: What is the objective?" Mr. Power then spoke with his own primary care doctor, who advised him to find a new specialist to oversee Mrs. Power's care. Under the new doctor's care, the regular testing stopped and Mrs. Power's condition stabilized. Now she sees the doctor only four or five times a year.

45. What is the main idea of this passage?
    (A) Treatments do not always cause harmful side effects.
    (B) Patients tend to believe more testing is better treatment.
    (C) Too much medical care may not be beneficial to patients.
    (D) Doctors generally recommend office visits that are necessary.

46. Which of the following was a problem for Mrs. Power during her medical treatment?
    (A) She had to be hospitalized for three weeks whenever she had a cold.
    (B) She didn't have any insurance, so she went broke because of her illness.
    (C) When test results showed she was fine, her doctor still ordered more tests.
    (D) Her doctor asked her to consult other specialists due to her constant complaints.

47. Who does "**they**" in the third paragraph most likely refer to?
    (A) Physicians.
    (B) Other patients.
    (C) Mr. and Mrs. Power.
    (D) The online support groups.

48. Which of the following best describes the author's attitude toward medical tests?
   (A) More tests than necessary are too much.
   (B) Medical tests are essential for disease prevention.
   (C) Many tests are needed for confirmation of diagnosis.
   (D) Doctors' interpretations of test results are seldom wrong.

第 49 至 52 題爲題組

　　Henri Cartier-Bresson (1908–2004) is one of the most original and influential figures in the history of photography. His humane, spontaneous photographs helped establish photojournalism as an art form.

　　Cartier-Bresson's family was wealthy—his father made a fortune as a textile manufacturer—but Cartier-Bresson later joked that due to his parents' frugal ways, it often seemed as though his family was poor.

　　Educated in Paris, Cartier-Bresson developed an early love for literature and the arts. As a teenager, Cartier-Bresson rebelled against his parents' formal ways of education. In his early adulthood, he even drifted toward communism. But it was art that remained at the center of his life.

　　Cartier-Bresson traveled to Africa in 1931 to hunt antelope and boar. And Africa fueled another interest in him: photography. He then wandered around the world with his camera, using a handheld camera to catch images from fleeting moments of everyday life.

　　Not long after World War II, Cartier-Bresson traveled east, spending considerable time in India, where he met and photographed Gandhi shortly before his assassination in 1948. Cartier-Bresson's subsequent work to document Gandhi's death and its immediate impact on the country became one of *Life Magazine*'s most prized photo essays.

　　Cartier-Bresson's approach to photography remained much the same throughout his life. He made clear his dislike of images that had been improved by artificial light, darkroom effects, and even cropping. The naturalist in Cartier-Bresson believed that all editing should be done when the photo is taken. In 1952, his first book, *The Decisive Moment*, a rich collection of his work spanning two decades, was published. "There is nothing in this world that does not have a decisive moment," he said.

In 1968, he began to turn away from photography and returned to his passion for drawing and painting.

49. Which of the following best describes Cartier-Bresson's family background?
    (A) His family was rich but was very economical.
    (B) His father went to Paris to open a textile factory.
    (C) His wealthy family went bankrupt and became poor.
    (D) His parents were very liberal in their ways of education.

50. Which of the following is true about Cartier-Bresson's career in photography?
    (A) He devoted himself to photography all his life.
    (B) He developed a passion for photography when he traveled to Africa.
    (C) He quit photography right after the publication of *The Decisive Moment*.
    (D) During World War II, he documented the everyday life of the Indian people.

51. What significance did Cartier-Bresson have to Gandhi of India?
    (A) He witnessed Gandhi's assassination in 1948.
    (B) He was the first photographer to take Gandhi's photo.
    (C) He used photos to document the effect of Gandhi's death on India.
    (D) His photos told the world who was guilty of assassinating Gandhi.

52. Which of the following is true about Cartier-Bresson's approach to photography?
    (A) He never waited for a decisive moment to shoot photos.
    (B) He preferred to edit his images carefully in his darkroom.
    (C) Most of his photos described things that happen every day.
    (D) He experimented with different ways and settled on being a naturalist.

第 53 至 56 題為題組

　　You've most likely heard the news by now: A car-commuting, desk-bound, TV-watching lifestyle can be harmful to our health. All the time that we spend rooted in the chair is linked to increased risks of so many deadly diseases that experts have named this modern-day health epidemic the "sitting disease."

　　Sitting for too long slows down the body's metabolism and the way enzymes break down our fat reserves, raising both blood sugar levels and blood pressure. Small amounts of regular activity, even just standing and moving around, throughout the day is enough to bring the increased levels back down. And those small amounts of activity add up—30 minutes of light activity in two or three-minute bursts can be just as effective as a half-hour block of exercise. But without that activity, blood sugar levels and blood pressure keep creeping up, steadily damaging the inside of the arteries and increasing the risk of diabetes, heart disease, stroke, and other serious diseases. In essence, fundamental changes in biology occur if you sit for too long.

　　But wait, you're a runner. You needn't worry about the harm of a **sedentary** lifestyle because you exercise regularly, right? Well, not so fast. Recent studies show that people spend an average of 64 hours a week sitting, whether or not they exercise 150 minutes a week as recommended by World Health Organization (WHO). Regular exercisers, furthermore, are found to be about 30 percent less active on days when they exercise. Overall, most people simply aren't exercising or moving around enough to counteract all the harm that can result from sitting nine hours or more a day.

Scared straight out of your chair? Good. The remedy is as simple as standing up and taking activity breaks.

53. What is the purpose of this passage?
    (A) To point out the challenges of the modern lifestyle.
    (B) To discuss how a modern epidemic may spread quickly.
    (C) To explore the effects of regular exercise to our body.
    (D) To explain the threat to our health from long hours of sitting.

54. What does the word "**sedentary**" in the third paragraph most likely mean?
    (A) Modern.　　　(B) Risky.　　　(C) Inactive.　　　(D) Epidemic.

55. What is the best way to bring down high blood sugar level and blood pressure?
    (A) Exercising for 150 minutes or more every week.
    (B) Getting rid of the habit of car commuting and TV watching.
    (C) Interrupting sitting time with light activity as often as possible.
    (D) Standing or moving around for at least two or three minutes every day.

56. Which of the following may be inferred about those who do serious exercise?
    (A) They often live longer than those who don't exercise.
    (B) They tend to stand or move around less on days they work out.
    (C) They generally spend less time sitting than those who are inactive.
    (D) They usually do not meet the standard of exercise recommended by WHO.

第貳部份：非選擇題（占 28 分）

說明： 本部分共有二題，請依各題指示作答，答案必須寫在「答案卷」上，並標明大題號（一、二）。作答務必使用筆尖較粗之黑色墨水的筆書寫，且不得使用鉛筆。

一、中譯英（占 8 分）

說明： 1. 請將以下中文句子譯成正確、通順、達意的英文，並將答案寫在「答案卷」上。

2. 請依序作答，並標明題號。每題 4 分，共 8 分。

1. 一個成功的企業不應該把獲利當作最主要的目標。

2. 它應該負起社會責任，以增進大眾的福祉。

二、英文作文（占 20 分）

說明： 1. 依提示在「答案卷」上寫一篇英文作文。

2. 文長至少 120 個單詞（words）。

提示： 下面兩本書是學校建議的暑假閱讀書籍，請依書名想想看該書的內容，並思考你會選擇哪一本書閱讀，為什麼？請在第一段說明你會選哪一本書及你認為該書的內容大概會是什麼，第二段提出你選擇該書的理由。

EVERYONE IS BEAUTIFUL:
Respect Others & Be Yourself

Caroline Strong

LEADERSHIP IS A CHOICE:
Conquer Your Fears &
You Can Be a Leader Too

Austin Young

104年度學科能力測驗英文科試題詳解

第壹部分：單選題

一、詞彙題：

1. (**D**) Nowadays many companies adopt a <u>flexible</u> work schedule which allows their employees to decide when to arrive at work—from as early as 6 a.m. to as late as 11 a.m.
   現在許多的公司採用彈性的工作時間，讓員工能自己決定何時到達公司——最早早上六點，最晚早上十一點。
   (A) relative〔'rɛlətɪv〕*adj.* 相對的
   (B) severe〔sə'vɪr〕*adj.* 嚴格的
   (C) primitive〔'prɪmətɪv〕*adj.* 原始的
   (D) ***flexible***〔'flɛksəbḷ〕*adj.* 有彈性的
   nowadays〔'nauə,dez〕*adv.* 現在　　adopt〔ə'dɑpt〕*v.* 採用
   schedule〔'skɛdʒʊl〕*n.* 時間表　　allow〔ə'lau〕*v.* 讓
   employee〔,ɛmplɔɪ'i〕*n.* 員工　　work〔wɝk〕*n.* 工作地點

2. (**C**) To teach children right from wrong, some parents will <u>reward</u> their children when they behave well and punish them when they misbehave. 為了教導孩子分辨是非，有些家長在孩子表現良好時會<u>給予獎勵</u>，行為不當時會給予懲罰。
   (A) settle〔'sɛtḷ〕*v.* 安頓　　　　(B) declare〔dɪ'klɛr〕*v.* 宣布
   (C) ***reward***〔rɪ'wɔrd〕*v.* 獎賞　(D) neglect〔nɪg'lɛkt〕*v.* 忽視
   teach sb. ***right from wrong*** 教導某人分辨是非
   behave〔bɪ'hev〕*v.* 表現　　punish〔'pʌnɪʃ〕*v.* 處罰
   misbehave〔,mɪsbɪ'hev〕*v.* 行為不檢點

3. (**C**) To stick to a tight budget, Robert bought a more <u>affordable</u> LED TV instead of a fancy, expensive 3D TV.
   為了堅守緊縮的預算，羅伯特買了一台較<u>負擔得起的</u>LED電視，而不是酷炫且昂貴的3D立體電視。
   (A) technical〔'tɛknɪkḷ〕*adj.* 技術的

(B) significant〔sɪg'nɪfəkənt〕*adj.* 意義重大的
(C) ***affordable***〔ə'fɔrdəbl〕*adj.* 負擔得起的
(D) expressive〔ɪk'sprɛsɪv〕*adj.* 表現的；表達的
stick to 堅持；堅守　　tight〔taɪt〕*adj.* 緊縮的
budget〔'bʌdʒɪt〕*n.* 預算　　fancy〔'fænsɪ〕*adj.* 華麗的；昂貴的

4. (**B**) David's new book made it to the best-seller list because of its
beautiful illustrations and amusing stories.　大衛的新書因爲有
美麗的插圖和有趣的故事，所以登上了暢銷書排行榜。
(A) operation〔ˌɑpə'reʃən〕*n.* 操作；手術
(B) ***illustration***〔ˌɪˌlʌs'treʃən〕*n.* 插圖
(C) engagement〔ɪn'gedʒmənt〕*n.* 訂婚
(D) accomplishments〔ə'kɑmplɪʃmənts〕*n. pl.* 成就
make it 成功；辦到　　best-seller〔'bɛst'sɛlə〕*n.* 暢銷書
amusing〔ə'mjuzɪŋ〕*adj.* 有趣的

5. (**D**) The airport was closed because of the snowstorm, and our departure
for Paris had to be delayed until the following day.
機場因爲暴風雪而關閉，而我們前往巴黎的班機也被延到了隔天。
(A) movement〔'muvmənt〕*n.* 動作
(B) registration〔ˌrɛdʒɪ'streʃən〕*n.* 登記；註冊
(C) tendency〔'tɛndənsɪ〕*n.* 傾向
(D) ***departure***〔dɪ'partʃə〕*n.* 出發
snowstorm〔'sno,stɔrm〕*n.* 暴風雪　　delay〔dɪ'le〕*v.* 延誤
the following day 隔天

6. (**A**) The moment the students felt the earthquake, they ran swiftly out of
the classroom to an open area outside.
學生們一感受到地震，就快速衝出教室，到戶外空曠處。
(A) ***swiftly***〔'swɪftlɪ〕*adv.* 快速地　　(B) nearly〔'nɪrlɪ〕*adv.* 幾乎
(C) loosely〔'luslɪ〕*adv.* 鬆鬆地　　(D) formally〔'fɔrmlɪ〕*adv.* 正式地
the moment 一…就～　　open〔'opən〕*adj.* 空曠的

7. (**D**) The maximum capacity of this elevator is 400 kilograms. For safety
reasons, it shouldn't be overloaded.
這部電梯最大的容量是四百公斤。爲了安全起見，它不應該超載。

(A) delicate〔'dɛləkɪt〕*adj.* 細緻的
(B) automatic〔,ɔtə'mætɪk〕*adj.* 自動的
(C) essential〔ɪ'sɛnʃəl〕*adj.* 必要的
(D) ***maximum***〔'mæksəməm〕*adj.* 最大的

capacity〔kə'pæsətɪ〕*n.* 容量　　elevator〔'ɛlə,vetɚ〕*n.* 電梯
kilogram〔'kɪlə,græm〕*n.* 公斤　　overload〔,ovɚ'lod〕*v.* 使超載

8. (**A**) An open display of <u>intimate</u> behavior between men and women, such as hugging and kissing, is not allowed in some conservative societies. 在某些保守的社會中，不允許男女之間，公開做出像是擁抱與親吻的<u>親密</u>行為。

(A) ***intimate***〔'ɪntəmɪt〕*adj.* 親密的
(B) ashamed〔ə'ʃemd〕*adj.* 羞愧的
(C) earnest〔'ɝnɪst〕*adj.* 認真的
(D) urgent〔'ɝdʒənt〕*adj.* 緊急的

open〔'opən〕*adj.* 公開的　　display〔dɪ'sple〕*n.* 展示
behavior〔bɪ'hevjɚ〕*n.* 行為　　hug〔hʌg〕*v.* 擁抱
allow〔ə'laʊ〕*v.* 允許　　conservative〔kən'sɝvətɪv〕*adj.* 保守的

9. (**C**) When taking medicine, we should read the instructions on the <u>labels</u> carefully because they provide important information such as how and when to take it. 我們吃藥時，應該小心閱讀<u>標籤</u>上的使用說明，因為它們提供了重要的資訊，像是服用方法及服用時間。

(A) medal〔'mɛdḷ〕*n.* 獎牌　　　　(B) quote〔kwot〕*n.* 引用文
(C) ***label***〔'lebḷ〕*n.* 標籤　　　　(D) recipe〔'rɛsəpɪ〕*n.* 烹飪法

instructions〔ɪn'strʌkʃənz〕*n. pl.* 使用說明
provide〔prə'vaɪd〕*v.* 提供

10. (**B**) The angry passengers argued <u>furiously</u> with the airline staff because their flight was cancelled without any reason. 因為航班被毫無理由地取消，所以生氣的乘客很<u>憤怒地</u>與航空公司的員工爭吵。

(A) evidently〔'ɛvədəntlɪ〕*adv.* 明顯地
(B) ***furiously***〔'fjʊrɪəslɪ〕*adv.* 狂怒地
(C) obediently〔ə'bidɪəntlɪ〕*adv.* 服從地
(D) suspiciously〔sə'spɪʃəslɪ〕*adv.* 懷疑地

argue〔ˈɑrgju〕v. 爭論　　airline〔ˈɛrˌlaɪn〕n. 航空公司
staff〔stæf〕n. 工作人員　　flight〔flaɪt〕n. 班機
cancel〔ˈkænsḷ〕v. 取消

11. (**C**) To <u>promote</u> the new product, the company offered some free samples before they officially launched it.
為了要<u>促銷</u>新產品，這間公司在正式推出商品前，提供了一些免費的樣品。

(A) contribute〔kənˈtrɪbjut〕v. 貢獻
(B) impress〔ɪmˈprɛs〕v. 使印象深刻
(C) ***promote***〔prəˈmot〕v. 促銷
(D) estimate〔ˈɛstəˌmet〕v. 估計

offer〔ˈɔfɚ〕v. 提供　　free〔fri〕adj. 免費的
sample〔ˈsæmpḷ〕n. 樣品　　officially〔əˈfɪʃəlɪ〕adv. 正式地
launch〔lɔntʃ〕v. 上市；發行

12. (**B**) I was worried about my first overseas trip, but my father <u>assured</u> me that he would help plan the trip so that nothing would go wrong.
我很擔心我的第一趟海外旅遊，但是我爸爸<u>向我保證</u>，他會協助規劃這趟旅程，使它萬無一失。

(A) rescue〔ˈrɛskju〕v. 拯救　　(B) ***assure***〔əˈʃur〕v. 向…保證
(C) inspire〔ɪnˈspaɪr〕v. 激勵　　(D) convey〔kənˈve〕v. 傳達
overseas〔ˈovɚˈsiz〕adj. 國外的　　***so that*** 以便於　　***go wrong*** 出錯

13. (**C**) The recent cooking oil scandals have led to calls for tougher <u>regulation</u> of sales of food products.
最近的食用油醜聞使我們必須更嚴格<u>管制</u>食品的銷售。

(A) tolerance〔ˈtɑlərəns〕n. 寬容
(B) guarantee〔ˌgærənˈti〕n. 保證
(C) ***regulation***〔ˌrɛgjəˈleʃən〕n. 管制；規定
(D) distribution〔ˌdɪstrəˈbjuʃən〕n. 分發

recent〔ˈrisṇt〕adj. 最近的　　***cooking oil*** 烹飪油
scandal〔ˈskændḷ〕n. 醜聞　　***lead to*** 導致
call〔kɔl〕n. 需要；必要　　tough〔tʌf〕adj.（法律、規則等）嚴格的
sales〔selz〕n. pl. 銷售

14. (**B**) John should <u>interact</u> more often with his friends and family after work, instead of staying in his room to play computer games.
約翰應該在下班後更常與他的家人朋友<u>互動</u>，而不是待在自己的房間玩電腦遊戲。

(A) explore〔ɪkˋsplor〕*v.* 探險；探索
(B) ***interact***〔͵ɪntɚˋækt〕*v.* 互動
(C) negotiate〔nɪˋgoʃɪ͵et〕*v.* 協商；談判
(D) participate〔parˋtɪsə͵pet〕*v.* 參加

instead of 而不是

15. (**A**) To prevent the spread of the Ebola virus from West Africa to the rest of the world, many airports have begun Ebola <u>screenings</u> for passengers from the infected areas.
為了預防伊波拉病毒由西非散播到全世界其他地方，所以許多機場已開始針對來自疫區的乘客進行伊波拉病毒<u>篩檢</u>。

(A) ***screening***〔ˋskrinɪŋ〕*n.* 篩檢　　(B) listing〔ˋlɪstɪŋ〕*n.* 列表
(C) clipping〔ˋklɪpɪŋ〕*n.* 修剪；剪報　(D) blocking〔ˋblɑkɪŋ〕*n.* 阻礙

prevent〔prɪˋvɛnt〕*v.* 預防　　spread〔sprɛd〕*n.* 散播
Ebola〔ɪˋbolə〕*n.* 伊波拉　　virus〔ˋvaɪrəs〕*n.* 病毒
rest〔rɛst〕*n.* 其餘之物　　infected〔ɪnˋfɛktɪd〕*adj.* 受感染的

二、綜合測驗：

第 16 至 20 題為題組

Tai Chi Chuan is a type of ancient Chinese martial art. People <u>practice</u>
₁₆
Tai Chi mainly for its health benefits. This centuries-old Chinese mind-body exercise is now gaining popularity in the United States.
太極拳是一種中國古代的武術。人們主要是為了健康而打太極拳。這個有數百年歷史的身心運動，現在在美國也越來越受歡迎。

Tai Chi Chuan 太極拳　　type〔taɪp〕*n.* 類型
ancient〔ˋenʃənt〕*adj.* 古代的　　***martial art*** 武術
mainly〔ˋmenlɪ〕*adv.* 主要地　　benefit〔ˋbɛnəfɪt〕*n.* 利益；好處
centuries-old〔ˋsɛntʃurɪzˋold〕*adj.* 悠久的；數百年歷史的
mind-body exercise 身心運動【包含身體運動與放鬆心靈】
gain〔gen〕*v.* 獲得　　popularity〔͵pɑpjəˋlærətɪ〕*n.* 受歡迎

16. (**A**) 依句意，應選 (A) ***practice*** 〔'præktɪs 〕 *v.* 做；執行 (= *perform*)。
而 (B) consult 〔 kən'sʌlt 〕 *v.* 請教；查閱，(C) display 〔 dɪs'ple 〕 *v.* 展示，
(D) manage 〔'mænɪdʒ 〕 *v.* 設法；管理，皆不合句意。

The most familiar aspect of Tai Chi Chuan is the hand form, which is a series of slow-flowing movements with poetic names <u>like</u> "dragons stirring
17
up the wind" and "wave hands like clouds." These movements, forming an exercise system, <u>allow</u> one to effortlessly experience the vital life force, or
18
the Qi energy, in one's body.

大家對太極拳最熟悉的方面，就是它的手形，那是一系列慢而流暢的動作，有著如詩般的名字，像是「龍攪拌風」、「雲手」等。這些動作形成了一個運動系統，讓人能毫不費力地體驗自己體內的生命力，也就是氣力。

> familiar 〔 fə'mɪljə 〕 *adj.* 熟悉的　　aspect 〔'æspɛkt 〕 *n.* 方面
> form 〔 fɔrm 〕 *n.* 形式　*v.* 形成　***a series of*** 一連串的；一系列的
> flowing 〔'floɪŋ 〕 *adj.* 流暢的　　movement 〔'muvmənt 〕 *n.* 動作
> poetic 〔 po'ɛtɪk 〕 *adj.* 充滿詩意的
> effortlessly 〔'ɛfətlɪslɪ 〕 *adv.* 不費力地；輕鬆地
> vital 〔'vaɪtl̩ 〕 *adj.* 生命的　***vital life force*** 生命力 (= *vital force*)
> or 〔 ɔr 〕 *conj.* 也就是　　Qi 〔 tʃɪ 〕 *n.* 氣
> energy 〔'ɛnədʒɪ 〕 *n.* 活力；精力

17. (**B**) 依句意，選 (B) ***like*** 〔 laɪk 〕 *prep.* 像是 (= *such as*)。
而 (D) regarding 〔 rɪ'gɑrdɪŋ 〕 *prep.* 關於，則不合句意。

18. (**A**) 主詞是 These movements，而分詞片語 forming…system 修飾 movements，故空格應填動詞，依句意為現在式，且主詞為複數，故選 (A) ***allow*** 〔 ə'lau 〕 *v.* 讓。

Tai Chi Chuan is not only a physical but also a <u>mental</u> exercise.
19
Psychologically, this exercise may increase communication between the body and the mind and enable one to deal with other people more effectively. It <u>reduces</u> stress and creates calmness and confidence. Relaxation and a feeling
20
of joy are among the first noticeable differences in a Tai Chi student.

太極拳不僅是身體的，也是心理的運動。就心理學而言，這種運動可以增加身體與心靈的溝通，而且能使人更有效地與別人溝通。太極拳能夠減少壓力，並創造平靜與信心。學太極拳的人最先會發現的明顯不同處，包含放鬆與快樂的感覺。

not only…*but* (*also*)~　不僅…而且~　　physical（ˈfɪzɪkl̩）*adj.* 身體的
psychologically（ˌsaɪkəˈlɑdʒɪkl̩ɪ）*adv.* 心理上
increase（ɪnˈkris）*v.* 增加　　communication（kəˌmjunəˈkeʃən）*n.* 溝通
enable（ɪnˈebl̩）*v.* 使能夠　　*deal with* 應付；處理；與~交往
effectively（ɪˈfɛktɪvlɪ）*adv.* 有效地　　stress（strɛs）*n.* 壓力
create（krɪˈet）*v.* 創造　　calmness（ˈkɑmnɪs）*n.* 平靜
confidence（ˈkɑnfədəns）*n.* 信心　　relaxation（ˌrilæksˈeʃən）*n.* 放鬆
joy（dʒɔɪ）*n.* 快樂　　noticeable（ˈnotɪsəbl̩）*adj.* 明顯的

19.（ **B** ）依句意，選 (B) *mental*（ˈmɛntl̩）*adj.* 心理的。而 (A) formal（ˈfɔrml̩）*adj.* 正式的，(C) social（ˈsoʃəl）*adj.* 社會的，(D) global（ˈglobl̩）*adj.* 全球的，則不合句意。

20.（ **C** ）依句意，選 (C) *reduces*（rɪˈdjusɪz）*v.* 減少。而 (A) impose（ɪmˈpos）*v.* 強加，(B) offend（əˈfɛnd）*v.* 冒犯，(D) disturb（dɪsˈtɝb）*v.* 打擾，則不合句意。

第 21 至 25 題為題組

Much like the dove and robin, the bluebird is considered a very lucky sign in most cultures, particularly when seen in the spring. <u>Similarly</u>, a
　　　　　　　　　　　　　　　　　　　　　　　　　　　　21
woodpecker, when seen near the home, is regarded as a good sign. In contrast, the peacock is not <u>universally</u> seen as lucky. In places like India,
　　　　　　　　　　　　　　　　　　22
the peacock is considered lucky because the great many "eyes" on its feathers are said to alert it to <u>approaching</u> evil.
　　　　　　　　　　　　　23

藍鳥像鴿子和知更鳥一樣，在大部份的文化中，被認為是非常幸運的象徵，尤其是在春天看到的時候。同樣地，在住家附近看到啄木鳥時，也被認為是個好兆頭。相較之下，孔雀並非普遍被認為是幸運的。像印度這樣的地方，孔雀被認為幸運，是因為牠羽毛上有許多「眼睛」，據說能使牠對即將接近的惡事提高警覺。

much like 很像　　*dove* 〔 dʌv 〕*n.* 鴿子　　*robin* 〔ˋrɑbɪn 〕*n.* 知更鳥
bluebird 〔ˋblu͵bɝd 〕*n.* 藍鳥　　*consider* 〔 kənˋsɪdɚ 〕*v.* 認為
sign 〔 saɪn 〕*n.* 象徵　　*particularly* 〔 pɚˋtɪkjələlɪ 〕*adv.* 尤其；特別是
woodpecker 〔ˋwʊd͵pɛkɚ 〕*n.* 啄木鳥　　*regard* 〔 rɪˋgɑrd 〕*v.* 認為
in contrast 相較之下　　*peacock* 〔ˋpi͵kɑk 〕*n.* 孔雀
a great many 許多的　　*feather* 〔ˋfɛðɚ 〕*n.* 羽毛　　***be said to*** 據說
alert 〔 əˋlɝt 〕*v.* 使警覺　　***alert sb. to sth.*** 使某人對某事提高警覺
evil 〔ˋivl̩ 〕*n.* 惡事

21. (**D**) 依句意，選 (D) ***similarly*** 〔ˋsɪmɪlɚlɪ 〕*adv.* 同樣地。
　　而 (A) therefore 〔ˋðɛr͵for 〕*adv.* 因此，(B) nevertheless 〔͵nɛvɚðɚˋlɛs 〕
　　adv. 然而，(C) roughly 〔ˋrʌflɪ 〕*adv.* 粗略地，則不合句意。

22. (**C**) 依句意，選 (C) ***universally*** 〔͵junəˋvɝslɪ 〕*adv.* 普遍地。
　　而 (A) officially 〔 əˋfɪʃəlɪ 〕*adv.* 正式地，(B) mutually 〔ˋmjutʃʊəlɪ 〕*adv.*
　　互相，(D) eventually 〔 ɪˋvɛntʃʊəlɪ 〕*adv.* 最後，則不合句意。

23. (**B**) 依句意，選 (B) ***approaching*** 〔 əˋprotʃɪŋ 〕*adj.* 即將接近的。現在分詞當
　　形容詞用，修飾後面的名詞 evil。

Peacocks are also highly valued in China and Japan, where they are kept as
symbols by the ruling families to <u>represent</u> their status and wealth. However,
24
the peacock receives only scorn from the rest of the world. The feathers of
peacocks are considered the most <u>unlucky</u> part of the bird because the
25
eye-shaped markings on them are associated with "evil eyes." To bring the
evil eye into the home is thus believed to invite trouble and sorrow.
孔雀在中國和日本也非常受到重視，牠們被統治家族養來當作代表地位和財富的
象徵。然而，孔雀在世界其他地方卻只受到蔑視。孔雀的羽毛被認為是牠們身上
最不幸的部分，因為上面像眼睛般的斑紋，被與「邪惡之眼」聯想在一起。因此
將邪惡之眼帶入家中，被認為會招來麻煩和悲傷。

highly 〔ˋhaɪlɪ 〕*adv.* 非常　　*value* 〔ˋvælju 〕*v.* 重視
keep 〔 kip 〕*v.* 飼養　　*symbol* 〔ˋsɪmbl̩ 〕*n.* 象徵
ruling 〔ˋrulɪŋ 〕*adj.* 統治的　　*status* 〔ˋstetəs 〕*n.* 地位
wealth 〔 wɛlθ 〕*n.* 財富　　*scorn* 〔 skorn 〕*n.* 蔑視；嘲笑

eye-shaped〔'aɪˌʃɛpt〕*adj.* 形狀像眼睛的　　marking〔'mɑrkɪŋ〕*n.* 斑紋
be associated with 被和…聯想在一起；與…有關
thus〔ðʌs〕*adv.* 因此　　invite〔ɪn'vaɪt〕*v.* 招來；引起
sorrow〔'sɑro〕*n.* 悲傷

24. (**D**) 依句意，選 (D) ***represent***〔ˌrɛprɪ'zɛnt〕*v.* 代表。而 (A) replace〔rɪ'ples〕
　　　v. 取代，(B) disguise〔dɪs'gaɪs〕*v.* 偽裝，(C) distinguish〔dɪs'tɪŋgwɪʃ〕
　　　v. 分辨，則不合句意。

25. (**A**) 依句意，選 (A) ***unlucky***〔ʌn'lʌkɪ〕*adj.* 不幸的。而 (B) illogical
　　　〔ɪ'lɑdʒɪkl̩〕*adj.* 不合邏輯的，(C) impossible〔ɪm'pɑsəbl̩〕*adj.* 不可能的，
　　　(D) unnecessary〔ʌn'nɛsəˌsɛrɪ〕*adj.* 不需要的，則不合句意。

第 26 至 30 題為題組

　　Nutritional products that can be collected from trees include fruits, nuts,
seeds, leaves, and bark.　Tree products have been an important part of diets
for thousands of years, from early humans <u>gathering</u> fruits and nuts to the
　　　　　　　　　　　　　　　　　　　　　　　　　　　　26
first cultivation of important trees, such as mango and apple.

　　能從樹上採集的營養品包括水果、堅果、種子、葉子，和樹皮。數千年來，
從樹上得到的產物一直是飲食重要的一部分，從早期人類採集水果和堅果，一直
到最初栽種一些重要的果樹，像是芒果樹和蘋果樹。

nutritional〔njuˈtrɪʃənl̩〕*adj.* 營養的
product〔'prɑdʌkt〕*n.* 產品；產物　　collect〔kəˈlɛkt〕*v.* 採集
nut〔nʌt〕*n.* 堅果　　seed〔sid〕*n.* 種子
leaf〔lif〕*n.* 葉子【複數形為 leaves】　　bark〔bɑrk〕*n.* 樹皮
diet〔'daɪət〕*n.* 飲食　　early〔'ɝlɪ〕*adj.* 早期的
human〔'hjumən〕*n.* 人　　cultivation〔ˌkʌltə'veʃən〕*n.* 耕種；栽培
apple〔'æpl̩〕*n.* 蘋果；蘋果樹　　mango〔'mæŋgo〕*n.* 芒果；芒果樹

26. (**D**) from A to B「從 A 到 B」，from 是介系詞，須接名詞或動名詞，故空格
　　　應填動詞 ***gathering***「採集」，選 (D)。也可寫成：…from early humans'
　　　gathering…。

　　The apple is one of the world's most cultivated fruit trees, <u>with</u> over
　　　　　　　　　　　　　　　　　　　　　　　　　　　　　　　　27
7,000 different kinds in existence.　Despite their great <u>variety</u>, however, most
　　　　　　　　　　　　　　　　　　　　　　　　　　　　　28

domesticated apples can be traced back to a common ancestor, the wild apple of Central Asia, *Malus sieversii*.

　蘋果樹是全世界最廣爲栽種的果樹，現存有超過七千多種不同的蘋果樹。然而，儘管種類很多，大部分被引進的蘋果樹，都可以追溯到共同的祖先，那就是中亞的野生蘋果樹—新疆野蘋果。

cultivate〔'kʌltə‚vet〕*v.* 栽培；栽種
in existence 現存的；存在著的　　despite〔dɪ'spaɪt〕*prep.* 儘管
domesticated〔də'mɛstə‚ketɪd〕*adj.* 引進的
can be traced back to 可追溯到（= *date back to*）
common〔'kɑmən〕*adj.* 共同的　　ancestor〔'ænsɛstə〕*n.* 祖先
Asia〔'eʒə, 'eʃə〕*n.* 亞洲　　*Central Asia* 中亞
Malus sieversii 新疆野蘋果【薔薇科蘋果屬的植物，分布在中亞細亞以及中國大陸的新疆等地】

27. (**B**) 依句意，選 (B) *with*「有」。

28. (**A**) 依句意，選 (A) *variety*〔və'raɪətɪ〕*n.* 種類；多樣性，*great variety*「種類很多」。而 (B) harvest〔'hɑrvɪst〕*n.* 收穫，(C) condition〔kən'dɪʃən〕*n.* 情況，(D) discovery〔dɪs'kʌvərɪ〕*n.* 發現，則不合句意。

Apples have been grown for thousands of years in Asia and Europe, and <u>were brought</u> to North America by European colonists in the 17th century. Today,
　29
apples are <u>regularly</u> eaten the world over and form the basis for multi-million
　　30
dollar industries. In 2005, at least 55 million tons of apples were grown worldwide, which generated a value of about \$10 billion.

蘋果樹在亞洲和歐洲已栽種了好幾千年，而在十七世紀時，被歐洲殖民者帶到北美洲。現在全世界的人都定期吃蘋果，替數百萬美元的產業打下基礎。在 2005 年，全世界共種植至少五千五百萬噸的蘋果，產值約一百億美金。

grow〔gro〕*v.* 栽種　　colonist〔'kɑlənɪst〕*n.* 殖民者
the world over 在全世界（= *all over the world*）
form〔form〕*v.* 形成　　basis〔'besɪs〕*n.* 基礎
form the basis for 爲…打下基礎
multi-million〔‚mʌltɪ'mɪljən〕*adj.* 數百萬的
industry〔'ɪndəstrɪ〕*n.* 產業　　*at least* 至少　　ton〔tʌn〕*n.* 公噸

worldwide〔'wɜld'waɪd〕*adv.* 在全世界
generate〔'dʒɛnə,ret〕*v.* 產生
value〔'vælju〕*n.* 價值　　billion〔'bɪljən〕*n.* 十億

29.（**C**）由句尾的 in the 17th century 可知，動詞應用過去簡單式，且依句意為被動，故選 (C) ***were brought***。

30.（**A**）依句意，選 (A) ***regularly***〔'rɛgjələlɪ〕*adv.* 定期地。而 (B) particularly〔pə'tɪkjələlɪ〕*adv.* 尤其；特別是，(C) permanently〔'pɜmənəntlɪ〕*adv.* 永久地，(D) barely〔'bɛrlɪ〕*adv.* 幾乎不；僅僅，則不合句意。

三、文意選填：

第 31 至 40 題為題組

A paperclip, made of steel wire bent into a hooped shape, is an instrument used to hold sheets of paper together. This common **31.** **(C) device** is a wonder of simplicity and function. But where did this simple, cheap, and indispensable invention come from?

由鋼絲彎成環狀所做成的迴紋針，是用來固定紙張的工具。這個常見的器具，是簡單又實用，很神奇的東西。但是這個簡單、便宜，而且不可或缺的發明，起源於哪裏？

paperclip〔'pepə,klɪp〕*n.* 迴紋針　　***be made of*** 由～製成
steel〔stil〕*adj.* 鋼鐵的　　wire〔waɪr〕*n.* 金屬線
bend〔bɛnd〕*v.* 使彎曲　　hooped〔hupt〕*adj.* 環狀的
instrument〔'ɪnstrəmənt〕*n.* 工具；器具
device〔dɪ'vaɪs〕*n.* 裝置；器具　　wonder〔'wʌndə〕*n.* 神奇的東西
simplicity〔sɪm'plɪsətɪ〕*n.* 簡單
function〔'fʌŋkʃən〕*n.* 功能；作用
indispensable〔,ɪndɪ'spɛnsəbl〕*adj.* 不可或缺的

In the late 19th century, the most common way to hold papers together was by using a pin. Although the pin was an inexpensive tool and was easily **32.** **(D) removable**, it would leave holes in the paper. Later, as steel wire became more common, inventors began to notice its elastic feature. With this feature, it could be stretched and **33.** **(H) twisted into** various clip-like objects. In the years just prior to 1900, quite a few paperclip designs emerged.

The name most frequently <u>34. (I) associated with</u> the paperclip invention is Johan Vaaler, a Norwegian inventor. However, Vaaler's clips were not the same as the paperclips currently in use. Specifically, they did not have the interior loop we see today. The <u>35. (A) familiar</u> looped design was invented by Gem Manufacturing Ltd. in England. This clip is therefore sometimes <u>36. (E) known as</u> the Gem clip.

在十九世紀末，用大頭針固定紙張是最普遍的方法。雖然大頭針是個便宜的工具，也容易拿下來，但卻會在紙上留下洞。後來，隨著鋼絲越來越普遍，發明家開始注意到它的延展性。因為有這樣的特性，所以它可以被拉長，並變成各式各樣像夾子的東西。就在 1900 年之前的幾年，出現了很多迴紋針的設計。最常和迴紋針這項發明聯想在一起的名字，是約翰•瓦萊，他是挪威的發明家。然而，瓦萊的迴紋針和現在的並不太一樣。明確地說，它沒有我們現在看得到的內環。我們所熟悉的環狀設計，是英國的傑姆製造有限公司發明的。因此，這樣的迴紋針有時候又被稱為 Gem clip。

late〔let〕 *adj.* 末期的	***hold together*** 使…在一起
pin〔pɪn〕 *n.* 大頭針	
inexpensive〔,ɪnɪk'spɛnsɪv〕 *adj.* 便宜的；不貴的	
removable〔rɪ'muvəbḷ〕 *adj.* 可除去的	
elastic〔ɪ'læstɪk〕 *adj.* 有彈性的	feature〔'fitʃə〕 *n.* 特性
stretch〔strɛtʃ〕 *v.* 延伸	twist〔twɪst〕 *v.* 使扭曲
various〔'vɛrɪəs〕 *adj.* 各式各樣的	clip〔klɪp〕 *n.* 夾子；迴紋針
object〔'ɑbdʒɛkt〕 *n.* 物體	***prior to*** 在…之前（= *before*）
quite a few 許多（= *many*）	emerge〔ɪ'mɝdʒ〕 *v.* 出現
associate〔ə'soʃɪ,et〕 *v.* 聯想	
Norwegian〔nɔr'widʒən〕 *adj.* 挪威的　*n.* 挪威人	
currently〔'kɝəntlɪ〕 *adv.* 目前	***in use*** 使用中的
interior〔ɪn'tɪrɪə〕 *adj.* 內部的	loop〔lup〕 *n.* 圈；環
manufacture〔,mænjə'fæktʃə〕 *v.* 製造	
Ltd.〔'lɪmɪtɪd〕 *adj.* 有限責任的【用於公司名稱後】	
be known as 被稱為	***the Gem clip*** 迴紋針

Because of Vaaler, the paperclip played an important <u>37. (J) historical</u> role in Norway. During World War II, Norway was occupied by the Nazis. Norwegians were prohibited from wearing any <u>38. (G) symbol</u> of their national unity, such as buttons with the initials of their king. Thus, in <u>39. (F) protest</u>, they started wearing paperclips to show their solidarity. The reason for doing this was simple: Paperclips were a Norwegian invention whose original function was to bind together. After the war, a giant paperclip statue was erected in Oslo to **40.** **(B) honor** Vaaler—even though his design was never actually manufactured.

因為瓦萊的關係，迴紋針在挪威扮演著一個重要的歷史角色。在二戰期間，挪威被納粹佔領。挪威人被禁止穿戴任何象徵他們國家團結的東西，例如有國王姓名起始字母的徽章。因此，為了表示抗議，他們開始配戴迴紋針，以象徵團結，這麼做的理由很簡單，迴紋針是挪威發明的，它原本的用途就是結合在一起。戰後，在奧斯陸豎立了一座巨大的迴紋針雕像，以向瓦萊致敬——即使他的迴紋針設計從來沒有被真正製造過。

> ***play an important role*** 扮演一個重要的角色
> historical〔hɪˈstɔrɪkḷ〕*adj.* 與歷史有關的　　Norway〔ˈnɔr,we〕*n.* 挪威
> occupy〔ˈɑkjə,paɪ〕*v.* 佔據　　Nazi〔ˈnɑtsɪ〕*n.* 納粹
> prohibit〔proˈhɪbɪt〕*v.* 禁止　　unity〔ˈjunətɪ〕*n.* 團結；統一
> ***national unity*** 國家團結　　button〔ˈbʌtn̩〕*n.* 鈕扣；徽章
> initial〔ɪˈnɪʃəl〕*n.*（姓名的）開頭字母　　protest〔ˈprotɛst〕*n.* 抗議
> solidarity〔,sɑləˈdærətɪ〕*n.* 團結
> original〔əˈrɪdʒənḷ〕*n.* 最初的；原本的　　***bind together*** 結合在一起
> giant〔ˈdʒaɪənt〕*adj.* 巨大的　　statue〔ˈstætʃu〕*n.* 雕像
> erect〔ɪˈrɛkt〕*v.* 豎立　　Oslo〔ˈɑslo〕*n.* 奧斯陸【挪威首都】
> honor〔ˈɑnɚ〕*v.* 向…致敬　　actually〔ˈæktʃuəlɪ〕*adv.* 真地

四、閱讀測驗：

第 41 至 44 題為題組

In 2009, the Taiwu Elementary School Folk Singers were invited to perform in Belgium, France, Germany, and Luxemburg. In 2011, they were voted as one of the world's top five performance groups by audiences of Japan Broadcasting Corporation's Amazing Voice program.

2009年，泰武國小古謠傳唱隊應邀前往比利時、法國、德國，和盧森堡演出。2011年，他們被日本 NHK 美聲節目的觀眾，評選為全世界前五名演出團體之一。

> folk〔fok〕*adj.* 民間的；民謠的　　Belgium〔ˈbɛldʒɪəm〕*n.* 比利時
> Germany〔ˈdʒɝmənɪ〕*n.* 德國　　Luxemburg〔ˈlʌksəm,bɝg〕*n.* 盧森堡

vote〔vot〕v. 投票；表決　　**top five**　前五名
performance〔pə'fɔrməns〕n. 表演　　audience〔'ɔdɪəns〕n. 觀衆
broadcasting〔'brɔd,kæstɪŋ〕n. 廣播；播放
corporation〔,kɔrpə'reʃən〕n. 公司
Japan Broadcasting Corporation　日本放送協會（*NHK*）
amazing〔ə'mezɪŋ〕adj. 令人吃驚的　　program〔'progræm〕n. 節目

Recalling the group's first tour in Europe, Camake Valaule, a physical education teacher and the founder of the Taiwu Elementary School Folk Singers, admitted that he felt very nervous. He was worried that the audience would fall asleep since most of the 75-minute performance was a cappella, that is, singing without instrumental sound. Surprisingly, the audience listened with full focus and high spirits. Camake said, "They told me afterward that through our performance, they had a vision of our country, our village, without having to visit it. This experience greatly boosted our confidence."

回想起他們在歐洲的第一次巡迴演出，泰武國小的體育老師兼泰武古謠傳唱隊的創始人查馬克‧法拉屋樂，承認他感到非常緊張。他擔心觀衆會睡著，因爲七十五分鐘的演出，大部分是人聲清唱，也就是沒有樂器聲音的歌唱。令人驚訝的是，全場觀衆都聽得聚精會神，而且興致高揚。查馬克說：「他們事後告訴我，透過我們的演出，他們就算沒有來過，也可以看見我們的國家、我們的村莊。這次的經驗大大地增強了我們的信心。」

recall〔rɪ'kɔl〕v. 回想起　　**physical education**　體育
admit〔əd'mɪt〕v. 承認　　nervous〔'nɝvəs〕adj. 緊張的
fall asleep　睡著　　cappella〔kə'pɛlə〕n. 無伴奏合唱
instrumental〔,ɪnstrə'mɛntḷ〕adj. 樂器的
surprisingly〔sə'praɪzɪŋlɪ〕adv. 令人驚訝地
focus〔'fokəs〕n. 焦點　　spirit〔'spɪrɪt〕n. 精神
afterward〔'æftəwəd〕adv. 之後；後來　　vision〔'vɪʒən〕n. 看見
village〔'vɪlɪdʒ〕n. 村莊　　experience〔ɪk'spɪrɪəns〕n. 經驗；經歷
boost〔bust〕v. 提高；增加　　confidence〔'kɑnfədəns〕n. 信心

According to Camake Valaule, singing traditional ballads has helped students and their parents to re-understand their culture. "It used to be that the only ones who could sing these songs were tribal elders aged between 50 and 60. Now with the children performing the pieces, parents are beginning to ask, 'Why do we not know how to sing these ballads?' Many times nowadays, it is the children who teach the songs to their parents, putting back **the pieces of a blurred memory**."

據查馬克・法拉屋樂的說法，唱傳統歌謠能幫助學生和家長重新認識自己的文化。「以前是只有50至60歲的部落長老才會唱這些歌曲。現在由孩子們表演這些作品，父母都開始在問：『為什麼我們不知道該怎麼唱這些歌謠？』如今，很多時候是孩子教他們的父母傳統歌謠，把模糊記憶的碎片拼湊回來。」

according to 根據…的說法　　traditional〔trə'dɪʃən!〕*adj.* 傳統的
ballad〔'bæləd〕*n.* 民謠
re-understand〔ri‚ʌndə'stænd〕*v.* 重新認識；重新了解
culture〔'kʌltʃə〕*n.* 文化　　*used to* 以前　　tribal〔'traɪb!〕*adj.* 部落的
elder〔'ɛldə〕*n.* 長者；前輩　　*aged~* ～歲的
piece〔pis〕*n.* 一首曲子　　nowadays〔'navə‚dez〕*adv.* 現在
put back 把…放回原處　　*a piece of* 一片；一塊
blurred〔blɝd〕*adj.* 模糊不清的　　memory〔'mɛmərɪ〕*n.* 記憶

Winning international fame, however, was neither the original intention nor the main reason why Camake founded the group in 2006. The most important thing was to make children understand why they sing these songs and to preserve and pass on their culture. Referring to the relocation of Taiwu Elementary School and Taiwu Village following Typhoon Morakot in August 2009, Camake said, "We could not take the forest or our houses in the mountains with us; but we were able to bring our culture along. As long as the children are willing to sing, I will always be there for them, singing with them and leading them to experience the meaning of the ballads."

然而，贏得國際聲譽既不是查馬克的初衷，也不是他在2006年創辦泰武國小古謠傳唱團隊的主要原因。最重要的事情，是讓孩子明白他們為什麼唱這些歌曲，以及保存和傳承自己的文化。談到2009年8月在莫拉克颱風之後，泰武國小搬遷和泰武村遷村，查馬克說：「我們不能帶著森林或山中的房子跟著我們；但我們能夠帶著我們的文化一起走。只要孩子們願意唱，我就會一直提供幫助，和他們一起唱歌，並且帶領他們體驗歌謠的意義。」

international〔͵ɪntɚˋnæʃənḷ〕*adj.* 國際的　　fame〔fem〕*n.* 名聲
neither…nor~ 既不…也不~　　original〔əˋrɪdʒənḷ〕*adj.* 最初的
intention〔ɪnˋtɛnʃən〕*n.* 企圖　　main〔men〕*adj.* 主要的
found〔faʊnd〕*v.* 創立　　preserve〔prɪˋzɝv〕*v.* 保存
pass on 傳遞　　***refer to*** 提到
relocation〔͵riloˋkeʃən〕*n.* 改變位置；遷往他處
following〔ˋfaləwɪŋ〕*prep.* 在…之後　　forest〔ˋfɔrɪst〕*n.* 森林
be able to V. 能夠~　　***bring…along*** 帶…一起
as long as 只要　　willing〔ˋwɪlɪŋ〕*adj.* 願意的
be there for sb. 在某人需要時提供幫助　　lead〔lid〕*v.* 帶領
experience〔ɪkˋspɪrɪəns〕*v.* 體驗

41. (**B**) 下列關於泰武國小古謠傳唱隊，何者正確？
　　(A) 該團體最初創立於 2009 年。
　　(B) 該團體是由一位體育老師所創立。
　　(C) 歌手們通常是唱流行民歌。
　　(D) 歌手們跟他們的父母學習唱歌。

　　establish〔əˋstæblɪʃ〕*v.* 設立；創辦

42. (**B**) 查馬克第一次去歐洲時，爲什麼他覺得觀衆可能會睡著？
　　(A) 觀衆的平均年齡是 50 到 60 歲之間。
　　(B) 大部分的表演都沒有用任何樂器伴奏。
　　(C) 沒有人能了解這些這些歌曲的語言和意義。
　　(D) 觀衆無法想像這些學童所唱的主題。

　　average〔ˋævərɪdʒ〕*adj.* 平均的　　accompany〔əˋkʌmpənɪ〕*v.* 伴奏
　　visualize〔ˋvɪʒʊə͵laɪz〕*v.* 想像　　theme〔θim〕*n.* 主題

43. (**D**) 在第三段中的「模糊記憶的碎片」最有可能是指什麼？
　　(A) 孩子們對自己文化的無知。
　　(B) 對老舊部落人們的褪色記憶。
　　(C) 學校所教的片段知識。
　　(D) 父母對於自己傳統並不是很了解。

　　ignorance〔ˋɪgnərəns〕*n.* 無知　　fading〔ˋfedɪŋ〕*adj.* 褪色的
　　broken〔ˋbrokən〕*adj.* 破碎的　　vague〔veg〕*adj.* 模糊的
　　understanding〔͵ʌndɚˋstændɪŋ〕*n.* 理解；認識
　　tradition〔trəˋdɪʃən〕*n.* 傳統

44. (**C**) 在莫拉克颱風的事件後，查馬克領悟到什麼？

    (A) 泰武國小搬遷的重要性。

    (B) 尊重自然的必要，以避免被自然摧毀。

    (C) 傳承傳統文化的重要性。

    (D) 在森林中建造房舍的後果。

realize〔ˈriəˌlaɪz〕v. 了解

significance〔sɪgˈnɪfəkəns〕n. 意義；重要性

need〔nid〕n. 需要；必要　　avoid〔əˈvɔɪd〕v. 避免

destroy〔dɪˈstrɔɪ〕v. 摧毀　　consequence〔ˈkɑnsəˌkwɛns〕n. 後果

第 45 至 48 題為題組

When it comes to medical care, many patients and doctors believe "more is better." But what they do not realize is that overtreatment—too many scans, too many blood tests, too many procedures—may pose harm. Sometimes a test leads you down a path to more and more testing, some of which may be invasive, or to treatment for things that should be left alone.

一談到醫療，許多病人和醫生都認為「越多越好」。但是他們並不知道，過度治療——太多掃瞄、太多驗血、太多療程——可能會造成傷害。有時候一項檢查會使你走向越來越多檢查的道路，有些檢查可能是侵入性的，或者是在對應該不予理會的情況加以治療。

when it comes to 一提到　　care〔kɛr〕n. 照料

medical care 醫療　　patient〔ˈpeʃənt〕n. 病人

overtreatment〔ˈovəˈtritmənt〕n. 過度治療

scan〔skæn〕n. 掃瞄　　blood〔blʌd〕n. 血液

test〔tɛst〕n. 檢查　　*blood test* 驗血

procedure〔prəˈsidʒə〕n. 程序　　pose〔poz〕v. 引起

harm〔hɑrm〕n. 傷害　　*lead~down* 引導某人走在~

path〔pæθ〕n. 小路　　invasive〔ɪnˈvesɪv〕adj. 侵入性的

treatment〔ˈtritmənt〕n. 治療　　*leave~alone* 不理會~

Terrence Power, for example, complained that after his wife learned she had Wegener's disease, an uncommon disorder of the immune system, they found it difficult to refuse testing recommended by her physician. The doctor insisted on office visits every three weeks, even when she was feeling well. He frequently ordered blood tests and X-rays, and repeatedly referred her to specialists for even minor complaints. Even when tests came back negative, more were ordered, and she was hospitalized as a precaution when she developed a cold. She had as many as 25 doctor visits during one six-month period. The couple was spending about $30,000 a year for her care.

例如,泰倫斯・鮑爾抱怨,他的妻子得知自己有韋格納病,一種罕見的免疫系統疾病之後,他們就覺得很難拒絕她的醫生所建議的檢查。醫生堅持每三週一次門診,甚至是當她覺得身體很健康時也如此。他常常指示要驗血和照X光,而且即使是較輕微的疾病,也反覆將她介紹給專科醫生。甚至當檢查結果是陰性時,還是要她做更多檢查,而且當她罹患感冒時,為了預防,還讓她住院。她在六個月的期間內,看醫生的次數多達25次。為了她的治療,這對夫婦一年內花了大約三萬美金。

complain〔kəmˈplen〕v. 抱怨　　learn〔lɜn〕v. 得知
disease〔dɪˈziz〕n. 疾病　　uncommon〔ʌnˈkɑmən〕adj. 罕見的
disorder〔dɪsˈɔrdɚ〕n. 疾病　　immune〔ɪˈmjun〕adj. 免疫的
immune system 免疫系統　　find〔faɪnd〕v. 覺得
refuse〔rɪˈfjuz〕v. 拒絕　　recommend〔ˌrɛkəˈmɛnd〕v. 建議
physician〔fəˈzɪʃən〕n. 醫生　　*insist on* 堅持
office〔ˈɔfɪs〕n. 診所　　visit〔ˈvɪzɪt〕n. 看診
office visit 門診　　order〔ˈɔrdɚ〕v. 命令;指示
X-ray〔ˈɛksˌre〕n. X光　　repeatedly〔rɪˈpitɪdlɪ〕adv. 反覆地
refer〔rɪˈfɜ〕v. 介紹　　specialist〔ˈspɛʃəlɪst〕n. 專科醫師
minor〔ˈmaɪnɚ〕adj. 較小的　　complaint〔kəmˈplent〕n. 疾病
negative〔ˈnɛgətɪv〕adj. 陰性的　　hospitalize〔ˈhɑspɪtlˌaɪz〕v. 使住院
precaution〔prɪˈkɔʃən〕n. 預防　　develop〔dɪˈvɛləp〕v. 患(病)
period〔ˈpɪrɪəd〕n. 期間　　couple〔ˈkʌpl̩〕n. 一對男女;夫婦

After several years of physical suffering and near financial ruin from the medical costs, the couple began questioning the treatment after consulting with other patients in online support groups. "It's a really hard thing to determine when **they**'ve crossed the line," Mr. Power said. "You think she's getting the best care in the world, but after a while you start to wonder: What is the objective?" Mr. Power then spoke with his own primary care doctor, who advised him to find a new specialist to oversee Mrs. Power's care. Under the new doctor's care, the regular testing stopped and Mrs. Power's condition stabilized. Now she sees the doctor only four or five times a year.

　　在歷經好幾年身體的痛苦，以及由於醫療花費而瀕臨破產，這對夫婦在線上的援助團體和其他病人商量後，開始對治療提出質疑。「要判定他們是不是太過份了，真的是很困難的事，」鮑爾先生說。「你認為她正接受全世界最好的醫療，但是過了不久，你就開始懷疑：目的是什麼？」鮑爾先生後來和他自己的主治醫生談，他建議鮑爾先生找一位新的專科醫生，來監督鮑爾太太的醫療情況。在新的醫生的照料之下，定期的檢查停止了，而且鮑爾太太的情況也已穩定下來。現在她一年只要看四或五次醫生。

physical〔'fɪzɪkḷ〕adj. 身體的　　suffering〔'sʌfrɪŋ〕n. 痛苦
financial〔fə'nænʃəl〕adj. 財務上的　　ruin〔'ruɪn〕n. 毀滅
cost〔kɔst〕n. 費用　　question〔'kwɛstʃən〕v. 質疑
consult〔kən'sʌlt〕v. 商量＜*with*＞　　online〔'ɑn,laɪn〕adj. 線上的
support〔sə'port〕n. 援助；支援　　determine〔dɪ'tɜmɪn〕v. 決定
cross the line 越線；做得太過份了
wonder〔'wʌndɚ〕v. 想知道；懷疑　　objective〔əb'dʒɛktɪv〕n. 目的
primary〔'praɪ,mɛrɪ〕adj. 主要的　　***primary care doctor*** 主治醫生
advise〔əd'vaɪz〕v. 勸告；建議　　oversee〔,ovɚ'si〕v. 監督
regular〔'rɛgjələ〕adj. 定期的　　condition〔kən'dɪʃən〕n. 情況
stabilize〔'stebḷ,aɪz〕v. 穩定　　time〔taɪm〕n. 次數

45. (**C**) 本文的主旨爲何？
　　(A) 治療不一定會造成有害的副作用。
　　(B) 病人多半會認爲更多的檢查是更好的治療。
　　(C) 太多的醫療可能不會對病人有益。
　　(D) 醫生通常會建議有必要的門診。

not always 未必；不一定　　harmful〔'hɑrmfəl〕adj. 有害的
side effect 副作用　　***tend to*** 易於；傾向於
beneficial〔,bɛnə'fɪʃəl〕adj. 有益的

46. (**C**) 在鮑爾太太接受醫療的期間，以下何者對她來說是個問題？
　　(A) 每當她得了感冒，她就必須住院三週。
　　(B) 她沒有任何保險，所以她就因爲生病而破產。
　　(C) 當檢查結果顯示她沒問題，她的醫生還是要她做更多的檢查。
　　(D) 由於她持續的生病，所以醫生要求她向其他的專科醫生求診。

insurance〔ɪn'ʃʊrəns〕n. 保險　　go〔go〕v. 變得 (= *become*)
broke〔brok〕adj. 沒錢的；破產的　　illness〔'ɪlnɪs〕n. 疾病
result〔rɪ'zʌlt〕n. 結果　　show〔ʃo〕v. 顯示
consult〔kən'sʌlt〕v. 請（醫生）診療
constant〔'kɑnstənt〕adj. 不斷的；持續的

47. (**A**) 第三段的「他們」最有可能是指誰？
　　(A) 醫生。　　　　　　　　　(B) 其他病人。
　　(C) 鮑爾夫婦。　　　　　　　(D) 線上援助團體。

　　refer to　是指

48. (**A**) 以下何者最能描述作者對於醫學檢查的看法？
　　(A) 非必要的檢查太多。
　　(B) 醫學檢查對於預防疾病是必要的。
　　(C) 許多檢查對於診斷的確認是需要的。
　　(D) 醫生對於檢查結果的解釋很少出錯。

　　essential〔ə'sɛnʃəl〕*adj.* 必要的
　　prevention〔prɪ'vɛnʃən〕*n.* 預防
　　confirmation〔,kɑnfə'meʃən〕*n.* 確認
　　diagnosis〔,daɪəg'nosɪs〕*n.* 診斷
　　interpretation〔ɪn,tɝprɪ'teʃən〕*n.* 解釋

第 49 至 52 題為題組

　　Henri Cartier-Bresson (1908-2004) is one of the most original and influential figures in the history of photography. His humane, spontaneous photographs helped establish photojournalism as an art form.

　　在攝影史上，享利・卡蒂爾－布雷松（1908-2004）是最有創意及影響力的人物之一。他充滿人性關懷、自然不做作的照片，使新聞攝影成為一種藝術。

　　original〔ə'rɪdʒən!〕*adj.* 有創意的
　　influential〔,ɪnflu'ɛnʃəl〕*adj.* 有影響力的
　　figure〔'fɪgjə〕*n.* 人物　　photography〔fə'tɑgrəfɪ〕*n.* 攝影
　　humane〔hju'men〕*adj.* 人道的
　　spontaneous〔spɑn'tenɪəs〕*adj.* 自發的；自然的
　　photograph〔'fotə,græf〕*n.* 照片　　establish〔ə'stæblɪʃ〕*v.* 建立
　　photojournalism〔foto'dʒɝn!,ɪzəm〕*n.* 新聞攝影

　　Cartier-Bresson's family was wealthy—his father made a fortune as a textile manufacturer—but Cartier-Bresson later joked that due to his parents' frugal ways, it often seemed as though his family was poor.

　　卡蒂爾－布雷松的家庭很富裕——他父親從事紡織製造業而致富——但卡蒂爾－布雷松後來開玩笑地說，因為父母生活方式非常節儉，所以他們家經常看起來好像很窮困的樣子。

wealthy (ˈwɛlθɪ) adj. 有錢的　　**make a fortune** 發財
textile (ˈtɛkstḷ) adj. 紡織的　　**textile manufacturer** 紡織製造業者
joke (dʒok) v. 開玩笑　　frugal (ˈfrugḷ) adj. 節儉的
as though 就好像

Educated in Paris, Cartier-Bresson developed an early love for literature and the arts. As a teenager, Cartier-Bresson rebelled against his parents' formal ways of education. In his early adulthood, he even drifted toward communism. But it was art that remained at the center of his life.

卡蒂爾－布雷松在巴黎受教育，很早就培養出他對文學與藝術的喜愛。他在青少年時期很抗拒他父母正規的教育方式。在他剛成年不久，他甚至漸漸向共產主義靠攏。不過藝術仍然是他生活的中心。

literature (ˈlɪtərətʃɚ) n. 文學　　rebel (rɪˈbɛl) v. 反抗 < *against* >
formal (ˈfɔrmḷ) adj. 正式的；正規的　　**early adulthood** 成年初期
drift (drɪft) v. 漂流；不知不覺陷入　　**drift toward** 逐漸走向
communism (ˈkɑmjuˌnɪzəm) n. 共產主義　　remain (rɪˈmen) v. 仍然

Cartier-Bresson traveled to Africa in 1931 to hunt antelope and boar. And Africa fueled another interest in him: photography. He then wandered around the world with his camera, using a handheld camera to catch images from fleeting moments of everyday life.

卡蒂爾－布雷松在1931年前往非洲，去獵捕鈴羊和野豬，而非洲就在他心中激發了另一個興趣：攝影。然後他便帶著他的相機到世界各地遊歷，用一台手持相機去捕捉日常生活中稍縱即逝的影像。

travel to 前往 (= *go to*)　　hunt (hʌnt) v. 獵捕
antelope (ˈæntḷˌop) n. 鈴羊　　boar (bor) n. 野豬
fuel (ˈfjuəl) v. 激發　　wander (ˈwɑndɚ) v. 流浪；遊歷
handheld camera 手持相機　　catch (kætʃ) v. 捕捉
image (ˈɪmɪdʒ) n. 影像　　fleeting (ˈflitɪŋ) adj. 短暫的；稍縱即逝的

Not long after World War II, Cartier-Bresson traveled east, spending considerable time in India, where he met and photographed Gandhi shortly before his assassination in 1948. Cartier-Bresson's subsequent work to document Gandhi's death and its immediate impact on the country became one of *Life Magazine*'s most prized photo essays.

　　二次世界大戰結束後不久，卡蒂爾－布雷松到東方旅行，在印度待了相當長的時間，他在1948年甘地被暗殺前不久，就遇到了甘地，並拍下他的照片。卡蒂爾－布雷松隨後為甘地的死亡，及他的死對印度造成的立即影響做了記錄，而這項作品就成了《生活雜誌》最珍貴的攝影專題之一。

> ***World War II*** 第二次世界大戰　　　east〔ist〕*adv.* 向東方
> considerable〔kən'sɪdərəbḷ〕*adj.* 相當多的　　India〔'ɪndɪə〕*n.* 印度
> Gandhi〔'gɑndi〕*n.* 甘地【印度民族運動領袖】
> assassination〔ə,sæsɪ'neʃən〕*n.* 暗殺
> subsequent〔'sʌbsɪ,kwənt〕*adj.* 隨後的　　work〔wɜk〕*n.* 作品
> document〔'dɑkjə,mɛnt〕*v.* 記錄　　immediate〔ɪ'midɪɪt〕*adj.* 立即的
> impact〔'ɪmpækt〕*n.* 影響　　prized〔praɪzd〕*adj.* 有價值的；珍貴的
> ***photo essay*** 圖片故事；攝影專題

Cartier-Bresson's approach to photography remained much the same throughout his life. He made clear his dislike of images that had been improved by artificial light, darkroom effects, and even cropping. The naturalist in Cartier-Bresson believed that all editing should be done when the photo is taken. In 1952, his first book, *The Decisive Moment*, a rich collection of his work spanning two decades, was published. "There is nothing in this world that does not have a decisive moment," he said.

　　卡蒂爾－布雷松對於攝影的看法，終其一生幾乎都沒有改變。他很清楚地表達，他不喜歡用人造光、暗室效果、甚至是照片裁切所修飾過的影像。他內心崇尚自然主義，相信所有的照片編輯，都應在照片被拍攝時就完成。在1952年，他的第一本書《決定性的瞬間》出版了，裡面收藏了他二十年來許多的攝影作品。「世上所有的東西都有其決定性的瞬間，」他說。

> approach〔ə'protʃ〕*n.* 方法；態度　　remain〔rɪ'men〕*v.* 依然；依舊
> ***much the same*** 大致相同　　***make clear*** 表明
> dislike〔dɪs'laɪk〕*n.* 討厭；不喜歡　　improve〔ɪm'pruv〕*v.* 改善
> artificial〔,ɑrtə'fɪʃəl〕*adj.* 人造的　　***darkroom effect*** （攝影）暗房效果
> cropping〔'krɑpɪŋ〕*n.* 裁切　　naturalist〔'nætʃərəlɪst〕*n.* 自然主義者
> editing〔'ɛdɪtɪŋ〕*n.* 編輯　　decisive〔dɪ'saɪsɪv〕*adj.* 決定性的
> rich〔rɪtʃ〕*adj.* 豐富的　　collection〔kə'lɛkʃən〕*n.* 收集；選集
> span〔spæn〕*v.* 跨越（時間）　　decade〔'dɛked〕*n.* 十年
> publish〔'pʌblɪʃ〕*v.* 出版

In 1968, he began to turn away from photography and returned to his passion for drawing and painting.

在1968年，他開始厭惡攝影，而回歸到他所熱愛的素描與繪畫。

> **turn away from** 厭惡　　passion〔ˋpæʃən〕n. 熱愛
> drawing〔ˋdrɔɪŋ〕n. 素描　　painting〔ˋpentɪŋ〕n. 繪畫

49. (**A**) 下列何者最能描述卡蒂爾－布雷松的家庭背景？
　　(A) 他們家有錢但很節儉。　　(B) 他爸爸到巴黎開紡織廠。
　　(C) 他有錢的家破產變窮了。　(D) 他父母的教育方式很開明。

> economical〔͵ikəˋnɑmɪkḷ〕adj. 節儉的
> bankrupt〔ˋbæŋkrʌpt〕adj. 破產的　　liberal〔ˋlɪbərəl〕adj. 開明的

50. (**B**) 下列關於卡蒂爾－布雷松的攝影生涯何者為真？
　　(A) 他一生都致力於攝影。
　　(B) 當他到非洲時，培養出對攝影的熱愛。
　　(C) 他出版《決定性的瞬間》後，立刻停止攝影。
　　(D) 在二次世界大戰期間，他記錄了印度人的日常生活。

> career〔kəˋrɪr〕n. 職業；生涯　　**devote** oneself **to** 致力於
> quit〔kwɪt〕v. 停止　　**right after** 在…之後立刻
> publication〔͵pʌblɪˋkeʃən〕n. 出版

51. (**C**) 卡蒂爾－布雷松對印度的甘地有什麼重要性？
　　(A) 他在 1948 年看見甘地被暗殺。
　　(B) 他是第一個為甘地拍照的攝影師。
　　(C) 他用照片來記錄甘地的死對印度的影響。
　　(D) 他的照片告訴世人誰犯了暗殺甘地的罪。

> significance〔sɪgˋnɪfəkəns〕n. 意義；重要性
> witness〔ˋwɪtnɪs〕v. 目擊；看見
> photographer〔fəˋtɑgrəfɚ〕n. 攝影師　　**take a photo** 拍照
> **the world** 世人　　guilty〔ˋgɪltɪ〕adj. 有罪的 < of >
> assassinate〔əˋsæsn͵et〕v. 暗殺

52. (**C**) 下列關於卡蒂爾－布雷松的攝影態度何者為真？
　　(A) 他拍照從來都不等待決定性的時間。
　　(B) 他偏好在暗房裡小心地編輯照片。
　　(C) 他大部分的照片都在描述每天發生的事情。
　　(D) 他實驗過不同的方法，然後決定要做一個自然主義者。

shoot〔ʃut〕*v.* 拍攝　　experiment〔ɪk'spɛrəmɛnt〕*v.* 實驗
settle on　決定

第 53 至 56 題為題組

You've most likely heard the news by now: A car-commuting, desk-bound, TV-watching lifestyle can be harmful to our health. All the time that we spend rooted in the chair is linked to increased risks of so many deadly diseases that experts have named this modern-day health epidemic the "sitting disease."

你很可能現在已經聽過這個新聞：搭車通勤、坐在書桌前、看電視的生活方式，可能對我們的健康有害。所有我們坐在椅子上的時間，都和許多致命疾病的風險增加有關，專家稱這個現代的流行病為「久坐症」。

commute〔kə'mjut〕*v.* 通勤
car-commuting〔'kɑr kə'mjutɪŋ〕*adj.* 搭車通勤的
bound〔baʊnd〕*adj.* 被綑綁的；被束縛的
desk-bound〔'dɛsk,baʊnd〕*adj.* 窩在書桌前的
lifestyle〔'laɪf,staɪl〕*n.* 生活方式
rooted〔'rutɪd〕*adj.* 固定的；（生了根般地）無法動彈的
be linked to　和⋯有關　　increased〔ɪn'krist〕*adj.* 增加的
risk〔rɪsk〕*n.* 風險　　deadly〔'dɛdlɪ〕*adj.* 致命的
expert〔'ɛkspɝt〕*n.* 專家　　epidemic〔,ɛpə'dɛmɪk〕*n.* 流行病
sitting disease　久坐症

Sitting for too long slows down the body's metabolism and the way enzymes break down our fat reserves, raising both blood sugar levels and blood pressure. Small amounts of regular activity, even just standing and moving around, throughout the day is enough to bring the increased levels back down. And those small amounts of activity add up—30 minutes of light activity in two or three-minute bursts can be just as effective as a half-hour block of exercise. But without that activity, blood sugar levels and blood pressure keep creeping up, steadily damaging the inside of the arteries and increasing the risk of diabetes, heart disease, stroke, and other serious diseases. In essence, fundamental changes in biology occur if you sit for too long.

　　坐太久會減緩身體的新陳代謝，並使酵素分解體內脂肪的能力下降，進而使血糖濃度及血壓上升。少量的規律活動，即使只是站立或四處走動，一整天下來，就足以使過高的血糖及血壓下降。而這樣少量的活動加起來——半小時少量活動，每次二至三分鐘，效果跟一次運動半小時是一樣的。但如果沒有這樣的活動，血糖跟血壓就會持續上升，進而持續傷害動脈內部及提高罹患糖尿病、心臟病、中風，以及其他重大疾病的風險。基本上，如果你坐太久，在生理上就會產生重大的變化。

slow down 減緩　　metabolism〔məˈtæbḷˌɪzəm〕*n.* 新陳代謝
enzyme〔ˈɛnzaɪm〕*n.* 酵素　　*break down* 分解
fat〔fæt〕*n.* 脂肪　　reserve〔rɪˈzɜv〕*n.* 儲藏
raise〔rez〕*v.* 提高　　*blood sugar* 血糖
levels〔ˈlɛvḷz〕*n. pl.* 濃度；含量　　*blood pressure* 血壓
regular〔ˈrɛgjələ〕*adj.* 定期的　　*move around* 四處走動
throughout the day 一整天　　bring〔brɪŋ〕*v.* 使
back down 退回去；倒退而下　　*add up* 加起來；合計
light〔laɪt〕*adj.* 輕微的　　burst〔bɜst〕*n.* 突發；爆發
effective〔əˈfɛktɪv〕*adj.* 有效的　　block〔blak〕*n.* 一組；一批；大量
creep〔krip〕*v.* 爬行　　steadily〔ˈstɛdəlɪ〕*adv.* 持續地
artery〔ˈartərɪ〕*n.* 動脈　　diabetes〔ˌdaɪəˈbitɪs〕*n.* 糖尿病
heart disease 心臟病　　stroke〔strok〕*n.* 中風
essence〔ˈɛsṇs〕*n.* 本質　　*in essence* 本質上；基本上
fundamental〔ˌfʌndəˈmɛntḷ〕*adj.* 基本的；重要的
biology〔baɪˈalədʒɪ〕*n.* 生物學；生理

But wait, you're a runner. You needn't worry about the harm of a **sedentary** lifestyle because you exercise regularly, right? Well, not so fast. Recent studies show that people spend an average of 64 hours a week sitting, whether or not they exercise 150 minutes a week as recommended by World Health Organization (WHO). Regular exercisers, furthermore, are found to be about 30 percent less active on days when they exercise. Overall, most people simply aren't exercising or moving around enough to counteract all the harm that can result from sitting nine hours or more a day.

　　但是等等，你是一個跑者。你不用擔心**久坐的**生活方式會造成的傷害，因為你都有在定期運動，對吧？嗯，先別這麼快下定論。最近的研究顯示，不論人們有沒有照著世界衛生組織建議的，一週做一百五十分鐘的運動，一週平均還是有六十四個小時坐著。此外，定期做運動的人，被發現在他們運動的那幾天，活動量會比平常少百分之三十。整體而言，大多數的人運動或四處走動的時間，都不足以抵銷他們整天坐九個小時甚至更久所造成的傷害。

> sedentary〔'sɛdn̩ˌtɛrɪ〕*adj.* 常坐著的；不愛活動的
> recommend〔ˌrɛkə'mɛnd〕*v.* 建議；推薦
> average〔'ævərɪdʒ〕*n.* 平均
> ***Wond Health Organization*** （聯合國）世界衛生組織
> furthermore〔'fɝðəˌmor〕*adv.* 此外　　active〔'æktɪv〕*adj.* 活動的
> overall〔ˌovə'ɔl〕*adv.* 整體而言　　counteract〔ˌkaʊntə'ækt〕*v.* 抵銷
> ***result from*** 起因於

Scared straight out of your chair? Good. The remedy is as simple as standing up and taking activity breaks.

嚇到直接從椅子上跳起來了嗎？很好。補救方法很簡單，只要站起來休息一下，做些活動就可以了。

> scared〔skɛrd〕*adj.* 害怕的　　straight〔stret〕*adv.* 直接地
> remedy〔'rɛmədɪ〕*n.* 治療法；補救方法　　***take a break*** 休息一下

53.(**D**) 本文的目的是什麼？
　(A) 指出現代生活方式的挑戰。
　(B) 討論現代流行病可能會如何快速蔓延。
　(C) 探討規律運動對我們身體的影響。
　(D) <u>解釋長時間坐著對我們健康的威脅。</u>

> ***point out*** 指出　　challenge〔'tʃælɪndʒ〕*n.* 挑戰
> spread〔sprɛd〕*v.* 蔓延　　explore〔ɪk'splor〕*v.* 探討
> effect〔ɪ'fɛkt〕*n.* 影響　　threat〔θrɛt〕*n.* 威脅
> hours〔aʊrz〕*n. pl.* 時間

54.(**C**) 第三段中的 sedentary 這個字，最接近哪個意思？
　(A) 現代的。　　　　　　　(B) 有風險的。
　(C) <u>不活動的。</u>　　　　　　(D) 傳染性的。

> risky〔'rɪskɪ〕*adj.* 有風險的　　inactive〔ɪn'æktɪv〕*adj.* 不活動的

55.(**C**) 什麼是降低高血糖和高血壓最好的方法？
　(A) 每週至少運動一百五十分鐘。
　(B) 擺脫搭車通勤以及看電視的習慣。

(C) 儘量常常中斷坐下來的時間，做些輕微的活動。

(D) 每天站著或四處走動至少二或三分鐘。

interrupt〔͵ɪntə'rʌpt〕*v.* 打斷；使中斷

56. (**B**) 對於那些認真做運動的人，我們可以推論出下列何者？

(A) 他們常比那些不運動的人活得久。

(B) 在他們要運動的那些日子，他們站著或四處走動的時間會比較少。

(C) 他們通常比那些不活動的人花比較少的時間坐著。

(D) 他們通常都不符合世界衛生組織建議的運動標準。

serious〔'sɪrɪəs〕*adj.* 認真的　　***tend to V.*** 易於；傾向於
work out 運動　　generally〔'dʒɛnərəlɪ〕*adv.* 通常
meet〔mit〕*v.* 符合　　standard〔'stændəd〕*n.* 標準

第貳部分：非選擇題

一、中譯英

1. 一個成功的企業不應該把獲利當作最主要的目標。

A successful $\begin{Bmatrix} \text{business} \\ \text{corporation} \\ \text{enterprise} \end{Bmatrix}$ should not

$\begin{Bmatrix} \text{make earning profits its} \begin{Bmatrix} \text{primary} \\ \text{principal} \\ \text{top priority.} \end{Bmatrix} \begin{Bmatrix} \text{objective.} \\ \text{goal.} \end{Bmatrix} \\ \text{take it as its} \begin{Bmatrix} \text{primary} \\ \text{principal} \\ \text{top priority} \end{Bmatrix} \begin{Bmatrix} \text{objective} \\ \text{goal} \end{Bmatrix} \text{to earn profits.} \end{Bmatrix}$

2. 它應該負起社會責任，以增進大眾的福祉。

It should $\begin{Bmatrix} \text{take (on)} \\ \text{shoulder} \\ \text{assume} \end{Bmatrix}$ social responsibility (in order) to

$\begin{Bmatrix} \text{improve} \\ \text{enhance} \\ \text{better} \end{Bmatrix}$ public $\begin{Bmatrix} \text{welfare.} \\ \text{well-being.} \end{Bmatrix}$

二、英文作文：

Summer Reading

For my summer reading, I would choose *Everyone Is Beautiful: Respect Others and Be Yourself* by Caroline Strong. The book is probably about how to be a good citizen by treating others the way you would want to be treated; *that is*, fairly and with compassion. *Also*, it most likely promotes a positive outlook on life, suggesting that by having respect for others, you may ultimately become more comfortable with yourself. *Above all*, the book may suggest that judging other people is both harmful to them and your own sense of well-being.

I chose this book because I am interested in personal communication. *There are times* in my life when I struggle with frustrations and obstacles that have been created by other people. This in turn makes me angry with myself. I think I could improve my interactions with others by fostering the respect the book probably talks about, *and at the same time*, improve my own sense of self-worth.

citizen (ˈsɪtəzn̩) *n.* 公民　　*that is* 也就是說
fairly (ˈfɛrlɪ) *adv.* 公平地　　compassion (kəmˈpæʃən) *n.* 同情心
promote (prəˈmot) *v.* 促進；倡導；鼓勵
positive (ˈpɑzətɪv) *adj.* 正面的　　outlook (ˈaʊtˌlʊk) *n.* 看法 < *on* >
suggest (sə(g)ˈdʒɛst) *v.* 指出　　ultimately (ˈʌltəmɪtlɪ) *adv.* 最後
above all 最重要的是　　judge (dʒʌdʒ) *v.* 批評 (= *criticize*)
sense (sɛns) *n.* 感覺　　well-being (ˈwɛlˈbiɪŋ) *n.* 幸福
personal (ˈpɝsn̩l) *adj.* 人的；有關人的
communication (kəˌmjunəˈkeʃən) *n.* 溝通
struggle (ˈstrʌgl̩) *v.* 掙扎；搏鬥
frustration (frʌsˈtreʃən) *n.* 挫折
obstacle (ˈɑbstəkl̩) *n.* 阻礙　　*in turn* 結果；後來
improve (ɪmˈpruv) *v.* 改善　　interaction (ˌɪntəˈækʃən) *n.* 互動
foster (ˈfɑstɚ) *v.* 培養　　*at the same time* 同時

104 年學測英文科試題出題來源

題　號	出　處
一、詞彙 第 1～15 題	所有各題對錯答案的選項，均出自大考中心編製的「高中常用 7000 字」。
二、綜合測驗 第 16～20 題 【Havard Magazine】	改寫自 Easing Ills through Tai Chi（透過太極減輕痛苦），描寫太極拳對身心上的好處好處，以及實踐的方式。
第 21～25 題	改寫自 A look at animal myths and superstitions（一瞥動物的神話和迷信），描寫各種動物在不同的文化脈絡下的意義和迷信。
第 26～30 題	改寫自 Global Trees Campaign（全球樹木活動），敘述樹木的用處，這裡選文為蘋果的樹的歷史和價值。
三、文意選填 第 31～40 題	改寫自 The Paperclip（紙夾），描寫紙夾的的歷史、來源，以及其用處。
四、閱讀測驗 第 41～44 題 【Taiwan Today】	改寫自 Paiwan folk singers keep culture alive through music（排灣古搖樂隊透過音樂保持文化），描述泰武國小古謠傳唱隊在國外獲獎，贏得國際名聲，並保持其古謠文化。
第 45～48 題 【New York Times】	改寫自 WELL: Overtreatment Is Taking a Harmful Toll（健康；過度治療正在造成損害），敘述太多的治療、檢驗，以及太多的程序，反而有反效果。
第 49～52 題	改寫自 Remembering the Henri Cartier-Bresson retrospective Exhibition at the MOMA（紀念亨利・卡蒂爾－佈雷松的紐約現代藝術博物館回顧展），描述亨利・卡蒂爾－佈雷松的生平、教育、攝影手法，以及他的攝影爲何成爲重要的指標。
第 53～56 題 【Economist】	改寫自 Sitting is the New Smoking—Even for Runners（坐著就是新式抽煙——即便是對跑步者），坐著的生活方式會降低新陳代謝，危害健康，即便是對有在跑步的人而言，也是有害。

104 年學測英文科試題修正意見

※104 年學測英文試題出得很嚴謹，只有六個地方建議修正：

題　　　號	修　　正　　意　　見
第 21～25 題 第 5 行	Peacocks are also highly valued in China and Japan, where they *are* kept as symbols by the ruling families to … → Peacocks are also highly valued in China and Japan, where they *were* kept as symbols by the ruling families to … ＊因爲中國已經沒有 ruling families（貴族），所以時態應該爲過去式。
第 21～25 題 第 7 行	To bring the evil eye into the home is *thus* believed to invite trouble and sorrow. → 去掉 thus。 ＊這句和上一句沒有因果關係，所以應該把 thus（因此）去掉。
第 31～40 題 第 8 行	The name most frequently ___34___ *the* paperclip invention is Johan Vaaler, a Norwegian inventor. → 去掉 the。 ＊paperclip invention（紙夾的發明）的 invention（發明）爲抽象名詞，不需要加定冠詞 the。
第 43 題	The fading memories *about* old tribal people. Vaaler, a Norwegian inventor. → The fading memories *of* old tribal people. Vaaler, a Norwegian inventor. ＊依照文意，應該是「逐漸消逝的古老部落人民的記憶」，故介系詞應改成 of。
第 49～52 題 第 9 行	He then wandered around the world *with his camera*, using a handheld camera to catch images from fleeting moments of everyday life. → 去掉 with his camera。 ＊with his camera（用他的相機）雖然文法沒錯，但是是贅字，因爲下面已經有説明 using a handheld camera（使用掌上型的相機）。
第 55 題	What is the best way to bring down high blood sugar *level* and blood pressure? → What is the best way to bring down high blood sugar *levels* and blood pressure? ＊high blood sugar level（高血糖量）爲可數名詞，故 level 應該成level<u>s</u>。

【104 年學測】綜合測驗：16-20 出題來源

—— http://harvardmagazine.com/2010/01/researchers-study-tai-chi-benefits

Easing Ills through Tai Chi

CATHERINE KERR has found an antidote for the hectic pace of laboratory life in the daily practice of tai chi. This centuries-old Chinese mind-body exercise, now gaining popularity in the United States, consists of slow-flowing, choreographed meditative movements with poetic names like "wave hands like clouds," "dragons stirring up the wind," and "swallow skimming the pond" that evoke the natural world. It also focuses on basic components of overall fitness: muscle strength, flexibility, and balance.

"Doing tai chi makes me feel lighter on my feet," says Kerr, a Harvard Medical School (HMS) instructor who has practiced for 15 years. "I'm stronger in my legs, more alert, more focused, and more relaxed—it just puts me in a better mood all around." Although she also practices sitting meditation and does a lot of walking, she says that the impact of tai chi on her mood were so noticeable—even after she was diagnosed with a chronic immune system cancer—that she has devoted her professional life to studying the effects of mind-body exercise on the brain at Harvard's Osher Research Center.

Kerr is careful to note that tai chi is "not a magic cure-all," and that Western scientific understanding of its possible physiological benefits is still very rudimentary. Yet her own experience and exposure to research have convinced her that its benefits are very real—especially for older people too frail to engage in robust aerobic conditioning and for those suffering from impaired balance, joint stiffness, or poor kinesthetic awareness.

⋮

【104 年學測】綜合測驗：21-25 出題來源

——http://www.essortment.com/animals-mythology-64889.html

A look at animal myths and superstitions

Much like the dove and robin, the bluebird is also considered a very lucky sign, particularly when seen in the spring. Likewise, a woodpecker, when seen near the home, is considered a good omen. But, quite in contrast, the peacock is not universally seen as lucky. Though considered lucky, because its multiplicity of "eyes" was said to alert it to approaching evil, in India, and held in esteem in China and Japan, where peacocks are kept as symbols of status and wealth by the ruling families, the peacock receives only scorn from the rest of the world. The peacock's feathers were considered the most unlucky part of the bird, because they end in round, brightly-coloured shapes that look much like eyes, which some call "evil eyes."

Perhaps the most majestic and lucky of all the birds, however, is the eagle. Universally seen as symbols of strength, swiftness and majesty, eagles have earned their place as the icons of some of the most powerful dynasties in all the world, including the Roman Empire itself, which sported an eagle as the imperial sigil.

⋮

【104 年學測】綜合測驗：26-30 出題來源

——http://globaltrees.org/threatened-trees/tree-values/food/

Food

People from all over the world gather nutritional products from trees including fruits, nuts, seeds, leaves, bark and even sap.

Tree products have been an important part of diets for thousands of years, from early humans gathering fruits and nuts (there is evidence of humans eating apples in the Neolithic period) to the first cultivation of important trees, such as mango (*Mangifera indica*) which has been grown in India for over 4,000 years.

Today, products such as apples, oranges, pistachios and brazil nuts are routinely eaten the world over and form the basis for multi-million dollar industries – the apple industry is estimated to be worth US $10 billion a year, for example.

At the local level, edible tree products are often highly valued by local communities as a core part of their diet, as an important supplement or to sustain them when food is seasonally scarce or when harvests are poor. This role as 'emergency' food sources is particularly important and there are several examples of entire communities surviving periods of famine by collecting food from trees.

There are thousands of tree species that provide important food products, but some good examples include:

The Brazil nut tree (*Bertholletia excelsa*)

This species takes a long time to reach maturity and cannot be grown on plantations. As a result, all Brazil nuts are collected from wild populations. One of the most valuable forest products in international trade, the collection of the Brazil nut has resulted in the species becoming threatened. It is currently classified as Vulnerable.

Maple trees (*Acer sp.*)

Trees from this genus produce a sugary sap that, certain species of which may be eaten, used for baking, or used as a flavouring and sweetener. This sap – commonly known as maple syrup – can only be produced in large enough quantities from two species: the sugar maple *Acer saccharum* and the black maple *Acer nigrum*.

Holes are bored in the trunk and a single tree can produce up to 100 litres of sap in one season. Canada is the largest producer of maple syrup and in 2008 the value of all maple products sold was estimated to be CAD$212 million. You can read about threatened maple species in the Red List of Maples, published by GTC in 2009.

Baobabs (*Adansonia sp.*)

Baobabs are found in mainland Africa, Australia and Madagascar. Both Grandidier's baobab (*Adansonia grandidieri*) and *Adansonia digitata* are extremely important food sources. The fruit of both species is rich in vitamins and very nutritious and is eaten raw and made into juice. The seeds can also be turned into oil, and the leaves of *A. digitata* may be eaten. Baobab fruit was called the new 'superfood' on the international market after it was approved for use in smoothies by the European Union in 2008.

Apples (*Malus sp.*)

Apples are one of the world's most cultivated fruit trees, with over 7,000 different varieties in existence.

Despite their great diversity, most domesticated apples can be traced back to a common ancestor, the wild apple – *Malus sieversii*. The wild species still exists in China, Kazakhstan, Kyrgyzstan and Tajikistan but is now, alongside a host of other fruit and nut species from Central Asia, threatened due to the loss of its forest habitat.

This species represents an important genetic storehouse of natural variation, which could include disease and pest resistance that may be important in the future.

【104 年學測】文意選填：31-40 出題來源

—http://itotd.com/articles/536/the-paperclip/

The Paperclip

⋮

Little Things Mean a Lot

About twenty-five years later, I started working for a computer accessories company called Kensington, which is a business unit of ACCO Brands—a major office-products manufacturer. I knew that ACCO made products like paperclips and binders, but what I did not know until I'd worked there for several years was that ACCO was originally short for "American Clip Company." The humble paperclip was largely responsible for the initial success of what is today a gigantic and extremely profitable business.

Where did this simple, cheap, and indispensable invention come from? Appropriately, the story is twisted.

As recently as the late 19th century, the most common way to hold papers together was by using a straight pin. This was an inexpensive and functional solution—and, unlike staples, easily removable. It did, however, leave holes in the paper (and occasionally in the finger). But as steel wire became more common, inventors began to notice that it had just the right amount of springiness to be formed into various sorts of effective cliplike devices. In the years just prior to 1900, quite a few paperclip designs emerged—both in the U.S. and in Europe. Some were patented, some not. There was at the time, and still is now, considerable disagreement about who devised which particular type of wire loop when.

The Norwegian Clipper

The name most frequently associated with the invention of the paperclip is Johan Vaaler, a Norwegian inventor who received patents on several designs—from Germany in 1899 and from the U.S. in 1901. However, Vaaler's clips were by no means the first, nor are they the same as what we think of today as the paperclip—they did not have an interior loop. The familiar double-U design was devised by Gem Manufacturing Ltd. in England; this clip is therefore sometimes known as the Gem clip. (Incidentally, despite the fact that ACCO made a name for itself with paperclips, the so-called ACCO Fastener is not a paperclip; it's a two-pronged brass fastener that was invented in 1912.)

Because the Gem clip itself was never patented, we don't know exactly when it first appeared. Some sources speculate that it may have been as early as 1890; in any case, it was certainly well before Vaaler's first patent in 1899.

In that year, a Connecticut man named William Middlebrook patented a machine for bending Gem-style clips. Such a device would be crucial to the paperclip's success, as it would enable the clips to be manufactured much more quickly and inexpensively.

⋮

【104 年學測】閱讀測驗：41-44 出題來源

—http://www.taiwantoday.tw/fp.asp?xItem=189516&CtNode=427

Paiwan folk singers keep culture alive through music

⋮

Camake Valaule's hard work over the years has paid off. In 2009, the Taiwu Elementary School Folk Singers were invited to perform in Belgium, France, Germany and Luxemburg. In 2011, they were voted one of the world's top five performance groups by audiences of Japan Broadcasting Corp.'s Amazing Voice program.

Recalling the group's first tour in Europe, Camake Valaule admitted that he felt very nervous. "People say Europe is the center of the arts. I was worried that the audience would fall asleep as most of our 75-minute performance was a cappella. The students were also anxious, especially after listening to bands that performed bel canto before us. They even thought the way we sang was weird and different from the others.

"Surprisingly, the audience listened with full focus and high spirits," Camake Valaule said. "They told me afterward that through our performance, they had a vision of our country, our village, without having to visit it. This experience greatly boosted our confidence."

According to Camake Valaule, singing traditional ballads has allowed students and their parents to re-understand their culture. "It used to be that the only ones who could sing these songs were tribal elders aged between 50 and 60. Now with the children able to perform the pieces as well, parents are beginning to ask, 'Why do we not know how to sing the ballads?' Many times nowadays, it is the children who teach the songs to their parents, putting back the pieces of a blurred memory."

To Camake Valaule, his original intention of forming the choir was not for the kids to perform, but to preserve and pass on their culture. Referring to the relocation of Taiwu Elementary School and Taiwu Village due to Typhoon Morakot in August 2009, he said, "We could not take the forest or our houses in the mountains with us; but we were able to bring our culture along. As long as the children are willing to sing, I will always be there for them, singing with them and leading them to experience the meaning of the ballads." (HZW)

【104 年學測】閱讀測驗：45-48 出題來源

——http://query.nytimes.com/gst/fullpage.html?res=9C02E6D7153DF93BA157 5BC0A9649D8B63

WELL: Overtreatment Is Taking a Harmful Toll

When it comes to medical care, many patients and doctors believe more is better.

But an epidemic of overtreatment—too many scans, too many blood tests, too many procedures—is costing the nation's health care system at least $210 billion a year, according to the Institute of Medicine, and taking a human toll in pain, emotional suffering, severe complications and even death.

"What people are not realizing is that sometimes the test poses harm," said Shannon Brownlee, acting director of the health policy program at the New America Foundation and the author of "Overtreated: Why Too Much Medicine Is Making Us Sicker and Poorer."

"Sometimes the test leads you down a path, a therapeutic cascade, where you start to tumble downstream to more and more testing, and more and more invasive testing, and possibly even treatment for things that should be left well enough alone."

Have you experienced too much medicine? As part of The New York Times's online seriesThe Agenda, I asked readers to share their stories. More than 1,000 responded, with examples big and small.

Some complained that when they switch doctors they are required to undergo duplicate blood work, scans or other tests that their previous doctor had only recently ordered. Others told of being caught in an unending maze of testing and specialists who seemed to have forgot the patient's original complaint. I heard from doctors and nurses, too— health professionals frustrated by a system that encourages these excesses.

Terrence Power of Breckenridge, Colo., said that after his wife, Diane, learned she had Wegener's disease, an uncommon autoimmune disorder, the couple found it difficult to refuse testing recommended by a trusted doctor. The doctor insisted on office visits every three weeks, even when she was feeling well. He frequently ordered blood tests and X-rays, and repeatedly referred her to specialists for even minor complaints. Even when tests came back negative, more were ordered, and she was hospitalized as a precaution when she developed a cold. During one six-month period, she had 25 doctor visits. The couple was spending about $30,000 a year out of pocket for her care.

"He was convincing enough that we felt we needed to have it done," said Ms. Power, 60, who recalls being sedated before an endoscopy procedure, one of the last tests she allowed her doctor to perform. "When they were getting ready to knock me out, I was thinking, 'Why am I doing this?' But we felt like the doctor knew what to do and we trusted him."

After several years of physical suffering and near financial ruin from the medical costs, the couple began questioning the treatment after consulting with other patients in online support groups. Mr. Power spoke with his own primary care doctor, who advised him to find a new specialist to oversee Ms. Power's care. "It's a really hard thing to determine when they've crossed the line," Mr. Power said. "You think she's getting the best care in the world, but after a while you start to wonder, what is the objective? He seemed caring, but he didn't really consider my wife's time and the suffering she was going through having all these tests done."

Under the new doctor's care, the regular testing stopped and Ms. Power was finally able to achieve remission. Now she sees the doctor only four or five times a year.

Sometimes the toll of too much medicine is brief, but emotional. Kara Riehman, 43, of Atlanta was vacationing in California when she lost a struggle with an ironing board in her hotel room and ended up with a black eye.

As the bruising peaked at around 10 days, she called her doctor to make sure everything looked normal. But instead of seeing her, the doctor, through a conversation with the nurse, ordered a CT scan. She had no symptoms other than a bruised eye, but the doctor never spoke with her or examined her. The scan came back with an ambiguous finding, and the nurse told her it could be a tumor. She was then given an M.R.I., and for two weeks while she waited for the results, she worried she had brain cancer. The nurse called to tell her the M.R.I. was fine.

：

【104 年學測】閱讀測驗：49-52 出題來源

——http://tweedlandthegentlemansclub.blogspot.tw/2011/10/remembering-henri-cartier-bresson.html

Remembering the Henri Cartier-Bresson Retrospective Exhibition at the MOMA

HENRI CARTIER-BRESSON AT THE MOMA
Henri Cartier-Bresson (1908–2004) is one of the most original, accomplished, influential, and beloved figures in the history of

photography. His inventive work of the early 1930s helped define the creative potential of modern photography, and his uncanny ability to capture life on the run made his work synonymous with "the decisive moment"—the title of his first major book. After World War II (most of which he spent as a prisoner of war) and his first museum show (at MoMA in 1947), he joined Robert Capa and others in founding the Magnum photo agency, which enabled photojournalists to reach a broad audience through magazines such as Life while retaining control over their work. In the decade following the war, Cartier-Bresson produced major bodies of photographic reportage on India and Indonesia at the time of independence, China during the revolution, the Soviet Union after Stalin's death, the United States during the postwar boom, and Europe as its old cultures confronted modern realities. For more than twenty-five years, he was the keenest observer of the global theater of human affairs—and one of the great portraitists of the twentieth century. MoMA's retrospective, the first in the United States in three decades, surveys Cartier-Bresson's entire career, with a presentation of about three hundred photographs, mostly arranged thematically and supplemented with periodicals and books. The exhibition travels to The Art Institute of Chicago, the San Francisco Museum of Modern Art (SFMOMA), and the High Museum of Art, Atlanta.

Henri Cartier-Bresson

Henri Cartier-Bresson (August 22, 1908 – August 3, 2004) was a French photographer considered to be the father of modern photojournalism. He was an early adopter of the 35 mm format, and the master of candid photography. He helped develop the "street photography" or "real life reportage" style that influenced generations of photographers who followed.

【104 年學測】閱讀測驗：53-56 出題來源

——http://www.economist.com/news/leaders/21576384-cars-have-already-chang
ed-way-we-live-they-are-likely-do-so-again-clean-safe-and-it

Sitting is the New Smoking-Even for Runners

You've no doubt heard the news by now: A car-commuting, desk-bound,
TV-watching lifestyle can be harmful to your health. All the time we
spend parked behind a steering wheel, slumped over a keyboard, or
kicked back in front of the tube is linked to increased risks of heart
disease, diabetes, cancer, and even depression—to the point where
experts have labeled this modern-day health epidemic the "sitting
disease."

But wait, you're a runner. You needn't worry about the harms of
sedentary living because you're active, right? Well, not so fast. A
growing body of research shows that people who spend many hours of
the day glued to a seat die at an earlier age than those who sit less—even
if those sitters exercise.

"Up until very recently, if you exercised for 60 minutes or more a day,
you were considered physically active, case closed," says Travis
Saunders, a Ph.D. student and certified exercise physiologist at the
Healthy Active Living and Obesity Research Group at Children's
Hospital of Eastern Ontario. "Now a consistent body of emerging
research suggests it is entirely possible to meet current physical activity
guidelines while still being incredibly sedentary, and that sitting
increases your risk of death and disease, even if you are getting plenty of
physical activity. It's a bit like smoking. Smoking is bad for you even if
you get lots of exercise. So is sitting too much."

Unfortunately, outside of regularly scheduled exercise sessions, active people sit just as much as their couch-potato peers. In a 2012 study published in the International Journal of Behavioral Nutrition and Physical Activity, researchers reported that people spent an average of 64 hours a week sitting, 28 hours standing, and 11 hours milling about (nonexercise walking), whether or not they exercised the recommended 150 minutes a week. That's more than nine hours a day of sitting, no matter how active they otherwise were. "We were very surprised that even the highest level of exercise did not matter squat for reducing the time spent sitting," says study author Marc Hamilton, Ph.D., professor and director of the inactivity physiology department at Pennington Biomedical Research Center. In fact, regular exercisers may make less of an effort to move outside their designated workout time. Research presented at the 2013 annual meeting of the American College of Sports Medicine from Illinois State University reports that people are about 30 percent less active overall on days when they exercise versus days they don't hit the road or the gym. Maybe they think they've worked out enough for one day. But experts say most people simply aren't running or walking or even just standing enough to counteract all the harm that can result from sitting eight or nine or 10 hours a day.

⋮

104 年學測英文科非選擇題閱卷評分原則說明

閱卷召集人：賴惠玲（國立政治大學英國語文學系教授）

　　104 學年度學科能力測驗英文考科的非選擇題型共有「中譯英」和「英文作文」兩大題。第一大題是「中譯英」，題型與過去幾年相同，考生需將兩個中文句子譯成正確、通順、達意的英文，兩題合計為 8 分。第二大題是「英文作文」，以至少 120 個單詞，從兩本書當中選擇其中一本設想該書可能的內容，再說明為什麼選擇該本書的理由。閱卷之籌備工作，依循閱卷標準程序，於 2 月 4 日先召開評分標準訂定會議，由正、副召集人及協同主持人共 14 人，參閱了約 3,000 份來自不同地區的答案卷，經過一整天的討論之後，完成評分標準訂定，選出合適的評分參考樣卷及試閱樣卷，並編製成《閱卷參考手冊》，以供閱卷委員共同參閱。

　　本年度共計聘請 171 位大學教授擔任閱卷委員。2 月 6 日上午 9：00 至 11：00 為試閱會議，首先由召集人提示評分標準並舉例說明；接著分組進行試閱，參與評分之教授須根據《閱卷參考手冊》的試閱樣卷分別評分，並討論評分準則，務求評分標準一致，以確保閱卷品質。為求慎重，試閱會議後，正、副召集人及協同主持人將進行評分標準再確定會議，確認評分原則後才開始正式閱卷。

　　評分標準與歷年相同，在「中譯英」部分，每小題總分 4 分，原則上是每個錯誤扣 0.5 分，相同的錯誤只扣一次。「英文作文」的評分標準是依據內容、組織、文法句構、詞彙拼字、體例五個項目給分，字數明顯不足的作文則扣總分 1 分。閱卷時，每份試卷皆會經過兩位委員分別評分，最後成績以二位閱卷委員給分之平均成績為準。如果第一閱與第二閱分數差距超過差分標準，則由第三位委員（正、副召集人或協同主持人）評閱。

　　今年的「中譯英」呼應最近社會發生的食安問題，提醒企業不應該以獲利為最主要目標，應該負起社會責任以增進大眾福祉，希望學生能以英文表達對社會現象的關心。評量的重點在於考生能否運用常用的詞彙與基本句型將兩句中文翻譯成正確、達意的英文句子，所測驗之句型爲高中生熟悉的範圍，詞彙亦控制在大考中心詞彙表四級內之詞彙，中等程度以上的考生，如果能使用正確句型並注意用字、拼字，應能得理想的分數。例如：「不應該把獲利當作最主要的目標」若譯成 should not regard making profit as its primary goal 即可得分；「以增進大衆福祉」則可翻譯爲to enhance public/the public's well-being/welfare 或者to enhance the well-being/welfare of the public。在選取樣卷時，我們發現有不少考生對於英文詞彙的語意及使用，以及英文拼字仍有加強的空間，如第一句的「獲利」指的是企業的利潤應該是profit(s) 而不是benefits；「福祉」應翻成well-being/welfare，也不是benefits；「最主要的目標」有考生翻譯爲the most main goal 重複了最高級的概念，多譯了most；「成功的企業」中的「成功的」應爲形容詞，有不少考生詞性用錯；「社會責任」social responsibilities 拼字錯誤的考生也不少，相當可惜。

今年的「英文作文」主題是要考生從兩本書擇一作答，一本是EVERYBODY IS BEAUTIFUL: Respect Others & Be Yourself，另外一本是LEADERSHIP IS A CHOICE: Conquer Your Fears & You Can Be a Leader Too，考生要根據書名猜測該書的內容並說明爲什麼選擇該本書，跳脫「看圖寫作」的模式。這種命題方式雖與過去四格漫畫敘述故事之方式不同，但本質仍爲引導式寫作，以書名及副標作爲提示，引導考生思考、寫作。題目要考生省思欣賞尊重他人，同時看重肯定自己，或者克服恐懼及培養領導能力的重要性，很符合社會對年輕人的正面期許。不論選擇哪本書，考生若能從不同的角度發揮想像力，清楚描述自己認爲書中可能的內容，同時條理說明選擇的理由，就能拿到不錯的分數。評分的考量重點爲作文內容與所選書籍之間關聯性是否緊密，並有足夠的細節支持，組織是否連貫合理，句構、語法及用字是否適切，以及拼字與標點符號是否正確得當。

104年學測英文考科試題或答案之反映意見回覆

※ 題號：6

【題目】

6. The moment the students felt the earthquake, they ran _____ out of the elassroom to an open area outside.
   (A) swiftly
   (B) nearly
   (C) loosely
   (D) formally

【意見內容】

loose 可解釋爲 "not rigidly organized"，選項 (C) loosely 應爲合理選項。

【大考中心意見回覆】

本題評量考生掌握詞彙 swiftly 的語意及其用法，作答線索在於空格前半句 the moment the students felt the earthquake 與空格後 ran…out of the classroom to an open area outside 之間的因果關係。loosely 應作爲 "not tightly"（「鬆散地」），語意上無法與 ran 搭配使用。根據上下文意及字詞搭配，最適當選項應爲選項 (A) swiftly。

※ 題號：9

【題目】

9. When taking medicine, we should read the instructions on the _____ carefully because they provide important information such as how and when to take it.
   (A) medals
   (B) quotes
   (C) labels
   (D) recipes

【意見內容】

選項 (D) recipes 可解釋爲「處方」，應爲合理答案。

【大考中心意見回覆】

本題評量詞彙label 的語意及其用法，作答線索在題幹 When taking medicine, we should read the instructions on the ⋯ carefully because they provide important information ⋯。根據字典的解釋，雖然 recipe 一詞有「處方（prescription）」之意，但使用情況多為古時候未經官方審核通過之民俗處方，與本題題幹所指市面上合法販售具使用說明之藥品並不一樣，而 on the recipes 的搭配用法通常僅使用在食譜方面。即使將語境置於古時的民間處方，本題題幹中若用了 recipes，就不會再用 instructions 一詞（兩者詞意重複）。

※ 題號：30

【題目】

第 26 至 30 題為題組

　　Nutritional products that can be collected from trees include fruits, nuts, seeds, leaves, and bark. Tree products have been an important part of diets for thousands of years, from early humans ___26___ fruits and nuts to the first cultivation of important trees, such as mango and apple.

　　The apple is one of the world's most cultivated fruit trees, ___27___ over 7,000 different kinds in existence. Despite their great ___28___, however, most domesticated apples can be traced back to a common ancestor, the wild apple of Central Asia, *Malus sieversii*. Apples have been grown for thousands of years in Asia and Europe, and ___29___ to North America by European colonists in the 17th century. Today, apples are ___30___ eaten the world over and form the basis for multi-million dollar industries. In 2005, at least 55 million tons of apples were grown worldwide, which generated a value of about $10 billion.

30. (A) regularly　　(B) particularly　　(C) permanently　　(D) barely

【意見內容】

選項 (A) Amazing 應爲合理選項。

【大考中心意見回覆】

本題評量考生掌握詞彙 regularly 的語意及其用法，作答線索在於空格前後的語意，及空格後下一句。regularly 意指「每天都會做的事情」或者作「經常地」解釋，根據空格前的文意可知，人們種植蘋果已有幾千年的歷史，今天，蘋果更成爲全世界人們經常食用的水果。因此，選項 (A) regularly 才符合上下文的發展。

※ 題號：34, 36

【題目】

第 31 至 40 題爲題組

A paperclip, made of steel wire bent into a hooped shape, is an instrument used to hold sheets of paper together. This common ___31___ is a wonder of simplicity and function. But where did this simple, cheap, and indispensable invention come from?

In the late 19th century, the most common way to hold papers together was by using a pin. Although the pin was an inexpensive tool and was easily ___32___, it would leave holes in the paper. Later, as steel wire became more common, inventors began to notice its elastic feature. With this feature, it could be stretched and ___33___ various clip-like objects. In the years just prior to 1900, quite a few paperclip designs emerged. The name most frequently ___34___ the paperclip invention is Johan Vaaler, a Norwegian inventor. However, Vaaler's clips were not the same as the paperclips currently in use. Specifically, they did not have the interior loop we see today. The ___35___ looped design was invented by Gem Manufacturing Ltd. in England.　This clip is therefore sometimes ＿＿36＿＿ the Gem clip.

　　Because of Vaaler, the paperclip played an important ＿＿37＿＿ role in Norway.　During World War II, Norway was occupied by the Nazis. Norwegians were prohibited from wearing any ＿＿38＿＿ of their national unity, such as buttons with the initials of their king.　Thus, in ＿＿39＿＿, they started wearing paperclips to show their solidarity.　The reason for doing this was simple: Paperclips were a Norwegian invention whose original function was to bind together.　After the war, a giant paperclip statue was erected in Oslo to ＿＿40＿＿ Vaaler—even though his design was never actually manufactured.

(A) familiar	(B) honor	(C) device	(D) removable
(E) known as	(F) protest	(G) symbol	(H) twisted into
(I) associated with	(J) historical		

【意見內容】

第 34 題與第 36 題答案可以互換。

【大考中心意見回覆】

第34 題評量考生掌握慣用語associated with 的語意，作答線索在於空格前後的 The name（指的是 Johan Vaaler）與 the paperclip 兩者的關係是「連結、聯想」（associated with），而非「同指一物」的 known as，因此本題答案為選項 (I)。

相對地，第 36 題評量考生掌握慣用語 known as 的語意，作答線索在空格前一句及空格本句前後的文意。重點在於空格前後 This clip 與 the Gem clip 指涉同一物品，故以 known as 為最佳答案。

※ 題號：46

【題目】

第 45 至 48 題為題組

When it comes to medical care, many patients and doctors believe "more is better." But what they do not realize is that overtreatment—too many scans, too many blood tests, too many procedures—may pose harm. Sometimes a test leads you down a path to more and more testing, some of which may be invasive, or to treatment for things that should be left alone.

Terrence Power, for example, complained that after his wife learned she had Wegener's disease, an uncommon disorder of the immune system, they found it difficult to refuse testing recommended by her physician. The doctor insisted on office visits every three weeks, even when she was feeling well. He frequently ordered blood tests and X-rays, and repeatedly referred her to specialists for even minor complaints. Even when tests came back negative, more were ordered, and she was hospitalized as a precaution when she developed a cold. She had as many as 25 doctor visits during one six-month period. The couple was spending about $30,000 a year for her care.

After several years of physical suffering and near financial ruin from the medical costs, the couple began questioning the treatment after consulting with other patients in online support groups. "It's a really hard thing to determine when **they**'ve crossed the line," Mr. Power said. "You think she's getting the best care in the world, but after a while you start to wonder: What is the objective?" Mr. Power then spoke with his own primary care doctor, who advised him to find a new specialist to oversee Mrs. Power's care. Under the new doctor's care, the regular testing stopped and Mrs. Power's condition stabilized. Now she sees the doctor only four or five times a year.

46. Which of the following was a problem for Mrs. Power during her medical treatment?
   (A) She had to be hospitalized for three weeks whenever she had a cold.
   (B) She didn't have any insurance, so she went broke because of her illness.
   (C) When test results showed she was fine, her doctor still ordered more tests.
   (D) Her doctor asked her to consult other specialists due to her constant complaints.

【意見內容】

1. 根據選文第二段第三句,選項 (D) Her doctor asked her to consult other specialists due to her constant complaints.,應為正確選項。

2. 根據文章內容,選項 (C) 並非正答選項。

3. 文章第二段…, even when she was feeling well.與選項 (C) When test results showed she was fine, …意思不同。

【大考中心意見回覆】

本題評量考生掌握文章細節的能力。根據文章第二段第三句 He frequently ordered blood tests and X-rays, and repeatedly referred her to specialists for even minor complaints. 的 complaints 一詞不是「抱怨」,而是「病痛」的意思,意指「即便她只提到輕微的病痛,醫生也一再將她轉診給專科醫師」,其中 repeatedly(經常,一再)所修飾的是醫師一而再再而三的轉診行為,而非 (D) 中所述 her constant complaints(她持續的抱怨),而 refer her to specialists 是指醫師將她轉診給專科醫師,而非叫她去諮詢其他專家,因此選項 (D) …asked her to consult other specialists … 句意與文中 … repeatedly referred her to specialists 語意不符，不能作為正答。

作答線索在第二段，尤其在第二句：The doctor insisted on office visits every three weeks, even when she was feeling well.，選項 (C) 才是正確選項。

※ 題號：47

【題目】

第 45 至 48 題為題組

　　When it comes to medical care, many patients and doctors believe "more is better." But what they do not realize is that overtreatment— too many scans, too many blood tests, too many procedures—may pose harm. Sometimes a test leads you down a path to more and more testing, some of which may be invasive, or to treatment for things that should be left alone.

　　Terrence Power, for example, complained that after his wife learned she had Wegener's disease, an uncommon disorder of the immune system, they found it difficult to refuse testing recommended by her physician. The doctor insisted on office visits every three weeks, even when she was feeling well. He frequently ordered blood tests and X-rays, and repeatedly referred her to specialists for even minor complaints. Even when tests came back negative, more were ordered, and she was hospitalized as a precaution when she developed a cold. She had as many as 25 doctor visits during one six-month period. The couple was spending about $30,000 a year for her care.

　　After several years of physical suffering and near financial ruin from the medical costs, the couple began questioning the treatment after consulting with other patients in online support groups. "It's a really hard thing to determine when **they**'ve crossed the line," Mr. Power said. "You think she's getting the best care in the world, but after a while you start to wonder: What is the objective?" Mr. Power then spoke with his own primary care doctor, who advised him to find a new specialist to oversee Mrs. Power's care. Under the new doctor's care, the regular testing stopped and Mrs. Power's condition stabilized. Now she sees the doctor only four or five times a year.

47. Who does "**they**" in the third paragraph most likely refer to?
    (A) Physicians.　　　　　　(B) Other patients.
    (C) Mr. and Mrs. Power.　　(D) The online support groups.

【意見內容】

選項 (C) 應該更符合文章的發展。

【大考中心意見回覆】

本題評量考生指代詞的意涵，作答線索在第三段。整篇文章都與過度醫療的議題相關，第二段舉例說明醫生對 Mrs. Power 的過度醫療行為，及第三段第一句 Mr. 與 Mrs. Power 開始質疑諸多（醫生）建議的醫療措施之必要性。題目焦點 "they" 所在的句子… when they've crossed the line（逾越常規律、過度）點出這些過度行為應是來自醫生。所以，此處 they 所指應該為選項 (A) Physicians。。

※ 題號：52

【題目】

第 49 至 52 題為題組

　　Henri Cartier-Bresson (1908−2004) is one of the most original and inf luential figures in the history of photography. His humane, spontaneous photographs helped establish photojournalism as an art form.

Cartier-Bresson's family was wealthy—his father made a fortune as a textile manufacturer—but Cartier-Bresson later joked that due to his parents' frugal ways, it often seemed as though his family was poor.

Educated in Paris, Cartier-Bresson developed an early love for literature and the arts. As a teenager, Cartier-Bresson rebelled against his parents' formal ways of education. In his early adulthood, he even drifted toward communism. But it was art that remained at the center of his life.

Cartier-Bresson traveled to Africa in 1931 to hunt antelope and boar. And Africa fueled another interest in him: photography. He then wandered around the world with his camera, using a handheld camera to catch images from fleeting moments of everyday life.

Not long after World War II, Cartier-Bresson traveled east, spending considerable time in India, where he met and photographed Gandhi shortly before his assassination in 1948. Cartier-Bresson's subsequent work to document Gandhi's death and its immediate impact on the country became one of *Life Magazine*'s most prized photo essays.

Cartier-Bresson's approach to photography remained much the same throughout his life. He made clear his dislike of images that had been improved by artificial light, darkroom effects, and even cropping. The naturalist in Cartier-Bresson believed that all editing should be done when the photo is taken. In 1952, his first book, *The Decisive Moment*, a rich collection of his work spanning two decades, was published. "There is nothing in this world that does not have a decisive moment," he said.

In 1968, he began to turn away from photography and returned to his passion for drawing and painting.

52. Which of the following is true about Cartier-Bresson's approach to photography?
   (A) He never waited for a decisive moment to shoot photos.
   (B) He preferred to edit his images carefully in his darkroom.
   (C) Most of his photos described things that happen every day.
   (D) He experimented with different ways and settled on being a naturalist.

【意見內容】

根據文章內容，選項 (A) 亦為合理答案。

【大考中心意見回覆】

本題評量考生掌握文章細節的能力，作答線索在於對全文文意的理解，尤其在第三、四、六段，從第四段內容最後一句 He then wandered around the world with his camera, using a handheld camera to catch images from fleeting moments of everyday life. 可以正確作答。其中，…images from fleeting moments of everyday life 呼應選項 (C) …things that happen every day。

而第六段內容則在描述他的攝影手法與哲學，重點在 "There is nothing in this world that does not have a decisive moment."，強調世上萬物皆有一個「決定性的瞬間」，而這瞬間必須在等待各項因素成熟之後，才果斷決定的。所以，第三句…all editing should be done when the photo is taken，意味等待光線、畫面配置皆成熟時，即是按下快門的「決定性瞬間」，而不需事後的暗房修補。由此可知，選項 (A) He never waited… 的句意與文章所說的意思不相符合，因此並非正答選項。

※ 題號：55

【題目】

第 53 至 56 題為題組

You've most likely heard the news by now: A car-commuting, desk-bound, TV-watching lifestyle can be harmful to our health. All the time that we spend rooted in the chair is linked to increased risks of so many deadly diseases that experts have named this modern-day health epidemic the "sitting disease."

Sitting for too long slows down the body's metabolism and the way enzymes break down our fat reserves, raising both blood sugar levels and blood pressure. Small amounts of regular activity, even just standing and moving around, throughout the day is enough to bring the increased levels back down. And those small amounts of activity add up—30 minutes of light activity in two or three-minute bursts can be just as effective as a halfhour block of exercise. But without that activity, blood sugar levels and blood pressure keep creeping up, steadily damaging the inside of the arteries and increasing the risk of diabetes, heart disease, stroke, and other serious diseases. In essence, fundamental changes in biology occur if you sit for too long.

But wait, you're a runner. You needn't worry about the harm of a sedentary lifestyle because you exercise regularly, right? Well, not so fast. Recent studies show that people spend an average of 64 hours a week sitting, whether or not they exercise 150 minutes a week as recommended by World Health Organization (WHO). Regular exercisers, furthermore, are found to be about 30 percent less active on days when they exercise. Overall, most people simply aren't exercising or moving around enough to counteract all the harm that can result from sitting nine hours or more a day.

Scared straight out of your chair? Good. The remedy is as simple as standing up and taking activity breaks.

55. What is the best way to bring down high blood sugar level and blood pressure?
    (A) Exercising for 150 minutes or more every week.
    (B) Getting rid of the habit of car commuting and TV watching.
    (C) Interrupting sitting time with light activity as often as possible.
    (D) Standing or moving around for at least two or three minutes every day.

【意見內容】

1. 選項 (B) 應為正確選項。
2. 文章內容均未提及選項 (C) 中的 as often as possible，命題有瑕疵，故本題應送分。

【大考中心意見回覆】

本題評量考生根據文章內容作適當推論的能力，作答線索在於第二段內容，尤其是第二句 Small amounts of regular activity, even just standing and moving around, throughout the day is enough to bring the increased levels back down.，由句中 regular activity 與 throughout the day 可推論出，這類小量、規律的活動，持續整天，而下一句亦提及此類活動可以「累積」（add up），更可推論出「次數越多越好」。因此，選項 (C) 為正答。

根據文章內容，選項 (B) 中的 car commuting 與 TV watching 僅是日常「久坐」活動的兩個例子，戒除此兩種活動，並非降低高血糖與高血壓的「最佳」方式，因此並非本題最適當的選項。

103 年大學入學學科能力測驗試題
英文考科

第壹部分：單選題（占 72 分）

一、詞彙（占 15 分）

說明：　第 1 題至第 15 題，每題有 4 個選項，其中只有一個是正確或最適當的
選項，請畫記在答案卡之「選擇題答案區」。各題答對者，得 1 分；
答錯、未作答或畫記多於一個選項者，該題以零分計算。

1. Lost and scared, the little dog ＿＿＿＿＿ along the streets, looking
for its master.
(A) dismissed　　(B) glided　　　(C) wandered　　(D) marched

2. On a sunny afternoon last month, we all took off our shoes and
walked on the grass with ＿＿＿＿＿ feet.
(A) bare　　　　(B) raw　　　　(C) tough　　　(D) slippery

3. It is both legally and ＿＿＿＿＿ wrong to spread rumors about other
people on the Internet.
(A) morally　　(B) physically　　(C) literarily　　(D) commercially

4. These warm-up exercises are designed to help people ＿＿＿＿＿ their
muscles and prevent injuries.
(A) produce　　(B) connect　　(C) broaden　　(D) loosen

5. Mei-ling has a very close relationship with her parents. She always
＿＿＿＿＿ them before she makes important decisions.
(A) impresses　　(B) advises　　(C) consults　　(D) motivates

6. The restaurant has a ＿＿＿＿＿ charge of NT$250 per person. So the
four of us need to pay at least NT$1,000 to eat there.
(A) definite　　(B) minimum　　(C) flexible　　(D) numerous

7. At the Book Fair, exhibitors from 21 countries will ＿＿＿ textbooks,
novels, and comic books.
(A) predict　　(B) require　　(C) display　　(D) target

8. Before John got on the stage to give the speech, he took a deep
   _____ to calm himself down.
   (A) order   (B) rest   (C) effort   (D) breath

9. Most young people in Taiwan are not satisfied with a high school
   _____ and continue to pursue further education in college.
   (A) maturity   (B) diploma   (C) foundation   (D) guarantee

10. Residents are told not to dump all household waste _____ into
    the trash can; reusable materials should first be sorted out and
    recycled.
    (A) shortly   (B) straight   (C) forward   (D) namely

11. Kevin had been standing on a ladder trying to reach for a book on
    the top shelf when he lost his _____ and fell to the ground.
    (A) volume   (B) weight   (C) balance   (D) direction

12. If student enrollment continues to drop, some programs at the
    university may be _____ to reduce the operation costs.
    (A) relieved   (B) eliminated   (C) projected   (D) accounted

13. People in that remote village feed themselves by hunting and
    engaging in _____ forms of agriculture. No modern agricultural
    methods are used.
    (A) universal   (B) splendid   (C) primitive   (D) courteous

14. The government issued a travel _____ for Taiwanese in response
    to the outbreak of civil war in Syria.
    (A) alert   (B) monument   (C) exit   (D) circulation

15. The baby panda Yuan Zai at the Taipei Zoo was separated from her
    mother because of a minor injury that occurred during her birth.
    She was _____ by zookeepers for a while.
    (A) departed   (B) jailed   (C) tended   (D) captured

二、綜合測驗（占 15 分）

說明：第 16 題至第 30 題，每題一個空格，請依文意選出最適當的一個選項，
　　　請畫記在答案卡之「選擇題答案區」。各題答對者，得 1 分；答錯、未
　　　作答或畫記多於一個選項者，該題以零分計算。

第 16 至 20 題爲題組

　　Aesop, the Greek writer of fables, was sitting by the roadside one day when a traveler asked him what sort of people lived in Athens. Aesop replied, "Tell me where you come from and what sort of people live there, and I'll tell you what sort of people you'll find in Athens." ___16___, the man answered, "I come from Argos, and there the people are all friendly, generous, and warm-hearted. I love them." ___17___ this, Aesop answered, "I'm happy to tell you, my dear friend, that you'll find the people of Athens much the same."

　　A few hours later, ___18___ traveler came down the road. He too stopped and asked Aesop the same question. ___19___, Aesop made the same request. But frowning, the man answered, "I'm from Argos and there the people are unfriendly, ___20___, and vicious. They're thieves and murderers, all of them." "Well, I'm afraid you'll find the people of Athens much the same," replied Aesop.

16. (A) Amazing　　　(B) Smiling　　　(C) Deciding　　　(D) Praying
17. (A) At　　　　　 (B) By　　　　　 (C) For　　　　　 (D) Into
18. (A) a　　　　　　(B) the　　　　　(C) other　　　　 (D) another
19. (A) Again　　　　(B) Indeed　　　 (C) Together　　　 (D) Moreover
20. (A) brave　　　　(B) lonely　　　 (C) mean　　　　　(D) skinny

第 21 至 25 題爲題組

　　Every year tens of thousands of tourists visit Mount Kilimanjaro, the highest mountain in Tanzania, Africa, to witness the scenes depicted in Earnest Hemingway's *The Snows of Kilimanjaro*. They are attracted by the American writer's ___21___ of the millennia-old glaciers. However, this tourist attraction will soon ___22___. According to the Climate Change Group, formed by environmentalists worldwide to document the effects of global warming, Mount Kilimanjaro's snows and glaciers are melting and are ___23___ to disappear by 2020. Not only will the summit lose its tourist attraction, but the disappearance of the snows will also cause major damage to the ecosystem on the dry African plains at its base. ___24___ the snow covering the peak, there will not be enough moisture and water to nourish the plants and animals below. Rising temperatures, an effect of global warming, ___25___ threaten the ecosystem of this mountain area. The loss of snows on the 5,892m peak, which have been there for about 11,700 years, could have disastrous effects on Tanzania.

21. (A) situations   (B) descriptions   (C) translations   (D) calculations
22. (A) operate   (B) expand   (C) recover   (D) vanish
23. (A) capable   (B) ready   (C) likely   (D) horrible
24. (A) Among   (B) Besides   (C) Inside   (D) Without
25. (A) thus   (B) just   (C) instead   (D) otherwise

第 26 至 30 題為題組

Most human beings actually decide before they think. When people encounter a complex issue and form an opinion, how thoroughly have they ___26___ all the important factors involved before they make their decisions? The answer is: not very thoroughly, ___27___ they are executives, specialized experts, or ordinary people in the street. Very few people, no matter how intelligent or experienced, can ___28___ all the possibilities or outcomes of a policy or a course of action within just a short period of time. Those who take pride in being decisive often try their best to consider all the factors beforehand. ___29___, it is not unusual for them to come up with a decision before they have the time to do so. And ___30___ an opinion is formed, most of their thinking then is simply trying to find support for it.

26. (A) conveyed   (B) examined   (C) solved   (D) implied
27. (A) whoever   (B) because   (C) whether   (D) rather
28. (A) set out   (B) turn out
    (C) put into practice   (D) take into account
29. (A) However   (B) Furthermore   (C) Conditionally   (D) Similarly
30. (A) though   (B) unless   (C) once   (D) even

三、文意選填（占 10 分）

說明： 第 31 題至第 40 題，每題一個空格，請依文意在文章後所提供的 (A) 到
(J) 選項中分別選出最適當者，並將其英文字母代號畫記在答案卡之「選
擇題答案區」。各題答對者，得 1 分；答錯、未作答或畫記多於一個選
項者，該題以零分計算。

第 31 至 40 題為題組

　　In English-speaking cultures, the choice of first names for children
can be prompted by many factors: tradition, religion, nature, culture,
and fashion, to name just a few.

　　Certain people like to give a name that has been handed down in the
family to show ___31___ for or to remember a relative whom they love
or admire. Some families have a tradition of ___32___ the father's first
name to the first born son. In other families, a surname is included in
the selection of a child's given name to ___33___ a family surname going.
It may be the mother's maiden name, for instance.

　　For a long time, ___34___ has also played an important role in
naming children. Boys' names such as John, Peter, and Thomas are
chosen from the Bible. Girls' names such as Faith, Patience, and
Sophie (wisdom) are chosen because they symbolize Christian qualities.
However, for people who are not necessarily religious but are fond of
nature, names ___35___ things of beauty are often favored. Flower and
plant names like Heather, Rosemary, and Iris ___36___ this category.

　　Another factor that has had a great ___37___ on the choice of names
is the spread of culture through the media. People may choose a name
because they are strongly ___38___ a character in a book or a television
series; they may also adopt names of famous people or their favorite
actors and actresses. Sometimes, people pick foreign names for their
children because those names are unusual and will thus make their
children more ___39___ and distinctive.

　　Finally, some people just pick a name the sound of which they like,

___40___ of its meaning, its origins, or its popularity. However, even these people may look at the calendar to pick a lucky day when they make their choice.

(A) drawn to (B) fall into (C) impact (D) involving
(E) keep (F) passing down (G) regardless (H) religion
(I) respect (J) unique

四、閱讀測驗（占 32 分）

說明：　第 41 題至第 56 題，每題請分別根據各篇文章之文意選出最適當的一個選項，請畫記在答案卡之「選擇題答案區」。各題答對者，得 2 分；答錯、未作答或畫記多於一個選項者，該題以零分計算。

第 41 至 44 題為題組

　　American writer Toni Morrison was born in 1931 in Ohio. She was raised in an African American family filled with songs and stories of Southern myths, which later shaped her prose. Her happy family life led to her excellent performance in school, despite the atmosphere of racial discrimination in the society.

　　After graduating from college, Morrison started to work as a teacher and got married in 1958. Several years later, her marriage began to fail. For a temporary escape, she joined a small writers' group, in which each member was required to bring a story or poem for discussion. She wrote a story based on the life of a girl she knew in childhood who had prayed to God for blue eyes. The story was well received by the group, but then she put it away, thinking she was done with it.

　　In 1964, Morrison got divorced and devoted herself to writing. One day, she dusted off the story she had written for the writers' group and decided to make it into a novel. She drew on her memories from childhood and expanded upon them using her imagination so that the characters developed a life of their own. *The Bluest Eye* was eventually published in 1970. From 1970 to 1992, Morrison published five more novels.

In her novels, Morrison brings in different elements of the African American past, their struggles, problems and cultural memory. In *Song of Solomon*, for example, Morrison tells the story of an African American man and his search for identity in his culture. The novels and other works won her several prizes. In 1993, Morrison received the Nobel Prize in Literature. She is the eighth woman and the first African American woman to win the honor.

41. What is the passage mainly about?
    (A) The life of black people in the U.S.
    (B) The life of an African American writer.
    (C) The history of African American culture.
    (D) The history of the Nobel Prize in Literature.

42. Why did Morrison join the writers' group?
    (A) She wanted to publish *The Bluest Eye*.
    (B) She wanted to fight racial discrimination.
    (C) She wanted to be a professional writer.
    (D) She wanted to get away from her unhappy marriage.

43. According to the passage, what is one of the themes in Morrison's works?
    (A) A search for African American values.
    (B) Divorced black women in American society.
    (C) Songs and stories of African Americans in Ohio.
    (D) History of African Americans from the 1970s through the 1990s.

44. Which of the following statements is true about Toni Morrison?
    (A) She has been writing a lot since her adolescent years.
    (B) She suffered from severe racial discrimination in her family.
    (C) What she wrote in her novels are true stories of African Americans.
    (D) No African American woman ever received a Nobel Prize in Literature before her.

Below is an excerpt from an interview with Zeke Emanuel, a health-policy expert, on his famous brothers.

Interviewer:	You're the older brother of Rahm, the mayor of Chicago, and Ari, an extremely successful talent agent. And you're a bioethicist and one of the architects of Obamacare. Isn't writing a book about how great your family is a bit odd?
Zeke:	I don't write a book about how great my family is. There are lots of idiocies and foolishness—a lot to make fun of in the book. I wrote *Brothers Emanuel* because I had begun jotting stories for my kids. And then we began getting a lot of questions: What did Mom put in the cereal? Three successful brothers, all different areas.
I:	To what do you attribute the Emanuel brothers' success?
Z:	I would put success in quotes. We strive. First, I think we got this striving from our mother to make the world a better place. A second important thing is you never rest on the last victory. There's always more to do. And maybe the third important thing is my father's admonition that offense is the best defense. We don't give up.
I:	Do you still not have a TV?
Z:	I don't own a TV. I don't own a car. I don't Facebook. I don't tweet.
I:	But you have four cell phones.
Z:	I'm down to two, thankfully.
I:	Your brothers are a national source of fascination. Where do you think they'll be in five years?
Z:	Ari will be a superagent running the same company. Rahm would still be mayor of Chicago. I will probably continue to be my academic self. The one thing I can guarantee is none of us will have taken a cruise, none of us will be sitting on a beach with a pina colada.

45. What does Zeke Emanuel have in mind when saying "What did Mom put in the cereal?"
　(A) The secret to bringing up successful kids.
　(B) The recipe for a breakfast food.
　(C) The difference among the brothers.
　(D) The questions from his kids.

46. What does Zeke Emanuel think of the modern conveniences mentioned in the interview?
　(A) Better late than never.
　(B) Practice makes perfect.
　(C) One can live without many of them.
　(D) They are great inventions.

47. According to Zeke Emanuel, which of the following is a reason for the brothers' success?
　(A) They defend themselves by attacking others.
　(B) They learn a lot from great people's quotes.
　(C) They are committed to glorifying their parents.
　(D) They keep moving forward even after a big success.

48. Which of the following best summarizes Zeke Emanuel's response to the last question?
　(A) The brothers look forward to a family trip on a cruise.
　(B) Nothing much will change in the near future for them.
　(C) Higher positions and more power will be their goals.
　(D) None of the brothers will go to the beach.

第 49 至 52 題為題組

　　MOOC, a massive open online course, aims at providing large-scale interactive participation and open access via the web. In addition to traditional course materials such as videos, readings, and problem sets, MOOCs provide interactive user forums that help build a community for the students, professors, and teaching assistants.

　　MOOCs first made waves in the fall of 2011, when Professor Sebastian Thrun from Stanford University opened his graduate-level artificial intelligence course up to any student anywhere, and 160,000 students in more than 190 countries signed up. This new breed of online classes is shaking up the higher education world in many ways. Since the courses can be taken by hundreds of thousands of students at the same time, the number of universities might decrease dramatically. Professor Thrun has even envisioned a future in which there will only need to be 10 universities in the world. Perhaps the most striking thing about MOOCs, many of which are being taught by professors at prestigious universities, is that they're free. This is certainly good news for **cash-strapped** students.

　　There is a lot of excitement and fear surrounding MOOCs. While some say free online courses are a great way to increase the enrollment of minority students, others have said they will leave many students behind. Some critics have said that MOOCs promote an unrealistic one-size-fits-all model of higher education and that there is no replacement for true dialogues between professors and their students. After all, a brain is not a computer. We are not blank hard drives waiting to be filled with data. People learn from people they love and remember the things that arouse emotion. Some critics worry that online students will miss out on the social aspects of college.

49. What does the word "**cash-strapped**" in the second paragraph mean?
    (A) Making a lot of money.　　　(B) Being short of money.
    (C) Being careful with money.　　(D) Spending little money.

50. Which of the following is **NOT** one of the features of MOOCs?
    (A) It is free to take the courses.
    (B) Many courses are offered by famous universities.
    (C) Most courses address artificial intelligence.
    (D) Many students can take the course at the same time.

51. What is the second paragraph mainly about?
    (A) The impact of MOOCs.　　　(B) The goal of MOOCs.
    (C) The size of MOOC classes.　　(D) The cost of MOOC courses.

52. Which of the following is a problem of MOOCs mentioned in the
    passage?
    (A) The disappearance of traditional course materials.
    (B) The limited number of courses offered around the world.
    (C) The overreliance on professors from prestigious universities.
    (D) The lack of social interaction among students and professors.

第 53 至 56 題為題組

　　Today the car seems to make periodic leaps in progress. A variety
of driver assistance technologies are appearing on new cars. A
developing technology called Vehicle-to-Vehicle communication, or
V2V, is being tested by automotive manufacturers as a way to help
reduce the number of accidents. V2V works by using wireless signals
to send information back and forth between cars about their location,
speed and direction, so that they keep safe distances from each other.
Another new technology being tested is Vehicle-to-Infrastructure
communication, or V2I. V2I would allow vehicles to communicate
with road signs or traffic signals and provide information to the vehicle
about safety issues. V2I could also request traffic information from a
traffic management system and access the best possible routes. Both
V2V and V2I have the potential to reduce around 80 percent of vehicle
crashes on the road.

　　More and more new cars can reverse-park, read traffic signs,
maintain a safe distance in steady traffic and brake automatically to
avoid crashes. Moreover, a number of firms are creating cars that drive
themselves to a chosen destination without a human at the controls. It is
predicted that driverless cars will be ready for sale within five years. If
and when cars go completely driverless, the benefits will be enormous.
Google, which already uses prototypes of such cars to ferry its staff
along Californian freeways, once put a blind man in a prototype and
filmed him being driven off to buy takeaway hamburgers. If this works,

huge numbers of elderly and disabled people can regain their personal mobility. The young will not have to pay crippling motor insurance, because their reckless hands and feet will no longer touch the wheel or the accelerator. People who commute by car will gain hours each day to work, rest, or read a newspaper.

53. Which of the following statements is true about V2V?
　(A) V2V communication has been very well developed.
　(B) Through V2V, drivers can chat with each other on the road.
　(C) V2V is designed to decrease crashes by keeping safe distances.
　(D) Through V2V, a car can warn cyclists nearby of its approach.

54. What does "**infrastructure**" in Vehicle-to-Infrastructure refer to?
　(A) Traffic facilities and information systems.
　(B) The basic structure of roads and bridges.
　(C) Knowledge and regulations about safe driving.
　(D) The traffic department of the government.

55. Which of the following is **NOT** a potential benefit of driverless cars?
　(A) The elderly will become more mobile.
　(B) "Drivers" can sleep in cars all the way to work.
　(C) People can race cars to their heart's content.
　(D) A blind man can get into a car and travel safely.

56. What can be inferred from the passage?
　(A) Cars will refuse to start if the driver is drunk.
　(B) The future may be a vehicle-accident-free era.
　(C) Everyone, including children, can afford a car.
　(D) The production of driverless cars is still far away.

第貳部份：非選擇題（占 28 分）

說明：　本部分共有二題，請依各題指示作答，答案必須寫在「答案卷」上，並標明大題號（一、二）。作答務必使用筆尖較粗之黑色墨水的筆書寫，且不得使用鉛筆。

一、中譯英（占8分）

說明： 1. 請將以下中文句子譯成正確、通順、達意的英文，並將答案寫在「答案卷」上。

　　　 2. 請依序作答，並標明題號。每題4分，共8分。

1. 有些年輕人辭掉都市裡的高薪工作，返回家鄉種植有機蔬菜。

2. 藉由決心與努力，很多人成功了，不但獲利更多，還過著更健康的生活。

二、英文作文（占20分）

說明： 1. 依提示在「答案卷」上寫一篇英文作文。

　　　 2. 文長至少120個單詞（words）。

提示： 請仔細觀察以下三幅連環圖片的內容，並想像第四幅圖片可能的發展，寫一篇涵蓋所有連環圖片內容且有完整結局的故事。

103年度學科能力測驗英文科試題詳解

第壹部分：單選題

一、詞彙題：

1. (**C**) Lost and scared, the little dog <u>wandered</u> along the streets, looking for its master. 迷路而受驚嚇的小狗，沿著街道徘徊，尋找牠的主人。
   - (A) dismiss〔dɪsˈmɪs〕*v.* 解散
   - (B) glide〔glaɪd〕*v.* 滑行
   - (C) *wander*〔ˈwɑndɚ〕*v.* 徘徊
   - (D) march〔mɑrtʃ〕*v.* 行進

   lost〔lɔst〕*adj.* 迷路的；不知所措的　　scared〔skɛrd〕*adj.* 害怕的
   look for 尋找　　master〔ˈmæstɚ〕*n.* 主人

2. (**A**) On a sunny afternoon last month, we all took off our shoes and walked on the grass with <u>bare</u> feet.
   在上個月一個晴朗的下午，我們都脫下了鞋子，赤裸著腳走在草地上。
   - (A) *bare*〔bɛr〕*adj.* 赤裸的
   - (B) raw〔rɔ〕*adj.* 生的
   - (C) tough〔tʌf〕*adj.* 困難的
   - (D) slippery〔ˈslɪpərɪ〕*adj.* 滑的

   sunny〔ˈsʌnɪ〕*adj.* 晴朗的　　***take off*** 脫下
   grass〔græs〕*n.* 草；草坪

3. (**A**) It is both legally and <u>morally</u> wrong to spread rumors about other people on the Internet. 在網路上散播有關他人的謠言，在法律上和道德上兩方面，都是錯的。
   - (A) *morally*〔ˈmɔrəlɪ〕*adv.* 道德上
   - (B) physically〔ˈfɪzɪkḷ〕*adv.* 身體上
   - (C) literarily〔ˈlɪtəˌrɛrəlɪ〕*adv.* 文學上
   - (D) commercially〔kəˈmɝʃəlɪ〕*adv.* 商業上

   legally〔ˈliglɪ〕*adv.* 法律上　　spread〔sprɛd〕*v.* 散播
   rumor〔ˈrumɚ〕*n.* 謠言

4. (**D**) These warm-up exercises are designed to help people <u>loosen</u> their muscles and prevent injuries.
   這些暖身運動是要幫助人們放鬆肌肉，避免受傷。
   - (A) produce〔prəˈdjus〕*v.* 生產；製造
   - (B) connect〔kəˈnɛkt〕*v.* 連接

(C) broaden〔'brɔdn̩〕v. 加寬；拓寬

(D) ***loosen***〔'lusn̩〕v. 鬆開；放鬆

warm-up〔'wɔrm,ʌp〕n. 暖身　　***be designed to V.*** 目的是爲了…

muscle〔'mʌsl̩〕n. 肌肉　　prevent〔prɪ'vɛnt〕v. 預防

injury〔'ɪndʒərɪ〕n. 傷害

5.(**C**) Mei-ling has a very close relationship with her parents. She always
<u>consults</u> them before she makes important decisions. 美玲與父母
的關係非常親近。她在做重要的決定之前，總是會<u>請教</u>他們。

(A) impress〔ɪm'prɛs〕v. 使印象深刻

(B) advise〔əd'vaɪz〕v. 勸告

(C) ***consult***〔kən'sʌlt〕v. 請教；查閱

(D) motivate〔'motə,vet〕v. 激勵

close〔klos〕adj. 親近的　　***make a decision*** 做決定

6.(**B**) The restaurant has a <u>minimum</u> charge of NT$250 per person. So
the four of us need to pay at least NT$1,000 to eat there.
該餐廳有每人新台幣 250 元的<u>最低</u>消費。所以我們四個人在那邊用
餐至少要付新台幣 1,000 元。

(A) definite〔'dɛfənɪt〕adj. 明確的；確定的

(B) ***minimum***〔'mɪnəməm〕adj. 最低的；最小的

(C) flexible〔'flɛksəbl̩〕adj. 有彈性的

(D) numerous〔'njumərəs〕adj. 許多的

charge〔tʃɑrdʒ〕n. 費用　　per〔pɚ〕prep. 每…　　***at least*** 至少

7.(**C**) At the Book Fair, exhibitors from 21 countries will <u>display</u>
textbooks, novels, and comic books. 在書展上，來自二十一個國家
的展覽商將會<u>展出</u>教科書、小說，和漫畫。

(A) predict〔prɪ'dɪkt〕v. 預測　　(B) require〔rɪ'kwaɪr〕v. 要求

(C) ***display***〔dɪ'sple〕v. 展示　　(D) target〔'tɑrgɪt〕v. 將…定作目標

fair〔fɛr〕n. 展覽會　　exhibitor〔ɪg'zɪbɪtɚ〕n. 展覽者

textbook〔'tɛkst,bʊk〕n. 教科書　　novel〔'nɑvl̩〕n. 小說

comic book 漫畫

8.(**D**) Before John got on the stage to give the speech, he took a deep
<u>breath</u> to calm himself down.
約翰在上台發表演說前，做個深<u>呼吸</u>，讓自己冷靜下來。

(A) order〔'ɔrdɚ〕n. 順序；命令　　(B) rest〔rɛst〕n. 休息
(C) effort〔'ɛfɚt〕n. 努力
(D) **breath**〔brɛθ〕n. 呼吸　　**take a deep breath** 做個深呼吸
stage〔stedʒ〕n. 舞台　　speech〔spitʃ〕n. 演講
give a speech 發表演說　　calm〔kɑm〕v. 使平靜
calm sb. **down** 使某人冷靜下來

9. (**B**) Most young people in Taiwan are not satisfied with a high school
<u>diploma</u> and continue to pursue further education in college.
在台灣大多數的年輕人對高中<u>文憑</u>感到不滿意，會繼續讀大學，接
受更進一步的教育。

(A) maturity〔mə'tʃʊrətɪ〕n. 成熟
(B) **diploma**〔dɪ'plomə〕n. 文憑；畢業證書
(C) foundation〔faʊn'deʃən〕n. 創立；基礎
(D) guarantee〔͵gærən'ti〕n. 保證；保證書
satisfy〔'sætɪs͵faɪ〕v. 使滿足　　**be satisfied with** 對…感到滿意
pursue〔pɚ'su〕v. 追求；從事　　further〔'fɝðɚ〕adj. 更進一步的

10. (**B**) Residents are told not to dump all household waste <u>straight</u> into
the trash can; reusable materials should first be sorted out and
recycled. 居民被告知不要<u>直接</u>將所有的家庭廢棄物丟到垃圾桶；
可再使用的物質應先被挑出來回收再利用。

(A) shortly〔'ʃɔrtlɪ〕adv. 不久　　(B) **straight**〔stret〕adv. 直接地
(C) forward〔'fɔrwəd〕adv. 往前　　(D) namely〔'nemlɪ〕adv. 也就是
resident〔'rɛzədənt〕n. 居民　　dump〔dʌmp〕v. 丟棄
household〔'haʊs͵hold〕adj. 家庭的　　waste〔west〕n. 廢棄物
trash can 垃圾筒　　reusable〔ri'juzəbl〕adj. 可再使用的
material〔mə'tɪrɪəl〕n. 物質　　sort〔sɔrt〕v. 分類
sort out 分類；挑出　　recycle〔ri'saɪkl〕v. 回收再利用

11. (**C**) Kevin had been standing on a ladder trying to reach for a book on
the top shelf when he lost his <u>balance</u> and fell to the ground. 當凱文
站在梯子上想伸手去拿放在架子最上層的書時，失去<u>平衡</u>跌倒在地。

(A) volume〔'vɑljəm〕n. 書籍；冊
(B) weight〔wet〕n. 重量　　(C) **balance**〔'bæləns〕n. 平衡
(D) direction〔də'rɛkʃən〕n. 方向
ladder〔'lædɚ〕n. 梯子　　**reach for** 伸手去拿
top shelf 架子的最上層

12. (**B**) If student enrollment continues to drop, some programs at the university may be <u>eliminated</u> to reduce the operation costs.
如果學生的註冊人數持續下降，有些大學的課程可能要<u>刪除</u>，以降低營運成本。

(A) relieve〔rɪˋliv〕*v.* 減輕；使放心
(B) ***eliminate***〔ɪˋlɪməˌnet〕*v.* 除去
(C) project〔prəˋdʒɛkt〕*v.* 投射
(D) account〔əˋkaʊnt〕*v.* 說明；解釋＜*for*＞

enrollment〔ɪnˋrolmənt〕*n.* 註冊人數　　drop〔drɑp〕*v.* 下降
program〔ˋprogræm〕*n.* 課程　　reduce〔rɪˋdjus〕*v.* 降低；減少
operation〔ˌɑpəˋreʃən〕*n.* 運作；經營

13. (**C**) People in that remote village feed themselves by hunting and engaging in <u>primitive</u> forms of agriculture. No modern agricultural methods are used.　在那個偏遠村莊的人，靠打獵和從事<u>原始</u>型態的農業養活自己。沒有使用現代的農業技術。

(A) universal〔ˌjunəˋvɝsl̩〕*adj.* 普遍的；一般的
(B) splendid〔ˋsplɛndɪd〕*adj.* 壯觀的；輝煌的
(C) ***primitive***〔ˋprɪmətɪv〕*adj.* 原始的
(D) courteous〔ˋkɝtɪəs〕*adj.* 有禮貌的

remote〔rɪˋmot〕*adj.* 遙遠的；偏僻的　　village〔ˋvɪlɪdʒ〕*n.* 村莊
feed〔fid〕*v.* 餵；養活　　hunting〔ˋhʌntɪŋ〕*n.* 打獵
engage in 從事　　form〔fɔrm〕*n.* 形式；型態
agriculture〔ˋægrɪˌkʌltʃɚ〕*n.* 農業
agricultural〔ˌægrɪˋkʌltʃərəl〕*adj.* 農業的
method〔ˋmɛθəd〕*n.* 方法

14. (**A**) The government issued a travel <u>alert</u> for Taiwanese in response to the outbreak of civil war in Syria.
政府因應敘利亞內戰的爆發，對台灣人民發佈了旅遊<u>警報</u>。

(A) ***alert***〔əˋlɝt〕*n.* 警報；留意
(B) monument〔ˋmɑnjəmənt〕*n.* 紀念碑
(C) exit〔ˋɛgzɪt〕*n.* 出口
(D) circulation〔ˌsɝkjəˋleʃən〕*n.* 循環；流通

issue〔ˋɪʃu〕*v.* 發佈　　***in response to*** 回應
outbreak〔ˋaʊtˌbrek〕*n.* 爆發　　***civil war*** 內戰
Syria〔ˋsɪrɪə〕*n.* 敘利亞【位於地中海東岸】

15. (**C**) The baby panda Yuan Zai at the Taipei Zoo was seperated from her mother because of a minor injury that occurred during her birth. She was <u>tended</u> by zookeepers for a while.

台北市立動物園的貓熊寶寶圓仔和牠的母親分開，因爲牠出生時有輕微的受傷，有一段時間是由動物園管理員負責<u>照顧</u>。

(A) depart〔dɪˋpɑrt〕*v.* 離開；出發

(B) jail〔dʒel〕*v.* 監禁　　　　　(C) ***tend***〔tɛnd〕*v.* 照顧

(D) capture〔ˋkæptʃə〕*v.* 捕捉

panda〔ˋpændə〕*n.* 貓熊　　separate〔ˋsɛpəˏret〕*v.* 使分開 < *from* >
minor〔ˋmaɪnə〕*adj.* 輕微的　　birth〔bɝθ〕*n.* 出生
zookeeper〔ˋzuˏkipə〕*n.* 動物園管理員

二、綜合測驗：

第 16 至 20 題爲題組

Aesop, the Greek writer of fables, was sitting by the roadside one day when a traveler asked him what sort of people lived in Athens. Aesop replied, "Tell me where you come from and what sort of people live there, and I'll tell you what sort of people you'll find in Athens." <u>Smiling</u>, the man answered,

16

"I come from Argos, and there the people are all friendly, generous, and warm-hearted. I love them." <u>At</u> this, Aesop answered, "I'm happy to tell

17

you, my dear friend, that you'll find the people of Athens much the same."

希臘的寓言作家伊索有一天坐在路邊時，一名旅行者問他，什麼樣的人會住在雅典。伊索回答說：「告訴我你從哪裡來，以及什麼樣的人住在那裏，我便會告訴你在雅典會發現什麼樣的人。」男士笑著回答說：「我來自阿哥斯，那裏的人很友善、很慷慨、很熱心，我很喜歡他們。」一聽到他這樣說，伊索回答：「親愛的朋友，我很高興告訴你，你會發現和雅典的人大致一樣。」

Aesop〔ˋisɑp〕*n.* 伊索【古希臘的寓言作家】
Greek〔grik〕*adj.* 希臘的　　fable〔ˋfebl̩〕*n.* 寓言
roadside〔ˋrodˏsaɪd〕*n.* 路邊
Athens〔ˋæθɪnz〕*n.* 雅典【希臘的首都】
reply〔rɪˋplaɪ〕*v.* 回答　　Argos〔ˋɑrgos〕*n.* 阿哥斯【古希臘國】
warm-hearted〔ˋwɔrmˋhɑrtɪd〕*adj.* 熱心的；慈愛的
generous〔ˋdʒɛnərəs〕*adj.* 慷慨的

16. (**B**) 依句意，應選 (B) *Smiling*，且現在分詞的結構表示主動的概念，描述男士帶著微笑回答。而 (A) amazing〔ə'mezɪŋ〕*adj.* 令人驚訝的，(C) decide〔dɪ'saɪd〕*v.* 決定，(D) pray〔pre〕*v.* 祈禱，則不合句意。

17. (**A**) 依句意，應選 (A) *At*「一聽到」。

A few hours later, <u>another</u> traveler came down the road.　He too
　　　　　　　　　　18
stopped and asked Aesop the same question.　<u>Again</u>, Aesop made the
　　　　　　　　　　　　　　　　　　　　　　19
same request.　But frowning, the man answered, "I'm from Argos and there
the people are unfriendly, <u>mean</u>, and vicious.　They're thieves and
　　　　　　　　　　　　　　20
murderers, all of them."　"Well, I'm afraid you'll find the people of Athens
much the same," replied Aesop.

幾個小時過後，另一位旅行者沿路走來，他也停下來問伊索同樣的問題。伊索提出同樣的要求，但男士皺著眉回答說：「我來自阿哥斯，那裏的人很不友善、很卑劣、很邪惡，他們全都是小偷跟兇手，所有都是。」伊索回答說：「嗯，恐怕你會發現雅典的人大致一樣。」

down〔daʊn〕*prep.* 沿著　　request〔rɪ'kwɛst〕*n.* 要求
frown〔fraʊn〕*v.* 皺眉　　unfriendly〔ʌn'frɛndlɪ〕*adj.* 不友善的
vicious〔'vɪʃəs〕*adj.* 邪惡的　　thief〔θif〕*n.* 小偷
murderer〔'mɝdərə〕*n.* 兇手　　***much the same*** 大致相同

18. (**D**) 依句意，選 (D) *another*「另一位」。而 (C) other「其他的」，通常接複數名詞，如 other people（其他的人），在此用法不合。

19. (**A**) 依句意，選 (A) *again*〔ə'gɛn〕*adv.* 再一次。而 (B) indeed〔ɪn'did〕*adv.* 的確，(C) together〔tə'gæðɚ〕*adv.* 一起，(D) moreover〔mor'ovɚ〕*adv.* 此外，皆不合句意。

20. (**C**) 依句意，選 (C) *mean*〔min〕*adj.* 卑劣的。而 (A) brave〔brev〕*adj.* 勇敢的，(B) lonely〔'lonlɪ〕*adj.* 寂寞的，(D) skinny〔'skɪnɪ〕*adj.* 骨瘦如柴的，皆不合句意。

第 21 至 25 題為題組

Every year tens of thousands of tourists visit Mount Kilimanjaro, the highest mountain in Tanzania, Africa, to witness the scenes depicted in

Earnest Hemingway's *The Snows of Kilimanjaro*. They are attracted by the
American writer's <u>description</u> of the millennia-old glaciers. However, this
　　　　　　　　　　21
tourist attraction will soon <u>vanish</u>. According to the Climate Change
　　　　　　　　　　　　　22
Group, formed by environmentalists worldwide to document the effects of
global warming, Mount Kilimanjaro's snows and glaciers are melting and
are <u>likely</u> to disappear by 2020.
　　23

　　　每年有數以萬計的觀光客，造訪位在坦尚尼亞的非洲最高峰吉利馬扎羅
山，為的是要一睹海明威在「雪山盟」中所描述的景象。他們是受到這位美國
作家對百萬年冰河描述的吸引。然而，這個觀光勝地將會很快消失。根據「氣
候變遷小組」，它是由世界各地的環保人士為記錄全球暖化影響所組成的，吉利
馬扎羅山的雪和冰河正在融化，而且有可能在 2020 年以前消失。

> ***tens of thousands of*** 數以萬計的　　　tourist〔'turɪst〕 *n.* 觀光客
> ***Mount Kilimanjaro*** 吉利馬扎羅山
> Tanzania〔,tænzə'niə〕 *n.* 坦尚尼亞【位於東非赤道以南的國家】
> Africa〔'æfrɪkə〕 *n.* 非洲　　witness〔'wɪtnɪs〕 *v.* 目睹
> scene〔sin〕 *n.* 景象　　depict〔dɪ'pɪkt〕 *v.* 描述
> ***Earnest Hemingway*** 厄尼斯特・海明威【美國著名作家】
> ***The Snows of Kilimanjaro*** 雪山盟【美國著名作家海明威作品】
> attract〔ə'trækt〕 *v.* 吸引
> millennia〔mə'lɛnɪə〕 *n. pl.* 千年【單數為 millennium】
> glacier〔'gleʃɚ〕 *n.* 冰河　　***tourist attraction*** 觀光勝地
> ***Climate Change Group*** 氣候變遷小組　　form〔fɔrm〕 *v.* 組成；成立
> environmentalist〔ɪn,vaɪrən'mɛntlɪst〕 *n.* 環保人士
> worldwide〔'wɝld'waɪd〕 *adv.* 在全世界
> document〔'dɑkjə,mɛnt〕 *v.* 記錄；證明　　effect〔ɪ'fɛkt〕 *n.* 影響
> ***global warming*** 全球暖化　　melt〔mɛlt〕 *v.* 融化
> disappear〔,dɪsə'pɪr〕 *v.* 消失

21.(**B**)依句意，選 (B) ***description***〔dɪs'krpʃən〕 *n.* 描述。而 (A) situation
　　　　〔,sɪtʃʊ'eʃən〕 *n.* 情況，(C) translation〔træns'leʃən〕 *n.* 翻譯，
　　　　(D) calculation〔,kælkjə'leʃən〕 *n.* 計算，則不合句意。

22.(**D**)依句意，選 (D) ***vanish***〔'vænɪʃ〕 *v.* 消失。而 (A) operate〔'ɑpə,ret〕 *v.*
　　　　操作，(B) expand〔ɪks'pænd〕 *v.* 擴大，(C) recover〔rɪ'kʌvɚ〕 *v.* 恢
　　　　復，則不合句意。

23. (**C**) 依句意,選 (C) *likely* 〔'laɪklɪ 〕 *adj.* 可能的。
　　　　而 (A) capable 〔'kepəbḷ 〕 *adj.* 能夠的,(B) ready 〔'rɛdɪ 〕 *adj.* 準備好
　　　　的,(D) horrible 〔'hɑrəbḷ 〕 *adj.* 可怕的,則不合句意。

Not only will the summit lose its tourist attraction, but the disappearance of
the snows will also cause major damage to the ecosystem on the dry African
plains at its base. Without the snow covering the peak, there will not be
　　　　　　　　　 24
enough moisture and water to nourish the plants and animals below. Rising
temperatures, an effect of global warming, thus threaten the ecosystem of
　　　　　　　　　　　　　　　　　　 25
this mountain area. The loss of snows on the 5,892m peak, which have been
there for about 11,700 years, could have disastrous effects on Tanzania.
積雪消失不只是山峰無法成為觀光勝地,對山下乾燥的非洲平原生態系統也造
成重大的危害。若沒有積雪覆蓋山頂,就沒有足夠的濕度和水滋養山下的動植
物。全球暖化所造成的氣溫上升,便因此威脅了山區的生態系統。位在五千八
百九十二公尺高山上,已有一萬一千七百年歷史的積雪的消失,可能會對坦桑
尼亞造成災難性的影響。

　　　 not only…but (also)～　不只…而且～
　　　 summit 〔'sʌmɪt 〕 *n.* 山峰　　　 major 〔'medʒɚ 〕 *adj.* 重大的
　　　 ecosystem 〔'ɪko,sɪstəm 〕 *n.* 生態系統　　　 plain 〔 plen 〕 *n.* 平原
　　　 base 〔 bes 〕 *n.* 基部;底部　　　 peak 〔 pik 〕 *n.* 山峰
　　　 moisture 〔'mɔɪstʃɚ 〕 *n.* 濕度;水氣　　　 nourish 〔'nɝɪʃ 〕 *v.* 滋養
　　　 rise 〔 raɪz 〕 *v.* 上升
　　　 temperature 〔'tɛmpərətʃɚ 〕 *n.* 氣溫　　　 threaten 〔'θrɛtn̩ 〕 *v.* 威脅
　　　 disastrous 〔 dɪ'zæstrəs 〕 *adj.* 災難性的　　　 effect 〔 ɪ'fɛkt 〕 *n.* 影響

24. (**D**) 依句意,「如果沒有」積雪覆蓋山頂,選 (D) *Without*。

25. (**A**) 依句意,選 (A) *thus* 〔 ðʌs 〕 *adv.* 因此。而 (B) just 〔 dʒʌst 〕 *adv.* 只是;
　　　　僅僅,(C) instead 〔 ɪn'stɛd 〕 *adv.* 反而,(D) otherwise 〔'ʌðɚ,waɪz 〕
　　　　adv. 否則,則不合句意。

第 26 至 30 題為題組

　　　 Most human beings actually decide before they think. When people
encounter a complex issue and form an opinion, how thoroughly have they
examined all the important factors involved before they make their decisions?
26

　　大部分的人都在思考之前做決定。當人們遭遇複雜的議題並且在腦中形成意見，做出決定之前，他們對於相關重要因素的檢驗有多全面？

> **human being** 人類　　actually〔ˋæktʃuəlɪ〕adv. 實際上；眞地
> encounter〔ɪnˋkauntɚ〕v. 遭遇
> complex〔kəmˋplɛks , ˋkɑmplɛks〕adj. 複雜的
> issue〔ˋɪʃju〕n. 議題；問題　　form〔fɔrm〕v. 形成
> opinion〔əˋpɪnjən〕n. 意見；看法
> thoroughly〔ˋθɝolɪ〕adv. 完全地；徹底地　　factor〔ˋfæktɚ〕n. 因素
> involved〔ɪnˋvɑlvd〕adj. 牽涉在內的；有關係的

26. (**B**) 依句意，選 (B) **examined**。　examine〔ɪgˋzæmɪn〕v. 檢查；審查
　　而 (A) convey〔kənˋve〕v. 傳達，(C) solve〔salv〕v. 解決，
　　(D) imply〔ɪmˋplaɪ〕v. 暗示，則不合句意。

The answer is: not very thoroughly, <u>whether</u> they are executives, specialized
　　　　　　　　　　　　　　　　　　27
experts, or ordinary people in the street. Very few people, no matter how
intelligent or experienced, can <u>take into account</u> all the possibilities or
　　　　　　　　　　　　　　　　　　　　　　28
outcomes of a policy or a course of action within just a short period of time.
答案是：不很全面，無論他們是主管、專家，或是街上的一般人。不管多聰明或多有經驗，很少人可以在短時間之內，將一個政策或是行為過程中的所有可能性與產生的結果都納入考量。

> executive〔ɪgˋzɛkjutɪv〕n. 主管
> specialized〔ˋspɛʃəl͵aɪzd〕adj. 專門的；專業的
> expert〔ˋɛkspɝt〕n. 專家
> ordinary〔ˋɔrdn͵ɛrɪ〕adj. 普通的；平常的
> intelligent〔ɪnˋtɛlədʒənt〕adj. 聰明的
> experienced〔ɪkˋspɪrɪənst〕adj. 有經驗的；經驗豐富的
> possibilities〔͵pɑsəˋbɪlətɪz〕n. pl. 可能性
> outcome〔ˋaut͵kʌm〕n. 結果　　policy〔ˋpɑləsɪ〕n. 政策
> course〔kors〕n. 做法；策略　　**course of action** 行動策略
> within〔wɪðˋɪn〕prep. 在…之內　　period〔ˋpɪrɪəd〕n. 期間

27. (**C**) 依句意，選 (C) **whether**「無論」。　**whether** A **or** B　無論 A 或 B
　　而 (A) whoever「無論是誰」，(B) because「因為」，(D) rather「更確切地說」，則不合句意。

28. (**D**) 依句意，選 (D) **take into account**「把…考慮在內」(= *take into consideration*)。而 (A) set out「出發」，(B) turn out「結果（成為）」，(C) put into practice「把…付諸實行」，則不合句意。

Those who take pride in being decisive often try their best to consider all the factors beforehand. <u>However</u>, it is not unusual for them to come up with a
    　　　　　　　　　　　　　　　29
decision before they have the time to do so. And <u>once</u> an opinion is formed,
    　　　　　　　　　　　　　　　30
most of their thinking then is simply trying to find support for it.

那些以果斷自豪的人們通常會盡力預先考量所有的因素。然而，在來不及做這些工作之前就必須做出決定的情形，對他們而言也並不罕見。意見一旦被形塑，之後所有的思考，其實都只是試圖支持自己的意見而已。

> ***take pride in*** 以…為榮 (= *be proud of*)
> decisive〔dɪ'saɪsɪv〕*adj.* 有決斷力的；果斷的
> ***try one's best*** 盡力　　　consider〔kən'sɪdɚ〕*v.* 考慮
> beforehand〔bɪ'for͵hænd〕*adv.* 事先
> unusual〔ʌn'juʒʊəl〕*adj.* 不尋常的　　***come up with*** 提出；想出
> thinking〔'θɪŋkɪŋ〕*n.* 思想；思考　　support〔sə'port〕*n.* 支持

29. (**A**) 依句意，選 (A) ***However***「然而」。
    (B) furthermore〔'fɝðɚ͵mor〕*adv.* 此外
    (C) conditionally〔kən'dɪʃənḷɪ〕*adv.* 有條件地
    (D) similarly〔'sɪmələlɪ〕*adv.* 同樣地

30. (**C**) 依句意，意見「一旦」被形塑，選 (C) ***once***。而 (A) though「雖然」，(B) unless「除非」，(D) even「甚至；即使」，則不合句意。

三、文意選填：

第 31 至 40 題為題組

    In English-speaking cultures, the choice of first names for children can be prompted by many factors: tradition, religion, nature, culture, and fashion, to name just a few.

    英語系國家之中，小孩子名字的選擇，受到諸多因素影響：傳統、宗敎、自然、文化、還有流行等等。

culture〔ˈkʌltʃə〕 n. 文化　　***first name*** 名字【last name　姓】
prompt〔prɑmpt〕 v. 促使；推動　　tradition〔trəˈdɪʃən〕 n. 傳統
religion〔rɪˈlɪdʒən〕 n. 宗教　　fashion〔ˈfæʃən〕 n. 流行
to name just a few 只舉出其中幾個例子；等等

Certain people like to give a name that has been handed down in the
family to show ^{31.} **(I) respect** for or to remember a relative whom they love
or admire.　Some families have a tradition of ^{32.} **(F) passing down** the father's
first name to the first born son.　In other families, a surname is included in the
selection of a child's given name to ^{33.} **(E) keep** a family surname going.　It
may be the mother's maiden name, for instance.

　　有些人喜歡幫小孩取家傳的名字，以緬懷自己所深愛或欣賞的親戚，並且
對他們獻上敬意。有些家庭有把父親名字傳承給長子的傳統。在某些其他的家
庭當中，姓氏也在小孩名字的選項之列，目的是讓家族的姓氏能夠繼續流傳下
去，例如母親的娘家姓，就是常見的選擇。

certain〔ˈsɝtn̩〕 adj. 某些　　***give a name*** 取名字
hand down 傳下　　respect〔rɪˈspɛkt〕 n. 尊敬
remember〔rɪˈmɛmbə〕 v. 記得；紀念　　relative〔ˈrɛlətɪv〕 n. 親戚
admire〔ədˈmaɪr〕 v. 讚賞；欽佩　　***pass down*** 將…傳給
surname〔ˈsɝˌnem〕 n. 姓（ = last name = family name）
include〔ɪnˈklud〕 v. 包括　　selection〔səˈlɛkʃən〕 n. 選擇
given name 名字（ = first name）　　keep〔kip〕 v. 使保持
go〔go〕 v. 流傳　　maiden〔ˈmedn̩〕 adj. 處女的；未婚的
maiden name （女子未婚前之）娘家姓氏
for instance 例如（ = for example）

For a long time, ^{34.} **(H) religion** has also played an important role in
naming children.　Boys' names such as John, Peter, and Thomas are chosen
from the Bible.　Girls' names such as Faith, Patience, and Sophie (wisdom)
are chosen because they symbolize Christian qualities.　However, for
people who are not necessarily religious but are fond of nature, names
^{35.} **(D) involving** things of beauty are often favored.　Flower and plant names
like Heather, Rosemary, and Iris ^{36.} **(B) fall into** this category.

　　長久以來，宗教也在小孩的命名中扮演很重要的角色。男生的名字像是
John、Peter 以及 Thomas 都出自聖經。女生的名字像是 Faith、Patience，以

及 Sophie（智慧），都是因爲象徵基督教標榜的特質而被選擇。然而，並不篤信宗教但卻熱愛大自然的人，往往偏好那些與美好事物有關的名字。花朵和植物的名稱，像是 Heather、Rosemary，或是 Iris 當屬此類。

play an important role 扮演一個重要的角色

name〔nem〕*v.* 給…命名　　*such as* 像是

Bible〔'baɪbḷ〕*n.* 聖經　　faith〔feθ〕*n.* 信念；信仰

patience〔'peʃəns〕*n.* 耐心　　Sophie〔'sofɪ〕*n.* 蘇菲【Sofia 的暱稱】

wisdom〔'wɪzdəm〕*n.* 智慧　　symbolize〔'sɪmbḷˌaɪz〕*v.* 象徵

Christian〔'krɪstʃən〕*adj.* 基督教的　　quality〔'kwɑlətɪ〕*n.* 特質；特性

not necessarily 未必；不一定　　religious〔rɪ'lɪdʒəs〕*adj.* 虔誠的

be fond of 喜歡　　nature〔'netʃə〕*n.* 大自然

involve〔ɪn'vɑlv〕*v.* 和…有關　　beauty〔'bjutɪ〕*n.* 美

favor〔'fevə〕*v.* 偏愛　　heather〔'hɛðə〕*n.* 石楠屬植物

rosemary〔'rozˌmɛrɪ〕*n.* 迷迭香　　iris〔'aɪrɪs〕*n.* 鳶尾科植物

fall into 屬於　　category〔'kætəˌgorɪ〕*n.* 類別；範疇

Another factor that has had a great [37.] **(C) impact** on the choice of names is the spread of culture through the media. People may choose a name because they are strongly [38.] **(A) drawn to** a character in a book or a television series; they may also adopt names of famous people or their favorite actors and actresses. Sometimes, people pick foreign names for their children because those names are unusual and will thus make their children more [39.] **(J) unique** and distinctive.

另外一個在名字選擇上有強大影響力的因素，是媒體所散播的文化。人們可能會因爲深受某本書，或是某個電視影集裡面的角色吸引而選擇名字；他們可能採用某個名人，或是自己最愛的男女演員的名字。有時候，人們會刻意爲自己的小孩選擇異國的名字，因爲那些名字很少見，所以可以讓他們的小孩更特別，也更有辨識度。

impact〔'ɪmpækt〕*n.* 影響

have a great impact on 對…有很大的影響

spread〔sprɛd〕*n.* 散播；流傳　　media〔'midɪə〕*n. pl.* 媒體

strongly〔'strɔŋlɪ〕*adv.* 強烈地　　draw〔drɔ〕*v.* 吸引

character〔'kærɪktə〕*n.* 人物

series〔'sɪrɪz , 'siriz〕*n.*（電視、電影等的）影集

adopt〔ə'dɑpt〕*v.* 採用　　favorite〔'fevərɪt〕*adj.* 最喜愛的

actor〔ˈæktɚ〕n. 演員　　actress〔ˈæktrɪs〕n. 女演員
pick〔pɪk〕v. 挑選　　thus〔ðʌs〕adv. 因此
unique〔juˈnik〕adv. 獨特的
distinctive〔dɪˈstɪŋktɪv〕adj. 獨特的；有特色的

　　Finally, some people just pick a name the sound of which they like,
40. **(G)** regardless of its meaning, its origins, or its popularity. However, even these people may look at the calendar to pick a lucky day when they make their choice.

　　最後，有些人選擇名字，只管聽起來順不順耳，完全不考慮名字的意義、起源，或是流行程度。然而，連這樣的人都可能會在日曆上挑出一個黃道吉日，再為小孩命名。

regardless of 不管；不論　　origin〔ˈɔrədʒɪn〕n. 起源
popularity〔ˌpɑpjəˈlærətɪ〕n. 受歡迎
calendar〔ˈkæləndɚ〕n. 日曆　　**make one's choice** 做選擇

四、閱讀測驗：

第 41 至 44 題為題組

　　American writer Toni Morrison was born in 1931 in Ohio. She was raised in an African American family filled with songs and stories of Southern myths, which later shaped her prose. Her happy family life led to her excellent performance in school, despite the atmosphere of racial discrimination in the society.

　　美國作家托妮・莫里森在1931年出生於俄亥俄州。養育她的是個非裔美國家庭，充滿著關於南方神話的歌曲與故事，為她日後的文章塑型。她快樂的家庭生活使她在校表現優秀，即使社會上有種族歧視的氛圍。

Ohio〔oˈhaɪo〕n.（美國）俄亥俄州　　raise〔rez〕v. 養育
African American 非裔美國人的
be filled with 充滿了　　myth〔mɪθ〕n. 神話
later〔ˈletɚ〕adv. 後來　　shape〔ʃep〕v. 塑造
prose〔proz〕n. 散文　　**lead to** 導致
performance〔pɚˈfɔrməns〕n. 表現　　despite〔dɪˈspaɪt〕prep. 儘管
atmosphere〔ˈætməsˌfɪr〕n. 氣氛　　racial〔ˈreʃəl〕adj. 種族的
discrimination〔dɪˌskrɪməˈneʃən〕n. 歧視

After graduating from college, Morrison started to work as a teacher and got married in 1958. Several years later, her marriage began to fail. For a temporary escape, she joined a small writers' group, in which each member was required to bring a story or poem for discussion. She wrote a story based on the life of a girl she knew in childhood who had prayed to God for blue eyes. The story was well received by the group, but then she put it away, thinking she was done with it.

從大學畢業後，莫里森開始任職教師，並在1958年結婚。幾年後，她的婚姻開始出問題。爲了暫時逃避，她加入了一個小型的寫作團體，團體中每個成員都被要求帶一則故事或詩文來討論。她寫了一則故事，是關於她兒時認識的一個女孩的生活，那女孩向上帝祈求一雙藍色的眼睛。那則故事在寫作團體中相當受歡迎，但她接著就把故事放在一旁，覺得已經了結了。

> graduate〔'grædʒʊ,et〕v. 畢業
> temporary〔'tɛmpə,rɛrɪ〕adj. 暫時的　　escape〔ə'skep〕n. 逃避
> member〔'mɛmbɚ〕n. 成員　　require〔rɪ'kwaɪr〕v. 要求
> **based on** 以…爲基礎；根據　　**pray to** sb. **for** sth. 向某人祈求某物
> **put** sth. **away** 把某物放在一旁　　**be done with** sth. 已了結某物

In 1964, Morrison got divorced and devoted herself to writing. One day, she dusted off the story she had written for the writers' group and decided to make it into a novel. She drew on her memories from childhood and expanded upon them using her imagination so that the characters developed a life of their own. *The Bluest Eye* was eventually published in 1970. From 1970 to 1992, Morrison published five more novels.

在1964年，莫里森離婚後投入寫作。有一天，她重拾了那則爲參加寫作團體而寫的故事，決定將它寫成小說。她憑藉著童年的記憶，並用想像力將它擴展，使得裡面的角色發展出自己的生命。終於在1970年，《最藍的眼睛》出版。從1970年到1992年，莫里森又出版了五本小說。

> divorce〔də'vors〕n.v. 離婚　　**devote** onself **to** 致力於
> **dust off** 拍掉灰塵；重拾　　**draw on** 憑藉著
> expand〔ɪk'spænd〕v. 擴大　　imagination〔ɪ,mædʒə'neʃən〕n. 想像力
> character〔'kærɪktɚ〕n. 角色；人物　　**of** one's **own** 自己的
> eventually〔ɪ'vɛntʃʊəlɪ〕adv. 最後　　publish〔'pʌblɪʃ〕v. 出版

In her novels, Morrison brings in different elements of the African American past, their struggles, problems and cultural memory. In *Song of Solomon*, for example, Morrison tells the story of an African American man and his search for identity in his culture. The novels and other works won her several prizes. In 1993, Morrison received the Nobel Prize in Literature. She is the eighth woman and the first African American woman to win the honor.

在她的小說裡，莫里森帶入了來自非裔美國人的不同元素，包括他們的過去、奮鬥、難題，以及文化記憶。例如在《所羅門之歌》一書中，莫里森述說了一位非裔美國男性尋找在他文化中的認同的故事。這些小說和其他作品爲她贏得了一些獎項。1993年，莫里森獲得了諾貝爾文學獎。她是獲得該獎的第八位女性，而且是首位非裔美國女性。

element〔ˈɛləmənt〕*n.* 要素　　struggle〔ˈstrʌgl〕*n.* 奮鬥
cultural〔ˈkʌltʃərəl〕*adj.* 文化的　　search〔sɝtʃ〕*n.* 搜尋；追求
identity〔aɪˈdɛntətɪ〕*n.* 認同；身分
work〔wɝk〕*n.* 作品　　***win sb. sth.*** 爲某人贏得某物
Nobel Prize in Literature 諾貝爾文學獎　　honor〔ˈɑnɚ〕*n.* 光榮

41.(**B**) 本文的主旨爲何？
　　(A) 美國黑人的生活。　　　　(B) 一位非裔美國作家的一生。
　　(C) 非裔美國文化的歷史。　　(D) 諾貝爾文學獎的歷史。

42.(**D**) 莫里森爲什麼要加入寫作團體？
　　(A) 她想要出版《最藍的眼睛》。　(B) 她想要對抗種族歧視。
　　(C) 她想要成爲專業作家。　　　　(D) 她想要逃離她不快樂的婚姻。

43.(**A**) 根據本文，哪一項是莫里森作品的主題之一？
　　(A) 非裔美國人對於價值觀的追尋。
　　(B) 在美國社會中離婚的黑人女性。
　　(C) 俄亥俄州非裔美國人的歌曲和故事。
　　(D) 非裔美國人自 1970 年代至 1990 年代的歷史。

44.(**D**) 下列哪一項關於托妮‧莫里森的敘述是正確的？
　　(A) 她從青少年時期就開始大量寫作。
　　(B) 她在家庭中遭到嚴重的種族歧視。
　　(C) 她在小說中寫的是非裔美國人的眞實故事。
　　(D) 在她之前，沒有任何一位非裔美國女性得到諾貝爾文學獎。

adolescent〔ˌædlˈɛsṇt〕*n.* 青少年
suffer〔ˈsʌfɚ〕*v.* 受苦；罹患 <*from*>　　severe〔səˈvɪr〕*adj.* 嚴重的

第 45 至 48 題爲題組

Below is an excerpt from an interview with Zeke Emanuel, a health-policy expert, on his famous brothers.

以下摘錄自和衛生政策專家紀克・伊曼紐爾的專訪，主題是關於他著名的兄弟。

Interviewer: You're the older brother of Rahm, the mayor of Chicago, and Ari, an extremely successful talent agent. And you're a bioethicist and one of the architects of Obamacare. Isn't writing a book about how great your family is a bit odd?

訪問者：你是芝加哥市長拉姆和非常成功的星探阿里的哥哥。而你是一位生物倫理學者，也是歐巴馬健保的設計者之一。寫一本關於你家族有多偉大的書不是有點奇怪嗎？

Zeke: I don't write a book about how great my family is. There are lots of idiocies and foolishness—a lot to make fun of in the book. I wrote *Brothers Emanuel* because I had begun jotting stories for my kids. And then we began getting a lot of questions: What did Mom put in the cereal? Three successful brothers, all different areas.

紀克：我不是寫一本關於我家人有多偉大的書。書裡有很多白癡和愚蠢的事—有很多的嘲弄。我寫《伊曼紐爾兄弟》是因爲我已經開始爲我的孩子們記下故事。而我們開始有很多問題：媽媽在早餐裡放了什麼？造就了三個成功的兄弟，而且全都是不同的領域。

I: To what do you attribute the Emanuel brothers' success?

訪問者：你把伊曼紐爾兄弟的成功歸因於什麼？

Z: I would put success in quotes. We strive. First, I think we got this striving from our mother to make the world a better place. A second important thing is you never rest on the last victory. There's always more to do. And maybe the third important thing is my father's admonition that offense is the best defense. We don't give up.

紀克：我會把「成功」加上引號。我們非常努力。首先，我認為這個努力來自於我們的母親，她讓這個世界變成一個更好的地方。第二件重要的事，就是你絕不能滿足於上一次的勝利。總是有更多的事要做。還有可能是第三重要的事，那就是我父親的訓誡，他說攻擊就是最好的防禦。我們都不會放棄。

I: Do you still not have a TV?

訪問者：你還是沒有電視嗎？

Z: I don't own a TV. I don't own a car. I don't Facebook. I don't tweet.

紀克：我沒有電視。我沒有車。我不上臉書。我不用推特。

I: But you have four cell phones.

訪問者：可是你有四隻手機。

Z: I'm down to two, thankfully.

紀克：謝天謝地，我剩下兩隻。

I: Your brothers are a national source of fascination. Where do you think they'll be in five years?

訪問者：你的兄弟是全國矚目的焦點。你認為五年後他們會在哪裡？

Z: Ari will be a superagent running the same company. Rahm would still be mayor of Chicago. I will probably continue to be my academic self. The one thing I can guarantee is none of us will have taken a cruise, none of us will be sitting on a beach with a pina colada.

紀克：阿里將會是經營同一間公司的超級星探。拉姆還會是芝加哥市長。我可能繼續當學者。我能保證的一件事，就是我們都不會去坐遊輪，我們都不會坐在海灘喝鳳梨可樂達雞尾酒。

---

below〔bə'lo〕*adv.* 以下　　excerpt〔'ɛksɜpt〕*n.* 摘錄
interview〔'ɪntə،vju〕*n.* 訪談
Zeke Emanuel 紀克・伊曼紐爾【美國科學家】
health〔hɛlθ〕*n.* 健康；衛生　　policy〔'pɑləsɪ〕*n.* 政策
expert〔'ɛkspɜt〕*n.* 專家　　famous〔'feməs〕*adj.* 有名的
Rahm Emanuel 拉姆・伊曼紐爾【美國芝加哥市長】

mayor〔ˋmeɚ〕*n.* 市長　　Chicago〔ʃɪˋkɑgo〕*n.* 芝加哥【美國第二大城】

Ari Emanuel 阿里‧伊曼紐爾【美國著名星探】

extremely〔ɪkˋstrimlɪ〕*adv.* 非常地

talent〔ˋtælənt〕*n.* 演藝圈人才　　agent〔ˋedʒənt〕*n.* 經紀人

talent agent 星探　　bioethicist〔͵baɪoˋɛθəsɪst〕*n.* 生物倫理學家

architect〔ˋɑrkə͵tɛkt〕*n.* 設計者；建築師

Obamacare 歐巴馬健保【美國總統歐巴馬所簽署的醫療法案，故得其名】

a bit 有些　　odd〔ɑd〕*adj.* 奇怪的

idiocy〔ˋɪdɪəsɪ〕*n.* 白癡（的言行）

foolishness〔ˋfulɪʃnɪs〕*n.* 愚蠢（的言行）

make fun of 嘲笑　　jot〔dʒɑt〕*v.* 記下

cereal〔ˋsɪrɪəl〕*n.* 穀類食品【尤指早餐時吃的，如玉米片等】

area〔ˋɛrɪə〕*n.* 領域　　attribute〔əˋtrɪbjut〕*v.* 將…歸因於

quote〔kwot〕*n.* 引號；引文　　***put sth. in quotes*** 把某物加上引號

strive〔straɪv〕*v.* 努力　　***rest on*** 停留在

admonition〔͵ædməˋnɪʃən〕*n.* 訓誡

offense〔əˋfɛns〕*n.* 攻擊　　defense〔dɪˋfɛns〕*n.* 防禦

give up 放棄　　thankfully〔ˋθæŋkfəlɪ〕*adv.* 感謝地

national〔ˋnæʃənḷ〕*adj.* 全國的　　source〔sors〕*n.* 來源

fascination〔͵fæsṇˋeʃən〕*n.* 魅力；令人著迷的事物

run〔rʌn〕*v.* 經營　　academic〔͵ækəˋdɛmɪk〕*n.* 學者

guarantee〔͵gærənˋti〕*v.* 保證　　cruise〔kruz〕*n.* 乘船旅行；遊輪

pina colada 鳳梨可樂達雞尾酒

45.（**A**）當紀克‧伊曼紐爾說「媽媽在早餐裡放了什麼？」時，他腦海中在想什麼？
　　(A) 養育出成功的小孩的秘訣。　　　(B) 做早餐的食譜。
　　(C) 三兄弟的不同之處。　　　　　　(D) 他小孩的問題。

secret〔ˋsikrɪt〕*n.* 秘訣　　***bring up*** 養育
recipe〔ˋrɛsəpɪ〕*n.* 食譜

46.（**C**）在這個訪談中提到的現代便利的設備，紀克‧伊曼紐爾有什麼想法？
　　(A) 遲做總比不做好。　　　　　　　(B) 熟能生巧。
　　(C) 沒有這些東西也沒關係。　　　　(D) 它們是偉大的發明。

conveniences〔kənˋvinjənsɪz〕*n. pl.* 便利的設備
mention〔ˋmɛnʃən〕*v.* 提到
Better late than never.【諺】遲做總比不做好。
Practice makes perfect.【諺】熟能生巧。
invention〔ɪnˋvɛnʃən〕*n.* 發明

47. (**D**) 根據紀克‧伊曼紐爾，以下何者是三兄弟成功的原因？

(A) 他們藉由攻擊別人來防衛自己。

(B) 他們從偉人的引用文句中學到很多。

(C) 他們致力於榮耀父母。

(D) <u>即使在非常成功之後，他們也會持續前進。</u>

be committed to V-ing 致力於…　　　glorify〔'glorə,faɪ〕*v.* 使榮耀

48. (**B**) 以下何者最能總結紀克‧伊曼紐爾對最後一個問題的回應？

(A) 三兄弟期待全家人可以搭遊輪旅行。

(B) <u>在不久的將來，他們不會有什麼改變。</u>

(C) 更高的地位和更多的權力將是他們的目標。

(D) 三兄弟都不會去海灘。

summarize〔'sʌmə,raɪz〕*v.* 總結　　　response〔rɪ'spɑns〕*n.* 回應
look forward to 期待　　　***in the near future*** 在不久的將來
position〔pə'zɪʃən〕*n.* 地位　　　power〔'pauɚ〕*n.* 權力
goal〔gol〕*n.* 目標

第 49 至 52 題為題組

MOOC, a massive open online course, aims at providing large-scale interactive participation and open access via the web. In addition to traditional course materials such as videos, readings, and problem sets, MOOCs provide interactive user forums that help build a community for the students, professors, and teaching assistants.

MOOC是一個大型的開放式線上課程，目標是提供大規模的互動參與，和網路上的開放途徑。除了傳統的課程資料，像是影片、文章，和問題集，MOOC也提供使用者互動論壇來幫助建立一個社群，供學生、教授和教學助理使用。

massive〔'mæsɪv〕*adj.* 大型的　　　open〔'opən〕*adj.* 公開的
online〔,ɑn'laɪn〕*adj.* 線上的　　　course〔kors〕*n.* 課程
aim at 目標是　　　provide〔prə'vaɪd〕*v.* 提供
scale〔skel〕*n.* 規模　　　interactive〔,ɪntɚ'æktɪv〕*adj.* 互動的
participation〔pɚ,tɪsə'peʃən〕*n.* 參與
access〔'æksɛs〕*n.* 接觸；途徑
via〔'vaɪə〕*prep.* 經由；透過　　　web〔wɛb〕*n.* 網路
in addition to 除了…之外（還有）

traditional〔trəˈdɪʃənḷ〕*adj.* 傳統的
material〔məˈtɪrɪəl〕*n.* 材料；資料　　***problem set*** 問題集；問題組
forum〔ˈfɔrəm〕*n.* 論壇　　community〔kəˈmjunətɪ〕*n.* 社區；社群
professor〔prəˈfɛsɚ〕*n.* 教授　　***teaching assistant*** 教學助理

MOOCs first made waves in the fall of 2011, when Professor Sebastian Thrun from Stanford University opened his graduate-level artificial intelligence course up to any student anywhere, and 160,000 students in more than 190 countries signed up. This new breed of online classes is shaking up the higher education world in many ways. Since the courses can be taken by hundreds of thousands of students at the same time, the number of universities might decrease dramatically. Professor Thrun has even envisioned a future in which there will only need to be 10 universities in the world. Perhaps the most striking thing about MOOCs, many of which are being taught by professors at prestigious universities, is that they're free. This is certainly good news for **cash-strapped** students.

MOOC第一次在2011年的秋天造成轟動，當時史丹佛大學教授，塞巴斯蒂安‧特隆，開放他的研究所程度的人工智慧課程，給任何地方的學生，所以有超過190個國家的十六萬名學生報名。這種新的線上課程在很多方面都撼動了高等教育界。因爲有好幾十萬的學生可以同時上課，大學的數量可能會大大地減少。特隆教授甚至預視未來全世界只需要十所大學。因爲MOOCs很多課程是由知名大學的教授所傳授，或許最引人注意的地方是，它們都免費的。這對經濟困難的學生來說，的確是個好消息。

make waves 引起轟動　　***Stanford University*** 史丹佛大學
graduate〔ˈgrædʒuɪt〕*adj.* 研究所的；研究生的
open up to 開放給…　　artificial〔ˌɑrtəˈfɪʃəl〕*adj.* 人工的
intelligence〔ɪnˈtɛlədʒəns〕*n.* 智力；智能　　***sign up*** 報名；註冊
breed〔brid〕*n.* 種類　　***shake up*** 撼動
higher education 高等教育　　world〔wɝld〕*n.*…界
hundreds of thousands of 數十萬的　　decrease〔dɪˈkris〕*v.* 減少
dramatically〔drəˈmætɪklɪ〕*adv.* 大大地
envision〔ɛnˈvɪʒən〕*v.* 想像；預見
striking〔ˈstraɪkɪŋ〕*adj.* 醒目的；引人注意的
prestigious〔prɛsˈtɪdʒəs〕*adj.* 有名望的
free〔fri〕*adj.* 免費的　　strap〔stræp〕*v.* 用皮帶捆
cash-strapped *adj.* 缺乏現金的；經濟困難的

There is a lot of excitement and fear surrounding MOOCs. While some say free online courses are a great way to increase the enrollment of minority students, others have said they will leave many students behind. Some critics have said that MOOCs promote an unrealistic one-size-fits-all model of higher education and that there is no replacement for true dialogues between professors and their students. After all, a brain is not a computer. We are not blank hard drives waiting to be filled with data. People learn from people they love and remember the things that arouse emotion. Some critics worry that online students will miss out on the social aspects of college.

關於MOOCs有很多興奮和恐懼。雖然有些人說，免費的線上課程是很好的方法，可增加少數族群學生的註冊人數，有些人說這些課程會使許多學生落後。一些批評者說，MOOCs 提倡了一個不切實際的高等教育通用模式，而且教授和學生之間眞實的對話是無法取代的。畢竟，人腦不是電腦，我們不是空白的硬碟等著裝載資料。人從他們愛的人身上學習，並記得觸動感情的事物。有些批評者擔心，參與線上課程的學生，會錯過大學能提供的社交機會。

excitement〔ɪkˈsaɪtmənt〕*n.* 興奮　　fear〔fɪr〕*n.* 恐懼
surround〔səˈraʊnd〕*v.* 與⋯相關　　increase〔ɪnˈkris〕*v.* 增加
enrollment〔ɪnˈrolmənt〕*n.* 註冊人數
minority〔maɪˈnɔrətɪ〕*adj.* 少數的；少數名族的
leave⋯behind 使⋯落後　　critic〔ˈkrɪtɪk〕*n.* 批評者
promote〔prəˈmot〕*v.* 促進；提倡
unrealistic〔ˌʌnrɪəˈlɪstɪk〕*adj.* 不切實際的
one-size-fits-all *adj.* 通用的　　model〔ˈmɑdl̩〕*n.* 模型
replacement〔rɪˈplesmənt〕*n.* 取代
dialogue〔ˈdaɪəˌlɔg〕*n.* 對話
after all 畢竟　　blank〔blæŋk〕*adj.* 空白的
hard drive 硬碟　　***be filled with*** 充滿了　　data〔ˈdetə〕*n. pl.* 資料
arouse〔əˈraʊz〕*v.* 喚起　　emotion〔ɪˈmoʃən〕*n.* 感情；情緒
miss out on 錯過　　social〔ˈsoʃəl〕*adj.* 社會的；社交的
aspect〔ˈæspɛkt〕*n.* 方面；（事物的某一）面

49. (**B**) 第二段的 "**cash-strapped**" 是什麼意思？
 (A) 賺很多錢。　　　　　　(B) 缺錢。
 (C) 小心用錢。　　　　　　(D) 花很少的錢。
 be short of 缺乏　　***be careful with*** 對⋯很小心；小心使用

50.(**C**) 以下何者不是 MOOCs 的特色之一？
　　(A) 上課是免費的。　　　　　　(B) 很多課程是知名大學所提供。
　　(C) 大多數的課程是講人工智慧。　(D) 很多學生可以同時上課。
　　feature〔ˈfitʃɚ〕 *n.* 特色
　　address〔əˈdrɛs〕 *v.* 演說；演講；處理（= *deal with*）

51.(**A**) 第二段主要是關於什麼？
　　(A) MOOCs 的影響。　　　　　　(B) MOOCs 的目標。
　　(C) MOOCs 班級的大小。　　　　(D) MOOCs 課程的費用。
　　impact〔ˈɪmpækt〕 *n.* 影響

52.(**D**) 下列何者是本文所提到關於 MOOCs 的問題？
　　(A) 傳統課程資料的消失。　　　　(B) 全世界提供的課程數量有限。
　　(C) 過度依賴知名大學的教授。
　　(D) 缺乏學生和教授之間的社交互動。
　　disappearance〔͵dɪsəˈpɪrəns〕 *n.* 消失
　　limited〔ˈlɪmɪtɪd〕 *adj.* 有限的　　offer〔ˈɔfɚ〕 *v.* 提供
　　overreliance〔͵ovɚrɪˈlaɪəns〕 *n.* 過度依賴 < *on* >　lack〔læk〕 *n.* 缺乏

第 53 至 56 題為題組

　　Today the car seems to make periodic leaps in progress. A variety
of driver assistance technologies are appearing on new cars. A developing
technology called Vehicle-to-Vehicle communication, or V2V, is being
tested by automotive manufacturers as a way to help reduce the number of
accidents. V2V works by using wireless signals to send information back
and forth between cars about their location, speed and direction, so that
they keep safe distances from each other.

　　現今汽車似乎是不斷地在大幅進步。新款的車輛配備中，已經出現各式各
樣的駕駛輔助科技。汽車製造商已經在測試，一項名為「車對車通訊」的研發
中科技，希望藉此能夠降低汽車事故的數字。「車對車通訊」是藉由使用無線信
號，在車輛間來回傳送地點、速度，和方向的訊息，如此車與車之間就能夠保
持安全距離。

　　periodic〔͵pɪrɪˈɑdɪk〕 *adj.* 週期性的；定期的
　　leap〔lip〕 *n.* 跳躍；遽增　　progress〔ˈprɑgrɛs〕 *n.* 進步
　　variety〔vəˈraɪətɪ〕 *n.* 多樣性　　*a variety of* 各式各樣的
　　vihicle〔ˈviɪkl〕 *n.* 車輛　　communication〔kə͵mjunəˈkeʃən〕 *n.* 通訊

automotive〔͵ɔtə'motɪv〕*adj.* 汽車的；自動的
manufacturer〔͵mænjə'fæktʃərə〕*n.* 製造商
number〔'nʌmbə〕*n.* 數目

Another new technology being tested is Vehicle-to-Infrastructure communication, or V2I. V2I would allow vehicles to communicate with road signs or traffic signals and provide information to the vehicle about safety issues. V2I could also request traffic information from a traffic management system and access the best possible routes. Both V2V and V2I have the potential to reduce around 80 percent of vehicle crashes on the road.

另外一項測試中的科技則稱爲「車對基本設施通訊」，可以讓車輛與道路標誌和交通號誌連線，並且提供車輛安全問題的資訊。車對基本設施通訊系統也會讀取交通管裡系統的交通資訊，並取得最佳路線。車對車通訊和車對基本設施通訊都將可能減少百分之八十的道路交通事故。

wireless〔'waɪrlɪs〕*adj.* 無線的   signal〔'sɪgnḷ〕*n.* 信號
back and forth 來回地
infrastructure〔'ɪnfrə͵strʌktʃə〕*n.* 基本設施   sign〔saɪn〕*n.* 告示
issue〔'ɪʃu〕*n.* 問題   management〔'mænɪdʒmənt〕*n.* 管理
access〔'æksɛs〕*v.* 取得   route〔rut〕*n.* 路線
potential〔pə'tɛnʃəl〕*n.* 潛力；可能性   crash〔kræʃ〕*n.* 相撞

More and more new cars can reverse-park, read traffic signs, maintain a safe distance in steady traffic and brake automatically to avoid crashes. Moreover, a number of firms are creating cars that drive themselves to a chosen destination without a human at the controls. It is predicted that driverless cars will be ready for sale within five years. If and when cars go completely driverless, the benefits will be enormous.

越來越多新的車子可以倒轉停車，讀取交通號誌，在穩定的車流中保持安全距離，並且可以自動煞車以避免相撞。此外，有一些公司正在製造無人駕駛，可以自動開往預定地點的車。一般預測，無人駕駛的車會在五年內量產上市。如果車子可以完全無人駕駛，那會有很多的好處。

reverse〔rɪ'vɚs〕*adj.* 倒轉的   reverse-park *v.* 倒車停車
steady〔'stɛdɪ〕*adj.* 穩定的   brake〔brek〕*v.* 煞車
automatically〔͵ɔtə'mætɪkḷɪ〕*adv.* 自動地
firm〔fɝm〕*n.* 公司   chosen〔'tʃozn̩〕*adj.* 被選上的
destination〔͵dɛstə'neʃən〕*n.* 目的地

controls〔kən'trolz〕*n. pl.*（車輛的）操縱裝置
predict〔prɪ'dɪkt〕*v.* 預測　　go〔go〕*v.* 變得
benefit〔'bɛnəfɪt〕*n.* 利益；好處
enormous〔ɪ'nɔrməs〕*adj.* 巨大的

Google, which already uses prototypes of such cars to ferry its staff along Californian freeways, once put a blind man in a prototype and filmed him being driven off to buy takeaway hamburgers. If this works, huge numbers of elderly and disabled people can regain their personal mobility. The young will not have to pay crippling motor insurance, because their reckless hands and feet will no longer touch the wheel or the accelerator. People who commute by car will gain hours each day to work, rest, or read a newspaper.

谷歌公司已經使用無人駕駛車，載運自己的員工行駛加州高速公路，他們曾經讓一位盲人坐在原形車的駕駛座，拍攝車子載他離開去買外帶漢堡的影片。如果這項計畫可以成功，許多的年長者和殘障人士就可以重獲移動能力。年輕人也不用再買造成嚴重損害的汽車事故險，因為他們魯莽的手腳將不會再碰到方向盤或油門。坐車的通勤族以後每天可以多幾個小時工作、休息，或看報紙。

prototype〔'protə,taɪp〕*n.* 原型　　ferry〔'fɛrɪ〕*v.* 載運
staff〔stæf〕*n.* 全體員工　　freeway〔'fri,we〕*n.* 高速公路
film〔fɪlm〕*v.* 拍攝　　*drive off* 開車離去
takeaway〔'tekə,we〕*adj.* 外帶的　　work〔wɝk〕*v.* 有效；行得通
elderly〔'ɛldəlɪ〕*adj.* 年長的　　disabled〔dɪs'cbḷd〕*adj.* 殘障的
regain〔rɪ'gen〕*v.* 恢復　　mobility〔mo'bɪlətɪ〕*n.* 機動性
crippling〔'krɪpḷɪŋ〕*adj.* 造成嚴重損害的
motor insurance 汽車險　　reckless〔'rɛklɪs〕*adj.* 魯莽的
wheel〔hwil〕*n.* 方向盤　　accelerator〔æk'sɛlə,retə〕*n.* 油門
commute〔kə'mjut〕*v.* 通勤　　gain〔gen〕*v.* 獲得

53.（**C**）以下對於 V2V 的敘述何者正確？
　(A) V2V 通訊已經發展得很完備。
　(B) 透過 V2V，駕駛人可以在路上互相聊天。
　(C) V2V 的設計是要藉由保持安全距離減少車禍。
　(D) 透過 V2V，車子可以警告在附近的腳踏車騎士車子正在靠近。
　warn sb. of sth. 警告某人某事
　cyclist〔'saɪkḷɪst〕*n.* 腳踏車騎士
　nearby〔'nɪr,baɪ〕*adj.* 附近的　　approach〔ə'protʃ〕*n.* 接近

54. (**A**) 在 Vehicle-to-Infrastructure 中的 infrastructure 指的是什麼？
   (A) 交通設施和資訊系統。　　(B) 道路和橋樑的基礎結構。
   (C) 安全駕駛的知識和規定。　　(D) 政府的交通部門。

   facilities〔fəˋsɪlətɪz〕*n. pl.* 設施　　structure〔ˋstrʌktʃɚ〕*n.* 結構
   regulation〔͵rɛgjəˋleʃən〕*n.* 規定
   department〔dɪˋpɑrtmənt〕*n.* 部門

55. (**C**) 下列何者不是無人駕駛車輛可能的好處？
   (A) 年長者會更有機動性。
   (B) 「駕駛人」可以在去上班途中一路睡覺。
   (C) 人們可以盡情賽車。　　(D) 盲人可以開車並且一路平安。

   the elderly 老人（= *elderly people*）　　mobile〔ˋmobḷ〕*adj.* 機動的
   content〔kənˋtɛnt〕*n.* 滿足　　***race cars*** 賽車
   to one's heart's content 盡情地　　travel〔ˋtrævḷ〕*v.* 行進

56. (**B**) 從這篇文章可以推論出什麼？
   (A) 駕駛人如果酒醉汽車會拒絕發動。
   (B) 未來可能是沒有車禍的時代。
   (C) 男女老幼都買得起車。　　(D) 無人駕駛車輛的生產還遙不可及。

   start〔stɑrt〕*v.* 發動　　drunk〔drʌŋk〕*adj.* 喝醉的
   free〔fri〕*adj.* 無⋯的　　era〔ˋɪrə〕*n.* 時代
   afford〔əˋford〕*v.* 負擔得起

第貳部分：非選擇題

一、中譯英

1. 有些年輕人辭掉都市裡高薪的工作，返回家鄉種植有機蔬菜。

   Some young people $\left\{\begin{array}{l} \text{quit} \\ \text{resigned from} \end{array}\right\}$ their high-paying/well-paid jobs
   in the city, and went back to their hometown to grow organic vegetables.

2. 藉由決心和努力，很多人成功了，不但獲利更多，還過著更健康的生活。

   $\left\{\begin{array}{l} \text{With} \\ \text{By means of} \end{array}\right\}$ determination and effort, many succeeded, not only
   $\left\{\begin{array}{l} \text{making more profit,} \\ \underline{\text{earning/making}} \text{ more money,} \end{array}\right\}$ but also $\left\{\begin{array}{l} \text{leading} \\ \text{living} \end{array}\right\}$ a healthier life.

二、英文作文：

Steve's Lucky Day

Irene and Steve were walking home from school. They each had their own iPhone. Irene liked to text and chat with her friends, while Steve enjoyed listening to music. This afternoon, they took a shortcut through the park. It wasn't their usual route. As they entered the park, Irene was texting with her friends and not paying attention to the path, which took a sharp turn to the left. Blissfully unaware of her surroundings, Irene bumped her head on a tree, and dropped her iPhone. Lost in his music, Steve continued walking without notice.

Several minutes later, Steve had to cross a busy street. Still listening to music at a dangerously loud level, he didn't look before stepping out into the roadway. An oncoming driver honked his horn and slammed on his brakes, otherwise he would have hit Steve with his car. *However*, unaware of the danger, Steve continued on his merry way. *Of course*, the driver was furious, and began shouting and cursing, but it was to no avail. It must have been Steve's lucky day.

text〔tɛkst〕v. 傳簡訊　　chat〔tʃæt〕v. 聊天
shortcut〔'ʃɔrt,kʌt〕n. 捷徑；近路　　route〔rut〕n. 路線
pay attention to 注意　　path〔pæθ〕n. 小道；小徑
sharp〔ʃɑrp〕adj. 急轉的　　*to the left* 向左
blissfully〔'blɪsfəlɪ〕adv. 幸福地；極快樂地
unaware〔,ʌnə'wɛr〕adj. 不注意的；未察覺的 <of>
surroundings〔sə'raʊndɪŋz〕n. pl. 周遭環境
bump〔bʌmp〕v. 使撞上 <on / against>
drop〔drɑp〕v. 掉落　　*be lost in* 沈迷於　　level〔'lɛvḷ〕n. 程度
at a ~ level 以~程度　　step〔stɛp〕v. 步行；踏出一步
roadway〔'rod,we〕n. 道路
oncoming〔'ɑn,kʌmɪŋ〕adj. 即將到來的；接近的
honk one's horn 按喇叭（= *sound one's horn*）
slam on one's brakes 緊急煞車（= *hit the brakes*）
merry〔'mɛrɪ〕adj. 快樂的　　*on one's way* 在路上
furious〔'fjʊrɪəs〕adj. 憤怒的　　curse〔kɝs〕v. 咒罵
to no avail 無效；枉然（= *in vain*）　　*must have + p.p.* 當時一定…

103 年學測英文科試題出題來源

題　　號	出　　　　　　　　　處
一、詞彙 第 1～15 題	所有各題對錯答案的選項，均出自大考中心編製的「高中常用 7000 字」。
二、綜合測驗 第 16～20 題	改寫自 Aesop's Fables（伊索寓言），敘述伊索和將去希臘旅遊的人的對話，表達他對希臘的觀點和評價。
第 21～25 題	改寫自 Global Warming Thaws Mount Kilimanjaro（全球暖化解凍吉力馬札羅山），全球暖化如何讓吉力馬札羅山失去長年以來的雪。
第 26～30 題	改寫自 Better Decision Making: From Who's Right to What's Right; A Computer-Aided Structured-Inquiry Method Offers a Better Way to Make Tough Decisions（做更好的決定：從誰是對的到什麼是對的；一個電腦輔助結構式探究方法提供更好的方式做困難的決定），敘述人們做決定的過程。
四、閱讀測驗 第 41～44 題	改寫自 Toni Morrison: biography（托妮·莫里森：傳記），描述非裔美國女作家妮·莫里森成為知名作家的經歷。
第 45～48 題	改寫自 10 Questions for Zeke Emanuel（十問齊克·伊曼紐爾），為一訪談，描述齊克兄弟的成功和其家庭的關係。
第 49～52 題	改寫自 Massive open online course（大型開放型線上課程），描述線上免費課程的出現和其衍生的影響。
第 53～56 題	改寫自 Clean, safe and it drives itself（乾淨又安全，自己會開車），描述新款的車，能夠接受無限訊號，自動開到目的地。

103 年學測英文科試題修正意見

※ 103 年學測英文試題出得很嚴謹，只有三個地方建議修正：

題　　號	修　　正　　意　　見
第 45～48 題 第 4 行	I *don't* write a book about how great my family is. → I *didn't* write a book about how great my family is. * 敘述過去的事，應用過去式，句尾的 is 不改，因為是現在的事。
倒數第 3 行	Rahm *would* still be mayor of Chicago. → Rahm *will* still be mayor of Chicago. * Ari *will be* a superagent… Rahm *will* still *be*… I *will* probably *continue*… 說話、寫文章都應有一致性。
第 53 題 (C)	V2V is designed to decrease crashes by keeping *safety distance*. → …*a safety distance between cars*. * 為了句意清楚，須將 safety distance 改成 *a* safety distance *between cars*。

【103 年學測】綜合測驗：16-20 出題來源

—— http://www.hltmag.co.uk/sep02/ex.htm

The railway ticket
Aesop's fable

1. There were eight of us in the carriage, and seven tickets were soon found and punched.

2. A few hours later a mean-looking travell- er came down the road, and he too stopped and asked Aesop, 'Tell me, my friend, what are the people of Athens like?'

3. Aesop, the Greek writer of fables, was sitting by the road one day when a friend- ly traveller asked him, 'What sort of people live in Athens?'

4. 'All tickets, please!' said the railway inspector, appearing at the door of the carriage.

5. Frowning, the man replied, 'I'm from Argos and there the people are unfriend- ly, mean, deceitful and vicious. They're thieves and murderers, all of them.'

6. 'Funny thing, absence of mind,' said the helpful traveller when the inspector had gone. 'Absence of mind?' said the old man.

7. But the old man in the corner went on searching through his pockets, looking very unhappy.

8. Aesop replied, 'Tell me where you come from and what sort of people live there, and I'll tell you what sort of people you'll find in Athens.'

9. So he was, and the inspector looked anything but pleased as he hastily punched the mangled ticket.

10. Smiling, the man answered, 'I come from Argos, and the people there are all friendly, generous and warm- hearted. I love them all.'

11. Again Aesop replied, 'Tell me where you come from and what people are like there and I will tell you what the people are like in Athens.'

12. 'I was chewing off last week's date!'

13. 'You haven't lost your ticket,' said the man next to him, helpfully. You're holding it in your teeth!'

14. At this Aesop answered, 'I'm happy to tell you, my dear friend, that you'll find the people of Athens much the same.'

15. 'I'm afraid you'll find the people of Athens much the same,' was Aesop's reply.

【103 年學測】綜合測驗：21-25 出題來源

——http://www.redorbit.com/news/science/135907/global_warming_thaws_ mount_kilimanjaro/

Global Warming Thaws Mount Kilimanjaro

LONDON (AFP)— Mount Kilimanjaro, the highest mountain in Africa, has been photographed stripped of its millennia-old snow and glacier peak for the first time, in a move used by environmentalists to show the perils of global warming.

The picture is the first time anyone has caught the Tanzanian mountain's dramatic change, according to the Climate Change group which led a project to document the effects of global warming across the world.

The launch of the photo project NorthSouthEastWest coincides with a meeting of environment and energy ministers from 20 countries at a British-sponsored conference on climate change that opened on Tuesday in London.

It also comes ahead of a further meeting of G8 ministers in Derbyshire, central England, later in the week.

Mount Kilimanjaro's crowning snow and glaciers are melting and likely to disappear completely by 2020, triggering major disruptions to ecosystems on the dry African plains that spread out at its feet below, scientists have warned.

The forests on Kilimanjaro's lower slopers absorb moisture from the cloud top hovering near the peak, and in turn nourish flora and fauna below.

"Rising temperatures threaten not only the ice-cap, but also this essential natural process," Climate Change warned.

The mountain, one of Africa's most stunning landscapes, was memorialized in Ernest Hemingway's 1938 short story "The Snows of Kilimanjaro". The story, and the 1952 film which followed, has brought tens of thousands of visitors to Tanzania for decades.

The loss of snows on the 19,330-foot (5,892-meter) peak, which have been there for about 11,700 years, could have disastrous effects on the Tanzanian economy, US researchers warned in a 2001 Science article warning about the melting.

The NorthSouthEastWest project also includes images from Magnum agency photographers of 10 "climate hotspots" including the Marshall Islands and Greenland, as well as Kilimanjaro, showing "the most dramatic examples of the impact of global warming", Climate Change's Denise Meredith told AFP Tuesday.

⋮

【103 年學測】綜合測驗：26-30 出題來源

——http://www.pbs.org/wgbh/aso/databank/entries/dh05te.html

Better Decision Making: From Who's Right to What's Right; A Computer-Aided Structured-Inquiry Method Offers a Better Way to Make Tough Decisions

⋮

The evidence for that way of making decisions and setting policies is not very reassuring. One only has to look at some of the more colossal failed decisions--the disastrous choice by American leaders to pursue the war in Vietnam, the pouring of billions of dollars of investment capital into imaginary dot-com businesses, and any number of misguided corporate mergers--to question the wisdom of decision making by advocacy. We must ask, If the various advocates of the conflicting options are all smart, experienced, and well-informed, why do they disagree so completely? Wouldn't they all have thought the issue through carefully and come to approximately the same--"best"--conclusion?

The answer to that crucial question lies in the structure of the human brain and the way it processes information.

First We Decide, Then We Justify

Most human beings actually decide before they think. When any human being--executive, specialized expert, or person in the street—encounters a complex issue and forms an opinion, often within a matter of seconds, how thoroughly has he or she explored the implications of the various courses of action? Answer: not very thoroughly. Very few people, no matter how intelligent or experienced, can take inventory of the many branching possibilities, possible outcomes, side effects, and undesired consequences of a policy or a course of action in a matter of seconds. Yet, those who pride themselves on being decisive often try to do just that. And once their brains lock onto an opinion, most of their thinking thereafter consists of finding support for it.

⋮

【103年學測】文意選填：31-40 出題來源

—http://answers.yahoo.com/question/index?qid=20080606000607AAdE5OS

How do you name your children?

The choice of first names for children can be prompted by many factors: Nationality; Tradition ; Politics; Religion; Beliefs; Culture; Social status; Fashion and trends; Fads; Popularity, to name but some.

One's ethnic origins come into play: people will in general choose for their children names that are comprehensible in their country or the society that they move in and that will not be a burden for them in life.

Certain people like to give a name that has been handed down the family either for sentimental reasons or as a tribute to a relative whom they love(d) or admire(d) (who may be alive or dead). Some families have a tradition of passing down the father's first name to the first born son. In certain families a surname is included in the selection of a child 's given names to keep an ancestral surname going. It may be the mother's maiden surname for instance.

Certain classes choose a certain kind of first name that is traditional to their class. There are names that are deemed to be aristocratic whilst others denote a working class origin.

For a long time religion had an important place and names were chosen from the Bible such as the names of apostles (John, Peter ,Thomas etc..) from the New Testament or those of characters from the Old Testament (David, Samuel, Josh, Rachel, Rebecca, Suzannah etc...). Saints names have always been popular, even amongst non believers, and tradition is a factor in the sense that though some names have been disputed as non genuine, they are still chosen (Saint Christopher's existence is now much in doubt for instance, yet the name "Christopher" is still very popular for to boys).

For a long time people liked to give their children names that embodied Christian qualities especially for girls: Faith, Charity, Patience, Sophie (wisdom) but which are constant in most religions or civilisations. Some people choose names from deities in antiquity (Juno, Venus), prophets, or beings with superhuman powers (Angel, Ariel, Gabriel, Michael).

Those that are not necessarily religious and are fond of nature pick names that evoke beautiful things: flowers or plants (Heather, Rosemary, Violet, Iris, Vinca etc..) or minerals (Amber, Opal, Pearl etc..) but this can run across social classes and even nationalities and simply reflect personal preferences.

⋮

【103 年學測】閱讀測驗：41-44 出題來源

——http://www.biography.com/people/toni-morrison-9415590

Toni Morrison: biography

Synopsis

Born on February 18, 1931, in Lorain, Ohio, Toni Morrison is a Nobel Prize- and Pulitzer Prize-winning American novelist, editor and professor. Her novels are known for their epic themes, vivid dialogue and richly detailed black characters. Among her best known novels are *The Bluest Eye*, *Song of Solomon* and *Beloved*. Morrison has won nearly every book prize possible. She has also been awarded honorary degrees.

Early Career

Born Chloe Anthony Wofford on February 18, 1931, in Lorain, Ohio, Toni Morrison was the second oldest of four children. Her father, George Wofford, worked primarily as a welder, but held several jobs at once to support the family. Her mother, Ramah, was a domestic worker. Morrison later credited her parents with instilling in her a love of reading, music, and folklore.

Living in an integrated neighborhood, Morrison did not become fully aware of racial divisions until she was in her teens. "When I was in first grade, nobody thought I was inferior. I was the only black in the class and the only child who could read," she later told a reporter from The New York Times. Dedicated to her studies, Morrison took Latin in school, and read many great works of European literature. She graduated from Lorain High School with honors in 1949.

At Howard University, Morrison continued to pursue her interest in literature. She majored in English, and chose the classics for her minor. After graduating from Howard in 1953, Morrison continued her education at Cornell University. She wrote her thesis on the works of Virginia Woolf and William Faulkner, and completed her master's degree in 1955. She then moved to Texas to teach English at Texas Southern University. In 1957, Morrison returned to Howard University to teach English. There she met Harold Morrison, an architect originally from Jamaica. The couple got married in 1958 and welcomed their first child, son Harold, in 1961. After the birth of her son, Morrison joined a writers group that met on campus. She began working on her first novel with the group, which started out as a short story.

Morrison decided to leave Howard in 1963. After spending the summer traveling with her family in Europe, she returned to the United States with her son. Her husband, however, had decided to move back to Jamaica. At the time, Morrison was pregnant with their second child. She moved back home to live with her family in Ohio before the birth of son Slade in 1964. The following year, she moved with her sons to Syracuse, New York, where she worked for a textbook publisher as a senior editor. Morrison later went to work for Random House, where she edited works for such authors as Toni Cade Bambara and Gayl Jones.

⋮

【103 年學測】閱讀測驗：45-48 出題來源

——http://content.time.com/time/magazine/article/0,9171,2139175,00.html

10 Questions for Zeke Emanuel

You're the older brother of Rahm, the mayor of Chicago, and Ari, an extremely successful talent agent. And you're a bioethicist and one of the architects of Obamacare. Isn't writing a book about how great your family is a bit unseemly?

I didn't write a book about how great my family is. There are lots of warts and idiocies and foolishness--a lot to make fun of in the book. I wrote Brothers Emanuel because I had begun jotting down stories for my kids. And then we began getting a lot of questions: What did Mom put in the cereal?

⋮

【103 年學測】閱讀測驗：49-52 出題來源

——http://faculty.washington.edu/chudler/ener.html

Massive open online course

A Massive Open Online Course (MOOC) is an online course aimed at unlimited participation and open access via the web. In addition to traditional course materials such as videos, readings, and problem sets, MOOCs provide interactive user forums that help build a community for students, professors, and teaching assistants (TAs). MOOCs are a recent development indistance education.

Although early MOOCs often emphasized open access features, such as connectivism and open licensing of content, structure, and learning goals, to promote the reuse and remixing of resources, some notable newer MOOCs use closed licenses for their course materials, while maintaining free access for students.

⋮

In the fall of 2011 Stanford University launched three courses. The first of those courses was Introduction Into AI, launched by Sebastian Thrun and Peter Norvig. Enrollment quickly reached 160,000 students. The announcement was followed within weeks by the launch of two more MOOCs, by Andrew Ng and Jennifer Widom. Following the publicity and high enrollment numbers of these courses, Thrun started a company he named

Udacity and Daphne Koller and Andrew Nglaunched Coursera. Coursera subsequently announced university partnerships with University of Pennsylvania, Princeton University,Stanford University and The University of Michigan.

Concerned about the commercialization of online education, MIT created the not-for-profit MITx. The inaugural course, 6.002x, launched in March 2012. Harvard joined the group, renamed edX, that spring, and University of California, Berkeley joined in the summer. The initiative then added the University of Texas System, Wellesley College and Georgetown University.

In November 2012, the University of Miami launched first high school MOOC as part of Global Academy, its online high school. The course became available for high school students preparing for the SAT Subject Test in biology.

⋮

【103 年學測】閱讀測驗：53-56 出題來源
——http://www.economist.com/news/leaders/21576384-cars-have-already-chang
ed-way-we-live-they-are-likely-do-so-again-clean-safe-and-it

Clean, safe and it drives itself

SOME inventions, like some species, seem to make periodic leaps in progress. The car is one of them. Twenty-five years elapsed between Karl Benz beginning small-scale production of his original *Motorwagen* and the breakthrough, by Henry Ford and his engineers in 1913, that turned the car into the ubiquitous, mass-market item that has defined the modern urban landscape. By putting production of the Model T on moving assembly lines set into the floor of his factory in Detroit, Ford drastically cut the time needed to build it, and hence its cost. Thus began a revolution in personal mobility. Almost a billion cars now roll along the world's highways.

Today the car seems poised for another burst of evolution. One way in which it is changing relates to its emissions. As emerging markets grow richer, legions of new consumers are clamouring for their first set of wheels. For the whole world to catch up with American levels of car ownership, the global fleet would have to quadruple. Even a fraction of that growth would present fearsome challenges, from congestion and the price of fuel to pollution and global warming.

Yet, as our special report this week argues, stricter regulations and smarter technology are making cars cleaner, more fuel-efficient and safer than ever before. China, its cities choked in smog, is following Europe in imposing curbs on emissions of noxious nitrogen oxides and fine soot particles. Regulators in most big car markets are demanding deep cuts in the carbon dioxide emitted from car exhausts. And carmakers are being remarkably inventive in finding ways to comply.

Granted, battery-powered cars have disappointed. They remain expensive, lack range and are sometimes dirtier than they look—for example, if they run on electricity from coal-fired power stations. But car companies are investing heavily in other clean technologies. Future motorists will have a widening choice of super-efficient petrol and diesel cars, hybrids (which switch between batteries and an internal-combustion engine) and models that run on natural gas or hydrogen. As for the purely electric car, its time will doubtless come.

⋮

103年學測英文科非選擇題閱卷評分原則說明

閱卷召集人：劉慶剛（國立台北大學應用外語學系教授）

　　103 學年度學科能力測驗英文考科的非選擇題題型共有「中譯英」和「英文作文」兩大題。第一大題是「中譯英」，題型與過去幾年相同，考生需將兩個中文句子譯成正確、通順、達意的英文，兩題合計為 8 分。第二大題是「英文作文」，考生須從三幅連環圖片的內容，想像第四幅圖片可能的發展，再以至少 120個單詞寫出一個涵蓋連環圖片內容並有完整結局的故事。

　　閱卷之籌備工作，依循閱卷標準程序，於 1 月 20 日先召開評分標準訂定會議，由正、副召集人及協同主持人共 14 人，參閱了約 3,000 份來自不同地區的試卷，經過一整天的討論之後，訂定評分標準，選出合適的評分參考樣卷及試閱樣卷，並編製成閱卷參考手冊，以供閱卷委員共同參閱。

　　本年度共計聘請 166 位大學教授擔任閱卷委員，1 月 22 日上午 9:00 至 11:00 為試閱會議，首先由召集人提示評分標準並舉例說明；接著分組進行試閱，參與評分之教授須根據閱卷參考手冊的試閱樣卷分別評分，並討論評分準則，務求評分標準一致，以確保閱卷品質。為求慎重，試閱會議後，正、副召集人及協同主持人進行評分標準再確定會議，確認評分原則後才開始正式閱卷。

　　評分標準與歷年相同，在「中譯英」部分，每小題總分 4 分，原則上是每個錯誤扣0.5 分。「英文作文」的評分標準是依據內容、組織、文法句構、詞彙拼字、體例五個項目給分，字數明顯不足的作文則扣總分 1 分。閱卷時，每份試卷皆會經過兩位委員分別評分，最後成績以二位閱卷委員給分之平均成績為準。如果第一閱與第二閱分數差距超過差分標準，則由第三位委員（正、副召集人或協同主持人）評閱。

今年的「中譯英」與「年輕人返鄉種植有機蔬菜」的趨勢有關，評量的重點在於考生能否能運用常用的詞彙與基本句型將兩句中文翻譯成正確達意的英文句子，所測驗之句型為高中生熟悉的範圍，詞彙亦控制在大考中心詞彙表四級內之詞彙，中等程度以上的考生，如果能使用正確句型並注意用字、拼字，應能得理想的分數。例如：「辭掉都市裡的高薪工作」若譯成（have）quit high-paying/well-paid job/jobs in the city 即可得分；「藉由決心與努力」則可翻譯為 through/with/because of determination and effort/efforts。在選取樣卷時，我們發現有不少考生對於英文詞彙的使用及英文拼字仍有加強的空間，如第一句的「返回家鄉」有考生翻譯為 backed to home，「成功了」有不少考生翻譯為 success 或 successed；在拼字方面，「更健康」healthier 有考生少寫了字母 "i"，「蔬菜」vegetables 這個字拼錯的考生也不少，相當可惜。

今年的「英文作文」主題與考生日常生活經驗相關，重點在於說明青少年若過度使用 3C 電子產品，甚至在走路時還像圖片二裡的女生忙著滑手機或像圖片三裡的男生沉迷於耳機裡的音樂中，將會造成意外，嚴重時還可能危及性命。大部分的考生應能從不同的角度發揮想像力，寫出一個涵蓋連環圖片內容並有完整結局的故事。評分的考量重點為作文內容是否切題，組織是否具連貫性、句子結構及用字是否適切、以及拼字與標點符號的使用是否正確得當。

103 年學測英文考科試題或答案之反映意見回覆

※ 題號：9

【題目】

9. Most young people in Taiwan are not satisfied with a high school _____ and continue to pursue further education in college.
   (A) maturity   (B) diploma
   (C) foundation   (D) guarantee

【意見內容】

選項 (C) foundation 有「基礎」的意思，應為合理選項。

【大考中心意見回覆】

本題測驗考生能否掌握詞彙 diploma 的語意及用法。作答線索為題幹中 …not satisfied with a high school 與 pursue a further education in college 之語意關係。foundation 當可 名詞時，為「機構」（基金會等，如 Pine High School Foundation）或「建築的基礎」（如：This lot has a sound foundation and good chimney built.）的意思，但並無 a high school foundation 的搭配用法。

※ 題號：12

【題目】

12. If student enrollment continues to drop, some programs at the university may be _____ to reduce the operation costs.
   (A) relieved   (B) eliminated
   (C) projected   (D) accounted

【意見內容】

選項 (C) projected 作為「提出某計畫」，應為合理選項。

【大考中心意見回覆】

本題測驗考生能否掌握詞彙 eliminate 的語意及用法。題幹中 student enrollment continues to drop（學生報到率降低）與 to reduce the operation costs（降低營運成本）之間的語意關係為本題作答線索。若 project 一詞依考生之解讀作為「提出某計畫」的意思，但因是被動語態，為求語意連貫，則應該是 some plans（計畫）或 some measures（措施）作為主詞而「被提出來」（be projected）；若選項 (C) 與本題幹主詞 some programs at the university（大學某些系所）一起使用，則跟上下文 student enrollment continues to drop（學生報到率降低）與 to reduce the operation costs（降低營運成本）之間的前後語意不連貫（原本題意為學生報到率降低與大學某些系所被刪減以降低營運成本之間的因果語意關係），因此選項 (C) 非本題正答選項。

※ 題號：15

【題目】

12. The baby panda Yuan Zai at the Taipei Zoo was separated from her mother because of a minor injury that occurred during her birth. She was _____ by zookeepers for a while.
　　(A) departed　　　　　　　　(B) jailed
　　(C) tended　　　　　　　　　(D) captured

【意見內容】

四個選項皆為合理選項，此題應送分。

【大考中心意見回覆】

本題主要測驗考生能否掌握詞彙 tend 的語意及用法。作答線索在於題幹中 …separated from her mother because of a minor injury…（因為小傷被迫與媽媽隔離）及 …by zookeepers…（由動物園的保育員……）之間的語意關係。除了 tended（照顧）外，其他選項與本句語意皆不符。

※ 題號：**16**

【題目】

第 16 至 20 題為題組

　　Aesop, the Greek writer of fables, was sitting by the roadside one day when a traveler asked him what sort of people lived in Athens. Aesop replied, "Tell me where you come from and what sort of people live there, and I'll tell you what sort of people you'll find in Athens." ___16___, the man answered, "I come from Argos, and there the people are all friendly, generous, and warm-hearted. I love them." ___17___ this, Aesop answered, "I'm happy to tell you, my dear friend, that you'll find the people of Athens much the same."

　　A few hours later, ___18___ traveler came down the road. He too stopped and asked Aesop the same question. ___19___, Aesop made the same request. But frowning, the man answered, "I'm from Argos and there the people are unfriendly, ___20___, and vicious. They're thieves and murderers, all of them." "Well, I'm afraid you'll find the people of Athens much the same," replied Aesop.

16. (A) Amazing　　　(B) Smiling
　　(C) Deciding　　　(D) Praying

【意見內容】

選項 (A) Amazing 應為合理選項。

【大考中心意見回覆】

Amazing（令人感到驚訝的）一詞通常用來修飾事物，若要修飾人應為 amazed，例：John was amazed at the news.，因此選項 (A) 非本題正答。

※ 題號：**17**

【題目】

　　Aesop, the Greek writer of fables, was sitting by the roadside one day when a traveler asked him what sort of people lived in Athens. Aesop replied, "Tell me where you come from and what sort of people live there, and I'll tell you what sort of people you'll find in Athens." ___16___, the man answered, "I come from Argos, and there the people are all friendly, generous, and warm-hearted. I love them." ___17___ this, Aesop answered, "I'm happy to tell you, my dear friend, that you'll find the people of Athens much the same."

　　A few hours later, ___18___ traveler came down the road. He too stopped and asked Aesop the same question. ___19___, Aesop made the same request. But frowning, the man answered, "I'm from Argos and there the people are unfriendly, ___20___, and vicious. They're thieves and murderers, all of them." "Well, I'm afraid you'll find the people of Athens much the same," replied Aesop.

17. (A) At　　　　　　　(B) By
　　(C) For　　　　　　　(D) In

【意見內容】

1. 請說明選項 (B) 與 (C) 不妥之處。

2. at 與 for 皆有「因爲、由於」的意義，因此選項 (C) 應爲合理選項。

【大考中心意見回覆】

本題測驗考生能否掌握片語 at this 在篇章中的用法。At this 的語意爲「Upon hearing this」（一聽到就回答……），故根據上下文意，選項 (A) 爲本題正答；其餘選項語意皆不符（By 語意爲「藉由……」；For 語意爲「因爲……」）。

※ 題號：**20**

【題目】

　　Aesop, the Greek writer of fables, was sitting by the roadside one day when a traveler asked him what sort of people lived in Athens. Aesop replied, "Tell me where you come from and what sort of people live there, and I'll tell you what sort of people you'll find in Athens."　　16　　, the man answered, "I come from Argos, and there the people are all friendly, generous, and warm-hearted. I love them."　　17　　this, Aesop answered, "I'm happy to tell you, my dear friend, that you'll find the people of Athens much the same."

　　A few hours later,　　18　　traveler came down the road. He too stopped and asked Aesop the same question.　　19　　, Aesop made the same request. But frowning, the man answered, "I'm from Argos and there the people are unfriendly,　　20　　, and vicious. They're thieves and murderers, all of them." "Well, I'm afraid you'll find the people of Athens much the same," replied Aesop.

20. (A) brave　　　　　　　　(B) lonely
　　(C) mean　　　　　　　　(D) skinny

【意見內容】

選項 (D) skinny 有「低劣的、吝嗇的」意思，應為合理選項。

【大考中心意見回覆】

本題測驗考生能否掌握詞彙 mean 之語意與能否掌握上下文意對比的關係：第一段內容中的 friendly、generous、warm-hearted 與第二段的 unfriendly、mean，以及 vicious。作答線索在於空格前後的 unfriendly 與 vicious，以及下一句 They're thieves and murderers, all of them.。此外，skinny 通常意指身體的瘦弱，考生所指 skinny

作爲「低劣、吝嗇」的語意並不常見，再者，根據本文全文文意，「低劣、吝嗇」的語意亦不妥適。

※ 題號：43

【題目】

第 41 至 44 題爲題組

American writer Toni Morrison was born in 1931 in Ohio. She was raised in an African American family filled with songs and stories of Southern myths, which later shaped her prose. Her happy family life led to her excellent performance in school, despite the atmosphere of racial discrimination in the society.

After graduating from college, Morrison started to work as a teacher and got married in 1958. Several years later, her marriage began to fail. For a temporary escape, she joined a small writers' group, in which each member was required to bring a story or poem for discussion. She wrote a story based on the life of a girl she knew in childhood who had prayed to God for blue eyes. The story was well received by the group, but then she put it away, thinking she was done with it.

In 1964, Morrison got divorced and devoted herself to writing. One day, she dusted off the story she had written for the writers' group and decided to make it into a novel. She drew on her memories from childhood and expanded upon them using her imagination so that the characters developed a life of their own. *The Bluest Eye* was eventually published in 1970. From 1970 to 1992, Morrison published five more novels.

　　In her novels, Morrison brings in different elements of the African American past, their struggles, problems and cultural memory.　In *Song of Solomon*, for example, Morrison tells the story of an African American man and his search for identity in his culture.　The novels and other works won her several prizes.　In 1993, Morrison received the Nobel Prize in Literature.　She is the eighth woman and the first African American woman to win the honor.

43. According to the passage, what is one of the themes in Morrison's works?
　(A) A search for African American values.
　(B) Divorced black women in American society.
　(C) Songs and stories of African Americans in Ohio.
　(D) History of African Americans from the 1970s through the 1990s.

【意見內容】

選項 (C) 應為合理選項。

【大考中心意見回覆】

本題測驗考生能否掌握文章內容細節之間的關係。作答線索在於第三段 …memories fromchildhood；第四段 …different elements of the African American past, their struggles, problems andcultural memory, search for identity in black culture 等字詞的提示。選項 (C) Songs and stories of African Americans in Ohio. 與第一段第二句 She was raised in an African American family filled with songs and stories of Southern myths… 之語意並不相符，故非合理之選項。

※ 題號：**45**

【題目】

第 45 至 48 題為題組

Below is an excerpt from an interview with Zeke Emanuel, a
health-policy expert, on his famous brothers.

> Interviewer: You're the older brother of Rahm, the mayor of
> Chicago, and Ari, an extremely successful talent
> agent. And you're a bioethicist and one of the
> architects of Obamacare. Isn't writing a book about
> how great your family is a bit odd?
>
> Zeke: I don't write a book about how great my family is. There
> are lots of idiocies and foolishness—a lot to make fun of
> in the book. I wrote *Brothers Emanuel* because I had begun
> jotting stories for my kids. And then we began getting a
> lot of questions: What did Mom put in the cereal? Three
> successful brothers, all different areas.
>
> I: To what do you attribute the Emanuel brothers' success?
>
> Z: I would put success in quotes. We strive. First, I think we got
> this striving from our mother to make the world a better place.
> A second important thing is you never rest on the last victory.
> There's always more to do. And maybe the third important
> thing is my father's admonition that offense is the best defense.
> We don't give up.
>
> I: Do you still not have a TV?
>
> Z: I don't own a TV. I don't own a car. I don't Facebook.
> I don't tweet.
>
> I: But you have four cell phones.
>
> Z: I'm down to two, thankfully.
>
> I: Your brothers are a national source of fascination. Where do
> you think they'll be in five years?

> Z: Ari will be a superagent running the same company. Rahm would still be mayor of Chicago. I will probably continue to be my academic self. The one thing I can guarantee is none of us will have taken a cruise, none of us will be sitting on a beach with a pina colada.

45. What does Zeke Emanuel have in mind when saying "What did Mom put in the cereal?"
   (A) The secret to bringing up successful kids.
   (B) The recipe for a breakfast food.
   (C) The difference among the brothers.
   (D) The questions from his kids.

【意見內容】

選項 (C) 應為合理選項。

【大考中心意見回覆】

本題測驗考生能否根據上下文推測 What did Mom put in the cereal? 的句意。作答線　在於第一段對答中提及三兄弟成功處之各句文意，尤其是在回應的最後一句 Three successful brothers, all different areas.。而後文的內容都與三兄弟的成功相關，例如：下一個問題為 To what do you attribute the Emanuel brothers' success?。全文並未提及三兄弟彼此間相異之處，且選項 (C) 的陳述未能表達成功的原因或秘訣，故選項 (C) 非合理選項。

※ 題號：50

【題目】

第 49 至 52 題為題組

　　MOOC, a massive open online course, aims at providing large-scale interactive participation and open access via the web.

In addition to traditional course materials such as videos, readings, and problem sets, MOOCs provide interactive user forums that help build a community for the students, professors, and teaching assistants.

MOOCs first made waves in the fall of 2011, when Professor Sebastian Thrun from Stanford University opened his graduate-level artificial intelligence course up to any student anywhere, and 160,000 students in more than 190 countries signed up. This new breed of online classes is shaking up the higher education world in many ways. Since the courses can be taken by hundreds of thousands of students at the same time, the number of universities might decrease dramatically. Professor Thrun has even envisioned a future in which there will only need to be 10 universities in the world. Perhaps the most striking thing about MOOCs, many of which are being taught by professors at prestigious universities, is that they're free. This is certainly good news for **cash-strapped** students.

There is a lot of excitement and fear surrounding MOOCs. While some say free online courses are a great way to increase the enrollment of minority students, others have said they will leave many students behind. Some critics have said that MOOCs promote an unrealistic one-size-fits-all model of higher education and that there is no replacement for true dialogues between professors and their students. After all, a brain is not a computer. We are not blank hard drives waiting to be filled with data. People learn from people they love and remember the things that arouse emotion. Some critics worry that online students will miss out on the social aspects of college.

50. Which of the following is **NOT** one of the features of MOOCs?
 (A) It is free to take the courses.
 (B) Many courses are offered by famous universities.
 (C) Most courses address artificial intelligence.
 (D) Many students can take the course at the same time.

【意見內容】

選項 (B) 應為合理選項。

【大考中心意見回覆】

本題測驗考生能否掌握文章主旨與細節之間的關係。作答線索在於第二段內容，尤其是第二句以後的 …the courses can be taken by hundreds of thousands of students at the same time、being taught by professors at prestigious universities、they're free 等字詞的提示，選項 (A)、選項 (B) 與選項 (D) 都是 MOOCs 的特質（feature）。其中，由第二段的內容 …many of which are being taught by professors at prestigious universities（許多課程由知名大學的教授授課），得知選項 (B) Many courses are offered by famous universities. 為特質之一；而根據文章第二段第一句，MOOCs 最初雖是由 Professor Thrun 所開設的artificial intelligence 課程造成後續風潮，但此並非 MOOCs 的特點，且選項 (C) 的敘述在文章中並未提及，與文意不符，因此選項 (C) 為本題正答。

※ 題號：51

【題目】

　　MOOC, a massive open online course, aims at providing large-scale interactive participation and open access via the web. In addition to traditional course materials such as videos, readings, and problem sets, MOOCs provide interactive user forums that help build a community for the students, professors, and teaching assistants.

　　MOOCs first made waves in the fall of 2011, when Professor Sebastian Thrun from Stanford University opened his graduate-level artificial intelligence course up to any student anywhere, and 160,000 students in more than 190 countries signed up. This new breed of online classes is shaking up the higher education world in many ways. Since the courses can be taken by hundreds of thousands of students at the same time, the number of universities might decrease dramatically. Professor Thrun has even envisioned a future in which there will only need to be 10 universities in the world. Perhaps the most striking thing about MOOCs, many of which are being taught by professors at prestigious universities, is that they're free. This is certainly good news for cash-strapped students.

　　There is a lot of excitement and fear surrounding MOOCs. While some say free online courses are a great way to increase the enrollment of minority students, others have said they will leave many students behind. Some critics have said that MOOCs promote an unrealistic one-size-fits-all model of higher education and that there is no replacement for true dialogues between professors and their students. After all, a brain is not a computer. We are not blank hard drives waiting to be filled with data. People learn from people they love and remember the things that arouse emotion. Some critics worry that online students will miss out on the social aspects of college.

51. What is the second paragraph mainly about?
　(A) The impact of MOOCs.
　(B) The goal of MOOCs.
　(C) The size of MOOC classes.
　(D) The cost of MOOC courses.

【意見內容】

　　根據字典，size 有「巨大」的意思，選項 (C) 應為合理選項。

【大考中心意見回覆】

本題測驗考生能否掌握段落大意。作答線索在於第二段全段文意，第二句 This new breed of online classes is shaking up the higher education world in many ways. （這類網路課程對於高等教育有震撼性的影響）為本段主題句，接下來的內容皆為支撐主題的細節，如：the number of universities might decrease （大學數量將大幅減少）。第二段內容雖然談及 Since the courses can be taken by hundreds of thousands of students at the same time…，但後半句 the number of universities might decrease dramatically 才是主要的重點，因此選項 (C) 並非本段大意。

※ 題號：56

【題目】

第 53 至 56 題為題組

　　Today the car seems to make periodic leaps in progress. A variety of driver assistance technologies are appearing on new cars. A developing technology called Vehicle-to-Vehicle communication, or V2V, is being tested by automotive manufacturers as a way to help reduce the number of accidents. V2V works by using wireless signals to send information back and forth between cars about their location, speed and direction, so that they keep safe distances from each other. Another new technology being tested is Vehicle-to-Infrastructure communication, or V2I. V2I would allow vehicles to communicate with road signs or traffic signals and provide information to the vehicle about safety issues. V2I could also request traffic information from a traffic management system and access the best possible routes. Both V2V and V2I have the potential to reduce around 80 percent of vehicle crashes on the road.

　　More and more new cars can reverse-park, read traffic signs, maintain a safe distance in steady traffic and brake automatically to avoid crashes. Moreover, a number of firms are creating cars that drive themselves to a chosen destination without a human at the controls. It is predicted that driverless cars will be ready for sale within five years. If and when cars go completely driverless, the benefits will be enormous. Google, which already uses prototypes of such cars to ferry its staff along Californian freeways, once put a blind man in a prototype and filmed him being driven off to buy takeaway hamburgers. If this works, huge numbers of elderly and disabled people can regain their personal mobility. The young will not have to pay crippling motor insurance, because their reckless hands and feet will no longer touch the wheel or the accelerator. People who commute by car will gain hours each day to work, rest, or read a newspaper.

56. What can be inferred from the passage?
   (A) Cars will refuse to start if the driver is drunk.
   (B) The future may be a vehicle-accident-free era.
   (C) Everyone, including children, can afford a car.
   (D) The production of driverless cars is still far away.

【意見內容】

文章中第一段內容只提到新的科技只能將車禍率降低百分之八十，因此選項 (B) 敘述不夠嚴謹，與文章敘述相違，建議送分。

【大考中心意見回覆】

本題測驗考生能否做適當的推論（inference）與判斷。作答線索在於對全文內容的理解。第一段最後一句 Both V2V and V2I have the potential to reduce around 80 percent of vehicle crashes on the road. 的語意可能還有約 20% 的機率產生車禍，選項 (B) 中用了 may be 正確且適度地表達了這個語意，是四個選項中對未來發展最合理的推論。根據第二段第一句至第三句，選項 (A) 與選項 (D) 皆非正確答案，而文章內容都未提及「所有的人都可以買車」這個概念，因此選項 (C) 亦非正解，故維持選項 (B) 為唯一正答。

102 年大學入學學科能力測驗試題
英文考科

第壹部分：單選題（占 72 分）

一、詞彙（占 15 分）

說明： 第 1 題至第 15 題，每題有 4 個選項，其中只有一個是正確或最適當的
選項，請畫記在答案卡之「選擇題答案區」。各題答對者，得 1 分；
答錯、未作答或畫記多於一個選項者，該題以零分計算。

1. It rained so hard yesterday that the baseball game had to be _____
   until next Saturday.
   (A) surrendered　　(B) postponed　　(C) abandoned　　(D) opposed

2. As more people rely on the Internet for information, it has _____
   newspapers as the most important source of news.
   (A) distributed　　(B) subtracted　　(C) replaced　　(D) transferred

3. Having saved enough money, Joy _____ two trips for this summer
   vacation, one to France and the other to Australia.
   (A) booked　　(B) observed　　(C) enclosed　　(D) deposited

4. Since I do not fully understand your proposal, I am not in the
   position to make any _____ on it.
   (A) difference　　(B) solution　　(C) demand　　(D) comment

5. Betty was _____ to accept her friend's suggestion because she
   thought she could come up with a better idea herself.
   (A) tolerable　　(B) sensitive　　(C) reluctant　　(D) modest

6. The bank tries its best to attract more customers. Its staff members
   are always available to provide _____ service.
   (A) singular　　(B) prompt　　(C) expensive　　(D) probable

7. John's part-time experience at the cafeteria is good _____ for running his own restaurant.
   (A) preparation   (B) recognition   (C) formation   (D) calculation

8. Women's fashions are _____ changing: One season they may favor pantsuits, but the next season they may prefer miniskirts.
   (A) lately   (B) shortly   (C) relatively   (D) constantly

9. Standing on the seashore, we saw a _____ of seagulls flying over the ocean before they glided down and settled on the water.
   (A) pack   (B) flock   (C) herd   (D) school

10. The book is not only informative but also _____, making me laugh and feel relaxed while reading it.
    (A) understanding (B) infecting   (C) entertaining (D) annoying

11. After working in front of my computer for the entire day, my neck and shoulders got so _____ that I couldn't even turn my head.
    (A) dense   (B) harsh   (C) stiff   (D) concrete

12. Getting a flu shot before the start of flu season gives our body a chance to build up protection against the _____ that could make us sick.
    (A) poison   (B) misery   (C) leak   (D) virus

13. The kingdom began to _____ after the death of its ruler, and was soon taken over by a neighboring country.
    (A) collapse   (B) dismiss   (C) rebel   (D) withdraw

14. Though Kevin failed in last year's singing contest, he did not feel _____. This year he practiced day and night and finally won first place in the competition.
    (A) relieved   (B) suspected   (C) discounted   (D) frustrated

15. Emma and Joe are looking for a live-in babysitter for their three-year-old twins, _____ one who knows how to cook.
    (A) initially   (B) apparently   (C) preferably   (D) considerably

二、綜合測驗（占 15 分）

說明： 第 16 題至第 30 題，每題一個空格，請依文意選出最適當的一個選項，
請畫記在答案卡之「選擇題答案區」。各題答對者，得 1 分；答錯、未
作答或畫記多於一個選項者，該題以零分計算。

An area code is a section of a telephone number which generally
represents the geographical area that the phone receiving the call is
based in. It is the two or three digits just before the local number. If
the number ___16___ is in the same area as the number making the call,
an area code usually doesn't need to be dialed. The local number,
___17___, must always be dialed in its entirety.

The area code was introduced in the United States in 1947. It was
created ___18___ the format of XYX, with X being any number between
2-9 and Y being either 1 or 0. Cities and areas with higher populations
would have a smaller first and third digit, and 1 as the center digit. New
York, being the largest city in the United States, was ___19___ the 212
area code, followed by Los Angeles at 213.

In countries other than the United States and Canada, the area code
generally determines the ___20___ of a call. Calls within an area code
and often a small group of neighboring area codes are normally charged
at a lower rate than outside the area code.

16. (A) calling   (B) being called
    (C) having called   (D) has been calling
17. (A) in fact   (B) to illustrate
    (C) at the same time   (D) on the other hand
18. (A) for   (B) as   (C) by   (D) in
19. (A) reserved   (B) assigned (C) represented (D) assembled
20. (A) cost   (B) format   (C) quality   (D) distance

For coin collectors who invest money in coins, the value of a coin is determined by various factors. First, scarcity is a major determinant. __21__ a coin is, the more it is worth. Note, however, that rarity has little to do with the __22__ of a coin. Many thousand-year-old coins often sell for no more than a few dollars because there are a lot of them around, __23__ a 1913 Liberty Head Nickel may sell for over one million US dollars because there are only five in existence. Furthermore, the demand for a particular coin will also __24__ influence coin values. Some coins may command higher prices because they are more popular with collectors. For example, a 1798 dime is much rarer than a 1916 dime, but the __25__ sells for significantly more, simply because many more people collect early 20th century dimes than dimes from the 1700s.

21. (A) Rare as   (B) The rare   (C) Rarest   (D) The rarer
22. (A) age   (B) shape   (C) size   (D) weight
23. (A) since   (B) while   (C) whether   (D) if
24. (A) merely   (B) hardly   (C) greatly   (D) roughly
25. (A) older   (B) better   (C) latter   (D) bigger

French psychologist Alfred Binet (1859-1911) took a different approach from most other psychologists of his day: He was interested in the workings of the __26__ mind rather than the nature of mental illness. He wanted to find a way to measure the ability to think and reason, apart from education in any particular field. In 1905 he developed a test in which he __27__ children do tasks such as follow commands, copy patterns, name objects, and put things in order or arrange them properly. He later created a standard of measuring children's intelligence __28__ the data he had collected from the French children he studied. If 70 percent of 8-year-olds could pass a particular test, then __29__ on the test represented an 8-year-old's level of intelligence. From Binet's work, the phrase "intelligence quotient" ("IQ") entered the English vocabulary. The IQ is the ratio of "mental age" to chronological age times 100, with 100 ___30___ the average. So, an 8-year-old who passes the 10-year-old's test would have an IQ of 10/8 times 100, or 125.

26. (A) contrary　　(B) normal　　(C) detective　　(D) mutual
27. (A) had　　(B) kept　　(C) wanted　　(D) asked
28. (A) composed of　　　　　　(B) based on
　　(C) resulting in　　　　　　(D) fighting against
29. (A) success　　(B) objection　　(C) agreement　　(D) discovery
30. (A) is　　(B) are　　(C) been　　(D) being

三、文意選填（占 10 分）

說明：第 31 題至第 40 題，每題一個空格，請依文意在文章後所提供的 (A) 到 (J) 選項中分別選出最適當者，並將其英文字母代號畫記在答案卡之「選擇題答案區」。各題答對者，得 1 分；答錯、未作答或畫記多於一個選項者，該題以零分計算。

　　Often called "rainforests of the sea," coral reefs provide a home for 25% of all species in the ocean. They are stony structures full of dark hideaways where fish and sea animals can lay their eggs and ___31___ from predators. Without these underwater "apartment houses," there would be fewer fish in the ocean. Some species might even become ___32___ or disappear completely.

　　There are thousands of reefs in the world; ___33___, however, they are now in serious danger. More than one-third are in such bad shape that they could die within ten years. Many might not even ___34___ that long! Scientists are working hard to find out what leads to this destruction. There are still a lot of questions unanswered, but three main causes have been ___35___.

　　The first cause is pollution on land. The pollutants run with rainwater into rivers and streams, which ___36___ the poisons into the ocean. Chemicals from the poisons kill reefs or make them weak, so they have less ___37___ to diseases.

Global warming is another reason. Higher ocean temperatures kill the important food source for the coral—the algae, the tiny greenish-gold water plants that live on coral. When the algae die, the coral loses its color and it also dies ___38___. This process, known as "coral bleaching," has happened more and more frequently in recent years.

The last factor contributing to the ___39___ of coral reefs is people. People sometimes crash into reefs with their boats or drop anchors on them, breaking off large chunks of coral. Divers who walk on reefs can also do serious damage. Moreover, some people even break coral off to collect for ___40___ since it is so colorful and pretty.

How can we help the reefs? We need to learn more about them and work together to stop the activities that may threaten their existence.

(A) resistance　　(B) identified　　(C) last　　　　(D) escape
(E) sadly　　　　(F) eventually　　(G) disappearance　(H) souvenirs
(I) endangered　　(J) carry

四、閱讀測驗（占 32 分）

說明：第 41 題至第 56 題，每題請分別根據各篇文章之文意選出最適當的一個
　　　選項，請畫記在答案卡之「選擇題答案區」。各題答對者，得 2 分；答
　　　錯、未作答或畫記多於一個選項者，該題以零分計算。

第 41 至 44 題為題組

The Swiss army knife is a popular device that is recognized all over the world. In Switzerland, there is a saying that every good Swiss citizen has one in his or her pocket. But the knife had humble beginnings.

In the late nineteenth century, the Swiss army issued its soldiers a gun that required a special screwdriver to dismantle and clean it. At the same time, canned food was becoming common in the army. Swiss generals decided to issue each soldier a standard knife to serve both as a screwdriver and a can opener.

It was a lifesaver for Swiss knife makers, who were struggling to compete with cheaper German imports. In 1884, Carl Elsener, head of the Swiss knife manufacturer Victorinox, seized that opportunity with both hands, and designed a soldier's knife that the army loved. It was a simple knife with one big blade, a can opener, and a screwdriver.

A few years after the soldier's knife was issued, the "Schweizer Offizier Messer," or Swiss Officer's Knife, came on the market. Interestingly, the Officer's Knife was never given to those serving in the army. The Swiss military purchasers considered the new model with a corkscrew for opening wine not "essential for survival," so officers had to buy this new model by themselves. But its special multi-functional design later launched the knife as a global brand. After the Second World War, a great number of American soldiers were stationed in Europe. And as they could buy the Swiss army knife at shops on military bases, they bought huge quantities of them. However, it seems that "Schweizer Offizier Messer" was too difficult for them to say, so they just called it the Swiss army knife, and that is the name it is now known by all over the world.

41. What is the main purpose of the passage?
    (A) To explain the origin of the Swiss army knife.
    (B) To introduce the functions of the Swiss army knife.
    (C) To emphasize the importance of the Swiss army knife.
    (D) To tell a story about the designer of the Swiss army knife.

42. What does "**It**" in the third paragraph refer to?
    (A) The Swiss army needed a knife for every soldier.
    (B) Every good Swiss citizen had a knife in his pocket.
    (C) Swiss knives were competing with imported knives.
    (D) Canned food was becoming popular in the Swiss army.

43. Why didn't the Swiss army purchase the Swiss Officer's Knife?
    (A) The design of the knife was too simple.
    (B) The knife was sold out to American soldiers.
    (C) The army had no budget to make the purchase.
    (D) The new design was not considered necessary for officers to own.

44. Who gave the name "the Swiss army knife" to the knife discussed in the passage?
    (A) Carl Elsener.　　　　　　(B) Swiss generals.
    (C) American soldiers.　　　　(D) German businessmen.

第 45 至 48 題爲題組

　　Space is where our future is—trips to the Moon, Mars and beyond. Most people would think that aside from comets and stars there is little else out there. But, since our space journey started we have left so much trash there that scientists are now concerned that if we don't clean it up, we may all be in mortal danger.

　　The first piece of space junk was created in 1964, when the American satellite Vanguard I stopped operating and lost its connection with the ground center. However, since it kept orbiting around the Earth without any consequences, scientists became increasingly comfortable abandoning things that no longer served any useful purpose in space.

　　It is estimated that there are currently over 500,000 pieces of man-made trash orbiting the Earth at speeds of up to 17,500 miles per hour. The junk varies from tiny pieces of paint chipped off rockets to cameras, huge fuel tanks, and even odd items like the million-dollar tool kit that astronaut Heidemarie Stefanyshyn-Piper lost during a spacewalk.

　　The major problem with the space trash is that it may hit working satellites and damage traveling spacecraft. Moreover, pieces of junk may collide with each other and break into fragments which fall back to the Earth. To avoid this, scientists have devised several ways for clearing the sky. Ground stations have been built to monitor larger pieces of space trash to prevent them from crashing into working satellites or space shuttles. Future plans include a cooperative effort among many nations to stop littering in space and to clean up the trash already there.

45. What was the first piece of man-made space trash?
    (A) A camera.　　　　　　　　(B) A tool kit.
    (C) A fuel tank.　　　　　　　　(D) A broken satellite.

46. Why were scientists **NOT** concerned about space trash in the beginning?
    (A) It no longer served any useful purpose.
    (B) It was millions of miles away from the Earth.
    (C) It did not cause any problems.
    (D) It was regarded as similar to comets and stars.

47. Which of the following statements is true about space junk?
    (A) It is huge, heavy machines.
    (B) It never changes position.
    (C) It floats slowly around the Earth.
    (D) It may cause problems for space shuttles.

48. What has been done about the space trash problem?
    (A) Scientists have cleaned up most of the trash.
    (B) Large pieces of space trash are being closely watched.
    (C) Many nations have worked together to stop polluting space.
    (D) Ground stations are built to help store the trash properly in space.

第 49 至 52 題為題組

　　An alcohol breath test (ABT) is often used by the police to find out whether a person is drunk while driving. In the United States, the legal blood alcohol limit is 0.08% for people aged 21 years or older, while people under 21 are not allowed to drive a car with any level of alcohol in their body. A "positive" test result, a result over the legal limit, allows the police to arrest the driver. However, many people who tested positive on the test have claimed that they only drank a "non-alcoholic" energy drink. Can one of these energy drinks really cause someone to test positive on an ABT? Researchers in Missouri set up an experiment to find out.

First, the amount of alcohol in 27 different popular energy drinks was measured. All but one had an alcohol level greater than 0.005%. In nine of the 27 drinks, the alcohol level was at least 0.096%. The scientists then investigated the possibility that these small levels of alcohol could be detected by an ABT. They asked test subjects to drink a full can or bottle of an energy drink and then gave each subject an ABT one minute and 15 minutes after the drink was finished.

For 11 of the 27 energy drinks, the ABT did detect the presence of alcohol if the test was given within one minute after the drink was taken. However, alcohol could not be detected for any of the drinks if the test was given 15 minutes after the drink was consumed. This shows that when the test is taken plays a crucial role in the test result. The sooner the test is conducted after the consumption of these drinks, the more likely a positive alcohol reading will be obtained.

49. For a person who just turned 20, what is the legal alcohol level allowed while driving in the US?
    (A) 0.000%.　　(B) 0.005%.　　(C) 0.080%.　　(D) 0.096%.

50. What is the purpose of the Missouri experiment?
    (A) To introduce a new method of calculating blood alcohol levels.
    (B) To discover the relation between energy drinks and ABT test results.
    (C) To warn about the dangers of drinking energy drinks mixed with alcohol.
    (D) To challenge the current legal alcohol limit for drivers in the United States.

51. What were the participants of the experiment asked to do after they finished their energy drink?
   (A) To line up in the laboratory.
   (B) To recall the drink brands.
   (C) To take an alcohol breath test.
   (D) To check their breath for freshness.

52. What is the most important factor that affects the ABT test result for energy drink consumers?
   (A) The age of the person who takes the test.
   (B) The place where the test is given.
   (C) The equipment that the test uses.
   (D) The time when the test is taken.

第 53 至 56 題爲題組

　　The majority of Indian women wear a red dot between their eyebrows. While it is generally taken as an indicator of their marital status, the practice is primarily related to the Hindu religion. The dot goes by different names in different Hindi dialects, and "bindi" is the one that is most commonly known. Traditionally, the dot carries no gender restriction: Men as well as women wear it. However, the tradition of men wearing it has faded in recent times, so nowadays we see a lot more women than men wearing one.

　　The position of the bindi is standard: center of the forehead, close to the eyebrows. It represents a third, or inner eye. Hindu tradition holds that all people have three eyes: The two outer ones are used for seeing the outside world, and the third one is there to focus inward toward God. As such, the dot signifies piety and serves as a constant reminder to keep God in the front of a believer's thoughts.

　　Red is the traditional color of the dot. It is said that in ancient times a man would place a drop of blood between his wife's eyes to seal their marriage. According to Hindu beliefs, the color red is believed to bring good fortune to the married couple. Today, people go with different colors depending upon their preferences. Women often wear dots that match the color of their clothes. Decorative or sticker bindis come in all sizes, colors and variations, and can be worn by young and old, married and unmarried people alike. Wearing a bindi has become more of a fashion statement than a religious custom.

53. Why did people in India start wearing a red dot on their forehead?
    (A) To indicate their social rank.
    (B) To show their religious belief.
    (C) To display their financial status.
    (D) To highlight their family background.

54. What is the significance of the third eye in Hindu tradition?
    (A) To stay in harmony with nature.
    (B) To observe the outside world more clearly.
    (C) To pay respect to God.
    (D) To see things with a subjective view.

55. Why was red chosen as the original color of the bindi?
    (A) The red dot represented the blood of God.
    (B) Red stood for a wife's love for her husband.
    (C) The word "bindi" means "red" in some Hindi dialects.
    (D) Red was supposed to bring blessings to a married couple.

56. Which of the following statements is true about the practice of wearing a bindi today?
    (A) Bindis are worn anywhere on the face now.
    (B) Bindis are now used as a decorative item.
    (C) Most Indian women do not like to wear bindis anymore.
    (D) Wearing a bindi has become more popular among Indian men.

第貳部份：非選擇題（占 28 分）

一、中譯英（占 8 分）

說明：　1. 請將以下中文句子譯成正確、通順、達意的英文，並將答案寫在「答案卷」上。

　　　　2. 請依序作答，並標明題號。每題 4 分，共 8 分。

1. 都會地區的高房價對社會產生了嚴重的影響。

2. 政府正推出新的政策，以滿足人們的住房需求。

二、英文作文（占 20 分）

說明：　1. 依提示在「答案卷」上寫一篇英文作文。

　　　　2. 文長至少 120 個單詞（words）。

提示：　請仔細觀察以下三幅連環圖片的內容，並想像第四幅圖片可能的發展，寫出一個涵蓋連環圖片內容並有完整結局的故事。

102年度學科能力測驗英文科試題詳解

第壹部分：單選題

一、詞彙：

1. (**B**) It rained so hard yesterday that the baseball game had to be <u>postponed</u> until next Saturday.
   昨天雨下得很大，以致於棒球比賽必須<u>延期</u>到下週六。
   (A) surrender〔sə'rɛndə〕v. 投降
   (B) ***postpone***〔post'pon〕v. 延期【92學測也考過】(= *put off*)
   (C) abandon〔ə'bændən〕v. 拋棄　　(D) oppose〔ə'poz〕v. 反對
   hard〔hɑrd〕adv. 猛烈地

2. (**C**) As more people rely on the Internet for information, it has <u>replaced</u> newspapers as the most important source of news.
   隨著有更多人依賴網路取得資訊，網路已經<u>取代</u>報紙，成為最重要的新聞來源。
   (A) distribute〔dɪ'strɪbjut〕v. 分配
   (B) subtract〔səb'trækt〕v. 減去；扣除
   (C) ***replace***〔rɪ'ples〕v. 取代【94學測也考過】
   (D) transfer〔træns'fɝ〕v. 轉移
   rely on 依賴　　***the Internet*** 網路
   information〔͵ɪnfɚ'meʃən〕n. 資訊　　source〔sors〕n. 來源

3. (**A**) Having saved enough money, Joy <u>booked</u> two trips for this summer vacation, one to France and the other to Australia. 在存夠錢之後，喬伊<u>預訂</u>了兩趟暑假的旅程，一趟去法國，一趟去澳洲。
   (A) ***book***〔buk〕v. 預訂　　　　(B) observe〔əb'zɝv〕v. 觀察
   (C) enclose〔ɪn'kloz〕v.（隨函）附寄
   (D) deposit〔dɪ'pɑzɪt〕v. 存（款）
   Australia〔ɔ'streljə〕n. 澳洲

4. (**D**) Since I do not fully understand your proposal, I am not in the position to make any <u>comment</u> on it.
   因為我並沒有完全了解你的提議，我沒有資格做任何<u>評論</u>。

(A) difference〔'dɪfərəns〕 *n.* 不同

(B) solution〔sə'luʃən〕 *n.* 解決之道

(C) demand〔dɪ'mænd〕 *n.* 要求

(D) ***comment***〔'kɑmɛnt〕 *n.* 評論　***make a comment on*** 評論

fully〔'fʊlɪ〕 *adv.* 完全地　　proposal〔prə'pozḷ〕 *n.* 提議

position〔pə'zɪʃən〕 *n.* 立場　***in a position to V.*** 有資格～；能夠～

5. (**C**) Betty was <u>reluctant</u> to accept her friend's suggestion because she thought she could come up with a better idea herself. 貝蒂<u>不願意</u>接受她朋友的建議，因為她覺得她自己可以想出更好的主意。

(A) tolerable〔'talərəbḷ〕 *adj.* 可容忍的

(B) sensitive〔'sɛnsətɪv〕 *adj.* 敏感的

(C) ***reluctant***〔rɪ'lʌktənt〕 *adj.* 勉強的；不願意的

(D) modest〔'mɑdɪst〕 *adj.* 謙虛的

come up with 想出

6. (**B**) The bank tries its best to attract more customers. Its staff members are always available to provide <u>prompt</u> service. 這家銀行竭盡所能來吸引更多顧客。職員們總是可以提供<u>即時的</u>服務。

(A) singular〔'sɪŋgjələ〕 *adj.* 單數的

(B) ***prompt***〔prɑmpt〕 *adj.* 迅速的；即時的

(C) expensive〔ɪk'spɛnsɪv〕 *adj.* 昂貴的

(D) probable〔'prɑbəbḷ〕 *adj.* 可能的

try *one's* ***best*** 盡力　　attract〔ə'trækt〕 *v.* 吸引

customer〔'kʌstəmə〕 *n.* 顧客　　staff〔stæf〕 *n.* 職員

member〔'mɛmbə〕 *n.* 成員

available〔ə'veləbḷ〕 *adj.* 可獲得的；有空的

provide〔prə'vaɪd〕 *v.* 提供

7. (**A**) John's part-time experience at the cafeteria is good <u>preparation</u> for running his own restaurant.

約翰在自助餐廳的兼差經驗，對經營自己的餐廳是很好的<u>事先準備</u>。

(A) ***preparation***〔,prɛpə'reʃən〕 *n.* 準備

(B) recognition〔,rɛkəg'nɪʃən〕 *n.* 認知；認可

(C) formation〔fɔr'meʃən〕 *n.* 形成

(D) calculation〔,kælkjə'leʃən〕 *n.* 計算

part-time〔,pɑrt'taɪm〕 *adj.* 兼差的　　run〔rʌn〕 *v.* 經營

8. (**D**) Women's fashions are <u>constantly</u> changing: One season they may favor pantsuits, but the next season they may prefer miniskirts.
女性時尚<u>不斷</u>在改變：這一季她們可能偏愛褲裝，但是下一季她們可能比較喜歡迷你裙。
   (A) lately〔'letlɪ〕*adv.* 最近　　(B) shortly〔'ʃɔrtlɪ〕*adv.* 不久
   (C) relatively〔'rɛlətɪvlɪ〕*adv.* 相對地
   (D) ***constantly***〔'kɑnstəntlɪ〕*adv.* 不斷地
   favor〔'fevɚ〕*v.* 偏愛　　pantsuit〔'pænt,sut〕*n.* 褲裝
   prefer〔prɪ'fɝ〕*v.* 比較喜歡　　miniskirt〔'mɪnɪ,skɝt〕*n.* 迷你裙

9. (**B**) Standing on the seashore, we saw a <u>flock</u> of seagulls flying over the ocean before they glided down and settled on the water. 站在海邊，我們看到一<u>群</u>海鷗滑翔而下，在水面上棲息，然後飛越海洋。
   (A) pack〔pæk〕*n.* (狗、狼等的)群
   (B) ***flock***〔flɑk〕*n.* (鳥)群【84 日大也考過】
   (C) herd〔hɝd〕*n.* (牛)群　　(D) school〔skul〕*n.* (魚)群
   seashore〔'si,ʃor〕*n.* 海岸　　seagull〔'si,gʌl〕*n.* 海鷗
   glide〔glaɪd〕*v.* 滑翔　　settle〔'sɛtl〕*v.* 棲息

10. (**C**) The book is not only informative but also <u>entertaining</u>, making me laugh and feel relaxed while reading it. 這本書不僅提供知識，也很<u>有趣</u>，當我閱讀的時候會使我發笑，覺得放鬆。
   (A) understanding〔,ʌndɚ'stændɪŋ〕*adj.* 體諒的
   (B) infect〔ɪn'fɛkt〕*v.* 感染
   (C) ***entertaining***〔,ɛntɚ'tenɪŋ〕*adj.* 有趣的
   (D) annoying〔ə'nɔɪɪŋ〕*adj.* 煩人的
   not only···but also~ 不僅···而且~
   informative〔ɪn'fɔrmətɪv〕*adj.* 提供知識的

11. (**C**) After working in front of my computer for the entire day, my neck and shoulders got so <u>stiff</u> that I couldn't even turn my head.
在我的電腦前面工作一整天後，我的脖子和肩膀<u>僵硬</u>到讓我連頭都沒辦法轉。
   (A) dense〔dɛns〕*adj.* 密集的；濃密的
   (B) harsh〔hɑrʃ〕*adj.* 嚴厲的　　(C) ***stiff***〔stɪf〕*adj.* 僵硬的
   (D) concrete〔kɑn'krit , 'kɑnkrit〕*adj.* 具體的
   in front of 在···前面　　entire〔ɪn'taɪr〕*adj.* 全部的
   neck〔nɛk〕*n.* 脖子　　shoulder〔'ʃoldɚ〕*n.* 肩膀

12. (**D**) Getting a flu shot before the start of flu season gives our body a chance to build up protection against the <u>virus</u> that could make us sick. 在流感盛行季節開始前打流感疫苗，能讓我們的身體有機會建立防護，以對抗可能讓我們生病的<u>病毒</u>。

(A) poison〔ˊpɔɪzn̩〕*n.* 毒藥　　　(B) misery〔ˊmɪzərɪ〕*n.* 悲慘

(C) leak〔lik〕*n.* 漏洞　*v.* 漏；漏水　(D) *virus*〔ˊvaɪrəs〕*n.* 病毒

flu〔flu〕*n.* 流行性感冒　　　shot〔ʃɑt〕*n.* 注射（疫苗）

season〔ˊsizn̩〕*n.* 季節；時期　　*build up* 建立

protection〔prəˊtɛkʃən〕*n.* 防護

13. (**A**) The kingdom began to <u>collapse</u> after the death of its ruler, and was soon taken over by a neighboring country.

該王國在統治者駕崩後開始<u>瓦解</u>，很快地被鄰國接管。

(A) *collapse*〔kəˊlæps〕*v.* 瓦解；倒塌

(B) dismiss〔dɪsˊmɪs〕*v.* 下（課）；解僱；解散

(C) rebel〔rɪˊbɛl〕*v.* 反叛　　　(D) withdraw〔wɪðˊdrɔ〕*v.* 撤退

kingdom〔ˊkɪŋdəm〕*n.* 王國　　　ruler〔ˊrulɚ〕*n.* 統治者

take over 接管　　　neighboring〔ˊnebərɪŋ〕*adj.* 鄰近的

14. (**D**) Though Kevin failed in last year's singing contest, he did not feel <u>frustrated</u>. This year he practiced day and night and finally won first place in the competition.

雖然凱文去年在歌唱比賽失敗，但是他並沒有感到<u>挫折</u>。今年他日以繼夜地練習，最後在比賽中贏得第一名。

(A) relieved〔rɪˊlivd〕*adj.* 放心的；鬆了一口氣的

(B) suspected〔səˊspɛktɪd〕*adj.* 受到懷疑的

(C) discount〔ˊdɪskaʊnt , dɪsˊkaʊnt〕*v.* 打折

(D) *frustrated*〔ˊfrʌstretɪd〕*adj.* 受挫的

contest〔ˊkɑntɛst〕*n.* 比賽　　*day and night* 日以繼夜地

first place 第一名　　competition〔ˌkɑmpəˊtɪʃən〕*n.* 比賽

15. (**C**) Emma and Joe are looking for a live-in babysitter for their three-year-old twins, <u>preferably</u> one who knows how to cook.

艾瑪和喬在為他們的三歲的雙胞胎找一位住在家裡的保姆，<u>最好</u>是會煮飯的人。

(A) initially〔ɪˊnɪʃəlɪ〕*adv.* 起初

(B) apparently〔əˊpærəntlɪ〕*adv.* 明顯地

(C) *preferably*〔'prɛfərəblɪ〕*adv.* 最好
(D) considerably〔kən'sɪdərəbḷɪ〕*adv.* 相當大地
look for 尋找　　live-in〔'lɪv'ɪn〕*adj.* 住在家裡的；宿於工作處的
babysitter〔'bebɪ,sɪtɚ〕*n.* 保姆　　twins〔twɪnz〕*n. pl.* 雙胞胎

二、綜合測驗：

　　An area code is a section of a telephone number which generally represents the geographical area that the phone receiving the call is based in.　It is the two or three digits just before the local number.　If the number <u>being called</u> is in the same area as the number making the call, an area code
　　　　16
usually doesn't need to be dialed.　The local number, <u>on the other hand</u> ,
must always be dialed in its entirety.　　　　　　　　　　　　17

　　區域號碼是電話號碼的一個部分，通常代表收訊的電話所處的地理位置。它是本地電話號碼之前的二到三碼。若是被撥打的電話與撥打的電話處在相同的區域，撥號時通常不需要輸入區域號碼。然而，本地號碼永遠必須被原封不動地輸入。

area code 區域號碼　　section〔'sɛkʃən〕*n.* 部分
generally〔'dʒɛnərəlɪ〕*adv.* 通常　　represent〔,rɛprɪ'zɛnt〕*v.* 代表
geographical〔,dʒiə'græfɪkḷ〕*adj.* 地理的
be based in 以…為基地　　digit〔'dɪdʒɪt〕*n.*（各個）阿拉伯數字
local〔'lokḷ〕*adj.* 當地的　　dial〔'daɪəl〕*v.* 撥（號）
entirety〔ɪn'taɪətɪ〕*n.* 全體　　*in its entirety* 原封不動；全部

16. (**B**) 依句意，「被撥打的」電話號碼，須用被動語態，故可用形容詞子句
which is called 修飾先行詞 number，也可省略關代 which，並將 be
動詞 is 改為現在分詞 being，故選 (B) *being called*。【101 指考也考過】

17. (**D**) 依句意，選 (D) *on the other hand*「另一方面；然而」。【87 學測也考過】
而 (A) in fact「事實上」，(B) to illustrate「為了要說明」，(C) at the
same time「同時」，均不合句意。

　　The area code was introduced in the United States in 1947.　It was created <u>in</u> the format of XYX, with X being any number between 2-9 and Y
　　　　　　　　　　　　　　18
being either 1 or 0.　Cities and areas with higher populations would have a

smaller first and third digit, and 1 as the center digit. New York, being the largest city in the United States, was <u>assigned</u> the 212 area code, followed by Los Angeles at 213.

19

　　區域號碼於 1947 年被引進美國。它以 XYX 的形式被創造出來，X 為 2 到 9 之間的任何數字，而 Y 為 1 或是 0。擁有較多人口的城市或區域的第一碼與第三碼數字會比較小，而中間的第二碼會是 1。美國最大城紐約的區域號碼被指定為 212，接著是洛杉磯的 213。

> introduce〔͵ɪntrə′djus〕v. 引進；採用　　create〔krɪ′et〕v. 創造
> format〔′fɔrmæt〕n. 形式；格式
> center〔′sɛntɚ〕adj. 中心的；中央的　　***followed by*** 接著就是

18.(**D**) ***in···format*** 以···形式

19.(**B**) (A) reserve〔rɪ′zɝv〕v. 預訂；保留
　　　　 (B) ***assign***〔ə′saɪn〕v. 分配；分派；指定
　　　　 (C) represent〔͵rɛprɪ′zɛnt〕v. 代表
　　　　 (D) assemble〔ə′sɛmbḷ〕v. 裝配；集合

　　In countries other than the United States and Canada, the area code generally determines the <u>cost</u> of a call. Calls within an area code and often

20

a small group of neighboring area codes are normally charged at a lower rate than outside the area code.

　　在美國與加拿大之外的國家，區域號碼往往決定了通話的費用。比起處於區域號碼之外的地區，區域號碼之內或是一小組鄰近區域號碼之間的通話，通常會被以比較低的費率計費。

> ***other than*** 除了···之外　　determine〔dɪ′tɝmɪn〕v. 決定
> neighboring〔′nebərɪŋ〕adj. 鄰近的；附近的
> normally〔′nɔrmḷɪ〕adv. 通常　　charge〔tʃɑrdʒ〕v. 收費
> rate〔ret〕n. 費用；價格　　outside〔aʊt′saɪd〕prep. 在···的外面

20.(**A**) 依句意，選 (A) ***cost*** 「費用」。而 (B) format 「方式；格式」，(C) quality 「品質」，(D) distance 「距離」，均不合句意。

　　For coin collectors who invest money in coins, the value of a coin is determined by various factors. First, scarcity is a major determinant.

The rarer a coin is, the more it is worth. Note, however, that rarity has
   21

little to do with the age of a coin. Many thousand-year-old coins often sell
                  22

for no more than a few dollars because there are a lot of them around, while
                                                         23

a 1913 Liberty Head Nickel may sell for over one million US dollars
because there are only five in existence.

　　對於把錢投資於硬幣的硬幣收藏家來說，有許多決定硬幣價值的要素。首
先，稀有度是一個主要的決定因素。一個硬幣越是稀有，就越是值錢。但是，
請注意，稀有度與硬幣的年份沒什麼關聯。很多千年古幣賣不了多少錢，因爲
到處都找得到，然而 1913 年的自由女神頭像五分硬幣售價可能超過一百萬美
金，因爲全世界只剩五枚。

> coin〔kɔɪn〕*n.* 硬幣　　collector〔kə'lɛktɚ〕*n.* 收集者；收藏者
> invest〔ɪn'vɛst〕*v.* 投資　　various〔'vɛrɪəs〕*adj.* 各種的；各式各樣的
> factor〔'fæktɚ〕*n.* 因素　　scarcity〔'skɛrsətɪ〕*n.* 缺乏；不足；稀少
> major〔'medʒɚ〕*adj.* 主要的
> determinant〔dɪ'tɜmənənt〕*n.* 決定因素
> worth〔wɝθ〕*adj.* 有…價值的　　note〔not〕*v.* 注意
> rarity〔'rɛrətɪ〕*n.* 稀有；罕見
> ***have little to do with*** 和…沒什麼關聯
> ***no more than*** 僅僅；只是（= *only*）
> around〔ə'raʊnd〕*adj.* 存在的；在大量出現
> liberty〔'lɪbɚtɪ〕*n.*（硬幣上的）自由女神像
> nickel〔'nɪkl̩〕*n.* 五分錢硬幣　　***in existence*** 現存的；存在著的

21. (**D**)　「the +比較級…the +比較級」表「越…就越～」，故選 (D) ***The rarer***。
　　　　rare〔rɛr〕*adj.* 稀有的

22. (**A**)　依句意，稀有性和硬幣的「年份」沒什麼關係，故選 (A) ***age***「年齡；
　　　　年代」。而 (B) shape「形狀」，(C) size「大小；尺寸」，(D) weight「重
　　　　量」，均不合句意。

23. (**B**)　表示「對比」，連接詞須用 ***while***「然而」，選 (B)。【84 學測考過 while
　　　　作「當…的時候」解；93 指考則考 while 作「雖然」解。】而 (A) since「自
　　　　從；既然；因爲」，(C) whether「是否；不論」，(D) if「如果」，均
　　　　不合句意。

Furthermore, the demand for a particular coin will also greatly influence
　　　　　　　　　　　　　　　　　　　　　　　　　　　　　24
coin values.　Some coins may command higher prices because they are
more popular with collectors.　For example, a 1798 dime is much rarer than
a 1916 dime, but the latter sells for significantly more, simply because many
　　　　　　　　　　25
more people collect early 20th century dimes than dimes from the 1700s.
此外，對某種特定硬幣的需求也將大大影響硬幣的價值。某些硬幣可以賣出比
較高的價錢，因為它們在收藏家之間較受歡迎。例如，一枚 1798 年的一角硬幣
遠比一枚 1916 年的一角硬幣罕見，但後者的售價卻高得多，僅僅只是因為收藏
二十世紀早期一角硬幣的人，比收藏十八世紀一角硬幣的人多得多。

> furthermore〔ˋfɝðɚˏmor〕*adv.* 此外；而且
> demand〔dɪˋmænd〕*n.* 需求　　particular〔pɚˋtɪkjəlɚ〕*adj.* 特定的
> influence〔ˋɪnfluəns〕*v.* 影響
> command〔kəˋmænd〕*v.*（商品）可賣（高價錢）
> dime〔daɪm〕*n.* 一角硬幣　　rare〔rɛr〕*adj.* 稀有的
> *the 1700s* 十八世紀

24. (**C**) 依句意，對特定硬幣的需求，會「大大地」影響硬幣的價值，故選
　　　 (C) *greatly*。而 (A) merely「僅僅；只是」、(B) hardly「幾乎不」、
　　　 (D) roughly〔ˋrʌflɪ〕*adv.* 粗略地；大約，均不合句意。

25. (**C**) 依句意，選 (C) *the latter*「後者」。

　　　French psychologist Alfred Binet (1859-1911) took a different approach
from most other psychologists of his day:　He was interested in the workings
of the normal mind rather than the nature of mental illness.　He wanted to
　　　 26
find a way to measure the ability to think and reason, apart from education
in any particular field.
　　　法國心理學家艾爾佛・比奈（1859-1911）與當時的大部分的心理學家採取
不同門徑：他的興趣在於正常心靈的運作而非精神疾病的性質。在任何特定領
域的教育之外，他想要找到一個方法，去衡量人類思考與推論的能力。

> psychologist〔saɪˋkɑlədʒɪst〕*n.* 心理學家
> Alfred Binet〔ˋælfrɛd bɪˋne〕*n.* 艾爾佛・比內【1857-1911，法國心理學家】
> approach〔əˋprotʃ〕*n.* 方法　　*of one's day* 某人的那個時代
> *be interested in* 對…有興趣

workings〔'wɜkɪŋz〕n. pl. 工作；運行；活動
rather than 而不是　　nature〔'netʃə〕n. 特質；特性
measure〔'mɛʒə〕v. 測量；衡量　　reason〔'rizn〕v. 推論
apart from 除了…之外　　field〔fild〕n. 領域

26. (**B**) 依句意，選 (B) ***normal***〔'nɔrml〕adj. 正常的；一般的。而 (A) contrary 〔'kɑntrɛrɪ〕adj. 相反的，(C) detective〔dɪ'tɛktɪv〕adj. 偵探的，(D) mutual〔'mutʃuəl〕adj. 相互的，則不合句意。

In 1905 he developed a test in which he <u>had</u> children do tasks such as follow
　　　　　　　　　　　　　　　　　　　　27
commands, copy patterns, name objects, and put things in order or arrange
them properly.　He later created a standard of measuring children's
intelligence <u>based on</u> the data he had collected from the French children he
　　　　　　　28
studied.　If 70 percent of 8-year-olds could pass a particular test, then
<u>success</u> on the test represented an 8-year-old's level of intelligence.
　29
1905 年，他發展出一套測試，在這個測試中，他要求孩童完成一些任務，像是
依指令行事、依模式模仿、指認物體、將物品依順序擺放或是妥善排列整理等
等。之後，依據從受測的法國孩童收集而成的數據，他創造了一套衡量孩童智
力的標準。如果百分之七十的八歲小孩能夠通過某項特定測試，則這項測試的
成功通過，便可代表八歲孩童的智力水準。

develop〔dɪ'vɛləp〕v. 研發　　task〔tæsk〕n. 任務；工作
follow〔'falo〕v. 遵守　　command〔kə'mænd〕n. 命令；指揮
copy〔'kɑpɪ〕v. 模仿；複製　　pattern〔'pætən〕n. 模式
name〔nem〕v. 說出…的（正確）名字
object〔'ɑbdʒɪkt〕n. 東西；物體　　order〔'ɔrdə〕n. 順序；次序
arrange〔ə'rendʒ〕v. 整理；排列　　properly〔'prɑpəlɪ〕adv. 適當地
later〔'letə〕adv. 後來　　standard〔'stændəd〕n. 標準
intelligence〔ɪn'tɛlədʒəns〕n. 智力
data〔'detə〕n. pl. 資料　　study〔'stʌdɪ〕v. 研究
represent〔.rɛprɪ'zɛnt〕v. 代表　　level〔'lɛvl〕n. 水平；程度

27. (**A**) 由受詞 children 後的原形動詞 do 可知，空格應填使役動詞，故選
(A) ***had***。　　***have sb. V.*** 叫某人（做）…
而 (B) kept「使…停留在（某種狀態）」，接受詞後須接補語，在此用
法與句意皆不合；(C) wanted「想要」和 (D) asked「要求」，為一般
動詞，接受詞後須接不定詞，用法不合。

28. (**B**) 依句意，選 (B) ***based on*** 「根據」。
   　而 (A) composed of 「由…組成」，(C) resulting in 「導致；造成」，
   　(D) fighting against 「與…作戰」，則不合句意。

29. (**A**) 依句意，「成功」通過測驗，選 (A) ***success***。
   　(B) objection〔əbˈdʒɛkʃən〕*n.* 反對
   　(C) agreement〔əˈgrimənt〕*n.* 同意；協議
   　(D) discovery〔dɪˈskʌvərɪ〕*n.* 發現

From Binet's work, the phrase "intelligence quotient" ("IQ") entered the
English vocabulary.　The IQ is the ratio of "mental age" to chronological
age times 100, with 100 <u>being</u> the average.　So, an 8-year-old who passes
　　　　　　　　　　　　　　　　　　　30
the 10-year-old's test would have an IQ of 10/8 times 100, or 125.
因為比奈的研究，智力商數（智商）這個用語進入了英語詞彙。智商，便是「心
理年齡」與實際年齡的比率乘上一百，而一百是平均值。因此，一個能夠通過
十歲測驗的八歲孩童，便擁有十除以八再乘以一百的智商，也就是智商一二五。

　　work〔wɜk〕*n.* 工作成果　　　phrase〔frez〕*n.* 片語；說法
　　quotient〔ˈkwoʃənt〕*n.* 商數
   　intelligence quotient 智力商數；智商（= *IQ* ）
   　vocabulary〔vəˈkæbjəˌlɛrɪ〕*n.* 字彙　　ratio〔ˈreʃo〕*n.* 比例
   　mental age 智力年齡；心理年齡
   　chronological〔ˌkrɑnəˈlɑdʒɪk!〕*adj.* 按年代順序的
   　chronological age 按時間計算的年齡　　times〔taɪmz〕*prep.* 乘以
   　average〔ˈævərɪdʒ〕*n.* 平均數；平均值　　or〔ɔr〕*conj.* 也就是

30. (**D**) with 表附帶狀態，其用法為：「with + O. + p.p 或 V-ing」，依句意為主
   　動，故選 (D) ***being***。【83 夜大也考過】

三、文意選填：

　　Often called "rainforests of the sea," coral reefs provide a home for
25% of all species in the ocean.　They are stony structures full of dark
hideaways where fish and sea animals can lay their eggs and [31](**D**) **escape**
from predators.　Without these underwater "apartment houses," there
would be fewer fish in the ocean.　Some species might even become
[32](**I**) **endangered** or disappear completely.

　　常有「海中雨林」美稱的珊瑚礁爲整個海洋百分之二十五的物種提供了家園。它們是充滿黑暗隱蔽處的堅硬結構，魚類及海洋生物可在其中產卵以及躲避掠食者。要是沒了這些海中的「公寓」，海裡的魚類可能會變少。有些物種甚至可能會瀕臨絕種或完全消失。

> rainforest (ˈrenˌfɔrɪst) *n.* 雨林　　coral (ˈkɔrəl) *n.* 珊瑚
> reef (rif) *n.* 礁　　***coral reef*** 珊瑚礁　　species (ˈspiʃɪz) *n.* 物種
> stony (ˈstonɪ) *adj.* 石頭的；非常堅硬的
> structure (ˈstrʌktʃʊ) *n.* 構造
> hideaway (ˈhaɪəˌwe) *n.* 躲藏處；藏匿處　　lay (le) *v.* 下（蛋）
> egg (ɛg) *n.* 蛋；卵　　***escape from*** 從…逃脫
> predator (ˈprɛdətʊ) *n.* 捕食者
> underwater (ˈʌndʊˌwɔtʊ) *adj.* 水中的
> apartment (əˈpartmənt) *n.* 公寓
> endangered (ɪnˈdendʒʊd) *adj.* 有危險的；瀕臨絕種的
> completely (kəmˈplitlɪ) *adv.* 完全地

There are thousands of reefs in the world; [33]**(E) sadly**, however, they are now in serious danger. More than one-third are in such bad shape that they could die within ten years. Many might not even [34]**(C) last** that long! Scientists are working hard to find out what leads to this destruction. There are still a lot of questions unanswered, but three main causes have been [35]**(B) identified**. 【98學測也考過】

　　世界上有數千種珊瑚礁；然而，悲傷的是，它們現在的處境極其危險。三分之一以上的狀態已經糟到可能會在十年之內死亡。很多可能甚至沒辦法撐那麼久！科學家努力要尋找造成此種毀滅的原因。目前仍有許多問題未解，但三個主因已被指認出來。

> sadly (ˈsædlɪ) *adv.* 可悲的是；遺憾的是　　***in danger*** 有危險
> ***one-third*** 三分之一　　shape (ʃep) *n.* 情形；狀況
> ***find out*** 查出　　last (læst) *v.* 持續；支撐；繼續存在
> ***lead to*** 導致；造成　　destruction (dɪˈstrʌkʃən) *n.* 破壞
> unanswered (ʌnˈænsʊd) *adj.* 無回答的　　main (men) *adj.* 主要的
> cause (kɔz) *n.* 原因　　identify (aɪˈdɛntəˌfaɪ) *v.* 辨識；確認

The first cause is pollution on land. The pollutants run with rainwater into rivers and streams, which [36]**(J) carry** the poisons into the ocean. Chemicals from the poisons kill reefs or make them weak, so they have less [37]**(A) resistance** to diseases.

　　第一個原因是陸地上的污染。污染物會隨著雨水流入河流與小溪，而溪流會將這些毒物帶入海洋。這些毒物中的化學物質會殺死或弱化珊瑚礁，讓它們對疾病的抵抗力變小。

pollution〔pəˋluʃən〕n. 污染　　pollutant〔pəˋlutənt〕n. 污染物
run〔rʌn〕v. 流　　rainwater〔ˋren͵wɔtɚ〕n. 雨水
stream〔strim〕n. 溪流　　carry〔ˋkærɪ〕v. 攜帶
poison〔ˋpɔɪzn̩〕n. 毒；毒藥　　chemical〔ˋkɛmɪkl̩〕n. 化學物質
weak〔wik〕adj. 虛弱的　　resistant〔rɪˋzɪstənt〕adj. 有抵抗力的
disease〔dɪˋziz〕n. 疾病

Global warming is another reason. Higher ocean temperatures kill the important food source for the coral—the algae, the tiny greenish-gold water plants that live on coral. When the algae die, the coral loses its color and it also dies [38](F) eventually. This process, known as "coral bleaching," has happened more and more frequently in recent years.

　　另一個原因是全球暖化。較高的海水溫度會殺死珊瑚的重要食物來源——海藻，也就是那些棲居於珊瑚上金金綠綠的微小水生植物。當海藻死去，珊瑚會失去顏色，然後最終也會死去。近年來，這個被稱為「珊瑚白化」的過程越來越常發生。

global warming 全球暖化　　reason〔ˋrizn̩〕n. 理由
temperature〔ˋtɛmpərətʃɚ〕n. 溫度　　source〔sors〕n. 來源
algae〔ˋældʒi〕n. pl. 海藻　　tiny〔ˋtaɪnɪ〕adj. 微小的
greenish〔ˋgriniʃ〕adj. 帶綠色的　　eventually〔ɪˋvɛntʃuəlɪ〕adv. 最後
process〔ˋprɑsɛs〕n. 過程　　*be known as* 被稱為
bleach〔blitʃ〕v. 漂白；變白　　*coral bleaching* 珊瑚白化
more and more 越來越　　recent〔ˋrisn̩t〕adj. 最近的

The last factor contributing to the [39](G) disappearance of coral reefs is people. People sometimes crash into reefs with their boats or drop anchors on them, breaking off large chunks of coral. Divers who walk on reefs can also do serious damage. Moreover, some people even break coral off to collect for [40](H) souvenirs since it is so colorful and pretty.

　　促使珊瑚礁消失的最後一個因素是人類。有時候人類會駛船撞上珊瑚礁，或是在珊瑚礁上落錨，讓珊瑚礁大塊大塊地剝落。那些在珊瑚礁上步行的潛水者也會對其造成嚴重損害。此外，因其多彩斑斕而賞心悅目，有些人甚至會扯落珊瑚礁當作紀念品收藏。

contribute to 促成；造成　　disappearance〔͵dɪsə'pɪrəns〕*n.* 消失
crash into 猛然撞上　　drop〔drɑp〕*v.* 放下
anchor〔'æŋkɚ〕*n.* 錨　*break off* 折斷　　chunk〔tʃʌŋk〕*n.* 厚塊
diver〔'daɪvɚ〕*n.* 潛水者　*do damage* 造成損害
souvenir〔͵suvə'nɪr〕*n.* 紀念品　　colorful〔'kʌləfəl〕*adj.* 五顏六色的

How can we help the reefs? We need to learn more about them and work together to stop the activities that may threaten their existence.

我們要如何幫助珊瑚礁？我們必須對它們有更加充分的認識，並且攜手停止那些可能威脅其生存的活動。

learn〔lɜn〕*v.* 知道　　*work together* 合作
activity〔æk'tɪvətɪ〕*n.* 活動　　threaten〔'θrɛtn̩〕*v.* 威脅
existance〔ɪg'zɪstəns〕*n.* 存在

四、閱讀測驗：

41-44 為題組

The Swiss army knife is a popular device that is recognized all over the world. In Switzerland, there is a saying that every good Swiss citizen has one in his or her pocket. But the knife had humble beginnings.

瑞士軍刀是個受歡迎的工具，受到全世界的認可。在瑞士，有一句話說，每位瑞士的公民的口袋裡都有一把瑞士刀。但是這刀子出身卑微。

Swiss〔swɪs〕*adj.* 瑞士的　　army〔'ɑrmɪ〕*adv.* 軍隊的　*n.* 軍隊
knife〔naɪf〕*n.* 小刀　*Swiss army knife* 瑞士軍刀
device〔dɪ'vaɪs〕*n.* 器具
recognize〔'rɛkəg͵naɪz〕*v.* 認可　*all over the world* 全世界
Switzerland〔'swɪtsəlænd〕*n.* 瑞士【歐洲中部的一聯邦共和國】
saying〔'se·ɪŋ〕*n.* 諺語；俗話　　citizen〔'sɪtəzn̩〕*n.* 市民；公民
pocket〔'pɑkɪt〕*n.* 口袋　　humble〔'hʌmbḷ〕*adj.* 卑微的
beginning〔bɪ'gɪnɪŋ〕*n.* 起源

In the late nineteenth century, the Swiss army issued its soldiers a gun that required a special screwdriver to dismantle and clean it. At the same time, canned food was becoming common in the army. Swiss generals decided to issue each soldier a standard knife to serve both as a screwdriver and a can opener.

在十九世紀晚期，瑞士軍隊發給每位士兵一支槍，這槍需要用專用的螺絲起子才能拆解並清理。同時，罐頭食品在軍隊裡變得普遍。瑞士的將軍們決定發給每位士兵一把標準規格的刀子，用來當作螺絲起子和開罐器。

century〔'sɛntʃərɪ〕 n. 世紀　　issue〔'ɪʃu〕 v. 發送；配給
soldier〔'soldʒɚ〕 n. 軍人；士兵　　gun〔gʌn〕 n. 槍
require〔rɪ'kwaɪr〕 v. 需要　　special〔'spɛʃəl〕 adj. 特殊的；專用的
screwdriver〔'skru,draɪvɚ〕 n. 螺絲起子
dismantle〔dɪs'mæntl̩〕 v. 拆解　　clean〔klin〕 v. 清理
at the same time 同時　　canned〔kænd〕 adj. 罐裝的
canned food 罐頭食品　　common〔'kamən〕 adj. 普遍的
general〔'dʒɛnərəl〕 n. 將軍　　standard〔'stændɚd〕 adj. 標準的
serve as 充當　　*can opener* 開罐器

It was a lifesaver for Swiss knife makers, who were struggling to compete with cheaper German imports. In 1884, Carl Elsener, head of the Swiss knife manufacturer Victorinox, seized that opportunity with both hands, and designed a soldier's knife that the army loved. It was a simple knife with one big blade, a can opener, and a screwdriver.

對於正奮力與德國廉價進口刀競爭的瑞士製刀商來說，這消息如同救星。在 1884 年，瑞士刀製造商維氏的總裁，卡爾・埃森納，抓緊了這個機會，並設計了受軍隊所愛的士兵用刀。這把小刀的構造很簡單，有一把大的刀身、一個開罐器和一個螺絲起子。

lifesaver〔'laɪf,sevɚ〕 n. 救星　　maker〔'mekɚ〕 n. 製造者
struggle〔'strʌgl̩〕 v. 掙扎；努力要
compete〔kəm'pit〕 v. 競爭　　German〔'dʒɝmən〕 adj. 德國的
import〔'ɪmport〕 n. 進口品
Carl Elsener 卡爾・埃森納【瑞士刀創始者】
head〔hɛd〕 n. 總裁
manufacturer〔,mænjə'fæktʃərɚ〕 n. 製造業者；製造公司
Victorinox 維氏【瑞士軍刀製造商，卡爾・埃森納以母親的名字維多利亞(Victoria)命名】
seize〔siz〕 v. 抓住　　opportunity〔,apɚ'tjunətɪ〕 n. 機會
with both hands 全力地　　design〔dɪ'zaɪn〕 v. n. 設計
blade〔bled〕 n. 刀片；刀身

A few years after the soldier's knife was issued, the "Schweizer Offizier Messer," or Swiss Officer's Knife, came on the market.

Interestingly, the Officer's Knife was never given to those serving in the army. The Swiss military purchasers considered the new model with a corkscrew for opening wine not "essential for survival," so officers had to buy this new model by themselves. But its special multi-functional design later launched the knife as a global brand. After the Second World War, a great number of American soldiers were stationed in Europe. And as they could buy the Swiss army knife at shops on military bases, they bought huge quantities of them. However, it seems that "Schweizer Offizier Messer" was too difficult for them to say, so they just called it the Swiss army knife, and that is the name it is now known by all over the world.

在發給士兵小刀幾年後，"Schweizer Offizier Messer"，也就是「瑞士軍官刀」，就上市了。有趣的是，軍官刀從來沒發給那些從軍的人。瑞士軍方的採買者認為這種附有開酒拔塞鑽的新刀款「對生存而言並非必要」，所以軍官想要這種新刀款的話，必須自掏腰包購買。但是這款獨有的多功能設計後來讓這款刀發售後，成為全球性的品牌。二次大戰後，很多美國士兵派駐在歐洲。而因為他們能夠在軍事基地的商店買到瑞士刀，他們便大量購買。然而，"Schweizer Offizier Messer"對他們來說似乎太難念了，所以他們就稱它為瑞士軍刀，這個名字也就聞名於全世界。

officer〔ˈɔfəsɚ〕 n. 軍官　　*on the market* 出售；上市
interestingly〔ˈɪntrəstɪŋlɪ〕 adv. 有趣地；有趣的是
serve〔sɝv〕 v. 任職；服役　　*serve in the army* 從軍
military〔ˈmɪləˌtɛrɪ〕 adj. 軍事的　　purchaser〔ˈpɝtʃəsɚ〕 n. 購買者
consider〔kənˈsɪdɚ〕 v. 認為　　model〔ˈmɑdḷ〕 n. 模型；款式
corkscrew〔ˈkɔrkˌskru〕 n. 拔塞鑽；螺絲錐
essential〔əˈsɛnʃəl〕 adj. 必要的；不可或缺的
survival〔səˈvaɪvḷ〕 n. 生存　　multi-〔ˈmʌltɪ〕 多…
functional〔ˈfʌŋkʃənḷ〕 adj. 功能的　　launch〔ˈlɔntʃ〕 n. 發行；發售
global〔ˈglobḷ〕 adj. 全球的　　brand〔brænd〕 n. 品牌
the Second World War 第二次世界大戰
a great number of 很多（= *many*）　　station〔ˈsteʃən〕 v. 派駐
base〔bes〕 n. 基地　　huge〔hjudʒ〕 adj. 龐大的
quantity〔ˈkwɑntətɪ〕 n. 數量　　*too～to*… 太～以致於不…
be known by 以…而知名

41. (**A**) 本文的主旨為何？

(A) 解釋瑞士軍刀的起源。

(B) 介紹瑞士軍刀的功能。

(C) 強調瑞士軍刀的重要性。

(D) 講述一個關於瑞士軍刀設計者的故事。

explain〔ɪkˈsplen〕v. 解釋　　origin〔ˈɔrədʒɪn〕n. 起源
introduce〔ˌɪntrəˈdjus〕v. 介紹
emphasize〔ˈɛmfəˌsaɪz〕v. 強調

42. (**A**) 第三段的 "It" 所指的是什麼？

(A) 瑞士的軍隊需要給每位士兵一把小刀。

(B) 每位瑞士公民口袋裡都有一把小刀。

(C) 瑞士刀和進口刀競爭。

(D) 罐頭食品在瑞士軍隊變得受歡迎。

imported〔ɪmˈportɪd〕adj. 進口的

43. (**D**) 為什麼瑞士軍方沒有購買瑞士軍官刀？

(A) 刀的設計太簡單。

(B) 刀子全賣給了美國士兵

(C) 軍方沒有預算購買。

(D) 新的設計對軍官來說被認為沒有擁有的必要。

sell out 售完　　budget〔ˈbʌdʒɪt〕n. 預算
purchase〔ˈpɜtʃəs〕n. 購買　　***make a purchase*** 購買

44. (**C**) 誰讓文中所討論的刀得到「瑞士軍刀」這個名字？

(A) 卡爾‧埃森納。　　　　(B) 瑞士的軍官。

(C) 美國士兵。　　　　　　(D) 德國商人。

45-48 為題組

　　Space is where our future is—trips to the Moon, Mars and beyond. Most people would think that aside from comets and stars there is little else out there. But, since our space journey started we have left so much trash there that scientists are now concerned that if we don't clean it up, we may all be in mortal danger.

我們的未來在太空——探索月球、火星和更遠地方的旅行。大多數的人會認為除了彗星和星星，沒有什麼其他的東西在太空中。可是，自從我們開始了太空之旅，我們已經在太空留下如此多的垃圾，而現在科學家擔心，如果我們不把它清理乾淨，我們可能全都有生命危險。

space〔spes〕*n.* 太空　　Moon〔mun〕*n.* 月球
Mars〔marz〕*n.* 火星
beyond〔bɪ'jɑnd〕*adv.* 在更遠處；往更遠處
aside from 除了⋯之外　　comet〔'kɑmɪt〕*n.* 彗星
concern〔kən'sɝn〕*v.* 擔心　　mortal〔'mɔrtl̩〕*adj.* 致命的

The first piece of space junk was created in 1964, when the American satellite Vanguard I stopped operating and lost its connection with the ground center. However, since it kept orbiting around the Earth without any consequences, scientists became increasingly comfortable abandoning things that no longer served any useful purpose in space.

第一個太空垃圾在西元 1964 年被創造出來，那時候是美國的先鋒 1 號衛星停止運轉而且失去與地面中心的連線。然而，因為它就這樣一直繞著地球運行而沒有造成任何不良後果，科學家們對於把失去用途的東西丟棄在太空中，也越來越不擔心了。

junk〔dʒʌŋk〕*n.* 垃圾　　satellite〔'sætl̩,aɪt〕*n.* 衛星
vanguard〔'væn,gɑrd〕*n.* 先鋒　　operate〔'ɑpə,ret〕*v.* 運轉
connection〔kə'nɛkʃən〕*n.* 連線
orbit〔'ɔrbɪt〕*v.* 繞⋯的軌道運行
consequence〔'kɑnsə,kwɛns〕*n.* 結果
increasingly〔ɪn'krisɪŋlɪ〕*adv.* 越來越
comfortable〔'kʌmfətəbl̩〕*adj.* 舒服的；自在的
abandon〔ə'bændən〕*v.* 拋棄　　***no longer*** 不再
serve〔sɝv〕*v.* 適合　　purpose〔'pɝpəs〕*n.* 用途

It is estimated that there are currently over 500,000 pieces of man-made trash orbiting the Earth at speeds of up to 17,500 miles per hour. The junk varies from tiny pieces of paint chipped off rockets to cameras, huge fuel tanks, and even odd items like the million-dollar tool kit that astronaut Heidemarie Stefanyshyn-Piper lost during a spacewalk.

　　目前估計有超過 50 萬件人造垃圾，以最高到每小時 1 萬 7 千 5 百英哩的速度，繞著地球的軌道運行。這些垃圾各異其趣，從火箭上剝落的小漆片，到相機、大型燃料箱，甚至有奇特的物品，像是太空人海德瑪莉‧史蒂芬妮欣—派柏在太空漫步時遺失的百萬元工具組。

estimate〔'ɛstə,met〕v. 估計
currently〔'kɝəntlɪ〕adv. 目前；現在
man-made〔'mæn,med〕adj. 人造的　　vary〔'vɛrɪ〕v. 不同
tiny〔'taɪnɪ〕adj. 很小的　　paint〔pent〕n. 油漆
chip〔tʃɪp〕v. 削去 < off >　　fuel〔'fjuəl〕n. 燃料
tank〔tæŋk〕n.（水、油、氣體等）箱
odd〔ɑd〕adj. 奇特的　　kit〔kɪt〕n. 一組工具
astronaut〔'æstrə,nɔt〕n. 太空人
spacewalk〔'spes,wɔk〕n. 太空漫步

The major problem with the space trash is that it may hit working satellites and damage traveling spacecraft. Moreover, pieces of junk may collide with each other and break into fragments which fall back to the Earth. To avoid this, scientists have devised several ways for clearing the sky. Ground stations have been built to monitor larger pieces of space trash to prevent them from crashing into working satellites or space shuttles. Future plans include a cooperative effort among many nations to stop littering in space and to clean up the trash already there.

　　太空垃圾的主要問題是，它可能會擊中運作中的衛星和損害旅途中的太空船。此外，垃圾可能會相撞並破成碎片，落回地球。爲了避免這樣的情況，科學家們已經想出幾個方法來清掃天空。建造地面站來監測大型太空垃圾，來阻止它們衝撞正在運作的衛星或太空梭。未來的計畫，包括許多國家在內的合作成果，要停止在太空亂丟東西，並將已經在那裡的垃圾清除乾淨。

major〔'medʒɚ〕adj. 主要的　　work〔wɝk〕v. 運作
damage〔'dæmɪdʒ〕v. 損害　　spacecraft〔'spes,kræft〕n. 太空船
moreover〔mor'ovɚ〕adv. 此外
collide〔kə'laɪd〕v. 相撞 < with >　　devise〔dɪ'vaɪz〕v. 想出
clear〔klɪr〕v. 從…除去～（障礙物）；把…打掃乾淨
monitor〔'mɑnətɚ〕v. 監測　　prevent〔prɪ'vɛnt〕v. 阻止
space-shuttle〔'spes'ʃʌtl〕n. 太空梭　　include〔ɪn'klud〕v. 包括

cooperative〔koˋɑpəˏretɪv〕*adj.* 合作的
effort〔ˋɛfət〕*n.* 努力的成果
among〔əˋmʌŋ〕*prep.* 在…之中　　litter〔ˋlɪtə〕*v.* 亂丟（東西）

45.（**D**）第一個人造太空垃圾是什麼？

(A) 一台相機。　　　　　　　　(B) 一組工具。
(C) 一個燃料槽。　　　　　　　(D) <u>一架壞掉的衛星。</u>

broken〔ˋbrokən〕*adj.* 損壞的

46.（**C**）爲什麼一開始科學家們「不」擔心太空垃圾？

(A) 它不再適合任何用途。　　　(B) 它離地球有幾百萬英里遠。
(C) <u>它沒有造成任何問題。</u>　　(D) 它被認爲像彗星和星星。

cause〔kɔz〕*v.* 造成　　regard〔rɪˋgɑrd〕*v.* 認爲
similar〔ˋsɪmələ〕*adj.* 類似的

47.（**D**）以下關於太空垃圾的敘述，哪一個是眞的？

(A) 它是大又重的機器。　　　　(B) 它從未改變位置。
(C) 它繞著地球緩慢飄浮。
(D) <u>它可能對太空梭造成問題。</u>

position〔pəˋzɪʃən〕*n.* 位置　　float〔flot〕*v.* 飄浮

48.（**B**）關於太空垃圾的問題，我們已經做了什麼？

(A) 科學家們已清除大部份的垃圾。
(B) <u>嚴密監看大型太空垃圾。</u>
(C) 很多國家一起合作來停止污染太空。
(D) 建造地面站來協助適當地儲存太空垃圾。

closely〔ˋkloslɪ〕*adv.* 嚴密地　　watch〔watʃ〕*v.* 監視
pollute〔pəˋlut〕*v.* 污染　　store〔stor〕*v.* 儲存
properly〔ˋprɑpəlɪ〕*adv.* 適當地

49-52 爲題組

An alcohol breath test (ABT) is often used by the police to find out whether a person is drunk while driving. In the United States, the legal blood alcohol limit is 0.08% for people aged 21 years or older, while people under 21 are not allowed to drive a car with any level of alcohol in their body. A "positive" test result, a result over the legal limit, allows the police to arrest the driver. However, many people who tested positive on the test have claimed that they only drank a "non-alcoholic" energy drink. Can one of these energy drinks really cause someone to test positive on an ABT? Researchers in Missouri set up an experiment to find out.

酒精呼氣測試常用於警察在查明一個人是否酒後駕車。在美國，21歲以上的人合法的血液酒精濃度限制為0.08%，而21歲以下的人不允許開車時體內有任何酒精。陽性的酒測結果，也就是超過合法範圍的結果，可以讓警察逮捕駕駛。然而，許多在測試中被測出陽性的人都聲稱他們只喝了「非酒精的」提神飲料。真的有某種提神飲料會導致某人在酒測時呈陽性反應嗎？密蘇里州的研究員精心設計了一項測試來查明。

alcohol〔'ælkə,hɔl〕*n.* 酒精　　breath〔brɛθ〕*n.* 呼氣
alcohol breath test (ABT) 酒精呼氣測試　　***find out*** 查明
drunk〔drʌŋk〕*adj.* 喝醉了的　　legal〔'ligḷ〕*adj.* 合法的
blood〔blʌd〕*n.* 血液　　limit〔'lɪmɪt〕*n.* 限制
result〔rɪ'zʌlt〕*n.* 結果　　allow〔ə'lau〕*v.* 允許
arrest〔ə'rɛst〕*v.* 逮捕　　test〔tɛst〕*v.* 檢驗
positive〔'pɑzətɪv〕*adj.* 陽性的　　claim〔klem〕*v.* 聲稱
non-alcoholic〔,nʌn,ælkə'hɔlɪk〕*adj.* 非酒精的
energy〔'ɛnɚdʒɪ〕*n.* 精力　　drink〔drɪŋk〕*n.* 飲料
energy drink 提神飲料　　cause〔kɔz〕*v.* 導致
Missouri〔mə'zurɪ〕*n.* 密蘇里州【美國中部之一州】
set up 精心策劃　　experiment〔ɪk'spɛrəmənt〕*n.* 實驗

First, the amount of alcohol in 27 different popular energy drinks was measured. All but one had an alcohol level greater than 0.005%. In nine of the 27 drinks, the alcohol level was at least 0.096%. The scientists then investigated the possibility that these small levels of alcohol could be detected by an ABT. They asked test subjects to drink a full can or bottle of an energy drink and then gave each subject an ABT one minute and 15 minutes after the drink was finished.

　　首先，測量總數為 27 種的提神飲料的酒精濃度。只有一種沒有超過 0.005%
的酒精濃度。27 種裡的 9 種飲料的酒精濃度至少有 0.096%。接下來科學家調
查了這些微量的酒精可以被酒測測出來的可能性。他們請被實驗者喝下一整罐
或一整瓶的提神飲料，然後在他們喝完後一分鐘及15分鐘時為每個受測者進行
酒測。

> amount〔ə'maʊnt〕*n.* 總數　　measure〔'mɛʒɚ〕*v.* 測量
> ***all but*** 幾乎　　great〔gret〕*adj.* 多的；大的
> investigate〔ɪn'vɛstə‚get〕*v.* 調查
> possibility〔‚pasə'bɪlətɪ〕*n.* 可能性　　detect〔dɪ'tɛkt〕*v.* 查出
> subject〔'sʌbdʒɪkt〕*n.* 被實驗者　　can〔kæn〕*n.* 罐
> bottle〔'bɑtḷ〕*n.* 瓶

　　For 11 of the 27 energy drinks, the ABT did detect the presence of
alcohol if the test was given within one minute after the drink was taken.
However, alcohol could not be detected for any of the drinks if the test
was given 15 minutes after the drink was consumed. This shows that when
the test is taken plays a crucial role in the test result. The sooner the test is
conducted after the consumption of these drinks, the more likely a positive
alcohol reading will be obtained.

　　27 種裡的 11 種提神飲料中，如果在喝完飲料的一分鐘測試的話，酒測確
實查出酒精的存在。然而，如果在飲料喝完的 15 分鐘時測試的話，沒有任何飲
料的酒精濃度會被測出。這顯示進行測試的時間點，在測試結果中扮演了很重
要的角色。在喝完這些飲料後越早執行測試，就越有可能得到陽性的度數。

> presence〔'prɛzn̩s〕*n.* 存在
> consume〔kən'sjum〕*v.* 消耗；吃；喝
> crucial〔'kruʃəl〕*adj.* 非常重要的
> ***play a crucial role*** 扮演很重要的角色
> conduct〔kən'dʌkt〕*v.* 執行
> consumption〔kən'sʌmpʃən〕*n.* 消耗
> likely〔'laɪklɪ〕*adj.* 有可能的
> reading〔'ridɪŋ〕*n.* 指示之度數
> obtain〔əb'ten〕*v.* 獲得

49. (**A**) 對一個剛 20 歲的人來說，在美國開車時允許的酒精濃度是多少？

    (A) <u>0.000%。</u>　　　　　　　　(B) 0.005%。

    (C) 0.080%。　　　　　　　　(D) 0.096%。

    turn〔tɜn〕v. 轉變；成為

50. (**B**) 密蘇里州的實驗目的是什麼？

    (A) 介紹一種新的計算血液酒精濃度的方法。

    (B) <u>發掘提神飲料和酒測結果之間的關係。</u>

    (C) 對喝提神飲料加酒的危險性做出警告。

    (D) 挑戰美國目前對駕駛的酒精濃度法規。

    method〔'mɛθəd〕n. 方法

    calculate〔'kælkjə,let〕v. 計算　　discover〔dɪ'skʌvɚ〕v. 發現

    relation〔rɪ'leʃən〕n. 關係　　mix〔mɪks〕v. 混合

    challenge〔'tʃælɪndʒ〕v. 挑戰

51. (**C**) 受實驗者在喝完飲料時被要求做什麼？

    (A) 在實驗室中排成一列。

    (B) 回想飲料的品牌。

    (C) <u>接受酒精呼氣測試。</u>

    (D) 測試他們呼氣的清新度。

    participant〔pə'tɪsəpənt〕n. 參與者　　***line up*** 排成一列

    laboratory〔'læbrə,torɪ〕n. 實驗室　　recall〔rɪ'kɔl〕v. 回想

    brand〔brænd〕n. 品牌　　freshness〔'frɛʃnɪs〕n. 新鮮

52. (**D**) 對提神飲料的消費者而言在接受酒測時什麼是最重要的因素？

    (A) 受測者的年紀。　　　　　　(B) 進行測試的地方。

    (C) 測試所用的儀器。　　　　　(D) <u>執行測試的時間點。</u>

    affect〔ə'fɛkt〕v. 影響　　consumer〔kən'sjumɚ〕n. 消費者

    equipment〔ɪ'kwɪpmənt〕n. 設備；儀器

53-56 為題組

　　The majority of Indian women wear a red dot between their eyebrows. While it is generally taken as an indicator of their marital status, the practice is primarily related to the Hindu religion. The dot goes by different names in different Hindi dialects, and "bindi" is the one that is most commonly known. Traditionally, the dot carries no gender restriction: Men as well as women wear it. However, the tradition of men wearing it has faded in recent times, so nowadays we see a lot more women than men wearing one.

大多數的印度女性在她們的眉間會點上一個紅點。雖然一般會被視爲是顯現她們的婚姻狀態，但這主要還是和印度的習俗有關。這個紅點在印度的方言中有很多不同的名稱，而 bindi 是最常見的說法。傳統上，這個點並不帶有性別的限制，男性女性都可以點。但是，近來男性已經漸漸不會去點它了，所以現在我們會看到眉間點紅點的女性遠多於男性。

> majority〔məˋdʒɔrətɪ〕*n.* 大部分；大多數
> dot〔dɑt〕*n.* 小點　　eyebrow〔ˋaɪˏbraʊ〕*n.* 眉毛
> ***be taken as*** 被視爲　　indicator〔ˋɪndəˏketɚ〕*n.* 指標
> marital〔ˋmærətḷ〕*adj.* 婚姻的　　status〔ˋstetəs〕*n.* 狀態
> practice〔ˋpræktɪs〕*n.* 習俗　　primarily〔ˋpraɪˏmɛrɪlɪ〕*adv.* 主要地
> Hindu〔ˋhɪndu〕*n.* 印度　　religion〔rɪˋlɪdʒən〕*n.* 宗敎
> go〔go〕*v.* 稱爲；叫作　　Hindi〔ˋhɪndi〕*adj.* 印度語的
> dialect〔ˋdaɪəˏlɛkt〕*n.* 方言
> bindi〔ˋbɪndi〕*n.*（印度婦女等的）眉心紅點；眉心飾記
> carry〔ˋkærɪ〕*v.* 具有　　gender〔ˋdʒɛndɚ〕*n.* 性別
> restriction〔rɪˋstrɪkʃən〕*n.* 限制　　***as well as*** 以及
> fade〔fed〕*v.* 凋謝；枯萎

The position of the bindi is standard: center of the forehead, close to the eyebrows. It represents a third, or inner eye. Hindu tradition holds that all people have three eyes: The two outer ones are used for seeing the outside world, and the third one is there to focus inward toward God. As such, the dot signifies piety and serves as a constant reminder to keep God in the front of a believer's thoughts.

眉心紅點有標準的位置：接近眉毛的前額中心點。它代表第三隻眼，或者說，內心之眼。印度的傳統習俗認爲所有的人都有三隻眼睛：兩隻外面的眼睛看外面的世界，第三隻眼睛向內觀照看神明。紅點本身代表虔誠，也一直提醒信徒們要把神明擺在第一位。

standard〔ˋstændəd〕*adj.* 標準的　　forehead〔ˋfɔr,hɛd〕*n.* 前額
represent〔,rɛprɪˋzɛnt〕*v.* 代表　　inner〔ˋɪnə〕*adj.* 內部的
hold〔hold〕*v.* 認為　　inward〔ˋɪnwəd〕*adv.* 向內
as such 就其本身而言　　signify〔ˋsɪgnə,faɪ〕*v.* 表示
piety〔ˋpaɪətɪ〕*n.* 孝順；虔誠
serve as 充當　　constant〔ˋkɑnstənt〕*adj.* 持續的
reminder〔rɪˋmaɪndə〕*n.* 提醒的人或物

　　Red is the traditional color of the dot.　It is said that in ancient times a man would place a drop of blood between his wife's eyes to seal their marriage.　According to Hindu beliefs, the color red is believed to bring good fortune to the married couple.　Today, people go with different colors depending upon their preferences.　Women often wear dots that match the color of their clothes.　Decorative or sticker bindis come in all sizes, colors and variations, and can be worn by young and old, married and unmarried people alike.　Wearing a bindi has become more of a fashion statement than a religious custom.

　　眉心上的點傳統顏色是紅色。據說在古代的時候，男性會滴一滴血在妻子的兩眼間，藉以鞏固他們的婚姻。根據印度信仰，紅色可以為夫妻帶來好運。現今，眉心上的點的顏色則是根據個人的喜好而定。女性會搭配衣服選顏色。裝飾或貼上去的點有各種大小尺寸，顏色和樣式，不管年紀大小，已婚或未婚都可以點上。眉心上的點已經比較像是時尚的展現，而不是代表宗教的習俗了。

drop〔drɑp〕*n.* 一滴　　seal〔sil〕*v.* 使堅固
fortune〔ˋfɔrtʃən〕*n.* 運氣　　***go with*** 適合；相配
depend upon 視…而定；取決於　　preference〔ˋprɛfrəns〕*n.* 偏好
decorative〔ˋdɛkə,retɪv〕*adj.* 裝飾的　　sticker〔ˋstɪkə〕*n.* 貼紙
variation〔,vɛrɪˋeʃən〕*n.* 變化
statement〔ˋstetmənt〕*n.* 陳述；聲明　　custom〔ˋkʌstəm〕*n.* 習俗

53. (**B**) 為何印度人開始在前額上點上紅點？
　　(A) 表示他們的社會階級。　　(B) 表示他們的宗教信仰。
　　(C) 表示他們的財務狀況。　　(D) 強調他們的家庭背景。
indicate〔ˋɪndə,ket〕*v.* 表示
belief〔bɪˋlif〕*n.* 信仰　　display〔dɪˋsple〕*v.* 展示
financial〔faɪˋnænʃəl〕*adj.* 財務的　　highlight〔ˋhaɪ,laɪt〕*v.* 強調

54.（**C**）在印度的傳統中第三隻眼的重要性爲何？
　　(A) 和大自然保持和諧。　　　　(B) 能把外面的世界看得更清楚。
　　(C) 尊敬神明。　　　　　　　　(D) 主觀看待事物。
　　harmony〔'hɑrmənɪ〕*n.* 調和；和諧　　***in harmony with*** 和…調和
　　subjective〔səb'dʒɛktɪv〕*adj.* 主觀的

55.（**D**）爲什麼人工痣本來是紅色？
　　(A) 紅點代表神明的血液。
　　(B) 紅色代表妻子對丈夫的愛。
　　(C) 在一些印度的方言中，bindi 這個字是紅色的意思。
　　(D) 紅色會對結婚的夫婦帶來好運。
　　stand for 代表　　　blessing〔'blɛsɪŋ〕*n.* 幸福；神恩

56.（**B**）以下對於現在點上眉心紅點的敘述何者正確？
　　(A) 眉心紅點可以點在臉上任何一個位置。
　　(B) 眉心紅點現在變成一種裝飾品。
　　(C) 大多數的印度女性已經不喜歡點眉心紅點了。
　　(D) 在印度的男性中，點眉心紅點已經越來越受到歡迎。

第貳部分：非選擇題

一、中譯英

1. 都會地區的高房價對社會產生嚴重的影響。
   The high prices of houses / High housing prices in urban / metropolitan
   areas have a serious effect / influence on society.

2. 政府正推出新的政策，以滿足人們的住房需求。
   The government is putting forth / proposing / launching new policies to
   meet / satisfy ⎰ people's housing demands / needs.
   　　　　　　 ⎱ people's demands / needs for housing.

二、英文作文：

　　In the past, George would sit in the Priority Seat while riding the
MRT.　Sitting there, he would bury his nose in his smartphone, unaware
that he was depriving others more deserving of the seat.　***For instance,***

an elderly man once had to stand for 15 minutes because George didn't care enough to give up his seat.

Then one day, George broke his ankle while playing basketball. His foot was in a cast and he had to walk with a crutch. ***The very next day***, George was on the MRT and couldn't find a seat. He noticed a young girl about his age sitting in a Priority Seat. He wondered, "Doesn't she see me standing here with a crutch?" Apparently, she did not. George was just about to say something when the elderly man sitting next to the girl spoke up.

"Excuse me, dear," the man said kindly to the girl, "but would you mind giving up your seat for that boy with the crutch?" The girl quickly stood up, offering her seat to George. As he sat down, George realized the importance of Priority Seats and learned a valuable lesson about consideration for others.

priority〔praɪˈɔrətɪ〕*n.* 優先權　　***priority seat*** 博愛座
the MRT 捷運（ = *the Mass Rapid Transit*）
bury〔ˈbɛrɪ〕*v.* 埋　　***bury*** *one's* ***nose in*** 埋首於；沈迷於
smartphone〔ˈsmɑrtˌfon〕*n.* 智慧型手機
unaware〔ˌʌnəˈwɛr〕*adj.* 不知道的；未察覺的
deprive〔dɪˈpraɪv〕*v.* 剝奪
deserving〔dɪˈzɝvɪŋ〕*adj.* 應得的< *of* >
for instance 舉例來說　　elderly〔ˈɛldɚlɪ〕*adj.* 年長的
give up *one's* ***seat*** 讓座　　ankle〔ˈæŋkl̩〕*n.* 腳踝
break *one's* ***ankle*** 跌斷腳踝　　cast〔kæst〕*n.* 石膏
in a cast 包石膏　　crutch〔krʌtʃ〕*n.* 拐杖
the next day（過去）隔天　　wonder〔ˈwʌndɚ〕*v.* 猜想
apparently〔əˈpærəntlɪ〕*adv.* 顯然
be (just) about to V. 即將～；正要～　　***speak up*** 大聲說
mind + V-ing 介意～　　offer〔ˈɔfɚ〕*v.* 提供
realize〔ˈriəˌlaɪz〕*v.* 了解；領悟
valuable〔ˈvæljəbl̩〕*adj.* 有價值的；珍貴的
learn a lesson 學到教訓
consideration〔kənˌsɪdəˈreʃən〕*n.* 體諒

102 年學測英文科試題修正意見

※ 今年試題製作嚴謹，只有兩個地方需要修正。

題　　號	修　　正　　意　　見
一、詞彙題 第 4 題	I'm not in *the* position to make any comment on it. → I'm not in *a* position to make any comment on it. * 根據句意，應用不定冠詞 a。
四、閱讀測驗 第 50 題	What *is* the purpose of the Missouri experiment? → What *was* the purpose of the Missouri experiment? * 因爲實驗已經做過，所以應用過去式。

※ 要特別注意，有人會認爲綜合測驗第 20 題答案 (D) distance 也可以，但是如果看到下一句，其中有 are normally charged at a lower rate（價格），就知道應選 (A) cost。

102 年學測英文科試題出題來源

題　　號	出　　　　　處
一、詞彙 第 1~15 題	所有各題對錯答案的選項，均出自大考中心編製的「學科能力英文常考字彙表」，像較難的單字 reluctant（不情願的）、stiff（僵硬的）、prompt（迅速的），都在其中。
二、綜合測驗 第 16~20 題	改寫自 Telephone Numbering Plan（電話數字計畫），敘述區域號碼產生的歷史。
第 21~25 題	改寫自 Determine the Value of a Coin（決定硬幣的價值），說明各種決定硬幣價值的方式。
第 26~30 題	改寫自 PEOPLE AND DISCOVERIES（人物與發現），敘述心理學家如何透過測驗研究孩童的智商。
三、文意選填 第 31~40 題	改寫自 Coral Reef（珊瑚礁），描述珊瑚礁目前所遭受的各種威脅，以及其重要性。
四、閱讀測驗 第 41~44 題	改寫自 From humble tool to global icon（從卑微的工具到全球品牌），描述瑞士軍刀如何從士兵的工具變成世界知名品牌。
第 45~48 題	改寫自 Trash…..In Space?（外太空的垃圾？），描述若垃圾丟到外太空，可能產生的問題。
第 49~52 題	改寫自 Neuroscience For Kids（孩童的神經科學），描述酒精測試的方法及過程。
第 53~56 題	改寫自 Why do Indians have red dots?（爲何印度人有紅點？），描述印度女性眉心紅點的宗教意涵，及相關歷史。

【102 年學測】綜合測驗：16-20 出題來源

—— http://en.wikipedia.org/wiki/Telephone_numbering_plan

Telephone Numbering Plan

Area codes are also known as Numbering Plan Area (NPA) codes and formerly known as Subscriber trunk dialling (STD) codes in the UK. These are typically necessary only when dialed from outside the code area, from mobile phones, and, especially within North America, from within overlay plans. Area codes usually indicate geographical areas within one country that are covered by perhaps hundreds of telephone exchanges, although the correlation to geographical area is becoming obsolete.

The area code is usually preceded in the dial string by either the national access code ("0" for many countries, "1" in USA and Canada) or the international access code and country code. However, this is not always the case, especially when 10-digit dialing is used. For example, in Montreal, where area codes 514, 438, 450 and 579 are in use, users dial 10-digit number (e.g. 514 555 1234), dialing a 1 before this results in a recording advising not to dial a 1 as it is a local call. For non-geographic numbers, as well as mobile telephones outside of the North American Numbering Plan area, the "area code" does not correlate to a particular geographic area. However, until the 1990s, some areas in the United States required the use of a "1" before dialing a 7-digit number within the same area code if the call was beyond the local area, indicating that the caller wished to make what was referred to as a "toll call."

Area codes are often quoted including the national access code, for example a number in London: 020 8765 4321. Users must then correctly interpret the "020" as the code for London. If they call from another number in London, they merely dial 8765 4321, or if dialing from another country, drop the "0" and dial: +44 20 8765 4321.

⋮

【102 年學測】綜合測驗：21-25 出題來源

——http://www.fleur-de-coin.com/articles/coin-value

Determine the Value of a Coin

How much is my coin worth?

Many collectors have come across a particular coin from time to time and wondered whether they had something of great value in their possession. As a matter of fact the age old question "How much is this coin worth?" is probably the most frequently asked question about coins by non-collectors today. In order to assess what your coins are worth, you have to take into account a number of factors or even seek advice from experienced coin collectors. Remember, however, that the mere fact that a coin does not have significant monetary value does not mean that it is not interesting or that it should not form part of your collection.

The factors influencing the value of a coin are the following: rarity, demand, supply, age, condition, and other external factors. Any of these factors can be significant in itself, or it may require some help from one of the other factors. A coin could be common in low grades, indicating a low rarity, but very rare in high grades making it what is called a condition rarity. In such a case, the value of the coin makes a great jump in price as it moves from a lower grade to a higher grade.

Age

Age doesn't always increase the value of a coin. It actually has little effect on it, as there are many coins from the last 20 years or so that are much more valuable than coins from 2,000 years ago. For example, given the choice between a 2,000 year old Roman denarius or a U.S. $20 Gold piece, most non-numismatists will pick the Roman coin as being worth more. Hoever, the U.S. $20 Gold piece is worth considerably more than the Roman denarius.

:

【102 年學測】綜合測驗：26-30 出題來源
——http://www.pbs.org/wgbh/aso/databank/entries/dh05te.html

A Science Odyssey: People and Discoveries

Binet pioneers intelligence testing 1905

French psychologist Alfred Binet (1859-1911) took a different tack than most psychologists of his day: he was interested in the workings of the normal mind rather than the pathology of mental illness. He wanted to find a way to measure the ability to think and reason, apart from education in any particular field.

In 1905 he developed a test in which he had children do tasks such as follow commands, copy patterns, name objects, and put things in order or arrange them properly. He gave the test to Paris schoolchildren and created a standard based on his data. For example, if 70 percent of 8-year-olds could pass a particular test, then success on the test represented the 8-year-old level of intelligence. From Binet's work, the phrase "intelligence quotient," or "IQ," entered the vocabulary. The IQ is the ratio of "mental age" to chronological age, with 100 being average. So, an 8 year old who passes the 10 year-old's test would have an IQ of 10/8 x 100, or 125.

Binet's work set off a passion for testing and in the enthusiasm, a widespread application of tests and scoring measures developed from relatively limited data. Tests based on Binet's test were used by the U.S. Army in sorting out the vast numbers of recruits in World War I. The questions, however, had much more to do with general knowledge than with mental tasks such as sequencing or matching. The results, released after the war, showed that the majority of recruits had a juvenile intelligence. This shocking news played into the hands ofeugenicists who argued that intelligence was an innate, inheritable trait limited to certain types (or nationalities) of people.

【102 年學測】文意選填：31-40 出題來源

——http://en.wikipedia.org/wiki/Coral_reef

Coral Reef

Coral reefs are underwater structures made from calcium carbonate secreted bycorals. Coral reefs are colonies of tiny animals found in marine waters that contain few nutrients. Most coral reefs are built from stony corals, which in turn consist of polypsthat cluster in groups. The polyps are like tiny sea anemones, to which they are closely related. Unlike sea anemones, coral polyps secrete hard carbonate exoskeletons which support and protect their bodies. Reefs grow best in warm, shallow, clear, sunny and agitated waters.

Often called "rainforests of the sea," coral reefs form some of the most diverseecosystems on Earth. They occupy less than 0.1% of the world's ocean surface, about half the area of France, yet they provide a home for 25% of all marine species, including fish, mollusks, worms, crustaceans, echinoderms, sponges, tunicates and other cnidarians. Paradoxically, coral reefs flourish even though they are surrounded by ocean waters that provide few nutrients. They are most commonly found at shallow depths in tropical waters, but deep water and cold water corals also exist on smaller scales in other areas.

Coral reefs deliver ecosystem services to tourism, fisheries and shoreline protection. The annual global economic value of coral reefs has been estimated at US$ 375 billion. However, coral reefs are fragile ecosystems, partly because they are very sensitive to water temperature. They are under threat from climate change, oceanic acidification,blast fishing, cyanide fishing for aquarium fish, overuse of reef resources, and harmful land-use practices, including urban and agricultural runoff and water pollution, which can harm reefs by encouraging excess algal growth.

:

【102 年學測】閱讀測驗：41-44 出題來源

——http://news.bbc.co.uk/2/hi/europe/8172917.stm

From humble tool to global icon

In Switzerland, there is a saying that every good Swiss citizen has one in his or her pocket.

It is an object that is recognised all over the world, and it is globally popular.

But the Swiss army knife had humble beginnings, and, at the start, it wasn't even red.

In the late 19th Century, the Swiss army issued its soldiers with a gun which required a special screwdriver to dismantle and clean it.

At the same time, tinned food was becoming common in army rations. Swiss generals decided to issue each soldier with a standard knife.

It was a life-saver for Swiss knife makers, who were, at the time, struggling to compete with cheaper German imports.

"My great-grandfather started a small business in 1884, 125 years ago," explains Carl Elsener, head of the Swiss knife manufacturer Victorinox.

"He was making knives for farmers, for in the kitchen and so on, and then he heard that the Swiss army wanted a knife for every Swiss soldier."

Carl Elsener senior seized that opportunity with both hands, and designed a knife that the army loved.

"It was a very simple thing," explains his great-grandson. "It had a black handle, one big blade, a tin opener and a screwdriver."
Global cult object

Now, to mark the 125th anniversary, that first knife is on display at an exhibition at the Forum for Swiss History, together with hundreds of other Swiss army knives.

⋮

【102 年學測】閱讀測驗：45-48 出題來源

——http://www.dogonews.com/2012/3/19/trashin-space/page/3

Trash……In Space?

Space is where our future is—Trips to the Moon, Mars and beyond. Most people would think that aside from a few meteors, asteroids, planets, comets and stars there is little else to stand in our way. But, over the last 55 years as humans have been venturing out in space they have left so many debris that scientists are now concerned that if we don't do something to clean it up, we may all be in mortal danger.

The first piece of space junk was created by mistake in 1964, when the connection with the American satellite Vanguard 1 was lost. However, since it kept rotating around the earth's orbit without any consequences, scientists became increasingly comfortable abandoning things that had outlived their use.

According to NASA, there are currently over 500,000 pieces of man-made trash orbiting the earth at speeds of up to 17,500 miles per hour. The debris vary from tiny flecks of paint chipped off of rockets to huge satellites and fuel tanks and even, odd items like the million dollar tool kit that NASA astronaut *Heidemarie Stefanyshyn Piper* lost, whilst on a space walk.

⋮

【102 年學測】閱讀測驗：49-52 出題來源

——http://faculty.washington.edu/chudler/ener.html

Alcohol, Energy Drinks and Breath Testing

Did you know that many popular energy drinks contain ALCOHOL? They do! Even those drinks that are supposed to be "non-alcoholic." In fact, some people who have tested positive on an alcohol breath test have claimed that they only drank a "non-alcoholic" energy drink. Can one of these energy drinks really cause someone to test positive on an alcohol breath test? Researchers in Missouri set up an experiment to find out.

First, the amount of alcohol in 27 different energy drinks was measured. The drinks tested included Red Bull, Full Throttle, andRockstar. All but one drink had a detectable alcohol level (greater than 0.005%). In 13 of the 27 drinks, the alcohol concentration was above 0.06% and in 9 of the 27 drinks, the alcohol concentration was at least 0.096%. (NOTE: In the United States, if the amount of alcohol in a drink is less than 0.5%, it does not have to be listed on the label.)

Although the amount of alcohol in the tested energy drinks was very low, the scientists investigated the possibility that these small levels of alcohol could be detected by a breath test. They asked test subjects to drink a full can or bottle of an energy drink and then gave each subject an alcohol breath test 1 minute and 15 minutes after the drink was finished.

⋮

【102 年學測】閱讀測驗：53-56 出題來源

——http://www.whycenter.com/why-do-indians-have-red-dots/

Why do Indians have red dots?

The majority of Indian women put a red dot between their eyebrows. The red dots signify their martial status—married women put a red dot, while unmarried girls put a small black dot on their forehead. The practice of putting a red dot on the forehead is primarily related to Hindu mythology.

It is believed that after marriage, the primary duty of the woman is to take care of her kin and kith. The red dot, in one hand, symbolizes the good fortune of a married woman, and on the other hand, it reminds her to uphold the sanctity of marriage. At one point of time, every married woman used to religiously follow this norm. However, with the passage of time, the thinking of people has changed dramatically. In the present day, women are educated and financially independent. Some of them do stringently follow the tradition, but for most of them, putting a red dot has become more of a fashion statement rather than a religious custom. Apart from red dot, women prefer the wear dots of different colors and styles, depending upon theirclothing.

⋮

The red dot also helps the Hindu woman or stand out in the crowd. In India, every religion is associated with some characteristic features. For instance, Muslim women compulsorily cover their face with a veil whenever they venture out. Likewise, the red dot on the forehead of a woman denotes that she is a Hindu.

In addition to women, Indian men also wear red dot. Again, this tradition is purely related to Hindu religious beliefs. Normally, after the performance of some rituals or religious ceremonies, the red dot is put on the forehead of men. Also, during festivals like Holi, Diwali, Dusshera and Raksha Bandhan, Indian men wear a red dot on their forehead. Whenever, men go for a long voyage or setup a new business venture or kick-start an important campaign, then too the red dot is placed on their forehead as a mark of good luck.

Priests, monks and saints also put a red dot on their forehead. It is believed that between the eyebrows is present the Ajna Chakra or the third eye, which is the center of spiritual energy. It is also called the Guru's (teacher) seat. By putting a red dot at this point, the monks and priests pay respect to their Guru, and seek their blessings to activate the Chakra and overcome the inner ego.

102年學測英文科非選擇題閱卷評分原則說明

閱卷召集人：劉慶剛（國立台北大學應用外語學系教授）

　　102 學年度學科能力測驗英文考科的非選擇題題型共有「中譯英」和「英文作文」兩大題。第一大題是「中譯英」，題型與過去幾年相同，考生需將兩個中文句子譯成正確、通順、達意的英文，兩題合計為 8 分。第二大題是「英文作文」，考生須從三幅連環圖片的內容，想像第四幅圖片可能的發展，再以至少 120 個單詞寫出一個涵蓋連環圖片內容並有完整結局的故事。

　　關於閱卷籌備工作，依循閱卷標準程序，於 1 月 30 日先召開評分標準訂定會議，由正、副召集人及協同主持人共 14 人，參閱了約 3,000 份來自不同地區的試卷，經過一整天的討論之後，訂定評分標準，選出合適的評分參考樣卷及試閱樣卷，編製成閱卷參考手冊，供閱卷委員共同參閱。

　　2 月 1 日上午 9：00 到 11：00 召開試閱會議，166 位大學教授與會，首先由召集人說明評分標準；接著分組進行試閱，根據閱卷參考手冊的試閱樣卷分別評分，並討論評分準則，務求評分標準一致，確保閱卷品質。為求慎重，試閱會議之後，正、副召集人及協同主持人進行評分標準再確定會議，確認評分原則後才開始正式閱卷。

　　評分標準與歷年相同，在「中譯英」部分，每小題總分 4 分，原則上是每個錯誤扣 0.5 分。「英文作文」的評分標準是依據內容、組織、文法句構、詞彙拼字、體例五個項目給分，字數明顯不足的作文則扣總分 1 分。閱卷時，每份試卷皆會經過兩位委員分別評分，最後成績以二位閱卷委員給分之平均成績爲準。如果第一閱與第二閱分數差距超過差分標準，將再由第三位委員（正、副召集人或協同主持人）評閱。

今年的「中譯英」與「高房價」有關，評量的重點在於考生能否能運用熟悉的詞彙與基本句型將中文翻譯成正確達意的英文句子，所測驗之句型爲高中生熟悉的範圍，詞彙亦控制在大考中心詞彙表四級內之詞彙，中等程度以上的考生，如果能使用正確句型並注意用字、拼字，應能得理想的分數。比如說，「都會區的高房價」若譯出 high house prices in city areas 即可得分；「對社會的嚴重影響」則可翻譯爲 serious effects on society。在選取樣卷時，我們發現有不少考生對於英文詞彙的使用及英文拼字仍有加強的空間，如第二句的「政府」和「政策」看起來是簡單的字，但有不少同學拼錯了，例如：government 少了中間的字母 n，policy 寫成 police 等，也有人把 satisfy 寫成 satisefy。

今年的「英文作文」主題與考生的生活經驗息息相關，大部分的考生應有不錯的發揮。根據作答提示，考生必須根據三幅連環圖片的內容，想像第四幅「空白圖片」可能的發展，寫出一個涵蓋連環圖片內容並有完整結局的故事，文長至少 120 個單詞。評分的考量重點爲作文內容應切題，組織具連慣性、句子結構及用字適切、拼字與標點符號的使用正確得當。

102 年學測英文科試題或答案之反映意見回覆

※ 題號：1

【題目】

1. It rained so hard yesterday that the baseball game had to be _____ until next Saturday.
   (A) surrendered　　　　　(B) postponed
   (C) abandoned　　　　　　(D) opposed

【意見內容】

選項 (C) abandoned 作「放棄」解釋時，應為合理選項。

【大考中心意見回覆】

Longman Dictionary of Contemporary English 的解釋，abandon 的定義是 to stop doing something because there are too many problems and it is impossible to continue。根據本試題題意，評量的是rain 與postpone the baseball game 之間的語意因果關係 (so…that…)，作答線索在空格後 …until next Saturday。選項 (C) abandoned 一詞與題幹until next Saturday 訊息不符，因此，選項 (C) 非正答選項。

※ 題號：6

【題目】

6. The bank tries its best to attract more customers. Its staff members are always available to provide _____ service.
   (A) singular　　　　　　(B) prompt
   (C) expensive　　　　　(D) probable

【意見內容】

1. 銀行外匯、放款、信託業務等幾乎都是個別的服務，尤其現在為了吸引更多的顧客，推出網路銀行提供個別的服務，因此選項 (A) singular 應為合理選項。再者，根據字典字義的解釋，選項 (A) 亦可作為合理選項。

2. 選項 (D) probable 作「可能的」解釋，應為合理選項。

【大考中心意見回覆】

1. 詞彙題的評量重點在於考生能否根據題幹說明，找出最符合題意的選項。本題的作答線索為題幹中 always available 與 prompt service 之間的語意關係。singular service 一詞在特定的情況下可用，但就本題題幹上下文（context），尤其是有 always（經常性）存在與對應的「語意」來觀照，prompt 是唯一「最適當」的答案。

2. probable 一詞的字義應該是「概率的、機率的」意思，並非作為「有可能的」解釋，與 possible 的意思不一樣，因此根據第六題題幹語意，選項 (D) probable 的字詞與題幹題意不符。

※ 題號：7

【題目】

7. John's part-time experience at the cafeteria is good _____ for running his own restaurant.
   (A) preparation　　　　　(B) recognition
   (C) formation　　　　　　(D) calculation

【意見內容】

選項 (C) formation 應為答案。

【大考中心意見回覆】

本題評量考生掌握 …preparation for… 的慣用語用法，考生除了需要掌握 preparation 的語意之外，空格後的介系詞 for 是另一個作答線索。formation 不可與 for 搭配使用，且與題幹語意不符，因此選項 (C) formation 非正答選項。

※ 題號：9

【題目】

9. Standing on the seashore, we saw a _____ of seagulls flying over the ocean before they glided down and settled on the water.
   (A) pack   (B) flock
   (C) herd   (D) school

【意見內容】

選項 (C) herd 應為答案。

【大考中心意見回覆】

本題評量 a flock of 的搭配語用法。考生必須了解並掌握 a flock of seagulls 的用法；空格後的 seagulls 是作答線索。選項 (C) herd 一詞指的是圈養在一起的動物（比如：牛、羊等），海鷗並不屬於此類之動物，因此非本題正答選項。

※ 題號：17

【題目】

An area code is a section of a telephone number which generally represents the geographical area that the phone receiving the call is based in. It is the two or three digits just before the local number. If the number __16__ is in the same area as the number making the call, an area code usually doesn't need to be dialed. The local number, __17__, must always be dialed in its entirety.

The area code was introduced in the United States in 1947. It was created ___18___ the format of XYX, with X being any number between 2-9 and Y being either 1 or 0. Cities and areas with higher populations would have a smaller first and third digit, and 1 as the center digit. New York, being the largest city in the United States, was ___19___ the 212 area code, followed by Los Angeles at 213.

In countries other than the United States and Canada, the area code generally determines the ___20___ of a call. Calls within an area code and often a small group of neighboring area codes are normally charged at a lower rate than outside the area code.

17. (A) in fact　　　　　　　(B) to illustrate
　　(C) at the same time　　　(D) on the other hand

【意見內容】

選項 (C) at the same time 比較有轉折的語氣，應為合理選項。

【大考中心意見回覆】

本題評量的是掌握連貫標記 on the other hand 在篇章中的用法。空格前一句 an area code usually doesn't need to be dialed 與後一句 The local number…must always be dialed in its entirety 之語意呈現對比關係，因此選項 (C) at the same time 非正答選項。

※ 題號：18

【題目】

An area code is a section of a telephone number which generally represents the geographical area that the phone receiving the call is based in. It is the two or three digits just before the local number. If the number ___16___ is in the same area as the number making the call, an area code usually doesn't need to be dialed. The local number, ___17___, must always be dialed in its entirety.

The area code was introduced in the United States in 1947. It was created ___18___ the format of XYX, with X being any number between 2-9 and Y being either 1 or 0. Cities and areas with higher populations would have a smaller first and third digit, and 1 as the center digit. New York, being the largest city in the United States, was ___19___ the 212 area code, followed by Los Angeles at 213.

In countries other than the United States and Canada, the area code generally determines the ___20___ of a call. Calls within an area code and often a small group of neighboring area codes are normally charged at a lower rate than outside the area code.

18. (A) for (B) as (C) by (D) in

【意見內容】

選項 (C) by 應為合理選項。

【大考中心意見回覆】

本題評量的是掌握慣用語 in the format 在篇章中的用法。空格後 …the format of XYX, with X being any number between 2-9 and Y being either 1 or 0；而動詞被動式之後若接 by，則標示其後為動作之主事者（agent），亦即「area code 乃是被 XYX 的形式所創造」，顯與此處上下文意不符，因此選項 (C) by 非本題正答選項。

※ 題號：19

【題目】

An area code is a section of a telephone number which generally represents the geographical area that the phone receiving the call is based in. It is the two or three digits just before the local number. If the number ___16___ is in the same area as the number making the call, an area code usually doesn't need to be dialed. The local number, ___17___, must always be dialed in its entirety.

　　The area code was introduced in the United States in 1947. It was created ___18___ the format of XYX, with X being any number between 2-9 and Y being either 1 or 0. Cities and areas with higher populations would have a smaller first and third digit, and 1 as the center digit. New York, being the largest city in the United States, was ___19___ the 212 area code, followed by Los Angeles at 213.

　　In countries other than the United States and Canada, the area code generally determines the ___20___ of a call. Calls within an area code and often a small group of neighboring area codes are normally charged at a lower rate than outside the area code.

19. (A) reserved　　　　　　　(B) assigned
　　(C) represented　　　　　(D) assembled

【意見內容】

選項 (C) represented 應為合理選項。

【大考中心意見回覆】

本題評量詞彙 assigned 在篇章中的意義和用法。作答線索在空格前一句 Cities and areas with higher populations would have a smaller first and third digit, and 1 as the center digit. 及本句 New York, being the largest city in the United States, was…the 212 area code… 之語意關係。

assign 為雙賓動詞（與 give 同類，如 to give NP1 NP2, to assign NP1 NP2），而根據本句句意和文法結構，New York 為原主動句式之間接賓語(NP1)，空格後之名詞 the 212 area code 則為其直接賓語(NP2)。而 represent 並非雙賓動詞，其被動式之後不能再接其他名詞片語做為賓語，因此語意及文法均不正確，因此選項 (C) represented 非正答選項。

※ 題號：**26**

【題目】

　　French psychologist Alfred Binet (1859-1911) took a different approach from most other psychologists of his day: He was interested in the workings of the ___26___ mind rather than the nature of mental illness. He wanted to find a way to measure the ability to think and reason, apart from education in any particular field. In 1905 he developed a test in which he ___27___ children do tasks such as follow commands, copy patterns, name objects, and put things in order or arrange them properly. He later created a standard of measuring children's intelligence ___28___ the data he had collected from the French children he studied. If 70 percent of 8-year-olds could pass a particular test, then ___29___ on the test represented an 8-year-old's level of intelligence. From Binet's work, the phrase "intelligence quotient" ("IQ") entered the English vocabulary. The IQ is the ratio of "mental age" to chronological age times 100, with 100 ___30___ the average. So, an 8-year-old who passes the 10-year-old's test would have an IQ of 10/8 times 100, or 125.

26. (A) contrary　　　　　　　(B) normal
　　(C) detective　　　　　　　(D) mutual

【意見內容】

　　選項 (C) detective 應為答案。

【大考中心意見回覆】

　　本題評量詞彙 normal 在篇章中的語意及用法。作答線索在空格前 ...the workings of ... mind 和空格後 ...rather than the nature of mental illness 之語意，尤其是 rather than 暗示前後的語意應是對比關係，因此只有選項 (B) normal 才符合本句語意。

※ 題號：27

【題目】

　　French psychologist Alfred Binet (1859-1911) took a different approach from most other psychologists of his day: He was interested in the workings of the ___26___ mind rather than the nature of mental illness.　He wanted to find a way to measure the ability to think and reason, apart from education in any particular field.　In 1905 he developed a test in which he ___27___ children do tasks such as follow commands, copy patterns, name objects, and put things in order or arrange them properly.　He later created a standard of measuring children's intelligence ___28___ the data he had collected from the French children he studied.　If 70 percent of 8-year-olds could pass a particular test, then ___29___ on the test represented an 8-year-old's level of intelligence.　From Binet's work, the phrase "intelligence quotient" ("IQ") entered the English vocabulary.　The IQ is the ratio of "mental age" to chronological age times 100, with 100 ___30___ the average.　So, an 8-year-old who passes the 10-year-old's test would have an IQ of 10/8 times 100, or 125.

27. (A) had　　　　　　　　(B) kept
　　(C) wanted　　　　　　 (D) asked

【意見內容】

選項 (D) asked 應為合理選項。

【大考中心意見回覆】

本題測驗詞彙 had 的使役動詞用法。作答線索在空格後...children do tasks such as follow commands, copy patterns, name objects, and put things in order or arrange them properly 之語意及該句中 do、copy、put 三個字詞皆爲原形動詞,因此空格中必須塡入使役動詞 had 一詞。若使用選項 (D) asked,則後面的動詞應爲不定詞用法(to + 原形動詞),因此選項 (D) asked 非本題正答選項。

※ 題號:**29**

【題目】

French psychologist Alfred Binet (1859-1911) took a different approach from most other psychologists of his day: He was interested in the workings of the ___26___ mind rather than the nature of mental illness. He wanted to find a way to measure the ability to think and reason, apart from education in any particular field. In 1905 he developed a test in which he ___27___ children do tasks such as follow commands, copy patterns, name objects, and put things in order or arrange them properly. He later created a standard of measuring children's intelligence ___28___ the data he had collected from the French children he studied. If 70 percent of 8-year-olds could pass a particular test, then ___29___ on the test represented an 8-year-old's level of intelligence. From Binet's work, the phrase "intelligence quotient" ("IQ") entered the English vocabulary. The IQ is the ratio of "mental age" to chronological age times 100, with 100 ___30___ the average. So, an 8-year-old who passes the 10-year-old's test would have an IQ of 10/8 times 100, or 125.

29. (A) success　　　　　　　　(B) objection
　　(C) agreement　　　　　　　(D) discovery

【意見內容】

1. 原本第 29 題空格後之 an 8-year-old's level 應為 the 8-year-old's level 較為合適；而 From Binet's work, the phrase "intelligence quotinet"("IQ") entered the English vocabulary. 不合英文語法，原文所用的句子 Following Binet's work, the phrase "intelligence quotinet"("IQ") entered the English vocabulary.，"following" 做為「由於」解釋，較符合文意。本題應不予計分。

2. 根據字典的字詞解釋，選項 (C) agreement 應為合理選項。

3. 選項 (B) objection 應為答案。

【大考中心意見回覆】

1. 空格後文字…an 8-year-old's level of intelligence 的 an 雖與原文使用的 the 不同，但因英文中的 an、a、the 皆可做為 generic（全部）使用，故在解讀與作答上並不會造成困難，因為本題之作答線索在於空格前的句子 If 70 percent of 8-year-olds could pass a particular test 與空格後的 …on the test represented an 8-year-old's level of intelligence 之語意連貫關係。再者，From Binet's work, the phrase "intelligence quotinet"("IQ") entered the English vocabulary. 之句構及語法並無不妥，亦不影響考生作答。

2. 選項 (C) agreement 語意無法與空格後的 on the test represented… 搭配使用，因為其語意將變成「對該測驗的意見/看法一致」，而非指測驗的結果。若要使用 agreement 一詞則可能需要加上 of the test results 等字詞較符合語法。

3. 本題之作答線索在於空格前的句子 If 70 percent of 8-year-olds could pass a particular test 與空格後的 …on the test represented

an 8-year-old's level of intelligence 之語意連貫關係。以英文一般常見的用法，didn't pass an exam 是 failure，pass a test 也就與 success on the test 密切呼應。選項 (B) objection 與文意發展不符，因此非本題正答。

※ 題號：30

【題目】

French psychologist Alfred Binet (1859-1911) took a different approach from most other psychologists of his day: He was interested in the workings of the __26__ mind rather than the nature of mental illness. He wanted to find a way to measure the ability to think and reason, apart from education in any particular field. In 1905 he developed a test in which he __27__ children do tasks such as follow commands, copy patterns, name objects, and put things in order or arrange them properly. He later created a standard of measuring children's intelligence __28__ the data he had collected from the French children he studied. If 70 percent of 8-year-olds could pass a particular test, then __29__ on the test represented an 8-year-old's level of intelligence. From Binet's work, the phrase "intelligence quotient" ("IQ") entered the English vocabulary. The IQ is the ratio of "mental age" to chronological age times 100, with 100 __30__ the average. So, an 8-year-old who passes the 10-year-old's test would have an IQ of 10/8 times 100, or 125.

30. (A) is   (B) are   (C) been   (D) being

【意見內容】

選項 (C) been 應為答案。

【大考中心意見回覆】

本題測驗分詞片語 with...being 之句法結構。空格前 The IQ is the ratio of "mental age" to chronological age times 100...，以及空格後 with 100... the average 之分詞片語結構。選項 (C) been 與此處文法及語意均不符。

※ 題號：**42**

【題目】

The Swiss army knife is a popular device that is recognized all over the world. In Switzerland, there is a saying that every good Swiss citizen has one in his or her pocket. But the knife had humble beginnings.

In the late nineteenth century, the Swiss army issued its soldiers a gun that required a special screwdriver to dismantle and clean it. At the same time, canned food was becoming common in the army. Swiss generals decided to issue each soldier a standard knife to serve both as a screwdriver and a can opener.

It was a lifesaver for Swiss knife makers, who were struggling to compete with cheaper German imports. In 1884, Carl Elsener, head of the Swiss knife manufacturer Victorinox, seized that opportunity with both hands, and designed a soldier's knife that the army loved. It was a simple knife with one big blade, a can opener, and a screwdriver.

A few years after the soldier's knife was issued, the "Schweizer Offizier Messer," or Swiss Officer's Knife, came on the market.

Interestingly, the Officer's Knife was never given to those serving in the army. The Swiss military purchasers considered the new model with a corkscrew for opening wine not "essential for survival," so officers had to buy this new model by themselves. But its special multi-functional design later launched the knife as a global brand. After the Second World War, a great number of American soldiers were stationed in Europe. And as they could buy the Swiss army knife at shops on military bases, they bought huge quantities of them. However, it seems that "Schweizer Offizier Messer" was too difficult for them to say, so they just called it the Swiss army knife, and that is the name it is now known by all over the world.

42. What does "It" in the third paragraph refer to?
　　(A) The Swiss army needed a knife for every soldier.
　　(B) Every good Swiss citizen had a knife in his pocket.
　　(C) Swiss knives were competing with imported knives.
　　(D) Canned food was becoming popular in the Swiss army.

【意見內容】

　1. 根據文章內容，選項 (D) 應為合理選項。
　2. 選項 (C) 應為答案。

【大考中心意見回覆】

　本題測驗考生是否能解讀上下文中指代詞（it）的篇章功能。作答線索是第二段最後一句 Swiss generals decided to issue each soldier a standard knife to serve both as a screwdriver and a can opener.。根據文章結構，第二段最後一個句子是第二段文意的總結，而第三段第一個句子中的 It 所回指的是第二段的文意總結，因此，除了選項 (A) 外，其餘選項皆與文意發展不符，非合理選項。

101 年大學入學學科能力測驗試題
英文考科

第壹部分：單選題（占 72 分）

一、詞彙（佔 15 分）

說明：第 1 題至第 15 題，每題有 4 個選項，其中只有一個是正確或最適當的
選項，請畫記在答案卡之「選擇題答案區」。各題答對者，得 1 分；
答錯、未作答或畫記多於一個選項者，該題以零分計算。

1. The ending of the movie did not come as a _____ to John because
he had already read the novel that the movie was based on.
(A) vision　　　(B) focus　　　(C) surprise　　　(D) conclusion

2. In order to stay healthy and fit, John exercises _____. He works
out twice a week in a gym.
(A) regularly　　　(B) directly　　　(C) hardly　　　(D) gradually

3. Traveling is a good way for us to _____ different cultures and
broaden our horizons.
(A) assume　　　(B) explore　　　(C) occupy　　　(D) inspire

4. The story about Hou-I shooting down nine suns is a well-known
Chinese _____, but it may not be a true historical event.
(A) figure　　　(B) rumor　　　(C) miracle　　　(D) legend

5. According to recent research, children under the age of 12 are
generally not _____ enough to recognize risk and deal with
dangerous situations.
(A) diligent　　　(B) mature　　　(C) familiar　　　(D) sincere

6. Helen let out a sigh of _____ after hearing that her brother was
not injured in the accident.
(A) hesitation　　　(B) relief　　　(C) sorrow　　　(D) triumph

7. Research suggests that people with outgoing personalities tend to be more _____, often expecting that good things will happen.
   (A) efficient (B) practical (C) changeable (D) optimistic

8. No one could beat Paul at running. He has won the running championship _____ for three years.
   (A) rapidly (B) urgently (C) continuously (D) temporarily

9. If you fly from Taipei to Tokyo, you'll be taking an international, rather than a _____ flight.
   (A) liberal (B) domestic (C) connected (D) universal

10. Jack is very proud of his fancy new motorcycle. He has been _____ to all his friends about how cool it looks and how fast it runs.
    (A) boasting (B) proposing (C) gossiping (D) confessing

11. The ideas about family have changed _____ in the past twenty years. For example, my grandfather was one of ten children in his family, but I am the only child.
    (A) mutually (B) narrowly (C) considerably (D) scarcely

12. The chairperson of the meeting asked everyone to speak up instead of _____ their opinions among themselves.
    (A) reciting (B) giggling (C) murmuring (D) whistling

13. Although Mr. Chen is rich, he is a very _____ person and is never willing to spend any money to help those who are in need.
    (A) absolute (B) precise (C) economic (D) stingy

14. If you want to know what your dreams mean, now there are websites you can visit to help you _____ them.
    (A) overcome (B) interpret (C) transfer (D) revise

15. The memory _____ of the new computer has been increased so that more information can be stored.
    (A) capacity (B) occupation (C) attachment (D) machinery

二、綜合測驗（占 15 分）

說明：第 16 題至第 30 題，每題一個空格，請依文意選出最適當的一個選項，
　　　請畫記在答案卡之「選擇題答案區」。各題答對者，得 1 分；答錯、
　　　未作答、或畫記多於一個選項者，該題以零分計算。

Kizhi is an island on Lake Onega in Karelia, Russia, with a beautiful
collection of wooden churches and houses. It is one of the most popular
tourist ___16___ in Russia and a United Nations Educational, Scientific,
and Cultural Organization (UNESCO) World Heritage Site.

The island is about 7 km long and 0.5 km wide. It is surrounded by
about 5,000 other islands, some of ___17___ are just rocks sticking out
of the ground.

The entire island of Kizhi is, ___18___, an outdoor museum of
wooden architecture created in 1966. It contains many historically
significant and beautiful wooden structures, ___19___ windmills,
boathouses, chapels, fish houses, and homes. The jewel of the architecture
is the 22-domed Transfiguration Church, built in the early 1700s. It is
about 37 m tall, ___20___ it one of the tallest log structures in the world.
The church was built with pine trees brought from the mainland, which
was quite common for the 18th century.

16. (A) affairs　　　(B) fashions　　　(C) industries　　(D) attractions
17. (A) them　　　　(B) that　　　　　(C) those　　　　(D) which
18. (A) in fact　　　(B) once again　　　(C) as usual　　　(D) for instance
19. (A) except　　　(B) besides　　　　(C) including　　　(D) regarding
20. (A) make　　　　(B) making　　　　(C) made　　　　(D) to make

There was once a time when all human beings were gods. However,
they often took their divinity for granted and ___21___ abused it. Seeing
this, Brahma, the chief god, decided to take their divinity away from
them and hide it ___22___ it could never be found.

Brahma called a council of the gods to help him decide on a place to hide the divinity. The gods suggested that they hide it ___23___ in the earth or take it to the top of the highest mountain. But Brahma thought ___24___ would do because he believed humans would dig into the earth and climb every mountain, and eventually find it. So, the gods gave up.

Brahma thought for a long time and finally decided to hide their divinity in the center of their own being, for humans would never think to ___25___ it there. Since that time humans have been going up and down the earth, digging, climbing, and exploring—searching for something already within themselves.

21. (A) yet　　　(B) even　　　(C) never　　　(D) rather
22. (A) though　(B) because　(C) where　　　(D) when
23. (A) close　　(B) apart　　(C) deep　　　　(D) hard
24. (A) each　　(B) more　　(C) any　　　　(D) neither
25. (A) look for　(B) get over　(C) do without　(D) bump into

In the fall of 1973, in an effort to bring attention to the conflict between Egypt and Israel, *World Hello Day* was born. The objective is to promote peace all over the world, and to ___26___ barriers between every nationality. Since then, *World Hello Day*—November 21st of every year— ___27___ observed by people in 180 countries.

Taking part couldn't be ___28___. All one has to do is say hello to 10 people on the day. However, in response to the ___29___ of this event, the concepts of fostering peace and harmony do not have to be confined to one day a year. We can ___30___ the spirit going by communicating often and consciously. It is a simple act that anyone can do and it reminds us that communication is more effective than conflict.

26. (A) skip over　(B) come across　(C) look into　　(D) break down
27. (A) is　　　　(B) has been　　(C) was　　　　(D) had been
28. (A) quicker　　(B) sooner　　　(C) easier　　　(D) better
29. (A) aim　　　(B) tone　　　　(C) key　　　　(D) peak
30. (A) push　　　(B) keep　　　　(C) bring　　　(D) make

三、文意選填（占 10 分）

說明：第 31 題至第 40 題，每題一個空格，請依文意在文章後所提供的 (A) 到
　　　(J) 選項中分別選出最適當者，並將其英文字母代號畫記在答案卡之「選
　　　擇題答案區」。各題答對者，得 1 分；答錯、未作答或畫記多於一個選
　　　項者，該題以零分計算。

　　Generally there are two ways to name typhoons: the number-based
convention and the list-based convention. Following the number-based
convention, typhoons are coded with ____31____ types of numbers such as
a 4-digit or a 6-digit code. For example, the 14th typhoon in 2003 can
be labeled either as Typhoon 0314 or Typhoon 200314. The ____32____
of this convention, however, is that a number is hard to remember. The
list-based convention, on the other hand, is based on the list of typhoon
names compiled in advance by a committee, and is more widely used.

　　At the very beginning, only ____33____ names were used because at
that time typhoons were named after girlfriends or wives of the experts
on the committee. In 1979, however, male names were also included
because women protested against the original naming ____34____ for
reasons of gender equality.

　　In Asia, Western names were used until 2000 when the committee
decided to use Asian names to ____35____ Asians' awareness of typhoons.
The names were chosen from a name pool ____36____ of 140 names, 10
each from the 14 members of the committee. Each country has its unique
naming preferences. Korea and Japan ____37____ animal names and China
likes names of gods such as Longwang (dragon king) and Fengshen (god
of the wind).

　　After the 140 names are all used in order, they will be ____38____. But
the names can be changed. If a member country suffers great damage
from a certain typhoon, it can ____39____ that the name of the typhoon be
deleted from the list at the annual committee meeting. For example, the
names of Nabi by South Korea, and Longwang by China were ____40____

with other names in 2007.　The deletion of both names was due to the severe damage caused by the typhoons bearing the names.

(A) request　　　(B) favor　　　(C) disadvantage　(D) composed
(E) recycled　　　(F) practice　　(G) replaced　　　(H) raise
(I) various　　　(J) female

四、閱讀測驗（占 32 分）

說明：　第 41 題至第 56 題，每題請分別根據各篇文章之文意選出最適當的一個
　　　　選項，請畫記在答案卡之「選擇題答案區」。各題答對者，得 2 分；答
　　　　錯、未作答或畫記多於一個選項者，該題以零分計算。

41-44 爲題組

　　The kilt is a skirt traditionally worn by Scottish men.　It is a tailored garment that is wrapped around the wearer's body at the waist starting from one side, around the front and back and across the front again to the opposite side.　The overlapping layers in front are called "aprons." Usually, the kilt covers the body from the waist down to just above the knees.　A properly made kilt should not be so loose that the wearer can easily twist the kilt around the body, nor should it be so tight that it causes bulging of the fabric where it is buckled.　Underwear may be worn as one prefers.

　　One of the most distinctive features of the kilt is the pattern of squares, or sett, it exhibits.　The association of particular patterns with individual families can be traced back hundreds of years.　Then in the Victorian era (19th century), weaving companies began to systematically record and formalize the system of setts for commercial purposes.　Today there are also setts for States and Provinces, schools and universities, and general patterns that anybody can wear.

　　The kilt can be worn with accessories.　On the front apron, there is often a kilt pin, topped with a small decorative family symbol.　A small knife can be worn with the kilt too.　It typically comes in a very wide variety, from fairly plain to quite elaborate silver- and jewel-ornamented designs. The kilt can also be worn with a sporran, which is the Gaelic word for pouch or purse.

41. What's the proper way of wearing the kilt?
    (A) It should be worn with underwear underneath it.
    (B) It should loosely fit on the body to be turned around.
    (C) It should be long enough to cover the wearer's knees.
    (D) It should be wrapped across the front of the body two times.

42. Which of the following is a correct description about setts?
    (A) They were once symbols for different Scottish families.
    (B) They were established by the government for business purposes.
    (C) They represented different States and Provinces in the 19th century.
    (D) They used to come in one general pattern for all individuals and institutions.

43. Which of the following items is NOT typically worn with the kilt for decoration?
    (A) A pin.　　　　　　　　　　(B) A purse.
    (C) A ruby apron.　　　　　　　(D) A silver knife.

44. What is the purpose of this passage?
    (A) To introduce a Scottish garment.
    (B) To advertise a weaving pattern.
    (C) To persuade men to wear kilts.
    (D) To compare a skirt with a kilt.

45-48 為題組

　　Wesla Whitfield, a famous jazz singer, has a unique style and life story, so I decided to see one of her performances and interview her for my column.

I went to a nightclub in New York and watched the stage lights go up. After the band played an introduction, Wesla Whitfield wheeled herself onstage in a wheelchair. As she sang, Whitfield's voice was so powerful and soulful that everyone in the room forgot the wheelchair was even there.

At 57, Whitfield is small and pretty, witty and humble, persistent and philosophical. Raised in California, Whitfield began performing in public at age 18, when she took a job as a singing waitress at a pizza parlor. After studying classical music in college, she moved to San Francisco and went on to sing with the San Francisco Opera Chorus.

Walking home from rehearsal at age 29, she was caught in the midst of a random shooting that left her paralyzed from the waist down. I asked how she dealt with the realization that she'd never walk again, and she confessed that initially she didn't want to face it. After a year of depression she tried to kill herself. She was then admitted to a hospital for treatment, where she was able to recover.

Whitfield said she came to understand that the only thing she had lost in this misfortunate event was the ability to walk. She still possessed her most valuable asset—her mind. Pointing to her head, she said, "Everything important is in here. The only real disability in life is losing your mind." When I asked if she was angry about what she had lost, she admitted to being frustrated occasionally, "especially when everybody's dancing, because I love to dance. But **when that happens** I just remove myself so I can focus instead on what I can do."

45. In which of the following places has Wesla Whitfield worked?
    (A) A college.　　　　　　　(B) A hospital.
    (C) A pizza parlor.　　　　　(D) A news agency.

46. What does "**when that happens**" mean in the last paragraph?

   (A) When Wesla is losing her mind.

   (B) When Wesla is singing on the stage.

   (C) When Wesla is going out in her wheelchair.

   (D) When Wesla is watching other people dancing.

47. Which of the following statements is true about Wesla Whitfield's physical disability?

   (A) It was caused by a traffic accident.

   (B) It made her sad and depressed at first.

   (C) It seriously affected her singing career.

   (D) It happened when she was a college student.

48. What advice would Wesla most likely give other disabled people?

   (A) Ignore what you have lost and make the best use of what you have.

   (B) Be modest and hard-working to earn respect from other people.

   (C) Acquire a skill so that you can still be successful and famous.

   (D) Try to sing whenever you feel upset and depressed.

49-52 為題組

Forks trace their origins back to the ancient Greeks. Forks at that time were fairly large with two tines that aided in the carving of meat in the kitchen. The tines prevented meat from twisting or moving during carving and allowed food to slide off more easily than it would with a knife.

By the 7th century A.D., royal courts of the Middle East began to use forks at the table for dining. From the 10th through the 13th centuries, forks were fairly common among the wealthy in Byzantium. In the 11th century, a Byzantine wife brought forks to Italy; however, they were not widely adopted there until the 16th century. Then in 1533, forks were brought from Italy to France. The French were also slow to accept forks, for using them was thought to be awkward.

In 1608, forks were brought to England by Thomas Coryate, who saw them during his travels in Italy. The English first ridiculed forks as being unnecessary. "Why should a person need a fork when God had given him hands?" they asked. Slowly, however, forks came to be adopted by the wealthy as a symbol of their social status. They were prized possessions made of expensive materials intended to impress guests. By the mid 1600s, eating with forks was considered fashionable among the wealthy British.

Early table forks were modeled after kitchen forks, but small pieces of food often fell through the two tines or slipped off easily. In late 17th century France, larger forks with four curved tines were developed. The additional tines made diners less likely to drop food, and the curved tines served as a scoop so people did not have to constantly switch to a spoon while eating. By the early 19th century, four-tined forks had also been developed in Germany and England and slowly began to spread to America.

49. What is the passage mainly about?
    (A) The different designs of forks.
    (B) The spread of fork-aided cooking.
    (C) The history of using forks for dining.
    (D) The development of fork-related table manners.

50. By which route did the use of forks spread?
    (A) Middle East→Greece→England→Italy→France
    (B) Greece→Middle East→Italy→France→England

(C) Greece→Middle East→France→Italy→Germany

(D) Middle East→France→England→Italy→Germany

51. How did forks become popular in England?

(A) Wealthy British were impressed by the design of forks.

(B) Wealthy British thought it awkward to use their hands to eat.

(C) Wealthy British gave special forks to the nobles as luxurious gifts.

(D) Wealthy British considered dining with forks a sign of social status.

52. Why were forks made into a curved shape?

(A) They could be used to scoop food as well.

(B) They looked more fashionable in this way.

(C) They were designed in this way for export to the US.

(D) They ensured the meat would not twist while being cut.

53-56 為題組

Animals are a favorite subject of many photographers. Cats, dogs, and other pets top the list, followed by zoo animals. However, because it's hard to get them to sit still and "perform on command," some professional photographers refuse to photograph pets.

One way to get an appealing portrait of a cat or dog is to hold a biscuit or treat above the camera. The animal's longing look toward the food will be captured by the camera, but the treat won't appear in the picture because it's out of the camera's range. When you show the picture to your friends afterwards, they'll be impressed by your pet's loving expression.

If you are using fast film, you can take some good, quick shots of a pet by simply snapping a picture right after calling its name. You'll get a different expression from your pet using this technique. Depending on your pet's mood, the picture will capture an interested, curious expression or possibly a look of annoyance, especially if you've awakened it from a nap. Taking pictures of zoo animals requires a little more patience. After all, you can't wake up a lion! You may have to wait for a while until the animal does something interesting or moves into a position for you to get a good shot. When photographing zoo animals, don't get too close to the cages, and never tap on the glass or throw things between the bars of a cage. Concentrate on shooting some good pictures, and always respect the animals you are photographing.

53. Why do some professional photographers NOT like to take pictures of pets?
    (A) Pets may not follow orders.
    (B) Pets don't want to be bothered.
    (C) Pets may not like photographers.
    (D) Pets seldom change their expressions.

54. What is the use of a biscuit in taking pictures of a pet?
    (A) To capture a cute look.
    (B) To create a special atmosphere.
    (C) To arouse the appetite of the pet.
    (D) To keep the pet from looking at the camera.

55. What is the advantage of calling your pet's name when taking a shot of it?
    (A) To help your pet look its best.
    (B) To make sure that your pet sits still.
    (C) To keep your pet awake for a while.
    (D) To catch a different expression of your pet.

56. In what way is photographing zoo animals different from
    photographing pets?
    (A) You need to have fast film.
    (B) You need special equipment.
    (C) You need to stay close to the animals.
    (D) You need more time to watch and wait.

第貳部份：非選擇題（占 28 分）

一、中譯英（占 8 分）

說明： 1. 請將以下中文句子譯成正確、通順、達意的英文，並將答案寫在「答
          案卷」上。
       2. 請依序作答，並標明題號。每題 4 分，共 8 分。

 1. 近年來，許多臺灣製作的影片已經受到國際的重視。
 2. 拍攝這些電影的地點也成為熱門的觀光景點。

二、英文作文（占 20 分）

說明： 1. 依提示在「答案卷」上寫一篇英文作文。
       2. 文長至少 120 個單詞（words）。

提示：你最好的朋友最近迷上電玩，因此常常熬夜，疏忽課業，並受到父母
      的責罵。你（英文名字必須假設為 Jack 或 Jill）打算寫一封信給他/
      她（英文名字必須假設為 Ken 或 Barbie），適當地給予勸告。

請注意：必須使用上述的 Jack 或 Jill 在信末署名，**不得使用自己的真實中文
         或英文名字**。

101年度學科能力測驗英文科試題詳解

第壹部分：單選題

一、詞彙：

1. (**C**) The ending of the movie did not come as a <u>surprise</u> to John because he had already read the novel that the movie was based on.
   這部電影的結局約翰並不<u>驚訝</u>，因為他已經看過這部電影的原著小說。
   - (A) vision〔'vɪʒən〕*n.* 視力
   - (B) focus〔'fokəs〕*n.* 焦點
   - (C) ***surprise***〔sə'praɪz〕*n.* 驚訝
   - (D) conclusion〔kən'kluʒən〕*n.* 結論

   be based on 以～為基礎

2. (**A**) In order to stay healthy and fit, John exercises <u>regularly</u>. He works out twice a week in a gym.
   為了保持健康，約翰<u>規律</u>運動。他一個禮拜去健身房運動兩次。
   - (A) ***regularly***〔'rɛgjələlɪ〕*adv.* 規律地
   - (B) directly〔də'rɛktlɪ〕*adv.* 直接地
   - (C) hardly〔'hɑrdlɪ〕*adv.* 幾乎不
   - (D) gradually〔'grædʒʊəlɪ〕*adv.* 逐漸地

   fit〔fɪt〕*adj.* 健康的　　***work out*** 運動　　gym〔dʒɪm〕*n.* 健身房

3. (**B**) Traveling is a good way for us to <u>explore</u> different cultures and broaden our horizons.
   旅行是個使我們<u>探索</u>不同文化和拓展視野的好方法。
   - (A) assume〔ə'sjum〕*v.* 假設
   - (B) ***explore***〔ɪk'splor〕*v.* 探索
   - (C) occupy〔'ɑkjə,paɪ〕*v.* 佔據
   - (D) inspire〔ɪn'spaɪr〕*v.* 激勵

   culture〔'kʌltʃɚ〕*n.* 文化　　broaden〔'brɔdn̩〕*v.* 拓展
   horizons〔hə'raɪzn̩z〕*n. pl.* 知識範圍

4. (**D**) The story about Hou-I shooting down nine suns is a well-known
Chinese <u>legend</u>, but it may not be a true historical event.
關於后羿射下九個太陽的故事，是中國著名的<u>傳說</u>，但是它可能不
是真正的歷史事件。
(A) figure〔'fɪgjɚ〕*n.* 人物　　　　(B) rumor〔'rumɚ〕*n.* 謠言
(C) miracle〔'mɪrəkḷ〕*n.* 奇蹟　　(D) ***legend***〔'lɛdʒənd〕*n.* 傳說
shoot down 射下　　well-known〔'wɛl'non〕*adj.* 著名的
historical〔hɪs'tɔrɪkḷ〕*adj.* 歷史的　　event〔ɪ'vɛnt〕*n.* 事件

5. (**B**) According to recent research, children under the age of 12 are
generally not <u>mature</u> enough to recognize risk and deal with
dangerous situations. 根據最近的研究，十二歲以下的孩童通常
還沒<u>成熟</u>到可以認清危險，以及處理危險的情況。
(A) diligent〔'dɪlədʒənt〕*adj.* 勤勉的
(B) ***mature***〔mə'tʃur〕*adj.* 成熟的　(C) familiar〔fə'mɪljɚ〕*adj.* 熟悉的
(D) sincere〔sɪn'sɪr〕*adj.* 真誠的
recent〔'risn̩t〕*adj.* 最近的　　research〔rɪ'sɜtʃ〕*n.* 研究
recognize〔'rɛkəg͵naɪz〕*v.* 認出　　risk〔rɪsk〕*n.* 危險
deal with 處理　　situation〔͵sɪtʃu'eʃən〕*n.* 情況

6. (**B**) Helen let out a sigh of <u>relief</u> after hearing that her brother was not
injured in the accident.
海倫聽到她的哥哥在這場意外中沒有受傷之後，<u>鬆了一口氣</u>。
(A) hesitation〔͵hɛzə'teʃən〕*n.* 猶豫
(B) ***relief***〔rɪ'lif〕*n.* 放心；鬆了一口氣
(C) sorrow〔'saro〕*n.* 傷心　　　　(D) triumph〔'traɪəmf〕*n.* 勝利
let out 發出　　sigh〔saɪ〕*n.* 嘆氣
injure〔'ɪndʒɚ〕*v.* 傷害；使受傷　　accident〔'æksədənt〕*n.* 意外

7. (**D**) Research suggests that people with outgoing personalities tend to
be more <u>optimistic</u>, often expecting that good things will happen.
研究指出，個性外向的人通常比較<u>樂觀</u>，常認為會有好事發生。
(A) efficient〔ɪ'fɪʃənt〕*adj.* 有效率的
(B) practical〔'præktɪkḷ〕*adj.* 實際的
(C) changeable〔'tʃendʒəbḷ〕*adj.* 多變的
(D) ***optimistic***〔͵ɑptə'mɪstɪk〕*adj.* 樂觀的

suggest〔sə'dʒɛst〕v. 顯示　　outgoing〔'aut,goɪŋ〕adj. 外向的
personality〔,pɜsn'ælətɪ〕n. 個性　　***tend to V.*** 傾向於～
expect〔ɪk'spɛkt〕v. 期待；預計會有

8. (**C**) No one could beat Paul at running. He has won the running
championship <u>continuously</u> for three years.
在跑步方面，無人能擊敗保羅。他已經<u>連續</u>三年贏得跑步冠軍了。
(A) rapidly〔'ræpɪdlɪ〕adv. 快速地
(B) urgently〔'ɜdʒəntlɪ〕adv. 迫切地
(C) ***continuously***〔kən'tɪnjuəslɪ〕adv. 連續地
(D) temporarily〔'tɛmpə,rɛrəlɪ〕adv. 暫時地
beat〔bit〕v. 打敗　　championship〔'tʃæmpɪən,ʃɪp〕n. 冠軍（資格）

9. (**B**) If you fly from Taipei to Tokyo, you'll be taking an international,
rather than a <u>domestic</u> flight.
如果你搭飛機從台北飛到東京，你將會搭乘國際航班，而非<u>國內</u>航班。
(A) liberal〔'lɪbərəl〕adj. 自由的
(B) ***domestic***〔də'mɛstɪk〕adj. 國內的
(C) connected〔kə'nɛktɪd〕adj. 連結的
(D) universal〔,junə'vɜsḷ〕adj. 全球的
fly〔flaɪ〕v. 搭飛機　　international〔,ɪntə'næʃənḷ〕adj. 國際的
rather than 而非　　flight〔flaɪt〕n. 班機

10. (**A**) Jack is very proud of his fancy new motorcycle. He has been
<u>boasting</u> to all his friends about how cool it looks and how fast it
runs. 傑克對於他的酷炫新摩托車感到非常驕傲。他一直向他所有
的朋友<u>誇耀</u>它有多酷，它能跑多快。
(A) ***boast***〔bost〕v. 誇耀　　　　(B) propose〔prə'poz〕v. 提議
(C) gossip〔'gasəp〕v. 說閒話　　*n.* 八卦
(D) confess〔kən'fɛs〕v. 招認
be proud of 以～為榮
fancy〔'fænsɪ〕adj. 昂貴的；花俏的；酷炫的

11. (**C**) The ideas about family have changed <u>considerably</u> in the past
twenty years. For example, my grandfather was one of ten
children in his family, but I am the only child.
家庭的觀念在過去二十年來已有<u>相當大的</u>改變。例如，我祖父生長
在一個有十個兄弟姊妹的家庭，但我是家裡的獨生子。

(A) mutually〔'mjutʃuəlɪ〕*adv.* 互相地

(B) narrowly〔'nærolɪ〕*adv.* 狹窄地；勉強地

(C) **considerably**〔kən'sɪdərəblɪ〕*adv.* 相當大地

(D) scarcely〔'skɛrslɪ〕*adv.* 幾乎不

past〔pæst〕*adj.* 過去的

12. (**C**) The chairperson of the meeting asked everyone to speak up instead of <u>murmuring</u> their opinions among themselves. 會議的主席要求大家大聲說出來，不要彼此之間<u>小聲地說</u>自己的意見。

(A) recite〔rɪ'saɪt〕*v.* 朗誦；背誦　　(B) giggle〔'gɪgl̩〕*v.* 吃吃地笑

(C) **murmur**〔'mɜmə〕*v.* 喃喃地說：小聲說

(D) whistle〔'hwɪsl̩〕*v.* 吹口哨

chairperson〔'tʃɛr,pɜsn̩〕*n.* 主席　　**speak up** 大聲說

opinion〔ə'pɪnjən〕*n.* 意見

13. (**D**) Although Mr. Chen is rich, he is a very <u>stingy</u> person and is never willing to spend any money to help those who are in need.
雖然陳先生很有錢，但他卻是個非常<u>小氣的</u>人，從不願意花任何錢幫助那些貧困的人。

(A) absolute〔'æbsə,lut〕*adj.* 當然的；絕對的

(B) precise〔prɪ'saɪs〕*adj.* 精確的

(C) economic〔,ikə'nɑmɪk〕*adj.* 經濟的

(D) **stingy**〔'stɪndʒɪ〕*adj.* 小氣的

willing〔'wɪlɪŋ〕*adj.* 願意的　　**in need** 貧困的

14. (**B**) If you want to know what your dreams mean, now there are websites you can visit to help you <u>interpret</u> them.
如果你想知道你的夢境是什麼意思，現在你可以瀏覽很多網站，幫助你<u>解夢</u>。

(A) overcome〔,ovə'kʌm〕*v.* 克服　　(B) **interpret**〔ɪn'tɜprɪt〕*v.* 解釋

(C) transfer〔træns'fɜ〕*v.* 轉移　　(D) revise〔rɪ'vaɪz〕*v.* 校訂

website〔'wɛb,saɪt〕*n.* 網站

15. (**A**) The memory <u>capacity</u> of the new computer has been increased so that more information can be stored.
新電腦的記憶體<u>容量</u>已經增加，所以可儲存更多的資料。

(A) *capacity* ﹝ kə'pæsətɪ ﹞ *n.* 容量

(B) occupation ﹝ ˌɑkjə'peʃən ﹞ *n.* 職業

(C) attachment ﹝ ə'tætʃmənt ﹞ *n.* 附件

(D) machinery ﹝ mə'ʃinərɪ ﹞ *n.* 機器

memory ﹝'mɛmərɪ ﹞ *n.* 記憶　　increase ﹝ ɪn'kris ﹞ *v.* 增加

store ﹝ stor ﹞ *v.* 儲存

二、綜合測驗：

Kizhi is an island on Lake Onega in Karelia, Russia, with a beautiful collection of wooden churches and houses. It is one of the most popular tourist <u>attractions</u> in Russia and a United Nations Educational, Scientific, and Cultural Organization (UNESCO) World Heritage Site.

> 基日島是一個小島，位在俄羅斯卡累利阿共和國的奧涅加湖，有大量的美麗木造教堂和房屋，是俄羅斯最受歡迎的觀光景點之一，也是聯合國教育科學暨文化組織的世界遺產地點。

island ﹝'aɪlənd ﹞ *n.* 島嶼　　Russia ﹝'rʌʃə ﹞ *n.* 俄羅斯

a collection of 大量的　　wooden ﹝'wʊdn̩ ﹞ *adj.* 木製的

popular ﹝'pɑpjələ ﹞ *adj.* 受歡迎的　　tourist ﹝'tʊrɪst ﹞ *adj.* 觀光的

United Nations Educational, Scientific, and Cultural Organization
　　聯合國教育科學暨文化組織（ = *UNESCO* ）

heritage ﹝'hɛrətɪdʒ ﹞ *n.* 遺產　　site ﹝ saɪt ﹞ *n.* 地點

World Heritage Site 世界遺產地點

16. (**D**) (A) affair ﹝ ə'fɛr ﹞ *n.* 事情；事件

(B) fashion ﹝'fæʃən ﹞ *n.* 流行

(C) industry ﹝'ɪndəstrɪ ﹞ *n.* 工業　　*tourist industry* 旅遊業

(D) *attraction* ﹝ ə'trækʃən ﹞ *n.* 吸引力；具吸引力的事物

　　tourist attraction 觀光景點

The island is about 7 km long and 0.5 km wide. It is surrounded by about 5,000 other islands, some of <u>which</u> are just rocks sticking out of the ground.

> 這座島大約七公里長，半公里寬，被大約五千座其他島嶼所圍繞，其中有一些只是從地面突出的岩塊。

surround ﹝ sə'raʊnd ﹞ *v.* 圍繞　　rock ﹝ rɑk ﹞ *n.* 岩石

stick ﹝ stɪk ﹞ *v.* 伸出；突出　　*stick out of* 從～突出

17. (**D**) 這裡需填上關係代名詞，來引導形容詞子句，用以修飾先行詞
　　　　islands，故選 (D) which。而 (B) that 雖也是關係代名詞，但因之前
　　　　有介系詞 of，故不能選；(A) 與 (C) 為代名詞，不能用以連接形容詞
　　　　子句，文法不合。

The entire island of Kizhi is, <u>in fact</u>, an outdoor museum of wooden
　　　　　　　　　　　　　　　18
architecture created in 1966. It contains many historically significant and
beautiful wooden structures, <u>including</u> windmills, boathouses, chapels, fish
　　　　　　　　　　　　　　19
houses, and homes.

　　　事實上，整座基日島就是一座戶外博物館，擁有 1966 年建造的木造建築，
包含許多史上重要的美麗木造建築，包括風車、船屋、教堂、漁屋和房舍等。

　　　　　entire〔ɪn'taɪr〕*adj.* 整個的　　　outdoor〔'aʊt,dor〕*adj.* 戶外的
　　　　　museum〔mju'ziəm〕*n.* 博物館
　　　　　architecture〔'ɑrkə,tɛktʃə〕*n.* 建築　　contain〔kən'ten〕*v.* 包含
　　　　　historically〔hɪs'tɔrɪkḷɪ〕*adv.* 歷史上地
　　　　　significant〔sɪg'nɪfəkənt〕*adj.* 重要的
　　　　　windmill〔'wɪnd,mɪl〕*n.* 風車　　boathouse〔'bot,haʊs〕*n.* 船屋
　　　　　chapel〔'tʃæpḷ〕*n.* 教堂　　　***fish house*** 漁屋

18. (**A**) (A) ***in fact*** 事實上　　　　　(B) once again 再一次
　　　　(C) as usual 如往常般　　　　　(D) for instance 例如

19. (**C**) (A) except〔ɪk'sɛpt〕*prep.* 除…之外（不包括…在內）
　　　　(B) besides〔bɪ'saɪdz〕*prep.* 除…之外（包括…在內）
　　　　(C) ***including***〔ɪn'kludɪŋ〕*prep.* 包括（= *inclusive of*）
　　　　(D) regarding〔rɪ'gɑrdɪŋ〕*prep.* 關於…

The jewel of the architecture is the 22-domed Transfiguration Church, built
in the early 1700s. It is about 37 m tall, <u>making</u> it one of the tallest log
　　　　　　　　　　　　　　　　　　　　　20
structures in the world. The church was built with pine trees brought from
the mainland, which was quite common for the 18th century.

建築之最是擁有 22 個圓頂的「變容教堂」，建造於十八世紀初期，大約 37 公尺
的高度讓它成為全世界最高的圓木建築之一，它是用歐洲大陸搬來的松木所建
造而成，這樣的情況在十八世紀相當常見。

jewel〔'dʒuəl〕n. 珠寶；最有價值的人（物）　　dome〔dom〕n. 圓頂
transfiguration〔͵trænsfɪgjə'reʃən〕n. 變形；改變容貌
log〔lɔg, lɑg〕n. 原木；圓木　　pine〔paɪn〕n. 松木
mainland〔'men͵lænd , 'menlənd〕n. 大陸

20.（ **B** ）此處原爲 which makes，因爲省略關代 which，之後的一般動詞須改
爲現在分詞，故選 (B) *making*。

There was once a time when all human beings were gods. However,
they often took their divinity for granted and <u>even</u> abused it. Seeing this,
　　　　　　　　　　　　　　　　　　　　　　　　21
Brahma, the chief god, decided to take their divinity away from them and
hide it <u>where</u> it could never be found.
　　　22
　　人類曾經一度都是神，然而，他們經常將自己的神性視爲理所當然，甚至
濫用它。衆神之王梵天看了這樣的情形後，決定從他們身上取走神性，並將它
藏在永遠無法找到的地方。

once〔wʌns〕adv. 曾經；一度　　human being　人類；人
take…for granted　視…爲理所當然
divinity〔də'vɪnətɪ〕n. 神性；神的特質
abuse〔ə'bjuz〕v. 濫用
Brahma〔'brɑmə〕n.（印度教主神）梵天
chief〔tʃif〕adj. 主要的

21.（ **B** ）依句意，講到當時人類將具有神的特質視爲理所當然，「甚至」濫用
它，故本題選 (B) *even*〔'ivən〕adv. 甚至。
(A) yet〔jɛt〕adv. 尚未；然而
(C) never〔'nɛvɚ〕adv. 從未
(D) rather〔'ræðɚ〕adv. 相當；頗；反之

22.（ **C** ）依句意，這裡需填上表示「在…地方」的連接詞 *where*，來引導後面
的子句，而 (A)「雖然」是表讓步的連接詞；(B)「因爲」是表因果關係
的連接詞；(D)「當…的時候」是表時間的連接詞，皆與文意不合。

Brahma called a council of the gods to help him decide on a place to
hide the divinity. The gods suggested that they hide it <u>deep</u> in the earth or
　　　　　　　　　　　　　　　　　　　　　　　　　　　　　　23

take it to the top of the highest mountain. But Brahma thought <u>neither</u>
₂₄
would do because he believed humans would dig into the earth and climb
every mountain, and eventually find it. So, the gods gave up.

　　梵天召開眾神會議，來幫祂決定一個地方來藏妥神性。眾神建議將它藏在
地底深處，或將它帶至最高的山頂上。但是梵天認為兩者皆不可行，因為他相
信人類會挖掘土地，並攀登每一座山，而終究會找到它。於是眾神放棄了。

　　　　call〔kɔl〕v. 召喚　　　council〔'kaʊnsl〕n. 會議
　　　　suggest〔sə'dʒɛst〕v. 建議　　　earth〔ɝθ〕n. 土地；地球
　　　　human〔'hjumən〕n. 人類；人（= human being）
　　　　dig〔dɪg〕v. 挖掘　　　eventually〔ɪ'vɛntʃʊəlɪ〕adv. 終究；最後
　　　　give up 放棄

23. (**C**) 依句意，「將它藏在地底深處」，應選 (C) ***deep***〔dip〕adv. 深深地。
　　　　(A) close〔klos〕adv. 緊密地；靠近地
　　　　(B) apart〔ə'part〕adv. 分開地
　　　　(D) hard〔hard〕adv. 努力地

24. (**D**) 此處依句意，須選擇「兩者皆不」，應用 ***neither***，故本題選 (D)。
　　　　(A) 每一者；(B) 更多者；(C) 任一者，均不合。

　　Brahma thought for a long time and finally decided to hide their
divinity in the center of their own being, for humans would never think to
<u>look for</u> it there. Since that time humans have been going up and down the
₂₅
earth, digging, climbing, and exploring—searching for something already
within themselves.

　　梵天想了很久，最後決定將神性藏在人類的內心深處，因為人們永遠想不
到要到那裡尋找。從那時起，人類就一直在地球上到處挖掘、攀登、探尋——
尋找那個已經存在他們內心的事物。

　　　　being〔'biɪŋ〕n. 存在；生命　　　explore〔ɪk'splor〕v. 探索
　　　　up and down 到處　　　***search for*** 尋找

25. (**A**) (A) ***look for*** 尋找　　　(B) get over 克服
　　　　(C) do without 沒有…也行　　　(D) bump into 撞上；偶遇

　　In the fall of 1973, in an effort to bring attention to the conflict between Egypt and Israel, *World Hello Day* was born.　The objective is to promote peace all over the world, and to <u>break down</u> barriers between every
26
nationality.　Since then, *World Hello Day*—November 21st of every year— <u>has been</u> observed by people in 180 countries.
27

　　在 1973 年秋天，爲了讓埃及與以色列的衝突受到關注，「世界你好日」誕生了。目標是爲了促進世界和平，打破各國間的藩籬。從那時起，「世界你好日」——每年的十一月二十一日——就有一百八十個國家的人在過。

> ***in an effort to + V.*** 努力要～；爲了要～
> attention (əˋtɛnʃən) *n.* 注意力　　conflict (ˋkɑnflɪkt) *n.* 衝突
> Egypt (ˋidʒɪpt) *n.* 埃及　　Israel (ˋɪzrɪəl) *n.* 以色列
> ***World Hello Day*** 世界你好日　　objective (əbˋdʒɛktɪv) *n.* 目標
> promote (prəˋmot) *v.* 促進；提倡　　peace (pis) *n.* 和平
> barrier (ˋbærɪə) *n.* 藩籬；障礙
> nationality (ˌnæʃənˋælətɪ) *n.* 國籍；國家
> observe (əbˋzɝv) *v.* 過 (節)

26. (**D**)　(A) skip over　略過；跳過　　(B) come across　偶遇
　　　　　　(C) look into　調查　　　　(D) ***break down***　打破；拆除；克服

27. (**B**)　從本句一開始的 since then「從那時起」，可以得知過世界你好日是從過去一直持續到現在，應該用「現在完成式」，故選 (B) ***has been***。

　　Taking part couldn't be <u>easier</u>.　All one has to do is say hello to 10 people
28
on the day.　However, in response to the <u>aim</u> of this event, the concepts of
29
fostering peace and harmony do not have to be confined to one day a year.

　　參加這個活動非常容易，你只要在當天跟十個人問好。然而，爲響應這個活動的目標，促進和平和和諧的觀念不必被侷限在一年中的一天。

> ***take part*** 參加　　***all sb. has to do is + V*** 某人所要做的是～
> response (rɪˋspɑns) *n.* 回應；反應　　***in response to*** 爲響應
> event (ɪˋvɛnt) *n.* 事件；活動　　concept (ˋkɑnsɛpt) *n.* 觀念
> foster (ˋfɔstə) *v.* 培養；促進　　harmony (ˋhɑrmənɪ) *n.* 和諧
> confine (kənˋfaɪn) *v.* 限制

28. (**C**)　「cannot/couldn't be + 形容詞比較級」表示「非常…；再…不過」，
　　　　依據文意，應選 (C) *easier*，表示「再容易不過；非常容易」的意思。

29. (**A**)　依句意，「為響應本活動的目標」，應選 (A) *aim*〔em〕*n.* 目標。
　　　　(B)　tone〔ton〕*n.* 語調；音調
　　　　(C)　key〔ki〕*n.* 鑰匙；關鍵；祕訣
　　　　(D)　peak〔pik〕*n.* 山峰；尖峰

We can <u>keep</u> the spirit going by communicating often and consciously. It is
　　　　　30
a simple act that anyone can do and it reminds us that communication is
more effective than conflict.
我們可以藉由經常且有意識地溝通，來讓這樣的精神持續下去，這是一個任何
人都能做的簡單行為，而且提醒我們，溝通比衝突更有效。

　　spirit〔'spɪrɪt〕*n.* 精神　　communicate〔kə'mjunə‚ket〕*v.* 溝通
　　consciously〔'kɑnʃəslɪ〕*adv.* 有意識地
　　simple〔'sɪmpl〕*adj.* 簡單的　　act〔ækt〕*n.* 行為
　　remind〔rɪ'maɪnd〕*v.* 提醒　　effective〔ɪ'fɛktɪv〕*adj.* 有效的

30. (**B**)　"keep + O. + V-ing" 表示「使～繼續下去」之意，故選 (B) *keep*。
　　　　(A) push〔puʃ〕*v.* 推擠　　　　(C) bring〔brɪŋ〕*v.* 帶來
　　　　(D) make〔mek〕*v.* 使得

三、文意選填：

　　Generally there are two ways to name typhoons: the number-based
convention and the list-based convention. Following the number-based
convention, typhoons are coded with [31](I) various types of numbers such as
a 4-digit or a 6-digit code. For example, the 14th typhoon in 2003 can be
labeled either as Typhoon 0314 or Typhoon 200314. The [32](C) disadvantage
of this convention, however, is that a number is hard to remember. The
list-based convention, on the other hand, is based on the list of typhoon
names compiled in advance by a committee, and is more widely used.

　　颱風命名的方式一般有兩種：以編號命名和以命名表命名。按照編號命名
的慣例，颱風會被編上不同種類的編號，像四位數或六位數。例如，2003 年第
十四個颱風，可能被稱為 0314 號颱風或是 200314 號颱風。然而，這種慣例的
缺點是數字很難記。另一方面，根據一個委員會事先制定的命名表來命名的方
式，則比較廣泛被使用。

generally〔'dʒɛnərəlɪ〕*adv.* 一般地；通常　　name〔nem〕*v.* 命名
typhoon〔taɪ'fun〕*n.* 颱風
convention〔kən'vɛnʃən〕*n.* 習俗；慣例；常規
follow〔'fɑlo〕*v.* 遵照；按照
code〔kod〕*v.* 把…編上編號　*n.* 編號
various〔'vɛrɪəs〕*adj.* 各種不同的
digit〔'dɪdʒɪt〕*n.*（各個）阿拉伯數字
label〔'lebḷ〕*v.* 把…分類（爲）；稱（爲）
either A as B 不是 A 就是 B　　disadvantage〔͵dɪsəd'væntɪdʒ〕*n.* 缺點
on the other hand 另一方面
compile〔kəm'paɪl〕*v.* 編輯　　*in advance* 事先；預先
committee〔kə'mɪtɪ〕*n.* 委員會　　widely〔'waɪdlɪ〕*adv.* 廣泛地

At the very beginning, only [33](J) female names were used because at
that time typhoons were named after girlfriends or wives of the experts on
the committee. In 1979, however, male names were also included because
women protested against the original naming [34](F) practice for reasons of
gender equality.

一開始只有女性的名字被使用，因爲那時候颱風都以委員會裡專家的女朋
友或妻子的名字命名。然而，在 1979 年，男性的名字也包含在內，因爲女性以
性別平等爲由，抗議原來的命名慣例。

female〔'fimel〕*adj.* 女性的　　*be named after* 以…的名字命名
expert〔'ɛkspɝt〕*n.* 專家　　male〔mel〕*adj.* 男性的
include〔ɪn'klud〕*v.* 包含　　protest〔prə'tɛst〕*v.* 抗議
original〔ə'rɪdʒənḷ〕*adj.* 原本的；最初的
practice〔'præktɪs〕*n.* 慣例　　reason〔'rizn̩〕*n.* 理由
gender〔'dʒɛndɚ〕*n.* 性別　　equality〔ɪ'kwɑlətɪ〕*n.* 平等

In Asia, Western names were used until 2000 when the committee
decided to use Asian names to [35](H) raise Asians' awareness of typhoons.
The names were chosen from a name pool [36](D) composed of 140 names,
10 each from the 14 members of the committee. Each country has its unique
naming preferences. Korea and Japan [37](B) favor animal names and China
likes names of gods such as Longwang (dragon king) and Fengshen (god
of the wind).

　　亞洲一直都使用西方名字爲颱風命名，直到 2000 年，委員會決定使用亞洲名字，以提高亞洲人對颱風的意識。颱風的名字由命名表中選出，這份命名表是由一百四十個名字組成，十四個會員國各提供十個名字。每個國家都有自己獨特的命名喜好。韓國和日本偏好動物名稱，而中國喜歡神的名字，例如「龍王」和「風神」。

Asia〔'eʒə〕n. 亞洲　　　　raise〔rez〕v. 提高
awareness〔ə'wɛrnɪs〕n. 意識　　pool〔pul〕n. 集合
be composed of　由…組成　　member〔'mɛmbə〕n. 會員
unique〔ju'nik〕adj. 獨特的　　preference〔'prɛfrəns〕n. 偏好
favor〔'fevə〕v. 偏好　　　　dragon〔'drægən〕n. 龍

After the 140 names are all used in order, they will be [38](E) recycled. But the names can be changed. If a member country suffers great damage from a certain typhoon, it can [39](A) request that the name of the typhoon be deleted from the list at the annual committee meeting. For example, the names of Nabi by South Korea, and Longwang by China were [40](G) replaced with other names in 2007. The deletion of both names was due to the severe damage caused by the typhoons bearing the names.

　　一百四十個名字都依序使用過後，還會被重新循環使用。但名字是可以改變的。如果颱風在某個委員國造成嚴重損害，該國可以在年度委員會會議上，要求將其除名。例如，由南韓命名的娜比颱風，由中國命名的龍王颱風，在 2007 年皆被以其他的名稱取代。兩者的除名都是由於名叫娜比和龍王的颱風所造成的嚴重損害。

in order　依照順序　　recycle〔ri'saɪkl̩〕v. 循環使用
suffer〔'sʌfə〕v. 遭受　　damage〔'dæmɪdʒ〕n. 損害；破壞
certain〔'sɝtn̩〕adj. 某個　　request〔rɪ'kwɛst〕v. 要求
delete〔dɪ'lit〕v. 刪除　　annual〔'ænjuəl〕adj. 年度的
replace〔rɪ'ples〕v. 取代　　deletion〔dɪ'liʃən〕n. 刪除
be due to　是由於　　severe〔sə'vɪr〕adj. 嚴重的
cause〔kɔz〕v. 引起；造成　　bear〔bɛr〕v. 擁有；帶有

四、閱讀測驗：

41-44 爲題組

　　The kilt is a skirt traditionally worn by Scottish men. It is a tailored garment that is wrapped around the wearer's body at the waist starting from one side, around the front and back and across the front again to the opposite side. The overlapping layers in front are called "aprons." Usually, the kilt covers the body from the waist down to just above the knees. A properly made kilt should not be so loose that the wearer can easily twist the kilt around the body, nor should it be so tight that it causes bulging of the fabric where it is buckled. Underwear may be worn as one prefers.

蘇格蘭裙是一種傳統上由蘇格蘭男士所穿著的裙子。它是一種訂製服，包覆著穿著者的腰際，從一側繞過前面到後面，再繞過前面到另一側。前面重疊的兩層被稱爲「圍裙」。通常，蘇格蘭裙遮蓋腰線以下到正好膝蓋上方的位置。一條以正確方式製作的蘇格蘭裙，不應該寬鬆到穿著者能夠輕易轉動，而也不應該緊到在裙子扣緊的地方造成鼓起的情形。裡面的內衣褲則可以依個人偏好來穿著。

kilt〔kɪlt〕*n.* 蘇格蘭裙　　traditionally〔trə'dɪʃənl̩ɪ〕*adv.* 傳統地
Scottish〔'skatɪʃ〕*adj.* 蘇格蘭的　　tailor〔'telɚ〕*v.* 縫製
garment〔'garmənt〕*n.* 衣服　　wrap〔ræp〕*v.* 包裹；圍繞
waist〔west〕*n.* 腰　　opposite〔'apəzɪt〕*adj.* 相反的
overlap〔‚ovɚ'læp〕*v.* 重疊　　layer〔'leɚ〕*n.* 一層
apron〔'eprən〕*n.* 圍裙　　cover〔'kʌvɚ〕*v.* 遮蓋
knee〔ni〕*n.* 膝蓋　　properly〔'prapɚlɪ〕*adv.* 適當地；正確地
loose〔lus〕*adj.* 寬鬆的　　twist〔twɪst〕*v.* 纏繞；扭轉
tight〔taɪt〕*adj.* 緊的　　bulge〔bʌldʒ〕*v.* 鼓起
fabric〔'fæbrɪk〕*n.* 織品；布料　　buckle〔'bʌkl̩〕*v.* 用扣環扣住
underwear〔'ʌndɚ‚wɛr〕*n.* 內衣褲　　prefer〔prɪ'fɝ〕*v.* 較喜歡

One of the most distinctive features of the kilt is the pattern of squares, or sett, it exhibits. The association of particular patterns with individual families can be traced back hundreds of years. Then in the Victorian era (19th century), weaving companies began to systematically record and formalize the system of setts for commercial purposes. Today there are also setts for States and Provinces, schools and universities, and general patterns that anybody can wear.

蘇格蘭裙最獨特的特點之一就是它所展示的方格花紋。特定的花紋和個別家族的關聯可以回溯到數百年前。在維多利亞時期（十九世紀）時，編織公司爲了商業用途，開始有系統地記錄這些樣式，並且使其形式化。今日有各種代表不同州、省份、學校和大學的花紋，還有任何人都可以穿著的一般圖案。

distinctive〔dɪ'stɪŋktɪv〕adj. 獨特的　　feature〔'fitʃɚ〕n. 特點

pattern〔'pætən〕n. 花樣；圖案　　square〔skwɛr〕n. 正方形

sett〔sɛt〕n. 河床四角形的鋪石；此指蘇格蘭裙的「方格花紋」

exhibit〔ɪg'zɪbɪt〕v. 展示　　association〔ə,soʃɪ'eʃən〕n. 關聯

particular〔pə'tɪkjələ〕adj. 特定的

individual〔,ɪndə'vɪdʒuəl〕adj. 個別的　　trace〔tres〕v. 回溯

Victorian〔vɪk'torɪən〕adj. 維多利亞時期的

era〔'ɪrə〕n. 時代　　weave〔wiv〕v. 編織

systematically〔,sɪstə'mætɪkl̩ɪ〕adv. 有系統地

formalize〔'fɔrml̩,aɪz〕v. 使形式化

system〔'sɪstəm〕n. 系統　　commercial〔kə'mɝʃəl〕adj. 商業的

purpose〔'pɝpəs〕n. 目的　　state〔stet〕n. 州

province〔'prɑvɪns〕n. 省份　　general〔'dʒɛnərəl〕adj. 一般的

The kilt can be worn with accessories. On the front apron, there is often a kilt pin, topped with a small decorative family symbol. A small knife can be worn with the kilt too. It typically comes in a very wide variety, from fairly plain to quite elaborate silver- and jewel-ornamented designs. The kilt can also be worn with a sporran, which is the Gaelic word for pouch or purse.

穿著蘇格蘭裙可以搭配配件。在前面的圍裙，通常會有一個裙子的別針，別針上蓋有小型裝飾性的家族象徵。穿蘇格蘭裙也可以配戴小刀，小刀通常有豐富的種類，從相當樸素到頗為細緻，還搭配銀飾和珠寶設計的都有。蘇格蘭裙也可搭配毛布袋，毛布袋就是蓋爾語裡的囊袋或錢包。

accessory〔æk'sɛsərɪ〕n. 配件　　front〔frʌnt〕adj. 前面的

pin〔pɪn〕n. 大頭針；別針　　top〔tɑp〕v. 加蓋

decorative〔'dɛkə,retɪv〕adj. 裝飾性的　　symbol〔'sɪmbl̩〕n. 象徵

typically〔'tɪpɪkl̩ɪ〕adv. 典型地；通常　　*come in* 有～

variety〔və'raɪətɪ〕n. 多樣　　fairly〔'fɛrlɪ〕adv. 相當地

plain〔plen〕adj. 樸素的　　quite〔kwaɪt〕adv. 相當地

elaborate〔ɪ'læbərɪt〕adj. 精巧的　　jewel〔'dʒuəl〕n. 珠寶

ornament〔'ɔrnə,mɛnt〕v. 裝飾　　design〔dɪ'zaɪn〕n. 設計；圖案

sporran〔'spɔrən〕n. 毛布袋　　Gaelic〔'gelɪk〕adj. 蓋爾語的

pouch〔pautʃ〕n. 囊袋

41.(**D**) 穿著蘇格蘭裙適當的方式為何？

　(A) 裡面應該穿著內衣褲。　　(B) 應該夠寬鬆以便旋轉。

(C) 應該長到可以遮住穿著者的膝蓋。

(D) 身體正面應該包覆兩層。

proper〔'prɑpə〕*adj.* 適當的
underneath〔ˌʌndə'niθ〕*prep.* 在～之下

42. (**A**) 下列何者是蘇格蘭裙方格花紋的正確描述？

(A) 它們曾經是不同蘇格蘭家族的象徵。

(B) 它們是為了商業目的而由政府建立的。

(C) 它們在十九世紀時代表不同的州和省份。

(D) 它們曾經有一種普遍的樣式讓所有的人和機構穿著。

description〔dɪ'skrɪpʃən〕*n.* 描述
establish〔ə'stæblɪʃ〕*v.* 建立　　represent〔ˌrɛprɪ'zɛnt〕*v.* 代表
used to V. 曾經　　individual〔ˌɪndə'vɪdʒuəl〕*n.* 個人
institution〔ˌɪnstə'tjuʃən〕*n.* 機構

43. (**C**) 下列何者通常不和蘇格蘭裙搭配來當作裝飾？

(A) 別針。　　　　　　　　(B) 錢包。

(C) 鮮紅色的圍裙。　　　　(D) 銀刀。

ruby〔'rubɪ〕*adj.* 鮮紅色的

44. (**A**) 本文的目的為何？

(A) 介紹一種蘇格蘭的衣服。　(B) 廣告一種編織的樣式。

(C) 說服男士穿著蘇格蘭裙。　(D) 比較一般的裙子和蘇格蘭裙。

advertise〔'ædvəˌtaɪz〕*v.* 廣告
persuade〔pə'swed〕*v.* 說服　　compare〔kəm'pɛr〕*v.* 比較

45-48 為題組

　　Wesla Whitfield, a famous jazz singer, has a unique style and life story, so I decided to see one of her performances and interview her for my column.

　　名爵士歌手薇絲拉・惠特菲爾有著獨特的表演風格，以及特別的人生故事，所以我決定去觀賞一場她的演出，並做訪談，以撰寫我的專欄。

unique〔ju'nik〕*adj.* 獨特的　　style〔staɪl〕*n.* 風格
performance〔pə'fɔrməns〕*n.* 表演
interview〔'ɪntəˌvju〕*v.* 訪談　　column〔'kɑləm〕*n.* (報紙) 專欄

　　I went to a nightclub in New York and watched the stage lights go up. After the band played an introduction, Wesla Whitfield wheeled herself onstage in a wheelchair. As she sang, Whitfield's voice was so powerful and soulful that everyone in the room forgot the wheelchair was even there.

我來到紐約的一家夜店，看著舞台燈光亮起。在樂團演奏完序曲後，惠特菲爾自己推著輪椅上舞台。當惠特菲爾開口唱歌時，她的聲音強而有力，而且充滿感情，在場的每個人甚至都忘了輪椅的存在。

> nightclub〔'naɪt,klʌb〕 *n.* 夜店；夜總會　　***go up***　（燈）亮起
> introduction〔,ɪntrə'dʌkʃən〕 *n.* 序曲；序文
> wheel〔hwil〕 *v.* 推動（有輪子的東西）
> onstage〔'ɑn'stedʒ〕 *adv.* 上舞台　　wheelchair〔'hwil'tʃɛr〕 *n.* 輪椅
> soulful〔'solfəl〕 *adj.* 充滿感情的

At 57, Whitfield is small and pretty, witty and humble, persistent and philosophical. Raised in California, Whitfield began performing in public at age 18, when she took a job as a singing waitress at a pizza parlor. After studying classical music in college, she moved to San Francisco and went on to sing with the San Francisco Opera Chorus.

五十七歲的惠特菲爾嬌小可愛，個性詼諧又謙卑，不輕言放棄而且相當豁達。加州長大的惠特菲爾，十八歲時開始在公開場合演出，那時她在披薩店擔任駐唱女服務生。惠特菲爾在大學主修古典音樂，畢業後搬到舊金山，接著就加入舊金山歌劇院合唱團。

> pretty〔'prɪtɪ〕 *adj.* 可愛的；漂亮的
> witty〔'wɪtɪ〕 *adj.* 機靈的；詼諧的　　humble〔'hʌmbḷ〕 *adj.* 謙虛的
> persistent〔pə'zɪstənt〕 *adj.* 堅忍不拔的
> philosophical〔,fɪlə'sɑfɪkḷ〕 *adj.* 達觀的；想得開的
> raise〔rez〕 *v.* 養育　　***in public***　公開地
> ***singing waitress*** 駐唱女服務生【服務客人並上台演唱的女服務生】
> parlor〔'pɑrlɚ〕 *n.* （某種職業的）店鋪
> classical〔'klæsɪkḷ〕 *adj.* 古典的　　***go on to V***. 接著～
> opera〔'ɑpərə〕 *n.* 歌劇；歌劇院　　chorus〔'korəs〕 *n.* 合唱團
> ***San Francisco Opera Chorus*** 舊金山歌劇院合唱團

Walking home from rehearsal at age 29, she was caught in the midst of a random shooting that left her paralyzed from the waist down. I asked how she dealt with the realization that she'd never walk again, and she confessed that initially she didn't want to face it. After a year of depression she tried to kill herself. She was then admitted to a hospital for treatment, where she was able to recover.

二十九歲那年，當她排練結束，走路回家的路上，遇到有人隨意開槍掃射，被流彈波及，使她從此腰部以下癱瘓。我問她知道自己再也不能走路時，她如何應付，她坦承一開始她無法面對。憂鬱了一年後，她企圖自殺，然後就被送到醫院治療，並在醫院康復。

rehearsal〔rɪˈhɝsḷ〕*n.*（戲劇等）排演
be caught in 遇到（不好的情況）
in the midst of 在…進行之中（= *in the middle of*）
random〔ˈrændəm〕*adj.* 漫無目的的；隨便的
random shooting（無特定目標的）亂槍掃射
paralyze〔ˈpærəˌlaɪz〕*v.* 使癱瘓　　waist〔west〕*n.* 腰部
deal with 處理；應付　　realization〔ˌrɪələˈzeʃən〕*n.* 認識；了解
confess〔kənˈfɛs〕*v.* 坦承　　initially〔ɪˈnɪʃəlɪ〕*adv.* 最初
depression〔dɪˈprɛʃən〕*n.* 憂鬱　　*kill oneself* 自殺
admit〔ədˈmɪt〕*v.* 送去（醫院）　　treatment〔ˈtritmənt〕*n.* 治療
recover〔rɪˈkʌvɚ〕*v.* 恢復

Whitfield said she came to understand that the only thing she had lost in this misfortunate event was the ability to walk. She still possessed her most valuable asset—her mind. Pointing to her head, she said, "Everything important is in here. The only real disability in life is losing your mind." When I asked if she was angry about what she had lost, she admitted to being frustrated occasionally, "especially when everybody's dancing, because I love to dance. But **when that happens** I just remove myself so I can focus instead on what I can do."

惠特菲爾說她後來了解到，在這場不幸的意外中，她唯一失去的東西就是行走的能力。她仍然擁有最有價值的資產——她的心智。她指著頭說：「重要的東西都裝在這兒。人生中唯一真正的殘障就是喪志。」當我問到她對已經失去的東西生不生氣時，她承認偶爾會感到沮喪，「尤其是當每個人都在跳舞的時候，因為我喜歡跳舞。但在那樣的情況下，我通常會離開現場，這樣我才能專注在我能做的事情上。」

misfortunate〔mɪsˈfɔrtʃənɪt〕*adj.* 不幸的　　event〔ɪˈvɛnt〕*n.* 事件
ability〔əˈbɪlətɪ〕*n.* 能力　　possess〔pəˈzɛs〕*v.* 擁有
valuable〔ˈvæljəbḷ〕*adj.* 有價值的　　asset〔ˈæsɛt〕*n.* 資產
disability〔ˌdɪsəˈbɪlətɪ〕*n.* 殘疾　　admit〔ədˈmɪt〕*v.* 承認
frustrated〔ˈfrʌstretɪd〕*adj.* 受挫的
occasionally〔əˈkeʒənḷɪ〕*adv.* 偶爾　　remove〔rɪˈmuv〕*v.* 移除
remove oneself 走開；離去　　*focus on* 專注於
instead〔ɪnˈstɛd〕*adv.* 作為代替

45. (**C**) 薇絲拉‧惠特菲爾曾在下列何處工作過？
　　(A) 大學。　　　　　　　　(B) 醫院。
　　(C) 披薩店。　　　　　　　(D) 通訊社。
　　news agency 通訊社

46. (**D**) 最後一段的「在那樣的情況下」指的是什麼？
　　(A) 薇絲拉喪志時。　　　　(B) 薇絲拉在台上演唱時。
　　(C) 薇絲拉坐輪椅出門時。　(D) 薇絲拉在看其他人跳舞時。

47. (**B**) 以下對薇絲拉‧惠特菲爾殘疾的敘述何者為真？
　　(A) 她的殘疾是由交通意外所引起。
　　(B) 一開始她很傷心而且沮喪。
　　(C) 她的殘疾嚴重影響她的唱歌生涯。
　　(D) 這是她在大學時發生的事。
　　physical〔'fɪzɪkl̩〕*adj.* 身體上的　　depressed〔dɪ'prɛst〕*adj.* 沮喪的

48. (**A**) 薇絲拉最有可能給其他殘障人士什麼建議？
　　(A) 不要理會你已經失去的，要充分利用你所擁有的。
　　(B) 要謙虛，而且努力以贏得他人的尊敬。
　　(C) 學習一項技術，你仍然可以成功成名。
　　(D) 每當覺得不高興或沮喪時，試著唱唱歌。
　　advice〔əd'vaɪs〕*n.* 忠告；建議　　disabled〔dɪs'ebl̩d〕*adj.* 殘障的
　　ignore〔ɪg'nor〕*v.* 忽視；不理　　***make the best use of*** 善加利用
　　modest〔'mɑdɪst〕*adj.* 謙虛的　　earn〔ɝn〕*v.* 贏得
　　acquire〔ə'kwaɪr〕*v.* 獲得；學得　　upset〔ʌp'sɛt〕*adj.* 不高興的

49-52 為題組

　　Forks trace their origins back to the ancient Greeks. Forks at that time were fairly large with two tines that aided in the carving of meat in the kitchen. The tines prevented meat from twisting or moving during carving and allowed food to slide off more easily than it would with a knife.

　　叉子的的起源可以追溯到古希臘人。當時的叉子很大，有兩條叉齒可在廚房用來協助切肉。叉齒可以在切肉時，固定肉不讓它扭動或移動，和用刀子比起來，也可以讓食物較容易滑落。

　　fork〔fɔrk〕*n.* 叉子　　trace〔tres〕*v.* 追溯
　　origin〔'ɔrədʒɪn〕*n.* 起源

ancient〔ˈenʃənt〕*adj.* 古代的　　Greek〔grik〕*n.* 希臘人
fairly〔ˈfɛrlɪ〕*adv.* 相當　　tine〔taɪn〕*n.* 叉；尖齒
aid〔ed〕*v.* 幫助　　carve〔kɑrv〕*v.* 切
prevent~from⋯ 使~不會⋯　　twist〔twɪst〕*v.* 扭曲
move〔muv〕*v.* 移動　　slide〔slaɪd〕*v.* 滑

By the 7th century A.D., royal courts of the Middle East began to use forks at the table for dining.　From the 10th through the 13th centuries, forks were fairly common among the wealthy in Byzantium.　In the 11th century, a Byzantine wife brought forks to Italy; however, they were not widely adopted there until the 16th century.　Then in 1533, forks were brought from Italy to France.　The French were also slow to accept forks, for using them was thought to be awkward.

到了西元七世紀，中東的皇室開始在餐桌上使用叉子用餐。從十世紀到十三世紀，在拜占庭的富人中，叉子的使用很普遍。在十一世紀，有一位拜占庭的婦人把叉子帶到義大利，然而，一直到十六世紀，叉子在那裡才被廣泛使用。之後，在1533年，叉子從義大利被帶到法國，法國人也是很慢才接受叉子，因為使用叉子被認為很笨拙。

A.D. 西元⋯年【拉丁文 Anno Domini，表示 in the year of our lord，原意為「主的紀年」】　　royal〔ˈrɔɪəl〕*adj.* 王室的
court〔kort〕*n.* 宮廷　　***the Middle East*** 中東【中東位於東西半球之間，地跨赤道南北，是亞洲與非洲相連接的地區。中東涵蓋阿拉伯半島及波斯灣區，東接土庫曼、阿富汗及巴基斯坦，南瀕阿拉伯海及印度洋，西臨波斯灣、埃及和地中海，北至黑海及大高加索山脈與歐洲相隔。】
common〔ˈkɑmən〕*adj.* 普遍的　　***the wealthy*** 富人
Byzantium〔bɪˈzæntɪəm〕*n.* 拜占庭【古羅馬城市，今稱伊斯坦堡】
Byzantine〔bɪˈzæntɪn〕*adj.* 拜占庭的
Italy〔ˈɪtḷɪ〕*n.* 義大利　　widely〔ˈwaɪdlɪ〕*adv.* 廣泛地
adopt〔əˈdɑpt〕*v.* 採用　　France〔fræns〕*n.* 法國
the French 法國人　　awkward〔ˈɔkwəd〕*adj.* 笨拙的

In 1608, forks were brought to England by Thomas Coryate, who saw them during his travels in Italy.　The English first ridiculed forks as being unnecessary.　"Why should a person need a fork when God had given him hands?" they asked.　Slowly, however, forks came to be adopted by the wealthy as a symbol of their social status. They were prized possessions made of expensive materials intended to impress guests. By the mid 1600s, eating with forks was considered fashionable among the wealthy British.

　　在1608年，叉子被湯姆斯・柯里亞特帶到英國，他是在義大利旅遊時看到叉子的。英國人一開始嘲笑叉子，覺得沒有必要。「當上帝已經賦予人雙手，人爲什麼要用叉子？」然而，慢慢地，叉子開始被有錢人使用，作爲他們社會地位的象徵。叉子是有價值的財產，是用昂貴的材料製成，要用來讓客人留下深刻印象。到了十七世紀中期，在有錢的英國人眼中，用叉子吃東西被視爲是很時尚的行爲。

> ridicule〔ˈrɪdɪˌkjul〕v. 嘲笑
> unnecessary〔ʌnˈnɛsəˌsɛrɪ〕adj. 不必要的
> **come to + V.** 開始…　　symbol〔ˈsɪmbḷ〕n. 象徵
> status〔ˈstetəs , ˈstætəs〕n. 地位　　**social status** 社會地位
> prized〔praɪzd〕adj. 非常有價值的；珍貴的
> possessions〔pəˈzɛʃənz〕n. pl. 財產；所有物
> **be made of** 由…製成　　material〔məˈtɪrɪəl〕n. 物質；材料
> intend〔ɪnˈtɛnd〕v. 打算
> **be intended to + V.** 目的是爲了…
> impress〔ɪmˈprɛs〕v. 使印象深刻　　mid〔mɪd〕adj. 中間的
> fashionable〔ˈfæʃənəbḷ〕adj. 流行的　　**the British** 英國人

Early table forks were modeled after kitchen forks, but small pieces of food often fell through the two tines or slipped off easily. In late 17th century France, larger forks with four curved tines were developed. The additional tines made diners less likely to drop food, and the curved tines served as a scoop so people did not have to constantly switch to a spoon while eating. By the early 19th century, four-tined forks had also been developed in Germany and England and slowly began to spread to America.

　　早期餐桌上用的叉子是仿造廚房的叉子做成的，但是小塊的食物會從兩齒中掉出，或是容易滑落。在十七世紀晚期的法國，較大的叉子，並帶有四支彎曲的叉齒研發出來；額外的叉齒讓用餐者較不會掉食物，而彎曲的叉齒也可充當杓子，如此一來，人們就不用一直在吃飯的時候改換用湯匙。到十九世紀早期，四齒叉子也在德國和英國發展出來，並開始慢慢擴及到美國。

　　model〔'madl〕 v. 製作；仿製 < after >　　slip〔slɪp〕 v. 滑落
　　curved〔kɜvd〕 adj. 彎曲的　　develop〔dɪ'vɛləp〕 v. 發展；研發
　　additional〔ə'dɪʃənl〕 adj. 額外的　　diner〔'daɪnɚ〕 n. 用餐的人
　　serve as 充當　　scoop〔skup〕 n. 杓子　 v. 舀取
　　constantly〔'kɑnstəntlɪ〕 adv. 不斷地
　　switch〔swɪtʃ〕 v. 轉換　　spread〔sprɛd〕 v. 傳播

49.(**C**) 這篇文章的主旨為何？
　　(A) 不同叉子的設計。　　　　　(B) 有叉子協助烹飪的擴張。
　　(C) 使用叉子用餐的歷史。　　　(D) 有關叉子的餐桌禮儀發展。
　　table manners 餐桌禮儀

50.(**B**) 叉子的使用是透過什麼路線發展？
　　(A) 中東→希臘→英國→義大利→法國。
　　(B) 希臘→中東→義大利→法國→英國。
　　(C) 希臘→中東→法國→義大利→德國。
　　(D) 中東→法國→英國→義大利→德國。
　　route〔rut〕 n. 路線

51.(**D**) 叉子是如何在英國變熱門？
　　(A) 有錢的英國人對叉子的設計印象深刻。
　　(B) 有錢的英國人認為用手吃飯很笨拙。
　　(C) 有錢的英國人送特別的叉子給貴族作為奢侈的禮物。
　　(D) 有錢的英國人認為用叉子用餐是社會地位的表徵。
　　noble〔'nobl〕 n. 貴族（常用複數）
　　luxurious〔lʌg'ʒʊrɪəs〕 adj. 奢侈的

52.(**A**) 為什麼叉子要做成彎曲的形狀？
　　(A) 它們也可以用來舀取食物。　 (B) 這樣看來比較時尚。
　　(C) 這樣設計可以出口給美國。
　　(D) 這樣可以確保在切肉的時候不會扭曲。
　　export〔'ɛksport〕 n. 出口　　ensure〔ɪn'ʃʊr〕 v. 保證

53-56 為題組

　　Animals are a favorite subject of many photographers. Cats, dogs, and other pets top the list, followed by zoo animals. However, because it's hard to get them to sit still and "perform on command," some professional photographers refuse to photograph pets.

　　動物是許多攝影師最愛的拍攝對象。前幾名是貓、狗以及其它寵物,然後是動物園裡的動物。然而,因為要讓牠們坐定並且「照命令演出」頗為困難,有些職業的攝影師拒絕拍攝寵物。

subject〔'sʌbdʒɪkt〕*n.* 主題;(照片)被拍攝的物體
photographer〔fə'tɑgrəfə〕*n.* 攝影師　　pet〔pɛt〕*n.* 寵物
top〔tɑp〕*v.* 位於…的頂端　　***top the list*** 位居排行榜的首位
followed by 接著就是　　still〔stɪl〕*adj.* 靜止的;不動的
sit still 坐著不動　　perform〔pə'fɔrm〕*v.* 表演;表現
command〔kə'mænd〕*n.* 命令;指揮
professional〔prə'fɛʃənḷ〕*adj.* 職業的
refuse〔rɪ'fjuz〕*v.* 拒絕　　photograph〔'fotə,græf〕*v.* 拍攝

One way to get an appealing portrait of a cat or dog is to hold a biscuit or treat above the camera. The animal's longing look toward the food will be captured by the camera, but the treat won't appear in the picture because it's out of the camera's range. When you show the picture to your friends afterwards, they'll be impressed by your pet's loving expression.

　　想拍出吸引人的貓或狗的照片,方法之一是拿一塊餅乾或小點心在照相機上方。動物看著食物的渴望眼神會被鏡頭捕捉,食物則因為落在鏡頭範圍之外而不會出現在照片裡。之後當你把照片秀給你的朋友看時,他們會因你的寵物那充滿愛意的眼光而感到印象深刻。

appealing〔ə'pilɪŋ〕*adj.* 吸引人的
portrait〔'portret〕*n.* 肖像畫;畫像;此指「照片」
hold〔hold〕*v.* 握住;拿著　　biscuit〔'bɪskɪt〕*n.* 餅乾
treat〔trit〕*n.* 美味食物　　camera〔'kæmərə〕*n.* 照相機
longing〔'lɔŋɪŋ〕*adj.* 渴望的　　look〔lʊk〕*n.* 眼神;樣子
toward〔tord〕*prep.* 對於　　capture〔'kæptʃə〕*v.* 捕捉
appear〔ə'pɪr〕*v.* 出現　　range〔rendʒ〕*n.* 範圍
show A to B 把 A 拿給 B 看
afterwards〔'æftəwədz〕*adv.* 之後;後來
impress〔ɪm'prɛs〕*v.* 使印象深刻
loving〔'lʌvɪŋ〕*adj.* 充滿愛的　　expression〔ɪk'sprɛʃən〕*n.* 表情

If you are using fast film, you can take some good, quick shots of a pet by simply snapping a picture right after calling its name. You'll get a different expression from your pet using this technique. Depending on your pet's mood, the picture will capture an interested, curious expression or possibly a look of annoyance, especially if you've awakened it from a nap.

如果你用的是感光快的底片，只要在叫喚你寵物的名字後馬上拍照，你就能拍出一些又快又好的照片。用這種技巧，你可以拍到寵物不同的表情。視寵物的心情而定，照片可能捕捉到牠們感興趣的、好奇的表情。或者，也可能是感到惱怒的表情，尤其當你吵醒小睡的牠們時。

film〔fɪlm〕n. 底片　　***fast film*** 感光快的底片
shot〔ʃɑt〕n. 照片（= *photograph*）　　***take a shot*** 拍照
simply〔'sɪmplɪ〕adv. 僅僅；只是　　snap〔snæp〕v. 喀擦一聲拍（照）
snap a picture 快速拍張照片　　technique〔tɛk'nik〕n. 技巧
depend on 視…而定；取決於　　mood〔mud〕n. 心情
interested〔'ɪntrɪstɪd〕adj. 感興趣的　　curious〔'kjurɪəs〕adj. 好奇的
annoyance〔ə'nɔɪəns〕n. 惱怒
especially〔ə'spɛʃəlɪ〕adv. 尤其；特別是
awaken〔ə'wekən〕v. 叫醒　　nap〔næp〕n. 午睡；小睡

Taking pictures of zoo animals requires a little more patience. After all, you can't wake up a lion! You may have to wait for a while until the animal does something interesting or moves into a position for you to get a good shot. When photographing zoo animals, don't get too close to the cages, and never tap on the glass or throw things between the bars of a cage. Concentrate on shooting some good pictures, and always respect the animals you are photographing.

拍攝動物園裡的動物照片需要更多一點的耐性。畢竟，你可不能去驚醒一隻獅子！你可能必須等上一陣子，等那些動物做出一些有趣的事，或是擺出可以讓你拍出好照片的姿勢。在拍攝動物園裡的動物時，不要太靠近籠子、拍打玻璃，或是從鐵籠的間隙丟東西進去。專心拍出好照片，而且永遠要尊敬你正在拍攝的動物。

require〔rɪ'kwaɪr〕v. 需要　　patience〔'peʃəns〕n. 耐心
after all 畢竟　　***wake up*** 叫醒
move〔muv〕v. 移動；改變姿勢　　position〔pə'zɪʃən〕n. 姿勢
cage〔kedʒ〕n. 籠子　　tap〔tæp〕v. 輕敲
bar〔bɑr〕n. 金屬條；柵欄
concentrate〔'kɑnsn̩ˏtret〕v. 集中；專心　　shoot〔ʃut〕v. 拍攝
respect〔rɪ'spɛkt〕v. 尊重

53. (**A**) 爲何有些職業攝影師不喜歡拍攝寵物的照片？
　　(A) 寵物可能不會遵守命令。　　(B) 寵物不想被打擾。
　　(C) 寵物可能不喜歡攝影師。　　(D) 寵物很少改變表情。

　　follow〔ˈfalo〕v. 遵守
　　order〔ˈɔrdɚ〕n. 命令　　bother〔ˈbɑðɚ〕v. 打擾

54. (**A**) 拍寵物照時，餅乾的作用爲何？
　　(A) 捕捉可愛的表情。　　(B) 製造特別的氣氛。
　　(C) 激起寵物的食慾。　　(D) 阻止寵物直視鏡頭。

　　cute〔kjut〕adj. 可愛的　　atmosphere〔ˈætməsˌfɪr〕n. 氣氛
　　arouse〔əˈraʊz〕v. 激起　　appetite〔ˈæpəˌtaɪt〕n. 食慾
　　keep…from 阻止…

55. (**D**) 拍寵物照時，叫喚寵物的名字有何好處？
　　(A) 幫助你的寵物展現最佳樣貌。
　　(B) 確保你的寵物坐定不動。
　　(C) 讓你的寵物暫時保持清醒。
　　(D) 捕捉你寵物的不同表情。

56. (**D**) 拍攝寵物與拍攝動物園裡的動物，在哪方面不同？
　　(A) 你需要有感光快的底片。　　(B) 你需要特殊設備。
　　(C) 你需要靠近動物。
　　(D) 你需要花更多時間觀望等待。

　　equipment〔ɪˈkwɪpmənt〕n. 設備；裝備

第貳部分：非選擇題

一、中譯英

1. 近年來，許多台灣製作的影片已經受到國際的重視。

　In recent years, many Taiwan-produced movies have gained
　international recognition/appreciation.

2. 拍攝這些電影的地點也成爲熱門觀光景點。

　The places where these movies were filmed have also become
　popular/hot tourist attractions/spots.

二、英文作文：

Dear Ken,　　　　　　　　　　　　　　　Jan.18, 2012

　　You know that I always support you but you've been spending far too much time playing video games—and suffering the consequences as a result. Of course, I love video games too and I understand how easy it is to get wrapped up in them. However, when the games begin to have an effect on your education and relationships, something has to give.

　　Moderation is the key to everything and video games are no exception. I'm not saying you should stop playing video games altogether but I am strongly suggesting you cut back a little, if for no other reason than to keep your parents off your back. You could try my method, which is to set a limit of two hours per day. I think you'll come to realize that life will be much easier when your parents aren't constantly scolding you. And besides, you really don't want to mess up your future, do you? Anyway, if there's anything I can do to help you, don't hesitate to ask.

　　　　　　　　　　　　　　　　　　Your Friend,
　　　　　　　　　　　　　　　　　　Jack

---

support〔sə'port〕v. 支持　　*video game* 電玩
suffer〔'sʌfɚ〕v. 遭受　　consequence〔'kɑnsə,kwɛns〕n. 後果
as a result 因此　　*be wrapped up in* 醉心於；迷戀
have an effect on 對…有影響　　education〔,ɛdʒə'keʃən〕n. 教育
relationship〔rɪ'leʃən,ʃɪp〕n. 關係
moderation〔,mɑdə'reʃən〕n. 適度；節制
key〔ki〕n. 關鍵　　*be no exception* ～也不例外
altogether〔,ɔltə'gɛðɚ〕adv. 完全　　*cut back* 減少
keep sb. off one's back 使某人不嘮叨
method〔'mɛθəd〕n. 方法
constantly〔'kɑnstəntlɪ〕adv. 不斷地　　scold〔skold〕v. 責罵
mess up 搞砸　　hesitate〔'hɛzə,tet〕v. 猶豫

101 年學測英文科試題修正意見

題　號	題　目	修　正　意　見
第 8 題	If you fly from Taipei to Tokyo, you'll be taking an international, rather than *a domestic flight.* → ... an international, rather than *a* an domestic, *flight*.	an international 和 a domestic 對等，修飾 flight，故須用逗點分隔對比的單字、片語或句子較佳。 【詳見「文法寶典」p.40】
第 9 題	The memory of *the new computer* has .... → The memory of *the computer* ...	依句意，應該是原來的電腦擴充記憶體，故須將 new 去掉。
第 16－20 題 第 5 行	...are just rocks sticking out of the *ground*. → ... are just rocks sticking out of the *water*.	依句意，島嶼散佈於海上，某些突出於「水面」，故須將 ground 改成 water 較佳。
第 26－30 題 第二段 第 2 行	However, *in response to the ___29___ of this event*, the concepts of fostering peace and harmony do not have to be confined to one day a year.... → However, the concepts of fostering peace and harmony do not have to be confined to one day a year....	in response to 意為「回應；響應」，但此句並沒有回應上句的意思，導致意義上的模糊不清，為多餘的資訊，故應將 in response to the ___29___ of this event 刪除。

題　　號	題　　　　目	修　正　意　見
第 31－40 題 第三段 第 1 行	In Asia, Western names were used until *2000 when* the committee …. → In Asia, Western names were used until *2000, when* the committee ….	「2000 年」為補述用法，when 引導的副詞子句前，應有逗點。 【詳見「文法寶典」p.244】
第 41－44 題 第二段 第 2 行	*Then in* the Victorian era (19th century) …. → *In* the Victorian era (19th century) ….	上下句並沒有表示時間前後的順序，故應把 Then 去掉。
第 41－44 題 第三段 第 2 行	*It* typically *comes* in a very wide variety …. → *Knives* typically *come* in a very wide variety ….	為了避免 It 的指涉模糊，因為可能指前句說的 knife，也可能指 sett，兩者皆為單數，故改成 Knives 以避免混淆。
第 41 題 (B)	It should *loosely fit* on the body *to be* turned around. → It should *fit loosely* on the body *so that it can* be turned around.	loosely 修飾動詞 fit，應放在後方；so that 表示「以便於」，較符合句意。
第 42 題	Which of the following is a correct description *about* setts? → Which of the following is a correct description *of* setts?	「description of + N」為固定用法。

101 年學測英文科考題出題來源

題　　號	出　　　　　　　　　　處
一、詞彙 第 1～15 題	所有各題對錯答案的選項，均出自「高中常用 7000 字」。
二、綜合測驗 第 16～20 題 第 21～25 題 第 26～30 題	改寫自 Wooden Miracle In Kizhi Island 一文。 改寫自 According to an old Hindu legend... 一文。 改寫自 World Hello Day 一文。
三、文意選填 第 31～40 題	出自 Digital Typhoon: Typhoon Names 一文。
四、閱讀測驗 第 41～44 題 第 45～48 題 第 49～52 題 第 53～56 題	取材自 Kilt 一文。 改編自關於歌手 Wesla Whitfield 的文章。 改寫自 A History of Dining Utensils 一文。 改寫自 Photographing Animals 一文。

【101 年學測】綜合測驗：16-20 出題來源——Blogspot

Wooden Miracle In Kizhi Island

Kizhi is an island on Lake Onega in the Republic of Karelia (Medvezhyegorsky District), Russia with a beautiful ensemble of wooden churches, chapels and houses. It is one of the most popular tourist destinations in Russia and a World Heritage Site.

The island is about 7 km long and 0.5 km wide. It is surrounded by about 5,000 other islands, most of which are very small. The world famous Kizhi Museum is one of the largest out-door museums in Russia – was founded in 1966.

The museum collections contain 83 pieces of the wooden architecture. The core of the collection is an outstanding sample of the wooden architecture – the architectural ensemble of the Kizhi Pogost of Our Savior built on Kizhi Island in the 18 th and the 19 th centuries. In 1990 the ensemble entered the World Heritage List of UNESCO. In 1993 the Kizhi Museum was entered the List of Cultural Objects of Special Value of the Peoples of the Russian Federation by Order of the President.

More than 150 thousand people visit the museum every year. More than 5 million people have visited the museum so far. The museum has very rich collections of the items connected with the cultural history, which demonstrate the subject environment of the past and reveal interrelations of the cultural traditions of the different peoples living in Karelia.

⋮

【101 年學測】綜合測驗：21-25 出題來源──Naute.com

According to an old Hindu legend…

..there was once a time when all human beings were gods, but they so abused their divinity that Brahma, the chief god, decided to take it away from them and hide it where it could never be found.

Where to hide their divinity was the question. So Brahma called a council of the gods to help him decide. "Let's bury it deep in the earth," said the gods. But Brahma answered, "No, that will not do because humans will dig into the earth and find it." Then the gods said, "Let's sink it in the deepest ocean." But Brahma said, "No, not there, for they will learn to dive into the ocean and will find it." Then the gods said, "Let's take it to the top of the highest mountain and hide it there." But once again Brahma replied, "No, that will not do either, because they will eventually climb every mountain and once again take up their divinity." Then the gods gave up and said, "We do not know where to hide it, because it seems that there is no

place on earth or in the sea that human beings will not eventually reach."
Brahma thought for a long time and then said, "Here is what we will do. We
will hide their divinity deep in the center of their own being, for humans
will never think to look for it there."

All the gods agreed that this was the perfect hiding place, and the deed
was done. And since that time humans have been going up and down the
earth, digging, diving, climbing, and exploring--searching for something
already within themselves.

【101 年學測】文意選填：26-30 出題來源──Wikipedia

World Hello Day

Every year, November 21 is World Hello Day. The objective is to say
hello to ten people on the day. By greeting others, the message is for world
leaders to use communication rather than using force to settle conflicts.
The event began in 1973 by Brian and Michael McCormack in response to
the Yom Kippur War. Since then World Hello Day has been observed by
people in 180 countries.

November 21, 2011 is the 39th annual World Hello Day. Anyone can
participate in World Hello Day simply by greeting ten people. This
demonstrates the importance of personal communication for preserving
peace. World Hello Day was begun in response to the conflict between Egypt
and Israel in the fall of 1973. Since then, World Hello Day has been observed
by people in 180 countries. People around the world use the occasion of
World Hello Day as an opportunity to express their concern for world peace.
Beginning with a simple greeting on World Hello Day, their activities send a
message to leaders, encouraging them to use communication rather than
force to settle conflicts. As a global event World Hello Day joins local
participation in a global expression of peace. 31 winners of the Nobel Peace
Prize are among the people who have realized World Hello Day's value as an
instrument for preserving peace and as an occasion that makes it possible for

anyone in the world to contribute to the process of creating peace. Brian McCormack, a Ph.D. graduate of Arizona State University, and Michael McCormack, a graduate of Harvard University, work together to promote this annual global event.

【101 年學測】閱讀測驗：31-40 出題來源

Digital Typhoon: Typhoon Names

Typhoons are named after number-based conventions and a list-based convention. The latter convention is more popular in most countries, such as human names for hurricanes, while the former is popular in Japan. Both conventions, however, share the same problem of ambiguity.

⋮

Number-based conventions are based on the sequential number from the beginning of a typhoon season. For example, Typhoon No. 14 is the 14th typhoon of the typhoon season. This kind of simplified 2-digit convention like "Typhoon No. 14" is very popular in Japan, often used in the media such as newspaper and television. This name does not the represent the year, because at the time of usage the current year is obvious.

⋮

List-based conventions are based on the list of typhoon names defined in advance by the committee of meteorological organizations worldwide. A new name is automatically chosen from the list upon the genesis of a typhoon. The list is defined for each basin and managed by the meteorological organization responsible for the respective basin. For example, Typhoon 200314 has a name "Maemi," which means a cicada or a locust in North Korea, and is an Asian name chosen from the list of typhoon names for the Western North Pacific basin.

⋮

【101 年學測】閱讀測驗：41-44 出題來源——Wikipedia

Kilt

The kilt is a knee-length garment with pleats at the rear, originating in the traditional dress of men and boys in the Scottish Highlands of the 16th century. Since the 19th century it has become associated with the wider culture of Scotland in general, or with Celtic (and more specifically Gaelic) heritage even more broadly. It is most often made of woollen cloth in a tartan pattern.

Although the kilt is most often worn on formal occasions and at Highland games and sports events, it has also been adapted as an item of fashionable informal male clothing in recent years, returning to its roots as an everyday garment.

⋮

【101 年學測】閱讀測驗：45-48 出題來源之一

Wesla Whitfield

Wesla Whitfield is a remarkable singer, with a deep love for that rich storehouse of musical treasures often identified as The Great American Popular Songbook.

Wesla has been developing her skills and learning her demanding craft for a number of years - by her own estimate, it's been ever since she "knew at age two-and-a-half that I would grow up to be a singer."

Her sound and approach would seem to place her somewhere in the intriguing area that borders on both jazz and that aspect of pop music which draws its material largely from the great standards and neglected gems of such as Cole Porter and Irving Berlin and Rodgers and Hart.

⋮

【101 年學測】閱讀測驗：49-52 出題來源

A History of Dining Utensils

⋮

Kitchen forks trace their origins back to the time of the Greeks. These forks were fairly large with two tines that aided in the carving and serving of meat. The tines prevented meat from twisting or moving during carving and allowed food to slide off more easily than it would with a knife.

By the 7th Century CE, royal courts of the Middle East began to use forks at the table for dining. From the 10th through the 13th Centuries, forks were fairly common among the wealthy in Byzantium.

⋮

In 1560, according to a French manners book, different customs evolved in different European countries. For eating soup, Germans are known for using spoons, Italians are known for using forks (presumably the fork assists in eating solid ingredients and the remaining liquid is drunk out of the bowl as it was in the Middle Ages). The Germans and Italians provide a knife for each diner, while the French provide only two or three communal knives for the whole table.

An Englishman named Thomas Coryate brought the first forks to England around 1611 after seeing them in Italy during his travels in 1608.

【101 年學測】閱讀測驗：53-56 出題來源

Photographing Animals

Animals are a favorite subject of many young photographers. Cats, dogs, hamsters and other pets top the list, followed by zoo animals and the occasional lizard.

Because it's hard to get them to sit still and "perform on command," many professional photographers joke that-given a choice-they will refuse to photograph pets or small children. There are ways around the problem of short attention spans, however.

One way to get an appealing portrait of a cat or dog is to hold a biscuit or treat above the camera. The animal's longing look toward the food will be captured by the camera as a soulful gaze. Because it's above the camera-out of the camera's range-the treat won't appear in the picture. When you show the picture to your friends afterwards, they will be impressed by your pet's loving expression.

If you are using fast film, you can take some good, quick shots of pets by simply snapping a picture right after calling their names. You'll get a different expression from your pets using this technique. Depending on your pet's disposition, the picture will capture an inquisitive expression or possibly a look of annoyance-especially if you've awakened Rover from a nap!

To photograph zoo animals, put the camera as close to the animal's cage as possible so you can shoot between the bars or wire mesh. Wild animals don't respond the same way as pets-after all, they don't know you! - so you will have to be more patient to capture a good shot. If it's legal to feed the animals, you can get their attention by having a friend toss them treats as you concentrate on shooting some good picture.

101年學測英文科非選擇題閱卷評分原則說明

閱卷召集人：賴惠玲（國立政治大學英文系教授）

　　101 學年度學科能力測驗英文考科的非選擇題題型共有兩大題，第一大題是中譯英，考生需將兩個中文句子譯成正確而通順達意的英文，題型與過去幾年相同，兩題合計八分。第二大題是英文作文，此次的題型爲書信寫作，評量考生運用所學詞彙、句法寫出切合主題，並妥適達成特定溝通目的的書信；此次的主題是，考生最好的朋友沈迷於電玩，因此常常熬夜，疏忽課業並受到父母責罵，考生需寫一封文長至少120個單詞（words）的信給他／她，給予適當勸告。作文滿分爲二十分。

　　關於閱卷籌備工作，在正式閱卷前，於1月31日先召開評分標準訂定會議，由正、副召集人及協同主持人共十四人，參閱了約3000份的試卷，經過一天的討論，訂定評分標準，選出合適的樣本，編製閱卷參考手冊，供閱卷委員共同參閱。

　　2月2日上午9：00到11：00，168位大學教授，分組進行試閱會議，根據閱卷參考手冊的樣卷，分別評分，並討論評分準則，務求評分標準一致，確保閱卷品質。爲求愼重，試閱會議之後，正、副召集人及協同主持人進行評分標準再確定會議，確認評分原則後才開始正式閱卷。

　　關於評分標準，在中譯英部分，每小題總分 4 分，原則上是每個錯誤扣 0.5 分。作文的評分標準是依據內容、組織、文法句構、詞彙拼字、體例五個項目給分，字數明顯不足則扣總分1分。

閱卷時，每份試卷皆會經過兩位委員分別評分，最後以二人平均
分數計算。如果第一閱與第二閱分數差距超過標準，將再由第三
位委員（正、副召集人或協同主持人）評閱。

　　今年的中譯英與國片有關，句型及詞彙皆為高中生所熟悉；
評量的重點在於考生能否能運用熟悉的詞彙與基本句型將中文翻
譯成正確達意的英文句子，所測驗之詞彙皆控制在大考中心詞彙
表四級內之詞彙，中等程度以上的考生如果能使用正確句型並注
意用字、拼字，應能得理想的分數；但在選取樣卷時發現，很多
考生對於英文詞彙的使用及中英文句構之間的差異，仍有加強的
空間，如中文裡「臺灣製作的影片」譯成英文時為 movies/films
produced in Taiwan，兩者詞序不同；「受到國際的重視」的翻譯
應為 have attracted international attention;「拍攝這些電影的地點」
譯成英文時的關係子句及被動語態結構 the locations where these
films were shot 與中文有差異，考生仍須加強這些用字及句構的
掌握。

　　英文作文題目的主題與考生的生活經驗息息相關，考生大多
能發揮，由於是書信寫作，如果書信格式使用不當或未按照規定
使用所提供之英文名字，會酌予扣分；書信內容是為了勸告最好
的朋友不要再沈迷於電玩，大部分考生均能就個人經驗表達，評
分的考量主要為內容是否能鋪陳書信的溝通目的並對朋友提出具
體勸告，組織連慣性、句子結構及用字適切與否、以及拼字與標
點符號的正確使用等。

101 年學測英文科試題或答案之反映意見回覆

※ 題號：30

【題目】

　　　In the fall of 1973, in an effort to bring attention to the conflict between Egypt and Israel, *World Hello Day* was born. The objective is to promote peace all over the world, and to ___26___ barriers between every nationality. Since then, *World Hello Day*——November 21st of every year——___27___ observed by people in 180 countries.

　　　Taking part couldn't be ___28___. All one has to do is say hello to 10 people on the day. However, in response to the ___29___ of this event, the concepts of fostering peace and harmony do not have to be confined to one day a year. We can ___30___ the spirit going by communicating often and consciously. It is a simple act that anyone can do and it reminds us that communication is more effective than conflict.

30. (A) push 　　　　　　　(B) keep
　　(C) bring 　　　　　　　(D) make

【意見內容】

　　選項 (C) 應為合理答案。文章可解釋為 We can bring the spirit (which is going) by communication often and consciously，亦符合文意。

【大考中心意見回覆】

　　本題評量考生能否掌握 keep *sth.* going 的用法。本題作答線索在於全文文意的理解以及空格後 …the spirit going。選項 (C) bring 無論在用法或者是語意上皆與本文無關，故非本題正答。

※ 題號：34

【題目】

Generally there are two ways to name typhoons: the number-based convention and the list-based convention. Following the number-based convention, typhoons are coded with __31__ types of numbers such as a 4-digit or a 6-digit code. For example, the 14th typhoon in 2003 can be labeled either as Typhoon 0314 or Typhoon 200314. The __32__ of this convention, however, is that a number is hard to remember. The list-based convention, on the other hand, is based on the list of typhoon names compiled in advance by a committee, and is more widely used.

At the very beginning, only __33__ names were used because at that time typhoons were named after girlfriends or wives of the experts on the committee. In 1979, however, male names were also included because women protested against the original naming __34__ for reasons of gender equality.

In Asia, Western names were used until 2000 when the committee decided to use Asian names to __35__ Asians' awareness of typhoons. The names were chosen from a name pool __36__ of 140 names, 10 each from the 14 members of the committee. Each country has its unique naming preferences. Korea and Japan __37__ animal names and China likes names of gods such as Longwang (dragon king) and Fengshen (god of the wind).

After the 140 names are all used in order, they will be ___38___. But the names can be changed. If a member country suffers great damage from a certain typhoon, it can ___39___ that the name of the typhoon be deleted from the list at the annual committee meeting. For example, the names of Nabi by South Korea, and Longwang by China were ___40___ with other names in 2007. The deletion of both names was due to the severe damage caused by the typhoons bearing the names.

(A) request　　(B) favor　　(C) disadvantage　　(D) composed

(E) recycled　　(F) practice　　(G) replaced　　(H) raise

(I) various　　(J) female

【意見內容】

選項 (B) 應為合理答案。選項 (B) favor 與選項 (D) practice 均各自有動詞、名詞形式，若第 34 題先填入 (B) favor，表示「(命名的) 偏好」，而第 37 題則填入 (F) practice 則表示「實行、實施」，更有解釋空間。

【大考中心意見回覆】

本題在於評量考生依據上下文意，掌握名詞 practice 的語意及用法。作答線索在於空格前文意的掌握，尤其是在第二段第一句 At the very beginning...were named after girlfriends or wives...。考生若能掌握 At the very beginning 呼應 original，而 named after girlfriends or wives 呼應 naming practice，便能正確作答。favor 無法與 naming 連用，亦無法與空格後 for reasons of gender equality 之文意相連貫，故本題最適當答案為選項 (F) practice。

※ 題號：42

【題目】

41-44 為題組

　　The kilt is a skirt traditionally worn by Scottish men. It is a tailored garment that is wrapped around the wearer's body at the waist starting from one side, around the front and back and across the front again to the opposite side. The overlapping layers in front are called "aprons." Usually, the kilt covers the body from the waist down to just above the knees. A properly made kilt should not be so loose that the wearer can easily twist the kilt around the body, nor should it be so tight that it causes bulging of the fabric where it is buckled. Underwear may be worn as one prefers.

　　One of the most distinctive features of the kilt is the pattern of squares, or sett, it exhibits. The association of particular patterns with individual families can be traced back hundreds of years. Then in the Victorian era (19th century), weaving companies began to systematically record and formalize the system of setts for commercial purposes. Today there are also setts for States and Provinces, schools and universities, and general patterns that anybody can wear.

　　The kilt can be worn with accessories. On the front apron, there is often a kilt pin, topped with a small decorative family symbol. A small knife can be worn with the kilt too. It typically comes in a very wide variety, from fairly plain to quite elaborate silver- and jewel-ornamented designs. The kilt can also be worn with a sporran, which is the Gaelic word for pouch or purse.

42. Which of the following is a correct description about setts?

(A) They were once symbols for different Scottish families.

(B) They were established by the government for business purposes.

(C) They represented different States and Provinces in the 19th century.

(D) They used to come in one general pattern for all individuals and institutions.

【意見內容】

根據文章中 Today there are also setts for States and Provinces, schools and universities, and general patterns that anybody can wear. 呼應選項 (D) They used to come in one general pattern for all individuals and institutions.，因此判斷選項 (D) 應為合理答案。

【大考中心意見回覆】

本題測驗考生掌握文章的內容細節的能力。作答線索在第二段，尤其是第二句 The association of particular patterns with individual families can be traced back hundreds of years.。根據文章第二段內容，選項 (D) 中 …one general pattern for all individuals and institutions 的敘述與本段文意不符，從最後一句 Today there are also setts for States and Provinces, schools and universities, and general patterns that anybody can wear. 即可判斷選項 (D) 非正確之選項，故選項 (A) 為本題正答無誤。

※ 題號：43

【題目】

41-44 為題組

The kilt is a skirt traditionally worn by Scottish men. It is a tailored garment that is wrapped around the wearer's body at the waist starting from one side, around the front and back and across the front again to the opposite side. The overlapping layers in front are called "aprons." Usually, the kilt covers the body from the waist down to just above the knees. A properly made kilt should not be so loose that the wearer can easily twist the kilt around the body, nor should it be so tight that it causes bulging of the fabric where it is buckled. Underwear may be worn as one prefers.

One of the most distinctive features of the kilt is the pattern of squares, or sett, it exhibits. The association of particular patterns with individual families can be traced back hundreds of years. Then in the Victorian era (19th century), weaving companies began to systematically record and formalize the system of setts for commercial purposes. Today there are also setts for States and Provinces, schools and universities, and general patterns that anybody can wear.

The kilt can be worn with accessories. On the front apron, there is often a kilt pin, topped with a small decorative family symbol. A small knife can be worn with the kilt too. It typically comes in a very wide variety, from fairly plain to quite elaborate silver- and jewel-ornamented designs. The kilt can also be worn with a sporran, which is the Gaelic word for pouch or purse.

43. Which of the following items is **NOT** typically worn with the kilt for decoration?

  (A) A pin.   (B) A purse.

  (C) A ruby apron.   (D) A silver knife..

【意見內容】

根據文章最後一段的敘述，pin 是配件，上面可以放置族徽等飾品，但沒指名 pin 就是飾品，因此選項 (A) 應為本題答案。

【大考中心意見回覆】

本題測驗考生能否掌握文章內容細節之間的關係。作答線索在第三段內容。第三段主題句 The kilt can be worn with accessories 已經點出本段相關細節內容。本題所問的是下列選項中何者不是蘇格蘭裙上的裝飾品，由第二個句子中的 ...there is often a kilt pin, topped with a small decorative family symbol 已可判斷選項 (A) A pin 為正確訊息，而第三句 a small knife 與第五句的 pouch or purse 顯示選項 (B) 與選項 (D) 為正確訊息，但全文內容並未提及 ruby apron 相關之訊息，故選項 (C) 為本題正答。

※ 題號：46

【題目】

45-48 為題組

Wesla Whitfield, a famous jazz singer, has a unique style and life story, so I decided to see one of her performances and interview her for my column.

I went to a nightclub in New York and watched the stage lights go up. After the band played an introduction, Wesla Whitfield wheeled herself onstage in a wheelchair. As she sang, Whitfield's voice was so powerful and soulful that everyone in the room forgot the wheelchair was even there.

At 57, Whitfield is small and pretty, witty and humble, persistent and philosophical. Raised in California, Whitfield began performing in public at age 18, when she took a job as a singing waitress at a pizza parlor. After studying classical music in college, she moved to San Francisco and went on to sing with the San Francisco Opera Chorus.

Walking home from rehearsal at age 29, she was caught in the midst of a random shooting that left her paralyzed from the waist down. I asked how she dealt with the realization that she'd never walk again, and she confessed that initially she didn't want to face it. After a year of depression she tried to kill herself. She was then admitted to a hospital for treatment, where she was able to recover.

Whitfield said she came to understand that the only thing she had lost in this misfortunate event was the ability to walk. She still possessed her most valuable asset——her mind. Pointing to her head, she said, "Everything important is in here. The only real disability in life is losing your mind." When I asked if she was angry about what she had lost, she admitted to being frustrated occasionally, "especially when everybody's dancing, because I love to dance. But **when that happens** I just remove myself so I can focus instead on what I can do."

46. What does "**when that happens**" mean in the last paragraph?
    (A) When Wesla is losing her mind.
    (B) When Wesla is singing on the stage.
    (C) When Wesla is going out in her wheelchair.
    (D) When Wesla is watching other people dancing.

【意見內容】

根據前兩段內容指出，Whitfield 有時會因爲失去控制雙腿的能力而感到生氣沮喪，「特別是」當大家都在跳舞時，由此並不能解讀只有在大家都跳舞才有這種想法，應該是前面文章所提的她仍有最有價值的 mind，選項 (A) 應爲最佳答案。

【大考中心意見回覆】

本題測驗考生根據上下文意掌握文中指代詞（anaphora）的能力。

作答線索在最後一段倒數第二句 When I asked if she was angry about what she had lost, ...especially when everybody's dancing, because I love to dance. But... ；本段前文的文意亦爲作答線索。選項 (A) When Welsa is losing her mind. 與本段文意不符，故選項 (D) When Welsa is watching other people dancing. 爲本題正答無誤。

※ 題號：49

【題目】

<u>49-52 爲題組</u>

Forks trace their origins back to the ancient Greeks. Forks at that time were fairly large with two tines that aided in the carving of meat in the kitchen. The tines prevented meat from twisting or moving during carving and allowed food to slide off more easily than it would with a knife.

By the 7th century A.D., royal courts of the Middle East began to use forks at the table for dining. From the 10th through the 13th centuries, forks were fairly common among the wealthy in Byzantium. In the 11th century, a Byzantine wife brought forks to Italy; however, they were not widely adopted there until the 16th century. Then in 1533, forks were brought from Italy to France. The French were also slow to accept forks, for using them was thought to be awkward.

In 1608, forks were brought to England by Thomas Coryate, who saw them during his travels in Italy. The English first

ridiculed forks as being unnecessary. "Why should a person need
a fork when God had given him hands?" they asked. Slowly,
however, forks came to be adopted by the wealthy as a symbol
of their social status. They were prized possessions made of
expensive materials intended to impress guests. By the mid 1600s,
eating with forks was considered fashionable among the wealthy
British.

Early table forks were modeled after kitchen forks, but small
pieces of food often fell through the two tines or slipped off easily.
In late 17th century France, larger forks with four curved tines were
developed. The additional tines made diners less likely to drop
food, and the curved tines served as a scoop so people did not have
to constantly switch to a spoon while eating. By the early 19th
century, four-tined forks had also been developed in Germany and
England and slowly began to spread to America.

49. What is the passage mainly about?
   (A) The different designs of forks.
   (B) The spread of fork-aided cooking.
   (C) The history of using forks for dining.
   (D) The development of fork-related table manners.

【意見內容】
根據文章第一段第一句 Forks at that time were fairly large with two
tines that aided in the carving of meat in the kitchen. ，以及最後一
段 …larger forks with four curved tines were developed 可知叉子設計
的改變，因此選項 (A) 應為合理答案。

【大考中心意見回覆】

本題測驗考生掌握文章主旨的能力。作答線索遍及全文，尤其各段的主題句提供了本題作答的關鍵。選項 (A) The different designs of forks 僅是本文內容的一部分並非全文主旨，因此選項 (C) The history of using forks for dining. 爲本題正答無誤。

※ 題號：54

【題目】

53-56 爲題組

Animals are a favorite subject of many photographers. Cats, dogs, and other pets top the list, followed by zoo animals. However, because it's hard to get them to sit still and "perform on command," some professional photographers refuse to photograph pets.

One way to get an appealing portrait of a cat or dog is to hold a biscuit or treat above the camera. The animal's longing look toward the food will be captured by the camera, but the treat won't appear in the picture because it's out of the camera's range. When you show the picture to your friends afterwards, they'll be impressed by your pet's loving expression.

If you are using fast film, you can take some good, quick shots of a pet by simply snapping a picture right after calling its name. You'll get a different expression from your pet using this technique. Depending on your pet's mood, the picture will capture an interested, curious expression or possibly a look of annoyance, especially if you've awakened it from a nap.

Taking pictures of zoo animals requires a little more patience. After all, you can't wake up a lion! You may have to wait for a while until the animal does something interesting or moves into a position for you to get a good shot. When photographing zoo animals, don't get too close to the cages, and never tap on the glass or throw things between the bars of a cage. Concentrate on shooting some good pictures, and always respect the animals you are photographing.

54. What is the use of a biscuit in taking pictures of a pet?
    (A) To capture a cute look.
    (B) To create a special atmosphere.
    (C) To arouse the appetite of the pet.
    (D) To keep the pet from looking at the camera.

【意見內容】

1. 選項 (C) 應為合理答案。

   (1) 選項 (A) To capture a cute look 為間接用途，選項 (C) 為直接用途。

   (2) 由該段最後一句中的 loving expression 回指第二句 …animal's longing look forward the food，因拍攝過程中餅乾的主要功能應為「引起寵物的食慾以吸引其注意」。

   (3) 小餅乾的直接用途應該是勾起寵物的食慾，間接讓牠們靜止不動，而不是拿來拍照。

   (4) Appetite 除了做「胃口」解釋外，也可代表「興致、愛好」的意思。文章中的 longing expression toward the food 應是對食物有了興致。

2. 選項 (A) 語意不清。

【大考中心意見回覆】

1. 本題測驗考生掌握文章內容細節之間關係的能力。作答線索在第二段第一句及最後一句 loving expression。本題題幹中已明白說明 the use of a biscuit in taking pictures，且根據第二段第一句 One way to get an appealing portrait of a cat or dog is to hold a biscuit or treat above the camera. 可知，拿著餅乾的目的不是引起寵物的食慾，而是拍得一張動人的照片（to get an appealing portrait）、捕捉可愛的表情（loving expression/a cute look）。再者，appetite 若要當「興致、愛好」解釋，應該與介系詞 for 搭配使用，而非介系詞 of 連用，因此本題選項 (C) 中的 appetite 一詞應單指「食慾」之意。

2. 「to」即有表達「目的」的意思，因此無論有沒有加 help 一詞，選項 (A) To capture a cute look 的語意皆明確、無誤。

※ 題號：非選擇題一、第 1 小題、第 2 小題

【題目】

1. 近年來，許多臺灣製作的影片已經受到國際的重視。
2. 拍攝這些電影的地點也成為熱門的觀光景點。

提示： 請仔細觀察以下三幅連環圖片的內容，並想像第四幅圖片可能的發展，寫出一個涵蓋連環圖片內容並有完整結局的故事。

【意見內容】

中譯英第 1、2 題參考答案之正確性。

【大考中心意見回覆】

非選擇題的評分標準說明將刊登於本中心網頁，敬請參考，謝謝。

100年大學入學學科能力測驗試題
英文考科

第壹部分：單選題（佔72分）

一、詞彙（佔15分）

說明：第1題至第15題，每題4個選項，其中只有一個是最適當的答案，畫記在答案卡之「選擇題答案區」。各題答對得1分；未作答、答錯、或畫記多於一個選項者，該題以零分計算。

1. All the new students were given one minute to _____ introduce themselves to the whole class.
   - (A) briefly
   - (B) famously
   - (C) gradually
   - (D) obviously

2. His dark brown jacket had holes in the elbows and had _____ to light brown, but he continued to wear it.
   - (A) cycled
   - (B) faded
   - (C) loosened
   - (D) divided

3. Everyone in our company enjoys working with Jason. He's got all the qualities that make a _____ partner.
   - (A) desirable
   - (B) comfortable
   - (C) frequent
   - (D) hostile

4. Eyes are sensitive to light. Looking at the sun _____ could damage our eyes.
   - (A) hardly
   - (B) specially
   - (C) totally
   - (D) directly

5. We were forced to _____ our plan for the weekend picnic because of the bad weather.
   - (A) maintain
   - (B) record
   - (C) propose
   - (D) cancel

6. Three people are running for mayor. All three _____ seem confident that they will be elected, but we won't know until the outcome of the election is announced.
   - (A) particles
   - (B) receivers
   - (C) candidates
   - (D) containers

7. If you _____ a traffic law, such as drinking and driving, you may not drive for some time.
   (A) destroy   (B) violate   (C) attack   (D) invade

8. Applying to college means sending in applications, writing study plans, and so on. It's a long _____, and it makes students nervous.
   (A) errand   (B) operation   (C) process   (D) display

9. Dr. Chu's speech on the new energy source attracted great _____ from the audience at the conference.
   (A) attention   (B) fortune   (C) solution   (D) influence

10. Everyone in the office must attend the meeting tomorrow. There are no _____ allowed.
    (A) exceptions   (B) additions   (C) divisions   (D) measures

11. To make fresh lemonade, cut the lemon in half, _____ the juice into a bowl, and then add as much water and sugar as you like.
    (A) decrease   (B) squeeze   (C) freeze   (D) cease

12. Buddhism is the _____ religion in Thailand, with 90% of the total population identified as Buddhists.
    (A) racial   (B) competitive   (C) modest   (D) dominant

13. When I open a book, I look first at the table of _____ to get a general idea of the book and to see which chapters I might be interested in reading.
    (A) contracts   (B) contents   (C) contests   (D) contacts

14. The children were so _____ to see the clown appear on stage that they laughed, screamed, and clapped their hands happily.
    (A) admirable   (B) fearful   (C) delighted   (D) intense

15. Typhoon Maggie brought to I-lan County a huge amount of rainfall, much greater than the _____ rainfall of the season in the area.
    (A) average   (B) considerate   (C) promising   (D) enjoyable

二、綜合測驗（佔 15 分）

說明：第 16 題至第 30 題，每題一個空格，請依文意選出最適當的一個答案，
　　　畫記在答案卡之「選擇題答案區」。各題答對得 1 分；未作答、答錯、
　　　或畫記多於一個選項者，該題以零分計算。

　　When it comes to Egypt, people think of pyramids and mummies,
both of which are closely related to Egyptian religious beliefs.　The
ancient Egyptians believed firmly in life ___16___ death.　When a person
died, his or her soul was thought to travel to an underworld, where it
___17___ a series of judgments before it could progress to a better life in
the next world.　For the soul to travel smoothly, the body had to___18___
unharmed.　Thus, they learned how to preserve the body by drying it
out, oiling and then ___19___ the body in linen, before placing it in the
coffin.　Egyptians also built pyramids as ___20___ for their kings, or
pharaohs.　The pyramid housed the pharaoh's body together with
priceless treasure, which would accompany him into the next world.

16. (A) for　　　　　(B) by　　　　　(C) after　　　　(D) into
17. (A) went through　(B) made up　　(C) changed into　(D) turned out
18. (A) remain　　　　(B) remind　　　(C) repair　　　　(D) replace
19. (A) wrapped　　　(B) wrapping　　(C) to wrap　　　(D) being wrapped
20. (A) galleries　　　(B) landmarks　(C) companies　　(D) tombs

　　On March 23, 1999, the musical MAMMA MIA! made its first
public appearance in London.　It ___21___ the kind of welcome it has
been getting ever since.　The audience went wild.　They were literally
out of their seats and singing and dancing in the aisles.

　　MAMMA MIA! has become a ___22___ entertainment phenomenon.
More than 30 million people all over the world have fallen in love with the
characters, the story and the music.　The musical has been performed in
more than nine languages, with more productions than any ___23___ musical.

Its worldwide popularity is mainly due to its theme music, which showcases ABBA's timeless songs in a fresh and vital way __24__ retains the essence of both pop music and good musical theater. It has __25__ so many people that a film version was also made. To no one's surprise, it has enjoyed similar popularity.

21. (A) is given   (B) was given   (C) has given   (D) had given
22. (A) worthy   (B) global   (C) sticky   (D) physical
23. (A) one   (B) thing   (C) other   (D) else
24. (A) how   (B) what   (C) where   (D) that
25. (A) appealed to   (B) presented with
     (C) resulted in   (D) brought about

Which is more valuable? Water or diamonds? Water is more useful to mankind than diamonds, and yet __26__ are costlier. Why? Called the diamond-water paradox, this is a classic problem posed to students of economics.

The answer has to do with supply and demand. Being a rare natural resource, diamonds are __27__ in supply. However, their demand is high because many people buy them to tell the world that they have money, __28__ as *conspicuous consumption* in economics. In other words, the scarcity of goods is __29__ causes humans to attribute value. If we __30__ surrounded by an unending abundance of diamonds, we probably wouldn't value them very much. Hence, diamonds carry a higher monetary value than water, even though we find more use for water.

26. (A) the above   (B) the former   (C) the following   (D) the latter
27. (A) traded   (B) weakened   (C) limited   (D) noticed
28. (A) term   (B) termed   (C) terms   (D) was termed
29. (A) what   (B) which   (C) why   (D) how
30. (A) be   (B) being   (C) to be   (D) were

三、文意選填（佔 10 分）

說明：第 31 題至第 40 題，每題一個空格，請依文意在文章後所提供的 (A) 到 (J) 選項中分別選出最適當者，並將其英文字母代號畫記在答案卡之「選擇題答案區」。各題答對得 1 分；未作答、答錯、或畫記多於一個選項者，該題以零分計算。

Popcorn is one of the snacks that rarely fail to make watching a movie more fun. However, the modern way of preparing this __31__ snack may carry an unhappy secret. Research by the U.S. government now reports that microwave popcorn may contain substances that can cause health __32__.

Researchers found that commercial popcorn companies often coat their microwave popcorn bags with a __33__ called perfluorooctanoic acid (PFOA) which has been found to cause both cancer and lung disease in laboratory animals. Making matters worse, the artificial butter substitute that generally __34__ with microwavable popcorn contains a common food-flavoring substance. This substance, according to health scientists, is __35__ for some serious lung diseases.

For an easy and __36__ alternative, nutritionists suggest that we pop our own popcorn. All that is __37__ is a large, high pot, about four tablespoons of vegetable oil and a small handful of organic popcorn kernels. When the kernels start __38__, shake the pot to let the steam escape and to let the unpopped kernels fall to the bottom. As soon as the popping slows down, __39__ the pot from the stove. Then pour the popcorn into a bowl and season with a small __40__ of real butter or olive oil and natural salt. And the healthy and fun snack is ready to serve.

(A) chemical　　(B) amount　　(C) popping　　(D) popular
(E) comes　　　(F) healthy　　(G) needed　　(H) responsible
(I) remove　　　(J) problems

四、閱讀測驗（佔 32 分）

說明：　第 41 題至第 56 題，每題 4 個選項，請分別根據各篇文章之文意選出最適當的一個答案，畫記在答案卡之「選擇題答案區」。各題答對得 2 分；未作答、答錯、或畫記多於一個選項者，該題以零分計算。

41-44 為題組

　　There is a long-held belief that when meeting someone, the more eye contact we have with the person, the better. The result is an unfortunate tendency for people making initial contact—in a job interview, for example—to stare fixedly at the other individual. However, this behavior is likely to make the interviewer feel very uncomfortable. Most of us are comfortable with eye contact lasting a few seconds. But eye contact which persists longer than that can make us nervous.

　　Another widely accepted belief is that powerful people in a society—often men—show their dominance over others by touching them in a variety of ways. In fact, research shows that in almost all cases, lower-status people initiate touch. Women also initiate touch more often than men do.

　　The belief that rapid speech and lying go together is also widespread and enduring. We react strongly—and suspiciously—to fast talk. However, the opposite is a greater cause for suspicion. Speech that is slow, because it is laced with pauses or errors, is a more reliable indicator of lying than the opposite.

41. Which of the following statements is true according to the passage?
　　(A) Rapid speech without mistakes is a reliable sign of intelligence.
　　(B) Women often play a more dominant role than men in a community.
　　(C) Speaking slowly is more often a sign of lying than speaking quickly.
　　(D) Touching tends to be initiated first by people of higher social positions.

42. What is true about fixing your eyes on a person when you first meet him/her?
(A) Fixing your eyes on the person will make him/her feel at ease.
(B) It is more polite to fix your eyes on him/her as long as you can.
(C) Most people feel uneasy to have eye contact for over a few seconds.
(D) It doesn't make a difference whether you fix your eyes on him/her or not.

43. Which of the following is **NOT** discussed in the passage?
(A) Facial expressions.   (B) Physical contact.
(C) Rate of speech.   (D) Eye contact.

44. What is the main idea of the passage?
(A) People have an instinct for interpreting non-verbal communication.
(B) We should not judge the intention of a person by his body language.
(C) A good knowledge of body language is essential for successful communication.
(D) Common beliefs about verbal and non-verbal communication are not always correct.

45-48 為題組

It is easy for us to tell our friends from our enemies. But can other animals do the same? Elephants can! They can use their sense of vision and smell to tell the difference between people who pose a threat and those who do not.

In Kenya, researchers found that elephants react differently to clothing worn by men of the Maasai and Kamba ethnic groups. Young Maasai men spear animals and thus pose a threat to elephants; Kamba men are mainly farmers and are not a danger to elephants.

In an experiment conducted by animal scientists, elephants were first presented with clean clothing or clothing that had been worn for five days by either a Maasai or a Kamba man. When the elephants detected the smell of clothing worn by a Maasai man, they moved away from the smell faster and took longer to relax than when they detected the smells of either clothing worn by Kamba men or clothing that had not been worn at all.

Garment color also plays a role, though in a different way. In the same study, when the elephants saw red clothing not worn before, they reacted angrily, as red is typically worn by Maasai men. Rather than running away as they did with the smell, the elephants acted aggressively toward the red clothing.

The researchers believe that the elephants' emotional reactions are due to their different interpretations of the smells and the sights. Smelling a potential danger means that a threat is nearby and the best thing to do is run away and hide. Seeing a potential threat without its smell means that risk is low. Therefore, instead of showing fear and running away, the elephants express their anger and become aggressive.

45. According to the passage, which of the following statements is true about Kamba and Maasai people?
    (A) Maasai people are a threat to elephants.
    (B) Kamba people raise elephants for farming.
    (C) Both Kamba and Maasai people are elephant hunters.
    (D) Both Kamba and Maasai people traditionally wear red clothing.

46. How did the elephants react to smell in the study?
    (A) They attacked a man with the smell of new clothing.
    (B) They needed time to relax when smelling something unfamiliar.

(C) They became anxious when they smelled Kamba-scented clothing.

(D) They were frightened and ran away when they smelled their enemies.

47. What is the main idea of this passage?
(A) Elephants use sight and smell to detect danger.
(B) Elephants attack people who wear red clothing.
(C) Scientists are now able to control elephants' emotions.
(D) Some Kenyan tribes understand elephants' emotions very well.

48. What can be inferred about the elephant's behavior from this passage?
(A) Elephants learn from their experiences.
(B) Elephants have sharper sense of smell than sight.
(C) Elephants are more intelligent than other animals.
(D) Elephants tend to attack rather than escape when in danger.

49-52 為題組

It was something she had dreamed of since she was five. Finally, after years of training and intensive workouts, Deborah Duffey was going to compete in her first high school basketball game. The goals of becoming an outstanding player and playing college ball were never far from Deborah's mind.

The game was against Mills High School. With 1:42 minutes left in the game, Deborah's team led by one point. A player of Mills had possession of the ball, and Deborah ran to guard against her. As Deborah shuffled sideways to block the player, her knee went out and she collapsed on the court in burning pain. Just like that, Deborah's season was over.

After suffering the bad injury, Deborah found that, for the first time in her life, she was in a situation beyond her control. Game after game, she could do nothing but sit on the sidelines watching others play the game that she loved so much.

Injuries limited Deborah's time on the court as she hurt her knees three more times in the next five years. She had to spend countless hours in a physical therapy clinic to receive treatment. Her frequent visits there gave her a passion and respect for the profession. And Deborah began to see a new light in her life.

Currently a senior in college, Deborah focuses on pursuing a degree in physical therapy. After she graduates, Deborah plans to use her knowledge to educate people how to best take care of their bodies and cope with the feelings of hopelessness that she remembers so well.

49. What is the best title for this passage?

  (A) A Painful Mistake   (B) A Great Adventure

  (C) A Lifelong Punishment   (D) A New Direction in Life

50. How did Deborah feel when she first hurt her knee?

  (A) Excited.   (B) Confused.

  (C) Ashamed.   (D) Disappointed.

51. What is true about Deborah Duffey?

  (A) She didn't play on the court after the initial injury.

  (B) She injured her knee when she was trying to block her opponent.

  (C) She knew that she couldn't be a basketball player when she was a child.

  (D) She refused to seek professional assistance to help her recover from her injuries.

52. What was the new light that Deborah saw in her life?
   (A) To help people take care of their bodies.
   (B) To become a teacher of Physical Education.
   (C) To become an outstanding basketball player.
   (D) To receive treatment in a physical therapy office.

53-56 爲題組

Redwood trees are the tallest plants on the earth, reaching heights of up to 100 meters. They are also known for their longevity, typically 500 to 1000 years, but sometimes more than 2000 years. A hundred million years ago, in the age of dinosaurs, redwoods were common in the forests of a much more moist and tropical North America. As the climate became drier and colder, they retreated to a narrow strip along the Pacific coast of Northern California.

The trunk of redwood trees is very stout and usually forms a single straight column. It is covered with a beautiful soft, spongy bark. This bark can be pretty thick, well over two feet in the more mature trees. It gives the older trees a certain kind of protection from insects, but the main benefit is that it keeps the center of the tree intact from moderate forest fires because of its thickness. This fire resistant quality explains why the giant redwood grows to live that long. While most other types of trees are destroyed by forest fires, the giant redwood actually prospers because of them. Moderate fires will clear the ground of competing plant life, and the rising heat dries and opens the ripe cones of the redwood, releasing many thousands of seeds onto the ground below.

New trees are often produced from sprouts, little baby trees, which form at the base of the trunk. These sprouts grow slowly, nourished by the root system of the "mother" tree. When the main tree dies, the sprouts are then free to grow as full trees, forming a **"fairy ring"** of trees around the initial tree. These trees, in turn, may give rise to more sprouts, and the cycle continues.

53. Why were redwood trees more prominent in the forests of North America millions of years ago?
    (A) The trees were taller and stronger.
    (B) The soil was softer for seeds to sprout.
    (C) The climate was warmer and more humid.
    (D) The temperature was lower along the Pacific coast.

54. What does a **"fairy ring"** in the last paragraph refer to?
    (A) Circled tree trunks.
    (B) Connected root systems.
    (C) Insect holes around an old tree.
    (D) Young trees surrounding a mature tree.

55. Which of the following is a function of the tree bark as mentioned in the passage?
    (A) It allows redwood trees to bear seeds.
    (B) It prevents redwood trees from attack by insects.
    (C) It helps redwood trees absorb moisture in the air.
    (D) It makes redwood trees more beautiful and appealing.

56. Why do redwood trees grow to live that long according to the passage?
    (A) They have heavy and straight tree trunks.
    (B) They are properly watered and nourished.
    (C) They are more resistant to fire damage than other trees.
    (D) They produce many young trees to sustain their life cycle.

第貳部份：非選擇題（佔 28 分）

一、中譯英（佔 8 分）

說明：1. 請將以下中文句子譯成正確、通順、達意的英文，並將答案寫在「答案卷」上。

　　　2. 請依序作答，並標明題號。每題 4 分，共 8 分。

1. 臺灣的夜市早已被認為足以代表我們的在地文化。

2. 每年它們都吸引了成千上萬來自不同國家的觀光客。

二、英文作文（佔 20 分）

說明：1. 依提示在「答案卷」上寫一篇英文作文。

　　　2. 文長約 100 至 120 個單詞（words）。

提示：請仔細觀察以下三幅連環圖片的內容，並想像第四幅圖片可能的發展，寫出一個涵蓋連環圖片內容並有完整結局的故事。

100年度學科能力測驗英文科試題詳解

第壹部分：單選題

一、詞彙：

1. (**A**) All the new students were given one minute to briefly introduce themselves to the whole class.

   全體新生都有一分鐘的時間向全班同學簡短地做自我介紹。

   (A) ***briefly*** 〔'briflɪ〕 *adv.* 簡短地【88 日大也考過】
   (B) famously 〔'feməslɪ〕 *adv.* 極好
   (C) gradually 〔'grædʒʊəlɪ〕 *adv.* 逐漸地
   (D) obviously 〔'abvɪəslɪ〕 *adv.* 顯然

   introduce 〔ˌɪntrə'djus〕 *v.* 介紹

2. (**B**) His dark brown jacket had holes in the elbows and had faded to light brown, but he continued to wear it.

   他深咖啡色的夾克在手肘部分有破洞，而且已經褪色成淡咖啡色，但他還是繼續穿。

   (A) cycle 〔'saɪkḷ〕 *v.* 循環　　(B) ***fade*** 〔fed〕 *v.* 褪色
   (C) loosen 〔'lusn̩〕 *v.* 鬆開　　(D) divide 〔də'vaɪd〕 *v.* 分割

   hole 〔hol〕 *n.* 洞；破洞　　elbow 〔'ɛl,bo〕 *n.* 手肘；（衣服的）肘部

3. (**A**) Everyone in our company enjoys working with Jason. He's got all the qualities that make a desirable partner.

   我們公司裡的每個人都喜歡和傑森工作。他擁有足以成爲理想夥伴的所有特質。

   (A) ***desirable*** 〔dɪ'zaɪrəbḷ〕 *adj.* 理想的
   (B) comfortable 〔'kʌmfə·təbḷ〕 *adj.* 舒服的
   (C) frequent 〔'frikwənt〕 *adj.* 經常的
   (D) hostile 〔'hɑstḷ, -tɪl〕 *adj.* 敵對的

   quality 〔'kwɑlətɪ〕 *n.* 特質
   make 〔mek〕 *v.* （因有某特點、品質等而）足以成爲
   partner 〔'pɑrtnə·〕 *n.* 夥伴

4. (**D**) Eyes are sensitive to light. Looking at the sun <u>directly</u> could damage our eyes. 眼睛對光很敏感。直視太陽可能會傷害我們的眼睛。

 (A) hardly〔'hɑrdlɪ〕*adv.* 幾乎不
 (B) specially〔'spɛʃəlɪ〕*adv.* 特別地
 (C) totally〔'totl̩ɪ〕*adv.* 全部地
 (D) *directly*〔də'rɛktlɪ〕*adv.* 直接地

 sensitive〔'sɛnsətɪv〕*adj.* 敏感的　　damage〔'dæmɪdʒ〕*v.* 損害

5. (**D**) We were forced to <u>cancel</u> our plan for the weekend picnic because of the bad weather.
　我們不得不取消週末野餐的計劃，因為天氣不好。

 (A) maintain〔men'ten〕*v.* 維持　　(B) record〔rɪ'kɔrd〕*v.* 記錄
 (C) propose〔prə'poz〕*v.* 提議
 (D) *cancel*〔'kænsl̩〕*v.* 取消【92 學測也考過】

 force〔fors〕*v.* 強迫；使不得不

6. (**C**) Three people are running for mayor. All three <u>candidates</u> seem confident that they will be elected, but we won't know until the outcome of the election is announced.
　有三個人競選市長。這三個候選人似乎都很有信心自己會當選，
　但是我們要到選舉結果宣布才會知道。

 (A) particle〔'pɑrtɪkl̩〕*n.* 粒子　　(B) receiver〔rɪ'sivɚ〕*n.* 聽筒
 (C) *candidate*〔'kændə,det〕*n.* 候選人
 (D) container〔kən'tenɚ〕*n.* 容器

 run for 競選　　mayor〔'meɚ〕*n.* 市長
 confident〔'kɑnfədənt〕*adj.* 有信心的　　elect〔ɪ'lɛkt〕*v.* 選舉
 outcome〔'aʊt,kʌm〕*n.* 結果　　election〔ɪ'lɛkʃən〕*n.* 選舉
 announce〔ə'naʊns〕*v.* 宣布

7. (**B**) If you <u>violate</u> a traffic law, such as drinking and driving, you may not drive for some time.
　如果你違反交通規則，例如酒醉駕車，你可能會有一段時間不能開車。

 (A) destroy〔dɪ'strɔɪ〕*v.* 破壞　　(B) *violate*〔'vaɪə,let〕*v.* 違反
 (C) attack〔ə'tæk〕*v.* 攻擊　　(D) invade〔ɪn'ved〕*v.* 入侵

 law〔lɔ〕*n.* 法律；法規　　drinking〔'drɪŋkɪŋ〕*n.* 喝酒
 drinking and driving 酒醉駕車

8. (**C**) Applying to college means sending in applications, writing study plans, and so on. It's a long <u>process</u>, and it makes students nervous.
申請大學意味著寄送申請書、撰寫讀書計畫等等。這是一個漫長的<u>過程</u>，而且會使學生緊張。

(A) errand〔ˋɛrənd〕*n.* 差事
(B) operation〔͵ɑpəˋreʃən〕*n.* 操作；手術
(C) *process*〔ˋprɑsɛs〕*n.* 過程　　(D) display〔dɪˋsple〕*n.* 展示

apply to 向⋯申請　　*send in* 郵寄；提出
application〔͵æpləˋkeʃən〕*n.* 申請書　　*and so on* 等等
nervous〔ˋnɝvəs〕*adj.* 緊張的

9. (**A**) Dr. Chu's speech on the new energy source attracted great <u>attention</u> from the audience at the conference.
朱博士對於新能源的演說非常吸引會議上聽眾們的<u>注意</u>。

(A) *attention*〔əˋtɛnʃən〕*n.* 注意
(B) fortune〔ˋfɔrtʃən〕*n.* 運氣；財富
(C) solution〔səˋluʃən〕*n.* 解決之道
(D) influence〔ˋɪnfluəns〕*n.* 影響

energy〔ˋɛnədʒɪ〕*n.* 能量　　source〔sors〕*n.* 來源
attract〔əˋtrækt〕*v.* 吸引　　audience〔ˋɔdɪəns〕*n.* 聽眾
conference〔ˋkɑnfərəns〕*n.* 會議

10. (**A**) Everyone in the office must attend the meeting tomorrow. There are no <u>exceptions</u> allowed.
辦公室裡的每個人明天都必須參加會議。不允許有任何<u>例外</u>。

(A) *exception*〔ɪkˋsɛpʃən〕*n.* 例外【82 夜大也考過】
(B) addition〔əˋdɪʃən〕*n.* 附加物
(C) division〔dəˋvɪʒən〕*n.* 劃分
(D) measure〔ˋmɛʒə〕*n.* 措施

attend〔əˋtɛnd〕*v.* 參加　　meeting〔ˋmitɪŋ〕*n.* 會議
allow〔əˋlaʊ〕*v.* 允許

11. (**B**) To make fresh lemonade, cut the lemon in half, <u>squeeze</u> the juice into a bowl, and then add as much water and sugar as you like.
要做新鮮的檸檬汁，將檸檬切成兩半，把汁<u>擠</u>入碗中，並依你的喜好加入水和糖。

(A) decrease〔dɪˋkris〕*v.* 減少
(B) *squeeze*〔skwiz〕*v.* 擠壓
(C) freeze〔friz〕*v.* 結冰
(D) cease〔sis〕*v.* 停止

lemonade〔ˌlɛmənˈed〕n. 檸檬汁　　*cut ~ in half* 把～切成兩半
juice〔dʒus〕n. 果汁　　bowl〔bol〕n. 碗
add〔æd〕v. 添加　　sugar〔ˈʃʊgɚ〕n. 糖

12. (**D**) Buddhism is the <u>dominant</u> religion in Thailand, with 90% of the
total population identified as Buddhists.
佛教在泰國是<u>主要的</u>宗教，有百分之九十的人口被確認是佛教徒。

(A) racial〔ˈreʃəl〕adj. 種族的

(B) competitive〔kəmˈpɛtətɪv〕adj. 競爭的

(C) modest〔ˈmɑdɪst〕adj. 謙虛的

(D) *dominant*〔ˈdɑmənənt〕adj. 主要的【88 日大的綜合測驗也考過】

Buddhism〔ˈbʊdɪzəm〕n. 佛教　　religion〔rɪˈlɪdʒən〕n. 宗教
Thailand〔ˈtaɪlənd〕n. 泰國　　population〔ˌpɑpjəˈleʃən〕n. 人口
identify〔aɪˈdɛntəˌfaɪ〕v. 確認　　Buddhist〔ˈbʊdɪst〕n. 佛教徒

13. (**B**) When I open a book, I look first at the table of <u>contents</u> to get a
general idea of the book and to see which chapters I might be
interested in reading. 當我翻開一本書，我會先看<u>目錄</u>以了解全書
大概的內容，看看哪些是我可能會有興趣閱讀的章節。

(A) contract〔ˈkɑntrækt〕n. 合約

(B) *contents*〔ˈkɑntɛnts〕n. pl. 內容；目錄
　　 the table of contents 目錄

(C) contest〔ˈkɑntɛst〕n. 比賽　　(D) contact〔ˈkɑntækt〕n. 聯絡
table〔ˈtebl〕n. 一覽表　　general〔ˈdʒɛnərəl〕adj. 總括的
chapter〔ˈtʃæptɚ〕n. (書籍的) 章節

14. (**C**) The children were so <u>delighted</u> to see the clown appear on stage
that they laughed, screamed, and clapped their hands happily.
孩子們看到小丑出現在舞台上時很<u>高興</u>，他們都大笑、尖叫，並
快樂地鼓掌。

(A) admirable〔ˈædmərəbl〕adj. 令人欽佩的

(B) fearful〔ˈfɪrfəl〕adj. 可怕的

(C) *delighted*〔dɪˈlaɪtɪd〕adj. 高興的
　　【86 日大考過 delight 當動詞的用法，作「使高興；使開心」解】

(D) intense〔ɪnˈtɛns〕adj. 強烈的
clown〔klaʊn〕n. 小丑　　stage〔stedʒ〕n. 舞台
scream〔skrim〕v. 尖叫　　clap〔klæp〕v. 鼓掌

15. (**A**) Typhoon Maggie brought to I-lan County a huge amount of rainfall, much greater than the <u>average</u> rainfall of the season in the area. 瑪姬颱風爲宜蘭縣帶來大量的降雨,比該地區當季<u>平均</u>降雨量還多很多。

    (A) ***average*** 〔'ævərɪdʒ〕*adj.* 平均的

    【83 日大則考過 average 當名詞用,作「平均數」解】

    (B) considerate 〔kən'sɪdərɪt〕*adj.* 體貼的

    (C) promising 〔'prɑmɪsɪŋ〕*adj.* 有希望的

    (D) enjoyable 〔ɪn'dʒɔɪəbḷ〕*adj.* 令人愉快的

    county 〔'kaʊntɪ〕*n.* 縣   huge 〔hjudʒ〕*adj.* 巨大的

    rainfall 〔'ren,fɔl〕*n.* 降雨;降雨量   season 〔'sizṇ〕*n.* 季節

二、綜合測驗:

When it comes to Egypt, people think of pyramids and mummies, both of which are closely related to Egyptian religious beliefs. The ancient Egyptians believed firmly in life <u>after</u> death.
16

一提到埃及,人們就會想到金字塔和木乃伊,兩者都跟埃及的宗敎信仰密切相關。古埃及人堅決相信死後有來生。

    when it comes to 一提到   Egypt 〔'idʒəpt〕*n.* 埃及

    think of 想到   pyramid 〔'pɪrəmɪd〕*n.* 金字塔

    mummy 〔'mʌmɪ〕*n.* 木乃伊   closely 〔'kloslɪ〕*adv.* 密切地

    be related to 和…有關

    Egyptian 〔ɪ'dʒɪpʃən〕*adj.* 埃及的   *n.* 埃及人

    religious belief 宗敎信仰   ancient 〔'enʃənt〕*adj.* 古代的

    believe in 相信有;相信…的存在   firmly 〔'fɝmlɪ〕*adv.* 堅定地

16. (**C**) ***life after death*** 死後的世界;來生

When a person died, his or her soul was thought to travel to an underworld, where it <u>went through</u> a series of judgments before it could progress to a
17
better life in the next world.

當一個人死的時候,一般認爲他(她)的靈魂會到陰間,在那裡經歷一連串的審判,然後才能進入來世,過更好的生活。

soul〔sol〕*n.* 靈魂　　travel〔'trævḷ〕*v.* 行進；前進
underworld〔'ʌndə,wɜld〕*n.* 陰間；冥府　　*a series of* 一串的
judgment〔'dʒʌdʒmənt〕*n.* 審判　　progress〔prə'grɛs〕*v.* 前進
the next world 來世（ = *another world* = *the other world*
　 = *the world to come* ）

17.（ **A** ）(A) *go through* 經歷　　　　　(B) make up 編造；化妝；組成
　　　　　(C) change into 變成　　　　　(D) turn out 結果成為

For the soul to travel smoothly, the body had to <u>remain</u> unharmed. Thus,
18
they learned how to preserve the body by drying it out, oiling and then
<u>wrapping</u> the body in linen, before placing it in the coffin.
19
為了要讓靈魂順利行進，屍體就必須不受損害。因此，他們學會保存屍體的方
法，要讓它完全乾燥、塗油，然後用亞麻布包裹，之後再放進棺材。

smoothly〔'smuðlɪ〕*adv.* 順利地　　body〔'badɪ〕*n.* 屍體
unharmed〔ʌn'harmd〕*adj.* 無損的；未受傷害的
thus〔ðʌs〕*adv.* 因此　　preserve〔prɪ'zɜv〕*v.* 保存
dry out 使完全乾燥　　oil〔ɔɪl〕*v.* 塗油　　linen〔'lɪnɪn〕*n.* 亞麻布
place〔ples〕*v.* 放置　　coffin〔'kɔfɪn〕*n.* 棺材

18.（ **A** ）(A) *remain*〔rɪ'men〕*v.* 保持；依舊
　　　　　(B) remind〔rɪ'maɪnd〕*v.* 提醒；使想起
　　　　　(C) repair〔rɪ'pɛr〕*v.* 修理　　(D) replace〔rɪ'ples〕*v.* 取代

19.（ **B** ）and 為對等連接詞，須連接文法地位相同的單字、片語，或子句，
　　　　　前面是動名詞 drying it out 和 oiling，故空格也應是動名詞，選
　　　　　(B) *wrapping*。【93 指考也考過和本題一樣的觀念】
　　　　　wrap〔ræp〕*v.* 包；裹

Egyptians also built pyramids as <u>tombs</u> for their kings, or pharaohs. The
20
pyramid housed the pharaoh's body together with priceless treasure, which
would accompany him into the next world.
埃及人也會為他們的國王，也就是法老王，建造金字塔，作為他們的墳墓。金
字塔存放了法老王的屍體，以及無價的寶藏，這些將會陪伴他進入來生。

or〔ɔr〕*conj.* 也就是　　pharaoh〔ˈfɛro〕*n.* 法老王
house〔haʊz〕*v.* 收容；收藏　　***together with*** 連同（*= along with*）
priceless〔ˈpraɪslɪs〕*adj.* 無價的；極為貴重的
treasure〔ˈtrɛʒɚ〕*n.* 寶藏；寶物　　accompany〔əˈkʌmpənɪ〕*v.* 陪伴

20.（**D**）(A) gallery〔ˈgælərɪ〕*n.* 畫廊　　(B) landmark〔ˈlændˌmɑrk〕*n.* 地標
　　　　(C) company〔ˈkʌmpənɪ〕*n.* 公司
　　　　(D) ***tomb***〔tum〕*n.* 墳墓

On March 23, 1999, the musical MAMMA MIA! made its first public
appearance in London. It <u>was given</u> the kind of welcome it has been
　　　　　　　　　　　　　　21
getting ever since. The audience went wild. They were literally out of
their seats and singing and dancing in the aisles.

1999 年三月二十三日，音樂劇 MAMMA MIA!在倫敦首度公開出演，當時
大受歡迎，而且至今歷久不衰。觀眾為之瘋狂，他們不誇張，真的是離開座位，
在走道上一起唱一起跳。

musical〔ˈmjuzɪkl̩〕*n.* 音樂劇
appearance〔əˈpɪrəns〕*n.* 出現；演出　　***ever since*** 從當時以來
audience〔ˈɔdɪəns〕*n.* 觀眾　　***go wild*** 瘋狂
literally〔ˈlɪtərəlɪ〕*adv.* 照字面地；實在地；不誇張地
out of *one's seat* 離開座位　　aisle〔aɪl〕*n.* 走道

21.（**B**）表示當時的這場表演「受到歡迎」，應該用過去式的被動語態，選 (B)
　　　　was given。【過去式的被動語態，在 88、89 學測，92 指考也考過】

MAMMA MIA! has become a <u>global</u> entertainment phenomenon.
　　　　　　　　　　　　　　22
More than 30 million people all over the world have fallen in love with the
characters, the story and the music. The musical has been performed in
more than nine languages, with more productions than any <u>other</u> musical.
　　　　　　　　　　　　　　　　　　　　　　　　　　　　　　23
MAMMA MIA!已經成為全球娛樂界的奇蹟。全世界超過三千萬人已經愛
上了劇中的角色、故事和音樂。這齣音樂劇演出的語言超過九種，演出場次比
起任何其他音樂劇還多。

entertainment〔͵ɛntɚˈtɛnmənt〕*n.* 娛樂
phenomenon〔fəˈnɑmə͵nɑn〕*n.* 現象；奇蹟
all over the world 全世界　　***fall in love with*** 愛上…
character〔ˈkærɪktɚ〕*n.* 人物；角色
perform〔pɚˈfɔrm〕*v.* 表演；演出
production〔prəˈdʌkʃən〕*n.* (戲劇) 演出；生產；製作

22. (**B**) (A) worthy〔ˈwɝðɪ〕*adj.* 值得的　　(B) ***global***〔ˈglobḷ〕*adj.* 全球的
　　　(C) sticky〔ˈstɪkɪ〕*adj.* 黏的
　　　(D) physical〔ˈfɪzɪkḷ〕*adj.* 身體的；物質的

23. (**C**) 依句意,「比任何其他的音樂劇還多」,應用 "more~ any ***other***",故
　　　本題選 (C)。(D) else 雖也表「其他的」但不與 any 連用,而是跟在疑
　　　問詞或 any-, no-, some- 的結合字之後。

Its worldwide popularity is mainly due to its theme music, which showcases
ABBA's timeless songs in a fresh and vital way <u>that</u> retains the essence of
　　　　　　　　　　　　　　　　　　　　24
both pop music and good musical theater.　It has <u>appealed to</u> so many
　　　　　　　　　　　　　　　　　　　　　25
people that a film version was also made.　To no one's surprise, it has
enjoyed similar popularity.

它會受到全世界的歡迎主要是因爲它的主題音樂,它將 ABBA 的永恆歌曲用嶄
新及充滿活力的方式展現出來,當中保留了流行音樂及音樂劇的精髓,這齣戲
已吸引了許多人,連電影版本也已完成。不讓人意外的是,它也同樣受到歡迎。

worldwide〔ˈwɝld͵waɪd〕*adj.* 全世界的
popularity〔͵pɑpjəˈlærətɪ〕*n.* 流行；受歡迎　　***be due to*** 由於
theme music 主題音樂　　showcase〔ˈʃo͵kes〕*v.* 展現；呈現優點
ABBA ABBA 合唱團【ABBA 是在 1970 前後成立的瑞典流行樂團,字母縮
寫 (ABBA) 源自於樂隊成員姓名的首字母。樂隊成員是昂內塔·費爾特斯
科格 (Agnetha Fältskog)、比約恩·奧瓦爾斯 (Björn Ulvaeus)、班尼·安
德森 (Benny Andersson)、和安妮福瑞德·來恩斯坦 (Anni-Frid Lyngstad)】
timeless〔ˈtaɪmlɪs〕*adj.* 永恆的
vital〔ˈvaɪtḷ〕*adj.* 充滿活力的；重要的　　retain〔rɪˈten〕*v.* 保留
essence〔ˈɛsns〕*n.* 本質；精華　　version〔ˈvɝʒən〕*n.* 版本
to one's surprise 令某人驚訝的是

24. (**D**) 這裡需填上關係代名詞，來引導一形容詞子句，用以修飾先行詞 a fresh and vital way，故選 (D) that。【that 當關係代名詞用，91 學測補考也考過】而 (A) 與 (C) 爲關係副詞，(B) 爲複合關係代名詞，文法及文意均不合。

25. (**A**) (A) *appeal to* 吸引　　(B) present with　贈予
　　　　(C) result in　導致　　　(D) bring about　引起；造成

　　Which is more valuable?　Water or diamonds?　Water is more useful to mankind than diamonds, and yet <u>the latter</u> are costlier.　Why?　Called the
　　　　　　　　　　　　　　　　　　　　　　26
diamond-water paradox, this is a classic problem posed to students of economics.

　　哪個比較有價值？是水還是鑽石？對人類來說，水比鑽石有用，但後者卻比較貴。爲什麼？這就叫做「鑽石與水悖論」，是經濟學學生都會被問到的經典問題。

　　　　have to do with 與 ～ 有關
　　　　valuable〔'væljəbḷ〕*adj.* 貴重的；有價值的
　　　　diamond〔'daɪəmənd〕*n.* 鑽石　　useful〔'jusfəl〕*adj.* 有用的
　　　　mankind〔mæn'kaɪnd〕*n.* 人類
　　　　costly〔'kɔstlɪ〕*adj.* 昂貴的；浪費的
　　　　paradox〔'pærə,dɑks〕*n.* 矛盾；似非而是的言論
　　　　diamond-water paradox 鑽石與水悖論【鑽石雖貴，卻並非生活必需品。
　　　　　相比之下，水是人類生活中的必需品，但是其市場價值卻非常低。這種強烈的
　　　　　反差，在經濟學中，就被稱爲「鑽石與水悖論」。這個問題連經濟學之父亞當·
　　　　　斯密都無法回答。直到 1871 年，經濟學家卡爾·門格爾（Carl Menger）發表
　　　　　一套理論，他相信價值完全是主觀的：商品的價值，是在滿足人類的慾望】
　　　　classic〔'klæsɪk〕*adj.* 經典的　　pose〔poz〕*v.* 提出（問題）
　　　　economics〔,ikə'nɑmɪks〕*n.* 經濟學

26. (**D**) 由文意判斷，水是指「前者」(the former)，而鑽石是「後者」(*the latter*)，故選 (D)。(A) the above「上述事物」，和 (C) the following「下列事物」均與句意不合。

　　The answer has to do with supply and demand.　Being a rare natural resource, diamonds are <u>limited</u> in supply.　However, their demand is high

because many people buy them to tell the world that they have money,
<u>termed</u> as *conspicuous consumption* in economics.
　28

　　答案跟供給與需求有關。作爲稀有自然資源的一種，鑽石的供應量很少。然而，他們的需求量卻很高，因爲很多人買鑽石的目的是要告訴世人他們有錢，這在經濟學上就叫做「炫耀性消費」。

　　have to do with 與～有關　　supply〔səˋplaɪ〕*n.* 供應（量）
demand〔dɪˋmænd〕*n.* 需求（量）　*supply and demand* 供給與需求
rare〔rɛr〕*adj.* 稀少的　　resource〔rɪˋsors〕*n.* 資源
natural resource 自然資源；天然資源
conspicuous〔kənˋspɪkjʊəs〕*adj.* 顯而易見的；引人注意的
consumption〔kənˋsʌmpʃən〕*n.* 消費
conspicuous consumption 炫耀性消費【經濟學術語，指富裕的上層階級，
　藉由大量購買商品價值超出實用價值的奢侈品，或是講究生活排場，利用不必
　要的浪費和鋪張，向他人炫耀和展示自己的金錢財力和社會地位，以及這種行
　爲帶來的榮耀、聲望和名譽】

27. (**C**)　(A) trade〔tred〕*v.* 貿易；交換　　traded *adj.* 交換的
　　　　　　(B) weaken〔ˋwikən〕*v.* 使衰弱　　weakened *adj.* 衰弱的
　　　　　　(C) *limit*〔ˋlɪmɪt〕*v.* 限制　　limited *adj.* 有限的
　　　　　　(D) notice〔ˋnotɪs〕*v.* 注意　　noticed *adj.* 受注意的

28. (**B**)　term 這個字在此爲動詞用法，表「稱爲；命名爲」的意思。整句文
　　　　意是說鑽石的需求很高，因爲很多人買它們來讓世人知道他們很有錢，
　　　　而這樣的現象就「被稱爲」經濟學所說的炫耀性消費，原本空格是
　　　　which is termed，因關代及 be 動詞可以省略，故選 (B) *termed*。
　　　　【關係子句省略關代及 be 動詞，只保留過去分詞的考型，84、93、95 學測
　　　　各出現一次。】

In other words, the scarcity of goods is <u>what</u> causes humans to attribute
　　　　　　　　　　　　　　　　　29
value. If we <u>were</u> surrounded by an unending abundance of diamonds, we
　　　　30
probably wouldn't value them very much. Hence, diamonds carry a higher
monetary value than water, even though we find more use for water.

　　換句話說，就是商品的稀少，致使人們賦予它們價值。假如我們身邊有取之不盡的大量鑽石，我們可能就不會把鑽石看得如此重要。因此，雖然我們覺得水對我們的用處較大，鑽石的商品價值還是比水高。

in other words 換句話說　scarcity〔'skɛrsətɪ〕*n.* 不足；缺乏；稀少
goods〔gʊdz〕*n. pl.* 貨物；商品　cause〔kɔz〕*v.* 導致
attribute〔ə'trɪbjut〕*v.* 歸因於…；認為有
surround〔sə'raʊnd〕*v.* 包圍　sunending〔ʌn'ɛndɪŋ〕*adj.* 無止盡的
abundance〔ə'bʌndəns〕*n.* 豐富；充裕　*an abundance of* 豐富的
probably〔'prɑbəblɪ〕*adv.* 或許（= *perhaps*）
value〔'væljʊ〕*v.* 重視　hence〔hɛns〕*adv.* 因此
carry〔'kærɪ〕*v.* 帶有　monetary〔'mʌnə,tɛrɪ〕*adj.* 金錢的
even though 即使　use〔jus〕*n.* 用處；功效

29. (**A**) 此處應用複合關係代名詞，選 (A) *what = the thing which*。用以引導
一名詞子句，作為整句話的主詞補語。【83、91、92、95 學測，94 指考也考
過】而 (B) 為關係代名詞，(C) 與 (D) 為關係副詞，文法及文意均不合。

30. (**D**) 此處為「與現在事實相反」的假設語氣，在 if 子句中的動詞應該用過
去式，故選 (D) *were*。【「與現在事實相反」的假設語氣，99 學測也考過】

三、文意選填：

Popcorn is one of the snacks that rarely fail to make watching a movie
more fun. However, the modern way of preparing this [31](D) popular snack
may carry an unhappy secret. Research by the U.S. government now
reports that microwave popcorn may contain substances that can cause
health [32](J) problems.

爆米花絕對是會讓看電影變得更好玩的小點心之一。然而，在現代，烹調
這種受歡迎的小點心的方法，可能隱含令人不開心的秘密。美國政府所做的新
研究指出，微波的爆米花可能含有引發健康問題的物質。

popcorn〔'pɑp,kɔrn〕*n.* 爆米花　snack〔snæk〕*n.* 點心
rarely〔'rɛrlɪ〕*adv.* 幾乎不　*fail to V.* 未能～
modern〔'mɑdən〕*adj.* 現代的　way〔we〕*n.* 方法；方式
prepare〔prɪ'pɛr〕*v.* 準備；烹調　popular〔'pɑpjələ〕*adj.* 受歡迎的
carry〔'kærɪ〕*v.* 帶有　unhappy〔ʌn'hæpɪ〕*adj.* 令人不滿的
research〔'risɜtʃ〕*n.* 研究　report〔rɪ'port〕*v.* 報告；呈報
microwave〔'maɪkrə,wev〕*adj.* 微波的
microwave popcorn（袋裝的）微波爆米花
contain〔kən'ten〕*v.* 包含　substance〔'sʌbstəns〕*n.* 物質
cause〔kɔz〕*v.* 導致

Researchers found that commercial popcorn companies often coat their microwave popcorn bags with a [33](A) chemical called perfluorooctanoic acid (PFOA) which has been found to cause both cancer and lung disease in laboratory animals. Making matters worse, the artificial butter substitute that generally [34](E) comes with microwavable popcorn contains a common food-flavoring substance. This substance, according to health scientists, is [35](H) responsible for some serious lung diseases.

研究者發現，生產的爆米花公司，常常會在微波爆米花的包裝袋表面，塗上一種稱為全氟辛酸銨（PFOA）的化學物質，而這種物質已被發現，會讓實驗室動物，罹患癌症還有肺部疾病。更糟的是，可微波的爆米花通常附有人造奶油替代品，這種奶油替代品內含一種常見的食品調味料。根據健康科學家所述，該調味料會造成某些嚴重的肺部疾病。

researcher (ri'sɜtʃə) n. 研究者

commercial (kə'mɜʃəl) adj. 商業的；大量生產的

company ('kʌmpənɪ) n. 公司　　coat (kot) v. 塗上；覆上

coat A with B 用 B 塗在 A 上　　bag (bæg) n. 袋

chemical ('kɛmɪkl̩) n. 化學物質

perfluorooctanoic (pɜ,fluəro'aktə,nɔɪk) n. 全氟辛的

acid ('æsɪd) n. 【化學】酸

perfluorooctanoic acid 全氟辛酸銨【這種人工合成物又稱作 C8，是不沾鍋的主要成份，也使用在爆米花的包裝袋。血液中該化合物的含量太高，會導致高血脂跟癌症】(= *PFOA*)

cancer ('kænsə) n. 癌症　　lung (lʌŋ) n. 肺

disease (dɪ'ziz) n. 疾病　　laboratory ('læbrə,torɪ) adj. 實驗室用的

laboratory animals 用來做實驗的動物

matter ('mætə) n. 事情；問題　　artificial (,artə'fɪʃəl) adj. 人工的

butter ('bʌtə) n. 奶油　　substitute ('sʌbstə,tjut) n. 代替（食）品

generally ('dʒɛnərəlɪ) adv. 通常　　***come with*** 伴隨…一起出現

microwavable (,maɪkrə'wevəbl̩) adj. 可微波的

common ('kamən) adj. 常見的

food-flavoring ('fud'flevərɪŋ) adj. 食物調味的

according to 根據　　scientist ('saɪəntɪst) n. 科學家

responsible (rɪ'spansəbl̩) adj. 負責任的

be responsible for 應負…的責任；是…的原因

serious ('sɪrɪəs) adj. 嚴重的

For an easy and [36](F) healthy alternative, nutritionists suggest that we pop our own popcorn. All that is [37](G) needed is a large, high pot, about four tablespoons of vegetable oil and a small handful of organic popcorn kernels. When the kernels start [38](C) popping, shake the pot to let the steam escape and to let the unpopped kernels fall to the bottom.

營養學家建議我們自己做爆米花，這是簡單又健康的替代方法。只需要一個又大又高的鍋子、大概四大湯匙蔬菜油，還有一小把有機玉米粒。玉米粒開始爆開的時候，要搖晃鍋子，讓蒸汽跑出來，並讓還沒有爆開的玉米粒沉到下面。

healthy (ˈhɛlθɪ) adj. 健康的
alternative (ɔlˈtɝnətɪv) n. 選擇；替代品
nutritionist (njuˈtrɪʃənɪst) n. 營養學家
suggest (səˈdʒɛst) v. 建議　　pop (pɑp) v. 爆炒（玉米等）
pot (pɑt) n. 鍋；壺　　tablespoon (ˈtebḷˌspun) n. 大湯匙
vegetable oil 蔬菜油　　handful (ˈhændˌful) n. 一把
a handful of 一些；一把　　organic (ɔrˈgænɪk) adj. 有機的
kernel (ˈkɝnḷ) n.（果實的）核仁　　shake (ʃek) v. 搖晃
steam (stim) n.（水）蒸汽　　escape (əˈskep) v. 漏出
unpopped (ʌnˈpɑpt) adj.（玉米）沒有爆開的
bottom (ˈbɑtəm) n. 底部

As soon as the popping slows down, [39](I) remove the pot from the stove. Then pour the popcorn into a bowl and season with a small [40](B) amount of real butter or olive oil and natural salt. And the healthy and fun snack is ready to serve.

一旦「爆」的速度變慢，就把鍋子從爐火上移開。然後把爆米花倒到大碗裡面，用少量真正奶油或橄欖油，以及天然鹽來調味。健康又好玩的點心就準備可以上桌了。

as soon as 一…就～　　*slow down* 變慢
remove (rɪˈmuv) v. 移開　　stove (stov) n. 爐子
pour (por) v. 倒　　bowl (bol) n. 碗　　season (ˈsizn̩) v. 調味
amount (əˈmaunt) n. 數量　　*a small amount of* 少量的
olive (ˈɑlɪv) n. 橄欖　　*olive oil* 橄欖油
salt (sɔlt) n. 鹽　　serve (sɝv) v. 將（食物）端上餐桌

四、閱讀測驗：

41-44 為題組

There is a long-held belief that when meeting someone, the more eye contact we have with the person, the better. The result is an unfortunate tendency for people making initial contact—in a job interview, for example—to stare fixedly at the other individual. However, this behavior is likely to make the interviewer feel very uncomfortable. Most of us are comfortable with eye contact lasting a few seconds. But eye contact which persists longer than that can make us nervous.

有一個人們長久以來相信的看法是，當我們跟別人見面，跟那個人有愈多的眼神接觸愈好。結果就是讓那些首先做出接觸的人有不幸的傾向——例如說在一個工作面試時——他們會牢牢盯著另一個人。然而，這樣的動作很可能讓面試者感到不自在。大部分的人對於幾秒鐘的眼神接觸感到自在，但持續超過這幾秒鐘的眼神接觸會讓我們緊張。

> long-held〔'lɔŋ'hɛld〕*adj.* 長期存在的
> belief〔bə'lif〕*n.* 信念；看法　　***eye contact*** 眼神接觸
> tendency〔'tɛndənsɪ〕*n.* 傾向　　initial〔ɪ'nɪʃəl〕*adj.* 首先的
> ***stare at*** 盯著　　fixedly〔'fɪksɪdlɪ〕*adv.* 牢牢地
> individual〔ˌɪndə'vɪdʒʊəl〕*n.* 個人　　persist〔pə'zɪst〕*v.* 持續

Another widely accepted belief is that powerful people in a society—often men—show their dominance over others by touching them in a variety of ways. In fact, research shows that in almost all cases, lower-status people initiate touch. Women also initiate touch more often than men do.

另一個被廣為人所接納的看法就是，社會上有力量的人——常常是男人——會藉由各種觸碰他人的方式展現自己的支配地位。事實上，研究顯示幾乎在所有個案中，總是地位較低的人先開始碰觸他人。女性比起男性更常開始觸碰的動作。

> dominance〔'dɑmənəns〕*n.* 支配　　***a variety of*** 各種
> status〔'stetəs〕*n.* 地位　　initiate〔ɪ'nɪʃɪˌet〕*v.* 開始

The belief that rapid speech and lying go together is also widespread and enduring. We react strongly—and suspiciously—to fast talk. However,

the opposite is a greater cause for suspicion. Speech that is slow, because
it is laced with pauses or errors, is a more reliable indicator of lying than
the opposite.

　　快速的說話跟說謊脫不了關係，這種想法也很普遍，且由來以久。我們總
是強烈地——而且猜疑地——對於快速的談話做出反應。然而，相反的狀況其實
更值得懷疑。說話速度慢，因爲其中穿插著停頓和錯誤，比起快速的談話，是
說謊更可靠的跡象。

　　　rapid〔'ræpɪd〕*adj.* 快速的　　　widespread〔'waɪd'sprɛd〕*adj.* 普遍的
　　　enduring〔ɪn'dʊrɪŋ〕*adj.* 持久的　　react〔rɪ'ækt〕*v.* 反應＜*to*＞
　　　suspiciously〔sə'spɪʃəslɪ〕*adv.* 懷疑地
　　　suspicion〔sə'spɪʃən〕*n.* 懷疑　　　***be laced with*** 穿插著
　　　reliable〔rɪ'laɪəbl̩〕*adj.* 可靠的　　indicator〔'ɪndə,ketɚ〕*n.* 跡象

41.(**C**) 根據本文下列敘述何者爲眞？
　　　(A) 快速講話不出錯是可靠的智慧象徵。
　　　(B) 在團體中女性比男性常扮演支配的角色。
　　　(C) 比起講話快，講話慢更常表示一個人說謊。
　　　(D) 觸碰的動作往往是由社會地位高的人開始。
　　　intelligence〔ɪn'tɛlədʒəns〕*n.* 智慧
　　　dominant〔'dɑmənənt〕*adj.* 支配的

42.(**C**) 關於注視第一次見面的人，何者爲眞？
　　　(A) 注視著那個人會讓他/她感到自在。
　　　(B) 注視那個人儘可能的久是比較禮貌的。
　　　(C) 大部分的人對於超過幾秒鐘的眼神接觸會感到不自在。
　　　(D) 不管你有沒有注視那個人都沒影響。
　　　fix *one's* ***eyes on*** 注視著　　***at ease*** 自在

43.(**A**) 下列何者本文**沒有**討論？
　　　(A) 臉部表情。　　　　　　(B) 肢體接觸。
　　　(C) 說話的速度。　　　　　(D) 眼神接觸。
　　　facial〔'feʃəl〕*adj.* 臉部的　　expression〔ɪk'sprɛʃən〕*n.* 表情

44.(**D**) 本文主旨爲何？
　　　(A) 人們有解釋非言語溝通的本能。
　　　(B) 我們不應該用一個人的肢體語言來評斷他的意圖。

　(C) 對於肢體語言的良好知識對於成功的溝通是極重要的。

　(D) <u>對於語言及非語言溝通的普遍看法不一定是正確的。</u>

instinct〔'ɪnstɪŋkt〕n. 本能　　interpret〔ɪn'tɝprɪt〕v. 解釋；詮釋

non-verbal〔nɑn'vɝbl̩〕adj. 非語言的　　intention〔ɪn'tɛnʃən〕n. 意圖

essential〔ə'sɛnʃəl〕adj. 必要的；極重要的

45-48 為題組

It is easy for us to tell our friends from our enemies. But can other animals do the same? Elephants can! They can use their sense of vision and smell to tell the difference between people who pose a threat and those who do not.

　　對我們來說，要辨別敵人跟朋友是很簡單的。但是其他動物也可以做到嗎？大象可以！牠們能用視覺及嗅覺來辨別哪些人會對牠們造成威脅，哪些人不會。

vision〔'vɪʒən〕n. 視覺　　pose〔poz〕v. 引起；造成

threat〔θrɛt〕n. 威脅　　***pose a threat*** 造成威脅

In Kenya, researchers found that elephants react differently to clothing worn by men of the Maasai and Kamba ethnic groups. Young Maasai men spear animals and thus pose a threat to elephants; Kamba men are mainly farmers and are not a danger to elephants.

　　在肯亞，研究人員發現大象對於馬賽人跟坎巴人兩種種族所穿的衣服，會有不同的反應。年輕的馬賽人會用矛攻擊動物，所以會對大象構成威脅；坎巴人主要是農夫，對大象而言不是危險。

Kenya〔'kɛnjə〕n. 肯亞共和國【位於東非中東部，屬大英國協一員，首都奈洛比 Nairobi】　　***Maasai*** 馬賽　　***Kamba*** 坎巴

ethnic〔'ɛθnɪk〕adj. 民族的

spear〔spɪr〕n. 槍；矛　v. 用槍（矛）刺

In an experiment conducted by animal scientists, elephants were first presented with clean clothing or clothing that had been worn for five days by either a Maasai or a Kamba man. When the elephants detected the smell of clothing worn by a Maasai man, they moved away from the smell faster and took longer to relax than when they detected the smells of either clothing worn by Kamba men or clothing that had not been worn at all.

　　在一個動物科學家所做的實驗之中，大象們被給予乾淨的衣服，或是馬塞或坎巴人穿了五天的衣服。比起當牠們聞到坎巴人的衣服或是乾淨衣服，大象聞到馬賽人所穿的衣服的氣味時，牠們會更快速地遠離那個氣味，也需要比較長的時間放鬆平復。

> conduct〔kən'dʌkt〕v. 實施；執行　　present〔prɪ'zɛnt〕v. 給予
> clothing〔'kloðɪŋ〕n. 衣物　　detect〔dɪ'tɛkt〕v. 察覺

Garment color also plays a role, though in a different way. In the same study, when the elephants saw red clothing not worn before, they reacted angrily, as red is typically worn by Maasai men. Rather than running away as they did with the smell, the elephants acted aggressively toward the red clothing.

　　服裝的顏色也有影響，不過方式不同。在同一個實驗當中，當大象看到沒被穿過的紅色衣服，牠們會有生氣的反應，因為馬賽人通常穿紅色。不像是面對氣味做出的逃跑動作，對於紅色衣服牠們會做出攻擊性的反應。

> garment〔'garmənt〕n. 服裝　　***play a role*** 扮演角色；有影響
> typically〔'tɪpɪklɪ〕adv. 典型地　　***rather than*** 而不是…
> aggressively〔ə'grɛsɪvlɪ〕adv. 有攻擊性地

The researchers believe that the elephants' emotional reactions are due to their different interpretations of the smells and the sights. Smelling a potential danger means that a threat is nearby and the best thing to do is run away and hide. Seeing a potential threat without its smell means that risk is low. Therefore, instead of showing fear and running away, the elephants express their anger and become aggressive.

　　研究人員相信大象不同的情緒反應，是因為牠們對於氣味跟景象有不同的解釋。聞到可能的危險代表威脅就在附近，而最好的作法就是逃跑躲起來。看到威脅但沒有氣味，代表危險性低。因此，不選擇表現恐懼然後逃跑，大象會展現憤怒，並且變得有攻擊性。

> ***due to*** 由於　　interpretation〔ɪn,tɝprɪ'teʃən〕n. 解釋
> potential〔pə'tɛnʃəl〕adj. 潛在的；可能的
> risk〔rɪsk〕n. 危險　　***instead of*** 而不是

45. (**A**) 根據本文，對於馬賽及坎巴人的敘述，下列何者爲眞？
    (A) 馬賽人對大象是一種威脅。
    (B) 坎巴人爲了農業飼養大象。
    (C) 坎巴人及馬賽人都是獵殺大象的人。
    (D) 坎巴人及馬賽人傳統上都穿著紅色衣服。

    raise〔rez〕*v.* 飼養

46. (**D**) 在研究中大象對氣味如何反應？
    (A) 牠們攻擊有新衣氣味的人。
    (B) 聞到不熟悉的氣味牠們需要時間放鬆平復。
    (C) 聞到有坎巴人氣味的衣服牠們會變得焦慮。
    (D) 聞到敵人的味道時，牠們會受到驚嚇然後逃跑。

    scented〔'sɛntɪd〕*adj.* 有…氣味的

47. (**A**) 本文主旨爲何？
    (A) 大象用視覺和嗅覺來察覺危險。
    (B) 大象攻擊穿紅色衣服的人。
    (C) 科學家現在已經有辦法控制大象的情緒。
    (D) 一些肯亞部落很了解大象的情緒。

    tribe〔traɪb〕*n.* 部落

48. (**A**) 關於大象的行爲，從本文何者可以被推論出來？
    (A) 大象從經驗中學習。
    (B) 大象的嗅覺比視覺敏銳。
    (C) 大象比其他動物聰明。
    (D) 遇到危險時大象傾向於攻擊而非逃跑。

    sharp〔ʃɑrp〕*adj.* 敏銳的　　intelligent〔ɪn'tɛlədʒnt〕*adj.* 聰明的
    tend to V. 傾向於~

49-52 爲題組

It was something she had dreamed of since she was five. Finally, after years of training and intensive workouts, Deborah Duffey was going to compete in her first high school basketball game. The goals of becoming an outstanding player and playing college ball were never far from Deborah's mind.

這是她從五歲的時候就一直夢想的事。最後，經過幾年的訓練和密集練習之後，黛波拉達菲要在她高中的第一場籃球比賽中出賽了。成爲頂尖球員以及在大學裡打球隊的目標，從未離開黛波拉的腦海。

> ***dream of*** 夢想　　　intensive〔ɪn'tɛnsɪv〕*adj.* 密集的
> workout〔'wɝk,aʊt〕*n.* 運動；練習
> compete〔kəm'pit〕*v.* 競爭
> outstanding〔aʊt'stændɪŋ〕*adj.* 傑出的　　***far from*** 遠離

The game was against Mills High School. With 1:42 minutes left in the game, Deborah's team led by one point. A player of Mills had possession of the ball, and Deborah ran to guard against her. As Deborah shuffled sideways to block the player, her knee went out and she collapsed on the court in burning pain. Just like that, Deborah's season was over.

那場比賽是和米爾斯高中對打。比賽還剩下一分四十二秒的時候，黛波拉那一隊領先一分。米爾斯高中的球員持球，黛波拉跑過去防守她。當黛波拉快步側身去阻擋她的時候，她的膝蓋脫臼了，她倒在球場上，非常痛苦。就這樣，黛波拉這個球季宣佈報銷。

> against〔ə'gɛnst〕*prep.* 對抗　　　lead〔lid〕*v.* 領先
> point〔pɔɪnt〕*n.* 一分　　　possession〔pə'zɛʃən〕*n.* 持有
> guard〔gɑrd〕*v.* 防守　　　shuffle〔'ʃʌfl〕*v.* 小步地走
> sideways〔'saɪd,wez〕*adv.* 側身地　　　block〔blɑk〕*v.* 阻擋
> knee〔ni〕*n.* 膝蓋　　　***go out*** 脫臼
> collapse〔kə'læps〕*v.* 倒下　　　burning〔'bɝnɪŋ〕*adj.* 猛烈的
> ***in pain*** 痛苦地　　　***just like that*** 正是如此

After suffering the bad injury, Deborah found that, for the first time in her life, she was in a situation beyond her control. Game after game, she could do nothing but sit on the sidelines watching others play the game that she loved so much.

膝蓋嚴重受傷之後，黛波拉生平第一次覺得，無法掌控自己的狀況。一場接一場的比賽過去，她只能坐在板凳區，看著其他人比賽自己最愛的籃球。

> suffer〔'sʌfɚ〕*v.* 遭受（痛苦）　　　injury〔'ɪndʒərɪ〕*n.* 傷害
> ***beyond*** one's ***control*** 無法控制　　　***do nothing but V.*** 只能～
> sideline〔'saɪdlaɪn〕*n.* 界外地區（提供觀眾或候補選手所坐的地區）

Injuries limited Deborah's time on the court as she hurt her knees three more times in the next five years. She had to spend countless hours in a physical therapy clinic to receive treatment. Her frequent visits there gave her a passion and respect for the profession. And Deborah began to see a new light in her life.

受傷限制黛波拉在場上的時間，因為她的膝蓋在接下來五年內，受傷超過三次。她必須花很多時間在物理治療診所接受治療。因為經常去那裡，因而激發她對這項專業的熱情和尊重。黛波拉漸漸找到人生的新方向。

countless〔'kauntlɪs〕adj. 無數的　physical〔'fɪzɪkl̩〕adj. 物理的
therapy〔'θɛrəpɪ〕n. 治療　clinic〔'klɪnɪk〕n. 診所
frequent〔'frikwənt〕adj. 經常的　passion〔'pæʃən〕n. 熱情
profession〔prə'fɛʃən〕n. 專業　light〔laɪt〕n. 方向

Currently a senior in college, Deborah focuses on pursuing a degree in physical therapy. After she graduates, Deborah plans to use her knowledge to educate people how to best take care of their bodies and cope with the feelings of hopelessness that she remembers so well.

黛波拉目前大四，專心攻讀物理治療的學位。畢業之後，黛波拉打算利用她的專業知識來教育人們，如何以最好的方式對待自己的身體，以及處理讓她最難以忘懷的無助感。

focus on 專注於　pursue〔pə'su〕v. 追求
cope with 處理

49. (**D**) 這篇文章最好的標題為何？
(A) 痛苦的錯誤　　　　　(B) 偉大的冒險
(C) 一輩子的懲罰　　　　(D) 人生的新方向
lifelong〔'laɪ,flɔŋ〕adj. 一生的

50. (**D**) 當黛波拉膝蓋剛受傷的時候她感覺如何？
(A) 興奮的。　(B) 困惑的。　(C) 慚愧的。　(D) 失望的。
ashamed〔ə'ʃemd〕adj. 慚愧的

51. (**B**) 關於黛波拉達菲下列何者正確？
(A) 初次受傷之後她就不再上場打球。
(B) 當她試圖要阻擋她的對手的時候膝蓋受了傷。

(C) 她小的時候就知道她不能成為籃球選手。
(D) 她拒絕接受專業的協助幫她復原。
initial〔ɪˋnɪʃəl〕 *adj.* 最初的　　opponent〔əˋponɛnt〕 *n.* 對手
assistance〔əˋsɪstəns〕 *n.* 協助

52.(**A**) 黛菠拉在她的人生中看到什麼新的方向？
(A) 幫助別人照顧身體。　　　 (B) 成為體育老師。
(C) 成為優秀的籃球選手。　　 (D) 在物理治療室裡面接受治療。
physical education 體育

53-56 為題組

　　Redwood trees are the tallest plants on the earth, reaching heights of up to 100 meters. They are also known for their longevity, typically 500 to 1000 years, but sometimes more than 2000 years. A hundred million years ago, in the age of dinosaurs, redwoods were common in the forests of a much more moist and tropical North America. As the climate became drier and colder, they retreated to a narrow strip along the Pacific coast of Northern California.

　　紅杉樹是世界最高的植物，高度可以達到一百公尺。它們也以長壽聞名，一般而言可達五百年至一千年久，但是有時會超過兩千年。一億年前，在恐龍時期，紅杉樹在北美潮濕熱帶地區的森林是很常見的。隨著天氣變得越來越乾，越來越冷，它們退到了加州北部太平洋沿岸的狹長地帶。

redwood〔ˋrɛdˏwʊd〕 *n.* 紅杉　　***on earth*** 地球上
reach〔ritʃ〕 *v.* 達到　　***up to*** 高達
be known for 以～聞名　　height〔haɪt〕 *n.* 高度
longevity〔lanˋdʒɛvətɪ〕 *n.* 長壽
typically〔ˋtɪpɪklɪ〕 *adv.* 典型地；通常
dinosaur〔ˋdaɪnəˏsɔr〕 *n.* 恐龍　　common〔ˋkɑmən〕 *adj.* 普遍的
moist〔mɔɪst〕 *adj.* 潮濕的　　tropical〔ˋtrɑpɪkḷ〕 *adj.* 熱帶的
climate〔ˋklaɪmɪt〕 *n.* 氣候　　retreat〔rɪˋtrit〕 *v.* 倒退
narrow〔ˋnæro〕 *adj.* 狹長的　　strip〔strɪp〕 *n.* 帶；條
along〔əˋlɔŋ〕 *prep.* 沿著　　***Pacific coast*** 太平洋海岸

　　The trunk of redwood trees is very stout and usually forms a single straight column. It is covered with a beautiful soft, spongy bark. This bark can be pretty thick, well over two feet in the more mature trees. It gives the older trees a certain kind of protection from insects, but the main benefit is that it keeps the center of the tree intact from moderate forest fires because of its thickness. This fire resistant quality explains why the giant redwood grows to live that long. While most other types of trees are destroyed by forest fires, the giant redwood actually prospers because of them. Moderate fires will clear the ground of competing plant life, and the rising heat dries and opens the ripe cones of the redwood, releasing many thousands of seeds onto the ground below.

　　紅杉樹的樹幹非常地粗壯，而且通常會形成很筆直的圓柱，同時被漂亮又柔軟、且富有彈性的樹皮所包覆。這樹皮可以很厚，較成熟的樹樹皮厚度可以超過兩英呎。這樣的樹皮對較年長的樹可以形成某種保護，以免昆蟲的侵害，但樹皮厚度主要的好處是在於，保持樹木中心的完好無缺，不受一般森林火災的傷害。這種抗火的特質解釋了，為何巨大的紅杉樹可以活得這麼久。當其他大部分的植物都被森林大火燒毀時，巨大的紅杉樹卻因為大火而欣欣向榮。一般火災會將互相競爭的植物的地面清除乾淨，而且上升的熱度將紅杉樹的成熟松果變乾並且打開，如此一來可以將數以千計的種子撒到地面上。

trunk (trʌŋk) *n.* 樹幹　　　stout (staut) *adj.* 堅強的
form (fɔrm) *v.* 形成　　　straight (stret) *adj.* 筆直的
column ('kaləm) *n.* 圓柱　　　cover ('kʌvɚ) *v.* 覆蓋
soft (sɔft) *adj.* 柔軟的　　　spongy ('spʌndʒɪ) *adj.* 富有彈性的
bark (bark) *n.* 樹皮　　　thick (θɪk) *adj.* 厚的
mature (mə'tjur) *adj.* 成熟的
protection (prə'tɛkʃən) *n.* 保護
benefit ('bɛnəfɪt) *n.* 好處　　　intact (ɪn'tækt) *adj.* 完好無缺的
moderate ('madərɪt) *adj.* 適度的；一般的
thickness ('θɪknɪs) *n.* 厚度　　　resistant (rɪ'zɪstənt) *adj.* 抵抗的
fire resistant 防火的　　　quality ('kwalətɪ) *n.* 特質
explain (ɪk'splen) *v.* 解釋　　　destroy (dɪ'strɔɪ) *v.* 損毀
prosper ('praspɚ) *v.* 繁榮　　　clear (klɪr) *v.* 清除
competing (kəm'pitɪŋ) *adj.* 互相競爭的；不能同時存在的
rising ('raɪzɪŋ) *adj.* 上升的　　　ripe (raɪp) *adj.* 成熟的
cone (kon) *n.* 松果　　　release (rɪ'lis) *v.* 釋放
seed (sid) *n.* 種子

New trees are often produced from sprouts, little baby trees, which form at the base of the trunk. These sprouts grow slowly, nourished by the root system of the "mother" tree. When the main tree dies, the sprouts are then free to grow as full trees, forming a "fairy ring" of trees around the initial tree. These trees, in turn, may give rise to more sprouts, and the cycle continues.

新樹通常是由新芽所生長出，也就是小樹，它是在樹幹的底部所形成。這些嫩芽長得很慢，從母樹的根部系統獲得養分。當主樹死了，嫩芽就可以自由地生長成高大的樹，環繞著原生的母樹形成「樹環」。這些樹接著會產生更多的嫩芽，而樹環也接續而生。

produce〔prə'djus〕v. 產生　　sprout〔spraʊt〕n. 嫩芽；新芽
base〔bes〕n. 底部　　nourish〔'nɝɪʃ〕v. 滋養　　root〔rut〕n. 根部
free〔fri〕adj. 自由的　　full〔fʊl〕adj. 高大的
fairy〔'fɛrɪ〕n. 小精靈　　***fairy ring*** 樹環；菌環
in turn 依序地；接著　　***give rise to*** 產生；造成
cycle〔'saɪkl̩〕n. 循環　　continue〔kən'tɪnju〕v. 持續；繼續

53.（**C**）在數百萬年前，為何紅杉樹在北美森林裡較佔有優勢？
　　(A) 因為樹比較高比較壯。　　(B) 土壤鬆軟，種子較容易發芽。
　　(C) 因為氣候較溫暖潮濕。　　(D) 在太平洋沿岸溫度較低。
　　prominent〔'prɑmənənt〕adj. 有優勢的
　　humid〔'hjumɪd〕adj. 潮濕的　　temperature〔'tɛmpərətʃɚ〕n. 氣溫

54.（**D**）最後一段的「fairy ring」指的是什麼？
　　(A) 圍成圈的樹木。　　(B) 連結在一起的樹根系統。
　　(C) 老樹周邊的昆蟲洞。　　(D) 年青樹環繞著成年樹。
　　circle〔'sɝkl̩〕v. 圍成圈
　　connect〔kə'nɛkt〕v. 連結　　surround〔sə'raʊnd〕v. 圍繞

55.（**B**）下列何者是在文章當中所提及的樹皮的功能之一？
　　(A) 使得紅杉樹得以生長種子。
　　(B) 保護紅杉樹免於昆蟲的侵害。
　　(C) 協助紅杉樹吸收空氣中的濕氣。
　　(D) 使得紅杉樹更漂亮更吸引人。
　　function〔'fʌŋkʃən〕n. 功能　　bear〔bɛr〕v. 生育
　　attack〔ə'tæk〕n. 攻擊　　absorb〔əb'sɔrb〕v. 吸收
　　moisture〔'mɔɪstʃɚ〕n. 濕氣　　appealing〔ə'pilɪŋ〕adj. 吸引人的

56. (**C**) 根據本篇文章，為何紅杉樹可活得這麼久？
　　(A) 它們有很厚很直的樹幹。　　(B) 它們被適度地澆水和滋養。
　　(C) <u>相較於其他植物，它們較能抵抗大火的損害。</u>
　　(D) 它們產生很多的小樹來維持生命週期。
　　water〔'wɔtɚ〕*v.* 澆水　　sustain〔sə'sten〕*v.* 維持

第貳部分：非選擇題

一、中譯英

1. 臺灣的夜市早已被認為足以代表我們的在地文化。

{ Taiwan's night markets / Night markets in Taiwan } have long been { regarded as / viewed as / seen as / considered (to be) }

a symbol of our local culture.

= …have long been thought to (be able to) represent our local culture.

2. 每年它們都吸引了成千上萬來自不同國家的觀光客。

They { attract / appeal to / draw } tens of thousands of tourists from { different / various }

countries every year.

二、英文作文：

Costume Party

Bill and Maryanne met at a costume party and it was love at first sight. Bill was especially attracted to Maryanne's beauty. When the party was over, they exchanged phone numbers and parted ways. However, Bill couldn't get Maryanne out of his mind. He decided to make a romantic gesture. Later that evening, he appeared outside Maryanne's apartment building with his guitar, prepared to sing a song declaring his love. He began to sing and play under a crescent moon. He thought Maryanne would certainly come to her window.

Unfortunately, Bill's serenade did not produce the reaction he was looking for. Within minutes, several angry residents came to their windows and shouted at Bill to stop making so much noise. "Get out of here," one woman shouted, "or I will call the police!" Bill was terribly embarrassed by his mistake. "I guess Maryanne doesn't live in that building," Bill said to himself. He quickly apologized and left the scene.

The next morning, Maryanne appeared at Bill's door. "I'm so sorry," Maryanne said. "That was my mother who shouted at you. She's very protective of me. I'm not allowed to have visitors after dark." Bill was relieved that his effort hadn't been wasted.

costume〔'kɑstum〕*n.* 服裝   ***costume party*** 化裝舞會
gesture〔'dʒɛstʃɚ〕*n.* 表示;動作
declare〔dɪ'klɛr〕*v.* 宣告   crescent〔'krɛsn̩t〕*n.* 新月
serenade〔͵sɛrə'ned〕*n.* 小夜曲   resident〔'rɛzədənt〕*n.* 居民
relieved〔rɪ'livd〕*adj.* 感到放心的

100 年學測英文科試題修正意見

題　　號	題　　　　目	修　正　意　見
第 7 題	If you violate a traffic law, such as *drinking and driving*, …. → … such as ***the one against drinking and driving*** …. 或→ such as ***the one that is against drinking and driving*** ….	這是典型的中式英文，中文不嚴謹，應改成「像是禁止酒駕的交通規則」，否則句意就錯。 drinking and driving（酒醉駕車）不是一條 traffic law。such as（＋名詞）＝ for example【詳見「文法寶典」p.125】
第 9 題	…attracted *great* attention …. → … attracted ***a lot of*** attention …. 或→ … attracted ***a great deal of*** attention ….	加在抽象名詞前表示「量」或「程度」的形容詞有 a great deal of，a good deal of，a lot of 等，但沒有 great。【詳見「文法寶典」p.167】
第 16－20 題 第 5 行	… by drying it out, *oiling* and then wrapping the body in linen …. → … by drying it out, ***oiling it*** and then wrapping the body in linen ….	雖然 oil 可當及物或不及物動詞，但根據句意，是「在它上面塗油」，應加上 it 才對。由 and 連接三個及物動詞片語，都有受詞，才有對稱性。【詳見「文法寶典」p.465】
第 26－30 題 第二段 第 2 行	… they have money, termed as *conspicuous consumption* in economics. → … they have money (termed as … in economics). 或→ … they have money, ***something that is*** termed as conspicuous consumption in economics. 或→ … they have money, ***what is*** termed as conspicuous consumption in economics.	本句錯在出題者改編時去掉了 money 後面的小括號。詳見網站 Business Line。用小括號括起與文意關係不太重要的插入語。【詳見「文法寶典」p.47】

題　號	題　目	修　正　意　見
第 31－40 題 第二段 第 2 行	… perflorootanoic acid (PFOA) *which* has …. → … perflorootanoic acid (PFOA)**,** *which* has ….	補述用法的形容詞子句，which 前應有逗點。【詳見「文法寶典」p.152】經查出題來源，同樣沒逗點。
第 42 題 (C)	Most people feel uneasy *to* have eye contact for *over* a few seconds. → Most people feel uneasy **when they** have eye contact for **more than** a few seconds. 或→ Most people feel uneasy **when they** have eye contact for **longer than** a few seconds.	不定詞片語當副詞用，可表「目的」、「結果」、「原因」、「理由」、「條件」，但是不可表「時間」。【詳見「文法寶典」p.413】over 改成 more than 或 longer than，句意才清楚。
第 52 題 (B)	To become a teacher of *Physical Education*. → To become a teacher of *physical education*. 或→ To become a *PE teacher*. 或→ To become a *gym teacher*.	physical education（體育）是一門學科，屬於抽象名詞，並非專有名詞。【詳見「文法寶典」p.65】
第 53－56 題 第一段 第 2 行	…, typically 500 to *1000* years, … than *2000* years. → …, typically 500 to *1,000* years, … than *2,000* years.	為了減少誤解，長的數字須用逗點隔開，年度則不須加逗點。【詳見「文法寶典」p.40, 41】
第 55 題 (B)	It prevents redwood trees from *attack* by insects. → It prevents redwood trees from *being attacked* by insects. 或→ It *protects* redwood trees from *attacks* by insects. 或→ It *protects* redwood trees from *being attacked* by insects.	prevent A from V-ing protect A from + N./V-ing 【詳見「文法寶典」p.576】

100 年學測英文科考題出題來源

題　　　號	出　　　　　　　　　處
一、詞彙 第 1～15 題	所有各題對錯答案的選項，均出自「高中常用 7000 字」。
二、綜合測驗 第 21～25 題 第 26～30 題	取材自關於音樂劇 MAMMA MIA!的文章。 改寫自 The diamond-water paradox(鑽石與水悖論)一文。
三、文意選填 第 31～40 題	出自關於微波的爆米花可能含有有害物質的文章。
四、閱讀測驗 第 41～44 題 第 45～48 題 第 53～56 題	取材自 The Truth Behind the Smile and Other Myths—When Body Language Lies 一文。 改編自關於大象（Elephants Use Sight and Smell to Know Friend From Foe）的文章。 改寫自 Flower Essence Society 及 Redwood World 網站關於紅杉樹的文章。

【100 年學測】綜合測驗：21-25 出題來源──thestar online

A global smash hit

A British journalist looks at the phenomenon that is Mamma Mia!, from its 1999 world premiere to today, where more productions are playing around the world than any other musical.

IT WAS on March 23, 1999, that the musical Mamma Mia! met its first and most crucial test when it was put in front of its first-ever paying audience in London and was given the kind of welcome it has been getting ever since, every night, at every one of the many productions that have since followed.

But on that early spring evening in London, it was still a completely unknown quantity. "We really had no idea how it was going to be received," reflects the producer Judy Craymer whose initial concept, exactly a decade earlier, had been to use existing Abba songs within the format of a new, original musical. But happily, she remembers: "The audience went wild. They were literally out of their seats and singing and dancing in the aisles and they still are. Every night."

And now, they are doing so all around the world. It has become a global entertainment phenomenon; but it is one that works on a far more elemental basis in which its creators have never lost sight of what they are seeking to achieve.

That is, the process of personalising a familiar repertoire of particular Abba songs in a fresh, vital and immediate way that simultaneously retains their pop integrity yet also does something more that is an essential requirement of good musical theatre: to advance an appealing story and comment on it.

⋮

【100 年學測】綜合測驗：26-30 出題來源——Busniess Line

The diamond-water paradox

B. Venkatesh

WHY is diamond costlier than water? Called the diamond-water paradox, this is a classic problem posed to students of economics. This issue is considered important because water is more useful to mankind than diamonds, and yet the latter is costlier. Why?

The answer has to do with utility and scarcity. Suppose you are in the middle of a desert, and dying of thirst. What if you are offered diamonds and a bottle of water and asked to pick one?

⋮

Now, suppose you are offered diamonds instead. You may hoard them in your bank locker. But what if you are offered more diamonds? Will your marginal utility for diamonds also diminish?

Yes, but at a lower speed than that of water. Why? The reason has to do with the demand and supply for diamonds.

Being a natural resource, its supply is limited. The demand is, however, high because people buy diamonds as a way to tell the world that they have money (termed as conspicuous consumption in economics).

The high demand and limited supply is the reason why the marginal utility for diamonds decreases at a lower rate than that of water. Hence, diamonds carry higher monetary value than water, even though we find more use for water.

If you are still not convinced, consider this: Assume your basic need for water is satisfied. You are now offered more water and plenty of diamonds. What will you choose?

【100 年學測】文意選填：31-40 出題來源──Natural Awakenings

Microwave Popcorn Toxicity Study

Modern preparation of favorite snack poses possible health hazards

Popcorn is one of the add-ons that rarely fails to make watching a movie more fun, but the modern way of preparing this popular snack may harbor an unhappy secret. Research by the U.S. government now reports that microwave popcorn may contain chemicals that can cause health problems.

At issue is that commercial popcorn companies often coat their microwave popcorn bags with a chemical called perfluorooctanoic acid (PFOA) which has been found to cause both cancer and lung disease in laboratory animals. Making matters worse, the butter substitute that generally accompanies microwavable popcorn contains a chemical called diacetyl, a common food-flavoring agent that, according to health scientists, is responsible for bronchiolitis obliterans, a serious, debilitating lung disease.

For an easy and fun healthy alternative, nutritionists suggest that we pop our own popcorn. All that's needed is a large, high pot, about four tablespoons of peanut or canola oil and a small handful of organic popcorn kernels. When the kernels start popping, shake the pot to let the steam escape and to let the unpopped kernels fall to the bottom. As soon as the popping slows down, remove the pot from the stove, pour the popcorn into a bowl, season with a small amount of real butter or olive oil and natural salt or brewer's yeast to taste, et voilà, happy eating.

【100 年學測】閱讀測驗：41-44 出題來源——Working Knowledge

The Truth Behind the Smile and Other Myths
—When Body Language Lies

⋮

2. When meeting someone, the more eye contact, the better. This long-held belief is the inverse of the idea that shifty-eyed people are liars. The result is an unfortunate tendency for people making initial contact—as in a job interview, for example—to stare fixedly at the other human. This behavior is just as likely to make the interviewer uncomfortable as not. Most of us are comfortable with eye contact lasting a few seconds, but any eye contact that persists longer than that can make us nervous.

⋮

5. High-status people demonstrate their dominance of others by touching them. Another widely accepted belief is that powerful people in society—often men—show their dominance over others by touching them in a variety of ways. In fact, the research shows that in almost all cases, lower-status people initiate touch. And women initiate touch more often than men do.

⋮

8. You can't trust a fast-talking salesman. The belief that speed and deception go together is a widespread and enduring one. From the rapid patter of Professor Hill in The Music Man to the absurdly fast speech of the FedEx guy in the TV commercial from a few years back, we react strongly—and suspiciously—to fast talk. People talk at an average rate of 125 to 225 words per minute; at the upper end of that range listeners typically find themselves beginning to resist the speaker. However, as Ekman says, the opposite is greater cause for suspicion. Speech that is slow, because it is laced with pauses, is a more reliable indicator of deception than the opposite.

⋮

【100 年學測】閱讀測驗：45-48 出題來源——Neuroscience For Kids

Elephants Use Sight and Smell to Know Friend From Foe

December 2, 2007

It is important to know your friends from your enemies. It's easy for us to do, but can other animals do the same? Elephants can! They use their sense of vision and smell to tell the difference between people who pose a threat and those who do not.

In Kenya, researchers found that elephants react differently to clothing worn by men of the Maasai and Kamba ethnic groups. Young Maasai men spear elephants and pose a threat to elephants; Kamba men are mainly farmers and are not a danger to elephants.

When the elephants detected the smell of clothing worn by a Maasai man, they moved away from the smell faster, traveled further from the smell, and took longer to relax than when they detected the smells of either clothing worn by Kamba men or clothing that was not worn at all. The elephants also always moved to tall grass after smelling Maasai-worn clothing, something they rarely did when they smelled Kamba-worn clothing. Maasai men typically wear RED clothing. When the elephants saw RED, unworn clothing, they reacted differently. Rather, than running away, the elephants acted aggressively toward the red clothing.

The researchers interpret these results to differences in the emotional reaction of the elephants to the smells and sights. Smelling a potential danger means that a threat is nearby and the best thing to do is run away and hide. Seeing a potential threat without its smell means that risk is low—perhaps a Maasai man was in the area, but has left. Therefore, instead of fear, the elephants show aggression.

：

【100 年學測】閱讀測驗：53-56 出題來源之一──Flower Essence Society

Plant Profile: The Redwood Tree

Redwood trees are ancient giants, the tallest living beings on the Earth, reaching heights of up to 360 feet (100+ meters). Redwoods are also known for their longevity, typically 500–1000 years, but sometimes more than 2000 years. Our contemporary Redwoods, however, are descendents from an even more ancient lineage. A hundred million years ago, in the age of dinosaurs, the primordial Redwoods were predominant in the forests of a much more moist and tropical North America. As the climate became drier and colder, the Redwoods retreated to a narrow strip along the Pacific coast of Northern California, where summer fog and mild winters contrast with harsher inland climates.

：

Although the Redwoods produce millions of seeds, few are fertile, and fewer still are able to produce viable seedlings. Those that do survive, however, are among the fastest growing trees in the world. They can often grow 30 feet (10 meters) in the first 20 years. New trees are often produced from sprouts which form at the enlarged base of the trunk.

These sprouts grow slowly, nourished by the root system and upper leaves of the "mother" tree. When the main tree dies, the sprouts are then free to grow as full trees, forming a "fairy ring" of trees around the stump of the initial tree. These trees in turn, may give rise to more sprouts, and the cycle continues. In that way some Redwoods may be the continuation of trees millions of years old.

⋮

【100 年學測】閱讀測驗：53-56 出題來源之二──Redwood World

Giant Redwood
(aka Wellingtonia, Sequoiadendron giganteum, Giant Sequoia)

⋮

The trunk of these trees is very stout, usually forming a single straight column, and with a marvellous tapering effect at the base. They are covered with a beautiful soft, spongy bark—so soft in fact that one can punch them quite hard and feel no pain.

This bark can be pretty thick, well over two feet thick in the more mature examples. This gives the older trees a certain amount of protection from insects, but the main benefit is its fire retarding properties. Whereas a forest fire is pretty much a disaster for the majority of trees, it seems that the giant redwood will not just shrug off such events, they actually need them in order to prosper. Moderate fires will clear the ground of debris and competing plant life, and the rising heat dries and opens the ripe cones, shortly afterwards releasing many thousands of seeds onto the well-prepared ground below. The crowns of the mature tree will, in a forest environment, be a long way from the ground, thus protecting the branches and foliage from destruction in the fire.

⋮

100年學測英文科非選擇題閱卷評分原則說明

閱卷召集人：張武昌（臺灣師範大學英語系）

　　100學年度學科能力測驗英文考科的非選擇題題型共有兩大題：第一大題是翻譯題，考生需將兩個中文句子譯成正確而通順達意的英文，這個題型與過去幾年相同，兩題合計八分。第二大題為英文作文，與去年的看圖作文相同，四格圖片中只畫了三格，並沒有提供結局，希望給考生更多的寫作發揮空間。今年圖片的主要內容是，一位年輕男子在化妝舞會上遇見一位讓他心儀的女子，及舞會後年輕男子所採取的追求行動，考生需依提供的連環圖片，寫一篇100至120個單詞（words）的作文。作文滿分為二十分。

　　至於閱卷籌備工作，在正式閱卷前，於2月9日先召開評分標準訂定會議，由正副召集人及協同主持人共十四人，參閱了約3000多份的試卷，經過一天的討論，訂定評分標準，並選出合適的樣本，編製了閱卷參考手冊，供閱卷委員共同參考，以確保閱卷之公平性。

　　2月10日上午9:00到11:00間，140多位大學教授，齊聚一堂進行試閱前的評分標準共識建立，並討論評分時應注意的事項及評分標準，再根據閱卷參考手冊的樣卷，分別評分。在試閱會議之後（11:00），正副召集人及協同主持人進行第一次評分標準再確定會議確認評分原則後，才開始正式閱卷。

　　關於評分標準，在翻譯題部分，每題總分4分，依文意及文法結構分成4部分，每部分1分。英文作文的評分標準是依據內容（5分）、組織（5分）、文法句構（4分）、字彙拼字（4分）、體例（2分）五個項目給分。若字數不足，則總分扣1分。

　　依慣例，每份試卷皆經過兩位委員分別評分，最後以二人之平均分數計算。如果第一閱與第二閱委員的分數在翻譯題部分的差距大於2分，或在作文題部分差距大於5分，則由第三位主閱（正副召集人或協同主持人）評分。

　　今年的翻譯題的句型與詞彙，皆為高中生應該熟習的，評量的重點在於考生是否能運用熟悉的字詞（比如：夜市 night markets、在地文化 local culture、吸引 attract、成千上萬 hundreds and thousands of、觀光客 tourists 或 visitors 等）與基本句型（如：have long been regarded as 等的用法），將中文句子翻譯成正確且達意的英文句子。所測驗之詞彙都屬於大考中心詞彙表四級內之詞彙，中等程度以上的考生如果能使用正確句型並注意拼字，應能得到理想的分數。但在選取樣卷時發現，很多考生對於拼字（如：把 night markets 寫成一個字 nightmarkets 或是把 culture 拼成 comture 等）、名詞單複數（如：把 from different countries 寫成 from different country）等的用法在掌握上仍有待加強。

　　英文作文部分，今年的看圖寫作，除了少數考生完全未作答繳交空白卷或故意抄寫閱讀測驗文章，意圖魚目混珠外，大都能針對圖意敘寫一篇簡短的英文作文；內容也多能與其生活經驗相結合，並適度發揮創意。評分的主要考量為考生的作文是否切題，組織是否具連貫性，句子結構及用字是否能妥適表達文意，及拼字與標點的使用是否正確等。

100年學測英文科試題或答案大考中心意見回覆

※ 題號：21

【題目】

　　On March 23, 1999, the musical MAMMA MIA! made its first public appearance in London. It ___21___ the kind of welcome it has been getting ever since. The audience went wild. They were literally out of their seats and singing and dancing in the aisles.

　　MAMMA MIA! has become a ___22___ entertainment phenomenon. More than 30 million people all over the world have fallen in love with the characters, the story and the music. The musical has been performed in more than nine languages, with more productions than any ___23___ musical. Its worldwide popularity is mainly due to its theme music, which showcases ABBA's timeless songs in a fresh and vital way ___24___ retains the essence of both popmusic and good musical theater. It has ___25___ so many people that a film version was also made. To no one's surprise, it has enjoyed similar popularity.

21. (A) is given　　　　　　(B) was given
　　(C) has given　　　　　 (D) had given

【意見內容】

　　選項 (D) 應為合理答案。

【大考中心意見回覆】

　　本題主要評量考生是否掌握動詞時態的能力。作答線索為上一個子句 On March 23, 1999, the musical MAMMA MIA! made its first public appearance in London。根據上下文意，此處 It 所指的是 MAMMA MIA! 音樂劇，第一次公演即「受到歡迎」，受歡迎一詞是需要使用被動式，和本句後半句 it <u>has been getting</u> ever since 相呼應，故正答選項為 (B) 無誤。(如果文中 It 改用 The audience 替代，才有可能用主動。)

※ 題號：**44**

【題目】

41-44 為題組

　　There is a long-held belief that when meeting someone, the more eye contact we have with the person, the better. The result is an unfortunate tendency for people making initial contact—in a job interview, for example—to stare fixedly at the other individual. However, this behavior is likely to make the interviewer feel very uncomfortable. Most of us are comfortable with eye contact lasting a few seconds. But eye contact which persists longer than that can make us nervous.

　　Another widely accepted belief is that powerful people in a society—often men—show their dominance over others by touching them in a variety of ways. In fact, research shows that in almost all cases, lower-status people initiate touch. Women also initiate touch more often than men do.

　　The belief that rapid speech and lying go together is also widespread and enduring. We react strongly—and suspiciously—to fast talk. However, the opposite is a greater cause for suspicion. Speech that is slow, because it is laced with pauses or errors, is a more reliable indicator of lying than the opposite.

44. What is the main idea of the passage?
　(A) People have an instinct for interpreting non-verbal communication.
　(B) We should not judge the intention of a person by his body language.
　(C) A good knowledge of body language is essential for successful communication.
　(D) Common beliefs about verbal and non-verbal communication are not always correct.

【意見內容】

選項 (C) 應爲合理答案。

【大考中心意見回覆】

本題主要評量考生是否掌握文章重點主旨。作答線索在於各段主題句中之 a long-held belief、widely accepted belief、the belief，以及各轉折詞 but、in fact、however 等。根據選文，從第一段至第三段各舉一個例子，說明長久以來人們對於肢體語言的看法與其背後眞正的意義是有所差異，整篇選文並未觸及肢體語言對於溝通是有幫助的內容，故正答選項爲 (D) 應無誤。

※ 題號：48

【題目】

45-48 爲題組

It is easy for us to tell our friends from our enemies. But can other animals do the same? Elephants can! They can use their sense of vision and smell to tell the difference between people who pose a threat and those who do not.

In Kenya, researchers found that elephants react differently to clothing worn by men of the Maasai and Kamba ethnic groups. Young Maasai men spear animals and thus pose a threat to elephants; Kambamen are mainly farmers and are not a danger to elephants.

In an experiment conducted by animal scientists, elephants were first presented with clean clothing or clothing that had been worn for five days by either a Maasai or a Kamba man. When the elephants detected the smell of clothing worn by a Maasai man, they moved away from the smell faster and took longer to relax than when they detected the smells of either clothing worn by Kamba men or clothing that had not been worn at all.

　　Garment color also plays a role, though in a different way. In the same study, when the elephants saw red clothing not worn before, they reacted angrily, as red is typically worn by Maasai men. Rather than running away as they did with the smell, the elephants acted aggressively toward the red clothing.

　　The researchers believe that the elephants' emotional reactions are due to their different interpretations of the smells and the sights. Smelling a potential danger means that a threat is nearby and the best thing to do is run away and hide. Seeing a potential threat without its smell means that risk is low. Therefore, instead of showing fear and running away, the elephants express their anger and become aggressive.

48. What can be inferred about the elephant's behavior from this passage?
   (A) Elephants learn from their experiences.
   (B) Elephants have sharper sense of smell than sight.
   (C) Elephants are more intelligent than other animals.
   (D) Elephants tend to attack rather than escape when in danger.

【意見內容】

選項 (B) 應為合理答案。

【大考中心意見回覆】

　　本題主要評量考生是否掌握文章內容並能做適當的推論，作答線索遍及全文。本篇選文第一段說明大象可利用其視覺與嗅覺來分辨危險，以後的各段則分別詳述一些實驗，說明大象的視覺與嗅覺對於危險的反應。全文內容並未刻意針對大象的視覺與嗅覺何者較為敏銳進行比較分析，因此正答選項為 (A) 並無異議。

※ 題號：50及52

【題目】

49-52 為題組

It was something she had dreamed of since she was five. Finally, after years of training and intensive workouts, Deborah Duffey was going to compete in her first high school basketball game. The goals of becoming an outstanding player and playing college ball were never far from Deborah's mind.

The game was against Mills High School. With 1:42 minutes left in the game, Deborah's team led by one point. A player of Mills had possession of the ball, and Deborah ran to guard against her. As Deborah shuffled sideways to block the player, her knee went out and she collapsed on the court in burning pain. Just like that, Deborah's season was over.

After suffering the bad injury, Deborah found that, for the first time in her life, she was in a situation beyond her control. Game after game, she could do nothing but sit on the sidelines watching others play the game that she loved so much.

Injuries limited Deborah's time on the court as she hurt her knees three more times in the next five years. She had to spend countless hours in a physical therapy clinic to receive treatment. Her frequent visits there gave her a passion and respect for the profession. And Deborah began to see a new light in her life.

Currently a senior in college, Deborah focuses on pursuing a degree in physical therapy. After she graduates, Deborah plans to use her knowledge to educate people how to best take care of their bodiesand cope with the feelings of hopelessness that she remembers so well.

50. How did Deborah feel when she first hurt her knee?
　(A) Excited.　　　　　(B) Confused.
　(C) Ashamed.　　　　(D) Disappointed.

52. What was the new light that Deborah saw in her life?
　(A) To help people take care of their bodies.
　(B) To become a teacher of Physical Education.
　(C) To become an outstanding basketball player.
　(D) To receive treatment in a physical therapy office.

【50題意見內容】

　1. 選項 (B) 應為合理答案。　　2. 選項 (C) 應為合理答案。

【50題大考中心意見回覆】

　　本題主要評量考生是否掌握細節的能力。作答線索在於第二段最後一句 Deborah's season was over、第三段 she was in a situation beyond her control. Game after game, she <u>could do nothing but sit on the sidelines watching others play</u> the game that she loved so much 及最後一段的最後一句 the feelings of hopelessness，說明了主角的失望之情，並非困惑（confused）或者慚愧（ashamed），故正答選項為 (D) 無誤。

【52題意見內容】

　1. 選項 (A) 之文字有瑕疵。　　2. 選項 (B) 應為合理答案。

【52題大考中心意見回覆】

　1. 本題主要評量考生是否掌握文章細節的能力，作答線索主要在第四段末與第五段。根據 *Longman Dictionary* 對於 educate 的解釋為：to give someone information about a particular subject, or to show people a better way to do something。因此，選項 (A) 在語意上並無不妥，故正答選項為 (A)。

　2. 根據選文內容最後一段的第一句：..., Deborah focuses on pursuing a degree in physical therapy 即可知道，主角想當的是物理治療師而非體育老師，故選項 (B) 並非正答。

※ 題號：54

【題目】

53-56 為題組

Redwood trees are the tallest plants on the earth, reaching heights of up to 100 meters. They are also known for their longevity, typically 500 to 1000 years, but sometimes more than 2000 years. A hundred million years ago, in the age of dinosaurs, redwoods were common in the forests of a much more moist and tropical North America. As the climate became drier and colder, they retreated to a narrow strip along the Pacific coast of Northern California.

The trunk of redwood trees is very stout and usually forms a single straight column. It is covered with a beautiful soft, spongy bark. This bark can be pretty thick, well over two feet in the more mature trees. It gives the older trees a certain kind of protection from insects, but the main benefit is that it keeps the center of the tree intact from moderate forest fires because of its thickness. This fire resistant quality explains why the giant redwood grows to live that long. While most other types of trees are destroyed by forest fires, the giant redwood actually prospers because of them. Moderate fires will clear the ground of competing plant life, and the rising heat dries and opens the ripe cones of the redwood, releasing many thousands of seeds onto the ground below.

New trees are often produced from sprouts, little baby trees, which form at the base of the trunk. These sprouts grow slowly, nourished by the root system of the "mother" tree. When the main tree dies, the sprouts are then free to grow as full trees, forming a **"fairy ring"** of trees around the initial tree. These trees, in turn, may give rise to more sprouts, and the cycle continues.

54. What does a "**fairy ring**" in the last paragraph refer to?

    (A) Circled tree trunks.　　(B) Connected root systems.

    (C) Insect holes around an old tree.

    (D) Young trees surrounding a mature tree.

【意見內容】

1. 選項 (D) 文字有瑕疵。

2. 選項 (A) 應為合理答案。

3. 選項 (C) 應為合理答案。

【大考中心意見回覆】

1. 根據最後一段的內容，the sprouts 的意思即是 young trees，而 the main tree 可解說成 the mature tree（第二段）、the "mother" tree 或者是 the initial tree（最後一段）。本題的作答線索是在 the sprouts are then free to grow as full trees, forming …<u>of trees around the initial tree</u>，因此選項 (D) 中的 mature tree 並未有用字不妥之虞。

2. 根據本篇選文最後一段，<u>the sprouts</u> are then free to grow as full trees, forming …of trees <u>around the initial tree</u>，即可判斷選項 (D) 為正答；雖然 "ring" 一詞有 "to surround something" 的意思，但根據上下文意並未提及環繞樹幹的相關內容，因此選項 (A) 並非本題正答。

3. 根據第二段與第三段的內容，尤其是第三段第三句，內容並未提及老樹的樹幹有很多昆蟲的洞穴，因此選項 (C) 並非正確答案。

※ 題號：非選擇題第二題

【題目】

說明：二、英文作文（占 20 分）

　　1. 依提示在「答案卷」上寫一篇英文作文。

　　2. 文長約 100 至 120 個單詞（words）。

提示：　請仔細觀察以下三幅連環圖片的內容，並想像第四幅圖片可能的發展，寫出一個涵蓋連環圖片內容並有完整結局的故事。

【意見內容】

圖畫的呈現不清，造成誤解。

【大考中心意見回覆】

對於繪畫的品質，大考中心將會持續改進；不過，對於圖片若有不同的解讀，只要言之成理，即使與主流的看法不同，亦不會影響其得分；換句話說，應該不會有「誤解」的問題。關於英文作文的評分標準，請詳見三月份選才英文考科非選擇題評分原則說明。

※ 題號：其他

【意見內容】

綜合測驗評量太過強調文法概念。

【大考中心意見回覆】

與往年試題相較，今年綜合測驗的文法試題比例的確不少，不過，所考的皆是基本、常用之文法概念；不過，「份量是否過重」這項議題，本中心將彙整相關意見提供給未來命題小組參考，希望試題可以兼顧評量各種不同的語言能力。

99 年大學入學學科能力測驗試題
英文考科

第壹部份：選擇題（佔 72 分）

一、詞彙（佔 15 分）

說明：第 1 至 15 題，每題選出最適當的一個選項，標示在答案卡之「選擇題答案區」。每題答對得 1 分，答錯不倒扣。

1. Mr. Lin is a very _____ writer; he publishes at least five novels every year.

   (A) moderate　　(B) temporary　　(C) productive　　(D) reluctant

2. Using a heating pad or taking warm baths can sometimes help to _____ pain in the lower back.

   (A) polish　　(B) relieve　　(C) switch　　(D) maintain

3. Peter stayed up late last night, so he drank a lot of coffee this morning to keep himself _____ in class.

   (A) acceptable　　(B) amazed　　(C) accurate　　(D) awake

4. Due to _____, prices for daily necessities have gone up and we have to pay more for the same items now.

   (A) inflation　　(B) solution　　(C) objection　　(D) condition

5. The government is doing its best to _____ the cultures of the tribal people for fear that they may soon die out.

   (A) preserve　　(B) frustrate　　(C) hesitate　　(D) overthrow

6. I could not _____ the sweet smell from the bakery, so I walked in and bought a fresh loaf of bread.

   (A) insist　　(B) resist　　(C) obtain　　(D) contain

7. Steve has several meetings to attend every day; therefore, he has to work on a very _____ schedule.
   (A) dense　　　(B) various　　　(C) tight　　　(D) current

8. Michael Phelps, an American swimmer, broke seven world records and won eight gold medals in men's swimming _____ in the 2008 Olympics.
   (A) drills　　　(B) techniques　　　(C) routines　　　(D) contests

9. Those college students work at the orphanage on a _____ basis, helping the children with their studies without receiving any pay.
   (A) voluntary　　(B) competitive　　(C) sorrowful　　(D) realistic

10. Studies show that asking children to do house _____, such as taking out the trash or doing the dishes, helps them grow into responsible adults.
    (A) missions　　(B) chores　　　(C) approaches　　(D) incidents

11. John has been scolded by his boss for over ten minutes now. _____, she is not happy about his being late again.
    (A) Expressively　(B) Apparently　(C) Immediately　(D) Originally

12. Since the orange trees suffered _____ damage from a storm in the summer, the farmers are expecting a sharp decline in harvests this winter.
    (A) potential　　(B) relative　　　(C) severe　　　(D) mutual

13. Typhoon Morakot claimed more than six hundred lives in early August of 2009, making it the most serious natural _____ in Taiwan in recent decades.
    (A) disaster　　(B) barrier　　　(C) anxiety　　　(D) collapse

14. Robert was the only _____ to the car accident. The police had to count on him to find out exactly how the accident happened.
    (A) dealer　　　(B) guide　　　(C) witness　　　(D) client

15. Badly injured in the car accident, Jason could _____ move his legs and was sent to the hospital right away.
(A) accordingly　(B) undoubtedly　(C) handily　(D) scarcely

二、綜合測驗（佔 15 分）

說明：　第 16 至 30 題，每題一個空格，請依文意選出最適當的一個選項，標示在答案卡之「選擇題答案區」。每題答對得 1 分，答錯不倒扣。

Anita was shopping with her mother and enjoying it. Interestingly, both of them ___16___ buying the same pair of jeans.

According to a recent marketing study, young adults influence 88% of household clothing purchases. More often than not, those in their early twenties are the more ___17___ consumers. There isn't a brand or a trend that these young people are not aware of. That is why mothers who want to keep abreast of trends usually ___18___ the experts — their daughters. This tells the retailers of the world that if you want to get into a mother's ___19___, you've got to win her daughter over first.

With a DJ playing various kinds of music rather than just rap, and a mix of clothing labels designed more for taste and fashion than for a precise age, department stores have managed to appeal to successful middle-aged women ___20___ losing their younger customers. They have created a shopping environment where the needs of both mother and daughter are satisfied.

16. (A) gave up　　(B) ended up　　(C) took to　　(D) used to
17. (A) informed　(B) informative　(C) informal　(D) informational
18. (A) deal with　(B) head for　　(C) turn to　　(D) look into
19. (A) textbook　(B) notebook　　(C) workbook　(D) pocketbook
20. (A) in　　　(B) while　　　(C) after　　　(D) without

Onions can be divided into two categories: fresh onions and storage onions. Fresh onions are available ___21___ yellow, red and white throughout their season, March through August. They can be ___22___ by their thin, light-colored skin. Because they have a higher water content, they are typically sweeter and milder tasting than storage onions. This higher water content also makes ___23___ easier for them to bruise. With its delicate taste, the fresh onion is an ideal choice for salads and other lightly-cooked dishes. Storage onions, on the other hand, are available August through April. ___24___ fresh onions, they have multiple layers of thick, dark, papery skin. They also have an ___25___ flavor and a higher percentage of solids. For these reasons, storage onions are the best choice for spicy dishes that require longer cooking times or more flavor.

21. (A) from   (B) for   (C) in   (D) of
22. (A) grown   (B) tasted   (C) identified (D) emphasized
23. (A) such   (B) much   (C) that   (D) it
24. (A) Unlike   (B) Through   (C) Besides   (D) Despite
25. (A) anxious   (B) intense   (C) organic   (D) effective

Many people like to drink bottled water because they feel that tap water may not be safe, but is bottled water really any better?

Bottled water is mostly sold in plastic bottles and that's why it is potentially health ___26___. Processing the plastic can lead to the release of harmful chemical substances into the water contained in the bottles. The chemicals can be absorbed into the body and ___27___ physical discomfort, such as stomach cramps and diarrhea.

Health risks can also result from inappropriate storage of bottled water. Bacteria can multiply if the water is kept on the shelves for too long or if it is exposed to heat or direct sunlight. ___28___ the information on storage and shipment is not always readily available to consumers, bottled water may not be a better alternative to tap water.

Besides these ___29___ issues, bottled water has other disadvantages. It contributes to global warming. An estimated 2.5 million tons of carbon dioxide were generated in 2006 by the production of plastic for bottled water. In addition, bottled water produces an incredible amount of solid ___30___. According to one research, 90% of the bottles used are not recycled and lie for ages in landfills.

26. (A) frightening　　(B) threatening　　(C) appealing　　(D) promoting
27. (A) cause　　　　　(B) causing　　　　(C) caused　　　　(D) to cause
28. (A) Although　　　　(B) Despite　　　　(C) Since　　　　　(D) So
29. (A) display　　　　　(B) production　　　(C) shipment　　　(D) safety
30. (A) waste　　　　　(B) resource　　　　(C) ground　　　　(D) profit

三、文意選填（佔 10 分）

說明： 第 31 至 40 題，每題一個空格，請依文意在文章後所提供的 (A) 到(J) 選項中分別選出最適當者，並將其英文字母代號標示在答案卡之「選擇題答案區」。每題答對得 1 分，答錯不倒扣。

Football is more than a sport; it is also an invaluable ___31___. In teaching young players to cooperate with their fellows on the practice ___32___, the game shows them the necessity of teamwork in society. It prepares them to be ___33___ citizens and persons.

Wherever football is played, the players learn the rough-and-tumble lesson that only through the ___34___ of each member can the team win. It is a lesson they must always ___35___ on the field. Off the field, they continue to keep it in mind. In society, the former player does not look upon himself as a lone wolf who has the right to remain ___36___ from the society and go his own way. He understands his place in the team; he knows he is a member of society and must ___37___ himself as such. He realizes that only by cooperating can he do his ___38___ in making society what it should be. The man who has played football knows that teamwork is ___39___ in modern living. He is also aware that every citizen must do his part if the nation is to ___40___. So he has little difficulty in adjusting himself to his role in family life and in the business world, and to his duties as a citizen.

(A) cooperation　(B) prosper　　　(C) teacher　　　(D) behave

(E) isolated　　(F) essential　　(G) better　　　(H) share

(I) field　　　(J) remember

四、閱讀測驗（佔 32 分）

說明：　第 41 至 56 題，每題請分別根據各篇文章之文意選出最適當的一個選項，標示在答案卡之「選擇題答案區」。每題答對得 2 分，答錯不倒扣。

41-44 為題組

　　On the island of New Zealand, there is a grasshopper-like species of insect that is found nowhere else on earth. New Zealanders have given it the nickname *weta*, which is a native Maori word meaning "god of bad looks." It's easy to see why anyone would call this insect a bad-looking bug. Most people feel disgusted at the sight of these bulky, slow-moving creatures.

　　Wetas are nocturnal creatures; they come out of their caves and holes only after dark. A giant weta can grow to over three inches long and weigh as much as 1.5 ounces. Giant wetas can hop up to two feet at a time.　Some of them live in trees, and others live in caves.　They are very long-lived for insects, and some adult wetas can live as long as two years.　Just like their cousins grasshoppers and crickets, wetas are able to "sing" by rubbing their leg parts together, or against their lower bodies.

Most people probably don't feel sympathy for these endangered creatures, but they do need protecting.　The slow and clumsy wetas have been around on the island since the times of the dinosaurs, and have evolved and survived in an environment where they had no enemies until rats came to the island with European immigrants.　Since rats love to hunt and eat wetas, the rat population on the island has grown into a real problem for many of the native species that are unaccustomed to **its** presence, and poses a serious threat to the native weta population.

41. From which of the following is the passage **LEAST** likely to be taken?
    (A) A science magazine.　　　(B) A travel guide.
    (C) A biology textbook.　　　(D) A business journal.

42. According to the passage, which of the following statements is true?
    (A) Wetas are unpleasant to the eye.
    (B) The weta is a newly discovered insect species.
    (C) The Maoris nicknamed themselves "Wetas."
    (D) The Europeans brought wetas to New Zealand.

43. Which of the following descriptions of wetas is accurate?
    (A) They are quick in movement.
    (B) They are very active in the daytime.
    (C) They are decreasing in number.
    (D) They have a short lifespan for insects.

44. Which of the following is the most appropriate interpretation of
   "**its**" in the last paragraph?
   (A) The rat's.　　　　　　(B) The weta's.
   (C) The island's.　　　　　(D) The dinosaur's.

45-48 為題組

　　The high school prom is the first formal social event for most
American teenagers. It has also been a rite of passage for young
Americans for nearly a century.

　　The word "prom" was first used in the 1890s, referring to formal
dances in which the guests of a party would display their fashions and
dancing skills during the evening's grand march. In the United States,
parents and educators have come to regard the prom as an important
lesson in social skills. Therefore, proms have been held every year in
high schools for students to learn proper social behavior.

　　The first high school proms were held in the 1920s in America. By
the 1930s, proms were common across the country. For many older
Americans, the prom was a modest, home-grown affair in the school
gymnasium. Prom-goers were well dressed but not fancily dressed up
for the occasion: boys wore jackets and ties and girls their Sunday
dresses. Couples danced to music provided by a local amateur band or
a record player. After the 1960s, and especially since the 1980s, the
high school prom in many areas has become a serious exercise in
excessive consumption, with boys renting expensive tuxedos and girls
wearing designer gowns. Stretch limousines were hired to drive the prom-
goers to expensive restaurants or discos for an all-night extravaganza.

Whether simple or lavish, proms have always been more or less traumatic events for adolescents who worry about self-image and fitting in with their peers. Prom night can be a dreadful experience for socially awkward teens or for those who do not secure dates. Since the 1990s, alternative proms have been organized in some areas to meet the needs of particular students. For example, proms organized by and for homeless youth were reported. There were also "couple-free" proms to which all students are welcome.

45. In what way are high school proms significant to American teenagers?
    (A) They are part of the graduation ceremony.
    (B) They are occasions for teens to show off their limousines.
    (C) They are important events for teenagers to learn social skills.
    (D) They are formal events in which teens share their traumatic experiences.

46. What is the main idea of the third paragraph?
    (A) Proper social behavior must be observed by prom-goers.
    (B) Proms held in earlier times gave less pressure to teenagers.
    (C) Proms are regarded as important because everyone dresses up for the occasion.
    (D) The prom has changed from a modest event to a glamorous party over the years.

47. According to the passage, what gave rise to alternative proms?
    (A) Not all students behaved well at the proms.
    (B) Proms were too serious for young prom-goers.
    (C) Teenagers wanted to attend proms with their dates.
    (D) Students with special needs did not enjoy conventional proms.

48. Which of the following statements is true?
    (A) Unconventional proms have been organized since the 1960s.
    (B) In the 1980s, proms were held in local churches for teenagers to attend.
    (C) Proms have become a significant event in American high schools since the 1930s.
    (D) In the 1890s, high school proms were all-night social events for some American families.

49-52 為題組

No budget for your vacation? Try home exchanges — swapping houses with strangers. Agree to use each other's cars, and you can save bucks on car rentals, too.

Home exchanges are not new. At least one group, Intervac, has been facilitating such an arrangement since 1953. But trading online is gaining popularity these days, with several sites in operation, including HomeExchanges. Founded in 1992, with some 28,000 listings, this company **bills** itself as the world's largest home exchange club, reporting that membership has increased 30% this year.

The annual fee is usually less than US$100. Members can access thousands of listings for apartments, villas, suburban homes and farms around the world. Initial contact is made via e-mail, with subsequent communication usually by phone. Before a match is made, potential swappers tend to discuss a lot.

However, the concept may sound risky to some people. What about theft? Damage? These are reasonable causes for concern, but equally unlikely. As one swapper puts it, "Nobody is going to fly across the ocean or drive 600 miles to come steal your TV. Besides, at the same time they're staying in your home, you are staying in their home."

Exchange sites recommend that swappers discuss such matters ahead of time. They may fill out an agreement spelling out who shoulders which responsibilities if a problem arises. It does not matter if the agreement would hold up in court, but it does give the exchangers a little satisfaction.

Generally, the biggest complaint among home exchangers has to do with different standards of cleanliness. Swappers are supposed to make sure their home is in order before they depart, but one person's idea of "clean" may be more forgiving than another's. Some owners say if they come back to a less-than-sparkling kitchen, it may be inconvenient but would not sour them on future exchanges.

49. What is the second paragraph mainly about?
    (A) How to exchange homes.
    (B) How home exchange is becoming popular.
    (C) The biggest home exchange agency.
    (D) A contrast between Intervac and HomeExchange.

50. Which of the following is closest in meaning to "**bills**" in the second paragraph?
    (A) advertises　　(B) dedicates　　(C) replaces　　(D) participates

51. How do home exchangers normally begin their communication?
    (A) By phone.　　　　　　　　(B) By e-mail.
    (C) Via a matchmaker.　　　　　(D) Via a face-to-face meeting.

52. What is recommended in the passage to deal with theft and damage concerns?
    (A) One can file a lawsuit in court.
    (B) Both parties can trade online.
    (C) Both parties can sign an agreement beforehand.
    (D) One can damage the home of the other party in return.

53-56 為題組

Bekoji is a small town of farmers and herders in the Ethiopian highlands. There, time almost stands still, and horse-drawn carts outnumber motor vehicles. Yet, it has consistently yielded many of the world's best distance runners.

It's tempting, when breathing the thin air of Bekoji, to focus on the special conditions of the place. The town sits on the side of a volcano nearly 10,000 feet above sea level, making daily life a kind of high-altitude training. Children in this region often start running at an early age, covering great distances to fetch water and firewood or to reach the nearest school. Added to this early training is a physical trait shared by people there—disproportionately long legs, which is advantageous for distance runners.

A strong desire burns inside Bekoji's young runners. Take the case of Million Abate. Forced to quit school in fifth grade after his father died, Abate worked as a shoe-shine boy for years. He saw a hope in running and joined Santayehu Eshetu's training program. This 18-year-old sprinted to the finish of a 12-mile run with his bare feet bleeding. The coach took off his own Nikes and handed them to him. To help Abate continue running, the coach arranged a motel job for him, which pays $9 a month.

Most families in Bekoji live from hand to mouth, and distance running offers the younger generation a way out. Bekoji's legend Derartu Tulu, who won the 10,000-meter Olympic gold medals in 1992 and 2000, is a national hero. As a reward, the government gave her a house. She also won millions of dollars in the races.

Motivated by such signs of success, thousands of kids from the villages surrounding Bekoji have moved into town. They crowd the classrooms at Bekoji Elementary School, where Eshetu works as a physical-education instructor. All these kids share the same dream: Some day they could become another Derartu Tulu.

53. Which of the following is NOT mentioned as a factor for the excellence of distance runners in Ethiopia?
    (A) Well-known coaches.
    (B) Thin air in the highlands.
    (C) Extraordinarily long legs.
    (D) Long distance running in daily life.

54. Which of the following is true about Bekoji?
    (A) It's the capital of Ethiopia.
    (B) It has changed a lot over the years.
    (C) It's located near a volcano.
    (D) It has trouble handling car accidents.

55. What is the goal of Bekoji's school kids?
    (A) To work as motel managers.
    (B) To win in international competitions.
    (C) To become PE teachers.
    (D) To perform well academically at school.

56. What can be inferred from this passage?
    (A) More distance runners may emerge from Bekoji.
    (B) Nike will sponsor the young distance runners in Bekoji.
    (C) Bekoji will host an international long-distance competition.
    (D) The Ethiopian government has spared no efforts in promoting running.

第貳部份：非選擇題（佔 28 分）

一、翻譯題（佔 8 分）

說明： 1. 請將以下兩題中文譯成正確而通順達意的英文，並將答案寫在「答案卷」上。

2. 請依序作答，並標明題號。每題 4 分，共 8 分。

1. 在過去，腳踏車主要是作為一種交通工具。

2. 然而，騎腳踏車現在已經成為一種熱門的休閒活動。

二、英文作文（佔 20 分）

說明： 1. 依提示在「答案卷」上寫一篇英文作文。

2. 文長至少 120 個單詞（words）。

提示： 請仔細觀察以下三幅連環圖片的內容，並想像第四幅圖片可能的發展，寫出一個涵蓋連環圖片內容並有完整結局的故事。

99年度學科能力測驗英文科試題詳解

第壹部分：單選題

一、詞彙：

1. (**C**) Mr. Lin is a very <u>productive</u> writer; he publishes at least five novels every year.
   林先生是一位非常<u>多產的</u>作家；他每年至少出版五本小說。
   (A) moderate〔'mɑdərɪt〕*adj.* 適度的
   (B) temporary〔'tɛmpə,rɛrɪ〕*adj.* 暫時的
   (C) *productive*〔prə'dʌktɪv〕*adj.* 多產的；有生產力的
   (D) reluctant〔rɪ'lʌktənt〕*adj.* 不情願的
   publish〔'pʌblɪʃ〕*v.* 出版　　*at least* 至少　　novel〔'nɑvl̩〕*n.* 小說

2. (**B**) Using a heating pad or taking warm baths can sometimes help to <u>relieve</u> pain in the lower back.
   使用電毯或洗熱水澡，有時候可以有助於<u>減輕</u>下背的疼痛。
   (A) polish〔'pɑlɪʃ〕*v.* 擦亮　　(B) *relieve*〔rɪ'liv〕*v.* 減輕
   (C) switch〔swɪtʃ〕*v.* 轉變　　(D) maintain〔men'ten〕*v.* 維持
   heating〔'hitɪŋ〕*adj.* 加熱的；供熱的　　pad〔pæd〕*n.* 墊子
   heating pad 小電毯

3. (**D**) Peter stayed up late last night, so he drank a lot of coffee this morning to keep himself <u>awake</u> in class.
   彼得昨晚熬夜到很晚，所以他今天早上喝了很多咖啡，讓自己在課堂上保持<u>清醒</u>。
   (A) acceptable〔ək'sɛptəbl̩〕*adj.* 可接受的
   (B) amazed〔ə'mezd〕*adj.* 驚訝的
   (C) accurate〔'ækjərɪt〕*adj.* 正確的
   (D) *awake*〔ə'wek〕*adj.* 醒著的；清醒的
   stay up 熬夜

4.(**A**) Due to <u>inflation</u>, prices for daily necessities have gone up and we
have to pay more for the same items now.

由於<u>通貨膨脹</u>，日常用品的價格已經上揚，現在我們必須付更多錢
買相同的物品。

(A) ***inflation*** 〔ɪnˈfleʃən〕 *n.* 通貨膨脹

(B) solution 〔səˈluʃən〕 *n.* 解決之道

(C) objection 〔əbˈdʒɛkʃən〕 *n.* 反對

(D) condition 〔kənˈdɪʃən〕 *n.* 情況

due to 由於   daily 〔ˈdelɪ〕 *adj.* 日常的
necessity 〔nəˈsɛsətɪ〕 *n.* 必需品   ***go up*** 上升
item 〔ˈaɪtəm〕 *n.* 物品

5.(**A**) The government is doing its best to <u>preserve</u> the cultures of the
tribal people for fear that they may soon die out.

政府正在盡力<u>保存</u>部落人民的文化，以免它們可能很快就會消失。

(A) ***preserve*** 〔prɪˈzɝv〕 *v.* 保存

(B) frustrate 〔ˈfrʌstret〕 *v.* 使受挫

(C) hesitate 〔ˈhɛzə‚tet〕 *v.* 猶豫

(D) overthrow 〔‚ovɚˈθro〕 *v.* 推翻

do one's ***best*** 盡力   culture 〔ˈkʌltʃɚ〕 *n.* 文化
tribal 〔ˈtraɪbḷ〕 *adj.* 部落的   ***for fear that*** 以免；惟恐
die out 逐漸消失；滅絕

6.(**B**) I could not <u>resist</u> the sweet smell from the bakery, so I walked
in and bought a fresh loaf of bread.

我無法<u>抵抗</u>麵包店傳來的香味，所以我就走進去買了一條新鮮的
麵包。

(A) insist 〔ɪnˈsɪst〕 *v.* 堅持

(B) ***resist*** 〔rɪˈzɪst〕 *v.* 抵抗；抗拒

(C) obtain 〔əbˈten〕 *v.* 獲得

(D) contain 〔kənˈten〕 *v.* 包含

sweet 〔swit〕 *adj.* 芳香的   smell 〔smɛl〕 *n.* 味道
bakery 〔ˈbekərɪ〕 *n.* 麵包店   loaf 〔lof〕 *n.* （麵包）一條

7. (**C**) Steve has several meetings to attend every day; therefore, he has to work on a very <u>tight</u> schedule.
史蒂夫每天都必須參加很多場會議；因此，他工作的時間表非常<u>緊湊</u>。

    (A) dense〔dɛns〕*adj.* 密集的；稠密的

    (B) various〔'vɛrɪəs〕*adj.* 各式各樣的

    (C) *tight*〔taɪt〕*adj.* 緊湊的；排得滿滿的

    (D) current〔'kɝənt〕*adj.* 目前的；現在的

    meeting〔'mitɪŋ〕*n.* 會議

    attend〔ə'tɛnd〕*v.* 參加　　schedule〔'skɛdʒul〕*n.* 時間表

8. (**D**) Michael Phelps, an American swimmer, broke seven world records and won eight gold medals in men's swimming <u>contests</u> in the 2008 Olympics.
美國游泳選手麥可·菲爾普斯，在 2008 年的奧運男子游泳<u>比賽</u>中，打破七項世界紀錄，並贏得八面金牌。

    (A) drill〔drɪl〕*n.* 反覆練習

    (B) technique〔tɛk'nik〕*n.* 技術

    (C) routine〔ru'tin〕*n.* 例行公事

    (D) *contest*〔'kɑntɛst〕*n.* 比賽

    medal〔'mɛdl̩〕*n.* 獎牌　　Olympics〔o'lɪmpɪks〕*n.* 奧運會

9. (**A**) Those college students work at the orphanage on a <u>voluntary</u> basis, helping the children with their studies without receiving any pay.
那些大學生<u>自願</u>在孤兒院服務，幫忙小孩的學業，沒有任何薪水。

    (A) *voluntary*〔'vɑlən,tɛrɪ〕*adj.* 自願的

       on a voluntary basis 自願地

    (B) competitive〔kəm'pɛtətɪv〕*adj.* 競爭激烈的

    (C) sorrowful〔'sɑrofəl〕*adj.* 悲傷的

    (D) realistic〔,riə'lɪstɪk〕*adj.* 現實的

    orphanage〔'ɔrfənɪdʒ〕*n.* 孤兒院　　basis〔'besɪs〕*n.* 基礎

    studies〔'stʌdɪz〕*n. pl.* 學業

    receive〔rɪ'siv〕*v.* 收到；接受　　pay〔pe〕*n.* 薪水

10. (**B**) Studies show that asking children to do house <u>chores</u>, such as
taking out the trash or doing the dishes, helps them grow into
responsible adults.
研究顯示，要求小孩做家事，像是倒垃圾或洗碗，能幫助他們長大
以後變成負責任的大人。

(A) mission〔ˋmɪʃən〕*n.* 任務

(B) *chores*〔tʃorz〕*n. pl.* 雜事

　　house chores 家事（ = *household chores* = *housework*）

(C) approach〔əˋprotʃ〕*n.* 方法　　(D) incident〔ˋɪnsədənt〕*n.* 事件

study〔ˋstʌdɪ〕*n.* 研究　　*take out the trash* 倒垃圾

do the dishes 洗碗　　*grow into* 長大成為

responsible〔rɪˋspɑnsəbḷ〕*adj.* 負責任的　　adult〔əˋdʌlt〕*n.* 成人

11. (**B**) John has been scolded by his boss for over ten minutes now.
<u>Apparently</u>, she is not happy about his being late again. 約翰現在
已經被老闆罵超過十分鐘了。顯然她對於他又遲到很不高興。

(A) expressively〔ɪkˋsprɛsɪvlɪ〕*adv.* 富於表情地

(B) *apparently*〔əˋpɛrəntlɪ〕*adv.* 似乎；顯然

(C) immediately〔ɪˋmidɪɪtlɪ〕*adv.* 立刻

(D) originally〔əˋrɪdʒənḷɪ〕*adv.* 本來；最初

scold〔skold〕*v.* 責罵

12. (**C**) Since the orange trees suffered <u>severe</u> damage from a storm in the
summer, the farmers are expecting a sharp decline in harvests this
winter.
由於柳橙樹在夏天遭受暴風雨<u>嚴重的</u>破壞，所以農民預計今年冬天的
收成會遽減。

(A) potential〔pəˋtɛnʃəl〕*adj.* 有潛力的

(B) relative〔ˋrɛlətɪv〕*adj.* 相對的

(C) *severe*〔səˋvɪr〕*adj.* 嚴重的　　(D) mutual〔ˋmjutʃuəl〕*adj.* 互相的

suffer〔ˋsʌfɚ〕*v.* 遭受　　expect〔ɪksˋpɛkt〕*v.* 預計；預料

sharp〔ʃɑrp〕*adj.* 急遽的　　decline〔dɪˋklaɪn〕*n.* 減少

harvest〔ˋhɑrvɪst〕*n.* 收穫（量）

13. (**A**) Typhoon Morakot claimed more than six hundred lives in early
August of 2009, making it the most serious natural <u>disaster</u> in
Taiwan in recent decades.
莫拉克颱風在 2009 年 8 月初奪去了超過六百人的性命，這使它成爲
台灣近幾十年來最嚴重的天<u>災</u>。

(A) *disaster* 〔dɪz'æstɚ〕 *n.* 災難　　*natural disaster* 天災
(B) barrier 〔'bærɪɚ〕 *n.* 障礙
(C) anxiety 〔æŋ'zaɪətɪ〕 *n.* 焦慮
(D) collapse 〔kə'læps〕 *n. v.* 倒塌

typhoon 〔taɪ'fun〕 *n.* 颱風　　claim 〔klem〕 *v.* 奪去
recent 〔'risṇt〕 *adj.* 最近的　　decade 〔'dɛked〕 *n.* 十年

14. (**C**) Robert was the only <u>witness</u> to the car accident. The police had to
count on him to find out exactly how the accident happened.
羅伯特是這場車禍唯一的<u>目擊者</u>。警方必須靠他查出這場意外究竟
是如何發生的。

(A) dealer 〔'dilɚ〕 *n.* 商人　　(B) guide 〔gaɪd〕 *n.* 導遊
(C) *witness* 〔'wɪtnɪs〕 *n.* 目擊者
(D) client 〔'klaɪənt〕 *n.* 客戶

count on 依靠　　*find out* 找出；查明
exactly 〔ɪg'zæktlɪ〕 *adv.* 究竟；到底

15. (**D**) Badly injured in the car accident, Jason could <u>scarcely</u> move his
legs and was sent to the hospital right away.
傑森在這場車禍中受重傷，他<u>幾乎不</u>能移動他的雙腳，所以馬上就
被送去醫院。

(A) accordingly 〔ə'kɔrdɪŋlɪ〕 *adv.* 因此
(B) undoubtedly 〔ʌn'daʊtɪdlɪ〕 *adv.* 無疑地
(C) handily 〔'hændɪlɪ〕 *adv.* 方便地；在手邊
(D) *scarcely* 〔'skɛrslɪ〕 *adv.* 幾乎不（= *hardly*）

badly injured 受重傷的　　move 〔muv〕 *v.* 移動
right away 馬上

二、綜合測驗：

Anita was shopping with her mother and enjoying it. Interestingly, both of them <u>ended up</u> buying the same pair of jeans.
16

艾妮塔和她的媽媽去逛街，她們逛得很開心。有趣的是，她們兩人最後買了同一條牛仔褲。

> interestingly〔'ɪntrɪstɪŋlɪ〕adv. 有趣的是【修飾整句】
> **the same pair of jeans** 同一條牛仔褲；指二條一模一樣的牛仔褲
> (= *two identical pairs of jeans*)

16. (**B**) (A) give up 放棄　　　　(B) **end up + V-ing** 以～結束；最後～
　　　　　(C) take to 熱中於；開始喜歡；開始做
　　　　　(D) used to + *V.* 以前～

According to a recent marketing study, young adults influence 88% of household clothing purchases. More often than not, those in their early twenties are the more <u>informed</u> consumers. There isn't a brand or a trend
17
that these young people are not aware of. That is why mothers who want to keep abreast of trends usually <u>turn to</u> the experts—their daughters.
18
This tells the retailers of the world that if you want to get into a mother's <u>pocketbook</u>, you've got to win her daughter over first.
19

根據最近一項行銷研究調查，一個家庭要購買衣服時，年輕人的影響佔了88%。二十出頭的年輕人，多半是比較有知識的消費者。沒有一個品牌或流行趨勢，是這些年輕人不知道的。這就是爲什麼想要跟上流行的媽媽們，通常會求助於專家——她們的女兒的原因。這也告訴了全世界的零售商，如果你想要賺到媽媽的錢，你必須先說服她的女兒。

> recent〔'risnt〕adj. 最近的　　　marketing〔'mɑrkɪtɪŋ〕n. 行銷
> study〔'stʌdɪ〕n. 研究　　　adult〔ə'dʌlt〕n. 成年人
> influence〔'ɪnfluəns〕v. 影響 (= *affect*)
> household〔'haus,hold〕adj. 家庭的
> clothing〔'kloðɪŋ〕n. 衣服　　　purchase〔'pɝtʃəs〕n. 購買

> ***more often than not*** 多半；常常（ = *as often as not* = *very often*）
> ***in one's early twenties*** 在某人二十歲出頭時
> consumer〔kən'sumə〕*n.* 消費者　　brand〔brænd〕*n.* 品牌
> trend〔trɛnd〕*n.* 流行；趨勢　　***be aware of*** 知道
> ***keep abreast of*** 不落後；跟得上　　expert〔'ɛkspɜt〕*n.* 專家
> retailer〔'ritelə〕*n.* 零售商　　***win over*** 說服

17. (**A**) 這一題主要考 informed 和 informative 的區別。
　　(A) ***informed***〔ɪn'fɔrmd〕*adj.* 有知識的；見聞廣博的
　　　　（ = *having a lot of knowledge* ）
　　(B) informative〔ɪn'fɔrmətɪv〕*adj.* 知識性的
　　　　（ = *giving information* ）
　　(C) informal〔ɪn'fɔrml̩〕*adj.* 非正式的
　　(D) informational〔ˌɪnfə'meʃənl̩〕*adj.* 新聞的；訊息的
　　　　（ = *about information* ）

18. (**C**) (A) deal with　應付；處理　　(B) head for　前往（某地）
　　(C) ***turn to sb.***　求助於某人　　(D) look into　往～裡面看；調查

19. (**D**) (A) textbook〔'tɛkst,bʊk〕*n.* 教科書
　　(B) notebook〔'not,bʊk〕*n.* 筆記本
　　(C) workbook〔'wɜk,bʊk〕*n.* 練習簿；作業簿
　　(D) ***pocketbook***〔'pakɪt,bʊk〕*n.* 錢包
　　get into a mother's pocketbook 字面意思是「進入媽媽的錢包」，
　　在此引申為「賺到媽媽的錢」，相當於 get her to buy your
　　product。

　　With a DJ playing various kinds of music rather than just rap, and
a mix of clothing labels designed more for taste and fashion than for a
precise age, department stores have managed to appeal to successful
middle-aged women <u>without</u> losing their younger customers. They have
　　　　　　　　　　　　　　　　20
created a shopping environment where the needs of both mother and
daughter are satisfied.

百貨公司請來 DJ，播放各種音樂，而非只有饒舌音樂，銷售各種品牌的衣服，是以品味和流行為設計主軸，而非只針對特定的年齡層，如此一來，他們設法吸引到成功的中年女性，也沒有失去較年輕的顧客。他們創造出一個購物環境，在這裡媽媽和女兒的需求都可以被滿足。

DJ〔'di͵dʒe〕*n.* 音樂播放人（= *disk jockey* = *deejay*）
various〔'vɛrɪəs〕*adj.* 各種的　　***various kinds of*** 各種的
rather than 而非　　rap〔ræp〕*n.* 饒舌音樂
mix〔mɪks〕*n.* 混合（= *mixture*）
a mix of 各種的（= *a variety of*）　　label〔'lebḷ〕*n.* 標籤
design〔dɪ'zaɪn〕*v.* 設計　　taste〔test〕*n.* 喜好；品味
fashion〔'fæʃən〕*n.* 流行；時髦　　precise〔prɪ'saɪs〕*adj.* 精確的
manage to* + *V. 設法～　　***appeal to*** 吸引（= *attract*）
middle-aged〔'mɪdḷ͵edʒd〕*adj.* 中年的　　create〔krɪ'et〕*v.* 創造
environment〔ɪn'vaɪrənmənt〕*n.* 環境　　satisfy〔'sætɪs͵faɪ〕*v.* 滿足

20.(**D**) 依句意，百貨公司吸引到中年女性，也「沒有」失去較年輕的顧客，故選 (D) *without*。

Onions can be divided into two categories: fresh onions and storage onions. Fresh onions are available <u>in</u> yellow, red and white throughout
                                            21
their season, March through August. They can be <u>identified</u> by their thin,
                                                    22
light-colored skin. Because they have a higher water content, they are typically sweeter and milder tasting than storage onions. This higher water content also makes <u>it</u> easier for them to bruise. With its delicate
                    23
taste, the fresh onion is an ideal choice for salads and other lightly-cooked dishes.

洋蔥可以分成兩種：新鮮洋蔥和儲藏的洋蔥。新鮮洋蔥盛產季節在三月到八月，整個季節可以買到黃色、紅色和白色的，看它們薄薄的、淺色的皮就知道是新鮮洋蔥。因為它們的水分含量較高，通常吃起來比儲藏的洋蔥甜，而且比較清爽。高含水量也使得新鮮洋蔥比較容易碰傷。因為味道爽口，所以新鮮洋蔥適合做沙拉，和其他烹煮清淡的菜餚。

onion〔'ʌnjən〕n. 洋蔥　　***be divided into*** 被分成
category〔'kætə,gorɪ〕n. 種類　　storage〔'storɪdʒ〕n. 儲藏；存放
available〔ə'veləbḷ〕adj. 買得到的；可獲得的
throughout〔θru'aʊt〕prep. 整個（時期）；自始至終
season〔'sizn̩〕n. 季節；當季；盛產期
through〔θru〕prep.（從～）到⋯
light-colored〔'laɪt,kʌləd〕adj. 淺色的
skin〔skɪn〕n.（人、動物、蔬果的）皮
content〔'kɑntɛnt〕n. 含量
typically〔'tɪpɪkḷɪ〕adv. 典型地；通常
mild〔maɪld〕adj. 溫和的；清淡的　　taste〔test〕v. 品嚐；吃起來
bruise〔bruz〕v. 淤傷；碰傷　　delicate〔'dɛləkɪt〕adj. 美味的
ideal〔aɪ'diəl〕adj. 理想的；適合的
lightly-cooked〔'laɪtlɪ,kʊkt〕adj. 烹煮清淡的
dish〔dɪʃ〕n. 菜餚

21.（**C**）表示「以～形式、顏色等」被買到，介系詞應用 *in*，故選 (C)。
　　　如：Cookies come *in* a box.（餅乾被裝在盒子裡出售。）

22.（**C**）(A) grow〔gro〕v. 生長；種植
　　　　　(B) taste〔test〕v. 品嚐；吃起來
　　　　　(C) ***identify***〔aɪ'dɛntə,faɪ〕v. 辨認；分辨
　　　　　(D) emphasize〔'ɛmfə,saɪz〕v. 強調

23.（**D**）這句話的主詞是 This⋯content，動詞 makes 之後需要受詞，
　　　easier 為受詞補語，而後面的不定詞 to bruise 是真正受詞，
　　　所以空格應填入虛受詞，選 (D) *it*。

Storage onions, on the other hand, are available August through April.
<u>Unlike</u> fresh onions, they have multiple layers of thick, dark, papery skin.
　24
They also have an <u>intense</u> flavor and a higher percentage of solids.　For
　　　　　　　　　25
these reasons, storage onions are the best choice for spicy dishes that
require longer cooking times or more flavor.

另一方面，儲藏的洋蔥在八月到四月買得到。不像新鮮洋蔥，它們有多層較厚、顏色較深、像紙一樣的皮。它們的味道也很強烈，固體物質含量較高。因為這些理由，儲藏的洋蔥是需要較長時間烹煮，或重口味辛辣菜色的最佳選擇。

> ***on the other hand*** 另一方面
> multiple〔ˈmʌltəpl̩〕*adj.* 多重的 (= *many*)
> layer〔ˈleɚ〕*n.* 層　　dark〔dɑrk〕*adj.* 深色的
> papery〔ˈpepərɪ〕*adj.* 如紙的　　flavor〔ˈflevɚ〕*n.* 味道；口味
> percentage〔pɚˈsɛntɪdʒ〕*n.* 百分比【前面不接數詞】
> solid〔ˈsɑlɪd〕*n.* 固體物質　　reason〔ˈrizn̩〕*n.* 理由
> spicy〔ˈspaɪsɪ〕*adj.* 辛辣的
> require〔rɪˈkwaɪr〕*v.* 需要 (= *need*)

24. (**A**) 儲藏的洋蔥的皮較厚、較深色，「不像」新鮮洋蔥，故介系詞選
 　　(A) *Unlike*。(B) through「穿過；經過」，(C) besides「除了～之外（還有）」，(D) despite「儘管」，均不合。

25. (**B**) 形容洋蔥的味道，應是很「強烈」，故選 (B) *intense*〔ɪnˈtɛns〕
 　　adj. 強烈的。
 　　(A) anxious〔ˈæŋkʃəs〕*adj.* 焦慮的
 　　(C) organic〔ɔrˈgænɪk〕*adj.* 有機的
 　　(D) effective〔əˈfɛktɪv〕*adj.* 有效的

 　　Many people like to drink bottled water because they feel that tap water may not be safe, but is bottled water really any better?

 　　Bottled water is mostly sold in plastic bottles and that's why it is potentially health <u>threatening</u>. Processing the plastic can lead to the
26
release of harmful chemical substances into the water contained in the bottles. The chemicals can be absorbed into the body and <u>cause</u> physical
27
discomfort, such as stomach cramps and diarrhea.

 　　許多人喜歡喝瓶裝水，因為他們覺得，自來水可能不太安全，但是瓶裝水真的比較好嗎？

　　瓶裝水大多裝在塑膠瓶裡販售，那就是為什麼可能威脅到健康的原因。加工塑膠瓶時，可能會導致有害的化學物質，被釋放到瓶中所裝的水裡。這些化學物質可能會被人體吸收，造成身體不適，例如急劇的腹痛和腹瀉。

> **bottled water** 瓶裝水　　tap〔tæp〕n. 水龍頭（= faucet）
> **tap water** 自來水　　plastic〔'plæstɪk〕adj. 塑膠的　n. 塑膠
> bottle〔'batḷ〕n. 瓶子　　potentially〔pə'tɛnʃəlɪ〕adv. 可能地
> process〔'prɑsɛs〕v. 加工　　**lead to** 導致；造成（= cause）
> release〔rɪ'lis〕n. 釋放　　harmful〔'hɑrmfəl〕adj. 有害的
> chemical〔'kɛmɪkḷ〕adj. 化學的　n. 化學物質
> substance〔'sʌbstəns〕n. 物質　　contain〔kən'ten〕v. 包含
> absorb〔əb'sɔrb〕v. 吸收　　physical〔'fɪzɪkḷ〕adj. 身體的
> discomfort〔dɪs'kʌmfɚt〕n. 不舒服
> cramp〔kræmp〕n. 抽筋；痙攣；(pl.) 急劇的腹痛
> diarrhea〔ˌdaɪə'riə〕n. 腹瀉

26. (**B**) (A) frighten〔'fraɪtṇ〕v. 使害怕　　frightening adj. 可怕的
　　　　　 (B) **threaten**〔'θrɛtṇ〕v. 威脅
　　　　　 health threatening adj. 威脅到健康的
　　　　　 (C) appeal〔ə'pil〕v. 吸引　　appealing adj. 吸引人的
　　　　　 (D) promote〔prə'mot〕v. 升遷；提倡

27. (**A**) 這個句子的主詞是 The chemicals，連接詞 and 應是連接兩個動詞，前面動詞是現在式複數，空格也應是，故選 (A) **cause**。

Health risks can also result from inappropriate storage of bottled water. Bacteria can multiply if the water is kept on the shelves for too long or if it is exposed to heat or direct sunlight. Since the information
28
on storage and shipment is not always readily available to consumers, bottled water may not be a better alternative to tap water.

　　健康的風險，也可能來自於瓶裝水的貯藏不當。如果瓶裝水放在架子上太久，或是接觸到熱源或受到陽光直接照射，細菌可能就會繁殖。因為有關貯藏和運送的資訊，消費者不一定能輕易獲得，所以瓶裝水可能不是比自來水更好的選擇。

　　　　　risk〔rɪsk〕n. 危險；風險（= danger = threat）
　　　　　result from 起因於【接原因；result in「導致」，接結果】
　　　　　inappropriate〔ˌɪnə'proprɪɪt〕adj. 不當的
　　　　　bacteria〔bæk'tɪrɪə〕n. pl. 細菌【單數為 bacterium〔bæk'tɪrɪəm〕】
　　　　　multiply〔'mʌltəˌplaɪ〕v. 繁殖（= reproduce）
　　　　　shelf〔ʃɛlf〕n. 架子【複數為 shelves〔ʃɛlvz〕】
　　　　　expose〔ɪk'spoz〕v. 暴露；使接觸 < to >　　heat〔hit〕n. 熱
　　　　　direct〔də'rɛkt〕adj. 直接的　　sunlight〔'sʌnˌlaɪt〕n. 陽光
　　　　　information〔ˌɪnfə'meʃən〕n. 資訊　　shipment〔'ʃɪpmənt〕n. 運送
　　　　　not always 未必；不一定　　　　readily〔'rɛdɪlɪ〕adv. 容易地（= easily）
　　　　　alternative〔ɔl'tɝnətɪv〕n. 選擇 < to >

28.（**C**）這個句子前後有兩個子句，可見空格應填入連接詞，依句意，「因
　　　　為」資訊不足，所以瓶裝水不見得比較好，故選 (C) *Since*，在此相
　　　　當於 Because。(A) although「雖然」，和 (D) so「所以」均為連接詞，
　　　　但句意不合；(B) despite「儘管」為介系詞，詞性、句意均不合。

Besides these <u>safety</u> issues, bottled water has other disadvantages.
　　　　　　　　　29
It contributes to global warming.　An estimated 2.5 million tons of
carbon dioxide were generated in 2006 by the production of plastic for
bottled water.　In addition, bottled water produces an incredible amount
of solid <u>waste</u>.　According to one research, 90% of the bottles used are
　　　　30
not recycled and lie for ages in landfills.

　　　　除了這些安全問題之外，瓶裝水還有其他缺點。它是促成全球暖化的原
因之一。在 2006 年，因為製造瓶裝水所需的塑膠，估計產生了 250 萬噸的二
氧化碳。此外，瓶裝水也造成了驚人數量的固態垃圾。根據一項研究，這些
被使用過的瓶子百分之九十都沒有被回收，而（因無法分解）會在垃圾掩埋
場裡埋上很久很久。

　　　　　besides〔bɪ'saɪdz〕prep. 除了～之外（還有）（= in addition to）
　　　　　issue〔'ɪʃju , 'ɪʃʊ〕n. 議題；問題
　　　　　disadvantage〔ˌdɪsəd'væntɪdʒ〕n. 缺點
　　　　　contribute〔kən'trɪbjut〕v. 貢獻；捐助；促成

contribute to 促成；是～的原因之一

global warming 全球暖化　　estimated〔ˋɛstəˏmetɪd〕*adj.* 估計的

ton〔tʌn〕*n.* 噸【重量單位】　　carbon〔ˋkɑrbən〕*n.* 碳【符號爲 C】

dioxide〔daɪˋɑksaɪd〕*n.* 二氧化物

carbon dioxide 二氧化碳（= *CO₂*）

generate〔ˋdʒɛnəˏret〕*v.* 產生；製造（= *produce*）

production〔prəˋdʌkʃən〕*n.* 生產；製造

in addition 此外（= *besides*）　　produce〔prəˋdjus〕*v.* 產生

incredible〔ɪnˋkrɛdəbl〕*adj.* 令人無法相信的；驚人的

amount〔əˋmaʊnt〕*n.* 數量　　solid〔ˋsɑlɪd〕*adj.* 固態的

according to 根據　　research〔ˋrisɝtʃ , rɪˋsɝtʃ〕*n.* 研究

recycle〔riˋsaɪkl〕*v.* 回收　　lie〔laɪ〕*v.* 躺；存在

for ages 很久（= *for a long time*）

landfill〔ˋlændˏfɪl〕*n.* 垃圾掩埋場

29.(**D**)　依句意，上一段所提的是「安全」問題，故選 (D) *safety*〔ˋseftɪ〕*n.*
「安全」。而 (A) display〔dɪˋsple〕*n.*「展示」，(B) production
「生產」，(C) shipment「運送」，均不合。

30.(**A**)　由最後提到垃圾掩埋場可知，瓶裝水會製造「垃圾」問題，故選
(A) *waste*〔west〕*n.* 廢物；垃圾。
而 (B) resource〔rɪˋsors〕*n.* 資源，(C) ground〔graʊnd〕*n.* 地面，
(D) profit〔ˋprɑfɪt〕*n.* 利潤，均不合句意。

三、文意選填：

Football is more than a sport; it is also an invaluable [31](C) teacher.
In teaching young players to cooperate with their fellows on the practice
[32](I) field, the game shows them the necessity of teamwork in society. It
prepares them to be [33](G) better citizens and persons.

　　足球不只是一項運動；它也是很寶貴的老師。在練習場上教導年輕球員要
和隊友合作時，足球比賽能讓他們明白，團隊合作在社會上的必要性。這能使
他們做好準備，成爲更好的公民和個人。

football〔'fut,bɔl〕n. 足球【足球、橄欖球，和美式足球的統稱】
more than 不只是　　invaluable〔ɪn'væljuəbl〕adj. 珍貴的
player〔'pleɚ〕n. 選手；球員　　cooperate〔ko'ɑpə,ret〕v. 合作
fellow〔'fɛlo〕n. 同伴　　***practice field*** 練習場
show〔ʃo〕v. 使…明白　　necessity〔nə'sɛsətɪ〕n. 必要（性）
teamwork〔'tim,wɝk〕n. 團隊合作
prepare〔prɪ'pɛr〕v. 使…有所準備
citizen〔'sɪtəzn̩〕n. 公民；國民

Wherever football is played, the players learn the rough-and-tumble lesson that only through the ³⁴(A) cooperation of each member can the team win. It is a lesson they must always ³⁵(J) remember on the field. Off the field, they continue to keep it in mind.

無論在哪裡踢足球，球員都能學到艱苦的教訓，那就是唯有透過每位成員的合作，球隊才能獲勝。這是他們在球場上必須永遠記得的教訓。離開球場後，他們還是會持續將這一點牢記在心。

> rough-and-tumble 是一個複合形容詞，字面的意思是「粗魯又跌倒」，源自足球是一項粗魯的比賽（rough game），球員會被撞倒、跌倒（tumble）。
> rough-and-tumble adj. 艱苦的【在字典上有很多解釋，但在此作「艱苦的」（= harsh = tough）解。】

lesson〔'lɛsn̩〕n. 教訓　　through〔θru〕prep. 透過
cooperation〔ko,ɑpə'reʃən〕n. 合作　　member〔'mɛmbɚ〕n. 成員
team〔tim〕n. 隊伍　　off〔ɔf〕prep. 離開
keep…in mind 將…牢記在心

In society, the former player does not look upon himself as a lone wolf who has the right to remain ³⁶(E) isolated from the society and go his own way. He understands his place in the team; he knows he is a member of society and must ³⁷(D) behave himself as such. He realizes that only by cooperating can he do his ³⁸(H) share in making society what it should be.

在社會上，以前踢過足球的人，不會認爲自己是有權利與社會隔絕、我行我素的獨行俠。他知道自己在球隊裡的地位；他知道自己是社會的一份子，必須要表現出應有的樣子。他了解唯有合作，才能盡自己的本分，使社會變成應該有的情況。

> former〔'fɔrmɚ〕*adj.* 以前的；前任的
> ***look upon*** A ***as*** B　認爲 A 是 B　　lone〔lon〕*adj.* 孤單的；孤獨的
> wolf〔wʊlf〕*n.* 狼　　***lone wolf*** 獨行俠；獨來獨往的人
> right〔raɪt〕*n.* 權利　　remain〔rɪ'men〕*v.* 依然；依舊
> isolated〔'aɪsḷ,etɪd〕*adj.* 孤立的；被隔離的
> ***go*** *one's* ***own way*** 我行我素　　place〔ples〕*n.* 地位；身分
> ***behave*** *oneself* 表現得
> such〔sʌtʃ〕*pron.* 如此的人或事物【在此指 a member of society】
> 【例】 I'm a gentleman and will be treated as ***such***.
> 　　【as such 的用法參照「文法寶典」p.124】　(*a gentleman*)
> realize〔'rɪəl,aɪz〕*v.* 知道；了解　　***do*** *one's* ***share*** 盡本分

The man who has played football knows that teamwork is [39](F) essential in modern living.　He is also aware that every citizen must do his part if the nation is to [40](B) prosper.　So he has little difficulty in adjusting himself to his role in family life and in the business world, and to his duties as a citizen.

踢過足球的人都知道，在現代生活中，團隊合作是非常重要的。他也知道，如果國家要興盛，每位國民都必須盡自己的本分。所以他能毫不困難地適應自己在家庭生活中和商場上的角色，以及身爲公民應盡的本分。

> essential〔ɪ'sɛnʃəl〕*adj.* 必要的；非常重要的
> living〔'lɪvɪŋ〕*n.* 生活　　aware〔ə'wɛr〕*adj.* 知道的；察覺到的
> ***do*** *one's* ***part*** 盡本分 (= *do one's share*)
> ***be to*** ***V.*** 預定要…　　prosper〔'prɑspɚ〕*v.* 繁榮；興盛
> ***have little difficulty in*** *V-ing* 在…方面沒什麼困難
> ***adjust*** *oneself* ***to*** 使自己適應　　role〔rol〕*n.* 角色
> ***business world*** 商業界；商場
> duty〔'djutɪ〕*n.* 義務；本分；責任

四、閱讀測驗：

41-44 為題組

On the island of New Zealand, there is a grasshopper-like species of insect that is found nowhere else on earth. New Zealanders have given it the nickname *weta*, which is a native Maori word meaning "god of bad looks." It's easy to see why anyone would call this insect a bad-looking bug. Most people feel disgusted at the sight of these bulky, slow-moving creatures.

紐西蘭島上有一種在世界上其他地方找不到，長得很像蚱蜢的昆蟲。紐西蘭人給他一個綽號叫 weta（沙螽），當地毛利語的意思是「難看之神」。很容易就可以知道，為什麼人們要說這樣的蟲很難看。大部分的人一看到這些巨大，且緩慢移動的生物，都會覺得很噁心。

island (ˈaɪlənd) *n.* 島　　*New Zealand* 紐西蘭
grasshopper (ˈɡræsˌhɑpɚ) *n.* 蚱蜢
grasshopper-like (ˈɡræshɑpɚˌlaɪk) *adj.* 像蚱蜢的
species (ˈspiʃiz) *n.* 物種　　insect (ˈɪnsɛkt) *n.* 昆蟲
on earth 在世界上　　*New Zealander* 紐西蘭人
nickname (ˈnɪkˌnem) *n.* 綽號　　weta (ˈwetə) *n.* 沙螽
native (ˈnetɪv) *adj.* 當地的
Maori (ˈmaʊrɪ) *adj.* 毛利人的；毛利語的　　looks (lʊks) *n.* 外表
bad-looking (ˈbædˈlʊkɪŋ) *adj.* 不好看的；醜的
disgusted (dɪsˈɡʌstɪd) *adj.* 感到厭惡的
at the sight of 一看見　　bulky (ˈbʌlkɪ) *adj.* 巨大的
slow-moving (ˈsloˈmuvɪŋ) *adj.* 行動緩慢的
creature (ˈkritʃɚ) *n.* 生物

Wetas are nocturnal creatures; they come out of their caves and holes only after dark. A giant weta can grow to over three inches long and weigh as much as 1.5 ounces. Giant wetas can hop up to two feet at a time. Some of them live in trees, and others live in caves. They are very long-lived for insects, and some adult wetas can live as long as two years. Just like their cousins grasshoppers and crickets, wetas are able to "sing" by rubbing their leg parts together, or against their lower bodies.

　　沙螽是夜行性生物；牠們在天黑後才從洞穴裡爬出來。大型的沙螽可以長到超過三吋長，重達 1.5 盎司。大型沙螽每次跳躍可高達兩呎高。牠們有些住在樹上，有些住在洞穴裡。牠們是很長壽的昆蟲，有些成蟲可以活長達兩年。沙螽跟牠的近親蚱蜢和蟋蟀一樣，能夠藉由摩擦腿部或是下腹部來「唱歌」。

> nocturnal〔nɑk'tɝnḷ〕*adj.* 夜間活動的　　　cave〔kev〕*n.* 洞穴
> hole〔hol〕*n.* 洞　　　***after dark*** 天黑之後
> giant〔'dʒaɪənt〕*adj.* 巨大的　　　weigh〔we〕*v.* 重～
> ounce〔aʊns〕*n.* 盎司（= 1/16 磅）　　　hop〔hɑp〕*v.* 跳躍
> ***up to*** 高達；多達　　　***at a time*** 一次
> long-lived〔'lɔŋ'laɪvd〕*adj.* 長壽的
> adult〔'ædʌlt , ə'dʌlt〕*adj.* 成熟的
> cousin〔'kʌzn̩〕*n.* 堂（表）兄弟姊妹；同類；密切相關的人或物
> cricket〔'krɪkɪt〕*n.* 蟋蟀　　　rub〔rʌb〕*v.* 摩擦

Most people probably don't feel sympathy for these endangered creatures, but they do need protecting. The slow and clumsy wetas have been around on the island since the times of the dinosaurs, and have evolved and survived in an environment where they had no enemies until rats came to the island with European immigrants. Since rats love to hunt and eat wetas, the rat population on the island has grown into a real problem for many of the native species that are unaccustomed to **its** presence, and poses a serious threat to the native weta population.

　　大多數人可能不會對這些瀕臨絕種的生物感到同情，但牠們的確需要保護。這些行動緩慢、醜陋而笨拙的沙螽，自從恐龍時代就已經存在於島上，在老鼠隨著歐洲移民來到島上之前，牠們一直演化，並生存在一個沒有天敵的環境中。由於老鼠喜歡捕食沙螽，島上的老鼠族群，對許多無法習慣牠們存在的當地物種而言，已成為一個很大的問題，而且對當地的沙螽族群造成了嚴重的威脅。

> sympathy〔'sɪmpəθɪ〕*n.* 同情
> endangered〔ɪn'dendʒəd〕*adj.* 瀕臨絕種的
> clumsy〔'klʌmzɪ〕*adj.* 笨拙而難看的

around〔ə'raʊnd〕*adj.* 存在的

times〔taɪmz〕*n. pl.* 時代；時期　　dinosaur〔'daɪnəˌsɔr〕*n.* 恐龍

evolve〔ɪ'vɑlv〕*v.* 演化　　survive〔sə'vaɪv〕*v.* 存活

enemy〔'ɛnəmɪ〕*n.* 敵人；天敵　　rat〔ræt〕*n.* 老鼠

immigrant〔'ɪməgrənt〕*n.* 移民　　hunt〔hʌnt〕*v.* 獵捕

population〔ˌpɑpjə'leʃən〕*n.* 某區域內生物的總數；族群；人口

unaccustomed〔ˌʌnə'kʌstəmd〕*adj.* 不習慣的

presence〔'prɛzn̩s〕*n.* 存在　　pose〔poz〕*v.* 引起；造成

threat〔θrɛt〕*n.* 威脅

41.(**D**) 本文最**不**可能出自下列何者？

　　(A) 科學雜誌。　　　　　　　(B) 旅遊指南。

　　(C) 生物課本。　　　　　　　(D) <u>商業期刊。</u>

biology〔baɪ'ɑlədʒɪ〕*n.* 生物學　　guide〔gaɪd〕*n.* 指南

textbook〔'tɛkstˌbʊk〕*n.* 教科書；課本

journal〔'dʒɜnl̩〕*n.* 期刊

42.(**A**) 根據本文，下列敘述何者正確？

　　(A) <u>沙螽令人看起來不舒服。</u>　(B) 沙螽是最近發現的昆蟲。

　　(C) 毛利人將自己暱稱爲 Wetas（沙螽）。

　　(D) 歐洲人將沙螽帶到紐西蘭。

unpleasant〔ʌn'plɛzn̩t〕*adj.* 令人不愉快的

newly〔'njulɪ〕*adv.* 新近；最近　　Maori〔'maʊrɪ〕*n.* 毛利人

nickname〔'nɪkˌnem〕*v.* 給…取綽號

43.(**C**) 下列對沙螽的敘述何者是正確的？

　　(A) 牠們行動快速。　　　　　(B) 牠們白天很活躍。

　　(C) <u>牠們的數量正在減少中。</u>

　　(D) 就昆蟲而言，牠們的壽命很短。

description〔dɪ'skrɪpʃən〕*n.* 描述

accurate〔'ækjərɪt〕*adj.* 正確的

movement〔'muvmənt〕*n.* 移動；動作　　active〔'æktɪv〕*adj.* 活躍的

daytime〔'deˌtaɪm〕*n.* 白天　　lifespan〔'laɪfspæn〕*n.* 壽命

44. (**A**) 下列何者是最後一段 its（牠的）的最佳解釋？

(A) 老鼠的。　　　　　　　(B) 沙蚤的。

(C) 島嶼的。　　　　　　　(D) 恐龍的。

* 因為 its 是單數型的所有格，也就代表 it 所指的是 the rat population。

appropriate〔ə'proprɪɪt〕adj. 適合的

interpretation〔ɪn,tɜprɪ'teʃən〕n. 解釋

45-48 為題組

The high school prom is the first formal social event for most American teenagers. It has also been a rite of passage for young Americans for nearly a century.

中學舞會是大部分美國青少年，第一次正式的社交活動。它也是將近一世紀以來，美國年輕人的成年禮儀。

prom〔prɑm〕n.（通常為隆重的）舞會（尤指高中或大學班級舉辦的）

formal〔'fɔrməl〕adj. 正式的

social〔'soʃəl〕adj. 社交的；聯誼的

event〔ɪ'vɛnt〕n. 事件；活動

teenager〔'tin,edʒɚ〕n. 青少年（13 至 19 歲的人）

rite〔raɪt〕n. 儀式　　　passage〔'pæsɪdʒ〕n. 通過；轉變

rite of passage　通過儀式【在某人的一生中，表示從一階段進入另一階段轉捩點的儀式或慶典，如從青少年進入成年】

The word "prom" was first used in the 1890s, referring to formal dances in which the guests of a party would display their fashions and dancing skills during the evening's grand march. In the United States, parents and educators have come to regard the prom as an important lesson in social skills. Therefore, proms have been held every year in high schools for students to learn proper social behavior.

「舞會」這個字最早用於一八九〇年代，指的是正式的舞會，而來賓會在晚上舞會盛大的開始儀式中，展示他們的時裝及舞蹈技巧。在美國，父母親和老師，已經把舞會認為是社交技巧中，重要的一課。因此，中學每年舉行舞會，好讓學生學會合適的社交行為。

 refer to　指的是 dance〔dæns〕*n.* 舞會
 display〔dɪ'sple〕*v.* 展示 fashion〔'fæʃən〕*n.* 時尚；時裝
 grand〔grend〕*adj.* 盛大的 march〔mɑrtʃ〕*n.* 行進
 grand march　(舞會上賓客繞場一周的) 開始儀式
 educator〔'ɛdʒəˌketə〕*n.* 教育家；教師
 come to　達到 (某種狀態)；結果是
 regard A as B　認為 A 是 B proper〔'prɑpə〕*adj.* 適當的
 behavior〔bɪ'hevjə〕*n.* 行為

 The first high school proms were held in the 1920s in America. By the
1930s, proms were common across the country. For many older Americans,
the prom was a modest, home-grown affair in the school gymnasium.
Prom-goers were well dressed but not fancily dressed up for the occasion:
boys wore jackets and ties and girls their Sunday dresses. Couples danced
to music provided by a local amateur band or a record player. After the
1960s, and especially since the 1980s, the high school prom in many areas
has become a serious exercise in excessive consumption, with boys renting
expensive tuxedos and girls wearing designer gowns. Stretch limousines
were hired to drive the prom-goers to expensive restaurants or discos for
an all-night extravaganza.

 美國最早的中學舞會，是在一九二〇年代舉辦的。到了一九三〇年代，舞
會在全國各地就很常見了。對於許多較年長的美國人而言，舞會是一種在學校
體育館裡，一件很樸實、又有本地特色的事。去參加舞會的人，會穿著考究，
但不會為了這個場合，很做作地盛裝打扮：男生會穿夾克、打領帶，而女生則
是穿上她們最好的衣服。舞伴們會隨著由當地業餘樂隊，或是電唱機所提供的
音樂翩翩起舞。一九六〇年代之後，尤其是自從一九八〇年代以來，許多地區
的中學舞會，已經變成一種重要的活動，而且會過度花費，男生租借昂貴的燕
尾服，而女生則穿著由設計師設計的禮服。租用加長型的大型豪華轎車，載送
去參加舞會的人到昂貴的餐廳，或是迪斯可舞廳，為的是參加整晚的盛大活動。

 across the country　在全國
 modest〔'mɑdɪst〕*adj.* 端莊的；樸素的
 home-grown〔'hom'gron〕*adj.* 本地的；有本地特色的

affair〔ə'fɛr〕 *n.* 事情　　gymnasium〔dʒɪm'nezɪəm〕 *n.* 體育館
well dressed〔ˌwɛl'drɛst〕 *adj.* 穿著考究的
fancily〔'fænsɪlɪ〕 *adv.* 做作地　　***dress up*** 盛裝打扮
occasion〔ə'keʒən〕 *n.* 場合　　jacket〔'dʒækɪt〕 *n.* 夾克
tie〔taɪ〕 *n.* 領帶

> ***Sunday dress***　(= *Sunday best*)
> ① 最好的衣服 (= *nicest dress*)
> ② 上教堂穿的衣服 (= *clothing worn to church*)
> 【因美國人習慣在星期天穿最好的衣服，上教堂做禮拜】

couple〔'kʌpəl〕 *n.* 夫妻；情侶；一對舞伴
to music 隨著音樂　　amateur〔'æməˌtʃʊr, -tʃɚ〕 *adj.* 業餘的
record player 電唱機　　especially〔ɛ'spɛʃəlɪ, ɪ'spɛʃ-〕 *adv.* 尤其
serious〔'sɪrɪəs〕 *adj.* 重要的　　exercise〔'ɛksɚˌsaɪz〕 *n.* 活動
excessive〔ɪk'sɛsɪv〕 *adj.* 過度的
consumption〔kən'sʌmpʃən〕 *n.* 消費　　rent〔rɛnt〕 *v.* 租借
tuxedo〔tʌk'sido〕 *n.* 燕尾服
designer〔dɪ'zaɪnɚ〕 *adj.* 由設計師專門設計的
gown〔gaʊn〕 *n.* 禮服
stretch〔strɛtʃ〕 *adj.* 車輛擴大座位區的；加長型的
limousine〔ˌlɪmə'zin, 'lɪməˌzin〕 *n.* 大型豪華轎車
【接送旅客的大型轎車，特指由專用司機駕駛的豪華轎車，有時乘客
　和駕駛座之間會相隔開】　　hire〔haɪr〕 *v.* 租用
disco〔'dɪsko〕 *n.* 迪斯可舞廳　　all-night〔ˌɔl'naɪt〕 *adj.* 整夜的
extravaganza〔ɪkˌstrævə'gænzə〕 *n.* 盛事；盛大慶典

　　Whether simple or lavish, proms have always been more or less
traumatic events for adolescents who worry about self-image and fitting
in with their peers.　Prom night can be a dreadful experience for socially
awkward teens or for those who do not secure dates.　Since the 1990s,
alternative proms have been organized in some areas to meet the needs of
particular students.　For example, proms organized by and for homeless
youth were reported.　There were also "couple-free" proms to which all
students are welcome.

　　無論是簡單或奢華,舞會對於擔心自我形象,以及和同輩可不可以合得來的青少年而言,或多或少都是痛苦的事情。對於在社交方面很笨拙的青少年,或是那些沒找到約會對象的人而言,舞會之夜可能是可怕的經驗。自從一九九○年代以來,在某些地區就籌辦過另類的舞會,來滿足特定學生的需求。例如,據報導,就有專為無家可歸的年輕人所舉辦的舞會。也有「無舞伴的」舞會,歡迎所有的學生參加。

> lavish〔ˈlævɪʃ〕*adj.* 奢華的　　***more or less*** 或多或少
> traumatic〔trɔˈmætɪk〕*adj.* 痛苦的
> event〔ɪˈvɛnt〕*n.* 事件;大型活動
> adolescent〔͵ædlˈɛsənt〕*n.* 青少年
> self-image〔ˈsɛlfˈɪmɪdʒ〕*n.* 自我形象　　***fit in with*** … 與…合得來
> peer〔pɪr〕*n.* 同輩;同儕　　dreadful〔ˈdrɛdfəl〕*adj.* 可怕的
> socially〔ˈsoʃəlɪ〕*adv.* 在社交上　　awkward〔ˈɔkwəd〕*adj.* 笨拙的
> teens〔tinz〕*n. pl.* 青少年(= *teenagers*)
> secure〔sɪˈkjur〕*v.* 找到;獲得　　date〔det〕*n.* (異性的)約會對象
> alternative〔ɔlˈtɜnətɪv〕*adj.* 供選擇的;另類的
> organize〔ˈɔrgə͵naɪz〕*v.* 組織;籌辦
> particular〔pəˈtɪkjələ〕*adj.* 特殊的;特定的
> homeless〔ˈhomləs〕*adj.* 無家可歸的
> -free 無…【構詞成分,用以構成形容詞和副詞】

45.(**C**)為什麼中學舞會對美國的青少年很重要?
　　(A)它們是畢業典禮的一部分。
　　(B)它們是青少年用來炫燿他們的大型豪華轎車的場合。
　　(C)它們是青少年學習社交技巧的重要活動。
　　(D)它們是青少年分享痛苦經驗的正式活動。

> significant〔sɪgˈnɪfɪkənt〕*adj.* 重要的
> graduation〔͵grædʒʊˈeʃən〕*n.* 畢業　　ceremony〔ˈsɛrə͵monɪ〕*n.* 典禮

46.(**D**)第三段的主旨為何?
　　(A)去參加舞會的人必須遵守適當的社交行為。
　　(B)早期所舉辦的舞會給青少年的壓力較少。
　　(C)舞會被認為很重要,因為每個人都為這個場合盛裝打扮。
　　(D)這些年來,舞會已經從很樸素的活動,變成很豪華的聚會。

> observe〔əbˈzɜv〕*v.* 遵守
> glamorous〔ˈglæmərəs〕*adj.* 豪華的;奢侈的

47. (**D**) 根據本文，是什麼導致另類的舞會的出現？
　　(A) 並不是所有的學生在舞會裡都舉止良好。
　　(B) 舞會太莊重了，不適合去參加舞會的年輕人。
　　(C) 青少年想要和他們的約會對象去參加舞會。
　　(D) <u>有特別需求的學生不喜歡傳統的舞會。</u>

conventional〔kən'vɛnʃənəl〕*adj.* 傳統的

48. (**C**) 下列敘述何者為眞？
　　(A) 自從一九六○年代以來，就一直在舉辦非傳統的舞會。
　　(B) 一九八○年代，會在當地的教堂舉行舞會，讓青少年參加。
　　(C) <u>自從一九三○年代以來，舞會在美國中學已經變成很重要的</u>
　　　　<u>活動。</u>
　　(D) 在一八九○年代，中學舞會對於一些美國家庭而言，是整晚的
　　　　社交活動。

attend〔ə'tɛnd〕*v.* 參加

49-52 為題組

　　No budget for your vacation? Try home exchanges—swapping houses with strangers. Agree to use each other's cars, and you can save bucks on car rentals, too.

　　沒錢去度假嗎？那就試試交換房屋 — 和陌生人交換房子。如果雙方同意可以用彼此的車子，那麼你也可以因此省下租車的錢。

budget〔'bʌdʒɪt〕*n.* 預算　　exchange〔ɪks'tʃendʒ〕*n.* 交換
swap〔swɑp〕*v.* 交換　　buck〔bʌk〕*n.* 一美元
rental〔'rɛntl̩〕*n.* 租金

　　Home exchanges are not new. At least one group, Intervac, has been facilitating such an arrangement since 1953. But trading online is gaining popularity these days, with several sites in operation, including HomeExchanges. Founded in 1992, with some 28,000 listings, this company *bills* itself as the world's largest home exchange club, reporting that membership has increased 30% this year.

　　交換房屋的活動早就有了。自 1953 年開始，至少已經有一個集團，也就是Intervac公司，在安排這樣的活動。不過，最近在網路上交易變得越來越普遍，有好幾個網站在營運，HomeExchanges就是其中之一。這家公司於 1992 年創立，有大約兩萬八千筆資料，大力宣傳自己是全世界最大的交換房屋俱樂部，他們表示，今年的會員已經成長了百分之三十。

　　group〔 grup 〕*n.* 集團　　facilitate〔 fə'sɪlə͵tet 〕*v.* 促進；幫助
arrangement〔 ə'rendʒmənt 〕*n.* 安排　　trade〔 tred 〕*v.* 交易
online〔'ɑn͵laɪn 〕*adv.* 在網路上　　gain〔 gen 〕*v.* 獲得；增加
popularity〔͵pɑpjə'lærətɪ 〕*n.* 流行；受歡迎
site〔 saɪt 〕*n.* 網站（= *website*）　　***in operation*** 營運中；運作中
found〔 faʊnd 〕*v.* 創立　　some〔 sʌm 〕*adv.* 大約
listing〔'lɪstɪŋ 〕*n.* 名單；名冊　　bill〔 bɪl 〕*v.* 宣傳（= *advertise*）
report〔 rɪ'port 〕*v.* 報導　　membership〔'mɛmbə͵ʃɪp 〕*n.* 會員

The annual fee is usually less than US$100. Members can access thousands of listings for apartments, villas, suburban homes and farms around the world. Initial contact is made via e-mail, with subsequent communication usually by phone. Before a match is made, potential swappers tend to discuss a lot.

　　年費通常不超過一百美元。會員可以瀏覽幾千張清單，搜尋世界各地的公寓、別墅、郊區的房子，以及農場。最初的接觸都是透過電子郵件，之後通常就會用電話聯繫。在配對成功之前，可能會交換房屋的人，都會經常進行討論。

　　annual〔'ænjʊəl 〕*adj.* 每年的　　fee〔 fi 〕*n.* 費用
access〔'æksɛs 〕*v.* 存取（資料）；使用　　villa〔'vɪlə 〕*n.* 別墅
suburban〔 sə'bɝbən 〕*adj.* 郊區的　　***around the world*** 全世界
initial〔 ɪ'nɪʃəl 〕*adj.* 最初的　　via〔'vaɪə 〕*prep.* 經由
subsequent〔'sʌbsɪ͵kwɛnt 〕*adj.* 之後的　　match〔 mætʃ 〕*n.* 配對
potential〔 pə'tɛnʃəl 〕*adj.* 可能的　　swapper〔'swɑpə 〕*n.* 交換者
tend to V. 傾向於；易於　　***a lot*** 常常（= *often*）

However, the concept may sound risky to some people. What about theft? Damage? These are reasonable causes for concern, but equally unlikely. As one swapper puts it, "Nobody is going to fly across the ocean or drive 600 miles to come steal your TV. Besides, at the same time they're staying in your home, you are staying in their home."

　　然而，這想法對某些人來說，或許聽起來有點冒險。如果發生偷竊怎麼辦？如果造成損害呢？這些顧慮的確很合理，但同樣是不太可能的。正如同一位交換房屋者所說的：「沒有人會飛越海洋，或開 600 哩的車去偷你的電視。此外，當他們住在你家時，你也正住在他們家。」

concept〔'kɑnsɛpt〕n. 觀念；想法
risky〔'rɪskɪ〕adj. 危險的；冒險的　　theft〔θɛft〕n. 偷竊
reasonable〔'riznəbl̩〕adj. 合理的　　cause〔kɔz〕n. 原因；理由
concern〔kən'sɝn〕n. 擔心　　equally〔'ikwəlɪ〕adv. 同樣地
unlikely〔ʌn'laɪklɪ〕adj. 不可能的
swapper〔'swɑpɚ〕n. 交換者（= exchanger）
put〔pʊt〕v. 說　　stay〔ste〕v. 暫住

　　Exchange sites recommend that swappers discuss such matters ahead of time. They may fill out an agreement spelling out who shoulders which responsibilities if a problem arises. It does not matter if the agreement would hold up in court, but it does give the exchangers a little satisfaction.

　　換屋仲介網站建議交換者要事先討論這些問題。他們可以填寫協議書，詳細說明問題發生時該由誰負責。該協議書是否具有效力並不重要，不過它的確能使交換者愉快一點。

recommend〔ˌrɛkə'mɛnd〕v. 推薦；建議　　*ahead of time* 事先
fill out 填寫　　agreement〔ə'grimənt〕n. 協議
spell out 詳細說明　　shoulder〔'ʃoldɚ〕v. 承擔
responsibility〔rɪˌspɑnsə'bɪlətɪ〕n. 責任　　arise〔ə'raɪz〕v. 發生
court〔kort〕n. 法庭
hold up in court 有法律效力（= be legally binding）
satisfaction〔ˌsætɪs'fækʃən〕n. 滿意；愉快

　　Generally, the biggest complaint among home exchangers has to do with different standards of cleanliness. Swappers are supposed to make sure their home is in order before they depart, but one person's idea of "clean" may be more forgiving than another's. Some owners say if they come back to a less-than-sparkling kitchen, it may be inconvenient but would not sour them on future exchanges.

　　一般說來，換屋者最大的抱怨，是和對整潔的標準不同有關。換屋者應該確保房屋在他們離開之前是井然有序的，但一個人對「整潔」的看法，可能比另一個人更寬鬆。有些屋主表示，如果他們回家時發現廚房不夠閃閃發亮，這或許會不太方便，但並不會使他們未來討厭進行交換。

> generally〔ˋdʒɛnərəlɪ〕adv. 一般說來
> complaint〔kəmˋplent〕n. 抱怨　　**have to do with** 和～有關
> standard〔ˋstændəd〕n. 標準　　cleanliness〔ˋklɛnlɪnɪs〕n. 清潔
> **be supposed to** 應該　　**in order** 整齊；井然有序
> depart〔dɪˋpɑrt〕v. 離開　　forgiving〔fəˋgɪvɪŋ〕adj. 寬容的
> sparkling〔ˋspɑrklɪŋ〕adj. 發亮的
> inconvenient〔͵ɪnkənˋvinjənt〕adj. 不方便的
> sour〔saʊr〕v. 使變得討厭

49. (**B**) 第二段的主旨為何？

(A) 如何換屋。　　　　　　　　(B) 房屋交換是如何變得普遍。
(C) 最大的換屋公司。
(D) Intervac 和 HomeExchange 這兩家公司的差異。

contrast〔ˋkɑntræst〕n. 對比；差異

50. (**A**) 下列哪一個字最接近第二段中的 **bills** 這個字？

(A) 宣傳　　　(B) 奉獻　　　(C) 取代　　　(D) 參與
dedicate〔ˋdɛdə͵ket〕v. 奉獻

51. (**B**) 換屋者通常如何開始溝通？

(A) 藉由電話。　　　　　　　　(B) 藉由電子郵件。
(C) 藉由媒人。　　　　　　　　(D) 藉由面對面的溝通。

matchmaker〔ˋmætʃ͵mekə〕n. 媒人

52. (**C**) 本文建議如何處理偷竊與損害？

(A) 可以向法院提出訴訟。　　　(B) 雙方可以在線上交易。
(C) 雙方可以事先簽訂協議書。
(D) 可以破壞另一方的房子作為報復。

deal with 處理　　concern〔kənˋsɝn〕n. 關心的事；事務
file〔faɪl〕v. 提出　　lawsuit〔ˋlɔ͵sut〕n. 訴訟
party〔ˋpɑrtɪ〕n. 一方　　sign〔saɪn〕v. 簽署
beforehand〔bɪˋfor͵hænd〕adv. 事先；預先　　**in return** 作為回報

53-56 為題組

　　Bekoji is a small town of farmers and herders in the Ethiopian highlands. There, time almost stands still, and horse-drawn carts outnumber motor vehicles. Yet, it has consistently yielded many of the world's best distance runners.

　　貝克基是一個位於衣索比亞高原，只有農民和牧者的小鎮。在這裡，時間幾乎靜止，馬車的數目比汽車還多。但是，它卻持續出產許多全世界最棒的長跑選手。

> Bekoji〔bɛˈkɔdʒɪ〕*n.* 貝克基【位於衣索比亞的小鎮，坐落於海拔四千
>   三百公尺的火山，世界許多優秀的長跑選手皆來自於此】
> herder〔ˈhɝdɚ〕*n.* 牧人
> Ethiopian〔ˌiθɪˈopɪən〕*n.* 衣索比亞人　*adj.* 衣索比亞的
> highland〔ˈhaɪlənd〕*n.* 高地；高原
> stand〔stænd〕*v.* 站立；處於⋯的狀態
> still〔stɪl〕*adj.* 不動的　　***stand still*** 停滯；不動
> horse-drawn〔ˈhɔrsˈdrɔn〕*adj.* 用馬拉的
> cart〔kɑrt〕*n.* 輕便馬車
> outnumber〔aʊtˈnʌmbɚ〕*v.* 比⋯多　　***motor vehicle*** 汽車
> consistently〔kənˈsɪstəntlɪ〕*adv.* 一貫地；一直；老是
> yield〔jild〕*v.* 出產；產生　　***distance runner*** 長跑選手

　　It's tempting, when breathing the thin air of Bekoji, to focus on the special conditions of the place. The town sits on the side of a volcano nearly 10,000 feet above sea level, making daily life a kind of high-altitude training. Children in this region often start running at an early age, covering great distances to fetch water and firewood or to reach the nearest school. Added to this early training is a physical trait shared by people there—disproportionately long legs, which is advantageous for distance runners.

　　當呼吸著貝克基稀薄的空氣時，會讓人很想注意到此地特殊的環境，這個小鎮坐落在高於海平面一萬呎的火山山腰處，讓日常生活都像是一種高海拔的訓練。這個地區的孩子往往在很小的時候就開始跑步，跑過很長的距離

去取水和柴薪，或是到達最近的學校。除了早年的訓練之外，這裡的人們都
有的另一個身體上的特色——就是不成比例的長腿，這對長跑選手而言是非常
有利的。

> tempting〔'tɛmptɪŋ〕adj. 吸引人的　　breathe〔brið〕v. 呼吸
> thin〔θɪn〕adj. 稀薄的　　*focus on* 專注於
> conditions〔kən'dɪʃənz〕n. pl. (週遭) 狀況；環境
> *sit on* 位於；坐落於　　side〔saɪd〕n. 山腰
> volcano〔val'keno〕n. 火山　　nearly〔'nɪrlɪ〕adv. 將近
> *sea level* 海平面　　*daily life* 日常生活
> altitude〔'æltə,tjud〕n. 海拔；高度
> region〔'ridʒən〕n. 地區　　cover〔'kʌvɚ〕v. 涵蓋；行走；走過
> fetch〔fɛtʃ〕v. 去拿　　firewood〔'faɪr,wud〕n. 柴薪
> physical〔'fɪzɪkl̩〕adj. 身體的　　trait〔tret〕n. 特徵
> disproportionately〔,dɪsprə'pɔrʃənɪtlɪ〕adv. 不成比例地
> advantageous〔,ædvən'tedʒəs〕adj. 有利的

A strong desire burns inside Bekoji's young runners. Take the case of
Million Abate. Forced to quit school in fifth grade after his father died,
Abate worked as a shoe-shine boy for years. He saw a hope in running
and joined Santayehu Eshetu's training program. This 18-year-old sprinted
to the finish of a 12-mile run with his bare feet bleeding. The coach took
off his own Nikes and handed them to him. To help Abate continue
running, the coach arranged a motel job for him, which pays $9 a month.

貝克基的年輕選手體內燃燒著一股強烈的渴望。以米利恩‧阿巴特為例，
他五年級的時候父親過世，被迫放棄學業，擔任擦鞋童很多年。他在跑步中看
到希望，加入山塔耶夫‧厄什圖的培訓計畫。這位十八歲的男孩跑了 12 英里，
用流著血的赤裸雙腳，全力衝刺跑向終點。教練脫下自己的耐吉球鞋，然後把
球鞋交給他。為了幫助阿巴特繼續跑步，教練幫他安排一份汽車旅館的工作，
每個月薪水九塊錢。

> desire〔dɪ'zaɪr〕n. 渴望　　burn〔bɜn〕v. 燃燒
> case〔kes〕n. 例子；情況　　*take the case of*… 舉…為例
> Million Abate〔'mɪljənɑ'bɑte〕n. 米利恩‧阿巴特

be forced to + V. 被迫~　　quit〔kwɪt〕v. 放棄；退（學）

grade〔gred〕n. 年級　　**a shoe-shine boy** 擦鞋童

for years 多年；很久　　running〔'rʌnɪŋ〕n. 賽跑；跑步

Santayehu Eshetu　n. 山塔耶夫・厄什圖【衣索比亞長跑教練】

program〔'progræm〕n. 計畫　　sprint〔sprɪnt〕v. 全力衝刺

finish〔'fɪnɪʃ〕n. 終結；終點　　run〔rʌn〕n. 賽跑

bare feet 光腳；打赤腳　　bleed〔blid〕v. 流血

coach〔kotʃ〕n. 教練　　**take off** 脫下

Nikes〔'naɪkis〕n. pl. 耐吉牌球鞋

hand sth. **to** sb. 將某物交給某人　　arrange〔ə'rendʒ〕v. 安排

motel〔mo'tɛl〕n. 汽車旅館　　pay〔pe〕v. 支付（薪水）

Most families in Bekoji live from hand to mouth, and distance running offers the younger generation a way out. Bekoji's legend Derartu Tulu, who won the 10,000-meter Olympic gold medals in 1992 and 2000, is a national hero. As a reward, the government gave her a house. She also won millions of dollars in the races.

在貝克基，大多數的家庭，生活都僅夠糊口，而長跑提供年輕的世代一個出路。貝克基的傳奇人物德拉圖・圖魯，在一九九二年和二○○○年，贏得一萬公尺的奧運金牌，成為全國英雄。衣索比亞政府給她一棟房子作為獎賞。她在競賽中也贏得了數百萬美元。

live from hand to mouth 生活僅夠糊口

distance running 長跑　　offer〔'ɔfɚ〕v. 提供

generation〔ˌdʒɛnə'reʃən〕n. 世代

a way out 解決問題的辦法；出路

legend〔'lɛdʒənd〕n. 傳奇人物

Derartu Tulu　n. 德拉圖・圖魯【1972-，衣索比亞人，全球第一位在
　奧運中奪得金牌的非洲黑人女子選手】

Olympic〔o'lɪmpɪk〕adj. 奧林匹克的

medal〔'mɛdl̩〕n. 獎牌　　**gold medal** 金牌

national〔'næʃənl̩〕adj. 全國的

reward〔rɪ'wɔrd〕n. 報酬；獎賞　　race〔res〕n. 賽跑；競賽

Motivated by such signs of success, thousands of kids from the villages surrounding Bekoji have moved into town. They crowd the classrooms at Bekoji Elementary School, where Eshetu works as a physical-education instructor. All these kids share the same dream: Some day they could become another Derartu Tulu.

這種成功的象徵，激勵貝克基周圍村落數以千計的小孩，紛紛搬進貝克基城內。孩子們擠滿貝克基國小的教室，厄什圖就是在這裡擔任體育老師。這些孩子都有個共同的夢想：將來有一天，他們會成為下一個德拉圖‧圖魯。

    motivate〔'motə,vet〕v. 激勵
    sign〔saɪn〕n. 象徵　　***thousands of*** 數以千計的
    village〔'vɪlɪdʒ〕n. 村莊　　surround〔sə'raʊnd〕v. 環繞
    crowd〔kraʊd〕v. 聚集在；使擠滿　　***elementary school*** 國小
    physical-education *adj.* 體育的（= PE）
    instructor〔ɪn'strʌktɚ〕n. 教師；指導者
    some day（將來）有一天

53.(**A**) 下列何者不是本文所提到，衣索比亞長跑選手會如此優秀的原因？
    (A) 著名的教練。　　　　　(B) 高原稀薄的空氣。
    (C) 特別修長的腿。　　　　(D) 日常生活中的長跑。
    factor〔'fæktɚ〕n. 因素
    well-known〔'wɛl'non〕adj. 著名的
    extraordinarily〔ɪk'strɔrdn,ɛrɪlɪ〕adv. 異常地；非常地

54.(**C**) 關於貝克基，下列何者為真？
    (A) 它是衣索比亞的首都。　　(B) 它在近年來有很大的變化。
    (C) 它位於火山附近。　　　　(D) 它在處理車禍方面有困難。
    capital〔'kæpətl〕n. 首都

55.(**B**) 貝克基學童的目標是什麼？
    (A) 要擔任汽車旅館的經理。　(B) 要贏得國際比賽。
    (C) 要成為體育老師。　　　　(D) 要在學校的學業上表現良好。
    competition〔,kɑmpə'tɪʃən〕n. 比賽　　perform〔pɚ'fɔrm〕v. 表現
    academically〔,ækə'dɛmɪklɪ〕adv. 在學術上

56.(**A**) 從本文可推論出什麼？

(A) 貝克基可能會出現更多的長跑選手。

(B) 耐吉會贊助貝克基的年輕長跑選手。

(C) 貝克基將主辦一場國際長跑比賽。

(D) 衣索比亞政府已經不遺餘力地推廣跑步。

emerge〔ɪˋmɝdʒ〕v. 出現　　sponsor〔ˋspɑnsɚ〕v. 贊助
host〔host〕v. 主辦　　spare〔spɛr〕v. 節省使用；吝惜
spare no efforts 不遺餘力

第貳部分：非選擇題

一、翻譯題

1. 在過去，腳踏車主要是作為一種交通工具。

   In the past, bicycles mainly acted as a means of transportation.

2. 然而，騎腳踏車現在已經成為一種熱門的休閒活動。

   However, $\left\{\begin{array}{l} \text{cycling} \\ \text{bicycle riding} \end{array}\right\}$ has become a (kind of) popular leisure activity now.

二、英文作文：

　　It was a typical morning in Mrs. Chen's noodle shop.　Mrs. Chen's son, Steven, sat at the counter doing his homework while a man ate noodles.　The man's bag sat on the stool between them.　When he finished his breakfast, the man paid and left the shop.　However, he forgot his bag on the stool.

　　Mrs. Chen and Steven opened the bag to find some identification.　To their surprise, the bag was filled with money.　"Run along to school, Steven," Mrs. Chen said.　"I'll take care of this."　Meanwhile, the man got to train station before he realized the bag was missing.　He quickly returned to the noodle shop where Mrs. Chen was holding the bag for him.

　　"I had a feeling you'd be back," Mrs. Chen scolded the man.　"Thank you so much," the man replied.　He reached into the bag and pulled out a stack of $1,000 NT notes.　"Please," the man said, "take this as a reward for your honesty."

typical〔'tɪpɪkḷ〕*adj.* 典型的
noodle〔'nudḷ〕*n.* 麵　　counter〔'kaʊntɚ〕*n.* 櫃台
sit〔sɪt〕*v.* 被放在　　stool〔stul〕*n.* 凳子
identification〔aɪ,dɛntəfə'keʃən〕*n.* 證件
to one's surprise 令某人驚訝的是
run along 走開　　*take care of* 處理
meanwhile〔'min,hwaɪl〕*adv.* 同時　　*get to* 到達
missing〔'mɪsɪŋ〕*adj.* 找不到的；遺失的
scold〔skold〕*v.* 責罵　　*reach into* 伸入
pull out 拿出　　stack〔stæk〕*n.* 一疊；一堆
note〔not〕*n.* 鈔票

99 年度學科能力測驗英文試題修正意見

題　號	題　　　　　目	修　正　意　見
第 4 題	..., *prices for* daily necessities.... → ..., ***the prices of*** daily necessities	「日用品的價格」該用所有格的形式。
第 10 題	... do *house* chores .... → ... do ***household*** chores	「家事」應該是 household chores 或 housework。
第 26 – 30 題 最後一行	According to one *research*, ... → According to one ***research study***, ... 或 According to one ***study***, ...	research 正常情況為不可數名詞，study 才是可數名詞，兩者都可作「研究」解。
第 31 – 40 題 倒數第 5 行	... must *behave himself* as such. → must ***behave*** as such.	出題原文是：conduct himself as such，改編錯誤，behave oneself 後面應接表稱讚的副詞。
第 41 – 44 題 最後一段 倒數第 3 行	*Since rats love to hunt and eat wetas, the rat population on the island has...native weta population.* → ***Since rats love to hunt and eat wetas, the rat population on the island poses a serious threat to the native weta population.*** 或→ ***The rat population on the island has grown into a real problem for many of the native species that are unaccustomed to its presence, and since rats love to hunt and eat wetas, they poses a serious threat to the native weta population.***	改編錯誤，不合邏輯，參照原文一看即知：The rat population on the island has burgeoned into a real problem for many of the native species who are unaccustomed to its presence, and has put a serious dent in the native weta population. Quite simply, rats love to hunt and eat wetas.
第 44 題 (A)	The *rat's*. → The ***rat population's***.	由前半句 Since rats love to hunt and eat wetas, the rat population on the island.... 可知，its 應是指 the rat population's。

第 45－48 題 第三段第 5 行	*After* the 1960s, and especially since the 1980s, the high school prom in many areas has become .... → *Since* the 1960s, and especially since the 1980s, the high school prom in many areas has become	由 and especially since the 1980s 及完成式動詞 has become 可知，*After* 應改成 *Since*。參照「出題來源」，就可知改編錯誤。
第三段 倒數第 2 行	... Stretch limousines *were* hired .... → Stretch limousines *are* hired	由倒數第 3 行的 has become 可知，應將過去式 *were* 改成現在式 *are*。
最後一段 倒數第 2 行	... for homeless youth *were* reported. → ... for homeless youth *are* reported.	
最後一段 倒數第 2 行	There *were* also "couple-free" proms *to* which all students are welcome. → There *are* also "couple-free" proms *at* which all students are welcome.	由句尾的 are welcome 可知，應將過去式 were 改成現在式 *are*，參照「出題來源」，即知改編錯誤。 須將介系詞 *to* 改成 *at*，因為：You are invited *to* a place. 或 You are welcome *at* a place.
第 49－52 題 第二段 第 1, 2 行	... such *an arrangement* .... → ... such *arrangements*	配合前一句的複數名詞 Home exchanges，「出題來源」本來就是複數 arrangements。
第五段 倒數第 2 行	*It does not matter if the agreement would hold up in court*, but .... → *The agreement may not hold up in court*, but	為了配合後面的連接詞 but，須改寫，句意才清楚。
最後一段 第 2 行	... make sure their *home*.... → ... make sure their *borrowed home*....	依句意，不是他們自己的房子，是「借來的」房子才對。
第 49 題 (B)	*How home exchange is becoming popular.* → *How popular home exchange is becoming.*	整句的回答，應該是名詞子句的形式，做 about 的受詞，How 引導名詞子句，應加上所修飾的字才對。
第 53－56 題 第三段第 2 行	He saw *a hope* .... → He saw *hope*	hope 正常情況為不可數名詞。

99 年度學測英文科考題出題來源

題　號	出　　　　　　　處
一、詞彙 第 1～15 題	所有各題對錯答案的選項，均出自「高中常用 7000 字」。
二、綜合測驗 第 16～20 題	改編自時代雜誌 2008 年 2 月 21 日的 Who's Holding the Handbag 一文，關於購物的文章。
第 21～25 題	出自 Onions for All Seasons and All Tastes 一文，關於洋蔥的文章。
第 26～30 題	改寫自 Should Bottled Water Be Included In A Healthy Diet? 一文，有關瓶裝水的文章。
三、文意選填 第 31～40 題	出自 Raise Your GPA 1 Full Grade 一書，其中一篇範例（More Than a Sport），關於足球對於運動員及社會影響的內容。
四、閱讀測驗 第 41～44 題	出自 Earth Invaded by Giant Insects 一文，關於紐西蘭特有昆蟲 weta 的文章。
第 45～48 題	出自 How did the tradition of high school proms start? 一文，關於美國高中舞會如何成為傳統的文章。
第 49～52 題	改編自時代雜誌 2009 年 8 月 3 日的 Home Exchange: Trading (Vacation) Places 一文，用和陌生人交換住所的方式來度假的報導。
第 53～56 題	改編自 Fast living in the Ethiopian highland town of Bekoji 一文，有關衣索比亞的 Bekoji 城市，由於地型因素造就了許多優秀的長跑者的文章。

【99 年學測】綜合測驗：16-20 出題來源——時代雜誌 2008 年 2 月 21 日

Who's Holding the Handbag?

On a recent Saturday afternoon in Manhattan, Anika, 26, an investment banker, was doing what many women of her generation do on weekends: she was shopping with her mother. And enjoying it. No surprise, either, that both mother and daughter ended up considering the same pair of J Brand jeans. Initially meant for Anika, the jeans caught her mother's eye too. "I'd wear those to your father's club with a blazer and heels," she said.

Retailers of the world, take note: If you want to get into a boomer's pocketbook, you've got to win her daughter over first. According to Resource Interactive, an Ohio-based marketing company, young adults influence 88% of household apparel purchases. It makes sense since members of the millennial generation—those born between 1980 and 2000—are closer to their parents than are members of any previous generation. Millennials and their parents not only take vacations together and text each other several times a day but also consult each other on what to buy. And more often than not, the millennials are the more informed consumers.

"They've never known life without a computer—they can take in 20 hours' worth of information in seven hours," says Nancy Kramer, CEO of Resource Interactive. "There isn't a brand or a trend these kids aren't aware of. "Which is why boomer mothers who want to keep abreast of the trends turn to the experts in discriminating shopping—their daughters. NPD Group's chief retail analyst, Marshal Cohen, estimates that the number of 18-to-24-year-olds shopping with Mom has grown 8% over the past three years. And what goes on in the dressing room is markedly different than in past generations. Unlike their mothers, boomer women don't want to adopt the ladies-who-lunch look, but at the same time they want to avoid that mutton-dressed-as-lamb look.

：

【99 年學測】綜合測驗：21-25 出題來源──National Onion Association

About Onions: Seasonality

Onions for All Seasons and All Tastes

Onions can be divided into two categories: spring/summer fresh onions and fall/winter storage onions.

Spring/summer Fresh Onions

Spring/summer fresh onions are available in yellow, red and white throughout their season, March through August. Fresh onions can be identified by their thin, light-colored skin. Because they have a higher water content, they are typically sweeter and milder than storage onions. This higher water content also makes them more susceptible to bruising.

With its delicate taste, the spring/summer onion is an ideal choice for salads and other fresh and lightly-cooked dishes.

Fall/winter Storage Onions

Fall/winter storage onions are available August through April. Also available in yellow, red and white, storage onions have multiple layers of thick, dark, papery skin. Storage onions have an intense flavor and a higher percentage of solids.

Storage onions are the best choice for savory dishes that require longer cooking times or more flavor.

The Color of Onions

Onions come in three colors–yellow, red, and white. Approximately 87 percent of the crop is devoted to yellow onion production, with about 8 percent red onions and 5 percent white onions.

Onion Sizes

Onions range in size from less than 1 inch in diameter (creamers/boilers) to more than 4.5 inches in diameter (super colossal). The most common sizes of onions sold in the United States are the medium (2 to 3 ¼ inches in diameter) and the jumbo (3 to 3 ¾ inches in diameter).

【99 年學測】綜合測驗：26-30 出題來源──BRIGHT HUB

Should Bottled Water Be Included In A Healthy Diet?

⋮

The production process of plastic can lead to the release of chemical substances into the water contained in the bottles. From there, the chemicals are absorbed into the body, where they can cause harm. The dangers of bottled water can be classified into chemical, microbial and physical. Chemical refers to the release of such poisonous substances as arsenic, lead or benzene. Microbial hazards are viruses, bacteria or parasites and physical can be tiny fragments of glass, metal or plastic which can find their way into the bottled water.

The chemical and microbial dangers can cause campylobacter infection which is the most widespread cause of bacterial gastroenteritis. Although it's highly unlikely that any of the above may lead to fatal illness, it can cause discomfort, cramps, diarrhea and sickness.

Health risks can also result from inappropriate storage. Bacteria can multiply if the water is kept on the shelves for too long or if it is exposed to heat or direct sunlight. It's very difficult to determine when a bottle you buy in the supermarket has been filled. Even if contamination has occurred, the effects depend on the quantity of water consumed.

The U.S. have a high standard of control and regulation laws as far as the production and supervision of bottled water is concerned, but the safety regulations for drinking water are even more strident. The same standards apply to the European Union, but many other countries are less strict. Information on the safety of drinking water is readily available locally, so there is no reason to prefer bottled water over tap water, However if you happen to live in or visit a country where tap water is unsafe, bottled water is the only sensible alternative.

⋮

【99 年學測】文意選填：31-40 出題來源

BOOK：Raise Your GPA 1 Full Grade

Football is more than a sport. It is an invaluable teacher. In teaching a young man to cooperate with his fellows on the practice field and in schedules games, it also shows him the necessity of team-work in society. It prepares him to be a better citizen and person.

The novice player first learns that football is not a one-man game, that he is but one member of an eleven-man team, and that in every play, either defensive or offensive, he has a particular job to do. If he fails to do it, the team suffers. If his task is to block the opposing right end, that job must be done. And he must do it alone, for every other man on the team has his own assignment in the play. The ends, tackles, guards, backfield men, and center must do their individual tasks if the play is to succeed.

⋮

Wherever football is played in the United States, on sandlot, high school field, college gridiron or in professional stadium, the players learn the invaluable rough-and-tumble lesson that only by the cooperation of each man can the team win. It is a lesson they do not forget on the field. Off the field, they duly remember it. In society, the former player docs not look upon himself as a lone wolf who has the right to create his individual moral code and observe his individual social laws. He understands his place in the scheme of things; he knows he is a member of society and must conduct himself as such. He realizes that only be cooperating, not shying off as a lone wolf, can he do his share in making society what it should be the protector and benefactor of all. The man who has played football knows that team-work is essential in modern living and that every citizen must do his part if the nation is to prosper. So he has little difficulty in adjusting himself to his role in family life and in the business world, and to his duties as a citizen in city, state and nation. In short, his football training helps make him a better citizen and person."

【99 年學測】閱讀測驗：41-44 出題來源——Extreame Science

Earth Invaded by Giant Insects!

⋮

The Dinosaur Insect

On the island of New Zealand, there is a grasshopper-like species of insect that is found nowhere else on earth. New Zealanders have dubbed it the weta, which is a native Maori "god of bad looks". It's easy to see why anyone would call this insect a bad-looking bug. Most People are repulsed at the sight of these bulky, slow-moving creatures. Most people don't feel sympathy for these endangered creatures, but they do need protecting. Europeans who came to Australia and New Zealand brought rats and cats with them. The slow and ungainly wetas have been around on the island since the dinosaurs roamed and have evolved and survived in an ecosystem that had no predators for the weta. Until the rats came to the island. The rat population on the island has burgeoned into a real problem for many of the native species who are unaccustomed to its presence, and has put a serious dent in the native weta population. Quite simply, rats love to hunt and eat wetas.

The photo below is of a rare tusked weta, that grows up to two inches (5cm) long. The Giant Weta can grow to over three inches (8 cm) long and weigh as much as 1.5 ounces (40 grams). Giant wetas can hop up to 2 feet (60cm) at a time. They are nocturnal creatures, venturing out of the safety of their holes and caves only after dark. Some Giant wetas live in trees, and others live in caves. Giant wetas are very long-lived for insects, the adults can live for over a year. Just like their cousins, grasshoppers and crickets, weta are able to "sing" (formally called stridulation) by rubbing their leg parts together, or against their abdomens.

【99 年學測】閱讀測驗：45-48 出題來源——BRIGHT HUB

How did the tradition of high school proms start?

⋮

The word "prom" was first used in the 1890s as a shortened form of "promenade," a reference to formal dances in which the guests would display their fashions and dancing (see entry under 1900sThe Way We Lived in volume 1) skills during the evening's grand march. In the United States, it came to be believed by parents and educators that a prom, or formal dinner-dance, would be an important lesson in social skills, especially in a theoretically classless society that valued behavior over breeding. The prom was seen as a way to instill manners into children, all under the watchful eye of chaperons.

The first proms were held in the 1920s. By the 1930s, proms were common across the country. For many older Americans, the prom was a modest, home-grown affair in the school gymnasium, often decorated with crepe-paper streamers. Promgoers were well dressed but not lavishly decked out: boys wore jacket and tie and girls their Sunday dress. Couples danced to music provided by a local amateur band or a record player. After the 1960s, and especially after the 1980s, the high-school prom in many areas became a serious exercise in conspicuous consumption, with boys renting expensive tuxedos and girls attired in designer gowns. Stretch limousines were hired to drive the prom-goers to expensive restaurants or discos for an all-night extravaganza, with alcohol, drugs, and sex as added ingredients, at least more openly than before.

Whether simple or lavish, proms have always been more or less traumatic events for adolescents who worry about self-image and fitting in with their peers. Prom night can be a devastating experience for socially awkward teens, for those who do not secure dates, or for gay or lesbian teens who cannot relate to the heterosexual bonding of prom night. In 1980, Aaron Fricke (1962) sued his school's principal in Cumberland, Rhode Island, for the right to bring Paul Guilbert as his prom date, and won. Since the 1990s, alternative proms have been organized in some areas for same-sex couples, as well as "couple-free" proms to which all students are welcome. Susan Shadburne's 1998 video, Street Talk and Tuxes, documents a prom organized by and for homeless youth.

【99 年學測】閱讀測驗：49-52 出題來源——時代雜誌 2009 年 8 月 3 日

Home Exchange：Trading (Vacation) Places

As the economy continues to flounder, many families are forgoing summer vacations in favor of staying at home. But there's a more interesting option that is just as cheap: vacationing in someone else's home. Growing numbers of people here and abroad are seeking a thrifty change of scenery by skipping all the hotels and looking instead to swap houses with strangers. Agree to use each other's cars, and you can save big bucks on rentals too.

Home exchanges are not new. At least one group, Intervac, has been facilitating such arrangements since 1953. But traffic online is particularly brisk these days, with several sites, including HomeExchange.com—which was founded in 1992 and, with some 28,000 listings, bills itself as the world's largest home-exchange club—reporting that membership has increased 30% or more this year. (See pictures of high-end homes that won't sell.)

For an annual fee that is usually less than $100, members can access thousands of listings for apartments, condos, villas, suburban homes and farms around the world. Initial contact is made through the sites via e-mail, with subsequent communication usually by phone. Before a match is made, potential swappers tend to talk a lot as part of a scoping-out phase that one exchange site likens to online dating.

⋮

Although home swappers often become such fans of the practice that they have a hard time paying for a hotel, the concept may sound dicey to the uninitiated. What about theft? Damage? Reasonable causes for concern, but equally unlikely. "Nobody is going to fly across the ocean or drive 600 miles to come steal your flat-screen TV," says Tony DiCaprio, president of 1stHomeExchange.com a four-year-old site that has seen membership increase 30% this year. Remember, he notes," at the same time they're staying in your home, you are staying in their home."

⋮

【99 年學測】閱讀測驗：53-56 出題來源——Ethiopian Review

Fast living in the Ethiopian highland town of Bekoji

⋮

It"s tempting, when breathing the thin air of Bekoji, to focus only on the confluence of geography and genetics. The town sits on the flank of a volcano nearly 10,000 ft. (3,000 m) above sea level, making daily life itself a kind of high-altitude training. Children in this region often start running at an early age, covering great distances to fetch water and firewood or to reach the nearest school. "Our natural talent begins at the age of 2," says two-time Olympic gold medalist Haile Gebrselassie, 35, who grew up in a village about 30 miles (50 km) north of Bekoji. Gebrselassie, who set a new marathon world record last year, remembers running over six miles (10 km) to and from school every day carrying his books, leaving him with extraordinary stamina—and a distinctive crook in his left arm. Add to this early training the physique shared by many members of the Oromo ethnic group that predominates in the region—a short torso on disproportionately long legs—and you have the perfectly engineered distance runner.

No formula, however, can conjure up the desire that burns inside Bekoji's young runners. Take the case of Million Abate, an 18-year-old who caught Eshetu's attention last year when he sprinted to the finish of a 12-mile (19 km) training run with his bare feet bleeding profusely. The coach took off his own Nikes and handed them to the young runner. Today, as he serves customers injera, the spongy Ethiopian flat bread, at a local truckers' motel, Abate is still wearing the coach's shoes. They are his only pair, though he confesses a preference for running in bare feet. "Shoes affect my speed," he says. And speed may be his only salvation. Forced to quit school in fifth grade after his father died, Abate worked as a shoe-shine boy before getting the motel job, which pays $9 a month. All along, he has never stopped running, chasing the dream of prosperity his mother imprinted on him shortly after his father's death, when she changed his name from Damelach to Million.

⋮

99 年度學測英文考科非選擇題評分標準說明

閱卷召集人：謝國平（靜宜大學英文系）

　　99 學年度學科能力測驗英文考科的非選擇題題型共有兩大題：第一大題是翻譯題，考生需將兩個中文句子譯成正確而通順達意的英文，這個題型與過去幾年相同，兩題合計八分。第二大題為英文作文，但與往年的看圖作文不太一樣，內容是顧客在麵店遺失金錢，但四格圖片中只畫了三格，並沒有提供結局，希望給考生更多的寫作發揮空間。今年考生需依提供的連環圖片，寫一篇至少120個單詞（words）左右的作文。作文滿分為二十分。

　　至於閱卷籌備工作，在正式閱卷前，於 1 月 31 日先召開評分標準訂定會議，由正副召集人及協同主持人共十四人，參閱了100 本約4000 多份的試卷，經過一天的討論，訂定評分標準，選出合適的樣本，編製了閱卷參考手册，供閱卷委員共同參考，以確保閱卷之公平性。

　　2 月 1 日上午 9:00 到 11:00 間，140 多位大學教授，分為12 組進行試閱會議，討論評分時應注意的事項及評分標準，再根據閱卷參考手册的樣卷，分別評分。在試閱會議之後（ 11:00），正副召集人及協同主持人進行第一次評分標準再確定會議確認評分原則後，才開始正式閱卷。求慎重起見，特別於下午六點加開第二次評分標準再確定會議，以求整體評分標準更為一致。

　　關於評分標準，在翻譯題部分，每題總分 4 分，依文意及文法結構分成幾部分，每部分 0.5 分至 1 分。英文作文的評分標準是依據內容（5 分）、組織（5 分）、文法句構（4 分）、字彙拼字（4 分）、體例（2 分）五個項目給分。若字數不足，則總分扣 1 分。

　　依慣例，每份試卷皆經過兩位委員分別評分，最後以二人之平均分數計算。如果第一閱與第二閱委員的分數在翻譯題部分的差距大於 2 分，或在作文題部分差距大於 5 分，則由第三位主閱（正副召集人或協同主持人）評分。

　　今年的翻譯題的句型與詞彙，皆為高中生應該熟習的，評量的重點在於考生是否能運用熟悉的字詞（比如：腳踏車 bicycle/bike、交通工具 a means of transportation、然而 however、休閒 leisure/recreational、活動 activity、主要 mainly 等）與基本句型翻譯成正確且達意的英文句子（如：served as/be used as、in the past、riding bicycles/bicycle-riding/cycling、has become 等的用法）。所測驗之詞彙都屬於大考中心詞彙表四級內之詞彙，中等程度以上的考生如果能使用正確句型並注意拼字，應能得到理想的分數。但在選取樣卷時發現，很多考生對於像動詞現在完成式、名詞單複數的用法的掌握仍有待加強。

　　英文作文部分，今年回復到多圖的看圖寫作題型，與去年學測的單圖看圖寫作略有不同，圖片內容主要為顧客在麵店遺失金錢。考生針對所提供之圖片，寫出一篇涵蓋連環圖片內容並有完整結局的故事，除了評量考生語法能力與敘述故事的能力（包括情節的安排及合理性）以外，更因為結局留白，提供學生相當大的發揮創意空間。

99 年度學測英文考科試題或答案之反應意見回覆

※ 題號：7

【題目】

7. Steve has several meetings to attend every day; therefore, he has to work on a very _____ schedule.
   (A) dense　(B) various　(C) tight　(D) current

【意見內容】

選項 (A) 應為合理答案。

【大考中心意見回覆】

　　本題所要評量考生掌握形容詞 tight 與名詞 schedule 之間的搭配（collocation）用法。作答線索為上一個子句 Steve has several meetings to attend every day。

※ 題號：17 及 19

【題目】

　　Anita was shopping with her mother and enjoying it. Interestingly, both of them ___16___ buying the same pair of jeans.

　　According to a recent marketing study, young adults influence 88% of household clothing purchases. More often than not, those in their early twenties are the more ___17___ consumers. There isn't a brand or a trend that these young people are not aware of. That is why mothers who want to keep abreast of trends usually ___18___ the experts — their daughters. This tells the retailers of the world that if you want to get into a mother's ___19___, you've got to win her daughter over first.

　　With a DJ playing various kinds of music rather than just rap, and a mix of clothing labels designed more for taste and fashion than for a precise age, department stores have managed to appeal to successful middle-aged women ___20___ losing their younger customers. They have created a shopping environment where the needs of both mother and daughter are satisfied.

17. (A) informed　　　　　(B) informative
　　(C) informal　　　　　(D) informational

19. (A) textbook　　　　　(B) notebook
　　(C) workbook　　　　　(D) pocketbook

【17 題意見內容】

選項 (B) 應為合理答案。

【17 題大考中心意見回覆】

　　Informed consumer 意指對於「消費資訊都能充分掌握的人士」，在語用及字詞搭配上只有 informed 是最適合的，故選項 (A) 為正答並無異議。

【19 題意見內容】

選項 (B) 應為合理答案。

【19 題大考中心意見回覆】

　　本題所要評量的是根據上下文意之發展，選出一個最適當的詞彙。四個選項中只有 pocketbook 與金錢或消費的概念相關，其餘三個選項皆與本段文意不符。

※ 題號：48

【題目】

<u>45-48 為題組</u>

The high school prom is the first formal social event for most American teenagers. It has also been a rite of passage for young Americans for nearly a century.

The word "prom" was first used in the 1890s, referring to formal dances in which the guests of a party would display their fashions and dancing skills during the evening's grand march. In the United States, parents and educators have come to regard the prom as an important lesson in social skills. Therefore, proms have been held every year in high schools for students to learn proper social behavior.

The first high school proms were held in the 1920s in America. By the 1930s, proms were common across the country. For many older Americans, the prom was a modest, home-grown affair in the school gymnasium. Prom-goers were well dressed but not fancily dressed up for the occasion: boys wore jackets and ties and girls their Sunday dresses. Couples danced to music provided by a local amateur band or a record player. After the 1960s, and especially since the 1980s, the high school prom in many areas has become a serious exercise in excessive consumption, with boys renting expensive tuxedos and girls wearing designer gowns. Stretch limousines were hired to drive the prom-goers to expensive restaurants or discos for an all-night extravaganza.

Whether simple or lavish, proms have always been more or less traumatic events for adolescents who worry about self-image and fitting in with their peers. Prom night can be a dreadful experience for socially awkward teens or for those who do not secure dates. Since the 1990s, alternative proms have been organized in some areas to meet the needs of particular students. For example, proms organized by and for homeless youth were reported. There were also "couple-free" proms to which all students are welcome.

48. Which of the following statements is true?
   (A) Unconventional proms have been organized since the 1960s.
   (B) In the 1980s, proms were held in local churches for teenagers to attend.
   (C) Proms have become a significant event in American high schools since the 1930s.
   (D) In the 1890s, high school proms were all-night social events for some American families.

【意見內容】

1. 選項 (C) 之文字有瑕疵。

2. 答案 (C) Proms have become a significant event in American high schools since the 1930s. 似乎與文義有出入。因為文章中的句子——The first high school proms were held in the 1920s in America. By the 1930s, proms were common across the country. 寫道的意思應為至 1930 年，高中舞會已很盛行，但答案 (C) 之意思為從 1930 年起，高中舞會已成為很重要的活動。兩者似乎有出入，即便答案無法更動，也希望得到相關答覆。

【大考中心意見回覆】

本題主要在於評量考生對於文章細節的理解，作答線索主要在第三段，尤其是在第二句 By the 1930s, proms were common across the country。本段的大意在於說明 prom 的發展，自 1930 年代就開始普及，第四句 Prom-goers were well dressed but not fancily dressed up for the occasion: boys wore jackets and ties and girls their Sunday dresses 皆顯示「與會者穿著正式」，因此可以判定 prom 為一項「盛會」(significant event)，因此選項 (C) 為正答並無異議。

※ 題號：49 及 51

【題目】

49-52 為題組

No budget for your vacation? Try home exchanges —— swapping houses with strangers. Agree to use each other's cars, and you can save bucks on car rentals, too.

Home exchanges are not new. At least one group, Intervac, has been facilitating such an arrangement since 1953. But trading online is gaining popularity these days, with several sites in operation, including HomeExchanges. Founded in 1992, with some 28,000 listings, this company **bills** itself as the world's largest home exchange club, reporting that membership has increased 30% this year.

The annual fee is usually less than US$100. Members can access thousands of listings for apartments, villas, suburban homes and farms around the world. Initial contact is made via e-mail, with subsequent communication usually by phone. Before a match is made, potential swappers tend to discuss a lot.

However, the concept may sound risky to some people. What about theft? Damage? These are reasonable causes for concern, but equally unlikely. As one swapper puts it, "Nobody is going to fly across the ocean or drive 600 miles to come steal your TV. Besides, at the same time they're staying in your home, you are staying in their home."

Exchange sites recommend that swappers discuss such matters ahead of time. They may fill out an agreement spelling out who shoulders which responsibilities if a problem arises. It does not matter if the agreement would hold up in court, but it does give the exchangers a little satisfaction.

Generally, the biggest complaint among home exchangers has to do with different standards of cleanliness. Swappers are supposed to make sure their home is in order before they depart, but one person's idea of "clean" may be more forgiving than another's. Some owners say if they come back to a less-than-sparkling kitchen, it may be inconvenient but would not sour them on future exchanges.

49. What is the second paragraph mainly about?
　(A) How to exchange homes.
　(B) How home exchange is becoming popular.
　(C) The biggest home exchange agency.
　(D) A contrast between Intervac and HomeExchange.

51. How do home exchangers normally begin their communication?
　(A) By phone.　　　　(B) By e-mail.
　(C) Via a matchmaker.　(D) Via a face-to-face meeting.

【49 題意見內容】

1. 選項 (B) 與文章所述不完全吻合。

2. 選項 (C) 應為合理答案。

3. 選項 (D) 應為合理答案。

【49 題大考中心意見回覆】

1. 由本段的主題句 Home exchanges are not new 可知本段主題為 home exchange 的發展,因此選項 (B) 的文字並未有與文章所述不吻合之處。

2. 由本段的主題句 Home exchanges are not new 可知本段主題為 home exchange 的發展,後續的句子都是在列舉其日漸普及的例證,故選項 (B) 為正答並無異議。本段中 HomeExchange 公司只是其中一個例證,選 (C) 可能僅是「見樹不見林」的觀察。

3. 本段內容並沒有刻意比較 Intervac 與 HomeExchange 兩家公司之間的差異,故選項 (D) 的對比並不存在。兩家公司只是在說明 home exchange 日漸受歡迎的例證。

【51 題意見內容】

選項 (A) 應為合理答案。

【51 題大考中心意見回覆】

　　本題在評量考生對於局部文意的理解。作答線索在第三段內容中 Initial contact is made via e-mail, with subsequent communication usually by phone。Contact 一詞本身包含各種溝通方式,因此,選項 (B) By e-mail 為正確答案。

※ 題號：54

【題目】

53-56 為題組

　　Bekoji is a small town of farmers and herders in the Ethiopian highlands. There, time almost stands still, and horse-drawn carts outnumber motor vehicles. Yet, it has consistently yielded many of the world's best distance runners.

　　It's tempting, when breathing the thin air of Bekoji, to focus on the special conditions of the place. The town sits on the side of a volcano nearly 10,000 feet above sea level, making daily life a kind of high-altitude training. Children in this region often start running at an early age, covering great distances to fetch water and firewood or to reach the nearest school. Added to this early training is a physical trait shared by people there— disproportionately long legs, which is advantageous for distance runners.

　　A strong desire burns inside Bekoji's young runners. Take the case of Million Abate. Forced to quit school in fifth grade after his father died, Abate worked as a shoe-shine boy for years. He saw a hope in running and joined Santayehu Eshetu's training program. This 18-year-old sprinted to the finish of a 12-mile run with his bare feet bleeding. The coach took off his own Nikes and handed them to him. To help Abate continue running, the coach arranged a motel job for him, which pays $9 a month.

　　Most families in Bekoji live from hand to mouth, and distance running offers the younger generation a way out. Bekoji's legend Derartu Tulu, who won the 10,000-meter Olympic gold medals in 1992 and 2000, is a national hero. As a reward, the government gave her a house. She also won millions of dollars in the races.

　　Motivated by such signs of success, thousands of kids from the villages surrounding Bekoji have moved into town. They crowd the classrooms at Bekoji Elementary School, where Eshetu works as a physical-education instructor. All these kids share the same dream: Some day they could become another Derartu Tulu.

54. Which of the following is true about Bekoji?
(A) It's the capital of Ethiopia.
(B) It has changed a lot over the years.
(C) It's located near a volcano.
(D) It has trouble handling car accidents.

【意見內容】

　　選項 (B) 應為合理答案。

【大考中心意見回覆】

　　第二段 The town sits on the side of a volcano 意思即代表 Bekoji 靠近火山，因此選項 (C) 為正答並無異議。第一段第二句 There, time almost stands still, and horse-drawn carts outnumber motor vehicles 已經說明 Bekoji 仍是變化不大的鄉村；因此，選項 (B) 並非正確選項。

84～106學年度學科能力測驗

英文科級分標準一覽表

年度＼標準	全均標	後均標	年度＼標準	全均標	後均標
84年	5	4	86年	4	3
85年	5	3	87年	5	4

年度＼標準	頂標	前標	均標	後標	底標
88年	12	10	8	6	
89年	12	11	8	6	
90年	12	10	7	5	
91年	13	11	8	6	4
92年	12	10	7	4	3
93年	12	11	8	5	4
94年	13	11	8	5	4
95年	13	11	8	5	4
96年	13	11	8	5	4
97年	14	13	10	6	4
98年	13	11	8	5	4
99年	13	11	8	5	4
100年	14	13	10	6	4
101年	14	12	10	6	4
102年	14	13	10	6	4
103年	14	12	10	6	4
104年	14	12	9	6	4
105年	14	12	9	6	4
106年	13	11	8	5	4

* 級分計分方式88學年由10級分改為15級分。

* 五標從91學年開始公布，84–87學年只公布全均標和後均標。

* 更多統計資料可上大考中心查詢：www.ceec.edu.tw/AbilityExam/
AbilityExamPaper.htm

「用會話背 7000 字 Unit 1 背誦比賽」得獎名單

名次	姓 名	學 校	班 級	名次	姓 名	學 校	班 級
1	陳國瑋	格致中學	普二信	51	關碩樸	劉毅英文	班務導師
2	洪唯晨	辭修高中	二年一班	52	賴柏盛	建國中學	二年十四班
3	林亮宇	新北高中	二年三班	53	劉承哲	花蓮明義	二年一班
4	陳少裔	百齡國小	六年三班	54	陳建希	花蓮中正	二年六班
5	謝予馨	景美女中	三年愛班	55	陳苡娟	花蓮中華	二年二班
6	曾紘瀅	中正高中	一年八班	56	鄭庭軒	花蓮明禮	三年忠班
7	黃佑家	景美女中	三年愛班	57	李思瑪	花蓮中原	三年一班
8	黃耀毅	私立復興中小學	七年信班	58	林楷晴	花蓮中正	三年孝班
9	張軒瑋	百齡國小	六年六班	59	陳德恩	花蓮明義	四年五班
10	許珽鈞	師大附中	二年十四班	60	鍾承曄	花蓮忠孝	五年孝班
11	張凱俐	中山女高	二年簡班	61	彭彥銘	花蓮國風	七年八班
12	謝佳沁	中正高中	二年十八班	62	林亮君	成淵高中	二年二班
13	江裪溙	方濟中學	二年信班	63	鍾宜閔	萬福國小	三年三班
14	陳 立	成淵高中	二年九班	64	劉雅拿	仁愛國小	四年二班
15	王喜鴻	華江高中	三年五班	65	劉雅列	仁愛國小	一年七班
16	翁菲蔓	西松高中	高二平班	66	張皓崴	百齡國小	三年七班
17	林郡毅	成淵高中	二年七班	67	徐可欣	新興高中	171
18	張淇鈺	景文高中	二年七班	68	黃耀陞	敦化國小	六年五班
19	程士垣	政大附中	三年五班	69	蘇宋易	景文高中	二年二班
20	張辛瑀	北一女中	二年樂班	70	鄭蜞瑩	文華國小	五年一班
21	黃詩博	華江高中	三年五班	71	陳品均	興隆國小	六年五班
22	吳牧城	中正高中	二年九班	72	谷憲霖	敦化國中	九年一班
23	曾偉紘	光復高中	二年二班	73	吳浩源	信義國中	九年七班
24	游家蓁	淡江大學	大學二年級	74	吳宇晏	南港高中	二年九班
25	陳宇翔	江翠國中	三年二十班	75	曾檍瑄	靜修女中	二年九班
26	孫家蔚	信義國中	三年五班	76	王懷仁	現役軍人	關指部
27	張爲綸	景美國中	三年十二班	77	袁博靖	青潭國小	三年三班
28	蔡育山	龍山國中	三年五班	78	袁詩閔	青潭國小	四年一班
29	陳元彬	百齡國中	三年五班	79	陳櫻丹	興隆國小	五年一班
30	林萬娣	龍安國小	五年八班	80	劉軒鳴	信義國中	九年九班
31	許哲齊	淡江國中	三年仁班	81	張鎧薇	敦化國中	九年八班
32	姜德昀	延平國中	二年四班	82	羅文妤	永和國中	九年四班
33	賴譽亳	板橋高中	一年十七班	83	楊舒棻	中正高中	二年二十一班
34	蔡昀倢	華江高中	二年七班	84	劉子郡	東山高中	九年九班
35	張詠琹	崇光女中	一年智班	85	蕭翊聖	東山高中	九年十班
36	陳瑾瑜	北一女中	二御	86	洪文棋	忠孝國中	九年六班
37	吳文心	北一女中	二禮	87	張譯勻	北市忠孝	九年一班
38	郭柏均	花蓮明義	四年九班	88	陳彥妤	忠孝國中	九年一班
39	吳欣臻	花蓮中原	四年三班	89	朱育正	萬華國中	九年六班
40	黃曄甯	花蓮中正	五年四班	90	李光浩	弘道國中	九年三班
41	張宸睿	花蓮明義	五年六班	91	劉懿萱	秀峰國中	九年三班
42	劉于瑄	花蓮明義	六年九班	92	陳 中	國北護長照	成人
43	馬亞恩	花蓮鑄強	六年忠班	93	陳虹樺	奎山國中	九年一班
44	郭恩妤	花蓮花崗	七年五班	94	張育瑋	蘆洲國中	九年二十九班
45	林楷芯	花蓮國風	七年十一班	95	陳彥龍	建國中學	一年十二班
46	黃惠心	花蓮國風	七年十四班	96	朱庭慧	金融業	上班族
47	李品瑤	花蓮國風	七年五班	97	游馨儀	進出口貿易業	上班族
48	黃暐哲	花蓮國風	七年八班	98	賴揚軒	新北高中	一年十四班
49	鄧清澄	花蓮慈濟	國一大愛班	99	崔宏燕	國文老師	學校老師
50	蕭仲軒	中正高中	二年九班	100	吳承達	建國中學	一年二十二班

劉毅英文家教班成績優異同學獎學金排行榜

姓 名	學 校	總金額	姓 名	學 校	總金額	姓 名	學 校	總金額
林子玄	建國中學	34999	劉星辰	松山高中	10000	洪子涵	縣明德國中	9000
李俊逸	建國中學	33532	郭子靖	麗山高中	10000	李安晴	衛理女中國中部	9000
李璨宇	建國中學	27666	陳均愷	大安高工	10000	陳鄞鄯	大安國中	9000
張心怡	北一女中	27666	黃義霖	高 中 生	10000	高梓馨	成淵國中	9000
范育馨	北一女中	27466	徐萱琳	大同高中	10000	李彥成	大同國中	9000
張文彥	建國中學	26666	游凱程	成功高中	10000	林彥凱	海山國中	9000
于辰欣	北一女中	26666	林于傑	松山高中	10000	高 行	仁愛國中	9000
汪汶姍	北一女中	26666	陳映綠	北一女中	10000	陳元彬	百齡國中	9000
劉可勤	建國中學	26666	楊承凡	敦化國中	10000	劉冠廷	海山國中	9000
周士捷	建國中學	26066	楊祐荃	福和國中	10000	黃長隆	師大附中	8333
許煥承	板橋高中	19000	朱庭萱	海山國中	10000	林佳璇	新莊高中	8000
顧存因	成功高中	18333	張世敏	興雅國中	10000	闕湘庭	士林高商	8000
陳彥龍	建國中學	18333	陳彥劭	南門國中	10000	陳詠恩	新店高中	8000
周 毅	南門國中	18333	呂佳壎	長安國中	10000	曾亭諺	大安高工	8000
游一心	建國中學	18333	曾煦元	誠正國中	10000	郭柏成	中正高中	8000
林佑達	建國中學	18333	陳冠綸	南門國中	10000	王紹宇	海山高中	8000
涂冠竹	師大附中	18333	陳柏旭	大安國中	10000	賴靜文	蘭雅國中	8000
吳承達	建國中學	18333	黃嵩文	西湖國中	10000	洪向霖	永平高中	8000
劉秉軒	建國中學	16666	袁國凱	永吉國中	10000	許珈瑜	海山高中	8000
呂沄諮	松山高中	16000	張為綸	景美國中	10000	康育菁	永春高中	8000
田國邑	成功高中	15000	郭家晉	成淵國中	10000	許定綸	明倫高中	8000
簡婕翎	延平中學國中部	15000	蔡知均	仁愛國中	10000	張詠智	宜蘭高中	8000
蔡佳頤	師大附中	15000	楊承凡	敦化國中	10000	賴禹彤	內湖高中	8000
謝旻臻	麗山高中	15000	萬承達	中正國中	10000	呂沛倢	東湖高中	8000
李承恩	成功高中	15000	陳宇翔	江翠國中	10000	陳彥升	和平高中	8000
劉奕均	新竹高中	15000	楊祐荃	福和國中	10000	陳孟婕	新莊高中	8000
康學承	恆毅中學國中部	15000	朱庭萱	海山國中	10000	蔡森旭	永平高中	8000
陳佩祺	板橋高中	15000	呂可弘	麗山高中	9000	翁穎程	再興中學	8000
吳彥霆	成功高中	15000	梁恩綺	景美女中	9000	王詠欽	仁愛國中	8000
許元愷	松山高中	15000	葉紹傑	復旦高中	9000	吳子恩	靜修女中國中部	8000
侯仲文	政大附中國中部	15000	李婕柔	華興國中	9000	鄭安璇	市中正國中	8000
廖珮妤	中山女中	14000	陳咸安	中崙高中	9000	李潔昀	萬華國中	8000
劉冠伶	景美女中	14000	簡彣熹	松山家商	9000	秦晨芳	興雅國中	8000
林子馨	板橋高中	14000	黃巧慧	海山國中	9000	陳宗震	內湖國中	8000
胡鈞涵	成功高中	14000	張喻珺	大同高中	9000	楊珮玲	市中山國中	8000
李昀浩	再興高中	14000	蘇知適	成淵高中	9000	楊傳芸	崇光國中	8000
袁輔瑩	松山高中	14000	陳映蓉	大同高中	9000	陳芊羽	陽明國中	8000
蔡禹萱	敦化國中	12000	賴譽亳	板橋高中	9000	蔡湘儀	金陵女中	8000
曹紘漾	中正高中	11000	石季韋	中和高中	9000	陳楡晴	永吉國中	8000
陳筱翎	中和高中	11000	陳鄞鄯	大安國中	9000	陳宗震	內湖國中	8000
張 晨	麗山國中	11000	李安晴	衛理女中國中部	9000	崔安綺	實踐國中	8000

※ 因版面有限，尚有領取高額獎學金同學，無法列出。

劉毅英文教育機構
台北本部：台北市許昌街17號6F（捷運M8出口對面·學善補習班）　TEL：（02）2389-5212
台中總部：台中市三民路三段125號7F（光南文具批發樓上·劉毅補習班）　TEL：（04）2221-8861
www.learnschool.com.tw

歷屆大學學測英文試題詳解②

主　　　編 / 劉　毅

發　行　所 / 學習出版有限公司　　　　☎ (02) 2704-5525

郵 撥 帳 號 / 05127272 學習出版社帳戶

登　記　證 / 局版台業 2179 號

印　刷　所 / 裕強彩色印刷有限公司

台 北 門 市 / 台北市許昌街 10 號 2 F　　　☎ (02) 2331-4060

台灣總經銷 / 紅螞蟻圖書有限公司　　　☎ (02) 2795-3656

本公司網址　www.learnbook.com.tw

電 子 郵 件　learnbook@learnbook.com.tw

售價：新台幣三百八十元正

2017 年 6 月 1 日初版

劉毅老師回答讀者的問題

1. 問：「用會話背7000字」和「一口氣背會話」有何不同？
   答：「用會話背7000字」是把「高中常用7000字」融入日常
   會話，背的會話越多，單字增加得越多。

2. 問： 我記憶力不好，怎麼辦？
   答： 每一句話大多在5個字以內，正
   好訓練你的記憶，記憶力不好的
   人，剛開始可能慢，會越背越快
   。背書有助於活化腦細胞。

3. 問： 為什麼要用會話背7000字？
   答： 說出來的單字才不容易忘記，背
   了句子，才知道單字如何用。

4. 問： 我唸「用會話背7000字」有助於我考大學嗎？
   答： 7000字是大學入學考試及高中課本的範圍，背完會話，
   說出來有信心，寫出來也有信心。

5. 問： 我小孩只有5歲，可以學嗎？
   答： 當然可以，你只要背給他聽，他跟著你唸，再聽CD，
   就自然會了。其實4歲以上即可，不需要給他看課本。

6. 問： 我是英文老師，我自己造句可以嗎？
   答： 自己造句太可怕了！合乎文法規則，不見得正確。背
   美國人口中說出來的句子，說起話來才像美國人。

唯有不忘記，才能累積

7. 問：我背完有機會用嗎？
   答：書中每一個句子，每天都可以主動對別人說。如：
   Holy cow!（天啊！）是不是可以天天說？背就要背用
   得到的句子。

8. 問：為什麼要背到2分鐘之內？
   答：脫口而出，變成直覺，才能終生不忘。唯有不忘記，
   才能累積，否則背到後面，前面會忘掉。

9. 問：什麼時間背書最好？
   答：早上起床和晚上睡覺前，是背書最好的時間。早上9
   點到11點，下午3點到5點，也是背書的好時間。

10. 問：背書有方法嗎？
    答：先聽CD以後再背，給自己限定10分鐘，背背看。背給
    別人聽，是最好的方法。

11. 問：我背了「用會話背7000字」，
    不會拼字怎麼辦？
    答：你寫作文的時候，用到你所背
    的句子，慢慢你就會說，也會
    寫了。如果你要密集背拼字，
    可參考我們新出版的「一分鐘
    背9個單字」。

12. 問：我討厭英文，我不想背，怎麼辦？
    答：英文是世界的語言，背一個單字的價值超過10萬元台
    幣，會說英文的廠長，可以賺到一般工人的50倍薪水。
    用背會話的方法，讓你說出來有信心，天不怕、地不
    怕，不會害羞。

不分年齡，人人都可背的一本書

13. 問：我的小孩是小學生，可以背嗎？

　　答：小學生潛力無限，記憶力最好。你只要給他適當的鼓勵，他就會喜歡背。小孩子會背這些深奧的句子，雖然不會用，以後慢慢就會了，背了這些句子，會使他終生受益。

14. 問：我是英文老師，該怎麼教？

　　答：小孩子不用課本，他跟你複誦即可。國、高中以上，可用「用會話背7000字教本」。

15. 問：「用會話背7000字」共1,080句，誰背得下來？

　　答：我們用「分組記憶法」編排，以三句為一組，九句為一回，12回為一個Unit，共108句為一個單元，你試試看，很容易！

這兩組編排相同，句子都是Be–Tell 開頭

開頭是 Don't

7. *Be sincere.*

Be *sincere*.	要真誠。
Tell only *facts*.	只說事實。
Give us the *details*.	告訴我們細節。
Be *honorable*.	要誠實。
Tell the *truth*.	說真話。
Speak from the *heart*.	說說心話。
Don't *boast*.	不要吹噓。
Don't *exaggerate*.	不要誇大。
Just tell what *happened*.	只說發生什麼事。

　　每個句子都精心編排，誰都能背得下來。最妙的是，每個句子都有一個較難的單字，說出這些精彩的句子，會讓美國人佩服你，中國人羨慕你。

跟著興趣走，身體會健康

16. 問： 有開「用會話背7000字班」嗎？

答：「劉毅英文」有開班，可打電話
詢問：(02) 2389-5212。
每個禮拜六下午2:00~5:00，
由曾文老師上課，目標是讓
你背完整本書。

17. 問： 在「用會話背7000字」中，有些難句我看不懂。

答： 你看不懂的地方，我們都有「背景說明」。
如：Don't quit.（不要放棄。）
Be persistent.（要堅持。）
Overcome!（克服困難！）
我們在「背景說明」中告訴你，*Overcome!* 源自
Overcome your problem!（克服你的困難！）

18. 問： 為什麼用*Overcome!* 一個字？

答： 句子短才背得下來，越短越好。學英文要先從背極短
句開始。小孩子剛開始學說話，都先說一個字。

19. 問： 我是國中生，可以學嗎？

答： 現在是你背單字最好的時間，上了高
中以後，記憶力逐漸減退，你的舌頭
會變硬。現在跟著CD背英文，你就會
有美國人的腔調。

20. 問： 我是地理老師，對英文有興趣，可當英文老師嗎？

答： 跟著興趣走，身體會健康。這本書人人能教，目標是
讓同學背下來。擊敗「啞巴英語」，拯救受苦受難學
英文的人，是劉毅老師的目標。